I0634750

THE YANKS ARE STARVING

A NOVEL OF THE BONUS ARMY

GLEN CRANEY

BRIGID'S FIRE PRESS

Published in the United States

FIRST EDITION

Library of Congress Cataloging-in-Publication Data
Craney, Glen
The Yanks Are Starving: A Novel of the Bonus Army

ISBN 978-0-9816484-4-6

1. Historical Fiction 2. Bonus March-Fiction. 3. World War One-Fiction. 4. Great Depression-Fiction. 5. Hoover, Herbert-Fiction. 6. MacArthur, Douglas-Fiction. 7. Gibbons, Floyd-Fiction. 8. Military-Fiction. 9. Bonus Army-Fiction

Brigid's Fire Press
www.brigidsfire.com

Praise for *The Yanks Are Starving*

Foreword Reviews Book-of-the-Year Finalist
indieBRAG Medallion Honoree

"[A] wonderful source of historical fact wrapped in a compelling novel.... Each of the characters is written in a depth that makes them come alive.... If you want to learn about one of America's darkest days, one that rarely gets any attention, this is a book that will both teach and entertain." — *Historical Novel Society*

"Glen Craney ... has drawn a vivid picture of not only men being deprived of their veterans' rights, but of their human rights as well. ...The Veterans Bonus March was a momentous event in American history and Craney performs a valuable service by chronicling it in this admirable book." — *Military Writers Society of America*

"Craney has written an outstanding social and military historical novel of the United States covering the crossing over from the nineteenth century mentality into the twentieth century. Simply put, an outstanding novel." — Joseph Spuckler, *Author Alliance* reviewer and Marine veteran

"One of the best and most memorable books I have ever read."
— Marine veteran Nathan Mercer, *Movies and Manuscripts*

"[C]hock full of really interesting historical figures. . . the writing is one of the most stand-out things about it. ...[H]istorical fiction readers will appreciate the great characters and very good detail within this book." — *A Bookish Affair*

"[I] know of no other fiction writer who has made this brave, tragic protest movement the main theme of a novel, until now. Glen Craney deserves praise for recognizing the significance and dramatic potential of the Bonus Army story and developing it in *The Yanks are Starving*." — Ruth Latta, *The Compulsive Reader Review*

For Harry Essex, who encouraged me to write it.

Here were they at the King's gates, and on every side environing them were many hostile cities and tribes of men. Who was there now to furnish them with a market? ... Haunted by such thoughts, and with hearts full of despair, but few of them tasted food that evening; but few of them kindled even a fire, and many never came into camp at all that night, but took their rest where each chanced to be.

— Xenophon, *Anabasis*

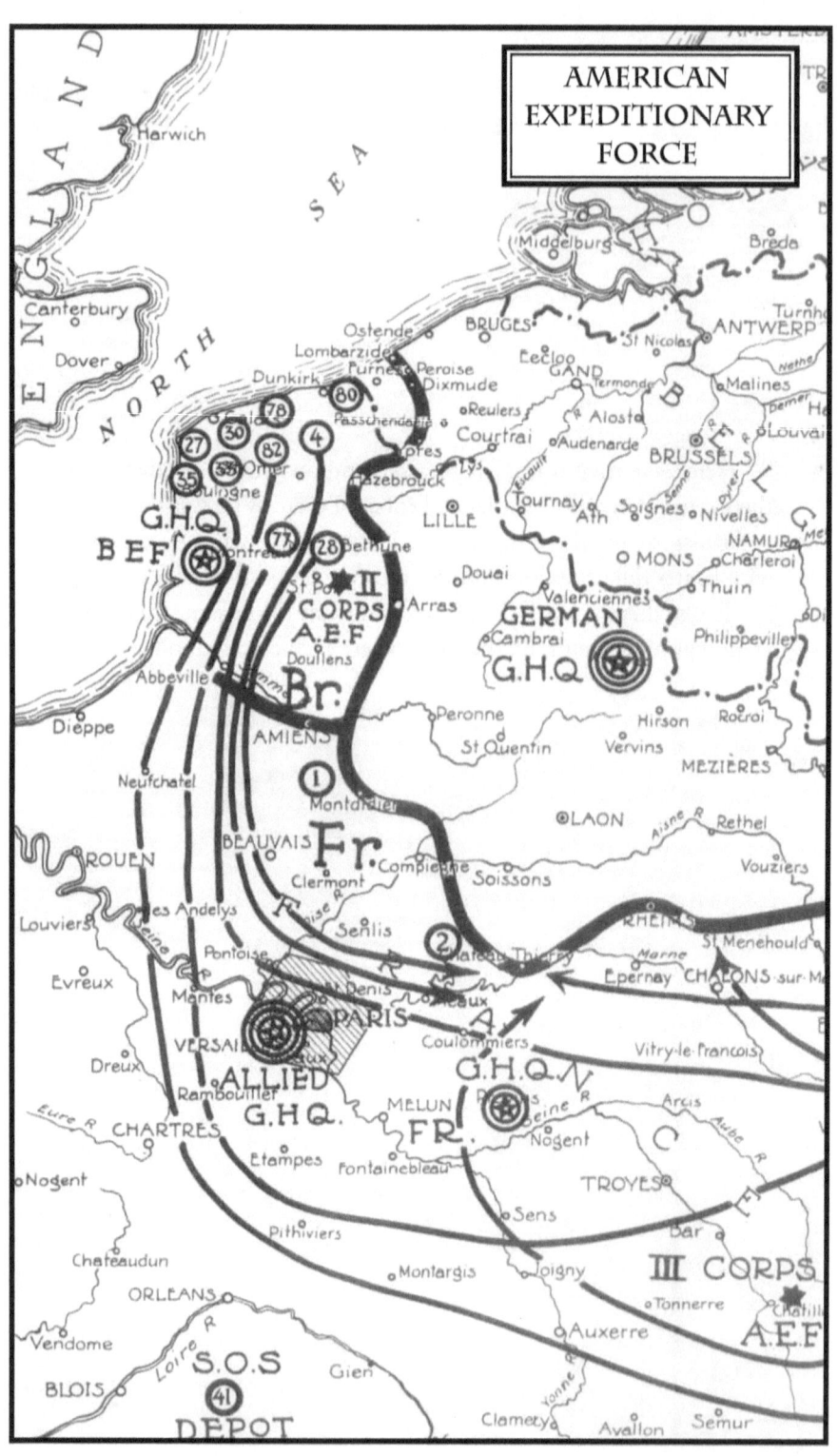

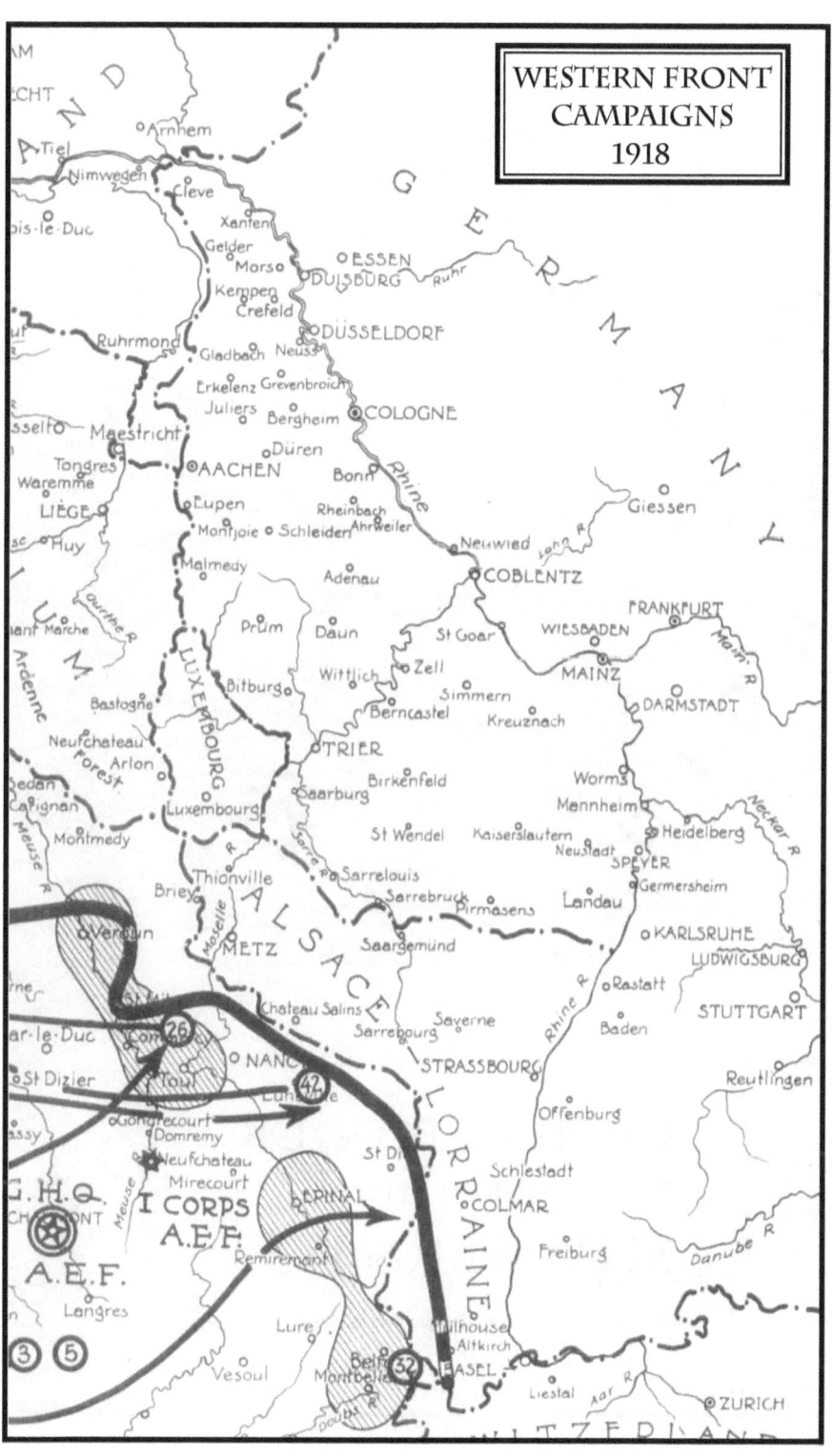

WESTERN FRONT
CAMPAIGNS
1918

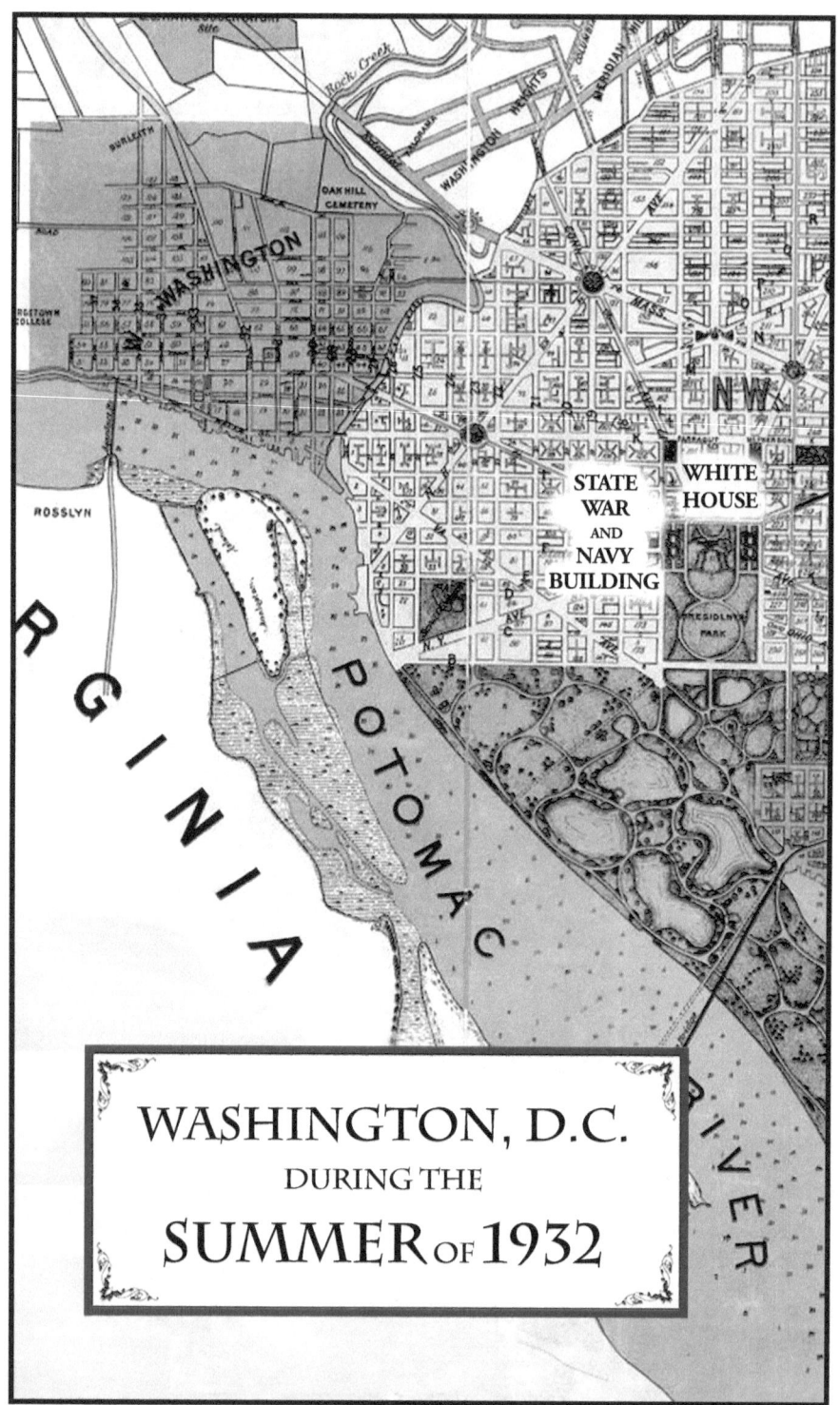

WASHINGTON, D.C.
DURING THE
SUMMER OF 1932

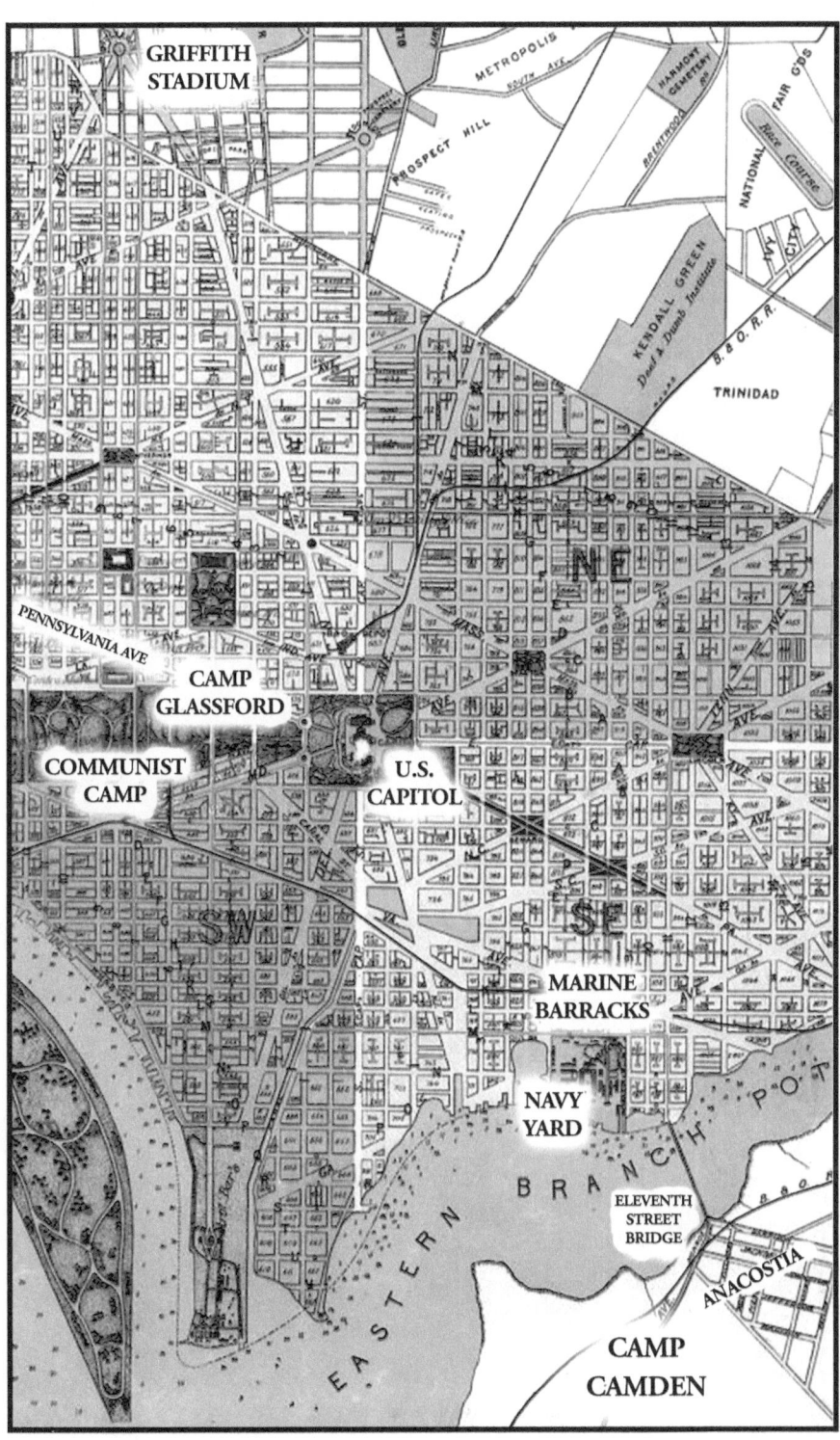

PROLOGUE

NORMAN, OKLAHOMA
DECEMBER 1941

"Get this sluice trough moving! If you don't put a gitty-up on, the war's gonna be over b-b-before we fire a shot!"

Lt. John Keyes shook his head at that pathetic yelp of false courage. He had heard dozens of boasts from the farm boys lining up that week at his induction station, but none sputtered with such an unstrung stammer. The way he figured it, anyone from around these parts trying to join the Navy had to be a little yellow anyway. Most of these dust-grimed crackers in overalls hadn't seen a body of water larger than a washbasin, and half of *them* couldn't swim. He wasn't fooled. All this bragging about steaming across the Pacific to Tokyo was just a cover to avoid the infantry.

"What's the d-d-damn hold-up?" demanded the same shuffling recruit at the head of the line.

The officer didn't bother to look up from the stack of NGCT intelligence tests that he was grading. "Keep your powder dry, cowboy. There'll be plenty of bullets to go around."

Ignored, the agitated recruit bit off an incoherent curse.

A few minutes later, the lieutenant leaned back in his metal chair to take a break from the paperwork. Chilled, he pushed his aviator sunglasses up the bridge of his red nose for cover, closed his eyes, and tried to warm his feet with the memory of Norfolk's sunny beaches. Crackerjack shore duty that had been, until the Japs had to go bomb Pearl Harbor and get him transferred to this Okie Siberia to process enlistments. He yawned and smiled at those Virginia dolls in their skimpy swimsuits, frolicking in the waves—

A frigid blast of prairie air walloped him harder than a Joe Louis left hook.

Roused from his daydream, the lieutenant returned to the test forms, and now his damn pen was frozen. If those pogue geniuses in Washington thought this country was ready to fight a war, they should bunk down a couple of nights at this cattle lick being passed off for a service base. Hell, the whole place was falling apart. Just that morning, wind gusts had collapsed a section of the Naval Training School's armory roof, forcing him to move this human cattle drive to the parade ground. He took out his frustration by thumping the pen's congealed tip against his desk. The cheap casing splintered. He tossed the remnants of the pen over his shoulder and wiped his ink-smeared hands on the brown grass around his boots, muttering a prediction that they'd all be eating out of rice bowls soon if those new anti-aircraft guns didn't last longer than these—

"Those Nips'll be in Frisco by the t-t-time you get us on the boats!"

The lieutenant shot to his feet to read the riot act to the dribble-mouthed hothead who kept hectoring him. His jaw dropped at what stood before him.

A gaunt codger sported a frayed khaki brownshirt, flared cavalry jodhpurs dappled with mud stains, and scuffed black jackboots that reached to his knees. The tall, lanky fellow seemed to be a nervous sort, constantly brushing his shocks of graying blond hair across his mottled head with fingers stained yellow from a chain of cigarette butts trailing behind him.

An ensign down the line stopped passing out medical forms. He raised his arms in mock surrender. "You'd better sound all-hands-on-deck, sir. I think we've been invaded by Mussolini."

The lieutenant stood grinning at what appeared to be a homespun fascist uniform worn by the grumpy sodbuster. "Nah, this one doesn't have enough flesh on the bone to be *El Duce*. I'm thinking he's the *Führer* in spy disguise. He must have cut off his mustache and painted his hair white."

The ensign walked up and fingered a rusty trench whistle that hung from a lanyard around the fellow's gizzard neck. He blew a couple of razzing toots. "You auditioning for the talkies, old-timer? I hear the Signal Corps is looking for a Hitler stand-in to make their movies for the war bonds campaign."

The craggy-faced volunteer glared damnation at the two officers from his steel-blue eyes. "You jabbering harebrains wouldn't have lasted a da-da-day in my army."

"*Your* army?" The lieutenant motioned up the other recruits. "Take a look, boys. Stonewall Jackson has arisen from the dead."

The geezer waited for the serenade of rebel yells behind him to fade. Then, he challenged the two chortling recruiters. "You g-g-gonna get on with this? Or you g-g-gonna keep performing your Abbott and Co-co-costello routine till the war's lost?"

The lieutenant wiped a tear of laughter from his cheek before it could freeze. "How old are you, gramps?"

The man cupped an unsteady hand to his ear. "What's that?"

"Your age!"

"Forty-three."

That claim drew puffs of disbelief from the other recruits.

The lieutenant realized the half-deaf yarn spinner was serious about joining up. He put a stop to the taunts and warned the man, "Lying under oath on a recruitment form is a federal offense."

The jittery volunteer pointed at a blank sheet of paper on the desk. "Write 'er down in duplicate. S-s-send one to Hirohito."

The lieutenant circled him to determine if he looked as gimpy from the rear. "What in God's name happened to you, partner? Appears you got one step in the grave already."

"I've been th-th-through a few rough patches with my health. But I can still fire an Enfield."

"What kind of rough patches?"

The volunteer kept staring at the ground. "It d-d-don't matter none."

"It matters to the U.S. Navy," the lieutenant said. "We're not going let some jag-off slip in just to freeload medical care. A lot of bums are trying to sponge off the government."

The older volunteer clasped his right hand to stifle a spasm. "There's more bums *in* the government these days, from what I've seen."

"You got the palsy?"

In a near whisper, the man admitted, "I was gassed."

"Did you say *gassed?* You forget to turn off your stove, or what?"

"On the Meuse."

The lieutenant stole a look of disbelief at his ensign. He scoffed at the volunteer. "You really expect us to believe that *you* fought in France?"

"Hundred F-f-forty-Sixth Field Artillery."

"And you were discharged?"

"Honorable."

The tale was getting so tall, the lieutenant could hardly see over it. "I suppose you had a rank, too."

"Sergeant."

The lieutenant knew the half-senile crank was just making it all up. Hell of a mess the Army would have to be in to promote such a clipped-winged cull to anything higher than a mess cook. He decided to let him down gently. "Sorry, doughboy, but you're just a bit over the age limit."

"I know my rights. The Navy is t-t-taking men up to age fifty. I ain't moving from this spot until I put my John Hancock on one of those killing contracts."

"Now listen here—"

"I'll go over your head to the stripe in charge of this playground!"

The lieutenant reddened. "You wouldn't pass the physical anyway. And you know it."

The veteran leaned in and squinted at the officer. "What if I f-f-fought in another war *after* France?"

The lieutenant rolled his eyes. "We don't have time for this nonsense. The country hasn't been in a war since 1918."

"The hell it ain't."

One of the boys in the rear of the line yelled up, "Hey Lieutenant, if we're not getting in today, I gotta catch the Greyhound back to Chickasha!"

Lt. Keyes debated how best to get rid of the pest. He was already behind again on the inductions, and the last thing he needed was to piss off the brass by not meeting the daily quota. This ornery buzzard seemed just trigger-happy enough to raise a holy ruckus if the MPs hauled him out. He decided to let the fellow make an even bigger fool of himself in the hope that the humiliation would drive him off. He ordered the other volunteers into a semi-circle, and played along by handing the man a form. "All right, *son*, what's your name?"

The fellow didn't seem to detect the sarcasm. "Walter Waters. Some f-f-folks call me Dubya-Dubya for short. But that ain't quite accurate, because my m-m-middle name is Warfield. Dubya-Dubya-Dubya would possess more authenticity. I'll answer to any of the three appellations that b-b-begin with Dubya."

The lieutenant licked his chapped lips, eager to send the blowhard out the gate with his tail dragging. "Sergeant Waters here—"

"Commander Waters."

"So now you're a commander? We'd better get this roll-call finished before you become emperor."

Waters cracked his knuckles as if itching to throw down. "You're a regular Will Rogers with all the jokes."

The lieutenant sighed at the vast and varied lunacies produced by the human race. He told the other recruits, "Commander Waters here is going tell us how he fought in the Great War of His Imagination." Then, he asked the man, "Who'd you square off against? Hannibal or Napoleon?"

Waters didn't wait to blink. "Mac."

One of the recruits yelled out, "General McClellan?"

Waters spun on the lippy Okie. "There's only one Mac, god-da-da-damn it! And you know who he is!"

Motioning the recruits to silence, the lieutenant shammed an interest. "You *fought* MacArthur. You fight *for* the Germans, did you, Herr Dubya-Dubya?"

The veteran's eyes filmed over, and he turned a woebegone gaze toward the railroad tracks in the distance. "Nah, I led the best American army that ever took the field. Worst thing about this c-c-country is it ain't got no memory for the important things that happen to it."

Baffled by the cryptic lament, the lieutenant glanced across the field and saw several drill squads looking over to see what all the commotion was about. He decided he'd better cut this little charade short before word started spreading downwind that he had lost control of his station. "Listen, Mr. Waters, or whoever you are. I'm going to have to order you to run along now. Or I'll have to call the mental hospital in town and—"

"I'll prove it."

The lieutenant, now really annoyed, set his hands on his hips. "You're going to prove to me that you fought General Douglas MacArthur with an *American* army? How exactly do you plan to do that?"

Waters puffed out his sunken consumptive chest to display two threaded military ribbons pinned to his breast pocket. "If I demonstrate my *bona fides* on the matter, will you let me t-t-take the oath?"

His first plan having backfired, the lieutenant reluctantly decided that letting the man blather his two cents' worth was probably the only way to get rid of him now. "You got five minutes before lunch call. Make it fast."

The other recruits moaned, forced to stay out in the cold even longer now.

The sniggering ensign piled more logs onto the fire in the oil drum.

Waters commandeered the chair behind the desk and placed it in front of the fire. Flicking away the butt of his last Lucky Strike coffin nail, he sat down and reached into his pocket for a plug of tobacco. He stuffed the chaw into his cheek and, satisfied at last with his preparations, waved the recruits forward. "Come on closer, maggots. I ain't g-g-gonna strip the gears in my throat educating your ignorance."

As the grousing recruits stepped in around him, Waters began singing the tune that had always helped calm the hitch in his words, an old big-band number by that top-hatted medicine man of jazz, Ted Lewis:

"There's a new day coming,
As sure as you're born,
A new day coming,
Start tootin' your horn,
The cobbler'll shoe, the baker'll bake,
When the brewer brews, folks,
We'll all get a break.
There's a new day coming,
Coming soon."

Finishing his jingle, Waters creaked up to his feet again and pointed toward the pole that towered over the camp. "In my army, we always c-c-commenced proceedings by honoring the glorious Stars and Stripes."

The lieutenant was still trying to figure out how Waters had sung the ditty without stuttering. He nodded for the younger recruits to humor the veteran, and they twitched off a few shivering, half-hearted salutes to the flag.

Forced to be satisfied with the lackadaisical effort, Waters sat back down and scooted the chair closer to the crackling logs to warm his rheumy knees. He prefaced his story with a condition. "Now listen up, shavetails. You're g-g-gonna promise me one thing."

"What's that, grandpa?" asked a recruit. "You need a latrine break already?"

Waters ran a warning finger across the seated ranks. "None of you's are gonna b-b-back outa serving after you hear what I got to say."

The volunteers traded confused glances. Finally, they nodded just to get on with whatever it was they were about to endure.

Waters wiped a seep of tobacco spittle from the corner of his mouth. "You ever heard those rich b-b-birds on Wall Street say teach a man to fish and you feed him forever?"

The recruits didn't have a clue what he was talking about.

Waters looked toward the sky, as if struck by a vision. "That d-d-day in Galilee, when the Good Lord gave His Sermon on the Mount, how come He d-d-didn't teach the multitudes to fish and bake bread, instead of just conjuring up those loaves and fillets of sole for them?"

The lieutenant was now worried the dotty veteran would start blaspheming on government property. He tapped on his wristwatch, signaling for Waters to tighten the reins and get on with it.

Yet Waters refused to be prodded off the winding trail of his sermon. "You figure Christ was a c-c-communist, do you? Not following the c-c-capitalist way? Distributing the dole like that to anyone who would listen to Him?"

"Hell, no!" shouted a recruit. "The Almighty ain't a Red!"

Waters picked a stick from the kindling pile. After examining it, he pulled out a pocketknife and began whittling away its bark. "What if the Great Shepherd had fed all the Romans in the world, but left His own d-d-disciples in want? You think the Galileans woulda followed Him to Jerusalem *then*?"

The recruits watched the oscillating pocketknife with alarm, half expecting the shaky veteran to slice off a finger. One of them complained, "This ain't Sunday school, pops! You ever gonna get to the point of this campfire story?"

Waters was sending the chips flying now. "There once lived such a man. A titan of history who f-f-fed a thousand times more multitudes than did Christ. But he couldn't bring himself to give sustenance to his own hungry folk."

"Some Bolshevik, was he?" asked another recruit.

Choked up from the memories, Waters brushed away the chips on the ground with his boot in a play to recover his voice. When he finally swallowed the frog in his throat, he stiffened his neck and insisted, "Farthest thing from it. Turned out he was just an orphan boy with a b-b-big heart. But he came to be surrounded by a dozen Judases for apostles."

"What was his name?"

Waters ballooned his cheeks and shot a black jet of tobacco juice at the ground, nearly splattering the front row. "Hoover."

"You talking about the suction sweeper fella?"

Waters aimed the pocketknife at the numbskull who had just asked that question. "No, junior. I am referring to the man who p-p-put all that Okie dirt *in* your momma's rug, not the one who took it out."

"*President* Hoover?"

Waters nodded. "But long before the d-d-dust twisters blew him into the White House, ol' Herbert found himself in another shitstorm halfway across the world. That's where it all started. With the great Quaker surrounded by millions of starving Chinamen."

Mystified, the recruits just sat staring up at the veteran.

The lieutenant figured he'd regret it, but he asked the question they were all pondering. "*What* started?"

Water reached the whittled end of his stick into the fire. When it took a flame, he flung the crackling stick like a live grenade over the heads of the ducking recruits. "The fight that came *that* close to sparkin' another American Revolution."

Principal Characters

(occupations and ages when first appearing in the main story)

Joe Angelo

Son of a miner in Hazleton, Pennsylvania; 14

Floyd Gibbons

Reporter for the *Minneapolis Daily News*; 20

Pelham Glassford

Plebe, U.S. Military Academy at West Point; 17

Herbert Hoover

Engineer and mining agent; 26

Douglas MacArthur

Yearling, U.S. Military Academy at West Point; 19

Anna Raber

Daughter of a Mennonite pastor in Indiana; 16

Ozzie Taylor

Street musician in Harlem; 12

Walter W. Waters

Son of an Idaho laborer and land agent; 10

PART ONE

NO MAN'S LAND
1900 – 1919

Don't fear, all is clear
That's the life of a stroll
When you take a patrol
Out in No Man's Land
Ain't it grand?
Out in No Man's Land

— lyrics by James Reese Europe and Noble Sissle,
369th Infantry Regiment (U.S.)

TIENTSIN, CHINA
JULY 1900

Tremble thee before the Lord.

Bert Hoover's fevered brain had been keening for hours with the admonition that his pastor mother always invoked when sending him as a boy to the Quaker meeting halls. Crouched behind a low mud wall, he examined the raised purple veins in his shaking hands and wondered if his soul was preparing to shed the flesh. His thoughts were clouded, and the periphery of his vision was starting to tunnel. Exhausted and unsteady from the vertigo, he placed a palm to his sweating forehead. Dysentery was spreading rapidly among the families of the Western diplomats and businessmen who remained trapped with him inside the besieged legation compound.

Was he fated to die just when his industry and perseverance were about to bear fruit? No, he could not accept that God would be so wasteful with His earthly resources. Once before, as a child, he had been mortally sick, infected with the croup. On that cold Iowa morning twenty-four years ago, he had given up his spirit, only to be resuscitated by his uncle, a physician. Blessed with that miracle, his birth parents, not long before their untimely deaths, came to believe that the Almighty had brought him back to serve some great purpose.

He fished the chained watch from his breast pocket and squinted at its hands under the diffused moonlight. It was nearly three a.m., that dreaded slough of morning when the fanatical occupiers of Tientsin often whipped themselves into a spiritual frenzy and stormed this suburban settlement. Posted here a year ago as the chief engineer for the London mining firm of Bewick, Moreing & Company, he could never have imagined that he would become trapped in the middle of a brutal civil war.

Now, fighting to stay awake, he peered out across the maze of lagoons and paddies toward the Old City. Thousands of Chinese had massed inside its walls, vowing to drive all foreigners from the country. Behind him, in the warehouse that served as their makeshift fortress, his new bride Lou gripped a pistol and stood guard over the other women and children. He worried how much longer she could—

"Thee is a fine Friend."

He recoiled into the shadows, startled by that discarnate voice. Had his dead father's Inner Light come forth to give praise that his son had finally been brought prostrate before the Almighty's terrible glory? Sensing a looming presence, he turned to find a shadowy figure emerge through the smoky haze. As the mists cleared, he released a held breath.

Kneeling down next to him was a young Marine lieutenant with slightly crossed eyes separated by a bruised, triangular nose that resembled a locomotive grille. "Didn't mean to fright you, Mr. Hoover. I thought a little humor might help."

Hoover braced against the wall to recover his balance. "I'm afraid you have me at a disadvantage on your meaning, Lieutenant."

"I come from Pennsylvania Quaker stock. My father was a congressman. Served on the House Naval Affairs Committee. One day, a fellow believer, disgusted with my father's involvement with war legislation, yelled at him, 'Thee is a fine Friend!'"

Hoover nodded. His own choice of a career in ore extraction, some of which made its way to the military, had confronted him with that same challenge of faith's demands. "And what did your father offer as a defense?"

"He told the constituent, '*Thee* is a damn Fool!'"

Hoover muffled a coughed laugh, the first one he had enjoyed in weeks.

The officer extended his hand. "Smedley Butler. One of the Brits in the compound mentioned that you were a Quaker. I decided to find you and make your acquaintance."

Heartened to find a fellow believer at such time of crisis, Hoover shook Butler's hand quickly, hoping to hide his unsteadiness. He studied the officer's wide grin that betrayed the brashness of youth. "If you don't mind my asking, Lieutenant, how old are you?"

"Officially… nineteen."

Hoover calculated that the officer must have been in the service for at least three years to attain that rank. "I guess you had a little congressional pull to get in under age."

Lt. Butler wouldn't looked at him directly, an admission of guilt.

"So, what *is* a pacifist Quaker doing in the Marines?"

"I come from the hot-tempered branch of the Society, I guess. Both of my grandpas joined the Union army to defend Gettysburg. My ma tried to drill the dream out of me, but I'd already heard too many battle stories. When the Spanish blew up the *Maine*, I was off the next day to the recruiting station."

Hoover smiled ruefully, remembering how his own mother, before leaving him an orphan at the age of nine, had told neighbors of her hope that he would devote his life to the ministry. "I suppose we've both disappointed our mothers with our chosen vocations."

Lt. Butler inched his eyes over the mud barricade. "Tell you the truth, ever since we got off the boat from the Philippines, I haven't had time to think about my ma, let alone put two thoughts together. You mind telling me what all this ruckus is about?"

Hoover was stunned. This officer and his nine hundred fellow Marines of the 9th U.S. Infantry, which had arrived in the port a few days ago, had apparently been kept in the dark about the deteriorating situation here. "Military plans still trickle down in drips, I see."

"The brass always plays its hand close to the vest."

Hoover found a stick and drew a crude map of Tientsin in the mud. "Short answer is, the entire country has gone insane. That city out there guards the approach to the imperial capitol at Peking, which is a three-day march up river. We're surrounded by a mob of zealots who call themselves Boxers."

"You mean … like prize fighters?"

Hoover nodded grimly. "They use their fists, all right, and any club they can find. They're mostly unemployed soldiers and dockworkers, abandoned by the Empress Dowager to starve. They practice martial arts in their temples and believe they make themselves invincible to bullets."

"Why doesn't the Chinese Army knock some heads?"

"The Dowager just sits in her Forbidden City eating candies while those anarchists out there murder Christian missionaries and converts. Many of the government soldiers have deserted to the Boxer side."

Informed of the difficulties facing him, Lt. Butler lost his grin. "Are you a God-fearing man, Mr. Hoover?"

Hoover thought back on the many nights when he had risked his life carrying fresh water for his fellow besieged civilians from the treatment plant outside these walls. "I've been getting some practice at it." Behind him, in the darkness, he heard the rustling of boots and rifles. "Why do you ask?"

Lt. Butler ratcheted the bolt on his carbine to confirm that it was in working order. "I have a confession. Making your acquaintance wasn't the only reason I came out here to find you. … In twenty minutes, we're going to launch a night assault."

Hoover nearly swore, but caught himself. "You can't be serious."

The officer nodded. "We've been ordered to attack the South Gate with the British, Japanese, and French troops. The Russians and Germans will circle around the city and attack the East Gate."

Hoover grasped the officer's shoulder to plead for him to reconsider. "There are fifty thousand Chinese inside that city. We have less than seven thousand troops. A frontal assault would be suicide. I've been calling for action for weeks, but that was before the Boxers brought in reinforcements. The wiser course now would be to get us out and march to Peking."

Lt. Butler could only shrug. He had no authority to countermand the order. Keeping his eyes trained on the walls a half-mile away, he confided, "You being an engineer and all, word back in the compound is that you know that ground out there better than anyone."

Hoover pointed him toward the most direct approach. "I've walked it many times. You'd have to navigate a dozen blocks of blind alleys and dangerous turns between the shacks. Then there's another miserable stretch of marshes followed by a narrow causeway. One misstep in this darkness and a man could fall and drown in one of those sinkholes out—" He froze with his mouth slacking, only then perceiving the real reason for the officer's confession.

"Major Waller was wondering if you'd be willing to guide us."

Before Hoover could press his protest, the wall on both sides of him filled with khaki-clad Marines, armed for battle. Hovering over his junior officer's shoulder, the major who had sent the request waited for an answer.

Hoover glanced down at his frayed black jacket and was struck by how slovenly he looked next to their crisp, clean khaki uniforms. Once the Marines hit open ground, the Boxers would ignite their torches on the walls, and he would stand out like a raisin in a bowl of oatmeal. He held no illusion about what would happen if he were captured. He had seen the mutilated bodies of Christian missionaries dangling from hooks in the pagan temples, flayed alive and left to hang upside down to slowly bleed to death. This wasn't exactly what he'd had in mind when he left Stanford eight years ago to find a life of adventure.

"Sir?" Lt. Butler prodded, reminding him of the need for a quick decision.

Hoover could hear his mother's stern voice reproaching him for even considering a breach of her Quaker principles. He stole a glance over his shoulder at the Victorian gables of Gordon Hall, where the American and British women and children, accompanied by hundreds of frightened Chinese Christian refugees, hurried down into the municipal crypt. They were singing *Nearer My God To Thee* to prepare for the coming onslaught of shells. Silently arguing with his mother, he asked her how he could allow these Marines to risk their lives while he cowered here in relative safety.

At last, despite feeling woozy from the fever, he nodded his agreement to guide them. "I suppose I, too, will be a damn fool, rather than a fine Friend."

Lt. Butler shook his new scout's hand in gratitude. Then, signaling to his fellow officers, he led Hoover toward the boarded entry to the no-man's land beyond the legation settlement. Behind them, the Marines filed up, two by two, checking their weapons one last time.

Before launching off, Hoover warned the leathernecks that the grassy stretch of open marshland ahead hid a thousand sinkholes and rice sluices. "Five hundred yards past low shacks, the Chinese snipers on the towers will see our movement. Once we reach the low ground near the arsenal, don't stop until you get under the range of their guns on the walls."

Major Waller tipped the brim of his cap, the command to advance.

The Marines fingered their triggers—and Lt. Butler kicked the settlement gate open. Hoover led them on the double-quick through the warren of shacks. Zigzagging from alley to alley, he heard the night sky open up with rifle cracks, first in dozens, then cascading to hundreds of bullets pinging the tin roofs and thudding the rotted wood. Cries erupted behind him. He turned and saw several Marines drop as if scythed at the ankles. Lt. Butler clasped his new scout's forearm and pulled him forward under rifle and artillery fire so heavy that it sounded like thunder.

Feeling his heart thumping in his chest, Hoover shouted, "Give me a rifle!"

An eerie calmness came over him. Had he just asked for a *weapon*?

Before he could question the morality of that spontaneous decision, one of the Marines retrieved an Enfield from a fallen comrade and thrust it into his hands. He stood frozen, expecting for God to test his bravado by bringing him face to face with a hatchet-armed Boxer. But his blood was up, and he was about to fall in with the closing ranks when someone shoved him off toward the rear shacks.

"Back thee go to the wall, Friend!" Lt. Butler shouted at him. "We'll take it from here!"

Bullets hissed around Hoover's ears, close enough to make the plastered hair on his scalp bristle. Needing no encouragement, he hurried back toward the settlement and ducked into an alley as the Marines surged toward the high walls around Tientsin. Relegated to the Western compound, he watched through a crack in the boards as Colonel Robert Meade, son of the hero of Gettysburg, walked courageously into battle wrapped like a mummy, his hands and feet so swollen that he had ordered them covered in gauze. A whirl of untold minutes passed as the Marines scrambled across the low rice fields, dodging the grave markers of a cemetery. Some sank knee deep in the mud, others abandoned their mired boots and, barefoot, charged on. He had never seen the flags of so many countries flying together for one cause.

A half-hour into the desperate fighting, the allied attack ground to a halt.

The surviving Marines now stood exposed, sucked down into the paddies and easy targets for the Boxer snipers. From his protected vantage, Hoover could only stand back and pray for the boys who just minutes earlier had been slapping his back appreciatively. Seeing the leathernecks falling in scores on their left flank, British troopers tried to come to their aid, but the heavy Chinese artillery on the walls repulsed their effort. The gates of the city were flung open, and hordes of death-defying Boxers poured out, raving to take prisoners. The remnants of the Marine unit regrouped and fought fiercely, but as the hours of bloodshed wore on, the broken allied lines were finally driven into a retreat.

Lt. Butler was one of the last of the leathernecks to fall back. He staggered toward the legation wall and dropped to his knees, grasping his thigh. Hoover rushed to the officer and motioned up two medics to help carry him back to the fortified warehouse.

"Your Yankee grandfathers would have been proud of you," Hoover whispered. "But I'm not so sure about your mother."

Roused from his slumber by that ambivalent praise, Lt. Butler opened his eyes and found Hoover sitting next to his bed in a makeshift hospital. "I was half-expecting to see a Chinese face."

"You're lucky to see a face at all," Hoover said. "Two of your men earned the Medal of Honor yesterday. I told Colonel Meade that you deserved one, but he said the Corps doesn't give them to officers. I guess you'll have to be satisfied with a new nickname."

"Whatever it is, please don't let it be—"

"The Fighting Quaker." Hoover grinned at the trouble that moniker would surely cause the young Marine during his promising military career.

Levering to his elbows, the officer looked around the ward and saw dozens of wounded Marines on both sides of him. "What happened? I blacked out."

"You'll be up before you know it," Hoover said. "Probably in time to join the march to Peking."

Lt. Butler's wan face suddenly brightened. "Peking? You mean ... we drove those bastards out of Tientsin?"

Hoover nodded, granting the brave Marine the right to indulge in a little coarse language. "Late last night, after we were thrown back, the Japanese circled the city and blew open the South Gate. The Boxers were so stunned, they ran north."

Lt. Butler thrust his fist in the air, but he quickly tempered his celebration when he noticed that Hoover seemed troubled. "What's the sour mug about?"

Hoover found it difficult to talk about what he had witnessed that morning when entering the shattered city with the allied troops. "The Chinese who fought on our side murdered their own people until the streets ran red with blood. The corpses were piled up to the windows. We found some of the defenders so starved, they were eating human flesh."

"I reckon people will do the unthinkable if they're hungry enough," Lt. Butler said. "I saw the same thing in the Philippines. A man's got to eat."

Hoover understood the barbaric effects of deprivation all too well, but he still had difficulty coming to terms with this madness. Only a few days ago, thousands of Chinese had joined the cruel Boxers for a few helpings of stolen food. Now, with the shocking fall of Tientsin, these same peasants and unemployed soldiers were turning on their defeated saviors, butchering them in the streets like cattle in a slaughterhouse. And the natives weren't the only ones fickle with their loyalty. Many of his fellow Westerners had abandoned their innocent Chinese servants, accusing them of treason and subjecting them to hysterical witch-hunts. During these past weeks, he had stared death in the face, and in the process, he had learned more about himself than he had ever wished to know. When his Quaker pacifism was tested, he had proven to be a damn poor Friend.

Hearing footsteps, he pushed his chair back and stood up to allow a medic to administer a dose of morphine to the wounded officer. The needle's plunge into Lt. Butler's leg shook Hoover from his self-pity; he braced his wounded friend with a hand to his shoulder until the painkiller eased the throbbing.

The officer smiled up at him, as if reading his mind. "Makes one glad to be an American, don't it, Mr. Hoover? Folks back home would never let their neighbors starve like those poor people out there."

Fighting the grip in his throat, Hoover shook the officer's hand to say goodbye. "That is why, Lt. Butler, we must toil tirelessly to spread the healing balm of capitalism and Christian industry around the world. These poor Chinese peasants have never tasted freedom and liberty. I still firmly believe that so long as a man is allowed to take full heed of his destiny, he will always turn to the better angel of his soul, even in times of trial."

2

WEST POINT, NEW YORK
DECEMBER 1900

Astrapping six-foot-three but just one month over seventeen, Pelham Glassford held the dubious distinction of being both the tallest and youngest member of his first-year class. Harassed constantly about his large head, jug-handle ears, and loping gait, he usually marched with the taller flankers. But on this cold morning, he had been reassigned to a squad filled with the shortest cadets, apparently to make him contemplate the likelihood that his impressive noggin would one day offer an inviting target for an enemy rifle sight. As he glided across the Plain with the woolen pom-pom of his tarbucket hat fluttering in the stiff Hudson breeze, he felt like a creaking sequoia towering above tumbling balls of sagebrush.

He took advantage of an "eyes right" command to steal a glance across the field where a yearling, Douglas MacArthur, strode with grim determination toward Cullum Memorial Hall. MacArthur always kept his slender, six-foot frame arched as if posing for a statue, and his haughty currant eyes, framed under a plaster of black hair parted down the middle like a trench, perpetually challenged other cadets to a silent duel of destinies. The Southerners particularly despised him, sensing in his cool condescension the bravado that his decorated father, Captain Arthur MacArthur, had displayed against their Confederate kinsmen atop Missionary Ridge.

Conger Pratt, Glassford's best friend, sniggered from the row marching behind him. "Look sharp, Hap. Boadicea of the Barracks is flanking us."

Glassford rolled his eyes. As if MacArthur's marble-soldier act wasn't arrogance enough, here now came his meddling mother, the ubiquitous Pinky, swishing up the path in her billowing skirts, ten paces behind the son she doted over. On the first day of MacArthur's matriculation, the overbearing woman had moved into Craney's Hotel to supervise his advancement and to make certain that her rival, the mother of Cadet Ulysses S. Grant III, did not pull rank. It had taken Pinky only a week to become mother hen to the cadets, cooking them lunches on Sundays while trawling for school gossip.

And yet, despite the jealous carpings of his classmates, Glassford secretly admired "Dauntless Doug," the nickname used only behind the cadet's back. He understood the pressures that MacArthur endured in coming from a military family. His own father, Col. William Glassford, had been a prominent Signal Corps officer in Apache country, and his older brother was a squid at Annapolis, on track to become an admiral.

Pratt, nearly stepping on Glassford's heels, whispered his best imitation of their engineering instructor's Dakota German twang. "Yooonga mahn, hal-lul many plebes dooos it take to deeg a luh-treen?"

Glassford nearly burst a neck vein trying not to lose his practiced marching face. Pratt was always scheming to get him nailed with another quill. Glassford was having enough trouble trying to keep his step consistent at thirty inches. Performing his best imitation of a ventriloquist through gritted teeth, he muttered back across his shoulder at Pratt, "Pipe down."

Yet Pratt persisted with the tight-lipped horseplay. "Hal-lul many?"

Marching aside Pratt, their bunkmate, Snitz Gruber, whispered the punch line. "None, suh. Latrine digging is a fourth-year course."

Glassford choked as he struggled to swallow his laughter.

"Cadet Happy of New Mexico!"

Glassford's square of cadets came to a shambling halt. Their drillmaster, a third-year cow, was now spitting mad. The provocative nickname "Spoons" had been pinned on the little Southern martinet in memory of its preceding owner, Union General Benjamin Butler, who, during his occupation of New Orleans, had commandeered for his personal profit all of the silver cutlery belonging to that Confederate city's wealthiest families. Glassford dared not look directly at Spoons, but on his periphery he caught a flash of the bile flaming up in the Southern cadet's liverish face.

Rising on his toes, Spoons crawled Glassford until their chinstraps nearly touched. "Did ah not pronounce your name correctly, Cadet Happy … ?"

"Glassford, sir."

"You're saying ah'm wrong?"

"Sir, no."

"Ah'm thoroughly confused, Cadet Happy. You certainly looked happy just a moment ago. Weren't you laughing?"

Glassford glanced at Pratt and Gruber, hoping for support, but neither flinched from their braced stances. Finally, he admitted, "Yes, sir."

"Ah'm told you ah quite the"—Spoons hissed the next word like a snake spitting venom—"ar-*teest.*"

Glassford silently vowed to ring Pratt's neck for getting him into this fix. He had already earned several demerits for prankstering, and now another one seemed inevitable. "I just doodle a bit, sir. Not very good at it."

"Nonsense! Modesty does not become such a famous painter. What is your specialty? Buxom nudes? Caricatures of upperclassmen, perhaps?"

"Landscapes, sir."

"Landscapes, you say?" Spoons drew his sword and handed it to Glassford to be used as a stylus. "Perhaps you would like to sketch for us the hallowed ground of Chancellorsville."

"Sir?"

"You remember Chancellorsville, don't you, Cadet Happy? Ah'd very much like to see a Yankee artistic rendition of that slope where General Lee broke the Union right flank."

From his position with the next platoon over, a first classman from Maine overheard the exchange. He walked up and, taking the sword from Glassford, shoved the weapon back into Spoons's sheath. With a sharp glare, he told his Southern classmate, "Until you earn *your* doctorate in history, Spoons, why don't you leave the Civil War lessons to Instructor Adams."

Spoons shunted the Maine cadet aside. "This is my platoon, Jenks."

The Maine cadet studied Glassford with evident sympathy, but finally waved off the confrontation as not worth the effort. He walked back to his own platoon, whose cadets stood watching the challenge with a mixture of anticipation and alarm.

Pleased at having held the field against the Northerner, Spoons turned a triumphant smirk back on Glassford. "If you don't feel like gracing us with your flourishes, Mr. Happy, perhaps you will regale us again with the chronicle of how you garnered your most distinctive appellation. Ah understand the story has become somewhat of a legend."

There was no way this was going to end well, Glassford knew. He had no control over his mannerism, didn't even know when he did it: but his bunkmates had warned him that he always grinned whenever he got nervous. Now, as the Louisiana cadet bellowed grits-laced breaths into his face, he did his damnedest to plaster a frown.

But a geyser of chuckling was again trying to force its way up his throat.

"Ah'll prime the pump for you, cognizant as ah am of your adorable shyness. It was your first day at the Point. You take it from there."

Glassford resolved to get the ordeal over with quickly as possible. "Sir, I had my hands full of my gear, sir! I dropped my shoes, sir! Reached down to pick them up and dropped my washbasin, sir! I managed to recover my shoes, but in the process I lost my basin, and I bent down to retrieve the item sir! But I dropped my mattress and broom, sir!"

"Sounds like you had the dropsies. Ah thought only poultry and Burnside's New York Irish scum at Fredericksburg got the dropsies. Or was it the runnsies first, then the dropsies?"

The Maine first classman stood listening to the ridicule from the next square over. Unwilling to endure any more of it, he ambled back to Spoons and, with a condescending smirk, whispered to the Southerner's ear, "You clay-for-brains cracker. Do you even know this plebe's first name?"

Spoons edged his hand toward his sword's hilt, itching to avenge the insult. "Of course ah know his first name. It's Pelham. What's it to you, Jenks?"

"Remind me again. Who manned the Confederate twelve-pounders on Marye's Heights at Fredricksburg?"

Invited to recite that cherished rebel lore, Spoons preened like a gray peacock and replied, "The best damned artilleryman in American history. The Gallant Pel—" Too late to avoid embarrassment, a synapse of discovery fired in his brain.

The other upperclassmen chortled at how Spoons had assumed all these many weeks that Glassford was a Northerner.

Glassford blenched. He had hoped to keep secret the fact that he had been named for his ancestor, John Pelham, the boy wonder of Lee's army. To steady himself, he fixed his gaze on the distant Doric column of Battle Monument, whose plaque had been cast from the melting of fifty Confederate cannon. He never passed it without wondering if its bronze had once been touched by his own flesh and blood. He exhaled a despairing sigh, knowing that he would now be subjected to the same harsh scrutiny suffered by cadets MacArthur and Grant.

Yet the revelation of Glassford's pedigree did not improve Spoons's mood. The drillmaster turned toward the target of his wrath again, glaring a silent accusation of treason at Glassford for not having admitted the connection sooner. "Do you remember my question, goat?"

"Yes, sir!"

"Get to the *dénouement*, then. We're all atwitter with anticipation."

"Sir, First Classman Burns tore into me that day for my clumsiness."

"And what was your response to such an unforgivable insult?"

Glassford braced for the usual reaction. "Sir, I began laughing and couldn't stop. I was then given the name 'Happy.'"

Spoons sneered at him. "Laughing can be a fatal weakness in a soldier. Some buffalo hunter may one day mistake you for a hyena."

Glassford coiled every facial muscle into a held frown. "Yes, sir!"

"Get back in line."

Glassford turned, gargling down another nervous laugh.

Spoons spun back on his heels. "Oh, one more thing, Cadet Happy. Ah'm told you engage, from time to time, in conversation with Cadet MacArthur. Has he become your mentor?"

A frisson of apprehension bristled through the ranks, and Glassford could feel the cadets squaring off in two opposing armies. His mind raced to come up with a defusing tactic. He saw Spoons shoot an apprehensive glance at the administration building, where MacArthur was heading with his mother. In minutes, MacArthur would be placed under oath to give testimony to a special military court of inquiry ordered by President McKinley into hazing of plebes, a tradition as old as the Corps itself. All hell had broken loose two weeks ago when a former cadet, Oscar Booz, died of injuries inflicted by upperclassmen. The scandal had enraged the nation, and now the Academy was under siege.

As he watched MacArthur approach Cullum Hall's arched doors, Spoons shouted an order at Glassford, "Recite the Code!"

"Never lie, sir."

"And more importantly?"

Glassford suddenly understood the purpose of this bracing. He was being singled out as a pretext for Spoons to launch a last sortie of desperation, the time-honored Southern tactic embraced in the trenches of Petersburg and on the killing fields of Franklin. The upperclassman apparently hoped that another repetition of the unwritten tenet here on the Plain would somehow reverberate through MacArthur's consciousness in that military courtroom.

After Booz, MacArthur had been the second most controversial hazing victim in the school's history. That previous year, a cadet friend of Spoons's—Albert Dockery of Mississippi—had led a group of upperclassmen in enforcing the infamous "soiree" on MacArthur. The ritual had involved bracing MacArthur rigid for hours, eagling him with deep knee bends over broken glass, and demanding that he recite over and over his father's military record. Overcome by convulsions, MacArthur had been in such grueling pain during the soiree that, unable to raise his arms, he had begged his tent mate to place a blanket in his mouth so that his screams could not be heard.

Now, months later, the politicians in Washington were calling for the heads of those cadets responsible for the abuse. And before this day was over, five generals sitting on the court of inquiry would demand that MacArthur identify their names. Newspapermen had been sniffing around the school all week to get a scoop on the hazing scandal. The entire nation was champing for retribution. If Congress and the president were not satisfied with the thoroughness of the investigation, budget appropriations for the Academy might be cut. Like every cadet on that field, Glassford wondered which code MacArthur would follow—the written or unwritten one?

"Well?" Spoons demanded with a hint of desperation in his voice. "Yell it out so that even the most distant cadet can hear."

"Sir!" Glassford shouted. "Never betray the Corps!"

Spoons glanced toward Cullum Hall to see if the reminder had hit its mark. But MacArthur walked on through the doors without turning, insolent in his refusal to acknowledge the veiled warning. Ignored by the one cadet who held the power to ruin his friend's career, Spoons angrily dismissed the plebes under his command to lunch.

While his classmates hurried off for the mess hall, Glassford held back and watched the windows of the courtroom. That summer, during his own Beast Barracks, he too had been hazed, forced to drink Tabasco sauce until he was so sick that he had to spend a week in the infirmary. MacArthur had visited him during that trying time, but neither had brought up the subject of hazing since that day. Despite the threats and demands from the superintendent, Glassford had never revealed the identity of the cadets who had forced him to gulp down the searing sauce that nearly ruined his stomach.

But standing up to a lone general was one thing; facing down the national press, Congress, and the President of the United States was quite another.

As Major General John R. Brooke gaveled the court of inquiry to order, MacArthur, sitting alone at the witness table, grimaced and fought back a surge of nausea. He had not slept for three nights, unstrung by the impossible dilemma before him. If he lied under oath, he could be found criminally liable, and worse, be denied a career in the military. Yet if he told the truth and gave up Dockery and the other cadets who had hazed him, he might be ostracized, never to realize his dream of becoming a respected leader of the Corps.

Under the inquiry rules, he had the right to be accompanied by counsel, but his mother had insisted on attending instead. He stole a glance over his shoulder at her, sitting three rows back. Fearing what she might blurt out against the judges, he prayed that she would not shame him as a son who required her constant protection. Seeking a brief distraction from his worries, he looked up at the towering walls that held paintings of famous Civil War generals. Staring down at him in judgment were Meade, Sedgwick, Slocum, and Thomas—the Rock of Chickamauga—whom his own father had served. He understood tactics well enough to know why the court of inquiry had been convened in this cavernous new hall. The judges were evoking the ghosts of glories past, hoping to cower him into breaking.

The side benches were filled with New York and Washington correspondents who had been filing daily front-page stories on the scandal. He tried to imagine his father, in Manila serving as that country's governor-general, reading the account of his testimony in the papers. He held himself rigid in the chair, setting his teeth to shove back the excruciating pain in his lower back, a constant companion from his boyhood. Hundreds of hours of special exercises had allowed him to overcome the spinal curvature that had threatened to deny him admission to the Academy.

And now that dream might be taken from him, through no fault of his.

"Mr. MacArthur," bellowed the mustachioed General Brooke, his hefty girth sashed and his chest festooned with medals. "We have heard the testimonies of other cadets regarding the hazing you suffered last summer. You understand that we are here by order of President McKinley?"

MacArthur pressed his soles against the floor under his table to quell his trembling. "Yes, sir."

"And that you are under oath?"

"Yes, sir."

"Do you remember the names of any of the upperclassmen who hazed you?"

"Yes, sir."

"Give their names."

MacArthur pulled a kerchief from his breast pocket and daubed the beads of sweat collecting on his brow. "General, is it absolutely necessary that I give these names, sir? I don't see that they have any bearing upon the investigation of Cadet Booz's death, sir."

The newspaper reporters scribbled down that protest in their note pads.

The military judges leaned forward, stunned that a cadet would dare to instruct them on what evidence was relevant. "This is not an ordinary examination, Mr. MacArthur," Lt. General Nelson Miles warned. "You are to reply to all of the questions as they are put to you."

MacArthur sat frozen in silence, his mind a blank, until he felt a tug at his sleeve. He turned to find one of the spectators in the row behind him passing up a folded sheet of paper.

"Do you require a moment to collect yourself?" General Brooke asked him.

MacArthur fumbled nervously with the message he had just been handed. "If I might refer to my notes, sir?"

"Quickly," General Brooke ordered.

Hiding it under the table, MacArthur unfolded a sheet of stationery from Craney's Hotel. On it, he found a poem, apparently written during these past few minutes by his mother:

Do you know that your soul is of my soul such a part
That you seem to be fiber and core of my heart?
None other can pain me as you, son, can do;
None other can please me or praise me as you.
Remember the world will be quick with its blame
If shadow or shame ever darken your name.
Like mother, like son, is saying so true.
The world will judge largely of mother by you.
Be this then your task, if task it shall be
To force this proud world to do homage to me.
Be sure it will say, when its verdict you've won
She reaps as she sowed: "This man is her son."

He saw that she had hastily added a postscript at the bottom of the page: *Never lie. Never tattle.* His hands shook as he refolded the paper and slid it into his breast pocket.

"Mr. MacArthur, may we have your answer?" General Brooke demanded. "Which upperclassmen hazed you?"

MacArthur clutched his mother's missive for strength. What would it really matter if he gave up one of the perpetrators? Everyone knew that Dockery had been an instigator of the hazing. Naming that troublemaker wouldn't really be tattling, not if the commandant already knew the guilty cadet's identity. Why should he suffer, and the real culprit go free? He had done nothing wrong. Finally, with his voice lowered, he answered, "Mr. Dockery, sir."

"Who else?"

"That is all I can say to you, sir. There were other cadets. They have since left the corps."

General Brooke was becoming visibly annoyed by this cat-and-mouse game of refusal and surrender. "Who were they?"

"Mr. Boswell, Mr. Barry, and Mr. Devall, sir."

The judges conferred, whispering with stern faces.

MacArthur tried to slow his breathing. Taught the ways of military politics by his father, he had chosen to walk the razor's edge, giving up a few names to appease them. These generals didn't want the full truth, any more than he wanted to reveal it. They simply needed a scapegoat to take back to Congress to show that they had extracted some flesh. The last three cadets he had just identified, all from the Class of 1902, had since left the Academy. They were quitters who didn't deserve protection. Only Dockery was still in school, and that hothead would be no great loss to the country, if it came to his dismissal. Other cadets would also be called to testify on the incident, perhaps even Dockery himself.

Yes, the Mississippi cadet was the burnt offering that God required of him for the survival of the Corps. Had his mother not always told him that he was divinely destined to lead armies in the defense of American freedom? There were times on the battlefield when a few soldiers had to be sacrificed to save the many. A blessed peace now came washing over him. He had held his ground by adopting a tenet of combat that Washington and Grant and Lee had been forced to accept many times. This, his first encounter with men who had stared down death at Antietam and Spotsylvania and—

The gavel banged, causing him to flinch.

"This court will stand recessed," General Brooke ordered. "Take the witness to quarters."

MacArthur came to his feet and arched his aching back to attention. Were they retiring to decide to place him under arrest for insubordination? Feeling faint, he looked over his shoulder again at his mother.

She stood radiant with the glow of approval.

That night in the mess hall, Glassford circled his table of ten standing cadets, serving as their gunner. As the waiters brought in pitchers of water and iced tea, he quickly inspected the plates to make sure the glazed images of the warrior goddess Athena were spotless. An upperclassman shouted for the cadets to be seated, and they perched on the front of their chairs, prepared for an order to rise at any moment.

Three bites into the meal, the din of conversation silenced.

Glassford risked turning his head in time to see MacArthur stride through the doors and take his usual seat at the table traditionally occupied by the baseball team. A murmur of surprise echoed across the hammer-beamed hall. Some of the cadets had expected him to be arrested or expelled for refusing to fully testify, never to step foot in this hall again. From across the aisle, Glassford tried to divine from MacArthur's steely expression the outcome of that afternoon's testimony. Did his return mean that he had given up the names? He stole a glance at the Southern cadets sitting at the next table over. Spoons and Dockery, wound tight as cannon fuses, kept their eyes pinned on their nemesis.

Assured that there were no instructors or tacs in the hall, the first captain of the Corps stood up and locked the doors. Then, he marched to the baseball table and, standing at the head, demanded, "You have a report for us, Cadet MacArthur?"

MacArthur pushed away his plate and rose slowly. He set his heels together, angling his toes at a forty-five degree angle and curling his fingers at attention. He waited for several seconds, like an actor building apprehension for a crucial scene. Careful not to reveal the specifics of his testimony, he announced, "I have not, nor will I ever, betray the Corps."

The cadets traded searching glances, not certain what that grand but oblique pronouncement meant. The first captain didn't seem eager to cross-examine MacArthur on the details of the inquiry, no doubt fearing a reprimand for trying to influence the proceedings. It crossed Glassford's mind that someone in MacArthur's position might view upholding the Corps as requiring the cadets in question to be sacrificed for the greater good. But he wasn't about to offer that suggestion, at least not to an upperclassman.

One by one, the cadets, choosing to believe that MacArthur had stonewalled the judges, took up their knives and the pounded the tables in approval.

MacArthur threw back his shoulders, beaming with pride at being boot licked for the second time in his career. The first honor had come during those days immediately after his hazing, when he had withstood the ordeal without complaint. As if this acclaim was sustenance enough, he walked across the hall without touching his food, stopping only at one table to nod an acknowledgment to the friend who had suffered a similar hazing.

Glassford reached out his hand in congratulations, but MacArthur waited until the appropriate gesture was offered. Remembering his place, Glassford shoved his neck into his collarbone and saluted the more senior cadet.

MacArthur jutted out his chin and returned the salute. "Always remember the Code, Cadet Glassford."

As MacArthur marched down the aisle toward the doors, Albert Dockery stood from his bench to confront his rival, trying to divine from his inscrutable eyes the truth of what had happened that afternoon. MacArthur merely stared back at the Mississippian in silent defiance. Finally, Dockery stepped aside and allowed MacArthur to walk from the mess hall.

Smiling with pride for his fellow victim of hazing, Glassford glanced over his shoulder at the Southern cadets. They were still glaring at the swinging doors, as if not sure what to make of the encounter.

3

WEISER, IDAHO
JUNE 1906

"*ust* my d-d-daggum luck … just *my* d-d-daggum luck."

Tented in hogwasher bib-alls three sizes too large, ten-year-old Walter Waters walked barefoot down the railroad spur that led to his mining town at the bend of the Snake River. He'd lost track of how many hours he'd been tramping over these barren hills that morning, mouthing the drill that Missus Parsons in the church choir had assigned him to smooth out his speaking hiccups. Just as she had instructed, he once again drew a long breath through his nose and, settling his tongue against the back of his teeth, changed the pedal pressure on his words.

"Just my *daggum* luck."

Yep, he was getting pretty dang good at spitting out *that* phrase with all its variations. Probably because he heard it growled every Friday night when his old man came home sheets to the wind from the fat chinaman's saloon.

Fact was, *Just my daggum luck* coulda been the motto for all of Weiser. Oughta just put that shibboleth right on the front-page banner of the *Signal-American,* truth be told. Work down in the shafts was hard to find these days, and it seemed not a week went by that he didn't hear about another ore vein being tapped out. The local populace was dwindling faster than the gold and timber, down to three thousand stubborn panners and the merchants, chinks, and whores who serviced them.

He once made the mistake of asking the old roosters down on the court-house stoop why Weiser wasn't booming like Huntington over in the next county. You'da thought the bartender at the Jolly Gem had just announced free sandwiches because those gum-flappers jumped to their feet and began hollering about crosses of gold and William-something-Bryan and legalized hooch. Best he could make out from their crazy cussing, a few decades before the turn of the century, the town had been slated to become the next San

Francisco when the Idaho Northern and the Union Pacific Company came into the state to haul the timber to the coast. Then the greedy land speculators stuck their snouts into the trough, and the railroad boys, knowing a thing or two about smacking noses, decided to build their own metropolis cheaper just across the Oregon border. And the rest of the sorry tale—as those courthouse vagrants insisted between their spitting and vows of damnation—was history.

Just then, a blast that sounded like a duck being attacked by a coyote nearly split his ears. Behind him, coming down the dirt road paralleling the rail tracks, appeared a ball of dust pushed by a black tin can on wheels. One of those newfangled Ramblers—he'd seen pictures in the newspaper ads—hissed and snorted as it clanked to a stop aside him. He could just make out on the door the faded outlines of the words *Fire Department,* rubbed down with linseed oil.

When the exhaust smoke dispersed, he stood staring at what appeared to be a giant insect sitting behind the steering wheel. But the driver in fact turned out to be a thickset fullback of a man crowned with wavy black hair greased back on his square head. Wrapped in a fur-lined trench coat with its collar fixed at his neck by a flapping red scarf, the man removed his smeared goggles to reveal twinkling blue irises that seemed designed to peer into secret places. He pulled a cigar from his pocket, cut its tip with a miniature guillotine, and lit up. After several puffs, he rolled the stogie to the corner of his mouth and thundered, "A young frontier Galahad appears at the very hour of my distress! Might you be so kind, valiant Grail quester, to point me towards Boise? I seem to have lost my way on my sojourn through the prairie desert of Sarras."

Waters figured the stranger was talking some kind of foreign language. All he understood from that blast of oratory was the name of the state capital. "If you're loo-loo-looking for Boise, mister, you made a wr-wr-wrong turn about an hour ago. It's b-b-back south, thataways."

"There are no wrong turns in my life, good squire. Only correct turns taken too soon. And be comforted in knowing that your tied tongue is not without historical precedent. So, too, did the masses of the Old World fail at words when finding themselves in the shadows of the Lionhearted and Alexander the Great. As your quaking humbleness so rightfully attests, I am fated for deeds of renown. And like Odysseus on his misty peregrinations through the Pillars of Hercules, I may *appear* to be cast adrift, but when the Akashic Records are read on the Day of Judgment, it shall be revealed that I was precisely where the divinities would have me."

When the fellow finally wound down his speech, Waters looked around at the bleak scape of tawny hillocks and inquired, "Mister, if you're s-s-so high and mighty, whatdya doing spinning circles out here in the m-m-middle of nowhere?"

The driver flashed another toothy grin lacquered with tobacco stains. "Well struck, lad! That piercing query was driven home with all the musketeering verve of a D'Artagnan! I think you may have the stuff of a newspaperman!"

"Heck, I can't speak the wo-wo-words right, let alone write 'em."

"Ah then, it's the editor's desk for you. Now, Master Pip of the Prairie, if you would be so kind as to direct me to the nearest temple dedicated to Bacchus, I shall gratefully bestow on you an honorary degree from the Fourth Estate." Seeing he had utterly baffled the boy, the driver lamented, "Gads, I buried the lede! I am, to put it with crass directness, in critical need of the two liquids that will fuel this new American century. Petrol and malt whiskey."

Waters felt his head starting to hurt from trying to follow the motorist's rapid-fire way of conversing. "There's a couple saloons in town, but they ain't much to write home about. And Mister Hawkins's livery might have some spare gas they use for the bit engines."

"Sounds like an oasis whose delights must not be missed. Your destination, as well, Pip?" Receiving a hesitant nod, the driver gunned the engine and ordered him to hop in.

Waters launched head over heels into the passenger seat and nearly suffered whiplash as the Rambler lurched off toward town. Now upright, he saw that the massive hands trying to wrestle the driving wheel into submission were stained black. "You out here prospecting for coal?"

The driver wiped a palm against his tan corduroys and offered it for a firm handshake. "Floyd Gibbons of the *Minneapolis Daily News*. International war correspondent." When that claim drew a beady glare of skepticism, the reporter spat a wad of cigar juice over the side door, barely avoiding spattering his goggles from the backdraft. "Working my way overseas. I'm on the crime beat at the moment. Just a temporary stepping-stone to the heights of Valhalla, where I intend to prick the generals who general the pricks."

Sniffing a foul odor, Waters looked over his shoulder into the rear compartment. He found a garbage stash of empty bottles, crumpled newspapers, and—most worrisome of all—a small ax. "Dang, what's that rotten smell?"

The driver scooped a handful of cigar butts at his feet and tossed them out into the dry scrub brush, apparently not concerned about igniting a grass fire. "*That* is the rarefied fragrance of freedom and liberty with justice for all." Met with a wrinkled look of exasperation, he edited down. "Newsprint."

Waters twisted his face. "That rot could gag a maggot."

Gibbons laughed at how the boy was pinching his nose. "I may have been too hasty in my assessment of your destiny, young Pip. If the opiate of press ink leaves you pekid, you'd best look for another enterprise to pursue your fame and fortune."

Waters couldn't quite figure where this traveler had gotten the cockeyed notion that he wanted to be a reporter, but he played along. "How exactly does someone b-b-become a newspaperman?"

"First, you quit college."

"The heck you say! I'll bet your pa thrashed you when he f-f-found out."

"I didn't stay around long enough to discuss the matter with him. I majored in supernatural pranks and higher spirits—the distilled variety—at that venerable papal academy for inquisitors known as Georgetown University. The Jesuits didn't find it particularly biblical when I greased the tracks at the campus train station and made the Army football team an hour late for a game. So much for the Christian command of forgiveness, eh?"

"You got kicked out?"

The driver winked a confession. "My buttocks still bear the Latin imprint of Saint Ignatius Loyola's holy seal."

"How old are you, anyways?"

"A mere tender shoot of twenty years. But I am an ancient soul, schooled in the artifices of scoundrels, senators, and priests. And yet, I now catch myself committing Rhetoric's cardinal sin."

"What's that?"

"Redundancy. Priests and scoundrels. Scoundrels and senators. Like ice and frozen water."

Waters scratched his head. He hadn't encountered anything so bizarre since the circus came through the county last summer. He stole another worried glance at the ax rattling in the trunk, and the thought crossed his mind that he might have just been kidnapped by a demented traveling murderer. "Far as I can tell, there's no war *or* crime g-g-going on out here."

Gibbons managed to miss about every third pothole on the dirt road, sending them both bouncing on the seat springs like two sacks of carrots. "There is *always* a war somewhere, Master Pip. We chroniclers of the great military conflict are like undertakers and whores. We never have to worry about employment, and we don't live long enough to require a pension."

"I ain't much on keeping t-t-track of world affairs. But I'm pretty sure the United States of America is at peace."

"Give it time," Gibbons promised. "As that great riverboat philosopher Sam Clemens observed, history may not repeat itself, but it rhymes. The Wall Street robber barons are smacking their lips for a taste of the tequila worm in Mexico. And I'll bet a nickel against those marbles you got jangling in your pocket that the Prussian princes on the Continent will soon be rattling their sabers again to earn their statues on the avenues in Vienna. But there is no need to wait. You have a war waging right now here in your own backyard."

"Now you're p-p-pulling my leg, fer sure. The Injuns were run off years ago."

"You've not heard of the Wobblies?"

"You mean them socialist union organizers?"

Gibbons nodded. "I'm on my way to Boise to cover the murder trial of Big Bill Haywood."

"I remember hearing the jackers d-d-down at the mill talking about a fella named Haywood. He's that thug that shot that old governor, ain't he?"

"I see the railroad oligarchs have already staked their claim inside your noggin. The Wobblies are fighting for decent wages for the workingman. It's a war, all right. And it's likely to get a lot hotter soon."

"My pa ain't got no use for s-s-socialist rabble-rousers. And I reckon I won't, either. We're red-blooded Americans, head to toe."

Gibbons shook his head, despairing at the propaganda being spread by the powerful and wealthy. "You'll need to grow a thicker carapace of cynicism, young Pip, if you expect to bring the religion of Truth to the heathen masses."

Waters passed the next twenty jouncing minutes listening to the newspaperman philosophize on topics ranging from how Teddy Roosevelt had won over the press by giving them their own room in the White House to the covert Masonic recipe used to make Kentucky bourbon. Before the boy could get another word in edgewise, they were rumbling down the mud sluice that served as Weiser's main street. Gibbons honked the horn to chase the horse carriages from his path and stopped at the saloon with the largest sign above its door. While the townsfolk ogled the steaming vehicle, the reporter pulled out two silver dollars from his pocket and flipped them to his new companion.

"What's this for?"

"Go quartermaster me a box of Cubans," Gibbons ordered.

"They oughta have some at the general store, but this would pay for a crate of 'em."

"Keep the change. Consider it your first day's wages as my newshawk."

Waters stared at the coins. "Dang, you must earn a mint."

"Expense account, the mother's milk of journalism." Gibbons pulled a pewter flask from his breast pocket and drained it. "Now, I must go foraging to replenish my stock of the traveling medicinal. Meet me back here in five minutes."

When the boy returned with the stogies, Gibbons, waiting by the auto, sniffed the box and gave him a thumbs-up. "Well done, scout!" He looked around and noticed that, in the span of minutes, the duckboards that served as sidewalks had become nearly deserted. "Is there an afternoon curfew?"

"Everyone's gone d-d-down to the ball yard. It's the biggest game of the year. The Kids are p-p-playing the Emmett Prune Pickers."

Gibbons tossed back his substantial head in disbelief as he squeezed his large frame into the driver's seat. "The Wall Street barons should outlaw baseball for being subversive to capitalist productivity. We have a hard and fast rule at my job, kid. A sign over the editor's door states: All requests for leave of absence on account of grandmother's funeral, sore throat, housecleaning, lame back, turning of the ringer, headaches, brain storm, cousin's wedding, general ailments or other legitimate excuses must be made out and handed to the boss not later than ten a.m. on the morning of the game."

Waters didn't know what to say, so he just nodded.

"The denizens of that fine watering hole gave me a lead on some petrol at a warehouse outside of town." The reporter started the engine and handed over a calling card with his name printed in fancy letters. "If the Sioux around here ever go back on the warpath, Master Pip, you call me at the paper." He was about to press the gas pedal to the floor when young Waters grabbed the steering wheel to delay him.

"You oughta st-st-stay and watch a couple innings," the boy said. "It's the championship of the Idaho Southern League."

Gibbons waved off the invitation. "Alas, I have a murder trial to turn into the third act of Hamlet."

"There's something gonna be there that you r-r-really oughta see. Could be a story in it."

Gibbons nearly stared a hole into him. "Think you've found my soft underbelly, do you, Pip?"

Waters pulled the remaining silver dollar from his pocket and flashed it. "Come watch the fir-fir-first inning. If you think it's a waste of your time, I'll give you the d-d-dollar back."

"Are you trying to sharp me with a wager?"

Waters put on his poker face. "You li-li-like what you see, I get double."

Stoked by the challenge, Gibbons waved the young usurer back into the Rambler, cranked it up again, and chugged toward the outskirts of town where the folks were herding toward a ballpark that sat next to the horse racetrack. The reporter paid twenty cents for seats down on the third-base line, where the Weiser team, known as the Kids, was warming up. He settled in on the hard bleachers, wiping the grime from his creases, and pulled another coin from his pocket. "Go get us a couple rats in hats."

Waters gawked at him blankly.

"Sausage dogs," Gibbons translated. "Slather mine with onions till it barks."

As Waters ran off on his errand, Gibbons pulled out his flask and sipped the local mash while lazily scanning the diamond. It looked populated by the typical muster of washed-up pensioners and bow-legged farm boys you'd find in any American town on a Saturday afternoon. He couldn't figure why the boy had dragged him here, or why every soul within a fifty-mile radius had gone to the trouble of rigging their buggies just to witness a semi-professional minor league game. The confines were packed to the gills and the mayor of Weiser was holding court atop a chicken coop behind home plate, taking wads of money as bonds for bets laid by the fervent supporters of both teams.

His gauzy gaze drifted toward the bare spot just beyond left field where the Weiser pitcher, a tall whippersnapper, was warming up. The Emmet traveling band had set up behind the poor bumpkin, and the trombone player, in an attempt to foul up the hurler's rhythm, would draw out his blare just as the pitch was released. When an occasional curveball hit the dirt, the cymbals player would celebrate with a great taunting clash. The Weiser catcher, who looked as if he'd weigh in north of three hundred pounds, was so ancient that every so often his young battery mate, twice as tall and a third his age, would have to walk up to the towel set down as a plate and help the old man back into his squat.

Gibbons laughed so loudly at the spectacle that several Weiser fans seated around him—many conspicuously armed with revolvers—singed him with glares. Not a moment too soon, young Waters returned with the sausage dogs. The Weiser faithful, seeing that the smirking stranger was with the local lad, eased their fingers off the triggers.

"We lucked out," Waters said. "Last two."

Gibbons slouched down to provide a smaller target. "I'm surprised there wasn't a shootout for them. Do your fellow Weezers always come to these contests armed like Texas Rangers?"

"There was a br-br-brawl at the game last month in Emmet. The sheriff there threw a hundred of our b-b-boys into jail. Might be a little payback today."

"Ah, forsooth, war doth perpetually nip at my heels." Gibbons sized up the opposing armies in the stands. "Who's your catcher, kid? He'd be in a coffin if they could find one large enough to hold him."

"That's Foxy Grandpa Uhrl. He played ball with Buffalo Bill."

"How old is the gray Foxy?"

"Fifty-three is what he admits to."

Gibbons took another swig and, shaking his head in futility, staggered to his feet to leave. "Hand over that silver dollar, Pip."

Waters looked up, confused, his mouth still stuffed with half his hotdog.

"I can see a dozen old Foxies in the carnivals," Gibbons scoffed.

Waters refused to part with the wagered coin. "Foxy Grandpa ain't w-w-why I brought you here. Keep the st-st-steam in your pipe and s-s-sit back down."

Impressed by the boy's guff, Gibbons collapsed back onto the bleacher, crashing onto his flask. Horrified, he carefully removed the holy reliquary from his back pocket and checked its cap. While examining it for leakage, he caught in his periphery the flash of an arm spinning like a windmill, followed by the crack of a ball hitting ancient leather. The sound most closely resembled the report of a musket echoing on a frosty autumn day.

Not trusting his sogged ears, Gibbons looked toward the Weiser bullpen again. The lanky Nordic slinger with the sad puss slowly brought his hands to the top of his head to introduce ball to glove, and when this ominous ascension reached its climax, he dropped both arms like the wings of an oil derrick and rotated the ball three-sixty before delivering it below his shoulder with a deceptive ease that belied the violence dealt to Foxy Grandpa's floppy mitt. The creaky catcher shook the numbness from his gloved hand and, wincing, lobbed the ball back, only to stoically descend and endure the ordeal again like a masked Sisyphus.

Gibbons risked another turn toward the stands to discover if anyone else had seen what he just witnessed. Every eye in the park was transfixed on the young pitcher. He looked down and found Waters grinning a big shiteater up at him. "Don't get too attached to that bullion, Rockefeller. Any carny freak can gin up a gimmicky delivery."

"Too Much is the real deal. He's gone forty innings straight without giving up a run."

"How'd he come by *that* moniker?"

"After every game, the newspapers in the n-n-neighboring towns print the same headline: 'It Was Too Much Johnson.'"

Gibbons was entranced by the pitcher's soothing but fatal delivery. "From where hails this reincarnated Thor?"

"California. The Pacific Coast League folded up and sold him to us. He's the best secret west of the Mississippi. And the town honchos here are gonna keep it that way. Word around the camps is they're dangling free hotel meals at Too Much to bait him on a new contract."

Gibbons snorted a puff of skepticism. His crime-blotter instincts told him that this mystery whiz kid had a skeleton somewhere in the closet; otherwise, the big league scouts would have bagged him by now. Probably a bum knee, or maybe he was running from the law and just didn't want to be discovered. He'd show these corn pones how a real reporter exposes the truth. He stood up and whispered from the corner of his mouth, "Bring that extra sausage dog and come with me."

Waters followed the reporter to the railing where one of the local deputies, a fat slob with more rolls than the Black Hills, was monitoring the crowd.

Gibbons put his arm around the deputy's shoulders. "My boy here would sell his left nut to get Too Much's John Hancock."

The deputy, sniffing high-octane moonshine on the stranger's breath, took a step away before somebody lit a match. "Find him after the game. He works over at the telephone company on his off days."

Gibbons slipped two fingers into his own breast pocket, and then shook the officer's hand. "I'm afraid we can't stay for the full nine. Our wagon train is leaving early."

The deputy stared down at the ten-dollar bill just planted into his palm. After a dangerous hesitation, as if debating whether to haul the stranger off to the jail for bribery, he nodded them onto the field. "Make it fast. First pitch is in fifteen minutes."

Gibbons and Waters dodged throws and curses as they angled through the outfielders. When they reached the battery warming up in the corner of the field, the reporter sidled up to the gargantuan catcher and offered him the last hotdog. "Foxy, you're this lad's hero. He bought this sausage for you, fearing you might need some sustenance chasing down that flamethrower over there."

Licking his lips, Foxy Grandpa grabbed the dog and devoured it in two bites. "Obliged."

Gibbons snapped his fingers back, as if he'd just fed a green apple to a chomping horse. "Would you mind regaling the lad on some of your exploits? I've told him before, but it would send him over the moon to hear a couple tips from the great Foxy himself."

Foxy had his game face on. "I gotta get my pitcher loose."

"Not a problem." Gibbons stole the catcher's glove and was checking its pocket before Foxy even knew it was off his hand. "I'll take a few throws to limber him up."

Befuddled by all the fast city talk, Foxy placed a hesitant paw on the boy's shoulder and began babbling about a game played back in 1880 when he used a musket stock for a bat.

Gibbons staggered down into a wobbly squat and winked for his young co-conspirator to keep Gramps occupied. He pounded the catcher's glove in a signal for the pitcher to resume his tosses. "Show me the hook, Too Much! Snap that baby off like your momma used to crack the green beans!"

The pitcher went into his windup and sent his right arm whipping across his lean torso.

Gibbons never saw the ball—but a searing bolt of pain shot up from his gloved palm to his shoulder. He gritted his teeth and snuck another swig from the flask for anesthesia, determined not to flap the sting from his hand for fear of alerting Foxy to his incompetence. He yelled at Too Much, "I called for the hook, not the heater!"

The pitcher glared at him. "That *was* the hook."

Gibbons counted himself fortunate to have guessed right about which of the three balls speeding at him to snag. He turned and squinted at the table set above the bleachers behind home plate. Several men in rumpled suits sat huddled together at the makeshift press box, scribbling fast in their notebooks. Muttering a "sonofabitch" under his breath, Gibbons walked the ninety feet up to Too Much and offered his right hand, the one that wasn't throbbing. "I'm Jack Warner."

The pitcher's square jaw dropped. "The catcher for the Nationals?"

Gibbons nodded while keeping one eye shifting toward the press table. "I came out to watch Foxy play. We're scouting him for my replacement. Down the road, of course."

"Foxy's a good fella. He calls a sharp game."

"He's paid his dues." Gibbons squeezed his burning left hand into a fist. "Might be time to give him a shot in the bigs. Don't say anything about this to old Foxy, though. I wouldn't want to make him nervous."

"Sure thing, Mr. Warner."

Gibbons began to walk away. Then, he turned back and asked casually, "Hey, Too Much, what's your baptized name?"

"Walter Johnson."

Gibbons monitored the press hounds in the stands, worried that any moment now one of them would run to the nearest phone and call in a scoop about this flamethrower. "Listen, Johnson. Do me a favor today, will you? Take it a little easy on Foxy with the hard stuff. Dial it down a couple notches so he doesn't look bad. I'd hate for his family to miss out on a good paycheck because he couldn't hold the pitches of a wild young buck like you."

"Sure thing, Mr. Warner."

Gibbons whistled for young Waters to leave with him. Waving goodbye to Foxy, the newspaperman turned back to Johnson and yelled, "Good luck with that telephone company job! Steady gigs like that are hard to come by in these hard times."

Johnson nodded as he let fly with another warm-up pitch to Foxy.

As Gibbons walked off the field with young Waters, he heard the thrown ball hitting the catcher's leather, this time with a muted thump. He stifled a satisfied grin as he paid off his bet by dropping another silver dollar into Waters's shirt pocket. Then, he headed fast for the exit.

"Ain't you g-g-gonna watch the game?" Waters asked.

Gibbons jumped the kissing gate that served as a turnstile. "I've seen enough." When they were outside the ball yard, the reporter took a swig from his flask and whispered, "You want your first lesson in journalism?"

Waters nodded hesitantly, not sure what the offer entailed.

Gibbons scanned the street across from the park, until his eyes fell on the lone telephone wire that stretched from a general store and ran south along the main road toward Boise. "Go fetch that ax from the Rambler and meet me behind this building in ten minutes."

Before Waters could question the reason for his assigned task, the reporter walked across the street and entered the general store alone. He tipped his panama hat to the lady behind the counter. "Our Lord does not grant us many glorious days like this one, ma'am."

"It is a blessing, indeed, sir. Are you in town for the big game?"

"Game? Oh, no, no. I'm on my way to Bozeman. My long-suffering mother lingers on her deathbed at the family homestead there. I hope to make it in time to hold her hand one last time before she goes to her heavenly reward."

"Dear man. Our prayers go with you."

"You are too kind." He turned away, as if trying to hide his grief. "Forgive me, but you do so remind me of Mama. I was hoping you might tell me if there is a pay phone in this county. I can no longer bear the agony, not knowing if she still holds on."

The lady took his hand and patted it to console him. "The Almighty has led you to us. We possess the only public phone this side of Caldwell. Most folk come here to use it for emergencies."

"Praise the Lord! Might I impose upon you to make a call? I will of course compensate you fully for the cost."

The woman led him to a back office. "I won't hear of it. You take as long as you need. Mabel over at the phone company will connect you."

"The angels will surely reward you."

When the door to the room closed, Gibbons quickly dialed the rotary and got the operator. He cupped a hand over his mouth and whispered, "Long distance for the District of Columbia. Collect call to Jake Stahl at the Washington Nationals or Senators or whatever the hell they're calling them this week. Floyd Gibbons of *The New York Times....* Of course he'll know me. He's still the manager there, isn't he?"

He threw a saddle blanket over his head to muffle the receiver. After several seconds, he heard a crusty voice come on the other end of the line.

"Stahl."

"Jakie Stahl, you over-the-hill monkey grinder! I thought they'd already fired you and hired Cantillon. You cost me two hundred bucks last year losing to the Yankees.... Hell no, I don't work for *The New York Times*. You been hitting the bottle again? Where'd you get an idea like that?"

He held the receiver from his ear while the voice on the other end ranted.

At last, he managed to interrupt the irate skipper. "Listen up, Jakie boy. I'm going to give you a tip that might save your overpaid ass. In return, all I'm going to take is a ten percent commission.... Hey, calm down. There's an interstate commerce law against swearing on the telephone lines. Have your sniff hounds check out a pitcher in the Idaho Southern League named Walter Johnson.... Hell, how do I know why he's out here in the boonies? Just tell that bookie parlor you call a front office to give him a look. And remember where you heard it.... Oh, and Jakie, you better keep tighter tabs on Warner. There's a rumor floating around out here that your catcher's been barnstorming on the side under an alias.... Yeah, I'd slap a fine on him."

After hanging up, Gibbons dipped his hand into a washbasin to flick a few fake tears on his cheeks. He staggered back into the front room of the store and shook his head, affecting sorrow to confirm that the Grim Reaper had not waited to gather his woeful harvest.

The lady behind the counter rushed over to offer him solace. "Our prayers go with you, sir!"

Gibbons raised his doused eyes to Heaven and blubbered an "amen" as he hurried out. Cleared of the store window's sightline, he ran around to the back of the establishment. Expecting his competitors in the press box to come rushing out of the ballpark any moment to call in their discovery, he motioned young Waters over and took the ax from him. "Now here's that journalism lesson I promised you."

Waters watched, confused, as the newspaperman stuffed the ax handle into his belt and strolled over to the pole that ran the telephone line into the store. With the dexterity of an acrobat, Gibbons clambered up the pole, pulled out the ax, and chopped the only telephone line that ran from Weiser to the outside world. He backtracked down the pole and cut a second piece of the line, rendering it impossible to splice. Armed with his souvenir of the purloined section of copper, the reporter hightailed it for the Rambler. Keeping his eyes peeled for the local cops, he reached into his pocket and flipped the boy the second dollar that he owed him. "You know what that old reb Nathan Bedford Forrest said was the secret to winning a newspaper war, don't you, Pip?"

Struck speechless by the vandalism, Waters could only shake his head.

Gibbons cranked up the roadster and jumped in. After cutting a circle around the boy in a cloud of dust, he sped out of town while yelling over his shoulder, "Always get there firstus with the mostest!"

4

RAGLESVILLE, INDIANA
APRIL 1910

While the congregation stood singing the second stanza of *When Peace Like a River*, Anna Raber slipped into the one-room Mennonite meetinghouse through the rear door. She found a seat at the end of the back pew, close enough to the opened window to enjoy the smells of the new planting year. The freshly broken sod, seeded in corn that week, was still pungent from the spread manure, and the crocuses and daffodils blanketed the gently rolling hay fields with a tangy whiff that nearly caused her heart to break with joy for God's goodness. Her departed mother had so loved southern Indiana in the spring, often commenting how it reminded her of southern Germany, where their Anabaptist forefathers had thrived before being persecuted by the Roman and Protestant churches for refusing to take oaths and baptize infants. Here, on this bountiful American land, their close-knit enclave had thrived for over a hundred years, living in harmony with the German and Irish Catholics who surrounded them.

But like a storm blowing in at the end of a sunny day, trouble was now threatening that peace.

Above the singing, she could hear her father's husky voice. To her dismay, he was speaking the Low German again. Engaged in an animated discussion with Ezekiah Knepp in the front row, Jacob Raber turned, as if sensing her disapproval. She shook her head in a gentle reminder that he should speak English. Many of the older members of the community still resisted this reform, even though the church had decided that because they were Americans and would inevitably have to deal with the outside world, the younger generations should be taught English as a first language.

She looked around, taking note of those present. The room was so swollen with latecomers that many had spilled out onto the yard beyond the doors.

The Sunday evening service was usually rotated from farmhouse to farmhouse, but this one promised to be so contentious that the elders had moved it to the communal hall, the largest building in the settlement. She had never seen so many believers gathered in one place, not even on the day they raised Ezra Yoder's barn, the largest in their Old Order farming community. That celebration, ten years ago, remained one of her earliest memories, and the fondest. The men on that hot July morning had clambered across the fresh-hewn beams of the looming framework with their hammers and saws while the bonneted women draped the long rows of tables outside with oilcloths and steeped them with platters of fried chicken, candied yams, and yeast rolls for lunch. Just six years old at the time, she had been assigned the task of chasing away the flies from the food with an oak branch.

That was when Micah Yoder gave her the nickname that stuck like sorghum. Shoofly Raber.

So pretty was her smile, the nervy boy had announced between bites on a drumstick at dinner on that hot afternoon, *even the flies enjoy her swats.* Fair as a white peach, she had blushed so intensely at the embarrassing compliment that the older men began to tease her mercilessly. In the years that followed, whenever a fly appeared on a windowsill, the elders would laugh and clap until she performed her divine-given gift.

Micah always seemed to show up at her most awkward moments. There was that time, for example, when she had to deliver a calf while her father was away at a biblical conference. To this day, she didn't know how Micah had known she needed help, but he came running over the snow-fluffed hills that December morning, not a minute too soon to unbreach the calf from the bawling cow. It was then that he had learned her shameful secret: She was squeamish at the sight of blood, couldn't even bear to dress a chicken. He had surely tattled this to the other men, for whenever she passed them now, she could almost hear the whispers about what a poor wife she would make.

The congregation launched into the final chorus of the hymn, shaking the whitewashed rafters. When they finished, her father arose from the front pew to deliver his sermon.

She fussed with smoothing her ankle-length dress, using her primping as a diversion to sneak another sidelong peek across the room. Micah had been stealing brazen glances back at her, flashing his teeth mischievously through his scraggly beard. She felt the heat rise in her cheeks again, a telling sign that only caused him to grin wider. She was doubly nervous because this eve promised to be one of the most important of her life. She could not deny another glance at Micah, but this time his smile had given way to a look of worry. The others sang with heavy hearts, their voices crackling from the tension that had pervaded the week.

Why did God have to bring darkness and division on her special night?

As the worshippers—women on one side, men on the other—finished their hymn, she felt a palpable jolt of trepidation. Standing before the congregation, her father cut the figure of an old German Moses in black as he bowed his head in humility, his long gray beard reaching to the navel of his white shirt and his knuckles pale from clutching his Ausbund hymnal. He no longer laughed as he once did, not since her mother had passed, for the horrid events of the past few days had taken a heavy toll on him. He was weary and burdened by a torrent of modern changes that he could no longer comprehend.

And there he was again, giving her that confused stare.

She used to become flustered whenever, addled by the tricks of age, her father looked at her as if expecting to find her mother. Yet in recent months, she had come to see the striking resemblance in the mirror: the long, strawberry blonde hair, so rare among their people, and worn in the same bun; the provoking cornflower eyes, which gave off her mother's same insistent gaze, the one that the English always mistook for suspicion; the fair skin susceptible to the sun, the naturally rouged cheeks, and the slender swan's neck—all frivolous features for a farm girl. Eager to negate the infuriating impression that she was vain about her appearance, she was always overcompensating by doing more grime work in the barns and fields than the other women.

Now, her father motioned forward Jonah Burkhardt, one of the elders who sat in the front row. For the first time, old man Burkhardt turned to face the congregation, and those who had not seen him since the unspeakable deed gasped in horror. Two days earlier, his beard had been crudely hacked away by violence and force. He still wore the scabs on his face and hands from the wounds suffered when he had tried to fight off the attackers—fellow Mennonites—who had broken into his home. Several of the women turned away, unable to look upon the poor soul. In their faith, a man's beard was a mark of his holiness and virility. Death was preferable to being mutilated in such a vile manner.

"I have failed my people in the eyes of the Lord," her father announced.

After a nettled silence, Ada Hostetler, the most senior of the women in the congregation, stood to testify. "We have all failed, Jacob. There is a pestilence of the soul sweeping over our land. The Devil has entered many hearts, even some in this assembly."

A younger man leapt to his feet in protest. "You talk as if some mysterious power did this deed! We all know who committed it! Amos Gingrich and his boys! This is not our sin. We have been too lenient with these criminals!"

"What would you have us do?" Anna's father asked him. "We have shunned them, but to no effect."

"Those men cannot be shamed!" a bearded elder insisted. "They laugh at our shunning and excommunication. They will not be satisfied until they tear us all down and humiliate us before the English."

"Evil not confronted rises like yeast," Ada Hostetler warned. "If we do not stop this abomination, soon there will be murder and more mayhem here!"

That prophecy horrified Anna's father. "You speak of murder, Sister Ada? There has not been such a crime since we came to this land."

"Persecution is the handmaiden of faith," Ada insisted. "We did not escape the English when we crossed the sea. The English will always be upon us, just as the Devil was always at Christ's side during His forty days in the desert."

"And how would you have us quash this madness?" Anna's father asked.

Ada did not flinch. "The heretics must be handed over to the police."

That demand spawned another surge of recriminations, and one of the men objected, "She would have delivered Our Lord unto the Romans!"

"It was not *your* home that was violated!" Ada reminded the man protesting her demand. "Your piety will fail soon enough when they shear you like a lamb at the slaughter!"

Jacob glanced helplessly at Anna as he tried to restore order. He spotted a hand raised in the far corner of the room asking for permission to speak. Smiling at the source of the request, Jacob nodded with a look of relief and said, "Yes, Micah. You have something to say?"

The elders murmured their astonishment that one so young—Micah was only a year older than Anna—would dare offer an opinion on such a grave matter of community governance.

Micah stood, taking a moment to find his courage. "You remember those five English boys awhile back who burned down my grandpa's barn?"

The congregation nodded, and some brushed back tears.

"They were out of their minds from drinking liquor," Micah reminded them. "The county sheriff begged my family to bring a charge in the English court. But Grandpa refused, and he forgave them. Those English boys came out here that summer and offered to help rebuild the barn. We all saw the miracle of their healing with our own eyes. Maybe the calves have to jump the fence a few times before they learn where the hay is on them cold winter days."

Anna had never heard him speak with such seriousness. Could this be the same carefree boy who was always cracking jokes and flirting with her?

As if sensing the doubt rising around him, Micah kept his eyes lowered to show humility. "I have been reading the Good Book on this matter. Did not Our Lord say that we must not resist one who is evil? Matthew Five-Nine.

Blessed are the peacemakers. Grandpa told me that turning aside in the face of violence is a kernel of our faith. I don't have a vote. But if you send Amos Gingrich and his wildings to the English law now, are we no better than those who afflicted suffering on the thousands of our martyrs who came before us?"

Many in the room nodded, and even those who had called for the unprecedented action of seeking English justice seemed moved by the young man's plea. Anna looked at her father and saw him beaming at Micah, as if sharing a secret knowledge between them.

Ada Hostetler stood again. "Our Lord sends breezes to warn of coming storms. If the church commands such a course of mercy, I too will turn aside. But I do not for a moment believe that by taking this path of meekness, we will escape greater trials of faith ahead."

Despite this warning, Anna's father gave his blessing to the course proposed by Micah. "He speaks wisely. Our Lord always counseled forgiveness."

"There was one sin for which Our Lord did *not* counsel forgiveness." Ada turned to another page in her Bible. "Mark Three-Twenty Nine. 'But he that shall blaspheme against the Holy Ghost hath never forgiveness, but is in danger of eternal damnation.' This abomination was not only a crime against Jacob Burkhardt. It was blasphemy against the Spirit and the command for our men to maintain themselves outwardly in Christ's example."

Troubled by these points, the congregation became silent again. Some of the worshippers turned to their prayer books for answers to their dilemma. Anna saw tears welling up in Micah's eyes. Why was he was taking this controversy so hard?

When sufficient time had been allotted for private prayer, Jacob stood again and called for a vote. "I would have the full congregation's guidance on this decision. Those in favor of handing the shunned over to the English court, please stand."

Only a third of the congregation came to their feet.

Micah's plea for forbearance had carried the day.

Anna's father raised his hands over the congregation. "Let us then pray for the Lord's intervention, that these stone hearts in our midst be softened."

That night, Anna lay shivering in the darkness of her upstairs bedroom. Before retiring, she had extinguished the fire in the kitchen stove, and already the house had grown cold. Covered from neck to heels in a woolen sack tied with drawstrings at her ankles and waist, she listened for the footsteps on the stairs, her teeth chattering more from nervousness than the spring frost on the window. When would he ask? Would he wait until those last hours before dawn, making her wait? She had practiced saying 'yes' a thousand times, sometimes delaying her answer for an extended moment to make him suffer in doubt, in retribution for those many times when he had teased her. She so wished she could see the anxiousness on his face. What if he snored? Or talked in his sleep? She would just have to act as if she never heard—

The stairwell door creaked open, and two sets of feet climbed the steps. Her skin tingled in anticipation. The latch to her room turned, and a rush of air entered from the hallway.

"Anna," her father whispered. "Are you settled?"

"Yes, father."

Denied the benefit of a lantern, Jacob Raber shuffled across the room blindly and found the board that he had rested against the wall. Working from feel and memory, he lifted the long two-by-four slat and slid it into the notched bracings constructed at the foot of the bed.

Anna heard the board screech down the middle of the straw mattress aside her, until the slat's planed facing came against her shoulders. She remained turned on her side, away from the door. A body compressed the mattress on the far side of the board, drawing groans and cracking from the bed supports. She felt the bed shaking—was that her, or *him*?

"Bless you, children," her father prayed. "Give thee both thanks to the Lord."

"Bless you, father," she said.

"B-b-bless you, sir," the young voice next to her stammered.

The door closed, and the room fell silent.

Should she speak first? Now, more than ever, she missed her mother, who would have given her instruction on the ways of bed courting, a biblical practice as old as Ruth and Boaz laying together all night on the threshing floor. But her mother had died before telling her of her own bundling with Papa, and what little Anna had learned about the ritual she had managed to glean from overhearing the grandmothers speak of it during the quilting bees.

No, she decided. She would make Micah speak first. She wasn't about to let him tease her again for saying something untoward. He could lay there mute all night if he wanted—

What was that buzzing in the corner? Was that the Holy Spirit filling her ears with the sound of holiness? The room became silent again. Seconds later, she heard a puffing, and then:

"Anna?"

He had spoken first.

She smiled, lording her first victory over him. "Yes?"

"I need you."

Her smile widened into a preening grin. This ritual was all the more enjoyable because her elation over his clumsy attempt at the proposal of marriage was hidden in the dark. She affected disgust and insisted, "You'll have to do better than that, Micah Yoder."

"No, I *really* need you."

She had waited all her life for this moment, and *that* flimsy effort wasn't going to cut it. She had beseeched her father for two months to allow the bundling to take place after her sixteenth birthday. Until this night, she and Micah had enjoyed only a couple of fleeting moments alone together, and this night would be the determining test of their compatibility.

"Did you hear me?"

She tried to decipher the depth of his love for her in the tenor of his voice. He sounded agitated. What was all that puffing and sputtering he was doing across the board? She would have to break him of that nasty habit, for sure. "Say it again."

"I … need … help!" he pleaded, emphasizing each word in rising desperation. *Help?*

He goes from needing *me* to needing *help?*

This was going to require more work than she had expected. "Needing is not enough, Micah Yoder. A woman wants to be wooed. I must know that I am the Lord's gift to you. That you cannot live without—" What in the heavens was he doing over there? The board between them was rattling, and it sounded as if he were thrashing inside his bundling shroud like a revived corpse fighting against the dirt thrown at him in the grave.

"I will recite every word in the Good Book," he begged, "if you will do one thing for me!"

Exasperated at the thick-headedness of men, she gave up her gentle coaxing and took firm control. "Yes, Micah Yoder! Yes, I will marry you! There, are you satisfied? Did my father tie the string around your tongue as well? Yes, yes, I will marry you despite your insufferable—"

"Marry?"

"What beclouds my very understanding is how a man who spoke like an angel before the entire church only hours ago can now find himself incapable of asking a simple question—"

"Marry?"

"Do you have a farm in mind for us? Ben Wagler's acres are rumored to be up for sale. It's a far piece from the road, but —"

"I wasn't trying to ask you to *marry* me!"

Stunned, she wiggled and struggled until she managed to sit upright like a woolly worm arching on its back. "What then *were* you asking?"

"There's a fly on my nose!"

In the span of seconds, Anna's kindled emotions caromed from befuddlement to anger to hilarity at their situation. They both broke out in laughter so loud that they heard her father stirring in the bedroom across the hall. She ducked back down behind the board. Sensing the danger in the moment, they stifled their giggling and tried to remain quiet, but their bodies were shaking with suppressed amusement against the bundling board.

"What would you have me do about it?"

"Blow on it," he begged. "My beard blocks my mouth."

With great effort, she managed to lever back up again and let loose with a blast. The blow was harsher than necessary to chase the fly, but it carried a silent message punishing him for turning the most important moment in her life into another story that would only entrench her nickname.

Rid of the pest, Micah edged against the board and whispered, "Thank you."

She huffed and turned her back toward him. "Don't try to butter me up! And don't you dare call me—"

"Shoofly."

She fell silent, fuming.

"I guess I really stepped in the cow pod this time."

"Do you know how many times a girl bundles in her life?"

"Once?"

"And how many times she gets to feel the first thrill of lying next to—"

"I love you, Anna."

Her burst of exasperation was rendered stillborn. Now she was the one tongue-tied. Her eyes filled with tears, and she could not find the words that matched her emotions.

"Did you hear me?"

She let loose on him with a torrent. "The Almighty busted the stir pole when he pushed you through the ice creamer, Micah Yoder! Two minutes ago, you could barely put two words together! And now you're gushing like a broken pipe! Do you not know when to give a girl time to savor the few moments in her life that might make the rest of the horror worth the effort?"

"Just in case that fly got stuck in your ear, I'll say it again. I love you. I fell for you the day you cut me that piece of cherry pie twice the size you served the others at the barn raising."

"I was hoping it would stifle your mouth for awhile."

"I did not come to ask you to marry me."

Her heart sank as swiftly as it had quickened. Swallowing her disappointment, she tried to remain calm, despite her confusion. "Why then did you ask my father to permit you to stay tonight?"

"There is something I have to tell ... to explain to you."

She pulled her legs into her chest, trying to quell the urge to sob.

"I feel God's calling," he said. "The same calling your father once felt."

That confession hit her like a pan to the forehead. Now she understood that knowing look her father had exchanged with Micah at the church earlier that night—*and* the uncharacteristic willingness of her father's surrender to the bundling.

"I tried to tell you earlier," Micah said. "But I couldn't find the right moment. Your father wrote to Goshen on my behalf."

"The bible college? That's two hundred miles away."

"The trustees have offered to help me with the tuition."

She used the sheets to brush away a tear. Had her father guided Micah toward the ministry only to keep her to himself? Coughing back a swell of emotion, she gathered up the courage to ask, "When do you go?"

"This summer. It will take ..." He hesitated. "Four years to get my degree."

She stifled a gasp. Four years seemed like a lifetime. Most of the other girls her age would be married by their eighteenth birthday. Her father was not in the best of health. What if she were left alone? While others were exploring the English world during *rumspringa*—their run-around time—she would be confined here.

"Anna, will you wait for me?"

There was only one thing she knew for certain: She loved him, too. After whispering a silent prayer for strength, she shoved her heartache deep inside and, inching her head over the bundling board, blew hard into his face.

He blinked from the unexpected blast. "What was that for?"

"For all the flies in Goshen."

Ozzie Taylor had just gone all in on the biggest dice throw of his young life. Now, as he jaunted up Broadway checking the keys of his new purchase for grease, he went over his daring plan again. Word around the Tenderloin District was that the Clef Club Orchestra was looking for an oboe player, so he'd decided to give his dream a shot by trading in his father's clarinet for the used oboe that had been collecting dust for months in the window of Old Man Groemann's Pawn Shop. The proprietor, a fat German who stank of vinegar and sauerkraut and once played tuba in a Prussian band for some big shot named Bismarck, had tried to chase him out, yelling through his bushy mustache that the oboe was a white man's instrument, too difficult for a colored boy with no proper musical schooling. But after an hour of badgering, Herr Grumps had finally thrown up his arms in surrender.

Ever since he could remember—and that was the last eight of the twelve years he'd been on this earth—Ozzie had set his heart on playing for the most famous Negro conductor in the world, Mister James Reese Europe. Big Jim, as he was known around the Tenderloin, took only the best black musicians into his Clef Club. But once you got signed, you made better wages than the white performers and played the private dance parties of the Astors and Vanderbilts. No washing dishes or moving pianos on the side, either. Rumor was that the Club raked in over a hundred thousand dollars in commissions last year alone. No sir, he'd never again have to shine shoes or play minstrel show tunes for street donations.

Yeah, Big Jim Europe was his ticket to the big time, all right. Big Jim and Li'l Ozzie had a nice ring to it. Kinda like Cole and Johnson, or Williams and Walker.

Buying that oboe had put one problem behind him, but another one still awaited solving. Even if he practiced day and night, how was he ever gonna get

Big Jim to notice him? When he talked about his dream, the older boys who threw pennies against the curb on 125th Street just laughed and scoffed that he'd have a better chance of getting a tryout for the Giants than weaseling past the bouncers down at the Marshall Hotel, where Big Jim held court.

Now that he thought about it, that famous brownstone establishment was only a couple of blocks away. Why not head over there for a little shoe-leather reconnaissance?

When he reached West 53rd Street, the situation looked bleak. Even if he somehow managed to con his way into the lobby of the Marshall, a gauntlet of Clef Club tough guys sat loitering around the stairway that led to Big Jim's second-floor suite, checking union cards and chasing off all the slummers and alley cats. Big Jim was so popular that he had to move in stealth whenever he traveled across the city. Rumor was that he would leave a concert in mid-set, hand the baton to his assistant director, and rush off to a waiting car to be whisked off to another concert in progress in another part of the city. Then he would enter the next venue with great fanfare and take the baton for a few sets before repeating the ritual. Yeah, Big Jim had performed his escape trick more times than Houdini.

Seeing how the Marshall's lobby entrance was guarded tighter than the Gates of Heaven, Ozzie slung his head in defeat and walked back north up Broadway toward Harlem. Tooting his oboe occasionally, he waited for the trolley car to pass, and when the street was clear again, he looked up and stared at a flyer posted on a lamppost:

Grand Musical Melange and Dance Fest
James Reese Europe and his Clef Club Orchestra
9 p.m. Manhattan Casino, West 155th Street and Eight Avenue
Tickets still available for tonight

Every big hat in the city would be there, he knew. He fantasized about sitting in the Casino pit, waiting for Big Jim to gesture the baton at him to come in strong for the finale of *Shoe-Fly Regiment*. He glanced over his shoulder, toward a drugstore across the street. Dodging traffic, he ran over and pressed his face against the window. The clock inside was about to chime nine. The guests in their snappy black-tie togs and flowing evening gowns would be arriving at the Casino any moment now, stepping out of their covered carriages and automobiles like European royalty.

He shook his head at the impossibility of the idea. Ducats for Big Jim's dance concerts ran up to fifty bucks, if you could find them. Heck, that was more than he'd ever made in a month. Man, but that basketball floor would be jammed and the foundations shaking tonight. He had been inside the Casino only once, to see some of the local legends take on the club team from the Abyssinian Baptist Church. His uncle, Clayton, used to hand out towels in the men's room and—

He stopped blowing the oboe in mid-note, struck by the invisible hand of genius. He took off north on a run, cradling the instrument in the crease of his left arm while checking his pocket to confirm that he still had his nickel.

Five blocks uptown, he slipped into the alley behind Gooden's Laundry. When no one was looking, he pilfered a small bale of linens from the delivery cart and hid it under his coat. A white cap with the establishment's name on the front rested on the driver's seat. He slapped it on his head and hurried down Broadway toward the Sixty-Sixth Street subway station. Flying down the stairs, he decided to save the nickel and ran past the ticket clerk. Before the grumpy Italian could corral him, he jumped on the arriving train bound for Harlem. As the doors closed behind him, several passengers stared at his bloated stomach.

He drove them toward the far end of the car by practicing a few notes.

Twenty minutes later, Ozzie bounded out the subway car and clambered up the stairs to 155th Street. At the top step, he stood staring at a herd of human glitter converging on the canopied entrance to the Manhattan Casino. Tapping the top of his head to make sure he was still wearing the Gooden Laundry cap, he hid the oboe under his jacket and stuffed the bale of linens under his arm. Now set for the dangerous foray, he elbowed his way through the crowd and shouted, "Delivery! Delivery!"

A guard at the door stopped him. "Where do you think you're going?"

"Linens."

"Who ordered linens?"

"Mister James Reese Europe."

The guard debated that unlikely claim. "Lemme see the invoice."

Ozzie put on his best street jive razzle-dazzle. "Invoice? You think we *charge* Mister Europe? Lord Almighty, if you're telling me we need to start charging Mr. Europe for his linens, well, then, I'll go back and tell my boss man. But I'm gonna need your name, 'cause there'll be a mighty ruckus stirred if Mr. Europe has to go out and perform without his linens. He sweats a mighty lot, they tell me, and if he don't have his linens handy, the pages of the music liable to get drenched, and if that happens, the notes on the page liable to run, and them musicians will get all off the tracks, and Lord Almighty, Mr. Europe is gonna wanna know why—"

"All right, all right!" The guard's eyes were nearly spinning from trying to follow the frenetic explanation. "If you're not back in ten minutes, popcorn mouth, this rumble stick is gonna be barking for your head."

Ozzie hid a wily grin as he darted into the dance auditorium. He walked ramrod straight to hide the oboe under his jacket behind his back. The scene on the Casino's parquet floor nearly took his breath away. The banisters and Arabian arches were hung with bunting, and the boards shimmered under the dozens of oriental lanterns that swung from the rafters. He reckoned at least three thousand people had already crammed inside, Negroes and whites both. Everyone was flitting from table to table, dancing and spinning with elegant drinks in their hands while the band stewards spread powder across the boards to keep them from becoming slippery. The couples looked to be trying out a new dance, cheek-to-cheek with slow steps mingled with quick retreats. The band was playing *Too Much Mustard*, but the number sounded different. More bounce and syncopation, with maybe a sassy uplift here from the fretted strings, followed by an occasional violin or cornet solo.

His eyes widened as they traveled across the array of musicians that he worshipped. Over yonder was Will Marian Cook, the eccentric composer and king of black musicals, tapping tables with his finger to correct the beat. And next to him stood Scott Joplin, drowning his bitterness at the bar with shots of whiskey. Jelly Roll Morton, up from New Orleans to play gigs, was glad-handing folks and setting up high-stakes pool games.

He migrated along the wall, staying out of sight, and at last he got a glimpse of the Clef Club musicians sitting below a raised platform at the far end of the auditorium. There had to be more than a hundred in the ensemble: eight violins, nine cellos, nearly thirty mandolins and banjos, all backed up by ten pianos. His heart raced: two clarinets sat where the oboe would be.

Big Jim hadn't filled the spot yet. And even better, an assistant conductor was still warming up the tune boys.

He rode the wave of dancers until he reached the door that led into the rear dressing room. He held up the bale of linens as evidence and with a devil-may-care attitude, marched toward the three bouncers. "Linens for Mr. Europe! Linens for Mr. James Reese Europe!"

One of the dragons guarding the cave stepped in front of the door. "I'll give them to him."

Ozzie debated his options. If he charged the pile driver, he knew his scraggly frame wouldn't put a dent into the dandied tough who stood festooned in baggy Oxford pants and sported a fedora slanted coolly across his head. But he hadn't come this far just to be turned away so close to the gold. "Okay, boss." He offered up the twined linens, and when they were nearly in the man's reach, he dropped them and feigned horror. "Oh, no. Mr. Europe ain't gonna like dirtied towels."

The door bouncer looked down in disgust at the white linens, soiled by the floor soot. He yelled at Ozzie, "You shit-for-brains little burrhead!"

Ozzie took a step back. "I'd best be gettin' back to my cart."

"The hell you will! I ain't taking these soiled wipers into Big Jim. He'd fire me on the spot." The bouncer picked up the linens and shoved them into Ozzie's hands. "Get in there and take the heat yourself."

Ozzie kept his gaze lowered in mock shame as he stepped inside. The door slammed behind him. The room was dark, lit only by a solitary candle on the corner desk. He looked up and saw, standing at the mirror, an image of what God Hisself mighta looked like if He were six-foot-five and wore a long cutaway tailcoat, a matching cummerbund, a bow tie, and striped trousers.

Big Jim turned slowly, his massive frame held as regally as a pharaoh. He set his fearsome large eyes, washed in red from fatigue, on the pint-sized stranger who stood at his door.

Ozzie's mouth went inoperative. Suddenly, recovering his wits, he dropped the bale of linens and pulled the oboe out from behind his back.

Big Jim's eyes bulged in terror. "Don't shoot me! I'll pay you double what Dab Jordan gave you! It was just one night, I swear! His wife came on sweet to me!"

Ozzie put the oboe's mouthpiece to his lips and began playing the *Clef Club Chant.*

Big Jim squinted across the dimmed room. His hands, clutching his chest, slowly migrated toward his ears, where they came to rest over his bulbous lobes. "Stop! Stop!"

Ozzie was tooting so loud that he didn't hear the command—until Big Jim came lunging across the room and yanked the oboe from his hands.

"Who are you?"

"My name's Oswald Taylor, sir, and—"

The door flew open. The sentry, hearing the noise, burst in. His eyes narrowed at the linens on the floor and the oboe in Big Jim's hands. "You okay, boss?"

"Collect your week's pay," Europe told the bouncer. "You're off the payroll."

The terminated guard glared a silent warning at Ozzie that they'd meet again, and soon.

When the door slammed, Big Jim poured himself a drink from a bottle of vodka to calm his nerves. "Oswald Taylor, you say? You're that urchin that plays for cup droppings down at the Armory. You need to undercut the third hole on that old clarinet of yours. It's out of pitch."

Ozzie was stunned. "How do you know *me?*"

"I make it my business to know every jiver from the Bowery to the Bronx who picks up an instrument. I also know when a street tooter is pulling my leg. You've never touched an oboe before today, have you, boy?"

"I'm a fast learner."

Europe pulled a sheet of music from a stack on his dresser and set it on a stand in front of Ozzie. "Play *that*, fast learner."

Ozzie stared blankly at the hieroglyphics on the page. "I plays from the heart. Like you do."

"Plays from the *heart?* Hell, you're no different than the damn white folk who think my orchestra's too damn stupid to read music." Big Jim bent down and got into Ozzie's face. "You spread the word out there to those horn sharkies on San Juan Hill! Nobody, and I mean *nobody*, gets into my band unless they *read!* And stand up straight and speak like a gentleman! Slouching all around like you're in a minstrel show! You know why I have so many mandolins and banjos in my orchestra?"

Ozzie braced to attention. "The boys around town say it's to kick the lift."

Outraged, Europe got into the boy's face again. "Kick the lift? Hell, I don't need to kick no lift! I have to employ so many goddamn strings because the white aristocrats like the Astors and the Vanderbilts don't want colored folk touching their grand pianos in the goddamn parlors!"

Ozzie heard the orchestra outside slide into the *Clef Club March,* the traditional moment when Big Jim always made his grand entrance. He knew he didn't have much time. "Give me a chance, Mister Europe."

"I don't hire alley honkers."

Ozzie felt the blood rise in his temples. This man, he realized, was nothing like his reputation for being magnanimous and caring for other musicians. He was just a money-grubber like Marian Cook and the rest of those Uncle Toms who'd made it big giving white folk what they wanted. If he was going to get kicked out to the bins, he figured might as well give Big Deal Jim a piece of his mind. "Good thing you weren't around here eight years ago."

Perplexed by that cryptic denunciation, Europe turned. "Why's that?"

"You wouldn't have hired yourself."

Europe narrowed his big eyes at the indictment, which was as nonsensical as it sounded. "You got some mouth on you, boy."

But Ozzie was on a righteous roll, figuring he had nothing to lose by testifying to the truth. "Yeah, you're all high and mighty now. But you weren't no better than me back in those days. Just an Alabama shucker, come up from Washington with your classical violin and thinking you were gonna burn down Carnegie Hall. Yeah, I know all about you! Couldn't get a job in an orchestra, either. So you pitched a tent on the Tenderloin streets and played saloons for meals. Got lucky, is all."

"Lucky?"

"Damn right!" Ozzie kicked the bale of linens across the room, sending towels flying everywhere. He grabbed his oboe back from Europe and huffed toward the door.

"Rag."

As Ozzie turned the doorknob, he spun back. "What'd you say?"

"Kicking a lift," Europe said calmly. "They're calling it Rag now. The white bands don't know how to do it. You learn the fundamentals, free yourself up tonally. The secret is in the way the instrument is handled. I couldn't teach it even if I wanted to. Comes from our ancestors in Africa. The spirits play through us." He cocked an ear to the music in the auditorium just beyond the wall. "What pattern do you hear out there?"

Ozzie listened for a moment. "AA … BB … A … CC … DD."

Europe nodded. "First strain uses fast sixteenth notes. Shifts between minor and major keys."

"The second section sounds like a march."

Big Jim was slapping his palms on his thighs. "Build them up, then give them the punch in the gut. Third strain. Let the instrumentation fight it out, and bring in the drums."

Ozzie tapped his foot to the beat. "Fourth coming now. Your mama's jam."

Big Jim picked up his baton and, closing his eyes, began conducting Ozzie as if he were the entire orchestra. "Keep the reins tight, but let 'em prance a bit."

Ozzie closed his eyes, feeling the oboe in his hands and playing it silently. "Here comes the cornet. Everything's relaxing, and yet it's building to the big boom. There's the drums."

Big Jim cut the air with a slash of his baton to bring in the wild climax. Smiling through a look of ecstasy, he opened his eyes and glared at the boy. He saw that Ozzie had tears from the effect of the music. "How old are you, Oswald Taylor?"

Ozzie wiped the mist of emotion from his eyes. "Twelve, sir."

"You can't play that oboe worth a damn."

"I knows it."

Europe pulled a business card from his vest pocket. "This will get you into the Marshall. You come hang around and pester the boys over there to teach you how to read the sheets."

Ozzie stared at the precious Clef Club ticket. "I don't know how to repay you, Mister Jim."

Europe took a last glance in the mirror to adjust his starched collar. "Oh, you'll repay me, all right. I'm a businessman first and a musician second. You seem to have a talent for getting past doormen. I want you to infiltrate the other colored concert halls and clubs. Report back to me on who sounds good and what the competition is playing."

"You mean ... like a spy?"

Bracing to be engulfed in a wave of wild applause, Europe tapped Ozzie on the head with his baton as he walked past. At the door, the bandleader turned with a wink. "That oboe of yours overblows at the octave. A clarinet overblows at the twelfth. Remember that, and you won't have to learn two different sets of fingerings."

Left alone in the Big Jim's dressing room, Ozzie was about to test that advice on the oboe when he caught a fleeting glimpse, through the cracked door, of the fired bouncer in the hall outside. The brute was flexing his meaty fingers in anticipation of getting revenge. Ozzie had hoped to watch Big Jim play the wand to the big crowd during a few numbers, but he decided it might be more advantageous for his budding career if he exited the casino on the quick through the small window above the radiator that led into the back alley.

6

HAZLETON, PENNSYLVANIA
JUNE 1910

Joe Angelo ran across the slag fields wondering if those grumpy riveters down at the rail yards were serious about cleaning their greasy knuckles on his scalp if he didn't stop telling tall stories about the Lattimer Massacre. But he swore to the Madonna of the Mountain that every time he passed the Pardee crossroads up ahead, he saw the ghosts of those unarmed Slovak miners who had been gunned down there fourteen years ago.

And there they were again.

He stopped and blinked hard, trying to chase the spirits off, but they wouldn't move. He'd been just a *bambino* when the Hazleton sheriff and his posse of Irish thugs had opened up with their Winchesters, killing nineteen strikers and wounding nearly fifty. Yet he could still hear the laughter of those lawmen on their trolley car as they shot those running Slavs as if hunting buffalo from an observation train. One of the murdered miners, a squabish Serb, had worn a bowler hat and black suit that day, as if knowing he was on his way to his own funeral. While leading four hundred marchers toward the anthracite breaker to demand better living conditions, the poor fellow had been carrying a large American flag when the mine's militia put the slugs into his chest.

Anthony Angelo, born in Naples and brought over to America by a *padroia* recruiter, had always dismissed his son's claims of seeing the Lattimer ghosts as just the fruits of a wild imagination. *Il bugiardo vuole buona memoria,* Joe's father used to say. *The liar needs a good memory.*

But his father changed his mind about the matter when, a year ago during the festival of the Cinti, an old *maga* just off the boat from Sicily read the cards for their family. The witch had warned the elder Angelo that she saw his son surrounded by the blood of others spilled from bullets. Asked if anyone in the family had witnessed a horror, Joe's mother, Emma, confessed that she'd been terrified while cradling him as a babe while her husband marched off that day to join the Lattimer strikers.

Il bambino succhia i ricordi della madre, the *maga* had insisted, pronouncing her verdict. *The child suckled the memories of the mother.*

Joe still shuddered at how the *maga* hag had sized him up with her Evil Eye. Shorter than a grapevine stake and just as slender, he had to admit he wasn't much to gaze upon. The other boys in town laughed at his mangled curls of black hair cut with sheep shears, and they called him "Cavo" because his raisin-like eyes sank so deep into their sockets and his thin lips were so flesh-less that his head resembled a skull. Apparently the *maga* had not been much impressed with him either, because she just shook her head and sent him away with the warning that he should say twenty Hail Marys each morning to ward off the approaching waves of misfortune.

The prayers had worked like magic.

A few weeks later, the tipple foreman at Mine Number Nine, hearing him singing, had pulled him from the hundreds of other whelps cracking anthracite in the breaker pits to ask him a few questions that sounded like a school examination. When he answered in passable English, the foreman had demanded to know how he'd come to learn the American tongue, suspecting him to be a spy for the union. He'd had to explain that his mama was from a place called Liverpool. Those words rose like holy smoke to God's ear, because the next day, the foreman assigned him the job of translator for the thousands of Italians who were arriving in Philadelphia and tromping their way out here into the coal fields.

The extra dollar a week was a gift from the saints, to be sure. But he hadn't yet told his papa of the promotion. All of Luzerne County seemed on the verge of exploding again. There was even talk in the union of another strike. Many of the miners feared that the hundreds of new immigrants being hauled in were for scabbing, and now he, *poco* Joey Angelo, was caught in the middle of the old Italians and the newcomers. He was thankful to be out of the pits—he crossed his breast and whispered *Grazie, Gesù Maria e Giuseppe*—but his loyalties were being pulled between these poor *miserabli* and the Pardee Company bosses who were paying him to tell their lies.

As he climbed to the next hill, leaving the Lattimer ghosts behind, he heard three sharp shrieks of the banshee from beyond the stripped valley, followed by the familiar chuffing of steam. That was the sound that every miner in Luzerne County waited each month to hear.

The paymaster's car was coming through the patches to hand out wages.

He broke into a run for the railroad spur to avoid being late for his new job of identifying the miners and confirming their names on the rolls.

Drawn by the signal, the miners rushed from their shacks and ran breathless for the tracks. Some stumbled and fainted from weakness, while others pushed desperately to the fore, all driven by the fear that the legal tender in the casement car would run out. If that happened, the miners in the rear of the lines would have to accept credit vouchers redeemable at the local stores, or wait for next month's car. Payday was held on Sundays to avoid loss of valuable work time, and the situation was always so tense that some of the men would inevitably panic and forget their own names. Most would not even understand when their names, mangled by the paymaster, were called. Two years ago, a riot had nearly broken out, so the Pardee bosses now employed hired gunmen to walk atop the cars and threaten to take down anyone who began politicking or fighting.

The locomotive pulled the armored car to a steaming halt.

The paymaster, a grizzled Ulsterman with a red cauliflower nose, stood atop the pay car. He caught sight of his reedy translator amid the scrum of miners hugging the tracks. "Hey, you sawed-off Wop! Get up here!"

The miners, eager to speed the transactions, hoisted Joe onto the roof of the pay car. After looking out over the sea of desperate faces, he took a deep breath and nodded his readiness for the onslaught.

"Giuseppe Russo!" the paymaster shouted. "Twenty days! Fifteen dollars! Sign the roll!"

Unable to understand the order, some of the miners began pushing and arguing about whose pay was being dispensed.

The paymaster elbowed Angelo to end the confusion.

Joe shouted the man's name again and translated his pay for that week, "*Venti giorni! Quindici dollari! Firma il rotolo!*"

One of the miners, ballooning red with anger, fought toward the car and shouted, "*No! Ho lavorato venticinque giorni!*"

Joe couldn't remember ever having translated for that particular fellow. Was he one of the new arrivals from the ships? There was something disturbingly familiar about his dark, round face and otherworldly eyes. Shaken for a reason he could not comprehend, Joe turned to the paymaster and translated the miner's protest, "He says he worked twenty-five days, not twenty."

The paymaster waved fifteen dollars in front of the irate miner. "Tell him he can take the money, or file a claim at the office and wait for the next car."

Joe couldn't bear to look at the miner as he translated the demand.

The miner fixed his deadened eyes on Joe as he scribbled his name in exchange for the fifteen dollars. Walking off with his paltry pay, he muttered, "*Chi parla in faccia non è traditore.*"

The paymaster turned to Joe. "What'd he say?"

Joe's face shaded lurid with dread. "A proverb from my country."

"Spit it out."

"He who speaks to your face is not a traitor."

The paymaster laughed and called the next name on the roll. As the miners stepped forward to sign to take their paltry tender, Joe kept watching the stranger who had cursed the disturbing indictment at him. The little man was wearing a black suit and a bolo hat from the old country. Suddenly, Joe gasped in recognition—*that* ghoulish face belonged to the murdered Slav who was always carrying the American flag in his visions.

Had the Lattimer ghost followed him down here from the grave?

Joe dropped to his knees and began babbling Hail Marys.

"What the hell's wrong with you?" the paymaster growled.

Joe jumped off the car and ran for the hills.

"You woolly-headed runt!" the paymaster shouted. "That extra dollar is goner than Caesar's shriveled dick!"

"Scorrere il dollaro in un flauto!" Joe shouted over his shoulder. *"Bastone su per il culo Mick, Danny Boy e giocare finchè le palle cadono!"*

Left without a translator, the paymaster searched the scrum of miners below him. "Any of you shit-for-brains speak English? There's two dollars a week more in it for you."

One of the miners raised his hand to offer his services.

The paymaster tested the volunteer's language skills. "What'd that two-bit Eyetie just say to me?"

The translator grinned as he translated Joe's curse. "He say that you can roll the dollar into a *flauto*, stick it up your Mick *asino*, and play Danny Boy *fino* your *testicoli* fall off."

7

SAN FRANCISCO, CALIFORNIA
JULY 1912

Happy Glassford sighed wistfully as he closed his eyes and turned his face toward the briny breeze that wafted up from Russian Hill and cooled the Art Institute studio. The cawing of the seagulls down at the wharf always transported him back to that morning years ago when, as a boy, he had sailed off to the Philippines with his father from those docks. Recovering to the present, he whipped up the last of his pigments with the linseed and eased up on the emulsifier. Painting here on the West Coast, he had learned, required a quicker stroke because the salty sea air dried the canvas in half the time. With his oils finally mixed, he set his palette under his easel, ready for his first day of his Landscape 304 class to begin.

Truth was, he hadn't felt so nervous since Beast Barracks. He looked around and nodded to a couple of the twenty senior students around him. But they just glared back at him, no doubt wondering what a six-foot-five, crew-cut newcomer was doing here amid their riotous collection of gypsy costumes, scraggly beards, and raffish headgear. If his old cadet buddies could see him now, they'd probably ping him all the way back to the Point on the double and hang him naked from Thayer Hall for going bohemian.

He loved donning his civvies and taking off on these recon missions. This time he hadn't even told the registrar that he was in the military. Assigned to the Presidio as a gunnery instructor, he had decided to spend that year's furlough studying painting techniques at one of the best art schools in the world. The year before, he had taken a job with the *San Francisco Examiner* as a reporter for a month, figuring he'd get some valuable lessons on how to deal with newspapermen. The editor who had hired him, a cynical old drunk, had decided to have a little fun by assigning him to cover the city morgue, and he ended up seeing more dead bodies during those few weeks on the crime beat than he had in all eight years since graduating from the Academy.

Fifteen minutes late, the door to the gallery finally flew open, and in loped a mournful-pussed instructor who could have passed for one of the Point's most notorious dropouts, Edgar Allen Poe. He had a crunched, sallow face and a long nose that seemed evolved for the sole purpose of inhaling opium incense. Wrapped at the throat with a red bandana, he didn't so much take steps as repeatedly confirm with surprise the existence of a floor supporting him. Glassford noticed that the other students had braced their easels with their hands as the fellow came near them, suggesting that more than a few canvases may have been lost to his altered senses and wobbly gait.

"You must become magicians!" the loopy instructor shouted at the class.

Glassford looked around, trying to figure out what all the ranting was about, but the other students had already taken up their brushes and were well into their first strokes.

"Perception imprisoned in two dimensions! The eye is the rabbit in the hat!"

He didn't have a clue what *that* meant. Shrugging, he dipped his brush into the blues he had blended to capture that unique hue of a Kansas sky nearing dusk, and began painting. He had decided to devote his first effort to recapturing the plains around Fort Riley, his assignment after leaving the Point. As he washed the top of the canvas in broad streaks of indigo and cobalt, the memory of that stunning Plains horizon quickly came back to him.

Sent west after graduation with cadets Danford, Dillard and Gruber, he had arrived at the remote cavalry post feeling his oats and hankering to launch an illustrious military career. To his surprise, instead of being treated as shavetails, the veterans there had welcomed them with a sumptuous feast of fried chicken and beer at the officer's club. When the evening of free drinks reached midnight, the old-timers had insisted that their new comrades sample the most famous delicacy in the region, the Geronimo jackdaw. That elusive bird, they had been told, could only be hunted during summer nights, and it just so happened that the week of their arrival was prime Geronimo jackdaw season. The veterans had recounted to them how Kit Carson still held the record for hauling in twenty-five jackdaws.

Brushing quicker strokes across his canvas now, he grinned as he recalled their excitement on the hunt that night, when Gruber had boasted that *their* class would break Carson's jackdaw record.

— We can nab more than five birds each, no sweat.

— They're damn slippery birds, Private Gruber.

— Fear not, sir. The Class of Oh-Four is about to be immortalized.

— You boys do seem brighter than the usual brood we get in here each year. You might be the ones to break ol' Kit's mark.

— Let's us at 'em.

He shook his head, still amused by it all. The officers at the post had been thoughtful enough to load up a wagon stocked with two cases of Budweisers on ice, and he and his buddies had sat like royalty on the boards while being escorted deep into the black Kansas wilderness. Along the way, as they had thrown their "dead soldiers" over their shoulders with each new pop of a cork, Snitz had insisted that those of us in the Field Artillery were long overdue for our own song. That was when Snitz revealed that he had been working on one secretly for months.

— Let's hear what you got so far.

— Over hill, over rivers, we will hit the dusty trail.

— What? You can't have a river next to a dusty trail!

— What da you know about trails? They got any trails in Chicago?

— He's right, Snitz. How about over hill, over dale? That rhymes.

— Dale? Hell, people'll think I'm some sort of English limp wrist!

— Go on. Give it a try.

Snitz took another swig and crooned:

> *Over hill over dale we will hit the dusty trail*
> *As the caissons go rolling along.*
> *Up and down, in and out, Countermarch and right about,*
> *And our caissons go rolling along.*
> *For it's hi-hi-hee in the Field Artillery,*
> *Shout out the number loud and strong.*

They had rolled on all that night, singing their new ballad until they got it just right. Then, the colonel in charge of their mounted entourage had back-tracked to the wagon and whispered:

— You boys better simmer down. We're getting near the migration path.

— Migration path? You mean these birds move like buffalo?

Gunnysacks and candles were tossed to them.

— What are these for?

The cavalrymen lit the candles with their cigars.

— The light draws the jackdaws in. When you hear the birds flapping near your ear, throw those sacks over them. They fight like mothers, so get ready.

With the sacks draped over their shoulders, he and his West Point buddies had staggered out of the wagon, clutching the last beers in one hand and their candles in the other.

— About five hundred yards yonder, the colonel directed them.

As he filled in the sky on his canvas, Glassford recalled how he had told the end of the jackdaw story at his recent class reunion: *We lurched blindly into the darkness, reaching out to look for cactus or other dangerous vegetation. Kept our ears cocked for sounds of the jackdaw, but all we heard was an occasional cackling* sound. *The night wind was picking up fierce, and it hadn't been more than five minutes before the candles went out. We stood alone, shivering and waiting for those birds to come hurling at us. After an hour or so, when we were feeling the full effects of all the beers, Runt made the observation that those ol' boys who'd escorted us out here had spent a fair amount of time on these plains, and wouldn't they have known that there was no way we were gonna keep these candles lit in this howler? Slowly, it dawned on us that four shavetails had been liquored up and taken for a snipe hunt. Six hours and ten miles later, we walked back into the fort, hung over and half-frozen, our legs looking like porcupines had bitten on us with all of the thistle needles. The officers had arranged the excursion so that we would stagger back just in time for Reveille.*

"What is *that*?"

Still reliving the experience at Fort Riley, Glassford grinned, remembering how he had been taught never to abandon equipment. "My sack, sir. It's my jackdaw sack."

"What?"

The art room erupted with laughter.

Roused from his musings of the jackdaw hunt, Glassford looked up to find the raffish California instructor hovering over him. The other students had evidently taken his misdirected answer in a sexual context. Recovering after a disoriented moment, he said to the instructor, "I'm sorry.... You were asking me something?"

"That crap you're painting. What is it?"

Glassford reddened at the insult. "Fort Riley."

"It looks like a horse just took a dump on the canvas. And take that watch off your wrist!"

Glassford felt the instructor's hand gripping his forearm.

"No professional paints with a watch on!"

"Sir, you'd best unhand me."

The instructor tightened his grip. "Who let you in this class, anyway?"

He wasn't about to be hazed again, especially by this opium-sotted jerk. He landed the teacher on his back with a jujitsu move. Looking around and finding the students staring at him with gaped jaws, he asked them with a challenging smile, "Anybody else think I should remove this watch?"

They shook their heads, suddenly filled with newfound respect for him.

He helped the dazed instructor to his feet. "We haven't been properly introduced. I'm Captain Pelham Glassford, United States Army. Now, would you really mind that much if I left my watch on while I painted?"

The instructor, terrified, looked down at the wet spot on his crotch. He managed a weak wave for the class—and Glassford—to carry on.

8

WASHINGTON, D.C.
JULY 1914

aptain Douglas MacArthur sat at his father's old roll-top desk in his fifth floor suite of the Hadleigh Apartments and ran his fingers across the thin War Department envelope that had just been delivered by an Army courier. All of the sacrifices—the physical and psychological suffering at the Point, the late nights studying with candles hidden under sheets after curfew, the grim determination to graduate first in his class, the grueling assignments and moves from outpost to outpost—all were about to be eclipsed by the contents of this letter inside. He slid the silver point of the opener into the crease, careful to avoid cutting what would surely become a precious document of American military history. He had been as steady as a rock when the bullets flew at Veracruz, but now he felt more on edge than when he had testified during the hazing scandal. Finally, with a quick, jagged stroke, he sliced open the envelope and—

"Not yet, Douglas. First, tell me again of Mexico."

He sighed with impatience. "Mother, I have recounted the story to you at least a dozen times."

Pinky MacArthur firmed her grasp on her son's shoulder. "Start at the beginning, darling, with General Wood. He has been so very kind to us."

He reluctantly dropped the letter, still folded, to the desk. In weak retaliation, he reached for a cigar in his humidor, eschewing the corncob pipe that he smoked as part of his carefully orchestrated military persona. Although he preferred stogies, he would never allow himself to be seen in public with one. General Grant had immortalized that image, and some might interpret cigar smoking as a crass attempt at imitation. Such accessories had to be adopted with subtlety. He had made a careful study of the great commanders of the past. A trait they had all shared was a keen understanding of the necessity for an identifying mannerism, one that the common soldiers could latch onto as a comforting symbol of victory and bravado. And so, he had decided the corncob pipe offered the perfect blend of frontier dash and American ingenuity.

"Douglas, your father died from that pernicious habit. You know I cannot abide the smoke in our house."

Our house?

This time, his sigh was resigned. Here he was, thirty-three years old and a member of the Army's General Staff, but still she treated him like a boy. He stole a last puff before putting the cigar out in the tray. He would humor her, as always, for any reminder of his father threatened to send her into a relapse of the mysterious invalidity from which she had only recently recovered.

Of course, he could only hope to approximate the sterling combat record, impeccable flair, and sense of timing that his father, the hero of Missionary Ridge and Manila, had demonstrated, even to the very end. Two years ago, while on the dais addressing the fiftieth reunion of the Twenty-fourth Wisconsin Regiment, Lt. General Arthur MacArthur had collapsed from a heart attack. The elderly surgeon of his father's Civil War unit had looked up from his knees to announce to his fellow veterans that their commander was dying. On that tragic night, ninety surviving comrades had stood around his father, crying and reciting the Lord's Prayer. When he was finally pronounced dead, they had wrapped him in the tattered regimental flag.

"You were fevering with malaria," Pinky reminded him, drawing him back to that time when destiny had first called him to Mexico.

"Tonsillitis."

Waving off his attempt to correct her, Pinky began pacing the room like a haunting ghost. "I was beside myself with the news. You had that same ghastly look of death that your brother Malcolm held before he passed from the measles. But the country needed you. General Wood told me that no other man could perform the task. I pulled myself together and told him that, early on in life, I knew that I was to be martyred repeatedly in my heart for the sake of the flag. If my son must be raised upon the cross, I wrote to him, I would stand willingly at the foot and suffer in silence.... Oh, Douglas, if you had been killed, no one would have known."

"That comes with the territory on spy operations," he said dryly, bemused at how she seemed to be hinting that she also deserved a medal.

Pinky catapulted the back of her hand to her forehead. "That monster! I cannot bear to think of how Huerta insulted the Stars and Stripes! If you had been placed in charge of the garrison instead of that blockhead Funston, we would welcoming Mexico into the Union!"

"Mother! How many times must I tell you? You *must* be more circumspect about what you say in this city!"

She spun on him with a crescendo of fury. "Every word of it is true! These insufferable colonials understand only the language of force! Your father found that out! That tub of lard Taft would not listen to him! If he had, General MacArthur could have won the Philippines for us!"

He set his jaw, sharing as he did her disdain for the insipid civilian liaisons who were always being sent off to rein in military commanders. "One day I will avenge that slight."

Pinky's eyes narrowed with ambition. "Yes ... yes, you will." She walked to the window and looked down across Dupont Circle, toward the White House and the Washington Monument towering over it. "The newspapermen will be calling you tomorrow. They will want an account of your heroism. It must be told in the appropriate tone. With humility, but with no details left out."

"The War Department will issue a press release."

She spun on him, aghast that he would even contemplate leaving such an important matter to those backstabbers at Fort Myer. "Absolutely not, Douglas! They must hear it from *you*, word for word. Practice telling it to me."

"I still have several hours of work left and—"

"Was I wrong when I required you to practice your oratories in my presence during your matriculation at the Point?"

One of the marks of a skillful military man, he had learned, was to know when to concede defeat. He stood obediently, as she had always insisted he do during their study sessions at the Point. Addressing an imaginary bank of reporters, he recited: "General Woods assigned me to undertake a solitary reconnaissance mission deep into Mexican territory with the objective of preparing the way for an invasion force to come to the salvation of the United States Marines in harm's way in the port of Veracruz."

She reached to his chin and lifted it. "Project your voice, dear."

Taking her cue, he elevated his carriage for a more Shakespearean delivery. "On the evening of June 3, armed with only a revolver, I absconded from Veracruz and walked deep into hostile territory—"

"Terrain once investigated by Robert E. Lee."

He nodded to confirm the importance of adding that comparison to the annals. "On my desperate Iliad through the Mexican barrens, I encountered numerous bandits and ruffians. I was forced to shoot my way out of several scrapes, including one with a band of horsemen, and my uniform suffered dearly with numerous bullet holes. Near morning, I made my way down a stream by canoe until I discovered an abandoned handcar on the rail tracks. I made my way another mile toward five locomotives and inspected the engines should we need to transport a relief army. Armed with the invaluable information, I made my way back toward Veracruz. The return, to put it succinctly, was a violent and bloody action."

"Don't forget the derringer."

"Ah, yes." Armed with that reminder, he continued the practiced report. "Having spent the bullets for my revolver, I was forced to resort to my last and only hope—a small derringer I carried in my vest pocket. I dropped two of the scoundrels and gave thanks to God for the aim He had given to me. As dawn rose, I scampered back over the walls of Veracruz. Those Marines were darned surprised to see me. And I was never so glad to see American faces in my life."

Pinky smoothed the wrinkles in his shirt, beaming at his performance. "Your father would have been so proud of you, Douglas. Now, my dearest son, you may open your reward."

He sat down again and pulled the letter from the envelope. He took a deep breath, having rehearsed this moment a thousand times. Then, he scanned the correspondence for the three most important words in a military man's life. His face reddened.

"What is wrong?"

He unbuttoned his collar, gulping for air.

Pinky stole the letter from his grasp and read it. "No.... this cannot be!"

He turned aside, trying not to let her see his tearing eyes. The last line of the letter was already seared into his brain: *To award Captain MacArthur the Medal of Honor might encourage any other staff officer, under similar conditions, to ignore the local commander, possibly interfering with the latter's plans with reference to the enemy.*

Pinky, outraged, circled behind him. "But General Wood recommended you! Those traitors on the awards committee!"

I should have seen this coming, he told himself.

Leonard Wood had ordered him not to tell General Funston, the commander at Veracruz, of the spy mission, lest Funston let it slip to junior officers who might reveal it inadvertently to the many Mexican agents in the city. Those bastards at the War Department despised him for his brilliance, and now they were conspiring to reverse his meteoric rise in the Army, latching onto this flimsy excuse to deny him his due. His father had suffered the same crime of jealousy when the Army denied him his Medal of Honor for thirty years.

We should have been the only father and son to ever receive the decoration.

Recovering to a steely composure, he picked up a pen and dipped it into the ink well.

"Douglas, what are you doing?"

He placed two clean sheets of his embossed stationery on the writing pad. "I am going to protest this injustice."

Alarmed, Pinky for once became the voice of reason. "You must not antagonize those inferior men in the War Department. Allow me to take care of this matter. You still have time."

"This was my only chance. There may never be another war in my lifetime."

"Douglas, please."

He ignored her plea. On the first letter, addressed to General Wood, he wrote: *I miss the inspiration, my dear general, of your own clear-cut, decisive methods. I hope sincerely that affairs will shape themselves so that you will shortly take the field for the campaign which, if death does not call you, can have but one ending—the White House.*

He titled the second letter, to the awards committee, an Official Memorandum, and in it he excoriated its members for what he termed their *rigid narrow-mindedness and lack of imagination.*

LONDON, ENGLAND
AUGUST 1914

Bert Hoover weaved through panicked crowds inside Victoria Station and confronted a scene of chaos that appeared all too familiar. Fourteen years earlier, he had witnessed that same pale look of terror on the faces of his fellow Westerners during the siege of Tientsin. The trains from Portsmouth that morning were disgorging thousands of American refugees from the Continent. Most hadn't even been given the time to collect their luggage before escaping France, and many had not eaten in two days. In the vertiginous span of a week, Austria-Hungary had declared war on Serbia for the assassination of the heir to the Austrian throne, and in retaliation, Russia, Germany, and France had mobilized their armed forces. Only a few hours ago, the wires had brought news that the Germans had invaded Belgium in a stunning flanking maneuver designed to encircle Paris. The Asquith government, he knew, would have no choice but to bring Great Britain into the war.

Like everyone else here, he had failed to foresee how swiftly the sinews of modern society in the West could be severed. Now, pitiful coveys of students, teachers, and vacationing women huddled in the main concourse of the station, destitute and frightened, not knowing when their next meal might come. He was convinced that the Kaiser had timed the onslaught at the height of the summer tourist season, when the European banks were closed for a three-day holiday. Even if the teller windows could be reopened, the cut telegraph lines and the prohibition against transporting bullion across borders had made transfers of funds between most Continental banks impossible. Traveler's cheques, money orders, and letters of credit—all had been rendered useless.

"Bert!"

He turned to find his wife Lou rushing at him from a queue at one of the ticket windows.

"Bert, thank God I found you!"

He pressed her hand into his, trying to calm her. "You shouldn't have come down here. Where are the boys?"

She was nearly breathless from rushing across the station. "Bertie is still at school. I left Allan with Mary Kent for an hour. I have good news."

"You'd be the only one in London, then."

Brushing aside his pessimism, she produced a document from her purse. "Our passage on the *Vaterland* is confirmed for the thirteenth. The Atlantic sailings haven't been canceled yet."

"The *Vaterland* is a German liner."

"It could be a Chinese junk for all I care," she said. "We're finally going home." When he avoided her eyes, she pressed him. "What's wrong?"

He glanced around the station at the throngs of abandoned Americans. "These people need my help."

Lou's shoulders sagged. "We've been away from home for fifteen years. You promised the boys we'd spend Christmas in California."

"You go on with Bertie and Allan. I'll come over as soon as I can."

She pinned him with a suspicious eye. "What have you got up your sleeve?"

"I've sent messages to Kent, Hetzler, and some of the other bankers. We're meeting at the Waldorf this afternoon. I think I can convince them to honor all American letters of credit without requiring collateral. We'll borrow on the gold reserves. Just enough to pay for the necessary passage tickets back to America."

"And what about those who don't have letters of credit?" When he did not answer her, but shifted his gaze, she demanded, "Bert?"

"The Lord has blessed us, Lou."

"You're going to loan them money from our *personal* funds?"

"Short term."

"How many will need our help?"

"The British Admiralty estimates about a hundred and twenty-five thousand Americans will be stranded here."

"What if they don't pay us back? We'll be bankrupted!"

"They will pay us back. And if they don't, well ... we can always earn more."

Exasperated, she began walking fast, until she had led him out of the station and east along the Strand.

He hurried to catch up with her. "Lou, I could not live with myself if—"

She turned back on him in hot anger. "Where am I supposed to go?"

"I'll wire ahead to New York and let Richard Jansen know that you and the boys will be staying at the apartment in—"

"No." She matched his determination. "I mean, where am I supposed to go to help *you* help these people?"

He was stunned by her offer. "You don't have to stay."

Lou hugged him. "This is why I married you, Bert Hoover. You never pass a soul in need without offering aid. You are a good man doing God's work. Now, tell me what role I will have in this great humanitarian endeavor, or I will embarrass you in front of all of these priggish Londoners."

Tears came to his eyes, and he brought his lips to her ear. "I think, instead, I will be the one to make *you* blush." He pressed a passionate kiss to her mouth, restraining her attempt to pull back while onlookers cheered. He would have stayed in her arms, but he felt a tapping on his shoulder.

"Are you Hoover?"

He turned from his embrace to find a gaggle of American women waiting for him in front of the Savoy Hotel. He doffed his hat to them. "I am. This is my wife, Lou. How can I help you ladies?"

Their self-designated spokesperson, a plump, cantankerous matron with a heated face that resembled a very ripe peach, inspected him from head to toe. "The hotel manager said you're the man to see about getting back to America."

Lou glared at her husband, informed only now that he had set his humanitarian plan into motion days before he had told her about it.

With a guilty smile, he nodded to the American women and opened his palms in a chivalrous gesture. "How many are in your party?"

"Fifteen," the lady spokesperson said before her companions could get a word in. "I'm traveling with my sister. We came over to do the Grand Tour."

He looked around the group for someone who might resemble her sibling. "Your sister must be the shy one in the family."

"Shy? Oh no, not Eleanor. She's in the lobby on a hunger strike."

"You mean your sister is not eating *on purpose*?" Lou exclaimed. "While thousands would give anything for a meal?"

"Those British bastards at Thomas Cook refuse to book us first class. The gall! These Normans expect us to return to the States in common steerage. Eleanor has vowed not to eat another bite until first-class tickets are issued."

Hoover grasped Lou's forearm to stifle a volcanic eruption. Before his wife could bite off a protest, he promised the demanding biddy, "I'll see what I can do about improving your accommodations on board. Is there anything else I can do to make your journey endurable?"

"As a matter of fact, there is. You can also give us a written guarantee that our ship will not be torpedoed by those German savages. Bonded by the full faith and credit of your mining company."

Hoover bowed, acting the part of a humble servant. "You'll have the instrument of guaranty in your travel documents before you depart."

Finally satisfied, the American woman turned and climbed the stairs to the hotel lobby, followed by her obedient fellow travelers.

Alone again with her husband, Lou cut loose. "You're going to provide that battle ax with a written promise that she won't be sent to the bottom of the ocean? Which, by the way, would be doing all of humanity a great service!"

"You must learn to think like a businessman, my dear. If the lady arrives home safely, she will tell all of her wealthy acquaintances in the States that Herbert Hoover accommodated her every need in a time of crisis."

"And if she doesn't arrive safely?"

He winked. "Well, then it won't really matter, will it?"

arry each other's burdens, and in this way you will fulfill the law of Christ. Bert Hoover drew solace from that promise from Galatians, but what he really needed was the biblical power to multiply the loaves and the fishes. And it wouldn't hurt if the Almighty also requisitioned for him a dozen or so cargo ships to carry the bounty across the Channel.

As he waited in the hall outside the Chancellor of the Exchequer's office, a servant presented him with a choice of bland crackers to take with his tea. He waved off the offer, having not recovered his appetite since returning from Belgium earlier that week. That dangerous journey through the front lines had been a surreal nightmare; twice he had been forced to strip naked and suffer humiliating searches. The Germans, understandably, were suspicious of an American coming through the blockade, even though the United States had proclaimed its neutrality. Yet the British had been just as harsh to him on his return to London, and he knew the scoundrel who was behind all of the harassment: That saber-rattling Churchill in Admiralty was lobbying to stop the food shipments from leaving Rotterdam. Quaker or no, he mulled, if left alone in a room with that royalist drunk, he would require all the restraint in his power not to throw a haymaker into the growing British Empire of his girth.

But none of that mattered now. His personal travails paled in comparison to the suffering of those starving Belgian children. He could not erase their drawn faces from his memory. Clad in rags and clutching their ration cards, the little ones had waited stoically for hours in the rain to receive a cup of weak gruel. Many were orphans, just as he had been. Around them had stood only burnt buildings and the ruins of once-proud towers, but still they would pass him, bow their heads, and whisper *Merci;* and then they would walk away barefooted under the threatening glowers of the German soldiers. Several times, unable to bear the sorrow, he had been forced to turn aside.

When the pressures became too much, he would sometimes dream of resigning from the Committee for the Relief of Belgium and leaving the mess to these Europeans who had created it. Had the war started a week later, he would be safe in San Francisco now, attending to his business fortune and spending time at his beloved Stanford University.

But the Almighty, it seemed, permitted no good deed to go unpunished. At the start of the war, he and Lou had been so successful in assisting the thousands of stranded Americans to get back home that an old Belgian business rival, Emile Francqui, had begged him to head up the effort to save his invaded country. Before the war, Belgium had produced only thirty percent of its own food, and now the tiny nation was caught in a vise, its fields left fallow and its harbors closed. He had called on every American and British business friend to trickle in enough grain to prevent bodies from piling high on the streets of Brussels, but he was fighting a losing battle. When an American newspaperman had asked him how the relief operation was progressing, he had described it as trying to feed a hungry kitten by means of a forty-foot bamboo pole, with the kitten confined in a barred cage occupied by two hungry lions.

The truth was, he had exhausted every stopgap measure at his disposal. And so, he had been forced to come here, hat in hand, to Downing Street. This meeting would determine if Belgium was to be thrown to the wolves.

A functionary opened the door. "The Chancellor will see you now."

He was escorted into a conference room where several Cabinet members sat around a long table. David Lloyd George, that Welsh stick of dynamite, chaired the meeting. Flanking him was Lord Kitchener, the lugubrious military hero, now Secretary of State for War, whose long hound's face and beckoning finger accosted everyone from recruiting posters all over Britain. The old warhorse looked deathly ill; his skin was the hue of slate and his usually meticulous mustache had grown wild.

From the far side of the table, Winston Churchill sat snorting contempt.

Hoover saw that the First Lord of the Admiralty had perched himself near Kitchener, no doubt hoping that the rays of respect and awe for the British ancient sun god would flatter his own liverish aura. The dozen or so other ministers in the room he did not recognize, but all stared at him with pinched, contemptuous eyes, evidently disgusted at being forced to waste war-planning time on an American with a ragged-shorn haircut whose family pedigree was no more elevated than that of the servant just dismissed from the chamber.

"That man is a son of a bitch," Churchill muttered to Lord Kitchener, who was so hard of hearing that he did not pick up on the aside.

Hoover considered ignoring the slight, but kowtowing wasn't in his nature, particularly on a day that would decide the fate of so many innocent civilians. "I wasn't aware that genealogy was one of your avocations, Lord Churchill. I suppose I owe my circumstance to our independence. In America, even a son of the lowest class of woman can rise up to help Europeans in need."

"In need?" Churchill cried in his infamous high-pitched lisp. "In this country, sir, we call what you are doing aiding and abetting the enemy."

Lloyd George glared Churchill to silence, and with one eye still on his irascible naval chief, told Hoover, "Mr. Churchill has an apology to offer."

The color took its time returning to Churchill's piggy face, but finally the shameless monarchist grumbled, "The charges were … premature."

Lloyd George rolled his crinkly eyes like a frustrated father. "I shall be more explicit than my colleague here. Mr. Hoover, the British Government expresses its deepest regrets that a warrant for corruption and espionage was issued against you in retaliation for your recent humanitarian endeavors. We were heartened to hear that the King's Bench dismissed the charges as groundless, and we can assure you that no such other infringements upon your duties will be countenanced in the future."

"Water under the bridge," Hoover said. "No time can be wasted arguing over past wounds. Every hour counts if we are to save Belgium from a catastrophe. I trust, after these many weeks, you have finally come round to my petition."

The British lowered their aristocratic glares, astonished by the bluntness and unwilling to accept a warning delivered by a man of such inferior station. Lloyd George cleared his throat and told Hoover, "Sir, we have indeed considered your request for financing of future food shipments to the Belgians. Given the exigencies of our war effort, however, I am afraid that we must decline to participate in your missionary work."

Seeing how much Churchill was enjoying the delivery of the rejection, Hoover took a moment to calm before locking onto Lloyd George. "May I be heard on this?"

Lloyd George glanced impatiently at the wall clock. "Do be brief, sir."

"Why is Britain fighting this war?"

Affronted by the curt question, the British officials straightened in their chairs, and even Kitchener lifted an inch from his slumbering hibernation. Churchill gave his Cabinet superior no time to respond. "We fight to save democracy and to preserve the sovereignty of smaller nations who cannot defend themselves."

Hoover scanned the table, looking into each set of haughty eyes. "What good does it do to send your boys off to die if the people in those democracies are all starved by the time you prevail?"

Kitchener's unkempt mustache fluttered with indignation. The old warhorse reached into a canvas campaigning bag at his feet and pulled out a rusted tin can, cut open at the top. He placed the can on the table and slid it down toward Hoover. "Do you know what *that* is?"

Hoover removed a handkerchief from his breast pocket and picked up the can to examine. "This is one of our milk containers."

"It *was* one of your milk containers," Kitchener said. "Our sappers retrieved it at Ypres. The Germans are converting them into grenades. The one you now hold was responsible for the death of four Yorkshire infantrymen."

Had the can still been a live explosive, Hoover might have given a second's thought to pulling the pin and taking out this entire cabal of puffering gray-heads. "I am told that both armies are melting down the crosses worn by the wounded and extracting the gold and iron."

"War necessitates salvage," Churchill insisted.

Hoover bored in on the bilious naval chief. "Why not then ban your soldiers from wearing crosses if the icons can be converted to bullets?"

Kitchener set his gold-capped teeth in anger. He summoned his waning strength and, as he was notorious for doing during staff meetings, stood up to deliver a condescending lecture on military strategy. "If the Germans are forced to feed the Belgians, sir, that will leave them less food to supply their own troops and people."

"The Germans will *not* feed the Belgians," Hoover warned. "They will save their own people first. And we will be responsible for a calamity of desolation against civilians—women and children and old men—the likes of which have never been witnessed."

Kitchener was unaccustomed to having his pronouncements challenged, and he shared a gape-jawed look at Churchill, his companion in indignation. The elderly general hovered unsteadily over the table for a few moments, fumbling for words, but finally he crumbled back into his seat and returned to the comfort of his briefing papers, which could not talk back to him.

Churchill came to his hero's assistance. "There are rumors that this relief boondoggle of yours is rife with profiteering and corruption."

Hoover did not flinch. He had expected from the start of his relief operation to eventually confront such charges. "Every penny from the transport of the food has been confirmed by an independent accounting firm. If you wish, Lord Churchill, I can arrange for you to inspect the Committee's books."

Checkmated, Churchill groused a curse into his glass of spirits.

Lloyd George finally broke the tense silence. "Even if these shipments were allowed, nothing would prevent the Germans from stealing the foodstuffs from the Belgians."

"The Germans have not seized any of the donations delivered during these past months," Hoover reminded them. "And the German ambassador has given me his word that his country will not violate the relief effort, provided Britain abides by the same rules."

Lloyd George seemed troubled by that news.

Knowing this would be his last chance to change their minds, Hoover leaned closer and dropped his voice, forcing the others in the room to cup their ears. "Sir, you have a reputation for caring about the less fortunate. Like Wales, Belgium is a small but proud nation. Through the centuries, your homeland has been no stranger to privation. Consider if it were Wales on the brink of disaster, and Belgium stood able to come to your aid, but chose to let you die."

Churchill slammed a fist to the table. "How dare you address us in such a churlish manner, sir! This is not one of your American barn disputations!"

Ignoring Churchill, Hoover remained fixed on Lloyd George, who was taking in the debate with owlish detachment. "I implore you to forgo whatever dubious military advantage might be seen in casting Belgium to the rocks. Think of the magnanimity that will outlast the bitterness of this war. To do otherwise would be to reach for an empty victory."

"War is a game that must be played with a smile," Churchill said with a snarl. "If you cannot smile, Mr. Hoover, then grin. If you cannot grin, keep out of our way until you can."

Hoover turned a judgmental gaze upon Churchill's vest, which had a bottom button undone to accommodate a small paunch. "Have *you* ever tried grinning on an empty stomach?"

Before Churchill could lob back one of his famous venomous retorts, Lloyd George banged his knuckles on the table. "I am convinced."

The British officials nodded and began shuffling papers, relieved that the crass American businessman would finally be sent on his way and they could get on with other business.

Lloyd George stood, walked to the far end of the table, and shook hands with Hoover. "You have my permission. The shipments will proceed."

Blindsided, the British officials fell silent, stunned by the policy change.

Hoover shook the Chancellor's hand in admiration for his courageous decision. Before walking out of the room, he reached for the decanter, poured two jiggers into a glass, and handed it to Churchill. "I promise not to deplete the Empire's supply of brandy."

10

CHIHUAHUA, MEXICO
MARCH 1916

Floyd Gibbons sped his armored Dodge touring car around the *zopilote* buzzards that were picking at the bean tins jettisoned by the five thousand American troops chasing Pancho Villa. Here on this rocky road sixty miles south of the New Mexico border, the hibiscus and bougainvillea fragrances encircling the haciendas had given way to the acrid stench of unburied horse carcasses and spent gunpowder. He smiled with anticipation, his nostrils flaring from the peppery aroma of black nitrate.

The holy incense of the war priests.

During the past two years, he had tramped all over Mexico interviewing swashbuckling revolutionaries and witnessing grisly executions in the hundreds, all for the pleasure of *Chicago Tribune* readers. Every hardscrabble village in these desolate Sierra Madres had its own torture house and dried mud wall that, depending on which *bandito* happened to be riding through that day, became a Golgotha for the local burghers or lowly laborers. He had even coined a new verb to describe this peculiarly Mexican spectacle of quasi-judicial murder: *To be adobed.*

Each morning at dawn, the chosen victims would be marched from their jail cells and stood against stones blackened from the dried blood of past victims. Dressed in their Sunday finest of white shirts, black suits, and bolo hats, the condemned would stroll to the designated spot with a jarring indifference, waving and joking with friends as if on a festival parade. Most enjoyed a few last puffs on a cigarette and, waving off an offered blindfold, opened their coats to expose their chests as a clear target. Then would come the shout calling for good aim—*En el pecho, mis amigos! En el pecho!*—and the firing squad, usually no more than fifteen feet away, would comply by riddling the victim's breast with a dozen rounds. Puffs of dust would fluff the adobe wall, and after nearly levitating for a split second, the brave *hombre* would spin on his heels and collapse.

The Mexicans had their own shibboleth for this daily ritual of dying with courage: *Hombrearse con la muerte.* To push death around.

The soldiers and families who had joined Villa's rebel armies were dirt poor, but no one could take away their dignity, not even at the bitter end. Some even went to their violent deaths singing. At Aguascalientes, he had watched the ruthless military commander Obregon hang all eighty members of Villa's famous musical band. Trombonists, guitarists, and trumpeters had been forced to play Villa's anthem, *La Cucaracha*, before being strung up on the trees lining the city's main boulevard with their instruments dangling at their feet.

The rhythmic banging of two Springfield rifles on the passenger floorboard interrupted his memories. Alerted by the cessation of the usual banter in the back seat, he looked over his shoulder and caught his fellow correspondents, Frank Elser of *The New York Times* and George Seese of the *Associated Press*, scribbling furiously in their journals. He slammed his foot on the brake and sent his two companions flying into the headboards, spattering their faces with ink.

"Son of a whoring bitch!" Seese, a tall scarecrow from Brooklyn, now resembled a painted Mayan. "You want to kill us all before Pershing gets the chance?"

Gibbons tossed a dirty oil rag to the back seat. "You boys wouldn't be trying to get the jump on me with your wire stories, would you now?"

Elser, a gifted novelist who could write the Devil out of Hell, sat glaring in horror at his latest page, now obliterated. "Damn you, Gibbons! That one was going to make it above the fold."

Gibbons fired up the sputtering Dodge again and resumed their invasion deep into the heart of Villista territory. Elser he could abide, barely, because the man had talent. But that goddamn Seese relied on pure luck to get his sappy stories. A couple months ago, while the other correspondents were out in the desert burning leather to rustle up anything worth filing, Seese had been sleeping off a bender in the Commercial Hotel at Columbus, New Mexico, when Villa had decided to burn the town on one of his wild raids. The *loco* firebrand had killed eighteen Americans in the debacle, and editors at every newspaper back home had been thrown into an uproar demanding firsthand accounts. As a result, through no effort of his own, Seese had become an overnight sensation with his wire stories filed from his "observation post" in the hotel window.

Gibbons kept grousing over that disastrous *coup;* the steam hissing from his ears could have powered the locomotive chugging down the tracks that ran aside this dirt road. How many times had he curried *El Jaguar's* favor with boxes of stogies? And then that bullet-festooned *bandito* bastard didn't even bother to send him advance warning of his sortie? Losing a story like that could cost a correspondent his career. He hated losing, especially to these Eastern assholes and their smug bylines; he was now more determined than ever to make a name for himself on this campaign so that he could demand to be shipped over to France to cover the real action.

"Gibbie," Seese purred. "You got anything to drink?"

"I'll stop and let you suck on one of those saguaro bushes. I hear that's how Geronimo survived out here."

Seese rustled around under the floorboards searching for a bottle. "Can you ferment cactus juice?"

Gibbons was already regretting his decision to pool their expense money to purchase this wheeled tin lizard. He preferred working alone, but the paper was paying him such a paltry *per diem* that he thought he might save a few dollars. "Let's go over the ground rules again," he said, not that he was about to follow them himself. "None of us touches the typewriters until Black Jack camps for the night. You keep your eyes and hands off my copy. I keep mine off yours."

"But *Fullll—llllloyd*," Elser moaned. "Your prose is so smooth and seductive, how can we help ourselves?"

"Yeah, Gib," Seese chimed in. "Tells us again of your ghost séances with President Madero before he bit the bullet. That story you wrote about his belief in astral conversations convinced me there *is* a God."

"You gin-sogged heathens think I made all that up. But I'll swear on St. Patrick's crosier that Madero was talking to the spirits when I interviewed him. He even told me that George Washington was standing over my shoulder and shaking his head at what I was writing."

"That's because old George couldn't tell a lie!" Seese said. "He saw that your notes were filled with them."

Gibbons ignored their taunts. "Let me ask you two hacks something. I've filed at least a hundred stories from down here. But that asshole Snelden on the desk in Chicago keeps bitching about my standard background graf. He says I don't explain this revolution so that the average American can understand it. How am I supposed to summarize this entire shithole war in one paragraph?"

Elser thought up a quick graf on the fly. "How about this one: 'Foreign fat cats came into Mexico and bought up all the land and utilities. When the old guard in Mexico City howled in protest, Uncle Sam gave weapons and money to bandits like Zapata and Villa to do its dirty work. Then that Puritan Woodrow Wilson got elected and decided revolution was dirty business, so he hung Villa out to dry. Villa retaliated by gutting a few gringos to avenge Mexico's honor.'"

Gibbons groaned. "The literary world should be thankful you didn't cover the Trojan War. Homer must be rolling over in his *tholos*."

Elser kicked at the seat. "Hell, Gib, your prose is so damn purple that even the rotting fish complain when they get wrapped in it."

"I can sum up the whole stinking business down here in one sentence," Seese insisted. "The meek shall inherit the Earth."

Gibbons laughed at their pathetic attempts to define morality for a hellhole like Chihuahua. "I've got an idea."

"I hope it's better than your last one," Elser said. "I think those whores in El Paso gave me the clap."

Gibbons spat out a ball of dust. "I say we come up with one background graf together and all take a vow to use it. That way, if one of our editors starts whining, we can point to the other's stories and say this was the only description of the war we could get past the Mexican censors."

Elser monitored the reaction from Gibbons's reflection in the rearview mirror. "Hey, Gib. Those reports you filed on Villa's defeat at Ceylaya. Did you have a prearranged code with your editor?"

Gibbons curled a devious grin. "Yeah, I knew old Pancho would read every word I wrote before he'd let me telegraph it home."

"Villa's illiterate," Seese reminded him.

Gibbons winked, putting the lie to that myth. "Right, I forgot. He must have been looking at the comics when I found him with his nose in those Mexico City newspapers."

"What *was* your secret code word?" Elser asked.

Gibbons revealed his secret adverb by writing it in the air. "'Apparently.'"

Elser shook his head in grudging admiration. "Yeah, I remember you writing that Villa had *apparently* won the battle. Brilliant. Villa couldn't understand the nuance. And all this time I thought you were just drunk when you filed that copy. That was the signal for your desk jockeys in Chicago to write a companion article stating that Villa had been routed."

Seese sounded jealous. "You won't pull stunts like that if you get to France."

"*When* I get to France. And no censor is going to stop me over—"

A rider on a gray horse came galloping up from the south in a dust cloud. Gibbons braked the automobile to a grinding halt and handed out the Springfields. He shielded his eyes from the low sun, but couldn't find the blue column of cavalry up ahead.

"Dammit, Gib," Elser groused. "You fell behind the horses' asses again. Nigger Jack's gonna flay us alive."

Gibbons cringed on hearing the racial slur that Pershing had earned for commanding the Negro Tenth Cavalry. "Better watch your mouth, Elser. If the general hears you call him that, he'll feed your balls to the scorpions. Now pay attention to those rocks over there."

The three correspondents nervously aimed their rifles at the approaching rider, fearful of being waylaid by the notorious Fierro, the psychopathic killer who tortured Villa's prisoners.

Gibbons squinted into the fading dusk light. "Oh, no."

Seese fingered his trigger. "One of Pancho's cutthroats?"

"Worse. It's that corn-cracker Patton."

Muttering curses, Elser and Seese lowered their weapons, but Gibbons lingered his barrel toward the horizon a bit longer, resisting the urge to let go with a couple of rounds at Pershing's gofer, Lt. George Patton. That foul-mouthed cockerel had been assigned to ride herd on the correspondents to make sure they portrayed this so-called Punitive Campaign in the most favorable light. Irascible and high-strung, Patton was also dyslexic, a condition that made him defensive and combative around newspapermen. Yet Gibbons did share a couple of traits with the officer: a preening ambition for fame, and an insatiable lust to get to the battlefields of France. The delicious irony was that Patton had been allowed to accompany the invasion force not because of his merit, which was undeniable, but because Pershing had become enamored with Patton's sister, who was waiting for the general back in El Paso. As the officer cantered up to the car, Gibbons whispered over his shoulder to his mates. "Let's have a little fun with Georgie boy."

Breathless from the forced ride, Patton circled the car and glared down at Gibbons. "I should have known *you'd* be at the wheel."

"Howdy, Lieutenant," Gibbons drawled like a cowboy. "What brings you to these parts? Somebody steal your saddle blanket again?"

Patton gritted his perfect teeth at having to deal with such uncouth scoundrels of inferior social class. "General Pershing is madder than a wet hen! He had to halt the column to wait for you people!"

Gibbons lit up a new cigar. "No need to wait for us, Jorge. We can follow the trail of canteens and soda bottles you soldier boys have been tossing behind to lighten your load. Are you fellas conducting a military expedition or seeding a new garbage dump?"

"Your orders are to maintain visual contact with the vanguard."

"Not our fault, Lew-tenant," Gibbons croaked between cigar puffs. "The telegraph operator on that train carrying your laundry flagged us over to deliver a message to headquarters."

Patton blinked his white-browed eyelids in confusion. "That is *my* assignment! I am to personally convey all communications to General Pershing."

"That's what I told the old warthead. But he said you were so far up Black Jack's ass that he couldn't find you."

Patton's freckled face bloomed crimson. "Just hand over the telegram."

"Oh, no, the message was too classified to put in writing. At least, that's what the telegraph operator told us."

Patton sat high in the saddle, agitating for his first military action. "The aeroplanes must have spotted Villa." His voice pitched higher, and he began talking so rapidly that his horse spooked.

"Careful there, Wellington. We wouldn't want another caparisoned steed to fall on you and break your flashlight again." Gibbons heard Elser and Seese sniggering behind him. Two days ago, Patton's pampered roan, unaccustomed to the Mexican heat, had collapsed atop him, but miraculously the officer had suffered no broken bones, only a bruised ego. Because of that embarrassing accident and a dozen others, Gibbons had early on concluded that this expedition was star-crossed. Hell, even Pershing had narrowly escaped injury in an automobile collision on the morning that the invasion force mustered to leave Columbus.

"Dammit, Gibbons, speak up!" Patton demanded. "Where is the Mexican felon hiding? I'll take a contingent of cavalry down there at once and surround him before he escapes."

Gibbons puffed away with lubricious delight. "No, no. The message is much more classified than mere enemy surveillance."

Patton, now even more bollixed, looked around to make sure no Villistas were lurking nearby to overhear the communiqué. "Well, out with it! There's no time to waste!"

Gibbons delayed to build to the crescendo. Finally, he cracked, "Your sister Nita said to tell your future brother-in-law that she would like him to bring some *tamales* home for dinner this evening. Not too spicy, though."

The two reporters in the backseat unleashed howls of laughter.

Patton was apoplectic. "Goddam you, Gibbons! I demand a duel of arms! You have besmirched the honor of my sister and my clan!"

Gibbons flipped the ashes of his stogie at the hooves of Patton's horse. "Soon as King Arthur can assemble the Knights of his Round Table, we'll have us a joust. But until then, let's you and I not disembowel each other before we reach the Flanders trenches. I shouldn't think it the destiny of a Patton to be shot by a lowly reporter in Chihuahua. You ought to wait for the next Waterloo or Gettysburg before you get yourself a memorial. Now, for what, may I ask, did you come back to us? Have you requisitioned those *cervezas* with the limes we ordered?"

Patton finally calmed down. With a look suggesting that he had swallowed castor oil, he grudgingly reported, "The general wishes to extend to you, Mr. Gibbons, an invitation to ride in his car with him for an hour."

"What the hell?" Seese yelped. "Why does Gibbons get an interview?"

Gibbons lorded a victorious grin over his fellow passengers. "I told you Black Jack's a military genius, boys. He knows the pecking order of a troop." He turned back to Patton. "I'll speak to the general on one condition."

Patton's eyes rounded. "*You* are making demands on *him*?"

"I didn't fall off the caisson yesterday," Gibbons said. "Pershing isn't looking to enjoy my *raconteur* wit, rare as it is. I'm the only *hombre* in this sorry exodus that has ever spent time with Villa. The general wants to prime me for information. I'm willing to be primed, of course, but I want a guarantee that he gives me the exclusive story about his strategy for the campaign."

"Bastard!" shouted Seese.

"After all we've done for you, Gib?" Elser whined. "And now you knife us in the back? What about our *rules*?"

Patton finally accepted the condition with a gruff nod, and Gibbons jumped out of the car before the two correspondents in the back seat could wrestle him down. He climbed atop the saddle behind the officer who only moments before had threatened to kill him. As they galloped off toward the invasion column, he waved a taunt at the two cursing reporters.

Arriving at the camp where the cavalry was resting, Gibbons leapt down from the saddle behind Patton and found Pershing sitting on a stool by the rear bumper of his car. The general, always a stickler for appearance, was peering into a mirror and shaving while his soldiers lay sprawled on the ground around him, catching a few rare minutes of sleep.

Despite his disdain for West Pointers and their airs, Gibbons liked Black Jack, even felt sorry for him. Pershing's nickname was apt, not because he had once commanded colored troops, but because a cloud of darkness seemed perpetually to hover over him. Just eight months ago, the general had received the horrifying news that his wife and three daughters were killed in a fire at their residence in the Presidio at San Francisco. Devastated, he had never fully recovered from the tragedy, nor had he been able to shake off the guilt of not bringing them out to live at Fort Bliss with him. He seemed determined to take out his anger at the world by pushing his men to their limits in the field.

Patton came marching up to cut off Gibbons. Reaching Pershing first, he formally reported to his superior, "Sir, I have delivered up the man that your Generalship summoned."

Pershing tossed his basin waters at Patton's feet, making him dance. He shook his head in weary bemusement at the officer's infuriating manner of always speaking as if he were a chamberlain in some medieval court. "Lieutenant, what would I ever do without you revealing the obvious to me?"

Patton was oblivious to the put-down. "Moreover, sir, I wish to lodge a complaint against Mr. Gibbons. He has besmirched the Army and our—"

"We'll deal with that later," Pershing snapped. "Leave us."

Curtly rebuffed, Patton saluted stiffly and marched off, his ruddy cheeks in full bloom.

Pershing wiped the streaks of shaving cream from his jaw with a towel. "Gibbons, do me a favor and lay off Patton. At least while I've got my hands full south of the border."

"He's all the entertainment I have out here."

Pershing arose from the stool and signaled for his adjutant to get the column rolling again. When the aide headed for the driver's side of the car, the general stopped him. "Let's let the newsman drive me for a while, Corporal."

The aide, astonished, retreated and found a horse at the strap line.

Gibbons got in behind the wheel and started up the engine. When Pershing gave the signal for the advance, they rumbled south with the horse column following behind them. Gibbons got right to the task before the general could set the agenda for the interview. "Whose idea was it for the Army to bring a traveling bordello on this campaign?"

Pershing's eyes narrowed. "How'd you find out about that?"

"Come on, General. I'm the all-seeing Eye of Whore Us for this invasion."

Pershing didn't find the play on words at all amusing. "Off the record?" Receiving a nod, the general revealed, "I figured we'd lose more men to gonorrhea than gunfire down here. This way, at least, I can keep the women clean."

Gibbons shifted uncomfortably in his seat, already starting to get a sore ass from the rough ride. "You need to check the tread on these tires."

"I'll change them after we catch Villa. There's no time to waste on pit stops. Some of the locals in the last town said the man was only ten miles away."

Gibbons shook his head at that naiveté. "You're not going to catch him."

Pershing clearly wasn't accustomed to being spoken to in such an irreverent manner. "Is every sonofabitch in the newspaper business a pessimist like you?"

"Villa will *always* be ten miles away. He was born running from the womb."

"You're a hell of an American, having an attitude like that."

Gibbons pressed the accelerator to punish Pershing with the thud of the faltering shock absorbers. "The United States Army chasing ol' Francisco is not much different than your boy Patton trying to mate with a porcupine."

Pershing frowned at the baffling comparison. "How's that, exactly?"

"It's a thousand pricks against one."

Pershing's expression hovered between disgust and concession.

Gibbons pulled his flask from his vest and reached it over to the general for a swig, but the offer was refused. He shrugged and took another hit. "Have you ever gone five days without eating?" Receiving the expected shake of the head, he explained the reason for his question. "Villa once fought a battle without having eaten for a week. He can live out here on nothing. And he's gonna lead you around like a snake drawing a rabbit into its hole."

"My reports say he vowed to shoot any gringo on sight. How is it you managed to get close enough to him to gain his trust?"

Gibbons grinned at the memory of their first meeting. "I was sent to Juarez to cover the prizefight between Jess Willard and Jack Johnson. I kept hearing about this charismatic Robin Hood of the Mexicans who traveled in style in a train across the northern outbacks and was trailed by Hollywood directors hoping to make a movie about him. So I bought an old railcar and fixed it up with a bathtub and a desk, then painted its side with big white letters declaring that I was a famous journalist come to sing the praises of the most famous *generalissimo* in all of Mexico. I had the festooned car pulled into his camp with six mules. He was so impressed with my monstrous *cojones* that he invited me to hook it onto his private car and join him on the campaign."

Pershing searched the parched desert for signs of his slippery prey. "Tell me about him."

"He sings himself to sleep at night."

Pershing huffed at the uselessness of that anecdote. "How does he find ammunition? We've dried up his sources north of the border, but he seems to have caches everywhere."

Gibbons laughed grimly. "He's very careful with his bullets."

"How so?"

"Well, when he captures prisoners, he stands them up nose to neck, five deep. That way he can shoot all of them in the head with one cartridge."

Pershing flushed. "What drives such a man? Greed? Sheer lunacy?"

"Honor."

Pershing winced. "Honor?"

"Villa only became a bandit after shooting the hacienda owner who raped his sister."

"If he had any real honor, he'd come out and fight like a man."

Gibbons was always grated by the ignorance of Americans, who could not understand the world unless it was clearly divided into heroes and villains. "Francisco Villa loves Mexico more than life itself. Last year, more than a hundred revolutionaries from all over the country met to decide the fate of the country. The delegates at the convention decided that the only way to gain a lasting peace was for both Carranza and Villa to resign from their positions of power. Do you know what Villa said in response to this suggestion?"

"He probably shot them."

Gibbons shook his head. "He agreed to resign. And then he suggested that both he and Carranza be executed to make sure that no one would expect their return to power."

Pershing shivered his mustache by blowing out his upper lip in disgust. After several moments of troubled contemplation, he asked, "What does the man like to eat?"

Gibbons wasn't sure he had heard correctly. "You planning to hold a feast for him?" When he saw that the general was serious about his inquiry, the correspondent answered, "He likes ice cream. Peanut brittle. Sautéed asparagus."

"Alcohol?"

"He doesn't touch the stuff. It's his only character flaw."

Pershing finally relented under Gibbon's inquisitive glare demanding the reason for such a question. "This is way off the record. We've been in contact with some Japanese businessmen who have access to Villa."

"And?"

"They've agreed to poison him for us."

Gibbons was a hard man to shock, but that made his jaw drop. When the general refused him a direct look, he shook his head, chastising himself for expecting better from an American army. "Well, I guess not everyone can be driven by honor. Particularly Woodrow Wilson."

"Watch your mouth. I won't put up with that kind of talk."

"You signed off on this culinary assassination?"

Refusing the reporter a direct look, Pershing shifted uncomfortably in his seat. "The decision was made in Washington."

Gibbons stopped the car, determined to finish the interview before moving another inch. "This so-called Punitive Expedition of yours will have repercussions beyond what you and the President can imagine."

"What the hell are you talking about?"

"The Kaiser watches every move the United States makes. His Prussian boot-lickers will be closely monitoring your military campaign down here, if that's what you call this ridiculous scorpion hunt. When you fail to catch Villa—and you *will* fail—the Germans will take it as a sign of weakness."

"That's a stretch, even for you," Pershing scoffed.

"Just wait and see."

"Whatever happens, you'll no doubt be safe under your reporter's hat."

"I'll make you a bet, General. A case of that moonshine you Missourians are so famous for says I get to the trenches in France before you do."

Pershing reached over to unlock the door latch, indicating that the interview was over. "In the unlikely event that we *are* ever over there together, make damn sure you stay out of my way."

That night, Gibbons sat alone under the stars of old Mexico, and with a spent flask at his side, pecked away on his typewriter. After an hour, he put the finishing touches on the last paragraphs of the story that he would deliver the next morning to the telegraph operator on the train:

They call it "The Gringo Hate." It is a well-named living, breathing thing, sometimes dormant, but never extinct. It is ever smoldering when it is not in flame. It never dies out. It is ever ready to rise up. It is admitted and recognized and cultivated.

That is the feeling Mexicans have toward Americans. For obvious reasons it does not appear in the diplomatic notes that reach Washington from the various revolutionary parties. On state occasions or in formal negotiations, especially where recognition by the United States is the desired object it is replaced by suave Latin politeness.

It may be said to the credit of the Mexican that he holds but little of the unreasonable prejudice against the Jew. The negro comes in for perfect equality among the lower classes. The chinaman is envied for his ability to save money and the Spaniard is disliked because he belongs to a nation that once ruled Mexico.

But the American is hated.

11

NOGALES, ARIZONA
JUNE 1916

Twenty-year-old Walter Waters rubbed his dry eyes as he peered across the sweltering darkness of the Sonoran desert. He had been standing guard at this border post for five lonely hours, with his rifle at the ready for the moment Pancho Villa and his bloodthirsty band came riding up. Only a few weeks earlier, and around this same time of night, that Mexican felon had raided Columbus, New Mexico, murdering seventeen Americans sleeping in hotels there.

He never thought he'd ever long for Weiser, but on this night he was downright homesick. With jobs at the timber camps drying up, he had finally gotten up the nerve to join the Idaho National Guard, hoping to catch a little excitement. Yet his unit had been sitting here on the border for four long months with twelve thousand other Guard call-ups, bored to death at dodging snakes and the Spanish flu. The only action he'd come close to seeing was the accidental wounding of a half-dozen tourists who had motored down on a weekend from Tucson to picnic along the Santa Cruz river and watch the Mexican government's patrols scuffle with the packs of bandits.

What he wouldn't give to be riding with Black Jack Pershing and the cavalry right now. Last week, in the local general store, he'd come across a copy of the *Chicago Tribune* that featured a story by none other than his old baseball buddy, Floyd Gibbons. He grinned at the memory of his boyhood encounter with that crazy ax-wielding reporter. It wouldn't surprise him if Gibbons ended up bringing back a dozen Mexican pitching phenoms and—

He heard a rustling in the scrub brush just ahead.

He lowered his rifle and ratcheted the bolt, making sure it was loaded. Shoot first at these dastardly Mexicanos and ask questions later, his sergeant had told him. He took careful aim at the lurker's lair.

"Waters!" came a whisper from the darkness.

Startled, Waters let go with a round.

"Hold your fire, you shit-for-brains!"

"Who-o-o-o-o-g-g-g-g-goes-th-th-th-there?"

His bunkmate, Goins Gavin, rushed up and yanked the gun from his hands. Gavin ratcheted the bolt to make sure there were no more bullets in the chamber and then threw the weapon to the ground in disgust. "You coulda splattered me halfway to Chihuahua!"

"You c-c-come up on me like Villa!"

"You think that sombrero-crowned sonofabitch talks like me? Hell, all you ever babble about is Pancho Villa this, Pancho Villa that. You'd think he was the goddamn Four Horsemen of the Apocalypse all rolled up into one! Give it a rest, will ya?"

Waters swallowed his heart back into his chest. "What are y-y-you doing out here?"

Gavin shook his head. "I don't know why they put you on guard patrol anyway. Half the goddamn Mexican army would be on us before you could spit out a warning." He reached into his pocket and handed Waters a folded piece of paper. "I'm taking over your watch."

"How come?"

"The striped buzzards have got a secret spy mission for you."

Waters got excited. "They want me to go on r-r-reconnaissance?"

"Just read the goddamn order, will ya?"

Waters struck a match for light and unfolded the paper. "S-s-soda water?"

Gavin tore up the order and scattered it to the wind. "The company is out of soda water."

"W-w-what am I supposed to do about it?"

"That Texarcana asshole who runs the hotel in town has a monopoly on the supply from El Paso. The boys are getting damn tired of paying out the nose for the drinks. Sarge wants you to go in undercover and bring back ten cases of the sparkly stuff."

"Why me?"

Gavin kept a deadpan glare. "I reckon you're the only one with the smarts and slipperiness to pull it off."

Waters broadened his chest. "I'm s-s-smelling a promotion."

"You're smelling, all right. Now skedaddle. Oh, and Waters…"

"Yeh?"

"It's a secret mission," Gavin warned. "The sergeant and I never knew nothin' about this, *comprende, compadre?*"

Waters nodded as he took off on a stealthy run toward town. Stalking from alley to alley, he slithered up behind the Bowman Hotel and found the back door locked. He picked up an abandoned tie rod, slid it into the crease of the hinge, and cracked it open. Leaving the door ajar to let in the light from the full moon, he slipped inside the storage room and rummaged through the crates until he located the bottles of soda water. It suddenly occurred to him that the spying order hadn't specified where the soda water should be delivered. He figured he'd earn a few bonus points by lugging the crates, one by one, over to Sergeant Bearson's tent in the encampment. Yeah, he'd leave them outside the flap for the Sarge to find in the morning.

When the heavy lifting was finally finished with no one the wiser, he hustled back into the encampment on the edge of town and slipped into his pup tent. Gavin was already fast asleep, so he crawled under his roll and dreamed about getting a weekend pass in reward.

Hours later, a commotion outside his tent woke him. He rushed out with Gavin and found the sergeant swearing at the top of his lungs and being led away in handcuffs. The Nogales police officers were carrying the pilfered soda water crates to a waiting wagon.

Gavin winked to his fellow Guardsmen who were now scrambling from their tents. Then, he slapped Waters on the back and whispered, "Well done, Private Waters. Secret mission accomplished."

When the conspiracy behind the nocturnal soda-water gambit had been exposed, the Guard brass punished the culprits and their unwitting dupe by transferring the entire Idaho company to the New Mexican outpost of Deming, a ramshackle town even more primitive than Nogales. There Waters and the prankstering Idahoans were assigned the dangerous duty of guarding the jail that held two Villistas condemned to be hanged for murder.

On the morning of the scheduled executions, the Idaho men, shouldering bayonet-fixed rifles, stood in ranks below a scaffold that had been set in the middle of the main street so that onlookers could gain a better view from their balconies. Hundreds of local Anglos, dressed in their Sunday best and armed with rifles, had commanded the preferred viewing spots before dawn. They had their gun chambers loaded, expecting Villa to make good on his promise to launch another raid across the border to prevent the hangings.

Waters watched with fascination as a deputy tested the trap door, sending it crashing against the beams and oiling its hinges until he was satisfied with its speed. He had never witnessed a hanging. Heck, he'd never even seen a man die peacefully, let alone by harsh means. But these hardened *nuevomexicanos* around him had seen so much bloodshed and brutality that jerking another Indian to Jesus was just all part of a day's work to them.

And then, a half-hour later, as the first needles of light sprang up over the desert, the sheriff escorted the two condemned Villistas from the jail. Waters had expected to see drooling brutes, but these two felons were just boys. The one named Sanchez looked about sixteen and couldn't have weighed more than a hundred pounds. The Anglo settlers shouted curses at the young Villistas and prayed the names of their relatives killed by their leader. Then, they listened for Spanish words of defiance that never came as the older of the two boys was set in place under the crossbeam. The Army captain in charge of the grisly affair read the death sentence and then asked the first condemned boy if he had anything to say.

The young *bandito* shook his head and muttered, "*Yo no quiero.*" Then he lowered his chin so that the black hood could be placed over his skull and the rope be tightened behind his ear.

While the others watched the noosed Mexican, Waters couldn't take his eyes off his co-conspirator, Sanchez, who stood only a few feet away, awaiting his turn to fly through death's door.

As if sensing the question now passing through Waters's mind, Sanchez turned to him and whispered, "*He seguido las órdenes. Que algún día entender.*"

Waters elbowed Gavin for a translation. "What did he say?"

"He followed orders. And that one day we would understand."

Before Waters could make sense of that prophecy, the trapdoor dropped. The first Mexican's neck snapped with a loud crack, and his spasming legs dangled a few feet above the ground. A doctor casually strolled over and placed a stethoscope to the corpse's chest. After ten seconds, the doctor turned and nodded to the captain. The dead Mexican was cut down and his hood removed, revealing his eyes and mouth still open. The crowd buzzed with satisfaction, and turned toward Sanchez to enjoy his reaction at having just witnessed what now awaited him.

Another rope was thrown over the beam, and the diminutive Sanchez, nursing a thigh wound suffered during the Columbus raid, limped up the stairs, prodded from behind. On the platform, the captain and sheriff conferred in animated whispers, arguing about some aspect of the ritual. Finally, the sheriff shook his head and stood aside. The captain positioned the inexpressive Sanchez on the reset trapdoor. Figuring the Mexican boy, like his co-conspirator, had nothing of any importance to say, the officer quickly fit him with the hood and set the noose.

The door hinged and Sanchez dropped, but this time there was no crack of the vertebrae. The young bandit writhed from the rope, gurgling and gasping. The sheriff glared a curse at the captain for not heeding his warning that the boy did not weigh enough for the length of the fall to do its work.

Waters turned aside, his stomach churning. As the Mexican boy near him struggled in agony, the crowd murmured, and some yelled suggestions on how to finish the grisly deed. The captain just stood there, dazed. Finally the sheriff pulled a knife and, standing atop a barrel rolled up for his assistance, cut Sanchez down. Still hooded, the boy collapsed to the ground, snorting for air and undulating like a worm.

"Well?" demanded the sheriff. "What do we do now?"

The captain's face was whiter than a shroud. "Get the damn judge down here."

Ten minutes later, the sheriff escorted the reluctant judge from his court-house office to the street. The judge glared at the captain, shaking his head with disgust. "This is what we get letting Washington tell us what to do."

"Do we let the boy live, or not?" the captain asked.

Sanchez had regained consciousness and was sitting up, gasping for breath through the hood.

Waters tried to imagine the terror the poor boy must be going through. Probably he was wondering if he had landed in some dark Limbo where the gringo English was spoken. Outraged by the cruelty, Waters shouted, "At least t-t-take his hood off while you ch-ch-chew the fat!"

The captain spun on his heels and pointed at him. "Silence, soldier!"

Waters stood steaming. Gavin shot him a glare of warning to shut up while the judge and town leaders continued to argue over what law applied to botched executions. Finally, the judge ordered the local telegraph office to send a wire to the governor asking for instructions. As they waited, the heat built into the day and fried the street, and poor Sanchez sat trembling and hooded, sweating and waiting for the Almighty to decide his fate.

An hour later, the telegraph operator came running down from his office waving a response from the state capitol. He stole a glance at Sanchez, who couldn't make out what was happening, and then reported to the sheriff, "The governor said hang him again."

The vengeful crowd, now reinvigorated for another swinging, abandoned the shade under the awnings and rushed to their favored spots under the gallows.

The sheriff shook his head in disgust at the captain. "How's he expect me to get a different result? That gallows you Army boys built isn't high enough." When the captain just shrugged and motioned for him to get on with the governor's orders, the sheriff searched the crowd and pointed to a burly rancher. "Jeffers! You want to earn ten dollars?"

"Doing what?" the rancher asked.

"I'm assigning you the position of hangman for the day."

"What does that mean?"

The sheriff glanced over at the hooded boy. Then, he told the drafted rancher, "Get it done."

The rancher dragged Sanchez up the stairs of the gallows. He wrapped the rope around the praying boy's neck and dropped him, with no more fanfare than if he were tossing a chicken from a coup in his barn. The crowd cocked their ears for the crack. They shook their heads as the boy just hung there again, kicking and fighting for breath.

"Goddammit!" the sheriff shouted. "It's down to five dollars now!"

Pissed off that his hangman's fee had been halved because of his failure, the giant Anglo waved his hand at the sheriff to keep his powder dry. For a third time, the local rawhider reeled up the Mexican boy through the drop hole and cradled him writhing in his arms. He turned Sanchez upside down and drove him through the hole as hard as he could, as if he were spearing a fish under a frozen lake. This time, finally, the good citizens of Deming heard their loud crack.

Waters didn't wait for permission to fall out. He rushed into an alley and lost the burrito he had eaten for breakfast.

12

MANHATTAN, NEW YORK
NOVEMBER 1916

"Boy, you're gonna bust my ears with that noise!"

Perched on a stool in the lobby of the Marshall Hotel, Ozzie Taylor stopped practicing his oboe and looked up to find Noble Sissle standing over him. He straightened his back and wetted his lips again, eager to demonstrate his improvement on the instrument for the only black composer who could rival Big Jim in prominence. After cutting loose with a series of riffs from *Shuffle Along* that would make a legless man dance, he asked, "Watcha think, Mr. Sissle?"

Sissle's face twisted as if he'd just bitten into a sour lemon. "I think the hotel management could find a better way of chasing off the rats."

"Big Jim says I'm coming along."

"He must be losing his hearing."

"Aw, now come on, Mr. Sissle. I ain't that bad."

Sissle kept glancing up at the staircase that led to the main suite. "How's he feeling?"

Ozzie debated how much he should reveal about Big Jim's weakened condition. "Oh, you know him, Mister Noble. Same ol' Boss."

Sissle glared right through him, clearly not buying the dumb act.

Ozzie figured Sissle's arrival from Indianapolis could mean only one thing: Big Jim was secretly planning another extravaganza at Carnegie Hall. Last year, the Boss and his Clef Club boys had made history by being the first jazz band to play in that hallowed venue. Even more shocking, Big Jim had insisted there be no segregated seating. Gussied up in tuxes and tails, the Who's Who of Harlem had come downtown that night to sit aside the Vanderbilts and Astors and soak up the new sound that was taking the country by storm. The band's performance had been a rousing success, so much so that even the white newspapers had given Big Jim rave reviews. In fact, Ozzie could think of only one downside to the whole evening: He hadn't been included in the band, hadn't even been allowed entry to attend. But now, with another big date in the works, he was more determined than ever to convince the boss to let him premiere the first oboe in the annals of Clef Club lore.

Sissle was still waiting for his answer. "I asked how the man was feeling."

Ozzie didn't rightly know what to say. Big Jim and Sissle were close friends, but he'd been ordered not to talk about how the Boss got tired more quickly and was always agitated and nervous. Big Jim had lost thirty pounds since Sissle had last seen him, and when the Boss took off his glasses nowadays, his eyes would bug from their sockets like they were being squeezed.

"I know what's going on."

Ozzie nodded a concession that he'd never been good at keeping a secret. "He don't laugh much anymore. You come to cheer him up, Mister Noble?"

Sissle twirled his hand at his pocket, a composer's nervous tic. "I'm not sure why I *am* here, to tell you the truth. I got an order from the armory—"

The din of activity in the lobby suddenly silenced, and Ozzie saw the Clef Club musicians who were playing cards jump to their feet in respect. A uniformed Army officer, a mustachioed white man with an aristocratic air about him, came walking down the wide corridor.

"Colonel Hayward!" Sissle said the name loud enough to remind everyone in the lobby that a celebrated guest had just arrived. "If I had known you issued the summons, I would have been here sooner."

The colonel grasped Sissle's extended hand. "I heard you left them begging for more at the Casino last Saturday night. You keep making a name for yourself, I may have to promote you to corporal to keep you from going AWOL."

"We gave them a show, all right."

Ozzie stared up at Sissle in confusion. "Promotion?"

Seeing the officer eye the boy suspiciously, Sissle made the introduction. "Ozzie Taylor, meet Colonel William Hayward, commander of the Fifteenth Infantry Regiment of the New York National Guard."

Stunned, Ozzie asked Sissle, "You joined up?"

The colonel, grinning, spilled the beans for his old friend from Indiana. "That's right, son. I convinced the Hoosier *maestro* here to bring his rat-a-tat-tat sounds to my machine-gun company."

"But we ain't in the war."

The colonel's eyes darted around the lobby, suggesting he wasn't eager to explain *that* buzzing fly in the ointment. The officer reached for the banister and began climbing the stairs with Sissle.

Ozzie followed the two men up the steps, until Sissle turned on him and asked, "Where do you think *you're* going?"

"Big Jim said I'm supposed to announce all visitors."

Sissle shook his head in disbelief. "You're pulling my leg."

"No, sir!" Ozzie shot up the stairway past Sissle and hurried to Big Jim's door. He knocked and bellowed, "Boss, you gotta couple of soldiers here to see you!"

Big Jim threw open the door and sized up his two guests with a wide grin. "Soldiers? All I see are a second-rate baton twirler and an Irish pol masquerading in Army khakis."

The men traded laughs and good-natured insults as they entered the suite.

Ozzie slithered in behind Sissle, hoping Big Jim wouldn't notice—

"Taylor!"

Ozzie froze at Big Jim's shout, his sortie to the corner intercepted.

"You played that oboe yet for Sissle?"

"Played?" Sissle protested. "I thought the boy was shooting off a twenty-one gun salute for the Colonel here. I'd rather face German artillery than have to suffer through that agony again."

Big Jim stomped his foot on the floorboards, giving vent to his mirth. "Maybe ol' Taylor here could be our secret weapon, Colonel. Five minutes of him screeching that oboe in the trenches and the enemy would come out waving the white flags."

"I ain't that bad, Big Jim," Ozzie said. "You said yourself I was getting better."

"You keep at it," Europe told him with a roll of his yellow-washed eyes. "The preachers say even Judas has a shot of getting into heaven. You might put five notes together yet. In the meantime, make yourself useful and offer the gentlemen here some refreshments."

Ozzie backpedaled to the decanter on the credenza and poured the Boss his usual libation, lemonade with a half-jigger of vodka, even though he knew Big Jim had been cutting down on the liquor because of his health. He took orders from Sissle and the colonel and brought them a couple of warmed apple ciders.

While sipping his beverage, the colonel watched Big Jim closely. "How are you holding up, Lt. Europe?"

Big Jim tried to stifle a cough, but the swallow got the better of him, and he hacked away until he finally caught his breath. "Fit as a bear, sir. You don't need to worry about me. When the boat sails, I'll be on it."

Ozzie turned so fast that he nearly dropped the tray—the Boss had joined the Guard, too?

"You sure, Jim?" Sissle bored in on his friend. "There been some rumors."

Big Jim shot to his feet and came towering over Sissle. "That's just slander being spread by Joplin and his vultures trying to cut in on my business! I haven't missed a concert date in two years." He turned to the colonel, determined to change the subject. "How's recruitment going?"

The colonel drew a weary breath as he turned to the window. "That's why I'm here. We're not making the numbers that I promised the governor. If we fail to get a good response, the entire country will say that … " He hesitated, clearly uncomfortable with the topic of discussion.

"Will say *what*?" Sissle demanded.

The colonel turned and looked at both men pointedly. "That the Negroes aren't pulling their weight on the war preparations."

Sissle turned indignant. "*We* aren't pulling *our* weight? You promised us uniforms! But we've been marching in the parks for six months in our topcoats. No guns. No ammunition. No place inside to drill."

"I've got a lease now on the second floor of the Lafayette Theatre," the colonel muttered, as if hoping the details of the location might slide past them.

"That dump on Hundred Thirty-Second Street?" Sissle asked.

"It's all we can afford," the colonel insisted.

Sissle, incredulous, looked to Big Jim for support in his protest. "What'd you get me into with this carny show? We're going to become the laughing-stock of Harlem."

Big Jim paced the suite in troubled thought, every so often gulping down a consumptive spasm of phlegm. Finally, he stopped and turned to remind the colonel, "Sissle and I agreed to join your regiment to raise the pride of our people. Some of those men I brought to you had grandfathers who fought with the Fifty-Fourth Massachusetts in the Civil War. Now we're being treated like second-class soldiers again."

"I can't deny it," the colonel said. "I've pleaded with the brass in Albany for new uniforms and rifles, but, frankly, they don't think you men will fight."

Sissle headed for the door. "I won't serve the rest of my enlistment tromping around Morningside Heights in dress shoes and carrying a broom."

"What choice do we have?" Big Jim asked Sissle. "We signed a contract with the government. There's nothing we can do about it now."

The colonel cleared his throat. "There is one thing that might spur recruitment and bring us the attention we need."

Europe and Sissle waited for the revelation, but the colonel glanced at Ozzie, worried that what he was about to say might travel beyond the room.

"The boy won't talk," Big Jim assured the officer.

The colonel rubbed a hand over his mouth to blunt the impact. "A band."

Sissle and Big Jim leaned forward, not certain if they had heard correctly.

"A regimental band," the colonel confirmed. "Led by the great James Reese Europe."

Big Jim's eyes rounded in revolt. "No, sir! I joined up to fight like every other soldier. I am in a machine-gun company. That's what we all agreed to."

"If you led a regimental band down Amsterdam Avenue with the best of your musicians, it would be worth a hundred machine-gun companies," the colonel said. "Recruits from all over the city would start pouring in by the hundreds to march off to war with the great Reese Europe. And I'm confident we'd get the funds for new uniforms and weapons. Every country in the world would come to know about Harlem. People would sit up and notice us." He stepped closer to Big Jim to drive home his point. "Then those old crows in Albany wouldn't have the guts to ignore us."

"I'm a classical composer," Big Jim reminded the officer. "Marching bands are too brassy and loud. Putting Sissle and me in one of those John Philip Sousa outfits would be like forcing the Kansas City Monarchs to play ball in some Sunday beer league."

"We all have to make sacrifices in time of war," the colonel said.

Sissle huffed. "Yes, but *some* folks sacrifice less than others."

"What are you implying, Private?" the colonel demanded, ruffled.

Sissle stood his ground. "There's something else you haven't told us about this band idea, isn't there?"

The colonel shifted away to deflect their demanding glares. Finally, he admitted to Europe, "Jim, you'd have to give up your officer's rank. The War Department doesn't allow a band leader to wear stripes."

Ozzie watched with bated breath as Big Jim limped over to the window and studied the bustle of automobiles gliding up Broadway. He'd seen the Boss have to swallow many slights from white folk, but this—giving up his commission—was intolerable.

After several moments of internal debate, Big Jim said without turning, "I'll do it, but on the following conditions."

"Let's hear them."

"You get me the funds I need to make this the best regimental band of its kind in the world. My musicians won't enlist for Regular Army pay. I won't have my name attached to a musical group that is not the class of the world."

The colonel's eyes narrowed at that brazen challenge. "Or maybe we can just wait until they are all drafted."

Big Jim refused to back down from that veiled threat. "If Harlem men *are* drafted, they'll be fingering guns, not instruments. I'll make damn sure of that."

The colonel swallowed hard, his bluff countered. "What else?"

"I want forty-eight instruments in the band."

"There's never been a United States Army band with more than twenty-eight," the colonel said. "That's regulation."

Big Jim remained uncompromising. "Then you'll just have to go around the regulation."

The colonel debated the stiff conditions. Finally, he nodded his agreement, smiling with grudging admiration for Big Jim's moxie. He shook the hands of the two musicians and turned for the door to leave.

"I've got a condition, too," Sissle added.

Having nearly escaped, the colonel closed his eyes in anticipation. "Yes?"

"Before we leave for France," Sissle said, winking at Europe, "we march down Fifth Avenue."

The colonel looked as if he thought the demand was a joke. "You sure you don't want to tromp through the White House, too?"

"We'll save that for our victorious return," Big Jim said.

Seeing that they were serious, the colonel saluted the men, and departed.

Ozzie hurried to the door. "I'll make sure he finds his way out."

"Yeah, you do that, Taylor," Big Jim said. "Just don't play that oboe for him."

Ozzie raced from the room and hurried down the stairs. He weaved through the lobby and caught up with the officer on the steps outside. "Colonel!"

The officer turned. "If Lt. Europe sent you with another demand—"

"No, it ain't that, sir. ... I want to join your regiment."

The officer held a bemused look. "How old are you, son?"

"Eighteen."

"You don't look more than fifteen."

"That's what they all say. But I can prove it."

"If Lt. Europe gives the okay, then he can muster you in."

Ozzie had to think fast, knowing that Big Jim was not about to let him go across the world to fight. "I'd like to surprise the Boss. Tell you the truth, Colonel, he's been holding off his best musicians from your regiment. He's afraid they're going to bust up their hands during the combat."

The officer slowed his retreat. "You don't say."

"Yes sir, I'm one of his prized players, his only oboe tooter. If I were to go up to ask him for permission to enlist, he'd just try to protect me. I bring in top dollar for him around town."

"You must be a real find."

"Not to be unhumble or nothing, but oboe players like me are pretty darn rare. I'd be a real gem in your marching band. And to tell you the truth, I kinda take care of Big Jim."

"His orderly."

Ozzie grinned. "Yeah, I'm kinda like his civilian orderly. He just wouldn't be able to get along if we were separated. He don't like to admit it, but that's the way it is."

The colonel glanced up at the window in the composer's suite. He broke a wily smile suggesting that he had found a way to get back at Big Jim for driving such a hard bargain. "I appreciate your passion to serve your country, young man. Tell you what. You show up at the recruiting station this afternoon, and we'll get you signed up. It'll make a nice surprise for Lt. Europe."

Ozzie snapped off an eager salute.

The colonel walked away, but then turned back. "Oh, and Private Taylor."

"Yes, sir?"

"Make sure you pack that oboe when we go overseas. I want you to play it for Lt. Europe every night in France. It'll help him get to sleep. And that's an order."

13

THE NORTH ATLANTIC
FEBRUARY 1917

"**D**on't you know that's unlucky?"

Floyd Gibbons smothered a smile at that female burst of exasperation from across the smoking lounge. Despite the warning, he continued spinning his forefinger around the inner edges of his glass to create a ringing sound. Hearing the expected harrumph of disgust, he lit his cigarillo on the bartender's match and lobbed a smirk of triumph at the ravishing American lady in her mid-twenties who, until that moment, had been pointedly ignoring him since their departure from New York a week ago.

At last, he'd found the crack in the ice: She had a fear of testing Fate.

He took another satisfying puff, then finished his drink at the bar of the RMS *Laconia* and strolled among the tables of the mostly British passengers who were engrossed in their evening games of bridge. He was almost within arm's reach of his heart's desire when the dragon guarding the princess—the young lady's mother—reappeared from the powder room.

"I cannot abide this tossing!" the plump matriarch cried as she waddled back into the lounge. "I've not been able to keep down a meal for days."

Winking at her daughter, Gibbons reached into his jacket and produced a sliver of ginger root. He drew a pocketknife from his pocket, carved a few shavings of the ginger into his palm, and offered the seasickness remedy to the mother. "Try chewing on these. Works wonders."

The mother, effusively grateful, nearly swooned from his attention. "Bless you, young man. At least there is one good soul on this ship who cares for the welfare of others." She shot a glower of accusation at the snooty bridge players who were ignoring her. "These redcoat limeys treat us like colonials. I was promised there would be more Americans."

"Only six of us lovers of liberty on board, by my count," he said. "More bread pudding to go around. That's how I look at it."

"How refreshing. An optimist like me." The mother offered her gloved hand for a formal introduction. "I don't believe we've met."

He cradled her wattled arm and pressed a kiss to the back of her wrist, drawing the first smile anyone had seen from her during the entire journey. Still bowed, he glanced up at the daughter and made sure she heard him announce his name, laying it on thick with a *faux* Irish brogue. Having prevailed in their private contest of stare-downs, he served up another dish of blarney. "Intrepid adventurers, you two. Sisters braving the high seas alone on a Cunarder."

"Oh my, no!" The mother blushed through several layers of rouge. "I am Mary Hoy. And this is *not* my sister, but my daughter, Elizabeth."

"Zeus be struck!" Gibbons exclaimed. "And to think I had mistaken you for college lasses off on holiday."

The mother batted her lashes at him like hummingbird wings and refused to let go of his hand. "We've been visiting relatives in Chicago."

He flashed his empty glass at the bartender and ordered a glass of wine for the daughter. He apologized to the mother, "I'd offer to buy you a drink, as well, young lady, but the spirits don't mix well with a testy stomach. So, tell me. What draws you two Grail princesses to the land of Merlin?"

"My husband is a physician. We moved to London two years ago to be with our son, who is an agent for the Sullivan machinery company. And you, sir? What brings you across the pond when everyone else seems to be fleeing west?"

He blew a ring of smoke toward the daughter. "The *Chicago Tribune* is paying me hard currency to get a firsthand look at the fireworks in France."

"A war correspondent!" the mother exclaimed. "How exciting!" She grasped her daughter's elbow to bring her closer. "Isn't that marvelous, Lizbeth?"

Elizabeth Hoy sized him up with all of the warmth of a cop studying a mug shot. "Frankly, I fail to see what is so admirable about sitting out the war pecking away on the keys of a typewriter miles behind the trenches. The British and French governments censor all stories coming from the front anyway, don't they, Mr. Gibbons? What's the use of reading your propaganda?"

"Lizbeth!"

He grinned, stoked to renew their battle. "Mrs. Hoy, I'm afraid your daughter doesn't approve of my profession."

The mother looked utterly mystified. "I must apologize, Mr. Gibbons. I fear the sea mist has corroded her manners. She is usually quite sociable."

Elizabeth kept her taunting eyes fixed on her puffing predator. "Mother, I have seen enough of Mr. Gibbons to know he is the type of man who lives to take unnecessary risks. It is neither prudent nor profitable to associate with such vainglorious fortune seekers."

"What has gotten into you, young lady?"

Gibbons received his refreshed glass of scotch and toasted Elizabeth's diagnosis of his character. "Now, don't be too hard on her, Mrs. Hoy. After all, it takes a risk-taker to know one."

Elizabeth bristled. "Whatever do you mean, sir?"

"Have you considered *why* so few Americans are with us on this ship?"

"Of course. They're afraid of being torpedoed by—" Elizabeth blanched, realizing that she had been tricked into proving his argument. She quickly went back on the offensive. "Maybe if you'd stop walking under ladders and spilling salt on board, we'd all have less to worry about."

Gibbons called over to one of his new acquaintances, a London solicitor who sat lapping an after-dinner brandy. "Mr. Chetham! My beautiful but superstitious friend from Chicago here was wondering what the odds are that we'll get bonked by one of the Kaiser's blowfish?"

The well-lubricated solicitor waved off that worry. "I should say no more than four thousand to one. Stiff upper lips, ladies. Britannia rules the lairs of Neptune with an iron fist."

A waxy diplomat sitting at the next table over wrote an arabesque in the air with his cigar smoke to challenge his fellow countryman's calculation. "We *are* carrying war matériel from the States, Chetham. I place it more in the neighborhood of two-fifty to one."

Before Mrs. Hoy could put a halt to their macabre game of tempting chance, Gibbons called out to the ship's commander walking through the lounge on his night rounds. "Captain Irvine! The Nelson of the twentieth century! When do we land, matey?"

The captain glared at the American reporter who had been pestering him nonstop during the crossing. "You ask that same bloody question every day, Gibbons. You think my answer is going to change? It's none of your damn bloody business! For all I know, you could be a Boche spy."

Several passengers suspended their card games and turned on Gibbons, regarding him anew, this time with suspicion.

"Touchy bloke," Gibbons whispered to Elizabeth.

"Stop riling him," she said. "Now you've got everybody leering at us."

Gibbons took that as his cue to further badger the dyspeptic British captain. "Oh, Admiral. Miss Hoy here wishes to lodge a complaint." Before she could deny that assertion, he announced loudly enough for all to hear, "Her mother is deathly ill from the way you are bobbing this giant Liverpool cork. She tells me the American liners are much smoother."

The captain's face ballooned redder than the Union Jack. "Did she now?"

Gibbons kept one eye on Elizabeth's foot, expecting at any moment to find her heel catapulting toward his shin. In his best Cockney accent, he called out again after the captain, who was now storming toward the exit. "Say, Blackbeard, any chance I could get a look at your sea charts?" When the door slammed in answer, Gibbons shrugged off the rebuff and confided to Elizabeth, "I hope you didn't have reservations at his table tomorrow tonight."

She glared at him. "As a matter of fact, we did."

"No loss. I've dined with him twice. He's a Tory and an insufferable bore."

She looked ready to explode. "Mr. Gibbons, will you kindly—"

Gibbons grasped her shoulders and jangled her gently, making it appear that, in an act of chivalry, he had caught her after she became unsteady from the roll of the ship. "My dear Miss Hoy, I fear the captain's bladdered steering has turned you a bit green in the gills. I must get you some fresh air." He turned to the mother with an appeal. "Would you grant me permission, Mrs. Hoy, to escort your daughter to the promenade to revive her?"

The mother beamed at the matchmaking potential. "Of course. She would be most grateful, wouldn't you, dear?"

Elizabeth tried to escape Gibbon's hand at her elbow. "That's not necessary."

Mrs. Hoy glanced at the bar clock. "Oh, it's nearly ten. Past my bedtime."

Elizabeth seized at the excuse to escape. "I'll accompany you to our—"

Gibbons walked Mrs. Hoy to the nearest bridge foursome finishing a hand. "Chetham, old chap, would you do your American cousins here a kindness?"

"Of course, Gib."

"Splendid. I may eventually forgive you and your fellow monarchists for burning down our White House and leaving the Madisons homeless. I'll consider penning an editorial lobbying against war reparations if you'll see Mrs. Hoy here to her stateroom. I have offered to reinvigorate Miss Hoy on deck with a few breaths of the same air that your inestimable Captain Cook inhaled on his way to his discoveries of the Pacific."

Having given the daughter no choice but to surrender to his ploy, Gibbons escorted her up the stairs, keeping a steadying but insistent hand at the small of her back. When they reached the promenade, he removed his coat and placed it around her shoulders. They stood at the railing in silence for several minutes, watching the waves crash against the bow and listening to the dull thrusts of the boiler pistons below. The promenade was dark, for the portholes had been curtained and the night-lights on the gangways had been extinguished to prevent easy spotting by the German subs.

Finally, forced to start the conversation, Elizabeth remarked dryly, "For a man who gets paid by the word, you've turned awfully quiet."

Gibbons felt for his hip flask, but he decided against fortifying his flagging courage. "The thing is, I can rattle off a dictionary when the bullets are flying around my head. But certain situations leave me despairing for description."

"Such as?"

"Standing next to a woman as smart as she is ravishing."

With her alluring profile set in sharp relief under the moonlight, Elizabeth gave him a sideways look of mistrust. "You had no problem describing those ladies on that traveling bordello with General Pershing's Mexican expedition. Weren't any of *them* smart and beautiful?"

Gibbons had to recalibrate his estimation of the reconnaissance and ammunition brought to the battle by this bewitching foe. "You saw that story?"

She punished him with a scoring smile. "They do teach girls in Chicago how to read. My father has the *Tribune* forwarded to our lodging in London. I knew who you were the moment you stepped on board. I read every newspaper report you filed from Mexico."

"And?"

"You can tell a lot about a man from the way he writes."

Now *he* was the one feeling queasy, and not from the roll of the deck. Fact was, he never did much care to be the one interrogated. "What did you think you found out about me from my dispatches?"

"For one thing, you don't believe in a Higher Power."

He let out an undignified snort. "Now you're really reading the tea leaves from the bottom of the cup! I've never scratched out a syllable about God."

She nodded. "Exactly my point. No descriptions of how the poor Mexican people prayed to the Virgin to save them from the war horrors? No crowding into the churches to beg Christ's protection while their husbands and sons were being slaughtered."

"I report every story with an objective eye."

The angle of her gaze slanted in a challenge. "No, you don't."

"Now look here, Miss Hoy—"

"You're telling me you didn't hear one prayer uttered in Mexico?"

"The Church betrayed those poor Indians. The bishops keep them poor by teaching them that they are helpless, that only a god who whispers to the pope can help them, and that this retooled Jupiter has placed them in miserable poverty and suffering for a greater purpose."

"So, you're an atheist.... An atheist *and* a socialist."

"I worship at the altar of hard facts. I report what I see and hear, and *only* what I see and hear."

"You write what you *think* you see and hear. But you filter all of it through your heart. You admired, maybe even loved, that horrid man Villa, despite the fact that he killed all of those innocent people."

He turned away to hide his discomfort at being so expertly exposed. Who did this woman think she was, his editor? "I admired what the man was trying to accomplish, bringing land and a decent life to the peasants. A lot of them put their faith in him, but…"

"But what?"

"Power turned him crazy. It does to all of them, eventually."

She lifted a hand to his cheek and brought his gaze back to hers. "You must find a faith greater than your belief in the power of reporting the truth, Mr. Gibbons. You will need it for what you will see in France."

"How can you possibly know what I'll see over there?"

"I've helped out with wounded soldiers in Britain. You have no idea what awaits you. But I *will* pray for you, even if you won't pray for your—"

He pressed his lips to hers and kissed her hard.

She surrendered, sinking into his embrace.

Then, she surfaced with a conflicted look. "I must go attend to Mother."

He refused to release her. "I want to call on you in London."

She wouldn't meet his eyes. "I cannot… Please, don't ask again."

"Why?"

She looked off into the sea. "My father… "

"You think I'm not in your social class?"

Stung by that accusation, Elizabeth broke away and ran for the stairwell. At the portal, she turned back. "Promise me you'll never write of what just happened. I hope you have honor enough to abide my request."

Too choked up to speak, he could only nod his agreement to her demand. When she had disappeared down the stairs, he walked aimlessly along the promenade, tremoring not from the cold, but the effect she'd had on him. Cast slump-shouldered by her rejection, he finally descended the stairwell and groped his way through the dark corridor. Returning to the card lounge, he heard the clock above the mirror strike ten-thirty, and several Brits stood from their tables, nodding to him as they retired for the night. A few of them lingered on, nursing their drinks and finishing up their bridge hands.

Feeling lower than he had in long time, he found his favorite spot at the bar and signaled for his usual. The scotch was nearly to his lips when the ship pitched sideways violently, sending glasses and bottles flying from the shelves behind the barkeep, whose complexion had suddenly turned ashen. The lounge fell silent—and then—the floor beneath their feet jolted, like an elevator lift slipping its gears.

"We're hit," the solicitor Chetham announced from his table, with no more apprehension in his voice than if he had just lost a trick in his bridge game.

Shaken, Gibbons held onto the edge of the bar. He watched the Brits in the lounge casually go about their conversations, as if by sheer refusal to acknowledge the dastardly strike they could turn back the German onslaught.

Mr. Jerome, the diplomat, calmly examined the fan of cards in his hand and then diligently played his lead. Only when he had raked in the cards for another deal did he answer Chetham, "Yes, that's what we've been waiting for."

Gibbons didn't know if the sardonic diplomat was referring to the explosion or the new card hand that he had just inspected.

Another Brit, sitting across from the diplomat, opined as he took the next trick, "What a lousy torpedo *that* one was. It must have been a fizzer."

Gibbons retrieved his glass at the far end of the bar, reassured by their indifference to the tremor. Shaking his head at his skittishness, he made quick work of what remained of the scotch not spilled. In celebration of their good luck, he ordered another round for everyone in the lounge and raised his glass in a toast. "To John Bull and St. George!"

"Here, here!" shouted a dozen Brits with raised glasses.

The ship lurched again—followed by five blasts of the warning whistle. This time, every man was on his feet and heading for the door. The herd of Brits finally broke into a run for the corridors and clambered up the stairwell. On the landing, the runway lights were out, and the passengers began stumbling into each other.

Bringing up the rear, Gibbons reached into his pocket and found the pen-size flashlight that he always carried. He snapped its bulb on, drawing appreciative murmurs, and led the passengers to the promenade. Outside, on the decks, they found the crewmen rushing to the lifeboats and unraveling the ropes from the davits.

"No worry!" the chief steward shouted. "The little devil hit us astern on the starboard! Missed the engines and dynamos! Evacuation is just precautionary."

Gibbons followed the Brits who, practiced from their many drills, filed calmly into queues alongside their assigned lifeboats. While waiting for his turn to disembark, he remembered he had left his notebook in his room. His editors would flay his hide if he didn't file a report of the crossing the very moment he reached France. He split off from the others and hurried back down the stairwell, toward the lower deck. Searching the door numbers with his penlight, he found Stateroom B-19 and darted inside. He retrieved his journal, along with his overcoat, a water bottle, and a special life preserver that the *Tribune* had given him. He was about to rush back into the darkened corridor when he heard the distant scream of a lady.

A familiar voice.

The Hoys.... He turned back, determined to make certain that Elizabeth and her mother had made it safely to the lifeboats.

A burly crewman blocked his path.

"I need to check on my friends," he explained, trying to get past.

The crewman refused him entry into the corridor. "They'll be fine, sir. I must ask you to return to the boats at once."

"But—"

"Orders, sir."

Denied, Gibbons reluctantly climbed back up the stairwell. When he reached the promenade deck, the ship began to angle up ominously, stern skyward. The crews struggled to lower the lifeboats and keep them level to allow the passengers to climb in. He kept looking over his shoulder and searching the dimly lit deck for Elizabeth, but there was no sign of daughter or mother. He fought a path through the panicking passengers to Captain Irvine, who was directing the disembarking operation from his perch near the aft.

"The Chicago women!" he shouted at the captain. "I can't find them!"

The captain stood unmoved with arms set akimbo, as if he were impersonating Lord Nelson at Trafalgar. Barely acknowledging the warning with an upturn of his chin, he advised, "The American ladies load on the other side of the ship, Mr. Gibbons. Now, if you will excuse me, I have more pressing matters to attend than the objects of your dalliances."

The insistent hands of two crewmen grabbed Gibbons from behind and drove him into a waiting lifeboat. Crowded around him sat several shivering men and a French actress who was threatening to tip the side with her standing and incoherent screaming. The liner groaned and tilted again, sending the hanging lifeboats askew and forcing the crew to untangle the drop ropes. A hiss of steam shot up overhead, and a rocket shot across the stack, illuminating the black sky with a streak of white light.

Were the Germans shooting up flares to gain a bead on their target?

He heard the order to lower away, and all across the length of the liner, lifeboats began jerking and lowering. He looked down, and for the first time saw the angry swells that would soon envelop them. The ropes holding the bow of his boat snagged, and the seaman in charge of its descent begged for a knife. From a bag in the stern, a hatchet was found and passed up.

The seaman cut the rope and sent the lifeboat plunging. Gibbons felt the air sucked from his throat. He surfaced breathless from the drop, drenched and cold from the sea wash, but still clinging to the side. As he and his frightened mates bobbed and dived, the crewman at the bow fought a losing battle to steer them into the wind by using an oar for a rudder. The French actress was now screaming like a banshee, and the men in tuxedos around her were on their knees, praying frantically. A hand clawed desperately at his wrist. He turned and found a half-blind little Jewish man, bereft of his glasses, begging him for help.

All would be lost, he saw, unless someone took charge of this heaving bedlam. He crawled toward the bow, and after several hasty inquiries, discovered that one of the refugees was an old salt named Captain Dear, a retired seaman who had been lodged in steerage. As the other passengers lurched and vomited, this ancient Ahab sat stoically, explaining with his lyrical Scouser accent how this was his third attempt to get home to Liverpool after his fishing schooner had split in half off Nova Scotia two months ago. The scruffy fellow's record on the high seas did nothing to inspire his confidence, but Gibbons decided that drowning beggars could not be choosers. So, in one breath, he nominated and seconded the codger to start giving orders for navigating the lifeboat. Informed that an experienced helmsman was now at the controls, the passengers calmed from their hysteria enough for them to harbor the hope that they might avoid flailing each other overboard.

After several harrowing minutes, the mood settled from delirium to frigid suffering. He searched the overcast horizon for the other lifeboats. The night had turned overcast, preventing him from seeing more than thirty feet around, but he could hear screams and cries through the mists. He listened for a young female voice above the crashing of the waves and the whistling wind.

"Elizabeth!" he called out repeatedly. "Lizbeth!"

He heard no response. If the Hoys had been lowered on the far side of the ship, they would likely be hundreds of yards adrift by now. For a moment, he thought of praying for her safety, but what good would that do, a prayer from a sinner and a scoffer too late to the dance? Then, there came a sucking sound from the distance, and a surge of waves rumbled toward his lifeboat boat and swept over it, dousing all inside with a chilling baptism.

"The old girl's down for good," the Irish fisherman at the helm muttered as he looked toward the sinking liner. "We got out of her wake just in the nick."

Gibbons shook his head at the bitter irony of it all. In preparation for a travel article, he had researched the origin of the liner's name before leaving New York. The *Laconia* had been christened after a region in Greece where the ancient Spartans had gained a reputation for speaking in a very concise manner. Now, as the night coldness sank into his bones, he became groggy, and the last thing he remembered thinking was if he drowned, those damned hacks on the editor's desk back in Chicago would have a field day with the headline:

Wordy Reporter Meets Watery End On Ship Named for Brevity.

Thirty hours later, after being rescued by a British minesweeper, Gibbons hurried down the docks of Queenstown to question the other survivors brought in to the port. Not finding the Hoys, he threaded past the honking ambulances and kept questioning the dazed passengers who only hours earlier had been engaged in their card games and speaking confidently of British dominance of the seas.

He shouted, "Has anyone seen the ladies from Chicago?"

The crew member who had stopped him from searching the staterooms staggered up in a daze. "I was with them on Boat Number Eight, sir."

He looked beyond the seaman's shoulders, toward the ship that had plucked many from the water. "Are they still on the *Laburnum*?"

"Our lifeboat was smashed during the lowering. The Hoy ladies…"

"Out with it! Where are they?"

"The stern cracked. We tried to bail it out, but the hole in its side was too large to patch. Every swell drove us deeper into the depths."

"The younger woman—"

The oyster-eyed man was in shock, trembling. "We tried to hold our breaths, but the water was so cold…just took the strength from you, it did. I begged them to hold on, but they got weaker and weaker. It was the cold, sir. I saw many a man give up sooner. They were brave lasses, they were, but it was so cold. … A wave came over us, and they were washed out. I tried to reach them, but they were… gone."

"But they wore lifejackets!"

"They just floated away. I tried to reach them, I swear I did. But they just floated away, lifeless like. I believe they were dead before they washed overboard. It was terrible cold out there."

Gibbons dropped his hands to his shaking knees. Exhausted and dehydrated from the hours of dry heaving, he nearly collapsed. Resolving not to pass out, he stumbled over to one of the ambulance drivers. "Where's the nearest telegraph office?"

The medic pointed him toward a municipal building perched above the port. "On Ferrell Street. But you need to warm up and get some fluids in you, chap."

"How many passengers are missing?"

"Thirteen."

Remembering that it was six hours earlier in Chicago, he staggered up the bluff toward the telegraph office. He still had time to make the evening deadline. As he pushed on up the street, the story took form in his mind. Yes, what he was about to write would be read in every drawing room across the nation. By God, he would make those damn politicians in Washington read it from the floor of the Capitol. The grafs were flowing in his mind now, and he had his lede:

> *I have serious doubts whether this is a real story. I am not entirely certain that it is not all a dream. I feel that in a few minutes I may wake up back in stateroom B-19 on the promenade deck of the Cunarder* Laconia *and hear my cockney steward informing me with an abundance of "and sirs" that it is a fine morning.*

His account of the sinking would be syndicated around the world. And he would spare the world no detail.

No detail but one.

He had promised Elizabeth that he would never write of the kiss that had caused him, for a brief moment, to wonder if there might be something more in life worth pursuing than headlines.

But no, not for him… not now.

Her eulogy would be just one cold line: *The latest information confirms the report of the death of Mrs. Hoy and her daughter.*

He vowed to finish the story with the words that would launch the United States into this war. *That* would be his vengeance against Elizabeth's God for taking her.

14

COLLINSVILLE, ILLINOIS
APRIL 1917

nna kept a tight rein on the balking horse as their black buggy trundled along the berm of the county road that led east from St. Louis. She and her father were forced to cover their mouths each time one of those new Ford Model Ts rushed past them trailing clouds of choking dust. The loud honks of the English trumpeting their superiority in speed always brought to her mind a verse from Job: *His children are far from safety, and they are crushed in the gate, neither is there any to deliver them.*

This world beyond Raglesville moved much too fast.

She studied her father, concerned why he was being so quiet. He looked haggard, and had eaten very little since leaving home. Despite her pleas that he not attempt the journey, he had insisted on attending his last Midwest Conference of Mennonite churches before retiring from the pulpit. It broke her heart to see him growing frailer and more despondent. She tried to lighten his mood with a bargain. "The rhubarb should be ripe by the time we get home. If you behave yourself and avoid that hard candy you always try to buy in Vincennes, I will make a pie."

His bearded chin remained glued to his chest. "Perhaps we should forgo the pies this year."

"But you love them."

"To everything there is a season."

Whenever something bothered him deeply, he always sought refuge in the verses of the Good Book. That particular passage from Ecclesiastes, however, was not one of her favorites, for it invariably caused her to feel dread and impending doom: *A time to be born, and a time to die; a time to plant, and a time to pluck up that which is planted; A time to kill, and a time to heal; a time to break down, and a time to build up.* She patted his fidgeting hand. "Father, what troubles you?"

"It does not seem proper that we enjoy sweets while other families send off their young men to go across the world and face death."

He was worrying about that horrible European war again. She knew little about it, except that several countries from the old land had been fighting for three long years. In St. Louis, the English folk had been swept up with excitement over America's joining the side of Great Britain and France. All that week, bands had been playing at the recruiting stations, where hundreds of boys had lined up to join the army, and bankers had been walking the sidewalks clamoring for people to buy Liberty Bonds to finance the guns. She tried to offer him some reassurance. "It has nothing to do with us."

"Wildfires do not honor fences."

Unable to cheer him, she turned her thoughts to Micah, and prayed that he had reached Raglesville by now. She had waited seven long years—the four he had spent studying at Bethel College and the three he had devoted to missionary work—for him to return and take over her father's ministry. Now, when at last they were about to join hands in marriage, this war—

A bloodcurdling scream echoed over the near hill.

Her father took the reins and snapped the horse into a hard canter toward the direction of the cry. Reaching the crest of the ridge, they saw a mob of a hundred or so men dragging a bound man toward a tree near a small courthouse. The victim, stripped to his underwear, had been wrapped in an American flag and was being forced to sing patriotic songs. Her father circled the horse into a retreat.

The abused man, seeing their buggy on the horizon, shouted in German at them for help. "*Helfen Sie mir!*"

Anna stuck her head out of the cab. Looking back, she saw the mob pummeling the poor man. "Father! I think he is calling to us."

Her father snapped the reins, sending the horse off into a harder canter. "It is an English matter. None of our concern."

She saw the mob throw a rope around the struggling man's neck. "They are going to kill him!"

"Turn from it, Anna!"

"But they don't understand what he's saying!"

"*Gehorche mir!*" He slipped into German, as he always did when flustered.

"What if that was Christ being taken to the Cross?"

Stung by that example, her father reluctantly halted the buggy and dropped his head. Finally, after muttering a prayer, he reined the buggy around and hurried it back down the hill into the town.

The victim, about to be strung up from the highest limb, pleaded in German again for their assistance.

The mob aimed their torches to discover what he was shouting at. One of them came closer to the buggy. "What do you clops want?"

Hearing her father stumble for words, Anna spoke for him. "That man you have taken is trying to tell you something important."

The ringleader examined her face. "How would you know?"

"I speak German."

The vigilantes surrounded the buggy.

"You a Kaiser lover, too?" the leader of the mob demanded.

The torches were now so close that she could feel the scorch of the heat. She felt her father's hand clutch at her wrist to demand her silence, so she demurred to him and lowered her gaze.

Jacob said, "My daughter learned a little of the old language in school."

"Yeah? Well then maybe she can tell this Boche traitor that he's about to learn which side of the war God is really on."

Anna could no longer remain mute. Disobeying her father, she spoke up again. "What wrong has the poor man done you?"

"He's a spy! And a Socialist rabble-rouser!"

Unable to comprehend why these people were so angry, she asked the prisoner in German if he spoke English. He shook his head and told her that he was a baker from Dresden. After immigrating to Philadelphia, he had come west and had tried to join the Navy, but was rejected because he was blind in one eye. Desperate for work, he had applied to join the United Mine Workers, but the union officials had refused to help him because he was unmarried. She tried to explain his innocence to the bloodthirsty crowd. "He says he came to this country before the war started. How could he be a spy?"

The mob's leader felt the questioning gazes around him. Incensed at being shown up, by a German girl no less, he pointed a threatening finger at her. "Maybe *you* were sent by the Kaiser to save him."

The knuckles on her hand gripped the reins so hard that they turned white. Had these English all gone mad? How could anyone possibly think that she and her father, descendants of Mennonite refugees from the kings and churches of the old country, would care anything for the current German leader? She looked beyond their torches and saw several policemen standing aside on a far street, unwilling to stop the lynching.

"You Krauts better get out of the way! Or you'll get the same treatment!"

She repulsed her father's attempt to take the reins. Refusing to move the buggy, she asked the ringleader, "Why have you wrapped him in a flag?"

The wild-eyed man laughed and swiped his torch at her horse to spook it. "He said he wants to be buried in it."

"I beg of you!" she cried, repulsing her father's grasp. "Don't kill him!"

"Get out of our way, you *fräulein* cow!"

The jeering throng pushed the buggy back, slapping at the flanks of the horse. When the grass under the tree had been cleared again, a hundred of hands began pulling on the rope and lifting the man off his feet.

Strangling, the German man rasped, *"Lassen Sie mich zu beten!"*

The mob's leader turned to Anna. "What did he say?"

She was frantic, struggling not to cry. "He asks to pray before he dies."

The instigator signaled for the German to be dropped. On his knees and clutching at his throat, the poor man mumbled prayers in his native tongue. When he was finished, he whispered another request to her.

"Does he want a last dance before his last dance?" the mob's leader asked.

She couldn't bring herself to look at the murderers. "He asks permission to write a letter to his parents. To tell them what happened to him."

The crowd roared its insistence that the request was an admission of guilt, and its leader nodded his permission for the letter. "Good idea! It'll let those Sauerkrauts know what's in store for them once we get to the Rhine."

One of the attackers thrust a handbill and a pencil into the kneeling German's shaking hands. Struggling to control the pencil, he managed to scribble a couple of lines, then handed the letter to Anna, thanking her in German, and nodded his readiness to die. The rope lifted him off his knees again and thrust him dangling to the sky. His feet thrashed for several minutes, and then, blessedly, it was finally over.

As the crowd dispersed with their bloodlust sated, Anna looked down through tears to see what the poor man had written. He had addressed the letter to Mr. and Mrs. Carl Henry Prager of Preston, Germany. She glanced around and saw a couple of the townspeople still lingering near their buggy, shaken by what they had allowed to happen. To shame them for their sin, she read the letter aloud to them in English:

> *Dear Parents, I must this day die. Please pray for me, my dear parents.*
> *This is my last letter. Your dear son, Robert Paul Prager.*

The next morning, after traveling all night in a state of shock and fright, Anna and her father reached Raglesville and found dozens of buggies parked at the meetinghouse. Anna couldn't understand why so many people were there on a Friday. And why was an American flag flying on a pole over the roof? The weather was clear, so everyone should have been in the fields. She searched the foddering horses, and her heart leapt.

There was Micah's roan, tied to the post.

She fussed at her bonnet, hoping for time to make herself presentable, but her father was insistent on learning without delay the reason for the gathering.

She helped him from the buggy, and together they opened the door. Micah stood at the front of the room addressing the congregation. She broke a wide grin, but resisted the urge to run into his arms. He had filled out, and his beard was now thick and wiry. She saw him catch her eyes, and she waited for the old mischievous smirk. But his glance, dark and foreboding, deflected from her and fell to the floor.

After all these years, did he not recognize her?

Her father shuffled down the aisle. "Could you not wait, Micah Yoder, for me to offer you the pulpit on Sunday?"

The congregation turned, their faces strafed with fear, and Micah reached for Anna's hands. "Praise the Lord you are back. The Almighty has commenced our days of trial."

She was hurt that he showed no joy in seeing her. "What do you mean?"

Ada Hostetler arose from her pew. "The English burned two of our barns near Jasper last night. Men from the government have been asking about the ages of our boys and demanding to know what we think of the Kaiser."

Anna's father pulled anxiously at his beard. "Men from the government? You mean the English sheriff?"

Micah shook his head. "No, they were with the military. The English politicians in Washington have passed a law making it a crime to say anything against this war. They confiscated all of our German Bibles and demanded that we fly their flag from the meetinghouse. I tried to explain that this was against our beliefs, but they threatened to padlock the doors if we refused."

Anna's father collapsed into a pew. "This is not possible. We were promised the freedom of speech and to practice our religion in peace."

Jared Wagler, a farmer, glared at him. "We should never have allowed the English police to come onto our lands and arrest those beard-cutting devils."

"We tried Micah's way, and it didn't work, "Ada said. "We had no choice."

Wagler shunted Ada aside, drawing protests at the act of discourtesy to his elder. But he would not be silenced. "I warned you, Jacob Raber. We were not harsh enough in dispensing punishment on our own. Now we will all pay dearly for bringing these English into our business. Our elders came here from the old country to escape this intrusion. We have gained nothing."

The congregation argued hotly, until Anna's father raised his hands in a plea for calm. Regaining their silence, he arose with difficulty and insisted, "We will weather this storm, as we have all others. We need only avoid saying anything about this war. We must stay out of it."

"I don't intend to remain silent," Jared Wagler said. "I have relatives in Germany. I'd rather see them win this war than those English out there who burn our barns and paint our houses yellow to vent their venom!"

"Enough of such talk!" Ada shouted. "You will put us all in danger!"

Another farmer in the congregation turned a look of hatred on Ada. "Maybe *you're* the one spying on us for the English. I've heard rumors that the government is paying people for information about what German-Americans say in private." He appealed to the rest of the congregation. "Does not anybody else notice how she has been leaving the services early this year?"

Ada clutched her hymnal to her bosom as if using it for a shield. "Where did you get the money to build that second new house of yours, Brother Wagler? If anyone is taking money on the side from the English, it is you."

Anna's father raised his hands weakly in a plea to stop the accusations. "Satan enters our hearts through the windows of suspicion and fear! We must remain steadfast in the faith that Our Lord will protect us."

"I am to blame for this," Micah said softly.

They all turned toward him, stunned by his confession.

Anna took a step closer. "Why do you say such a thing, Micah?"

He would not look at her directly. "The government has been investigating graduates of Bethel for violations of the Sedition Act. Many of us there swore a pact of nonresistance in this war. These government agents are here because I came home. They are looking for German sympathizers. Some of my fellow pastors in Ohio and Pennsylvania have already been arrested."

"Arrested for what?" Anna asked.

"Conspiracy and unpatriotic behavior."

Horrified, she turned to her father for an explanation of this injustice.

Her father tried to assure them that such prosecutions could never be enforced. "I promise you, if we tend to our own business and do not get drawn into these English arguments, this war will not ensnare us."

"The war has already ensnared us," Micah warned. "The government has created a draft to compel civilians to become soldiers. All men between the ages of twenty-one and thirty must report to the local boards to register."

Anna felt certain that Micah must have misunderstood the law. "But that is surely only for the English and—

"I have been called to report to their draft board," Micah said. "Six other men from Raglesville have also received orders."

Anna turned toward her father again, unable to accept that such a violation of their faith could stand. She had waited seven years for Micah to come back, and now this? Had her father let him go to Bethel knowing this might happen? Could this have been prevented if he had allowed her to marry Micah years ago? When he would not meet her demanding eyes, she turned back to Micah. "The English must give you an exemption."

Micah set his eyes askance, silently denying that possibility. "The government has ruled that all men, including Mennonites, must serve."

Jacob stumbled, and Anna braced his arm to prevent him from falling. Nearly blind with despair, she felt as if everything she loved was crumbling around her. She turned back to Micah and begged him, "Don't go."

"I have no choice," Micah said. "None of us do. You needn't worry. We will register with the conscription authorities. If the English require us to travel to the military camps, we will declare ourselves conscientious objectors and refuse to drill. The worse that can happen is that we will be required to delay our happiness in life together for a few more weeks."

Anna looked around the room. They were all nodding, taking refuge in a dream, but she could not banish from her memory the horrid lynching in Collinsville. That poor German man had come to America taking refuge in a dream, too. And what had his dreaming gotten him? She had seen how war fever turned people into animals. She no longer shared her father's belief that the divine spark in people would always burn to chase the Devil's darkness. She grasped Micah's hands and pleaded with him. "Listen to me. If you leave our protection here, the government can do what it will with you. If you stay as pastor of this settlement, you will have the strength of numbers and prayers."

"The English can force us to report," he said. "But they cannot force us to fight. We will resist and remain silent with humility, just as Christ remained silent and resisted Pilate."

Unable to sway him from this course, she turned in desperation to her father. "You can order him not to do this."

But Jacob sat dazed, as if he could no longer hear her.

Anna had waited for two hours outside the infirmary at Camp Zachary Taylor in Kentucky, but there was still no word if she would be allowed admittance. Earlier that week, the corpse of one of the Mennonite men reporting to the Army had been brought back in a coffin, a victim of the Spanish flu that was ravaging the military encampments. During the funeral, the deceased man had twitched, revealing to the horror and then relief of all that he was still alive.

It was then that she had decided to come here and bring Micah home.

She had not heard from him in three months. With her father now too ill to travel, she had made the long, terrifying journey alone. She was feeling faint, having not eaten since leaving Raglesville, and it had taken all of her waning strength just to persuade the gate guard to grant her a pass. After entering the camp that morning, she had learned to her distress that Micah was not housed with the other Mennonite men in the CO detention barracks, but was being kept under medical care.

Finally, the barracks door opened, and a soldier motioned her inside. "Ten minutes."

Her heart raced as she passed through a door and walked down the aisle of sickbeds. She searched for Micah's face among the sleeping and unconscious patients, but she couldn't find him. Convinced that a mistake had been made, she was about to leave when one of the prostrate boys, his eyes closed in an agitated sleep, captured her wrist.

"Mama! Mama!" he cried. "Don't leave me!"

She tried to escape, but the boy, caught in a nightmare, wouldn't let go.

In the next bed over, an older man with burred gray hair and a toneless, pocked face shouted across the gape. "Amos! Wake up!"

The fever-addled boy looked up at Anna with rounded eyes, as if unable to understand why he was staring at a woman.

"He has these spells," the older patient explained. "He hasn't been in his right mind for weeks."

The boy finally eased back into a fitful sleep, and she escaped his clawing grasp. She asked the coherent man next to him, "Do you know Micah Yoder?"

"Are you his sister?"

"No, we are to be married."

After regarding the door, the older man sat up, wincing. He levered to his feet and, limping down the aisle, led her to another patient who lay unconscious, his legs chained to the bars of the footer.

Anna stared into the twisted face of the emaciated soldier. He was apparently out of his mind, his lips constantly moving but making no sound. Relieved, she shook her head. "No, my Micah has a beard. This is not him."

"The officers sheared him. They sheared us all like this."

She stared down at the shackled patient again—and stifled a gasp. She had not recognized him. His beardless face, sunken and wan from malnourishment, was bruised and marred with cuts. He looked ten years older than when she had last seen him.

"He's been out for two days."

She brought her fist to her mouth and turned away, trying not to let the other patients in the ward see her fall apart. Recovering enough to speak, she turned to the man who had helped her. She looked deeply into his deadened eyes and asked, "Are you one of us?"

The man shook his head. "I am a Hutterite pacifist. They dragged ten of us here from North Dakota. They despise me and my people, all right, but Micah has gotten the worst of it."

She stroked Micah's arm, at a loss how to help him. "But why him? He never hurt a living thing."

"They found out he was a man of the cloth. I guess they figured if they could break him, the rest of us would follow. They tried to make us drill, but we refused. Then they drove us out to load ammunition onto wagons. Micah told them that transporting armaments was no different than firing them. He held up pretty good for a while, better than most of us. Beatings. Kickings. Cuttin' us with bayonets. He kept us going. But then... "

She couldn't bear to hear more, but she knew she must. "What happened?"

"They forced him to dig a grave. And they buried him alive."

She braced against the wall to avoid collapsing.

The Hutterite man helped her sit on Micah's bed. "They dug him up before he stopped breathing. Then they threw him into the latrine cesspool and pushed his head under. They were mocking Christ's baptism. After that... well, he goes in and out now."

She stared down at Micah, hoping that her touch would heal his fractured mind, but his eyes remained closed. "I have to get him out of here."

"The Army ain't let one CO go from this camp. They're making an example of us for the rest of the country."

She wrung out a cloth with warm water in a basin that sat on a table next to the bed. As she washed the grime and dried blood from Micah's face, she prayed to God for guidance. None of these men around her were being cared for properly. She handed the basin to the Hutterite and gestured for him to follow her. She went from bed to bed, washing the abused faces of the objectors and asking their names so that she could contact their families back home.

After doing what she could for all of them, she retreated to a window to find fresh air. Through the pane, she saw a sign across the base pointing the way toward the office of the commandant. She whispered to the Hutterite objector who had helped her, "What is the name of the man who governs this place?"

"Colonel Riggins."

She handed him the washcloth and marched out of the infirmary.

A round-bellied officer with cropped red hair that looked like wheat stubble sat lounging behind his desk with his feet kicked up. He slapped at a fan, trying to speed its blades in the stifling heat. When that didn't work, he rolled up the short sleeves of his drab uniform, revealing biceps tattooed with images of profligate women and satanic-looking insignias. "So, you plan to marry that German slacker, huh? Maybe you can talk some sense into him."

Anna's skin crawled with revulsion at the officer's crudeness. "Our people don't believe in war."

"Nah, you let the others do the fighting while you sit safe on your farms and enjoy prosperity. You think evil just slinks away because of prayer? Your Boche kinfolk across the pond are starving babies and raping Belgian women."

"How could there be more evil over there than what is being done here?"

The officer reddened. "You go blabbing to the papers, lady, and I'll make it even worse on that copperhead coward of yours."

"Micah Yoder is a good man. He will die if he is forced to stay here."

"That's his choice."

She felt utterly helpless. Her father had always promised her that the Light of the Almighty resided in every human soul, and that sometimes one just needed to search deeper for its source. Micah had sacrificed everything here for his faith. How could she stand by and do nothing while letting him suffer? She had prayed and prayed during this last hour, but God had given her no answer on a way to stop this madness. Seeing that she could say nothing more to convince this Godless man to show mercy, she stood to leave.

"Wait."

At the door, she turned, expecting the officer to hurl more threats at her.

"That Bible thumper will go to his grave before he agrees to drill. I've seen enough of his blind stubbornness to know it. But I can't let him off without paying a price. Every coward in the country would yelp his name in protest."

"He has given everything for his faith."

"Not everything."

"What more can you take from him than his life?"

The officer lit up a cigarette and savored a couple of puffs. "During the Civil War, rich folk were allowed to pay for some fool immigrant off the boat to take their place in the draft. That doesn't seem fair to me, but I don't make the rules. Does that seem fair to you?"

She shook her head, unable to understand his point.

He lifted his boots off his desk and, pulling a document from under a stack of papers, waved it at her. "Congress just passed a law giving base commanders the discretion to furlough a few conscientious objectors to perform farm work for the duration of the war. Not the way I would have handled the problem, but I just take orders and pass them along. The furlough would require the CO to work at least fifty miles from his home."

She allowed herself a prayer of hope. "Why are you telling me this?"

"That sonofabitch thinks he's beaten me. But I won't be humiliated in my own camp."

She took a cautious step closer. "I can promise you, sir, that he meant no—"

"I'll give your fiancé one of these precious furloughs. On one condition."

She waited, expecting a demand that Micah make a public apology. She would convince him to do it, anything to get him out of this hell on—

"The guards at the infirmary told me you were a regular angel of mercy."

"Sir?"

"Cleaning those slackers up. Washing their faces. Almost like you had a gift for healing."

"I was just tending to their cuts. I didn't mean to—"

"No, I think you've got what it takes to be a military nurse. There's nothing in your faith that says you can't tend to wounded, is there?"

"I don't have any training."

His smile widened into an evil grin. "You'll learn quick enough. Instinct takes over the first time you see a man's jugular gushing blood."

"I haven't seen any other women here. Where would I live?"

"Here?" The colonel guffawed. "No, you'll be going to France."

She stared at him in disbelief. "This is the farthest I've ever been from home. I have an elderly father who needs me."

The colonel bounced to his feet and came shambling around the desk to loom over her. "That's the deal. That bastard Yoder is about to find out that the Army has other ways to break a yellow sloper. I don't give a damn if you take his place or not. Go back to your farm and tend your chickens, then come pick up his coffin when it's Judgment Day."

"Please—"

"Or we can do it my way. When we get confirmation from the Brits that you've arrived at the Front, I'll release your preacher boy on furlough. And you won't be allowed to see him until the war is over. You people are big on sacrificing for penance. I'd pay to see Yoder's face when I tell him what his pigheadedness cost him."

She closed her eyes to dam the tears. If this was the Lord's wish, why had He delivered it to her through the Devil?

15

HASKELL, NEW JERSEY
APRIL 1917

One spark, and Joe Angelo knew he'd be scrap meat for the gulls that trolled the garbage flotsams down on the Brandywine River. He rolled the nitrate car into the blending factory of the Dupont Powder Works and carefully dumped the blacklead grain into the hopper of the glazing barrel, where it would be polished like glass. Only lunatics took this job, but the hiring men said they found him more than qualified. Everywhere, in the magazines and on the barges waiting to be hauled off to Europe, the combustible granules lay in great black heaps. The hundreds of laborers who worked in this giant explosives grinder kept a constant watch on him, making sure he watered the grooves on the wheels.

The foreman, a puffy Irishman with a face redder than a poppy, shot him the evil eye. "Sop those rails, Wop! I want them wetter than the cunt of that whore who birthed ye!"

Angelo grumbled a Calabrian curse as he ran the mop down the line. He often fantasized about lighting up a cigarette and sending that Guinness-swilling mick into the clouds along with the other mamelukes here who constantly tormented him. Hell, most of them had walked in right off the boats, just like his father. Slovaks, Sicilians, fucking Germans even. Some of them couldn't even speak a word of English. And who did they think they were, always yanking his chain about his short height? If somebody sneezed, a dozen of 'em would step forward thinking their name had been called out. And that *spacone* Celt slave driver thought he was the high king of this whole damn herd of *stunad* leprechauns.

Only three months ago, the entire plant had nearly been blown to smithereens in what the government agents suspected was a Teutonic plot. Lucky for him, the detonation had happened the week before he was hired on. The old Welshman he replaced had been vaporized, not a bone of his body found to bury. Hundreds of houses in the towns nearby had been crushed, and telegraph and telephone lines all over New Jersey and New York had snapped. The fuse boys who survived the conflagration had told him it was the worst munitions disaster since those Boche agents blew up the depot on Black Tom Island in New York Harbor the year before. Ever since that explosion, everyone had been on edge and suspecting fellow workers of being spies for the Kaiser.

"Hey, L'il Caesar!" A former miner from some place called Birmingham yelled over from his station on the grating bins. "Are all the Dagos in the Italian army as puny as you?"

The taunter's pal, another English immigrant, howled with laughter at that jibe. "I heard the Kaiser took one look at them and said, no thanks! We'd rather fight on our own!"

Through the powdery haze, Angelo heard the foreman's voice boom an order. "Shut the feck up over there, you Cockney parrots! Stop distracting the Wop! You trying to get us all killed?"

He grinned grimly at the hilarious spectacle of those two scousers being reamed out by an Irishman. From what he was hearing, their snooty British Empire was getting its nose bloodied over in a place called Flanders. Hell, the whole damn world was being turned upside down. The Italians in his neighborhood argued day and night over who really *was* the enemy. The old country had been allies with the Germans, but then the king decided to remain neutral; that didn't last long, and now all the Angelos in Calabria were fighting on the side of the British and French. And just last week, President Wilson had sent America into it on the Allied side. The *melanzana* Germans had told the Mexicans that they'd give them back Texas and California when the war was over. No way those American tycoons were going to let the Boche steal the land they'd stolen in the first place. All he knew was that this war was booming business for the gunpowder racket, and he was getting paid three dollars a day, more than twice what his father had earned in the Hazleton mines.

"Hey, Angelo!" the foreman shouted. "You an Alpine or a Mediterranean?"

"He's a Wopalonian, boss," one of the Brits said.

"Did I ask you?" the foreman snarled at the Cockney wiseass.

Angelo shook his head like a snorting bull while muttering more curses. The ugly mick was at it again, pestering him with that damn book about the races that he read and quoted more than the Bible.

"I'm guessing he's a Mediterranean," the second Brit said. "They're the lowest form of human excrement, aren't they, boss?"

"Yeah, I was going over that very evidence from *The Passing of the Great Race* just last night," the foreman said. "That book oughta be required reading for every real American."

"The guy that wrote it knows what he's talking about, from what I hear," said the first Brit. "He's a zoologist lawyer, right?"

The foreman nodded. "The book says you gotch your Alpines, your Mediterraneans like Angelo there, and your Nordics like me."

"Like *you*? How come *you're* a Nordic?"

"You brain-curdled sot! Don't you know the Vikings settled the Emerald Isle? I happen to be descended from the pure race of ferocious warriors."

"What about us?" the second laborer asked.

"You two Cockney halfwits appear to be Alpine scum. But at least you're not Mediterraneans," the foreman said. "This war is pushing us toward a racial abyss. Wops like Angelo over there are coming in off the boats and diluting our strong American blood with the weak and mentally crippled."

"The Wopalonians are yellow, all right," the second Brit insisted. "The paper says they're getting their olive-dripping asses kicked back to Rome by the German militias."

"That right, Angelo?" the foreman asked. "Your relatives hiding in the vines over there?"

All the rage that Angelo had kept bottled up from the months of abuse came spewing out like a blown gasket. He charged at the mouthy foreman and latched onto his thick neck. "I ain't no goddam yellow, goddam it!"

Thrown onto his heels, the foreman growled like a bear. He finally dug Angelo from his throat and threw him to the ground. "You Wop pissant! You're fired!"

"Hell, I quit!"

"I'll make damn sure you don't get a job for a hundred miles from here!"

Angelo lunged at the foreman's bum knee. "Blabbering potato mashers! All talk and no fists! What war did you micks ever win?"

The foreman's ruddy face flamed as they wrestled. "By God, I'll use that tongue of yours for a fuse."

Pushed off, Angelo stood for another charge, though his head didn't reach the foreman's chin. "You think you got more fight in you than me?"

The foreman took a John L. Sullivan stance, bowing his legs and balling his fists. "I'm about to prove it."

The other men, eager for a match, formed a circle around them.

Angelo yanked off his cap and slapped the powder from its brim. "All right, then. Let's see who's yellow and who ain't."

The foreman tore off his shirt. "Throw the first one."

Angelo grinned at the stupid paddy—and turned to walk out.

"There's a Mediterranean for you! Showing us his olive-stained arse!"

Angelo spun back on the foreman. "You coming, or not?"

The foreman and the two scousers traded confused glances.

"Coming where?" the foreman asked.

"To join up," Angelo said. "I'm going down to the recruiting station and put my signature on a contract to fight the Boche. Any of you don't follow me are yellower than the piss stains on Mickey Finn's trousers there."

He walked out of the factory.

Afraid of losing face around the other workers, the foreman and his two Cockney parrots sheepishly followed the Mediterranean Wopalonian across the street and toward the sign that offered free sandwiches to those who scratched an "X' on a piece of paper.

16

WASHINGTON, D.C.
MAY 1917

Certain the next hour would determine the fate of his military career, Major Douglas MacArthur stepped out of his top-floor office at the Army's Bureau of Information and walked with pensive determination down the corridor of the old State, War and Navy Building. Before reaching the Secretary of War's corner suite, he paused at a window to glance down at the White House across the street. There, in the flickering shadows of the West Wing, he could just make out the bent silhouettes of President Wilson and his closest advisor, Colonel Edward House. The two men stood huddled over a map, no doubt planning the country's intervention in the European war.

A blast of wind rattled the rows of panes in the drafty hallway. MacArthur rubbed his hands together for warmth while recalling the many cold nights he had suffered in the West Point barracks. This late winter had hung over Washington for so long that even the new cherry trees along the Potomac, a gift from the mayor of Tokyo, had failed to bloom. He tapped an ancient radiator to draw some heat, but the rusted pipes clanged hollow. Built in the style of the French Second Empire, this cast-iron building was so gloomy and frigid that the journalist Henry Adams had once dubbed it an architectural insane asylum.

But MacArthur knew better, having served here for two years as the Army's chief public-relations officer. This was not an asylum. No, it was a mausoleum, where soldiers who didn't make the grade were buried to serve out their careers behind desks. And he was desperate to avoid becoming one of them.

The Army bulls had been called to Washington that afternoon for a meeting. Rumor was Newton Baker had finally decided on a commander for the American Expeditionary Force. The Administration's first choice, Major General Frederick Funston, had suffered a fatal heart attack three months ago, leaving a scrum of lesser-ranking generals elbowing and clawing for the assignment.

President Wilson cared little for the minutiae of military matters, he knew. So, the cold Princetonian had likely accepted Baker's recommendation.

MacArthur conceded that being stuck in the military's bureaucracy did offer one advantage. As the War Department's publicity front man, he had expertly navigated the treacherous terrain of Army politics by applying the lessons learned from watching his father deal with civilian meddlers in the Philippines. Now, he used his position to garner valuable tidbits of intelligence from, among other sources, the office typing pool. Just that morning, one of the girls had let slip that Secretary Baker took home two large binders with background briefings on several generals. The first victory a soldier must win, his father had advised him, was to latch onto the right mentor in the senior ranks. Every officer in the Army was lobbying hard now to be sent overseas with the first contingent of troops. Only a few would get the assignment; the choice of AEF commander would make or break dozens of West Point careers.

He had thus made it a point to devote the same detailed analysis to this matter that he would for any military campaign. Truth was, the diminutive War Secretary—bespectacled, soft-spoken, and averse to conflict—was the last person suited to run the nation's military operations. As a lawyer and former mayor of Cleveland, Newton Baker was such an avowed pacifist that he had declined an offer to run the Boy Scouts because he felt the organization was too martial in its indoctrination of young men. An odd conviction, considering that Baker's father had been a Confederate cavalryman who rode with Jeb Stuart. Had there been something in the old man's humiliating defeat that caused the son to despise war? One thing was certain: Baker was the typical political appointee who had risen to his heights by avoiding risk and making decisions popular with the public.

Yes, Baker could be counted on to make the safe choice.

Nodding confidently to the officers he passed in the corridor, MacArthur went over in his mind again the odds that he had placed for the candidates. Peyton March, an aide to his father in the Philippines, had hurt his chances by being cold and brutal in his performance assessments of junior officers in Mexico and Manchuria. March's chief rival, Jim Harbord, a tough Kansan at the War College, was not a West Pointer, and the brotherhood would never allow a regular soldier to rise to such heights. Hugh Scott, the Chief of Staff, was a personal friend of the president, but he was also a relic of the Indian wars, too old to lead a new Army overseas. And his colleague on the Army Staff here, Tasker Bliss, was just as old and out of shape as Scott.

Some in the press were trumpeting Jack Pershing, but MacArthur dismissed that possibility. Pershing had fumbled his chance by failing to catch Pancho

Villa, a fiasco that had embarrassed Wilson in the eyes of the world. And when MacArthur got wind of Pershing privately criticizing Wilson's Mexican policy to his staff, he had made certain that the indiscretion was passed around at the most posh Georgetown parties.

Yes, MacArthur told himself, smiling with anticipation. The Black Jackass was about to learn the cost of crossing swords with him over a woman. A month ago, at a soiree, he had been engrossed in private conversation with one of the most beautiful ladies in the city, Louise Cromwell Brooks, a flapper socialite stuck in a dead-in marriage to a wealthy Baltimore contractor. No sooner had he offered to order her another drink than Pershing, standing off on the other side of the ballroom, had moved in to steal the lady to the dance floor, even though he was still courting that Patton woman. Such a flagrant behavior would have been grounds for a brawl at the Point.

No, it would not be Pershing. He was forever tarnished by Mexico.

Good riddance.

That left, as the obvious choice, Leonard Wood, the general who had assigned him with the secret mission to garner intelligence at Veracruz. He was not only a hero to every American, but also a clever politician. A Republican like himself, Wood was the Rough Rider stalwart of San Juan Hill, a comrade of Teddy Roosevelt, and the creator of the Selective Service System.

It would be Wood.

And *he*, the general's protégé, would be assigned to the HQ staff in France.

He reached Newton's lobby and was ushered in by an aide to the Secretary's office. He scanned the room and saw Generals March and Scott, along with several junior officers. Then, he felt the blood drain from his face—Leonard Wood was not present. And Jack Pershing was sitting next to Baker.

He lost his smile. *What in God's name is he doing here?*

"Ah, Major MacArthur," Baker said. "Come join us, please. We were just discussing the condition of the National Guard units."

MacArthur saluted his superiors, cutting off the last one stiffly at Pershing, who was burning him with a lording smirk.

Baker pushed his spectacles higher on his nose as he shuffled through some papers. "I was telling General Pershing about your idea. Fill him in, Major."

MacArthur stumbled for the words. "Of course…"

Baker, slow to perceive the source of MacArthur's discomfort, finally realized his neglect. "I may have failed to tell you, Major. General Pershing will be commanding our troops in France. The president signed off on my recommendation this morning. I thought we'd discuss a few issues before we announced it to the newspapers this afternoon."

Pershing kept MacArthur pinned with a bemused eye. "I'm surprised you hadn't heard, Major. You have a reputation of knowing everything that goes on in this building."

MacArthur steadied himself. Had Pershing been ruthlessly lobbying for the post in secret all this time, sowing seeds of doubt about the other candidates? The man was proving once again what a cold-blooded sonofabitch he could be. He had heard stories of how, in the Philippines, Pershing had forced captured Muslim insurrectionists to dig their own graves and pour pig entrails into the holes before being executed, letting them believe that they would be going to their deaths denied Paradise because of the Koran's taboo. He had dismissed the account as apocryphal, spread by soldiers with wild imaginations. But now, feeling the heat from Pershing's steely eyes, he wasn't so sure. He shrugged, affecting indifference to the stunning decision to elevate Pershing, and replied, "I try to stay informed, sir. One of the duties of my position."

"I'd very much like to hear your idea about the Guard," Pershing said dryly, his drifting attention belying that assertion.

MacArthur forced a thin smile. He knew the observation was meant to rub in his nose his relative lack of importance now in the grand scheme of the AEF operations. "Sir, I merely mentioned in passing to Secretary Baker that we might consider federalizing a division with units from all the states, rather than separating the divisions by region."

General March tapped his cane to indicate agreement. "A fine idea. We don't want our Northern and Southern boys fighting Gettysburg all over again in the training camps. We need to integrate the recruits and prevent them from reforming old regiments."

MacArthur stole a glance at Baker to see if the reference to the battle that doomed the Confederacy had offended him. Yet Baker seemed oblivious to any slight; he merely turned to Pershing to receive his new commander's assessment of the recommendation.

"Workable," Pershing grunted.

"The Major has even suggested a name for the division," Baker said.

The corner of Pershing's mouth twitched. "He's quite the dynamo."

Baker spared MacArthur the embarrassment of stating it himself. "The Rainbow Division. Because it will stretch across the country like a rainbow."

Pershing's mustache fluttered under a muted snort. "Major MacArthur can name all of the divisions, for all I care. My paramount concern is getting them equipped and trained. We have only twenty-five thousand Regular Army soldiers on the rolls. If you want four hundred thousand men in France, we've got a hell of task on our hands. Those National Guard boys I had in Mexico are rough around the edges. Shooting at bandits is one thing. Facing down veteran German divisions will be a shock to them."

"Are you telling me you can't do the job?" Baker asked him.

Pershing stole a preemptive glance at MacArthur. Then, he glared at Baker and said, "I told you I would get it done. And I will."

Baker nodded at Pershing's confident tone. "The French and British will try to use our boys for cannon fodder. We're not going to be cut up piecemeal just to plug their holes in the trenches. Bottom line, the president wants a fully independent American army."

Pershing's eyes narrowed. "And where will this independent American army obtain rifles and artillery? We don't have enough stock in the armories to outfit five regiments."

"The allies will supply us weapons when we get over there," Baker said.

General Scott, alarmed by that decision, spoke up for the first time. "That means we'll be training with weapons we won't be using."

"Our troops won't be stateside long," Baker promised. "If we don't get to France soon, there won't be a war left to fight."

"Mr. Secretary," MacArthur interjected. "There is another concern that I'm afraid we haven't considered. Thousands of French *poilus* are reported to be mutinying each week on the Front. Entire divisions have been listed as missing in action. We need to prepare for what the witnessing of such acts will do to the morale of our own men."

"What do you propose?" Baker asked.

"We should impose strict censorship on the newspaper correspondents," MacArthur said. "Nothing gets out from the front without our permission."

"Good luck with that," Pershing said with a dismissive puff. "You can start by putting a muzzle on that burrowing mole Gibbons at the *Chicago Tribune*."

Baker waved off the suggestion. "We can't single out individuals for special retribution or repression. The press would raise a ruckus."

"I'm damn serious," Pershing warned Baker. "Keep a tight rein on Floyd Gibbons, or he'll create problems for us."

General March cleared his throat. "Speaking of problems."

"Yes?" Baker asked.

"What about the coloreds?"

MacArthur and the others glanced at Pershing, anticipating his reaction because of his controversial history in commanding Negro cavalry troops.

"They'll ship with the rest of the Army," Pershing said, sounding defensive.

"We can't put them in close quarters with the white boys," March insisted.

Pershing glared at March. "The Negro soldiers will fight."

"That's what I'm worried about," March said. "They'll fight our white boys first, and our white boys will fight them. We just can't have it."

The War Secretary fidgeted in his chair, clearly uncomfortable with the issue. "The president is of the opinion that the troops should remain segregated."

MacArthur saw a cloud of disgust pass over Pershing's face, but Pershing chose not to press his protest.

Baker stood to indicate the present business was finished. Walking the military men to the door, he told Pershing, "I've instructed the General Staff to make arrangements for you to leave for France within the week on the RMS *Baltic*. Form up your staff quickly, and take no more than two hundred officers with you. The sailing is to be kept top secret. Portholes and windows will be covered. Two destroyers will escort you. I'll be damned if I'm going to let you get torpedoed and have to go through this hell again." Baker turned to MacArthur and ordered, "Major, see to the arrangements for getting out the press release on the appointment. That will be all, gentlemen."

MacArthur opened the door to allow the senior officers to leave first.

Baker motioned him out, too. "Major, would you give me a moment with General Pershing?"

"Yes, sir." MacArthur shot a suspicious glance at Pershing while closing the door behind him.

Alone now with his new commander, Baker motioned Pershing to the far window, away from prying ears in the lobby outside. "I sensed some tension between you and Major MacArthur. Do you have a problem with him?"

"Frankly, the man has kissed every ass in the Army, and more than a few over there in the White House. He's a fawning rank climber."

"And what kind of soldier is he in the field?"

"Fearless. On the verge of reckless."

Baker came to his desk and pulled a letter from a pile of correspondence. "I have the misfortune of knowing his mother socially. Not a month goes by that she doesn't write a missive importuning me to promote her son to a general-ship." His face soured as he read from Pinky MacArthur's latest correspondence: "'This officer is an instrument ready to hand for large things if you see fit to use him. My heart's wish is that you might see your way clear to bestow upon him a Star.'"

Pershing's forehead flashed crimson at the woman's brazen arm-twisting.

Baker set the letter aside. "What do you think I should do? She's quite influential on the Hill. And persistent."

Pershing took a moment to choose his words. "Did you know Jim Harbord never got into West Point?"

"What does Harbord have to do with MacArthur?"

Pershing walked to the window and studied the Washington monument in the distance. "General Harbord is one of the best damn soldiers I've ever had the privilege to serve with. He was a poor farm boy in Kansas when he applied for an appointment to the Academy. He was denied admission so that another applicant with connections could go instead. A boy with connections, just like Douglas MacArthur had connections. That boy who took Harbord's slot is still a colonel. He remains Harbord's junior in rank by twelve files."

"Your point, General?"

Pershing regarded the door, as if imagining MacArthur still on the far side of it, waiting to beg Baker for a spot with the first wave of AEF officers to sail to France. "I've got only one condition for taking this job. I want the freedom to appoint the officers I trust and send them where they're needed. Harbord's going to be my chief of staff. You do whatever you want with MacArthur. Hell, put him with his damn Rainbow Division, for all I care. Just don't assign him to my headquarters. I won't have him spying on me for you or anybody else."

17

SAUMUR, FRANCE
JUNE 1917

Standing with a dozen of his fellow American officers behind a battery of howitzers on the firing range of the Ecole de cavalerie, Colonel Pelham Glassford was having trouble concentrating on Capitaine Goudreau's lecture about range procurement. The problem was not the diminutive Toulousian's English, which was quite good, but the ghosts that kept riding across the historic landscape behind the presentation platform. This famous cavalry school, recently converted into an artillery academy to indoctrinate arriving Americans on French bombardment tactics, stood on the same Loire slopes where Joan of Arc had led her troops against the English Burgundians. And there, across the river in the towering tenth-century château, Protestant Huguenots had held out against King Louis XIII during the Wars of Religion. All around him, the green ridges were dotted with Druid dolmens and menhirs that marked the silent graves of Gallic warriors who had died two thousand years ago trying to repulse another invader, that one from Rome.

It was all heady stuff for Glassford, who had arrived with the first contingents of American officers in August. Rumor was that once the French handed over this school, General Pershing intended to name him commandant, with the critical task of instructing the American field artillery brigades that would soon be disembarking at Le Havre and other ports. Still, he had doubts about whether their green troops would be ready in time for the daunting task that lay ahead.

After three years of suffering horrific casualties in open-field assaults, the British, French, and German armies had become mired in a muddy artillery standoff on a line of trenches that stretched from the North Sea to the Swiss frontier. As part of his introduction to the new realities of trench fighting, he had recently been escorted by his French liaison to the Aisne, northeast of Paris, to witness a diversionary assault conducted by elements of the French Fifth

Army. The bloodshed he had expected, but what shocked him was the crushed morale of the French *poilus* and the stupefying manner in which the French high command was employing its heavy guns by pounding the German lines for three or four days before launching an assault. After witnessing a week of this insanity, he had decided that such so-called preparation bombardments were not only a waste of shells, but they gave the Germans advance warning of the sector targeted and allowed them to mass their machine guns.

Now, Goudreau, the little veteran of Verdun, kept strutting back and forth pontificating about the same artillery maxims that had led the Allies to the brink of annihilation. Most of the American officers were checking their watches, eager to escape this martinet who had the maddening habit of mixing in references to how the Marquis de Lafayette had won the American Revolution for George Washington.

Glassford ignored the lecture and instead fixed his loving attention on the 75 mm French field gun being manned by its crew on the terrace below. The magnificent piece was spitting out shells at an impressive rate of fifteen rounds a minute and throwing them five miles. He shook his head in wonderment; his bolt-action Springfields back home couldn't come close to knocking them off that rapidly. He desperately wanted to get his hands on that gun's magical heart, a hydro-pneumatic recoil mechanism that kept the trail and wheels perfectly still during the firing sequence, dispensing with the necessity of sighting the aim again after each shot. But every time he got near one of the guns, Goudreau would chase him away. The French deemed the 75mm's design to be such a precious state secret that they refused to allow American manufacturers to reproduce it. Pershing had expressed outrage at this lack of trust, to no avail. The French had begged them to come over here and spill their guts to save them, but Glassford knew they'd surrender to the Germans first before giving up their—

"Attention!" Goudreau barked at him. "*Vous n'écoutez pas!*"

The other officers sniggered at seeing Glassford singled out for a Gallic scolding. "Better watch out, Hap," whispered Maj. Steer Jeffers. "Another demerit and you'll be back in plebe class at the Point."

Capitaine Goudreau kept carping at his tall, wayward student. "You seem to think you know all there is to know about *artillerie*, Colonel Glassford. Tell us, *s'il vous plaît*, what is the optimum duration of shell firing to prepare enemy ground for infantry penetration?"

"Two hours."

Goudreau stopped his strutting. "I will not be made the butt of jokes! Every gunner knows that four days minimum of firing is required to suppress German capabilities and destroy the barbed wire in front of their trenches."

"You can fire these 75s until Kingdom Come," Glassford said. "But they won't destroy wire. Major Jeffers here grew up in Kansas. He'll tell you. Wire has to be cut."

Jeffers glared at Glassford for trying to drag him into this confrontation.

Goudreau tried to get up into Glassford's face, but even standing on his toes, he barely reached the American officer's chin. "How many battles have you fought, *monsieur?*"

"We Americans have been in so many battles, Capitaine, we don't count those we fought," Glassford said. "We have enough trouble just keeping track of how many we've *won*. I'll be a gentleman and not ask how many *you've* won."

When the French instructor turned to assess the reaction to that outrage, Jeffers elbowed Glassford to shut up. "What the hell are you doing, Hap?"

Goudreau spun and thrust his riding crop into Glassford's hand. Standing aside with an air of exaggeration, he proclaimed, "Very well, sir. You are smarter than even Clausewitz, it seems. *You* teach the class."

Glassford accepted the baton of authority with an insouciant shrug. To the astonishment of the Frenchman, who had obviously devised the gesture to humiliate him, Glassford strolled in front of his American colleagues and spoke to them casually. "I did a little reading on the ship over. Any of you boys heard of the Baltic port of Riga?" When he received the expected shake of heads, he revealed the purpose for his question. "Ludendorff's Eighth Army took the port in three hours after a surprise bombardment. The Russians had expected the barrage to last several months."

"Great, Hap," Jeffers grumbled. "You can wax eloquent about it in your Eastern Front lecture at the Point. Let the Frog finish his tune so that we can get some lunch."

"Aren't you fellows curious how the Germans did it?" Glassford asked his fellow officers.

Jeffers took the bait. "Yeah, well?"

"According to intelligence that the British shared with us, Ludendorff has been promoting a junior officer named Bruchmüller after each victory. This Bruchmuller fellow studied shelling innovations during the Russo-Japanese War. He's been applying some rather unorthodox tactics with his artillery."

Goudreau ruffled his quills on hearing that Teutonic name. "The Germans are desperate! They are resorting to conjurers and ass-kissers!"

Glassford had been warned the French were much stricter on the protocol of rank than the Germans. "Maybe, but this Bruchmuller is getting results."

"Napoleon taught us all there is to know about artillery!"

"He didn't fight in trenches," Glassford reminded the French instructor. "If we're going to help you win this war, Capitaine, then we have to coordinate our artillery better with the infantry. Neutralization of the enemy is all we require, not destruction of their guns."

Jeffers suddenly became more interested. "Hap, are you suggesting we dispense with counter-battery measures?"

Glassford nodded. "Artillery duels are a thing of the past. How can you duel an enemy you can't see? We need to become more adaptable, and fast. Surprise is the key."

"And how would you create this surprise?" Goudreau demanded.

"We should send out advance observers to communicate coordinates back to our artillery," Glassford said. "Then, short but furious neutralization fusillades, and at night only. No extended registrations on fixed schedules. They just chew up the fields and slow our advance. Send the infantry in quickly, before the Germans can get their batteries back into position from their protected pits in the rear. Our scouts can send back more timely target data by using pigeons, dogs, and lanterns. When the infantry goes over the top, we follow them up with double creeping barrages."

The other officers grimaced and shook their heads, aware of the dangers inherent with using such unconventional tactics.

"Double creeping!" Goudreau cried in dismay. "You will obliterate our own foot soldiers!"

"Not if control of the artillery is handed over to the infantry at zero hour for the assault," Glassford said. "Mobile batteries can follow up faster and more effectively if they are directed by the infantry officers on the field."

"Damn it, Hap!" Jeffers said. "Are you trying to put us all out of a job?"

Another American officer protested, "I'll go to Hell first before I transfer command of my battery to a bunch of Army grunts."

From the corner of his eye, Glassford caught the French instructor smirking and enjoying the protests, but he had saved his most damning statistic for his last salvo. "It won't put us out of a job. It'll save our jobs, and probably several thousands of lives."

"How do you figure?" Jeffers demanded.

"I did a little research on French artillery degradement. Turns out that eighty percent of the French guns destroyed during infantry assaults resulted from their fixed positions being exposed by extended bombardments. The Germans get a reading from the flashes. Then, they take out the French batteries with their longer-range cannon." He turned on Goudreau to drive home his point. "Long-range cannon that you French choose not to mass-produce because Napoleon didn't use them."

The AEF officers waited for the French instructor to refute that claim, but Goudreau merely stormed off and screeched, "Americans! Insufferable!"

18

LONDON, ENGLAND
JUNE 1917

Anna felt certain there had to be a mistake. She opened her bag and pulled out the letter with the address where she had been ordered to report. There it was, the Aldwych, just like the sign said. Yet this vast stone building she stood staring up at looked more like some ancient temple than a nursing barracks. Weary from the overnight train journey from Liverpool, she found an empty bench in a small park across the street and sat for a moment, trying to escape the bustle and noise of strange accents to collect her thoughts. This foreign city felt suffocated under a great cloud of sadness mixed with manic frivolity. Only two blocks away, top-hatted men and expensively dressed women exited laughing from theatres and walked aside veiled widows and mourning mothers in black. It almost seemed that half the British population had resolved to do everything it could to avoid thinking about the other half.

Across the street, the uniformed doorman caught her eye and nodded to her with a knowing smile. He strolled over and bowed. "Madam, might you be the nurse from America?"

She was shocked that a stranger knew of her arrival. "Yes, but—"

Before she could stop him, the doorman took her suitcase. "Worry not, Miss Raber. I have seen that same fuddled look many times this week. Welcome to the Waldorf Hotel. Please, follow me."

Trailing him to the entrance, she shuffled hesitantly through the revolving glass doors, fearful of catching her coat hem on the moving frame that chased her heels. Inside the hotel, she stood gawking in awe at a spacious courtyard planted with a garden and surrounded by a marble terraced lit in pale green and white. In one of the open ballrooms, couples were dancing to the music of an orchestra, stopping only to enjoy cups of tea and cookies. At the doorman's behest, she resumed walking down a broad, carpeted corridor toward the registration desk. As she passed, every bellboy and guest turned and, smiling at her, offered a slight bow as if she were the queen being escorted through Buckingham Palace.

Seeing her approach, an elderly gentleman at the registry came to attention and produced a key. "Ah, you must be Miss Raber. We have been expecting your arrival with great anticipation. Room Four Nineteen. The lift is that way."

"Lift?" Before she could ask what that meant, the clerk snapped his fingers, signaling for the doorman to show her the way. Moments later, she heard a great crash, and the door opened on its own, revealing a small box lit with gas lanterns inside. She stepped back. "What is this?"

Her reaction amused him. "I think you call it an elevator in America. It rises and lowers between floors." He gestured for her to step inside. "Perfectly safe, I assure you."

She inched a toe across the crack to test the contraption's stability. The doorman dragged her trunk in, and when the doors closed behind them, he dropped a lever. She felt an exhilarating sensation as they slowly ascended. The grinding and groaning caused her to wonder if some poor beast of burden in a stall below ground was being forced to drag the box up on pulleys. Finally they came to a jolting stop, and the door folded open. She followed him down the shadowed hall, until he stopped at one of the rooms and knocked.

The room door opened. Greeting her stood a petite, attractive young woman with wavy, dark brown hair and limpid green eyes that seemed at once warming and melancholic. The diffuse London light from the far window cast her in a soft, gilded penumbra, giving her a spiritual, almost ephemeral, quality. "You must be Anna. They've put us in the room together." She offered her hand in greeting, then thought better of it and came in for an embrace. "I'm Helen Fairchild."

Anna quickly escaped from the hug, uncomfortable with the intimacy. "Pleased to meet you."

"Anything you require, Miss Raber," the doorman said. "Please let us know."

Anna suddenly remembered the English practice of tipping, a tradition about which she had been sternly lectured by one of the crew on the Cunard crossing. She fumbled for some coins in her purse.

The doorman waved off her effort. "Not necessary. We're all very grateful to you ladies for offering to help our chaps at the Front." He bowed and departed, closing the door behind him.

Helen retreated to a large mirror to adjust the collar of her crisp blue uniform. "We were afraid you missed the train. Isn't this room just grand? The Brits are treating us like royalty. We've even had tea with Lady Astor at Cliveden."

Anna nodded warily, pretending to know who Lady Astor was. Before leaving home, she had resolved to try her best to hide her ignorance of the outside world. And after seeing what had happened to Micah in the military camp in Kentucky, she also thought it best not to reveal her Mennonite upbringing and faith. She prayed that she would receive enough training in France to avoid suspicion about her lack of nursing experience.

Helen finished putting the final touches on her hair. "I'm afraid I don't have much time to show you around the city. We received our disposition orders this morning. We're to cross the Channel to Dieppe tomorrow at midnight. They say a night crossing is safer."

Anna tried not to betray alarm. "Do you know where we'll be assigned?"

"Colonel Johnston hasn't told us. There are only sixty-four of us here at the moment. I've heard rumors that they intend to spread us out. Some to the hospitals behind the lines. Others to the clearing stations up near the fighting. Oh, I nearly forgot. The colonel left your uniform here."

Helen rushed over to the dresser and pulled out a long, one-piece pinafore that dropped to the ankles. The cloth was heavy dark blue serge, with big broad pleats over the shoulders, white bands around the collar and sleeves, and rows of large black buttons down both sides. Accessories included a broad buckled belt, black shoes with short heels, and a flat-brimmed blue hat.

Anna lifted the uniform to the window light. "They expect us to wear *this* in the hospital? It looks like you can hardly move in it."

Helen regarded her quizzically. "Of course not. These are our street uniforms. For work, they'll give us white cotton dresses that can be washed easily. But believe me, you'll want to wear this one wherever you go when off-duty."

"Why? It looks hideous."

Helen winked. "Take my word. It will protect you. The men won't paw at you—"

"Paw?"

"And you'll get free meals. Try it on. We'll go out and give it a test."

Anna reluctantly changed into the uniform. Its itchy wool chafed her skin. How would she ever get used to such a stiff garment?

Helen put a nurse's cap on Anna's head, tipping it a bit for a little fashion. "The others went to the theatre, but I found a great little restaurant on Charing Cross Road. Let's dine in style before we have to start eating military rations."

Anna's charming new roommate threaded arms with her, and together they hurried down the stairs and out the hotel. As they walked along the Strand, Helen reached into her handbag for a few crumbs of bread to throw at gulls hovering along the banks of the Thames. As she fed the birds, she asked Anna, "How many years have you nursed?"

Anna prayed that the Almighty would forgive her the lie. "A couple."

"They didn't tell us much about you. Only that you were from Indiana."

"What about you?" Anna asked, trying to deflect the attention.

"Most of us worked at hospitals in Pennsylvania. We organized and decided to come over to help. What caused you to come?"

Anna yearned to reveal the real reason she had taken the assignment, but she knew it was too dangerous for Micah's safety. "I just felt the need."

"Well, you come highly recommended," Helen said. "Colonel Johnston said he received a glowing letter from the commandant of Camp Taylor on your work there."

Anna didn't know what to say without violating the biblical strictures against lying and bearing ill words against another, so she remained silent. As they turned and walked north toward Leicester Square, she saw a homeless British veteran curled up in the corner of an alley, his head dipped to his knees. She gasped at the pitiful sight.

"You'll see a lot of them here," Helen whispered. "Broken souls."

Anna inched closer to the poor man. "He's shaking."

Helen put a hand on the slumped soldier's neck. He appeared to be semi-conscious. She opened the collar of his frayed uniform to ease his labored breathing. "He's running a fever."

"Maybe we should get him to a hospital."

Helen shook her head. "They won't take him. He has no limbs missing. The government shuns these men as shirkers. They don't believe one can be wounded in the mind."

Anna was horrified by the callous attitude caused by the war. "We have to do something. Help me lift him to his feet."

When the man finally managed to stagger up with help, he opened his eyes and, looking up at Anna with a glance of terror, tried to crawl away.

She gently restrained him. "Wait, can you walk?"

The soldier blinked hard, only then realizing that they were nurses, not alley thugs. He nodded hesitantly. "I walked all the way to Albert."

Anna lifted the man to his feet.

Helen looked down both ends of the street. "Where are we taking him?"

Anna didn't reveal what she had in mind, but together they helped the man shuffle back down the street toward the Strand. When they reached the park bench where she had rested earlier, she motioned for Helen to stay with the veteran while she approached her favorite doorman to whisper a request.

The doorman glanced at Helen clutching the veteran. Despite the risk to his employment, he nodded and motioned them to the rear of the building. "Bring him around back to the loading dock."

Waiting until no passersby were around, Anna and Helen helped the veteran limp into the side alley next to the hotel. The doorman assisted the veteran onto a small trolley and placed a canvas over him. They wheeled him toward the delivery lift used only by the employees and took the elevator to the fourth floor.

The doorman rolled the trolley to their room and lifted the veteran onto one of the beds. "I'll send up some broth."

"Could you spare some ice, as well?" Helen asked the doorman.

He nodded as he departed and shut the door behind him.

Helen rushed into the bathroom to soak some towels. "Get his shirt off. We have to cool him down with packs."

Anna unfastened the man's smelly drab tunic, which still held mud and blood stains. She shot the back of her hand to her mouth. "My God!"

Helen came running from the bathroom. "What's wrong?"

Standing over the prone veteran, both nurses stared down at two female breasts.

"He's a woman," Anna said.

Stunned, Helen stroked her cheeks until she woke. "Who are you?"

The woman on the bed looked up at them with heavy-lidded eyes. "My name's Dorothy Lawrence."

Anna fingered the regulation buttons on the woman's sleeves. "Why are you in a uniform?"

"They don't believe me."

Helen washed the grime from the woman's face. "Who doesn't believe you?"

"The government. I told them I fought in the trenches, but they don't want anyone to know it. They tell people I'm daft."

Helen shook her head at Anna, silently communicating her suspicion that they had rescued a mentally ill person masquerading as a veteran. "I'll call the Lunacy Commission."

Anna searched the pockets of the woman's uniform to search for some identification. She found a photograph of the woman in the very uniform she was now wearing. On the reverse side was written: *Sapper Dorothy Lawrence, taken at Albert, France, 1915. By her fellow sapper mate, Tommy Dunn.* "Wait, I think she may be telling the truth."

Helen examined the photograph. "How did you manage this?"

The female veteran exposed her crooked tombstone incisors in a grin. "You'll tell them for me, won't you, matron? You tell them that I was the only woman who ever fought on the Front."

Anna opened the last couple of buttons on the woman's uniform and saw that a binding of cotton bandages had slid down to her stomach. "She wrapped her breasts to fool them."

"What on earth possessed you to do such a thing?" Helen asked the woman.

The female sapper gazed up at the nurses with a look of comradeship. "The same thing that's possessing the both of you to go over there now, I'd wager."

"That's different," Helen insisted.

"All my life, I wanted to be a correspondent," the homeless woman explained. "I wrote a few articles for the *Times*. But the editors there just laughed at me when I said I wanted to go to France and cover the war. That's a man's business, they said. So I went on my own. I was an orphan, no family, so what did I have to lose? Hang it if I was going to miss out."

"But how did you get into the lines?" Anna asked.

Dorothy was eager to recount her adventure. "I met a few boys who thought a girl ought to have a chance to kill the Boche, too. A couple of Scotties gave me this uniform, and I cut me hair and ran a razor across me face a few times to raise a stubble. I took the ferry to Boulogne and then rode a bicycle to Senlis. The Frenchies arrested me, but I escaped into the forest and spent a few nights with the rats until me accomplices got me into the tunnels at Albert."

Anna gasped. "Tunnels?"

Dorothy took a shuddering breath, nodding to confirm the horror of the underground war there. "That's when the damn ruperts caught up with me and interrogated me like I was a spy. Six generals gave me the dirty look-over and kept me under wraps until they lost the Battle of Loos. I came back home with nary a pence to my name. Every time I try to tell my story on paper, the bullies over at the Ministry of Defence censor it. Everyone shuns me now, even my own village. They'd prefer I just died so they don't have the suffragettes coming around demanding to go over there like I did."

Glancing at Helen, Anna wondered if the Almighty had arranged this miraculous encounter to firm her own courage for what lay ahead.

19

SPARTANBURG, SOUTH CAROLINA
OCTOBER 1917

Ozzie Taylor waited nervously for his big chance as he sat in the front pew of the Cleveland Chapel Baptist Church. Fanning air to his mouth, he looked down at his olive shirt and saw to his horror that he had sweated right through the armpits. It was nine o'clock on a Sunday evening and the sun was long gone, but the night heat down here could roast a rabbit on the run. He still hadn't got use to these new uniforms. The pants flared out at the sides, making him feel like a waddling duck when he walked, and the collar was so tight he could barely move his vocal cords. The itchy wool cocoons might come in handy during the French winters, but here in Dixie they made the nights long and the days longer. He scratched at his neck and fidgeted his feet nervously, until Big Jim, enthroned at the organ, shot him a stern glare to settle down.

Up front near the choir, Noble Sissle finished playing *Amazing Grace* on a violin, and Big Jim followed his composer buddy on the keyboard with an encore of *Say Brothers, Will You Meet Us?* When the final notes were struck, the packed Negro congregation rose to its feet with such ecstatic applause that the little church seemed on the verging of levitating.

Big Jim stood from the organ and bowed in gratitude for the acclaim. "We soldiers of the 369th Infantry want to express our appreciation for your kind invitation. Noble and I have felt the presence of the Lord here in your house of worship tonight. We all have received from you the blessings of the Almighty in song and music."

"God bless *you*, Jim!" cried a local woman from the pews.

"You boys are gonna bring 'em to their knees over there!" an old man shouted, spawning another round of testifying and praise-giving.

Ozzie watched Big Jim lower his luminous white eyes as if in humility, but in reality to steal a few gulps of dripping air. The Boss had been finding it more and more difficult to breath in this Southern heat. Earlier that year, before leaving New York, he had undergone two operations for his neck goiter, and he hadn't quite been himself since. The doctors said he could die of strangulation if he didn't get his throat glands working, but he kept right on pushing, drilling and training like the rest of them. Some of the boys had been whispering that Colonel Hayward and the Army doctors were looking the other way, unwilling to discharge Big Jim because he was needed for the recruitments.

The applause heightened, finally causing Big Jim to plead, "You folk are going make me cry now! I feel the work of the Lord working here in Spartanburg. You've made us feel right at home."

Ozzie caught Sissle rolling his eyes. He knew they were both thinking the same thing. This cracker town was a lot of things, but hospitable wasn't one of them. These few black folk who lived in the shacks on the far side of the railroad tracks had done all they could to make existence bearable for the unit. But in the week since they'd been transferred to Camp Wadsworth, tensions with the white residents had been running high. Two months ago, at Camp Logan in Texas, the all-Negro 24th Infantry had been goaded into a riot. Sixteen whites had been killed, and more than fifty Negro soldiers had been hanged or imprisoned in retaliation. Now the mayor down here was going around town making noises that the same thing was going happen in Spartanburg. Just to be safe, Colonel Hayward had warned the men to keep their noses clean, even if the taunts started flying fast.

"We have one last special treat for you tonight," Big Jim told the congregation. "One of our fine soldiers, Private Ozzie Taylor there in the front row, has been lugging around a new oboe for awhile. Now, folks, an oboe player is about as rare in these parts as a bad pulled pork sandwich, so I hope you'll indulge me in this request. Private Taylor has been dogging me for months to let him play in public. I'd like to give him that chance tonight, if you're willing."

"We ain't use to rubbing elbows with such high-class fare, Jim!" an elderly woman shouted, drawing laughter. "Go on and let the child play some of his city sounds for us!"

Big Jim winked at Ozzie, the signal for him to stand up and ascend the podium step. "All right. The Good Lord, I trust, will forgive us putting a little rag in our step to finish out the night and take His Gospel to the vastness of His Creation. Private Taylor is going to play a solo rendition of *Slipping Through My Fingers*."

Ozzie tried to soak the double reed in his mouth, but his tongue was dry enough to file down sandpaper. He wrapped his tremoring lips around the heart of the reed, its thickest point, and let go. He felt as if he were standing outside his own body; he heard a flurry of loud notes and realized that he was blowing too hard and creating harsh sounds instead of the oozing melodies he usually managed. Try as he might, he couldn't force himself to ease off the air. His heart was thumping in his chest, and he tried to calm down by closing his eyes, but the Devil himself had taken over his body—in a church, of all places. Finally, blessedly, he came to the end, and lowered the oboe from his lips, keeping his eyes down.

Dead silence, and then the church echoed with a smattering of applause.

"One thing's certain," said the elderly woman who only moments before had clamored for the performance. "Christ and His Saints ain't sleeping this hour."

"Not tonight they ain't!" agreed one of the old men sitting behind her.

The worshippers arose from the pews and filed by, hugging Big Jim and Sissle and gifting them with prayers for their safety in the war. Most of them stopped in front of Ozzie, reached for his hands, and patted them silently, like mourners at a funeral. When Big Jim and Sissle finally managed to escape the well-wishers, they walked out of the church and donned their regulation flat-brimmed campaign hats. The soldiers strolled down the darkened street toward the center of town, which led back toward Camp Wadsworth.

Ozzie trailed a step behind the two officers, packing his oboe on his shoulder and wondering if Big Jim was ever going to comment on his performance. They had walked a quarter of a mile with the suspense nearly killing him, and he finally blurted, "Well, what'd you think, Big Jim?"

Big Jim lost his broad smile. "Lt. Europe, soldier!"

Ozzie was taken aback by the Boss's sudden return to formality. "Yes, sir."

They walked another ten steps, and Big Jim, sounding irritated, remarked in a low voice to Sissle, "What'd we learn back there?"

Sissle shrugged. "I don't know, Jim. What *did* we learn?"

"We learned that the Army is going to throw us into that fight over there in France before we're good and ready."

Sissle stopped. "How'd we learn *that* from a church service?"

"You saw what happened when I let Private Taylor here talk me into letting him embarrass me. I spent twenty years building up my reputation in the business. Now those folks are going home thinking I'm a fool! Thinking I don't know what a professional is!"

Tears flooded into Ozzie's eyes. "But, Boss—"

Big Jim swung around and loomed over Ozzie. "Lt. Europe, damn it! How many times do I have to tell you, Private? You think all of this is a lark?"

"Easy now, Jim," Sissle said. "Don't get your blood rushing."

Big Jim bent over, gasping and heaving for breath. Finally, he recovered enough to complain, "The damn government is doing the same thing to us. All this puffering and hollering about how tough we are and how we're going to go over there and give the Germans a lesson. We're gonna get our heads handed to us, just like this Amsterdam Avenue street barker did tonight!"

As his two heroes walked on ahead, Ozzie trailed behind with his chin to his chest, his spirit crushed. He had been practicing every spare minute he could find, but now he had ruined his lone chance. He could never ask Big Jim for another chance to show what he could do.

Ignoring Ozzie, Big Jim kicked at the dirt. "Damn, Siss. I miss New York."

"I hear you."

"The Castles opened their new show on Broadway last night."

"First one without you," Sissle said. "I'd bet a steak dinner that Verne and Irene now realize how you were the straw that stirred the drink."

Big Jim began coughing and hacking again. He stopped to drop his hands to his knees, desperate for air.

"You sure you're okay?" Sissle asked. "We should get you to the infirmary."

Big Jim looked over to a corner, where several dozen men from his regiment were standing around a sandwich stand operated by two local Negroes. He called out to them, "Hey, any of you know where I can buy a New York newspaper?"

Ozzie, a few steps behind, perked up. "Some of the boys bought one this afternoon at that hotel across the street, Lieutenant."

Sissle looked at him with a skeptical glare. "That's a white hotel, isn't it?"

One of the Negro sandwich vendors overheard them. "They don't necessarily cotton to us locals, but I seen some of your soldiers go in there to buy newspapers from time to time. I've waited tables in there. Ain't hearda no problems."

Ozzie saw his chance to make amends. "I'll go in there for you, Lieutenant."

Big Jim pulled a dollar from his pocket. "No, Siss, you go."

Sissle bristled. "Why are you sending me?"

Before Big Jim could answer Sissle, the man behind the stand, learning for the first time that it was the famous James Reese Europe in his presence, stepped out. "If he's afraid to go, Jim, I'll go in there for you."

Ozzie watched as Big Jim eyed down Sissle, as if testing his friend to determine if he was the type of man who could be counted on in a hot spot.

Sissle angrily grabbed the dollar. "Come on, Taylor. Let's get the officer's damn newspapers for him."

Sissle marched across street, with Ozzie hurrying to keep up. When they reached the hotel's front porch, Sissle peered inside the large glass window.

Ozzie pressed his nose against the pane and saw several white officers at the bar. The paper stand stood next to the lounge. "Lot of white folks in there, Mister Siss."

"You stay here."

Ozzie watched through the window as Sissle walked inside. Unable to hear anything, he slinked around toward the door and watched as Sissle made his way down the long corridor toward the newsstand. Several of the white officers, sitting in chairs, nodded to Sissle, who pulled out a couple of papers from the stand and paid for them. Ozzie breathed a sigh of relief. He was about to run back across the street and tell Big Jim the good news—

"Hey, nigger! Don't you know enough to take your hat off?"

Ozzie turned and saw a white man in a bartender's vest grab Sissle at the collar from behind. Every other soldier in the hotel had his hat on. Sissle reached down to retrieve his hat, which had been knocked off his head. The white bartender kicked him and swore again. Sissle looked dazed. Ozzie didn't know whether he should run in and help Sissle or go back to the lunch stand for help. Before Ozzie could decide, Sissle climbed to his feet to confront his attacker.

"Do you realize you are abusing a United States soldier?" Sissle said. "That is government property you knocked to the floor."

"Damn you *and* the government!" the white bartender gruffed. "No nigger can come into my place without taking his hat off."

Seeing how Sissle needed help, Ozzie scampered off to call for the other men of the Fifteenth hovering around the food stand. "Mister Noble's in trouble!"

Big Jim came running up. "What happened?"

"The white man who owns the hotel is roughing him up!"

Big Jim and the other men started marching toward the hotel when Sissle came staggering out and looking for a car to take him back to the camp in a hurry. "Siss! You all right?"

"Leave it be, Jim," Sissle begged. "Let's don't start another Brownsville."

A white soldier no taller than Ozzie came running down the hotel steps. "That peckerwoo kicked him around."

Big Jim saw that the soldier reporting the incident was wearing one of those skullcaps that the Jews back home sported. "Who are you?"

"I'm with the Twenty-Seventh," the boy said. "I'm gonna go get some of my buddies. We'll teach these rednecks they can't treat us like that."

"Us?"

"New Yorkers!" the Jewish soldier shouted as he ran off for help.

Big Jim traded confused glances with Sissle and Ozzie, stunned that white soldiers were offering to fight other whites for the honor of Negroes. He nodded his determination to handle the situation alone, and began walking into the hotel. "You men stay here."

Ozzie risked another chewing out by sneaking into the lobby behind the Boss. Come hell or high water, he was going to be there at his side if needed.

He hid behind a chair as Big Jim walked toward the proprietor, who was still ranting and cursing. The white officers in the bar had gathered around and were regarding the raving Southerner as one might a dangerous animal at a zoo.

Big Jim approached the white hotel owner, who was now tending bar. "What's the problem, sir?"

The owner pointed toward the door. "That nigger came in here and didn't remove his hat."

Big Jim slowly removed his own hat and held it at his chest. "I'll take off mine just to find out what crime Private Sissle committed. Did he commit any unlawful offense?"

"No, I told you. He didn't take off his hat."

Several military police, including white soldiers from the 27th Infantry, burst into the lobby, prepared for trouble. The white officers watching the confrontation from the bar shook their heads at the bigoted owner.

Big Jim just stood there, hat in hand.

The white officers made a point of saluting him, rubbing the gesture of rank and equality in the face of the bewildered Southern proprietor. "Well done," one of them whispered, praising Big Jim's restraint. "I suggest you get your men back to camp before the Klan shows up."

Ozzie looked up from his hiding niche to see dozens of his buddies from the 369th pressing toward the door, itching for retribution. He waited for Big Jim to give the signal for the fisticuffs to commence. Instead, Big Jim drew the hotel owner aside to speak privately to him. Ozzie crawled from chair to chair, eager to hear their confrontation.

"I'm not going to belittle you in front of your people, like you did my friend," Big Jim warned the hotel owner. "But if you ever lay hands on one of my men again, I won't be so charitable."

"Go to hell, and get out of my establishment! This country's in a damn fix if we have to send niggers to fight the Germans."

Big Jim put his hat on in front of the white man, making a point, and then turned to walk out of the lobby. From the corner of his eye, he spied Ozzie huddled in the corner behind a lamp.

Caught disobeying orders, Ozzie slowly came out, expecting to be punished.

"Thanks for covering me, Private Taylor," Big Jim whispered.

Ozzie brightened like the first day of Creation.

"I'm gonna need an orderly when we get to France. You up for the job?"

Ozzie straightened and saluted, beaming with pride.

"Just one rule," Big Jim said. "No more oboe playing in my presence. I'd at least like to come back from the war with my hearing intact."

LORRAINE, FRANCE
OCTOBER 1917

onfined to a crumbling château a few kilometers east of Nancy, Floyd Gibbons was indulging one of his favorite pastimes, entertaining his fellow war correspondents who for weeks had been caged together like a pack of rabid skunks. He leaned over the shoulder of an imaginary telegraph operator and impersonated Damon Runyon dictating a cable back home. "Now most any doughboy will be thrilled to fight aside the ever-in-the-future-tense Runyon! And any French doll will be begging him to give her a tumble when the fighting is finished!"

Runyon, a sports hack and wannabe poet on assignment for the *New York American*, paced the room, annoyed. "Give it a rest, Gibbons!"

"Yeah, Bad News," said Heywood Broun of the *New York Tribune*. "Lay off little Alfred here before he pulls out his shiv and carves your snoot no little and quite some."

As the reporters began pulling out their well-honed Runyonisms, Gibbons lit a cigar. He reveled in his new nickname of Bad News, awarded to him because the worst of times always seemed await his byline wherever he landed.

Westbrook Pegler of the *United Press* piped out another of their Runyon favorites. "And don't forget the one and all!"

"Go to hell, you overpaid boiler-room ink monkeys!" the thin-skinned Runyon snarled, incensed at being mocked. "I will come over there and kick every one of your mustard-gas spewing asses!"

Gibbons slipped a hundred bucks off his money clip and waved the stash like a red flag in front of the snorting bulls. "Ten to one says I see the first American shot fired in this war."

Runyon, an incurable gambler, went bug-eyed. "Easy money. I am in."

Pegler snorted. "'I am in?' Don't you ever talk in contractions like sane people, Runyon? Come on, let's hear just one 'y'all' or 'don'tcha.'"

"Pegler is begging for the old roscoe!" Broun warned. "Here comes the old equalizer! The old snub-nosed Gatling! The old heater! The old flame rod!"

Gibbons poured more flammable on the fire with another of his favorite Runyon idioms. "Loathe and despise! Despise and loathe!"

Assaulted from all sides, Runyon spun on Broun. "To mention *your* rod and contraction in the same sentence, Mr. *Hale*, would be redundant."

Broun suddenly lost his smirk. "You leave my wife out of this!"

Runyon curled a dime-novel gangster's grin. "I am sorry, did I get it wrong? I always forget. Was it your ever-loving feminist doll that kept *her* last name? Or did *you* take *hers*?"

As fisticuffs erupted around him, Gibbons took a step back to enjoy the fruits of his mischief. Again he was reminded—as Runyon himself might have written—that there is always that brief but liminal moment when the flickering match will hit the kerosene, and everybody will be watching and waiting and wondering if the spark will find enough hydrocarbons to do its job.

He and the boys had been edgy for weeks, elbowing and gnawing at the Army's leash, desperate to know which American unit would be the first to go into battle. The first to file the story back to the States would be immortalized—which was why he had tried to get the jump across the Channel in the cargo bay of a captured Zeppelin. At the time, he had figured it at fifty-fifty that he'd make it to Rouen before freezing. Unfortunately, the Brits discovered him in mid-flight and hauled him back to London. It would have been a hell of a story; he had even cabled his final report ahead with orders to run it if he fell into the Atlantic: *American Correspondent Dies Invading France By Air.*

No, even better: *Icarus Of Ink Defies Gravity For War News.*

He took a load off in a dusty old chair while his competitors threw more pulled punches and launched stinging verbal incendiaries. Amid the mayhem, he lifted the journal from his hip pocket and began jotting down every delectable detail of the scene he had just fathered.

Since landing here with the first elements of the American Expeditionary Force, he had been taking notes for a humorous exposé on the drunkards, racetrack tip-sheeters, and purple-prosed sports columnists that the world's greatest newspapers had sent over to cover the bloodiest war in history. The quickest way to get good copy, he had found, was to mimic aloud the irascible Runyon's writing style, avoiding the past tense and throwing in the absurd slang that only imaginary gangsters and lowlifes would speak. If that didn't light the fuse, which was rarely, he could always stir up Broun by claiming that left-wing European syndicalists had started the war, or that the Brooklyn Dodgers were baseball's equivalent of Belgium, just standing in the way of the Yankees and Giants and never hitting anything thrown at them. And Pegler, the youngest of the bunch, was too easy a mark to parody; the pompous scribe was forever portraying himself as a crusading muckraker, so they all took turns leaving steaming piles of horse manure under his bed at night.

The door slammed open, and a miasma of expensive cologne wafted in.

Junius Wood of the *Chicago Daily New*, the short, bow-tied elder statesman of the news pool, was followed by his usual entourage, Irvin Cobb of the *Saturday Evening Post* and Raymond Carroll of the *Philadelphia Public Ledger*, a loner who had earned the nickname "Hermit Crab." Wood took one look at the scattered furniture and shook his head at their juvenile regression. He retreated to the door with a huff of disdain, making it known that such crass violence was beneath his presence.

"Junie!" Runyon stopped his brawling long enough to wipe a trickle of blood from his mouth. "Any word when we are heading out of this dump?"

The elegant Wood turned back with his chin held high. As always, he stood at attention, as if addressing an august gathering of the National Press Club. "The Army is not giving us any information on troop movements."

"Pershing's lips are puckered tighter than Patton's ass," griped Cobb, a crusty Kentucky blueblood who paraded around with a walking cane, as if he were overlording the plantation once owned by his Confederate ancestors. "That old warhorse is playing us for fools. Feeding us finger food whenever he wants some good press."

"Then what the hell are we all doing over here, anyway?" Pegler demanded. "Every time I file a story, the damn Army censors cut half my copy, the French cut another half, and the British cut another half. And that's just from interviews with that sonofabitch Palmer."

"I say we do something about this outrage!" Broun demanded. "We'll have more clout if we all go to Pershing and complain together."

Wood tugged at his expensive cuffs. "And just how will your superiors feel about forfeiting those ten thousand dollar bonds that we all had to post to insure our good behavior?"

"The First Amendment is being trampled upon by hobnailed fools!" Runyon insisted. "I say we write up a letter of protest to be printed in all of our papers and sign it. It is about time the public knows they are not getting the full broadside on this war."

"I'm all for it!" Pegler said.

Wood pondered the proposed tactic. "The vote must be unanimous."

"Let's let Gib write the manifesto," Cobb said. "If anyone can shine shit into brass, it's the Bard of Old Mexico."

Broun agreed. "Yeah, besides, Black Jack owes him a favor. Hell, Gib was the entire intelligence operation on that Punitive Expedition joy ride."

Wood tapped his fist against his palm to bang an imaginary gavel. "All right, then, it's settled. Floyd will be our Thomas Jefferson."

With vaudevillian flair, Runyon fell to his knees in front of Cobb as if begging for his freedom. "Hey, Massa Cobb. Best hide your slave women."

Affronted by the dig at the founding father's horn-dogging ways with the plantation help, Cobb was about to lay into his Yankee target with his cane when Runyon turned toward the shadowy corner. The chair where Gibbons had been sitting was empty. The reporters slowly realized that Bad News had disappeared while they were caucusing.

Runyon catapulted to his feet. "Where is that Irish bastard?"

Broun ran upstairs. Seconds later, he returned looking like a man who had just seen a ghost. He shook his head, unable to utter what he had discovered.

Wood was furious. "Damn it, Runyon! I told you not to let Gibbons out of your sight!"

"Junie, I got distracted. He was here just a second ago."

Pegler kicked a milk can across the room. "He's probably off filing another cable at the double urgent rate, getting the jump on us."

"Woowee!" exclaimed the Hermit Crab in one of his rare utterances. "That's seventy-five cents a minute!"

"You brain-dead numbskull!" Runyon snapped at the introverted Carroll. "We all know what the double-urgent rate is! You do not have to tell us! We have one hand tied behind our backs trying to beat that scofflaw Gibbons! He just files stories whenever he wants and lets the green eyeshades scream in Chicago! He knows Bertie McCormick and Joe Patterson are not going to fire the gringo who licked the balls of Pancho Villa and lived to lie about—"

A distant tune came from outside, and the correspondents perked their ears. The music was accompanied by a rumbling of wheels. They shoved in a scramble through the door and found a procession of caissons and 75mm French field guns hurrying down the lone cobblestone street. The newsmen huddled like schoolboys watching a parade. They all squinted, trying to make out the insignias on the passing uniforms.

"What unit is that?" Wood asked.

"The Sixth Field Artillery," Pegler said.

Runyon snorted. "That is the first scoop you have had in France."

"They're probably just on practice maneuvers," Broun said.

Wood gave a doubtful nod. "Strange that they'd be heading east, though."

As the correspondents herded back to their assigned prison, Runyon spotted an extra soldier on the last caisson passing through the town. That man wasn't wearing a uniform—and he was waving at them with a shit-eating grin.

"Son of a bitch!"

Hearing Runyon's curse, the other correspondents turned. Two French sentries who had been posted outside the château restrained the reporters from running after the battery.

"That's Gibbons!" Runyon shouted. "That's goddam *Gibbons!*"

The sentries merely shrugged.

The other corespondents stood frozen with their jaws slacked, not knowing what shocked them more: That Gibbons had snookered them again with another daring escape—or that their slippery competitor had finally caused Runyon to utter a contraction.

An old but familiar tingle crawled up Gibbons's neck as he thudded across the rolling Lorraine countryside with his adopted gunnery company. He hadn't felt such an unerring warning of imminent action since he rode into battle with Pancho Villa. Unbeknownst to those suckers back at the château, he had spent the last month secretly training with the 6th Field Artillery. While Broun and Pegler had been off sampling every bottle of French wine they could scavenge within a hundred miles of Paris, he had been learning how to load high-explosive shells into a 75mm French canon. In the process, he had formed a close bond with these doughboys, and they had returned the trust by giving him a heads-up that orders had been issued to move out to the Front.

This time, he knew it was going to be the real deal.

Two miles from the old French-German border, the artillery unit reached the churned approach to the trenches near a village called Bathelémont. The roar of the German guns became more distinct, and the three American batteries, each with six guns, began splitting off and fanning out to prepare for forward deployment under fire.

As the crews flushed with the anticipation of at last getting into a real fight, Gibbons knew the most important decision of his life was now at hand: Which battery would gain the honor of the first shot? He couldn't follow all three batteries. He had to rely on his intuition, place a gamble on which one would reach its range line first. He scanned the gunners as they unhitched their pieces and began rolling them toward the near ridge.

It was a three-way race for fame. Battery A took the early lead, so he went with them. He ran toward its lead gun and began helping the crew push it up the gentle ascent. As he heaved, he looked across the field and saw Company C become mired knee-deep in mud. *Poor bastards.* Once again, his instincts had been right. His new mates reached the ridge and staked the tail into the ground to prevent it from rolling back down the ridge. The German shelling was getting hotter. But instead of bringing up the shell that would win him fame, the doughboys picked up shovels and began digging.

"What the hell are you boys doing?" he cried.

"Orders," huffed one of the gunners. "Gotta dig a pit first."

"Just put a damn shell in the gun and fire it, for God's sake!"

"Can't do it, sir."

So close to immortality, Gibbons looked to his right and saw that Battery C had extricated its lead gun from the morass. That crew now seemed possessed by the devil as it rolled its field gun up the hill. Those boys were heading toward old French gun pits. They wouldn't have to pull their trench shovels and dig redoubts first. He waved goodbye to the burrowing fellows in Company A and began running across the field. "Good luck, lads! I'll see you in Germany!"

"Where you going, Gib?"

"To the victor go the spoils!" he shouted over his shoulder. He ducked explosions as he slogged toward Battery C. Those fellas had already staked their gun into the first pit. Before he could reach them, one of the battery's doughboys, a little fellow named Alex Arch from Indiana, carried up a shell and slammed it into the rear of the barrel.

The Hoosier soldier grinned over at him—and pulled the lanyard.

As the casing ricocheted to the rear, Gibbons stopped in his muddy tracks and watched the projectile arc toward the German lines. For a split second, he considered making a mad dash into this no-man's land in the Lunéville sector of old Germany to retrieve what remained of the first shell. But as more concussions pinged all around him, he quickly thought better of that idea.

The American officers were yelling at him to go back, but he knew he had to find something, anything, that he could take back as a souvenir to prove that he had witnessed the first shot. As the crew reloaded the field gun, he staggered toward the spent casing, several feet behind them. He fell to his knees and covered it. Cradling the smoking relic to his chest like a newborn babe, he felt cooled by a shadow, and looked up.

An Army major—accompanied by five military policemen—stood over him. "Mr. Gibbons, you are under arrest."

Two months later, Gibbons chugged across the Vosges in the second-hand taxi that he had rented in Nancy. It was Christmas Eve, and he felt confident that the armies on both sides of the trenches would hold their fire for the next forty-eight hours to honor of the birth of that two-thou-sand-year-old Levantine pacifist who would have been horrified by all of the bloodshed being inflicted in His Name. Dead tired, he decided to look for a quiet little spot here in the rear of the Front and catch up on his sleep.

As he drove, he grinned at the thought of his fellow hacks stuck back in Paris. After his little AWOL escapade at the château, he had spent two days under detention for flagrantly violating the Army's rules for the news pool. But a telegram from one of the *Tribune*'s owners—who may or may not have possessed some salacious information about General Pershing's dalliances in the City of Light—had gained his release, just in time for him to rejoin his artillery buddies for the big push that might end the war.

And even better, to the acclaim of the nation back home, the *Tribune* had run his thrilling eyewitness account of the first American shot, showering him with more accolades and making a hero of Sgt. Alex Arch—whose family, it turned out, had decided to do the very American deed of shortening its name from Archkiewicx. To add a sweet twist to the *coup*, Broun and Pegler, hounded by their editors to learn the identity of the first shooter, had demanded that the Army press office reveal the hero's name. A shrugging flack, not knowing the answer, had quipped that it was undoubtedly some Irishman. Left with the embarrassing alternative of having no story to file, Broun and Pegler had conspired to send puffed dispatches about the "red-headed Irishman" who had loaded the gun and pulled the lanyard.

He laughed at the marvelous devilry he had spawned. When his story revealed the true identity of the now-famous artilleryman, Broun and Pegler had been forced to scramble to clean up their embarrassing journalistic mess. He made a mental note to send those two blowhards a bottle of wine with a note congratulating them on their retraction. Now, as he approached a small village, he noticed several American soldiers sneaking into a barn on the snow-dusted outskirts. Were they planning a nocturnal assault on this holiest of nights?

He stopped the car, got out, and slithered from tree to tree toward the barn. Under the loft, he inched his eyes over the sill and saw some of the doughboys busy cooking over portable stoves. Others were stuffing boots and gunnysacks with candy and trinkets. Into the middle of this bizarre workshop stood a stumpish soldier being helped into a red Santa Claus suit.

He shook his head in admiration. Dressed as St. Nick and his elves, these clever doughboys were planning to walk right into that German village across the lines. Then, in a sled-and-reindeer version of the Trojan-Horse caper, they would open fire on the unsuspecting Boche, spreading good cheer all around.

He licked his lips, eager for another scoop. This would make his story of the first shot look like rookie crime-blotter copy. Seeing a spare elf costume hanging on a peg near the window, he stealthily reached for it, pulled it through the window, and disguised himself as one of the elf raiders. As the armed munchkins followed their Santa out the barn and down the deserted street toward the distant trenches, he fell in with them, unnoticed.

Launched on their dangerous mission, the death-dispensing elves were laughing and trading Christmas stories with so much *élan* that their courage brought tears to his eyes. As they passed the square, the merry line of disguised doughboys suddenly made a left turn and burst into the *maison*. Were the Germans hiding in *this* village? He felt for the pistol at his belt under his costume, making sure it was loosened from its holster. He followed the breach-breakers into the conflagration, expecting to hear the screams of attack and crack of bullets any moment.

Seventy French children, sitting on their haunches, stared up at him.

After finding his breath again, he laughed at himself. Instead of his pistol, he pulled out his notebook and wrote a description of the remarkable scene that now played out before him:

> *The real daddies and big brothers and uncles of those seventy young-sters have been away from Saint-Thiebault for a long time now—yes, this is the fourth Christmas that the urgent business in northern France has kept them from home. They may never return but that is unknown to the seventy young hopefuls.*

An American regimental band marched in from the back door and struck up a rousing rendition of *Dixie*. The rotund doughboy playing Santa Claus—*Père Noël* to the French—walked around the circle of raptured faces, handing out gifts of hair ribbons, toy cannons, wool capes, paper airplanes, mittens, and miniature warships carved with American flags, all purchased with dona-tions collected by the Americans. A quartet of doughboys sang *Down in the Coal Hole*, and the regimental band led the children outside. Moments later, the sky lit up with a barrage of fireworks arranged by the American artillery battery on the ridge above the village.

When the holiday show was finally over, the village priest came forward and, first in French and then in flawless English for the benefit of the soldiers, explained to the children: "These Americans have come to our country to fight side by side with your fathers and your big brothers and your uncles. These Americans want to take their places today. In doing these things for you, they are thinking of their own little girls and little boys back across the ocean." At the priest's signal to rise, the children rushed into the arms of the doughboys and hugged the surrogates for the fathers and brothers that they would likely never see again.

Gibbons was now finding it difficult to scribble down his thoughts, and not because of the dim light from the lampposts outside. Finally, when his eyes cleared, he managed to put together the final graf of the Christmas report that he would file to the *Tribune* that night:

> *The red glare illuminated the upturned happy faces of American and French together. Our men learned to love the French people. The French people learned to love us.*

21

CAMP DE SOUGE, BORDEAUX, FRANCE
JANUARY 1918

While his buddies huddled around a pair of rolling dice, Walter Waters stood behind the gambling scrum and studied the observation balloon that hovered in the sky over their AEF encampment. Ever since he had set sail from Hoboken with the 146th Field Artillery—the unit to which his Idaho National Guard company had been assigned—he had witnessed several marvels of technology, including the churning boiler room of the ironclad S.S. *Lapland* liner that had saved him from the German submarines in the Atlantic. Yet none had captured his imagination like that giant gasbag overhead piloted by the daredevils of the 43rd Balloon Company.

He wished he were up there in that wicker basket with them, peering through their binoculars toward the Mediterranean and reporting to the ground by radio on the coordinates of practice targets set miles away. He had even asked about volunteering for the new unit, but the doctors told him his eyes weren't sharp enough. Maybe it was a blessing. Most of those balloon jockeys didn't last long anyway, and it was an ongoing bone of contention which job was more hazardous, standing up there in those tossing duck blinds while getting shot at, or flying the busting planes that dived out of the clouds and tried to get close enough to take out the bags with machine-gun fire without getting incinerated by the explosion.

"Hey, Dubya!" Goins Gavin barked. "You in the game, or not?"

Waters kept ogling the sky. "How c-c-come rifle bullets don't b-b-bring them balloons down?"

The craps game suspended momentarily, and the men stared at Waters as if he were a Martian who had just landed in their midst.

"What in God's name are you blathering about now?" Gavin asked.

"I was t-t-talking to that Frog trench instructor y-y-yesterday. He said r-r-rifle bullets don't bring a balloon d-d-down. I don't rightly understand that."

Hurley Bratt, a cattle herder whose hands looked like they'd been swaddled in the crib with barbed wire, was hankering and snorting to the shoot the dice. "You and the Frog conversing? That must have been a regular parlorvous chicken-clucking exercise in hilarity. I hope he don't think we all talk like you."

"If y-y-you're so d-d-damned smart," Waters said, "explain it."

Bratt sent the dice flying again, not about to let his run of luck be waylaid by a discussion on the physics of gasbags *by* gasbags. "Little Joe from Kokomo!" he shouted as he hit a favorable number. "They use some kind of special balloon hide. Bullets can't pierce it."

"What k-k-kind of hide?"

"Prolly some kind of seal skin," Bratt said.

"Hurls, you're hotter than a skillet!" Gavin kept one eye on the stash of money being clutched by the banker. "Keep those bones sizzling!"

"I w-w-went and seen that dang balloon up close," Waters said. "Them b-b-bullets go right through the fabric. I'm t-t-telling ya I seen the holes."

Bratt ignored Waters and set the dice between his thumb and index finger, holding them high enough for all the boys to witness his secret tossing technique. "Prepare to weep, young'uns."

"You measuring Billup's pecker?" snapped one of the men on the losing side of the Pass Line. "Or you gonna throw the goddam boxcars while we're still collecting pay scrip?"

"I'm t-t-telling ya," Waters insisted. "Them b-b-bullets go right through it."

"It's got somethin' to do with the gas inside," Gavin explained as he followed the carom of the dice. "It's like if we stuck a fork in Conlin's fat ass, his miraculous sphincter valve would miraculously close over the fork holes to seal up the beans fermentation inside him. It's a miracle of nature."

"The Lord works in mysterious ways," Conlin pronounced.

A sudden smell sent the men searching for their masks, until they realized that Conlin had unleashed his version of a high-energy chemical explosion.

"Aw, shit!" shouted one of the men, as the others around him turned their noses, all the while keeping watch that Bratt didn't try to set them in one of his notorious cheat holds on the dice.

Gavin gagged between hacking coughs. "Dammit, Conlin! Nobody asked for a goddam scientific demonstration."

"Bone app-eh-teet." Sporting a relieved look on his face, Conlin let out a moan and lifted one of his buttocks in a threat. "Pipe down, vermin, or there'll be a return engagement."

"The Frogs oughta take you up in that balloon and dump you over the Boche lines," Bratt said. "The war'd be over in a week."

Gavin waved off the fetid air hovering over the dice game. "You're a god-damn rolling barrage of legume fumes, Conlin! Give me the Boche mustard any time over your butt fusillades."

"Those b-b-bullets go in one side and out the oth-th-ther," Waters said. "That's what I th-th-think."

Bratt sent the dice spinning again. "Ada from Decata!"

Conlin growled, "If I have to spend another week in this stinking cowpen, I'm gonna blow my own brains out and save the krauts the bullet."

Bratt blew on the returning dice. "What the hell's Black Jack waiting on, anyway? He can't seem to take a shit without holding a parade down the streets of Paris first."

"I hear the Frogs are trying to break us up," Gavin said.

Waters was scratching his head. "Maybe those d-d-dum-d-d-dum bullets'd take 'er down."

"By the way, Dubya," Bratt said. "Congratulations on having a bullet named for you."

"Whatdaya mean, break us up?" Conlin asked Gavin.

"Old Man Joffre wants us to fill the holes in his regiments around Verdun," Gavin said. "Pershing's been throwing a shit fit trying to keep us together as an American army."

Bratt sent the dice airborne. "I ain't taking orders from no Frog. They'll leave us hanging high and dry. Hell, the poilies are already shooting each other."

Gavin leaned in to whisper a solemn demand. "Listen, once we get to the Front, we stay together. Nobody gets left behind. We in agreement on that?"

"What-ch-ch-cha mean, Goinsie?" Waters asked.

Gavin looked around to make sure no officers were watching them. "Word is that the Boche have been crucifying the prisoners that they capture between the lines."

The craps game came to a stop.

Gavin motioned them closer. "The brass don't want us to know about it. You remember those Brit officers here last week checking out the camp? I happened to get into a conversation with one of their orderlies. Little Cockney sonofabitch with a nose like a ship's derrick."

"Yeah, I remember the guy," Collins said. "Sniffing all the time. Like a dog on a skunk."

Gavin whispered, "He told me the word was, last month the Hun nailed a couple Canadian boys to crosses above the trenches at Ypres. In full goddamn view of their own regiment. Nailed the hands and feet of those poor bastards with bayonets. Took 'em five hours to die."

"Shit," Bratt muttered.

"Th-th-that ever h-h-happens to me," Waters begged, "you boys sh-sh-shoot me. Promise me you'll shoot me in the ticker."

"Why wait and take the chance," Collins said. "I'll shoot you right now. I'd put the goddamn bullet in your brain, but it would just rattle around in there like a seed in a coconut."

"That ain't the worst of it," Gavin added. "The little Cockney also said the Germans built a cadaver factory working day and night behind their lines."

"A *what?*" asked one of the Idahoans.

Gavin angled his shoulder to shield his next revelation from the howling wind. He looked up at each of his mates in warning. "The Krauts are so desperate for animal fat, they've been retrieving enemy bodies at night and feeding them into a maw mill that oozes out tallow and nitroglycerine for their bombs."

After another horrified silence, Waters pleaded, "You boys p-p-promise me. P-p-promise you'll shoot me and put me outa my misery."

"You ain't got nothin' to worry about, Dubya," Bratt said. "If they ever made a bomb out of your scrawny frame, it'd be a fizzler. Go off half-cocked with your tongue flapping for a rudder."

"Nobody gets left behind," Gavin insisted. "Nobody."

The men nodded to seal their vow.

Shaken by the story, Bratt finally shook off the gloom and scooped up the dice, determined not to think about what awaited them at the Front. "Let's shoot some friggin' craps before I have to go resurrect myself after the third friggin day! What's the pot, Riggins?"

Riggins the banker counted his collection. "Four and a half bucks."

"All right, then." Bratt sent the dice hurdling toward the blanket.

Waters blurted, "You b-b-boys promise m-m-me!"

The dice landed snake eyes, crapping Bratt out.

The men backed away as Bratt turned toward Waters with fists balled. "You gear-slipping monkey! You just cost me a week's pay! You know better than to blabber your nonsense while the bones are in the air!"

Gavin tried to calm him. "Take it easy, Bratt."

"Hell, he jinxed me! His yammering and stammering hexed my run!" Bratt started after the backpedaling Waters. "Get the hell out of here!"

"I'm s-s-sorry, Bratt."

"Don't ever come around me again when I'm shootin' the bones! Spookin' the vibrations with all that ner-ner-nervous jibbering! I'll ship you to the Kaiser's fat factory myself! Bleach your useless skull for talcum powder and smear it all over my sack, you goddamn carny freak!"

Waters stormed off with his head low and his hands dug deep into his empty pockets. He kicked at the dirt as he headed up toward the high copse of trees that overlooked the camp, the only place in this hardscrabble prison where he could always find time alone to think.

Hell, he could scare the crap out of those boys with stories, too, but he wasn't much at spinning long yarns. Nobody had the patience to listen to him for very long. If he coulda smooth out his talking, he would have told them how their French cook in the mess, a scarecrow with caterpillar eyebrows who hailed from a place called Minerve, had warned him never to go out alone in no-man's land when he got to the trenches. That cook told him that deserters from both sides had formed a new army of scavengers that lived in the tunnels and caves below the trenches. Unrecognizable in long beards and rags, they came out only at night, in the hundreds, foraging for food tins and dragging stragglers back into their subterranean kingdom, where they lived like packs of wild animals. The General Staff would deny the existence of this miserable rabble, but those generals never got close enough anyway to—

Waters stopped walking. Up ahead, an officer was sitting in the shade under his favorite tree, writing in what appeared to be a book of blank pages. The bars on his sleeve indicated he was a captain. When the officer saw him, Waters came to attention and saluted the ranked intruder, but inside he was steaming mad. Those sonofabitches had their own clubs and quarters. Did they have to go around squatting on the only places the enlisted men had to escape?

"At ease," the officer said. "Nice spot."

"You d-d-don't look f-f-familiar, sir."

"I just transferred in from the Yale Ambulance Unit."

"You a medic, sir?"

"I was, until last week." The officer offered his hand. "Archie MacCleish."

"Walter Waters, sir. If y-y-you don't mind my asking, wh-wh-what ya do to get kicked into a fighting unit?"

MacCleish motioned Waters to sit with him under the old oak. "My brother's in the Air Corps. The guilt started gnawing at me. I decided that if he is going to be up there fighting, I should be down here fighting."

"Kinda ir-r-ronic."

"How's that?"

"I just g-g-got booted to medic. I guess I'll b-b-be carrying a stretcher, too."

"Conscientious objector?"

"Naw, I just don't t-t-talk real easy. The stripes are af-f-f-fraid I wouldn't be able t-t-to relay orders when th-th-things get hot."

"One of the greatest orators of history had the same trouble."

"You're p-p-pulling my leg."

"Demosthenes. In ancient Greece, he overcame his hesitancy by filling his mouth with pebbles to practice projecting his voice in the theatres."

"I'd p-p-probly just swallow 'em and choke to death." Waters glanced down at the long column of verses that the officer was writing. "You a poet?"

"The jury is still out on that question. My father thinks I'm a lawyer. Or at least a lawyer in the making. You mind if I try this poem out on you?"

"I'm a little shy on the education."

"All the better. In days of yore, poetry was written to inspire the everyman." MacLeish held his journal toward the sunlight. "I'm thinking of calling this one 'The Silent Slain.'" He studied Waters for an extended moment, as if contemplating a suggestion. Then, he handed Waters the journal. "Read it aloud for me, will you?"

Waters suspected the officer was trying to humiliate him. "Now listen, sir. I don't take no indignity from any m-m-man, enlisted or otherwise."

"Just try it."

Waters looked down at the page. Bracing for embarrassment, he started reading the poem aloud. "'We too, we too, descending once again, the hills of our own land, we too have heard.'" He stopped, not quite believing what he had just heard. He hadn't mangled a single word. He glared at the officer, wondering if the man was some kind of magician.

"Keep going," MacLeish said.

Waters drew a deep breath. "'Far off—Ah...'"

MacLeish helped him with the rest of the line. "'*Que ce cor a longue haleine.*'"

"What does that mean?"

MacLeish smiled. "This horn has a long breath."

Waters shrugged, clueless about what that meant. He recited the rest of the poem and struggled with the end. "'Of swords, of horses, the disastrous war. And crossed the dark defile at last, and found at Ronce—'"

"Roncevaux," MacLeish pronounced.

"'At Roncevaux upon the darkening plain, the dead against the dead and on the silent ground, the silent slain.'" Waters, stunned, took a moment. "Why didn't I hitch the words?"

MacLeish held a distant look. "Poetry is the language of the gods. Our first language, I think. And the gods do not stutter."

"You're saying that when I just read that poem, I was a god?"

"Do you stumble when you sing?"

Waters thought back to his bathtub-warbling days. "I reckon not."

"There's your answer, then. Poetry is, at its essence, music."

Waters studied the poem again, mouthing the words silently this time and then singing them in his mind. "What does it all mean?"

"Wrong question."

"What's the r-r-right question?"

"How does the poem *feel?*"

"Feels like someone else is talking through me."

"Maybe someone was."

Waters pondered the poem. "Who is this Roland guy, anyway?"

"A warrior who served a famous king named Charlemagne. When the king was on a desperate retreat, Roland blew his rallying horn until his brain hemorrhaged. He gave up his life so that others might live."

Waters looked down the hill at his buddies, who were still shooting craps. He wondered how many of them would give up their lives for *him*, and if he would have the courage to sacrifice himself for them. He studied this Captain MacLeish, and suddenly it occurred to him what this poem was all about. "You w-w-wrote this for your b-b-brother, didn't you?"

The officer coughed back emotion as he stood and closed his notebook. "*Que ce cor a longue haleine*, Private Waters," he said softly. He began to walk off, but turned back. "Remember, in times of great trial, the gods speak through you. And the gods never stutter."

BOURG, FRANCE
JANUARY 1918

Joe Angelo ratcheted open the door of the dark cattle car and hopped out. Gripping his Enfield rifle, he fell in with his company from the 42nd Infantry Division as it ran along an embankment toward a jagged row of freshly dug trenches. In the distance, to the north, he could hear the faint booms of the big guns starting up with the first light of morning. He figured the cannonade duel was being waged somewhere near Verdun, the meat grinder where hundreds of thousands of French *poilus* and German iron-heads had been mashed into a morass of mud and guts.

He looked around, trying to get his bearings. He couldn't see much difference between this part of France and the fields in southern Pennsylvania. The sweeping farmland here looked a lot like the homesteads in Lancaster County, except that the houses were a lot older and made of stone. His unit had been sent east overnight from Rolampont with orders not to ask the local Frogs about where they were going. All during the rumbling journey, most of them had prayed to the Madonna while they wrote what figured to be their last letters home.

He followed Johnny Campio and his other buddies in a single file down into the earth. They hunched their backs to avoid snipers and spurred to a double-quick along a vertical supply trench that led toward the forward position. This was nothing like what he had been led to expect for his first battle. The Frog veterans in the training camps had warned there'd be a deafening roar, but he heard only a scary silence broken by the occasional chirp of a swallow. Where was the mud that was supposed to be thick enough to drown rats? These trench boards were bone dry and efficiently buttressed with fresh sandbags.

Something didn't add up.

He whispered to Campio, "What the hell's going on?"

"Quiet!" their sergeant shouted up the line. "Any soldier who breaks the order for silence again will be denied leave for a month!"

Denied leave? Who'd give a damn about leave now?

The men took their positions just as they'd been trained, stepping up to the revetments and waiting for the command for the slots on the boltholes to be opened to allow them to fire at the charging Krauts. They checked their rifles one last time, making sure the chambers were loaded.

"Remove all bullets," the sergeant ordered.

What the hell? Angelo couldn't understand why they would face the enemy without ammunition. Were they going to make a sneak charge over the top? He and the other men reached for their bayonets, but they were ordered sheathed.

The sergeant checked each man's gun to make certain the chambers were empty. "Eyes straight on the ground above you!"

A distant rumbling sounded like a herd of spooked cattle coming at them. Angelo resisted the urge to step up on the mounting parapet to see what was causing all the commotion. Did the Boche roar like savages? The snorting grind became louder and—

Suddenly, teethed loop tracks lurched onto the trench overhead.

He and his buddies stared at the bizarre intruder rocking violently above them. At last, with a mighty grunt, the mechanical contraption became unstuck and staggered forward, until its tracks straddled both sides of the trench. Its engine rattled and puffed smoke before dying.

A high-strung major with a ruddy face and white caterpillars for eyebrows popped up atop the trenches and stared down at them, as if expecting a reaction other than bewilderment. When they just stared back up at him, the major slapped his thigh with a riding crop and shouted in a rage, "Why the hell aren't you sonofabitches running back to your mommas?"

Angelo snuck a confused glance at Campio. Had Black Jack sent them here to guard the *boombots* farm where the Frenchies hid the poor fellas who'd gone jelly from shell shock?

The combustible major climbed atop the broken-down contraption and began cursing at its driver. While the officer was distracted, Angelo edged up to peer into the valley. This still didn't look anything at all like the descriptions he'd heard of the Front. A dozen boxes like the one now trapped over their trench were crawling across the rolling countryside, zagging and reversing and nearly crashing into each other. He reckoned they were about the size of the mausoleums that the rich folk buried themselves in back home at Evergreen Cemetery. As they crisscrossed the field, the boxes resembled a giant game of bocce being played with square balls.

The sun rose higher, chasing the shadows, and he discovered that the smoking contraptions were in fact tractors scaffolded with cross beams and draped in sheets of canvas. Their wheels had been fitted with caterpillar tracks and three slits had been cut into their front coverings, forcing the men hidden under them to rely on direct line of sight. Several of these mechanized units sat coughing gas, run aground by burst carburetors, snapped tracks, broken axles, and drivers overcome by fumes.

He and the other doughboys climbed up out of the trenches and watched the major dart from tractor to tractor, slamming his riding crop against the engines in what appeared to be some form of code. Messengers with flags flapped signals and released carrier pigeons that alighted and splattered the canvases with shit. The expletive-spewing officer tapped the heads of the drivers who wore leather helmets like football players, and the tin-can jockeys popped up from their hidden seats to salute him repeatedly.

Angelo shook his head in amazement. How would he ever convince those coots back at the powder factory that the United States was planning to beat the Kaiser with rolling tents?

The crazy major turned and strode back toward the trench while flailing at his thigh with his riding crop. It was a wonder that the officer's leg wasn't beaten to a bloody pulp. "Tanks!" the major screeched in his dog-whistle voice as he got directly into the face of Johnny Campio. "Tanks!"

Campio blinked hard, baffled. "Sir?"

"I heard you asking what those rattle wagons are."

"Sir, I swear I didn't say nothing."

The major doused Campio in flying spittle. "Did I say you *said* anything, soldier?"

"No, sir. I just assumed—"

"I can read your goddamn reptile mind!" The officer walked up and down the line like a constipated rooster. "I can read every one of your goddamn minds! I am a goddamn clairvoyant savant! Caesar campaigned with a host of seers and bone throwers who told him what the gods wanted him to do! I don't have the benefit of a goddamn army of seers! Do you see any Druids boiling newts around here, soldier?"

Campio looked ready to piss his pants. "No, sir."

"Goddamn right you don't! But I don't need a gaggle of oracle-yelping priests! I can read the future myself! I knew three months ago that those goddamn Frenchies wouldn't get me those goddamn Renault tanks on time! Do you know why I knew that, soldier?"

"No, sir."

"Because the goddamn Frenchies don't give a rat's *sautéed* ass if you boys go over the top gripping nothing but your fine American dicks for weapons!"

"Yes, sir."

The major pointed toward the spires of a cathedral high on a promontory about a mile away. "You know who once camped on that ground, soldier?"

Campio seemed to get the drift of the officer's obsession. "Caesar?"

The officer grinned. "You're goddamn right! You may make an officer yet!"

Campio relaxed, pleased with himself. "*No problemo.*"

The major buzzed around poor Campio like a bee intent on sapping a wilting flower. "No *problemo*? You speak American to me, soldier! And don't you *ever* address me without saying 'sir'! Do you understand! Flatten that collar! You think you're some goddamn primeval Gaul?"

"No, sir."

Angelo remained at attention during Campio's grilling. From the corner of his eye, he saw a gaggle of brass watching with binoculars from the far ridge. It then dawned on him why he and the boys had been dragged out here from Roulampont on the sly. The Army was employing them as guinea pigs in an experiment to see how soldiers in the trenches would react when surprised by these giant rolling outhouses with machine guns. Apparently Black Jack had resorted to using camouflaged tractors for training to mimic the rolling tin lizzies that the Brits had used at Cambrai. He figured the major's foul mood was due to the fact that they hadn't retreated in fright. Probably would be hard for him to explain that to headquarters, especially if the stunning effect on the enemy had been trumpeted to justify the expense of new tanks.

"You see that high rock up there, soldier?" the major shouted at Campio.

Campio squinted into the sun. "Yes, sir."

"The Gaulish hordes set their defenses on that rock. Caesar's generals told him it was impregnable. Couldn't be taken! You know what Caesar did?"

"Didn't listen to his generals?"

"You're goddamn right he didn't listen to his goddam toga-crapping generals! He ordered a night attack and took those tattoo-painted Gaul bastards before they knew what hit 'em! Threw the sonofabitches off that cliff in the hundreds!"

The lunatic major gazed longingly at the distant crag. Finally, rousing from his wistful reverie of ancient times, he demanded in an ominously calmed voice, "You know how I know that, soldier?"

"You learned it in history class, sir?" pipped Campio, his voice tremoring.

"I was with goddamn Caesar when he captured those goddamn heights, that's how I know! And I ought to march the whole lot of you up there and drive you off the goddamn cliffs in a sacrifice to Mars!"

Angelo stole another glance at his mates. Maybe they *were* at the Army's mental hospital—and this albino-looking major was just one of the internees.

The officer kept slamming the riding crop against his thigh as he strode like a Roman emperor across the ranks of his legions. "Now, you men were sent to me for a top-secret mission. Until I get my goddamn Renaults from the goddamn Paris bureaucrats, you're going to keep those tractors down there in operational order so that my tank knights can drill."

Angelo cursed under his breath. *Top-secret mission, my ass. This sonofabitch thinks he's going to requisition us from the fighting to serve as his mechanics and oil teamsters.*

"First order of business," the major barked. "Under my command, no soldier will report to duty with stains on his uniform."

Angelo looked down at his trousers, which were dappled with boxcar grime and horse manure. How the hell did the Army expect him to stay spotless in the middle of a damn Boche fight?

"Who can tell me the most important use for petrol in war?"

Campio raised his hand. "Fuel for the engines, sir."

"On your knees, private!"

Campio slowly descended, wondering if the major would produce a sword and behead him.

"Stand up!"

Campio did as ordered. Tracking the gazes of the other men, he saw a couple of brown stains now marring his knees. The major nodded toward the marooned tractor, and the driver, as if clairvoyantly sensing a silent order, jumped off the vehicle, doused a hanging rag with gasoline from one of the strapped cans, and handed the rag to the major. Strutting like a magician about to perform a trick, the major finally made his move and rubbed the gasoline-soaked rag on Campio's knees. To their amazement, the stains disappeared.

"Petrol is a goddamn solvent!" the major shouted. "As you see—"

A loud explosion on the field below them caused the major to nearly leap out of his boots.

Ducking down, Angelo risked a glance over his elbow. One of the tractors practicing maneuvers had just rear-ended another fake tank that had extra gas cans strapped to its rear bumper. The impact had caused a spark to detonate the gasoline, and now both tractors were ablaze. The drivers crawled from their fake tanks and a fire crew ran to extinguish the flames.

The major turned to find the men snickering at his skittishness. He seemed so nervous and tightly winched that Angelo wondered how he would ever endure a battle. Rattled by the disaster, the major, now white-faced, glanced worriedly at the generals watching from afar. As if hoping to divert blame for the screwup, he shouted at the doughboys, "You're dismissed until Fourteen Hundred! Don't return until you've read your tactics manuals!"

The men fell out, relieved to escape the clutches of this loony martinet.

Angelo hung back. "Major? Permission to speak, sir?"

The other doughboys froze at Angelo's shouted request.

When the officer nodded, Angelo said, "Sir, it looks to me like you're loading them fake tanks of yours with their own gas supply and repair parts."

The major narrowed his owlish eyes. "That's standard tactical procedure."

The other men groaned at Angelo for delaying their midday mess.

"I used to service the rail trucks for the Hazleton coal mines. We ran into the same problem. One car would bust into another and explode the gas cans. Not real pleasant down in a hole when that happened."

"You got a point to this little tale, Private?"

"I came up with a solution at the mines you might find useful. If I was you, I'd try something else."

Standing behind the major, a couple of the men balled their fists in a silent threat that Angelo had better shut up and let them get the hell out of there.

But Angelo persisted. "Put all your gas cans and repair gear on one tank. Have it follow the other tanks. That way, you'd always have your supply, but only one tank can get blown up."

The major stared at him for a dangerous moment. "What's your name?"

He gulped, now realizing that he'd made a big mistake. "Angelo, sir."

"How tall are you?"

He figured he was being measured for a solitary-confinement hole. "The doctors at the recruiting station said Five-Six, sir. But they got me on a bad day. I was slouching from eating some bad navy beans. The grub they served at the camp in Hoboken wasn't fit for chinamen."

The other men were smirking, waiting for Angelo to get the hammer.

The major kept staring at Angelo like Beelzebub sizing up a sinner. "You see that farthest oak down there?"

"Yes, sir."

"Count its limbs for me."

He did the sums in his head. "Seventeen."

The major pulled an ivory-handled pistol form his holster, causing the other men to back away. "Run down there and grab some bark, then hightail back here with it as fast as you can."

Always eager for a challenge, Angelo got into a crouch. The major looked at his wristwatch, and fired the starting shot. Angelo set off like a rabbit, dodging the tanks and debris strewn across the churned valley. The men howled with laughter at their clueless comrade who didn't realize that he was being punished. He reached the tree and, huffing and puffing, staggered back up the hill. He delivered the bark as ordered and dropped his hands to his knees.

The major looked up from his watch. "Two minutes. Thirteen seconds."

"Make him do it again, sir!" one of the men yelled. "He can break two minutes easy!"

"Can you write, soldier?"

Angelo nodded. "I learned the scrip for the pay days down at the mines."

The major pulled out an order pad and pencil from his pocket. He wrote something on one of the sheets and then handed the pad to Angelo.

Angelo read what the officer had written: *Pfc Joe Angelo is hearby comisioned as batman for Majer George S. Patton.*

"Write down what I just wrote," the major ordered. "Do it right. Fix it up."

Stumped, Angelo wondered if this was some kind of reverse aptitude test. Did this officer really not know how to spell, or was he being goaded into the correction so that he'd be reamed out? And what the hell is a batman anyway? He took a deep breath and accepted the pencil. An order was an order. *Do it right*—and suffer the consequences. He wrote: *Pfc. Joe Angelo is hereby commissioned as batman for Major George S. Patton.* He handed the pad back.

The officer studied what Angelo had written. He signed the page, tore it out, and handed it to Angelo. "Give this to your commanding officer. And get a damn haircut. You're an American soldier, not some Frog poet." He drew Angelo aside, out of earshot of the other men. "If you grow another inch, I'll bust you back down to shoveling shit in latrines. I want you slipping in and out of my tank turrets like a mouse through a soup can. And if you ever tell anyone that I have dyslexia and can't spell, I'll cut off those Italian olives you call gonads and use them for ball bearings. That is if I ever get my sonofabitchin' tanks delivered to me."

The officer marched off, leaving Angelo staring at the order, not knowing what to make of it. The other men gathered around to see what the officer had written. Reading the lines, they let out a collective gasp of disbelief.

Campio slapped off Angelo's helmet. "You stupid Wop!"

"What's a batman?" Angelo asked.

Campio shook his head in amazement at his buddy's stupidity. "Thanks to your big mouth, Angelo, you just became the orderly for that striped madman. I give you a week before he blows your brains out with that Wyatt Earp revolver he carries with him."

23

SAINTE-NAZAIRE, FRANCE
JANUARY 1918

Standing in line at the mess station, Ozzie Taylor waited for his two metal plates to be slopped with a breakfast of corned beef and gravy that looked more like pea soup. He could barely remember what a home-cooked meal tasted like. Heck, he hadn't had a hot serving of anything green with life since getting off the boat a month ago, and like most of the men in the 15th Regiment, he had already lost ten pounds. All this rushing to get over here to save civilization, and now all they did was wait and waste away.

"One plate."

He turned toward the speaker of that twangy command, a white private carrying a rifle who stood three men behind him. He nodded politely and showed him his second plate. "This one here's for Lt. Europe."

"Europe? Hell of a name for a nigger. Is his asshole called Africa?"

Ozzie looked around and realized that he had failed to abide Big Jim's first rule: always have at least six members of the regiment with you wherever you went. Willie Graham and Sgt. White were in the hall, but they stood on the far side, too far away to offer him help. "The Lieutenant is back in the barracks finishing up some paperwork. He ordered me to bring his breakfast to him."

"I don't give a shit if you're getting cornbread for Uncle Tom. You fill one plate. Eat the damn serving. Then get back in line for the second helping for that bootlicker you clean the bedpans for."

Inside, Ozzie was shaking, but he tried to put up a strong front. "Now I can't have you talking that way about my superior officer."

The white soldier pushed him aside. "Get behind me."

At that moment, two conflicting commandments were struggling for dominance inside Ozzie's head. Colonel Hayward had ordered them to avoid confrontation with the Southern boys, warning that their Harlem regiment would always get the worse of it from headquarters. But Big Jim had told him that if he ever slouched from an indignity, he would no longer have him as his orderly. He was going to get the worst of the fight, that was a given, but he had to stand up for the regiment. He asked another soldier to hold his plates, not wanting to get them dirty. Then, he charged at the mouthy cracker and latched onto him in a bear hug, trying to deny him the use of his arms. They staggered locked together across the mess hall, chest-to-chest, resembling two drunks slow dancing.

The other soldiers laughed at the uproarish spectacle. The white soldier who had instigated the brawl held a look of horror, embraced in a clench by a descendant of the African race. He finally shook off Ozzie and raised the butt of his rifle to smash in his skull. On his knees, Ozzie curled his head into his hands and waited for the blow that would send him to his Maker. When several seconds passed and he didn't hear the harp strings of Heaven, he looked up.

Sgt. White was standing in front of the white soldier. "Give me your weapon, Private."

"I ain't handing over my rifle to no nigger."

"You're speaking to an officer. You'll do as ordered, or you'll face a court-martial."

The white soldier cocked his ear as if listening for guidance from the spirits of his departed Confederate ancestors. Finally, with a huff of disgust, he surrendered the Springfield.

Sgt. White unloaded the bullets from the magazine and handed the rifle back to the soldier. Standing nose to nose with the lippy redneck, he ordered Ozzie, "Now, go fill those plates, Private Taylor."

The cook behind the mess station was so impressed with Ozzie's courage that he tossed an extra helping of gravy on each biscuit. With his dangerous mission accomplished, Ozzie hurried out of the mess hall, trailed by Graham and Sgt. White, who was rolling those confiscated bullets in his hand like marbles. They made a beeline for the barracks and found Big Jim sitting on his bed.

Sgt. White nodded for Ozzie to make his costly delivery. "Europe, you might want to get your own breakfast from now on."

"You get out on the wrong side of the cot this morning, Primrose?"

"Your orderly here almost got his noggin busted for those biscuits. I hope they're worth it."

Big Jim shot to his feet. "What happened?"

"What always happens happened."

Big Jim grasped Ozzie's chin to check him over. "You all right, Taylor?"

"I left him bruised, Lieutenant."

Big Jim looked around the barracks, shaking his head and trying to keep the steam from exploding through his ears. He whirled and kicked a shovel halfway down the aisle between the cots. "Sonofabitches! We've been here a month and we don't even have guns! Shoveling and digging. Digging and shoveling. That's all they got us doing!"

"Yeah, but that dam we're building is going to be mighty pretty." Sgt. White shot a knowing smile at Ozzie, as if conspiring to egg Big Jim on.

Ozzie picked up Big Jim's boots and wiped them with a rag. "We better get started down there, sir. That colonel gets a might choleric if we show up to the worksite late."

Big Jim stole the boots and slammed them onto his feet. He stood and marched toward the tent flap. "We won't be shoveling dirt today."

"Where the hell you going, Jim?" Sgt. White demanded.

"Come along and see."

Ozzie and the sergeant followed Big Jim across the camp until they reached the building where the top brass kept their desks. The place was off-limits to non-regular officers and enlisted men without a written order. But Big Jim strode up the stairs and down the hall as if he owned the place and was about to demolish it.

A short adjutant stood from his desk, not rising much rise above it. "What's this about, sir?"

Big Jim hovered over the rattled soldier. "Colonel Hayward wants to see Lt. Europe."

The adjutant stared down at his appointments journal. "Sir, I don't—"

Big Jim walked right past the colonel's aide. Without turning, he waved for Ozzie and Sgt. White to follow him. Ozzie shrugged at the stunned adjutant as he tiptoed past.

Big Jim made a tight left into one of the offices. "'You'll fight like the rest of them.' You remember telling us that before we shipped over?"

Colonel Hayward looked up from his desk. Seeing who was standing in front of him, the white officer dropped his eyes and sat back into his chair, a slouching figure of fatigue and defeat. He waved in the other two members of the regiment, who were lingering just behind the door. "Shut it."

Big Jim waited until the door was closed. Then, he reminded the colonel, "Every other unit in this army has been assigned to a division."

Colonel Hayward arose from his chair and opened a cigar box on his desk. "I shouldn't be offering you one of these."

"Because I'm a Negro?"

"No, because you're a wheezing asthmatic."

Big Jim reached into the box and dug out three stogies. He stuck one in his mouth and gave the others to Sgt. White and Ozzie, lighting their tips with a match. The room soon became filled with smoke.

The colonel waited until the nicotine did its soothing work. "Pershing would have you on the line tomorrow. You know that. But certain congressmen—"

"And the President," Big Jim insisted.

The colonel sighed. "Yes, and the President. They won't allow Pershing to mix in our Negro regiments with the whites."

"You mean they don't intend to let us fight?"

The colonel flicked his ashes into a spittoon and stared at the floor. "There may be one way to force their hands."

"I'm waiting," Big Jim said.

"You're not going to like it."

"Sounds like I got no choice."

"Headquarters has been hounding me to send your band to Aix-les-Bains."

"What's there?"

"It's a spa town. The French have given it to us temporarily to serve as a leave haven for those troops who have put in their two weeks in the trenches."

Big Jim took a step closer. "You want us to entertain them with *concerts?*"

"Hear me out," the colonel said. "I think I can convince the brass to first send you and your band on a promotional tour to drum up morale for the French. You'd be playing in some of the finest concert halls in the country."

Big Jim stole a glance at Ozzie and Sgt. White, as if not believing what he'd just heard. "How is *that* going to get us into battle?"

"The French don't suffer the same prejudices," the colonel said. "If you can impress Joffre and his staff, I think I may be able to work something out."

"You mean… "

The colonel nodded. "Fight with the French Army."

Looking through the window, Big Jim watched the men of their regiment lugging shovels down to the French dam to work like laborers. "Taylor!"

Ozzie stepped forward, his face green from his first stogie. "Yes, sir."

"You willing to fight with the French?"

"Will they let me play my oboe?"

Big Jim broke a wide grin. "What do you think, Colonel?"

"Hell, they may be desperate enough to allow even that."

Two weeks later, Ozzie stood out of sight, stage left, on the boards of the grand old opera house of Nantes. He snuck a peek through the curtains at the packed audience and saw only French faces—*white* faces—crowning black tuxes and evening gowns. There was no Nigger Heaven here, the name applied to the balcony in concert halls back in the States where black folks were forced to sit.

He gave the thumbs-up to Big Jim, who stood waiting in front of the seated regimental band. The Boss had been worried that nobody would come to their first performance, especially in the midst of the war. But this night the place was dazzling with jewels and finery. He had begged Big Jim to let him join the band for the event, even auditioning with the oboe again, but the Boss had denied his request by lifting a finger to his chin, his indication that he needed work on his posture and windpipe position. As a result, he had been left to do his usual duties as stage runner, holding extra copies of the music charts, rushing out glasses of water between sets, and making sure there was an ample supply of batons.

While waiting to go on stage, Big Jim shrugged his shoulders to loosen up his uniform for the coming effort. The other band members shuffled their feet nervously, wetting their reeds and blowing out saliva. Then, as they all settled back into their seats, they lidded their eyes in meditation on the importance of what they were about to attempt.

Ozzie realized they were preparing as if going into battle. In truth, they were: Their futures—perhaps, for many, their lives—rested on this night. At Big Jim's signal, he pulled the cords and drew back the curtains.

Presented to France for the first time, the Boss cut the air with his famous wand and sent the band into a ragtime rendition of the tune they'd been practicing day and night since arriving here. The cornet and clarinet players swayed with the rising rhythms, and the drummers bounced with their syncopated raps. The entire stage looked like an ocean of black waves.

The spectators sat on their hands, ominously silent.

Ozzie's heart raced, and he could see that Big Jim was alarmed, too. Had they made a terrible mistake? He was already calculating how many days it would take before Col. Hayward sent them back home in disgrace, not having fired one bullet against the Germans. He'd be back on the streets in Harlem, tooting for pennies and—

"La Marseillaise!" shouted an elderly lady in the fifth row.

The crowd erupted from the seats with thunderous applause.

Big Jim shot a grin of relief at Ozzie. These Frenchies, they both now realized, had never heard such music before. It had taken several notes before they understood that the band was playing their national anthem. The audience began to sway now, and even the French generals in the front row were tapping their feet. Ozzie marveled at how Big Jim seemed to become young again, flowing like the limb of a willow tree and aiming his baton at the anxious trombone players and let them loose their slides with a shuddering crack that would have made the Kaiser soil his britches.

All of a sudden, the lady who had identified the anthem elbowed her way into the aisle and started "Walking the Dog," a dance move that the honeys back at the Manhattan Casino had perfected. The Frenchies were now laughing and roaring with delight. The good times were back again, and for the moment, everyone seemed to forget that there was a war on. The Dog-Walking lady high-stepped onto the stage and began jitterbugging with Big Jim. Her bold sortie spurred the soldiers in the band to stand from their chairs and let go on the double-loud.

By God, Ozzie whispered to himself, if those shimmying French generals in the front row had anything to say about it, they'd all be singing the *Marseillaise* together in the trenches before long. Hell would freeze over before they'd ever see Black Jack Pershing cut loose like that. Maybe their regiment *did* belong with these life-lovin' *c'est la vie* people.

The French lady dancing on the stage with Big Jim was downright possessed now, inflicted by a seizure of the soul.

Ozzie knew that disease, all right. He had seen it catch hold of many a victim back home. France had just become infected with Ragtimitis.

24

LE TREPORT, FRANCE
JANUARY 1918

As the train from Le Havre steamed doggedly toward the black tails rising from hundreds of coastal chimneys, Anna lowered her seat's window for a better view of the towering chalk cliffs that sheltered her new home from the harsh Normandy gales. Her first impression of the seaport village, aspersed now by the dimming light of dusk, was how thoughtful the French had been to brighten the track platforms with planters filled with white magnolias and lilies. Yet when the locomotive rumbled closer to the small station, her appreciation turned to horror. The rectangular flowerbeds were not planters at all, but rows and rows of wounded men shrouded in blankets and linens.

Behind them, at the far end of the platform, sat stacks of pine coffins waiting to be transported across the Channel. This very car, she realized, would soon be filled with bodies bound for grieving loved ones in England. The wheels of the train hissed to a crawl, and she looked down at the bandaged faces passing below her. A few soldiers looked up and smiled weakly at her, but most just stared blankly off into the distant waves of the Atlantic.

The train finally jerked to a stop, and she climbed down from the stairwell. Accompanied by thirty fellow reserve nurses from America, she hurried for the exit, passing the hundreds of British wounded who had been brought here to Base Hospital Number Ten from the Flanders Front. She searched the civilians huddled around their piles of trunks and portmanteaus, hoping that Helen Fairchild, who had been sent over in July, might have come to greet her.

Finding no sign of her friend, she carefully stepped around the prostrate men, offering a hand of comfort whenever a groan stopped her short. There was none of the order and discipline here that she had become accustomed to in the military hospital in London. Many of these broken soldiers looked to be only a few days from the battlefield; some fidgeted nervously, flailing at imaginary enemies and yelling commands as if still in the trenches; others sat or lay inert, as if the flame of hope inside them had been extinguished.

She was grateful now that God, altering her orders, had not sent her over with Helen and the first volunteers. The officer in charge of medical support in London had assigned her to Queen Alexandra Hospital, and there the Brits had been so short of medical staff that the chief nurse had endured her ignorance, blaming it on poor American training. During these past weeks, she had managed to pick up the bare rudiments of nursing by secretly studying a borrowed training book at night.

She and the nurses rode up the precipice to the cliffs on a precarious cable car pulled by chains. Reaching the summit, they stepped out onto a green flatland filled with tents and wooden medical barracks. Hooded and bent against the gusts, the others headed straight for the nursing barracks, but she lingered behind. Curious to know what awaited her in the morning, she took a detour and walked around the perimeter of a tent marked *Surgery*.

She lifted the flap and stepped inside. The place looked like a macabre puppet show. Rows of cots were lined up against both sides of the pavilion, with just enough space between them for one person to stand. Hundreds of men— she assumed they were men, for most were so bandaged that she could not see their faces—lay in various contortions, with their cast-encased limbs dangling from ropes. Some had wounds that were being disinfected with tubes dripping sodium hypochlorite from bags. The poor fellows were constantly shifting and struggling to find respite from their agonies, giving the place an unsettling white shimmer. At the far end of the tent, a doctor worked over a convulsing, gray-cheeked soldier who looked to be no older than sixteen. A nurse assisting the procedure at the operating table tried to restrain the wounded soldier long enough for a rancid bandage to be removed from his thigh.

Anna raised a sleeve to her mouth. The wound gash, dark and puffy, gave off a sickening smell, like that of a dead mouse. All around her, other soldiers who were waiting on cots for their turn under the knife began praying the Lord's Prayer. The doctor stopped his digging into the boy's leg and stood mute with arms folded, but the attending nurse continued to work furiously, pressing her thumb against the flesh of the wounded soldier, just above his knee. His skin crackled, as if bubbles under it were being popped.

The writhing boy heard the snapping on his leg, and became eerily still. He looked up at the doctor and begged, "Please, sir, don't take it off!"

The doctor shook his head wearily. "Not coming off, lad. It's too late for that." He turned and walked on down the aisle as if he had done nothing more than prescribe a dose of aspirin.

The soldier wouldn't let go of the nurse's hand. "What's he saying, mum?"

The nurse knelt down aside the cot. "You have gas gangrene, Alfred. You don't have more than an hour, I'm afraid."

Anna hurried to a bucket and vomited.

The nurse turned, only then aware of another presence. "Anna?"

Anna wiped her mouth, ashamed. How did this nurse know her name?

"Are you ill?"

Anna blinked with sudden recognition. Before she could utter the name, the doctor shouted from the far end of the pavilion. "Fairchild!"

She grasped Helen's hands and felt them trembling. Her friend had lost a frightening amount of weight, and her face was a sickly shade of yellow; she looked as if she had aged twenty years. "What has happened to you?"

"Tetanus shot!" the doctor shouted at Helen. "Bed Fifty-Eight!"

Helen rushed Anna down the aisle with a hand at her elbow. "Stay with me. We're short of nurses. I'm sorry I couldn't get away to meet you."

They stopped at the bed of a soldier whose head was bent back, his neck arched in pain. His throat muscles were spasming, and his dirty teeth were bared like those of a snarling dog. The doctor loaded up a syringe with the serum, and handed it to Helen.

Helen turned aside to prevent the soldier from overhearing them. "Why put him through the suffering?"

Anna put a hand up to shield her eyes, unable to watch. "What is happening to him?"

The doctor glared suspiciously at her. "Who is this?"

Helen tried to calm the manic soldier in the bed. "One of our new nurses."

The doctor snorted his disgust. "Another American lass has come looking for a war adventure. Saint George help us."

Helen kept pleading against giving the soldier the painful tetanus shot. "He's in the advanced stages of lockjaw. The injection will do nothing for him now. All we can do is to ease his suffering as best we can."

"Give it to him. There is a chance it may spark the antibodies."

Another patient down the row cried out for help.

The doctor turned, distracted. "Fairchild, come with me." He nodded toward Anna. "Let her give him the injection." He spun on his heels and marched down the row toward the screaming soldier.

Helen slipped the tetanus syringe into her own pocket and brought out another needle. She secretly gave the second syringe to Anna and whispered, "Morphine. Give him the full dose." She took off running for the doctor.

Left alone with the dying soldier, Anna stood terrified with the needle thrumming in her hand. The poor boy stared pleadingly at her, his mouth stretched in a silent scream. She managed to restrain his flailing arm and turned it over to look for a vein, just as the training manual had demonstrated in the drawings. She was so dizzy with nervousness that she couldn't stop her own tremors long enough to get the needle to the thin blue line. Finally, she took a deep breath and whispered, "Lord, please help me." Opening her eyes, she plunged the needle into the suffering boy's arm. She pressed on the syringe, but the morphine refused to release.

My God!

She had bent the needle on the man's skin, tough as leather. Breathing hard, she finally managed to pull the needle out. She saw another syringe on the table. Helen and the doctor were walking back toward her. She yanked the needle from the man's arm and quickly snapped the new one onto the morphine syringe. With no time to hesitate, she drove the second needle into the vein and plunged the morphine into the man's bloodstream.

Blessedly, his spasms eased.

The doctor was now only a few steps away. She extracted the needle and dropped it into her pocket. And then she remembered: she hadn't emptied the other syringe. She slipped her hand into her pocket and drained the tetanus fluid as the doctor and Helen arrived. She pulled out the empty syringe and affected indifference as she dropped it into the kidney dish on the table.

The doctor glared at her, then walked away.

Helen pulled her aside, away from the patients. "We don't have much time. Another barge came in this morning with two hundred wounded." Anger thrummed in her hoarse voice. "The winter fighting is usually slower, thank God. They're casualties from the practice shelling and the useless sorties ordered when the officers get bored. The generals call it normal wastage. They give sanitized names to every horror to keep the poor folks back home from knowing what really happens here."

Anna was already lost. "You said we don't have much time. For what?"

Helen's eyes were fluttering, windows to her racing heart. "Staff Headquarters could send you to an advance clearing station any hour now. You'll be the only nurse there. I won't let them put you through what I endured."

"I've learned—"

"You've learned nothing!" Helen walked faster down the aisle, talking frenetically. "Forget everything they taught you. Nothing prepares you for what you will face out there."

Anna was frightened by her frenetic behavior. "Helen, you need to rest."

Helen stopped at the bed of a soldier who appeared asleep. She picked up his limp hand and gestured for Anna to feel it in a test. "First thing, when the men are brought in to the clearing stations, sort the dying from those who are near death but can be saved. You won't have time for laboratory tests. Many will be in shock. They will seem dead, but their bodies have just retreated into a cocoon of protection. You must learn to triage them by touch alone. All will come in feeling cold. Some will be cold from just the chill of the night. Others will be cold because their life force is ebbing away. Don't use your mind. Think with your fingers. And don't second-guess yourself. Delay costs lives."

Anna struggled to comprehend the rapid-fired instructions. They came to a man resting on his side with his back exposed. Helen gently removed a corner of a large bandage that covered the crease between his left buttock and upper thigh. Under the gauze lay a seething white mass. Anna nearly gagged. "Are those… maggots?"

Helen sprayed the larvae with a can of ether. "If a soldier comes in with these blessed creatures, leave them on the wound for twenty-four hours. They help fight the gangrene." Anna hurried to keep up as Helen rushed from bed to bed. "Vaseline for the burned ones. Drop almond oil on their eyelids. Sometimes they will come in with their skin stuck to the stretchers. You have to soak them first with warm water before trying to move them. If you see blue crosses on their body, the *poilus* found them. That's the French sign for wounds." Helen held up her right hand, revealing one of the fingers swollen with a cut. "Wear gloves. Worse thing that can happen to you is a septic finger. You're no good for weeks. If you get an infection, bathe it in iodine. If you don't have iodine, use urine." Her thrumming voice was rising in stridency. "Many times you will have to inflict a lot of pain early to save them months of pain later."

"Please, Helen. Sit down a moment."

Helen found a pack of cigarettes on a bed table. Pulling one out, she dipped it in a bottle of vinegar and thrust it into Anna's mouth. Anna tried to spit it out, revolted by the taste, but Helen demanded that she endure it. "Give one of these to each gas victim when they first arrive. If they do what you just did, they are lying about being gassed. The mustard masks their taste of vinegar."

"But—"

"They will put you in the *Salle de Morte* first."

"The what?"

"The Death Room. It's where they keep the hopeless ones." Helen's quivering lips came to Anna's ear. "Some doctors will tell you to save the morphine. The good ones, the ones who would have given Christ the hyssop on the Cross to ease His suffering, will tell you to be free with it."

"You mean… "

Helen stopped her cold with a hard look warning against easy judgment about the merciful speeding of life's end. "When you draw the night shift, you must be on guard around four in the morning. That is the time hemorrhages are mostly likely to—" She doubled over in pain.

Anna helped her to a chair. "What's wrong?"

Helen coughed up blood. She lurched back and fainted.

"Doctor!" Anna screamed.

The flap flew open, and the physician who had dismissed her so callously before came running. He checked Helen's pulse and felt along the front and sides of her abdomen.

"I don't think she has slept in days," Anna said.

The doctor motioned the orderlies up with a stretcher. "It's not from lack of sleep."

Two weeks later, Anna and the other nurses brightened with relief when Helen opened her eyes in the recovery room of the operating tent. Called over with the good news, the surgeons arrived and hovered over Helen, testing her vitals and checking the X-rays.

"Nothing to worry about," Anna assured her groggy friend. "They found a gastric ulcer blocking your stomach valve. No doubt caused by too much worrying. You are finally going to get that rest you deserve."

Helen smiled weakly; then, her face shadowed. "How many have died?"

Anna patted her hand. "You mustn't think about that right now."

"How many?"

Anna sighed, driven to the admission. "Thirty-seven since you went under. Lt. Cornishon in Tent Eight was asking about you this morning. He said the men stayed up all night praying."

The surgeon brought down the X-ray from the light. "The obstruction is gone. Now we must let the healing take place."

Helen looked up at him with an admonishing glare. "I have a bitter taste in my mouth. Chloroform. You should have saved it for the men."

The surgeon smiled. "Fairchild, I'm surprised you didn't rise up on the table during the operation and tell me which knife to use."

The nurses nodded at the friendly reminder of Helen's perfectionism.

"Right," the surgeon said. "Let's give her some rest. Do you ladies of the cape not have other patients to attend, or did the Kaiser suspend the war for Miss Fairchild's benefit?"

As the other nurses filed out of the tent, Helen held onto Anna's wrist. "Stay a moment with me, won't you?"

Anna looked to the surgeon for permission.

"Not long." He departed and shut the flap behind him.

Helen indicated for her to pull a chair up. "Do you remember that theatrical we saw on Charing Cross Road?"

Anna nodded, sitting aside the bed. "'Maid of the Mountains.'"

"Yes, that's the one. How wonderful an evening it was."

Anna smiled. "As I recall, you let loose with a catcall so loud that the lead actor halted his performance and gave you the evil eye."

"He deserved it with that lackluster effort."

Anna fussed at her nurse's apron, still a little ashamed that she had allowed Helen to talk her into seeing such a profane performance. If her father or Micah ever learned that she had spent good money on such frivolous nonsense, they might shun her for a year.

Helen turned serious. "Anna, you must protect yourself."

"I wash my hands after every patient."

"No. I mean… you must protect your heart."

"My heart? Helen, I told you in London. I am betrothed to Micah. He will be waiting for me when I return. He is the reason I am doing this."

"I am not speaking of romance. You will become the mother of every soldier who is brought to you now. They will call for you with their final breaths. You have to find a way to rise above it all, to look down on what you will endure as if you are watching that play on Charing Cross. Try to treat it as just a bad dream. One that you will soon awake from."

"You're scaring me with talk like this."

"In my trunk, there is a letter I wrote to my mother. I meant to post it, but didn't have a chance. Would you mind sending it for me?"

"Of course."

Helen's eyes lidded. "I think I'll sleep a little now, if I can remember how."

Anna pressed a kiss to her forehead. "I will look in on you in the morning."

Late into that night, Anna awoke from a nightmare. She looked around, not knowing where she was, but then saw the other nurses in their cots, sound asleep. She wondered how the soldiers slept in a different hole every night. In the horrid dream that she had just escaped, seven medics had been walking down the aisle of the gassed pavilion, firing off corks from wine bottles in a twenty-one-gun salute. The poor faceless boys in the ward had sat up in their cots to sing the Star-Spangled Banner with Cockney accents, and the worst injured of the lot, a Leicester boy whose bottom jaw was blown off, had brought a bugle to the gaping hole in his face to play "Taps" through his nose.

She shivered with dread from the lingering effects of the vision. Then, she remembered promising Helen that she would mail her letter before the train left that morning. Fearful of forgetting, she climbed from her cot and walked softly across the tent to Helen's small station. She lit a candle and quietly opened the trunk, careful not to wake the others. She dug through the toiletries until she found a single folded page. There was no envelope with it. She hoped the address for Helen's mother was written on the return for the letter. She opened it to find the address. She couldn't help but read it, holding her breath on the last paragraphs:

> *Gee but I'll be glad to see you all by the time this war is over, but at the same time I am glad to be here to help take care of these poor men, and I'll be doubly glad when our own U.S. boys will be with us, for they will be so far from home, and they will have no one but us American nurses to really take any genuine interest in them, for their own friends will not be able to reach them.*
>
> *What the Red Cross and the YMCAs are doing for us here means so much to us. Really, it would be awful to get along without the things they send us. Most of the pleasure that the troops get are the ones provided by the YMCA.*
>
> *If you could only see what the boys here have to go through sometimes, you would see they need all the comfort possible. Without the supplies sent to us by the Red Cross Society, we could not do half as much for them as we are.*
>
> *Please tell me what it was that everyone seems to have heard concerning me at home. Of course, whatever it was, as you know, is not correct, for as I have told you often, anytime anything should happen, you would be notified.*
>
> *Heaps of love, your very own, Helen.*

"Miss Raber."

Startled, Anna straightened on her knees and turned to find Major Mitchell, the chief surgeon, standing behind her. The other nurses, awakened, climbed from their cots and came hovering around the surgeon.

"I'm sorry to report that Miss Fairchild has slipped into a coma."

A week later, Anna stood with the ranks of British and American nurses as a military honor guard lowered Helen's casket into the frozen ground of Mont Huon Cemetery. Helen was being given the full salute reserved for soldiers killed in action, and every officer who could be spared that morning had come to see her buried in her uniform. The British nurses whispered that it was the most well-attended funeral they had ever witnessed on the Front. Against orders of the doctors, several of the recuperating men in the wards had insisted on coming out. Limping and bundled against the cold, they supported each other with hands to their shoulders.

Acute failure of the liver had been the official cause of death, but several of the nurses said they knew better. No one dies from an ulcer. Helen's constant exposure to the mustard gas at the clearing station in Passchendaele had eviscerated her immune system. They had witnessed the same grisly fate played out in thousands of wounded soldiers in the hospital. About a month ago, one of the boys who survived the Third Battle of Ypres had come back again. After seeing the jaundice in Helen's eyes, he had cried a tearful admission that she had given up her gas mask after he had lost his.

Anna, you must protect yourself.

She had seen many dreadful things since arriving in France, but what scared her most now had nothing to do with blood and guts. She didn't know why, but she was having trouble remembering Micah's features. She had looked into so many mangled and mutilated faces during these past weeks that something inside her seemed to be turning off the capacity to see him.

As the honor guard turned to depart, she lingered near Helen's casket and raised a cheek toward the sea to let the howling wind dry her tears. She reached into her jacket and pulled out a letter that had arrived that morning from Chaumont. She had delayed reading it, fearing that it would contain what seemed inevitable. But now, feeling Helen's prodding presence, she forced herself to open it.

Her eyes fell upon the last paragraph: The Army Nursing Corps of the AEF was transferring her to a base hospital in a town called Rimaucourt near the Marne River. The American boys were coming over by the thousands, the order advised, and they would soon be going into action. Looking down at Helen's grave again, she wondered what she would encounter at this place called the Marne. It had a peaceful-sounding name, at least. Whatever was waiting for her there, she was certain it could be no worse than what she had witnessed here at Le Treport.

25

ROLAMPONT, FRANCE
FEBRUARY 1918

olonel MacArthur shook his head at the slovenly appearance of the grumbling *poilus* trampling past him. No wonder the armies of the Allies were in such desperate straits. With their stringy long hair curling under their helmets and their unkempt beards and mustaches caked with bread crumbs and the stew they'd eaten that evening, these French infantrymen moving forward to take the ladder positions for their nightly raid across no man's land looked more like Slav coal miners than soldiers.

After several weeks of persistent requests to GHQ, he had finally procured an assignment to the Front, ostensibly to observe fighting tactics. He enjoyed an inward chuckle at that conceit; as if the *Frogs* had anything to teach *him* about combat. That desk jockey Pershing believed a divisional chief of staff should remain behind the lines, but he would not be holed up in some crumbling château ten miles to the rear, shuffling orders and sending messages by carrier pigeons. He was no George McClellan. His destiny would be found here, amid the whistle of bullets and the taste of fresh blood. He paced the duckboards of this rear supply trench, agitated and anxious to see some action. He had suffered his fill of what the French called "training" in these stinking earthworks. These disease-infested sluice troughs would have made Lee's defenses at Petersburg seem luxurious.

Right on time, the big German guns in the Luneville sector ahead opened up with their nightly serenade, peppering the moonless agate sky with distant concussions. Seconds later, the French howitzers to his rear retaliated.

Several *poilus* trying to sleep lurched up from their cubbyholes. But he had not flinched, and they saw it. At the Point, he had taught himself that trick of willful steadiness by having his mother slam pans together behind his ear at unannounced moments. Now, while others ducked under overhanging bluffs, he casually kicked the globs of mud from his right heel and reached his boot up against an embrasure to stretch his aching lower back. The curvature in his spine was acting up, his unerring warning that someone somewhere was stabbing him in the back.

George Marshall and those bastards at headquarters were out to get him again, merely because he had felt duty-bound to make an end run around Pershing when his sycophants threatened to break up the 42nd and disperse its regiments to the French lines like scrap wire to patch holes in an old fence. General Menoher was still officially in command of the Rainbow, but its soldiers knew who really ran the operation. And they would be eternally grateful when they discovered how he had lobbied their congressmen and senators back home. It had been hard work, the hours of writing cables to Washington, but his strategy had paid off. Inundated by newspaper editorials and complaints from the Hill, Pershing had finally backed down on his dispersal plan.

History will remember me as the savior of the best damn division in this war.

Yet because of his defense of his beloved division, he now had two fights on his hands—a frontal attack against the Boche, and a rear guard action against GHQ at Chaumont. He had to do something, and soon, to thwart those conspirators from poisoning his name to get him sent home. He had just the solution: Even Pershing would not think of burying in the Army bureaucracy the first American officer who went over the top.

No, the press would never allow it.

He retreated into the small bunker that served as his quarters and quickly changed into the uniform that he had designed for this long-awaited moment. Instead of a steel helmet and regulation overcoat, he donned his favorite smashed-down cap—which gave him just the air of dash and insouciance he desired—and wrapped his shoulders in a heavy wool cardigan sweater crowned with a turtleneck collar. He pondered wearing his old Army letter sweater instead, but decided the meaning of the large 'A' on its breast would be lost on the French. He kept on his jodhpurs and traded his trench boots for a pair of black cavalry boots that had been spit-polished to give off a gleam.

Fully attired now for glory, he took out a small mirror from his toiletry kit and stared at his creation with approval. Something was still missing, though, an accessory to finish the look. He searched his canvas bag, and nodded. He gathered up his silver cigarette holder and thrust it into the side of his mouth, moving it around it until he found the most carefree angle. He glanced at the mirror again and set his chin in defiance.

Yes, this will show the French and Germans how an American goes to war.

He walked out of the bunker and strode with determination down the duck-boards. A few steps from the front trench, the thought occurred to him that he would need a witness for the deed. He backtracked, and in the next dugout found Captain Thomas Handy, one of General Menoher's aides. "Handy, I'm going on the picnic tonight with the Frogs. Care to join me?"

The captain held the look of a man who wanted to say no, but didn't dare. He stoically stood up and followed his superior out. The sloe-eyed *poilus* looked up in disbelief at the foppish American colonel and his reluctant captain parading past. The two officers looked like a doughboy version of Don Quixote and Sancho Panza. MacArthur nodded to them, aware that they had never seen such a dapper presentment. He led Handy past the whispers until he found General Georges de Bazelaire, the brave French field officer in charge of this sector.

Bazelaire blinked, as if not quite understanding what he was staring at.

MacArthur saluted the general. "*Bonsoir,* General. Captain Handy and I request permission to join your fine troops on their raid this evening."

Bazelaire smelled MacArthur's breath to determine if he was drunk. "This is not a sortie for officers who cannot be lost."

"An officer who cannot be lost is not worth a damn."

While listening to the exchange, the *poilus* sat daubing mud on their faces in preparation for the mission. Amused, they watched the two officers continue to argue, wondering if the two Americans were playing one of their infamous betting games, each trying to conquer the other in pointless bravery.

Bazelaire, who spoke fine English, pulled MacArthur aside. "Colonel, I have not received authority from your commander to allow this."

MacArthur slung his four-foot red muffler across his neck in a gesture of determination. "I cannot fight the Boche, sir, if I cannot see them. If I am to be asked to send my soldiers into those lines in defense of France, I must know what they will face."

"General Menoher has approved this?"

MacArthur knew there was no time to get permission from his superior, and even if he tried, the answer would likely be no. General Menoher would be watching the raid from the observation post on the next hill. He had to trust that, if spotted, he would not be called back. He qualified his answer, hoping the French general would not detect its nuance in English. "Captain Handy is General Menoher's aide. He will confirm that the general encourages his officers to be bold and informed when it comes to troop deployments."

Bazelaire turned to Handy for a confirmation of that claim. Receiving an uncertain nod, he shrugged at the mystery of this American obsession for glory and ordered his officer in charge of the raid: "Give them pistols."

MacArthur declined the offer. With a dramatic flair, he reached into his thick sweater and pulled out a riding crop. "I have the only weapon I need."

The *poilus*, now even more incredulous, grinned through their mustaches.

Handy took MacArthur aside, out of earshot of the others. "Sir, you know as well as I do that General Menoher hasn't approved this."

MacArthur stretched his neck in a gesture of insistence. "Handy, it's the orders you disobey that make you famous."

Before Handy could press his protest, General Bazelaire beckoned up a pair of wire cutters and a trench knife. He forced the implements on his two American volunteers. "The signal for the attack will be a hand grenade thrown by one of my men. If you do not come back, I know nothing of this conversation." He looked at his watch. "Five minutes, you shall go."

Following the example of the experienced *poilus*, MacArthur rubbed mud on his face, a concession to his initial strategy of forcing the Germans to witness the same American intrepidness demonstrated by Confederate General Patrick Cleburne on the bloody field of Franklin. With his first true battle action now only moments away, a hundred thoughts raced through his mind. Those many nights at his father's knee listening to stories of the Civil War had been but preparation for this moment, as had his hazing at the Point. He took comfort from the memory of his convulsions in Beast Barracks. After surviving those horrid hours, he had come to accept that he was invulnerable, protected by a mystical force. So long as he kept the faith in his destiny, he would always be safe.

Death was not what frightened him. No, what he prayed for was the strength to look the Elephant straight in the eye, and not waver.

I think the boy may have the makings of a soldier.

Those words, spoken when he was ten, remained seared into his memory. Was Father watching him now, whispering that prediction to his ear again?

He recalled a British veteran of the Somme telling him over tea one afternoon in Chaumont of his first time over the top. The Brit commander, a Captain Nevill, had seen fear in the faces of his 8th East Surreys recruits. So, before the assault, he had brought out four rugby balls and had handed one to each of his platoons. When the whistle for the surge sounded, Neville had offered a prize to the platoon that managed to kick their ball all the way to the German lines. One of the infantrymen had climbed to the top of the parapet and had let fly with a kick that would have made the Preston North Enders proud. And off they all went to die, cheering the progress of those balls as if at a match. Captain Nevill had been killed instantly, but two of the balls eventually found their way back to the British trenches.

The survivor of the Somme kicking competition had written a poem about that day. Now, as MacArthur prepared to go over the top, he whispered it to himself, having memorized it for this moment:

On through the hail of slaughter,
Where gallant comrades fall,
Where blood is poured like water,
They drive the trickling ball.
The fear of death before them
Is but an empty name.
True to the land that bore them—
The Surreys play the game.

He interrupted Handy's meditation with an elbow to his ribs. "Do you know anyone who brought a football over from the States?"

Handy stared at him, wondering how anyone could think about football at such a moment. Before he could ask the reason for the strange question, the *poilus* went up the ladders in grim silence.

Handy made a move to follow them, but MacArthur held him back and took the lead. He scrambled to the top of the trench, bracing for the night that would, in the words of his beloved Robert Burns, send him to his gory bed, or to victory.

The next morning, General Bazelaire, standing in the forward trench, looked out across no man's land through his elevated periscope and saw his raiding party walking back across the open field. With them were Handy, bloodied and bedraggled, and MacArthur, who wielded his riding crop as a prod as he herded up a captured German colonel.

Welcoming them into the trench, the French general chortled with delight. "Well, Colonel MacArthur! How did you find your first taste of war?"

"Success is ours, General. And I have brought you a gift."

Bazelaire offered a cigarette to MacArthur's downcast German prisoner. "You must not be ashamed, *Herr* Colonel. You have been captured by the d'Artagnan of the American Expeditionary Force. You are the first prisoner of the Americans. You will go down in history."

That news did not brighten the German officer's mood.

When MacArthur turned to ensure that his fellow raiders were all present and accounted for, the French soldiers around him in the trench burst into good-natured laughter.

Seeing what so amused his men, Bazelaire fluttered his drooping mustache with mirthful puff. "Colonel MacArthur, it seems you have lost the seat to your riding britches!"

MacArthur looked over his shoulder. His buttocks were exposed. Not one to let a moment of his triumph be sullied, he announced to the delight of the *poilus*, "I can assure you, my friends, that this prisoner will be the only Boche who ever sees my *derriere!*"

When the laughter finally quieted, Bazelaire stepped forward and braced MacArthur with hands to his shoulders. "And I can assure *you*, my brave American comrade, that you will win your country's precious Silver Star for this feat." He motioned up an aide and took a medal out of a box. "Until then, you will have to be satisfied with this." The general pinned a Croix de Guerre on MacArthur and kissed him on both cheeks.

Taking his practiced statuary pose, MacArthur raised an acknowledging hand to the applauding *poilus*. "Lafayette, we have returned!"

26

ARGONNE FOREST, FRANCE
MAY 1918

O zzie Taylor bounded up from his trench bench and stomped at the duckboards. "Goddamn rats!"

Perched on their stools below the embankment, the French *poilus* laughed and passed around a bottle of wine as they watched their new black friend from America try to chase off the giant vermin that were more plentiful—and, so far, more dangerous—than the Germans who were facing them across the field that night. "Foxtrot!" one of the French soldiers shouted, rocking his shoulders to imitate Ozzie's gyrations.

Sitting with them, Big Jim gave a thumbs up to confirm that they had correctly identified the American dance that his rodent-phobic orderly seemed to be performing. Catching the beat of Ozzie's heels, he whistled a rendition of *Everybody's Doing It Now*. "Taylor, I think you've invented a new one. The Rat Step. If you ever catch the ol' gal with the tail, hold her tight and show the polies here how we tango in Harlem."

Not the least amused, Ozzie stuck his hands under his armpits to prevent them from being gnawed off. "If I wanted to chase biting weasels, I'da saved myself the suffering of boot camp and just stayed in Harlem to sweep up the Casino after your concerts."

The French soldiers slapped Ozzie on the back in commiseration. But this time, instead of joining them and lobbing another jibe at his orderly, Big Jim pulled up his stool and walked a few steps away to sit alone, whispering words as if conjuring a new tune. Ozzie regretted his outburst, seeing how the reminder of those glory days had thrust Big Jim into another of his melancholic spells. The Boss hadn't been the same since word came a week ago that his old friend and concert headliner, Vernon Castle, had been killed in a plane crash. Ozzie had never witnessed a closer friendship between a Negro and a white man. At the start of the war, the slender, elegant Castle had gone back to his home in Great Britain with his wife Irene to join the Royal Flying Corps. Two months later, Vernon had been dancing the skies with the same verve and grace, shooting down two German aircraft and winning the Croix de Guerre.

But Castle's luck finally gave out. And it didn't help Big Jim's mood that their New York unit—renamed the 369th Infantry Regiment—had been cast off to the French army because the racists in Pershing's headquarters didn't want them using the same latrines with the whites. As a result, the Harlem men had been hunkered down in these putrid trenches in the Argonne Forest for more than a month, still waiting to see action. They weren't even allowed to use their own rifles. The French insisted they trade their Springfields for Lebels, which were slow to load and had a tendency of shoving a rear round in the magazine into the primer of the cartridge in front and blowing the face off the man trying to aim—

"Grenade!"

Ozzie hit the mud face down, clinging to the rim of his helmet. While he waited for the concussion to blow his brains across the trench, all he could think about was those big-toothed varmints making lunch out of what remained of his innards. Several seconds passed, but he heard nothing. Slowly, he risked raising his eyes. Big Jim and the Frenchies were standing over him, fingering what looked like an iron pomegranate.

"Must be a dud," Big Jim said.

Ozzie ran to the spot where the grenade had hit. He squatted and folded his arms over his chest for protection.

"What in Hallelujah's name are you doing, boy?" Big Jim asked.

Ozzie looked up over his forearm. "Boss, you told me those whiz-bangs never land in the same place twice. So I figured the safest place to be was right here where the first one landed."

One of the Frenchies reached down to examine the gutted grenade. He pulled out a broadsheet with letters stenciled in ink by a duplicating machine. He read what had been written, then shook his head and handed it to Big Jim with the declaration that it was *pour vous*.

Big Jim inspected the German message: *African comrades! You fight for American slave masters! Join our side and be free of humiliation!* He angrily crumpled the sheet into a ball and smashed it under his heel. "The sonsabitches are trying to turn us into traitors."

Ozzie saw the French soldiers watching Big Jim with suspicion, as if thinking the Germans might have a point. "What you gonna do?"

Big Jim was boiling mad. "Somebody give me a *real* grenade."

The Frenchies shook their heads, refusing him.

Their officer waved off Big Jim's itch to retaliate. "Too far. They shot it with a launcher. We have none."

Still steaming, Big Jim walked down the trench toward several men of the 369th who were hunched around a blanket, playing cards. "Jefferson!"

Junie Jefferson, a strapping six-foot-four, snapped to attention. "Yes, sir."

"Come with me."

Big Jim led Jefferson back to the French officer. He held out us hand, waiting for the grenade he had requested. The officer, shaking his head at the unbounded temerity of his American volunteers, finally gestured for one of his men to bring up an explosive.

"Ever seen a baseball game?" Big Jim asked the officer.

The officer made a swiping gesture of contempt. "Slapping a sphere with a stick. Our fur traders watched your savages play this absurd game long before it became, how do you now call it, your national waste time?"

Big Jim curled that same devilish smile of anticipation he'd always shown when announcing an encore number to catapult his audiences to the dance floor. "How about wagering. You Frenchies don't have a problem with *that* sport, do you?"

The French officer suddenly became more interested. "Ah, challenges of chance. *Oui*, my country excels the rest of the world in the *élan* of risk. Napoleon was the consummate champion of chance."

Big Jim looked up at the clear night sky. "Well, here's a bet for you. If Private Jefferson here can hit those Boche trenches with this grenade, I get to tag along next time you go on one of your Boche scavenger hunts."

The French officer puffed out his chest. "But there is no sport in such a wager. The deed you propose is impossible. The Allemande are more than a hundred meters away."

Big Jim offered his hand. "Deal?"

The officer smirked as he shook it. "*Un accord.*"

Big Jim took Junie Jefferson into one of the communication trenches that ran ninety degrees toward the front trench, out of earshot of the Frenchies. "When I pull the pin on this baseball, you get yourself a running start and heave this baby like you did when you threw out Cap Mullins from center field that day at Dexter Park. You hear me now?"

"Yes, sir."

"Get loose. I got a lot riding on this."

Windmilling his arm, Junie Jefferson nodded and got into his centerfield stance, waiting for the ball to drop into his glove hand. Big Jim was the picture of steadiness as he took his position a few paces ahead of Junie down the trench. All the Frenchies and the Harlem men of the 369th were crowding the duck-boards, leaving just enough room for Junie to make his run.

"Bottom of the ninth!" Big Jim shouted as if announcing the game, to get Junie into the mind-frame for the feat. "Rube Foster hits a mighty shot deep to center. Junie Jefferson, the Stuyvesant Scooper, is on the run. He catches the ball and turns for the throw—" He pulled the pin on the grenade and tossed it high into the air.

Junie shot forward on a sprint. He caught the live grenade in his left glove hand, transferred it to his right paw, and took three mighty leaps down the duckboards before heaving it toward the German lines on a magnificent arc. The *poilus* arched their necks in disbelief as they watched the grenade disappear into the night sky.

Big Jim silently counted off the seconds... One... Two... Three... Four.

An explosion rocked the ground in the distance, followed by groans and German curses.

The *poilus* cheered wildly. Impressed by the feat, their officer ordered up a new bottle of wine from the case being protected in the bunker like the crown jewels. He pulled out a corkscrew from his pocket and opened his delivery. He took a drink, and offered the bottle to Big Jim to do the same. As the Boss enjoyed his tasty swig, the French officer kissed him on each cheek. Ozzie and the other men of the 369th stood staring in amazement, having never seen one of their own be kissed by a white man. The officer pulled a small pistol from his holster and gifted it to Big Jim.

"What is this for?" Big Jim asked.

The officer gestured for an aide to bring up a spare Gallic uniform and a cloth skullcap. "I always pay my wagers promptly. We go this night."

Big Jim's distended eyes bugged even wider. "Go where?"

A raiding party of ten *poilus* strolled up from the communications trench and, looking no more concerned than if they were preparing for a stroll down the Champs-Élysées, waited at the ladders for the signal to go over the top.

The officer called Big Jim's bluff. "You want a tour of no man's land? I will be proud to accompany the first American Negro officer to lead men into this war."

Big Jim swallowed hard and glanced at Ozzie, silently admitting that his big talk had gotten him into a hell of a pickle. Shrugging, he removed his drab olive coat, handed it to Ozzie for safekeeping, and squeezed into the French uniform. Fingering the pistol that looked no larger than a cap shooter, he nodded his readiness. "Goddamn, let's go, boys!"

ig Jim had come staggering back from his first raid that night still in one piece. And ever since, his Harlem men hadn't been able to shut him up about how he had traded punches with a startled German who had called him "Black Death."

But a month later, the Boss hadn't been so lucky. Near a place called Château-Thierry, German gas bombs had left him gagging so violently that he had to be evacuated to a field hospital in Gézaincourt, a few miles behind the lines. Now, blessed with a rare lull in the bombardment, Ozzie and Noble Sissle walked into the hospital tent unannounced, having wheedled a twenty-hour leave from the trenches. To their relief, they found Big Jim sitting up in his bed and writing in his musical notebook.

Every few breaths, Big Jim began hacking and coughing, until one of the nurses rushed over to offer him a few hits from an oxygen tank. Seeing his buddies through his horn-rimmed glasses, he grinned from ear to ear and barked with gravelly voice, "Shouldn't you boys be in Berlin by now?"

"How you doing, Lieutenant?" Ozzie asked.

"Hell, I'm so bored, I'd almost be willing to hear you play that damn oboe. With emphasis on the 'almost'."

"You've lost some weight," Sissle said.

Big Jim waved off his friend's concern. "How are the boys?"

"We been kicking some Boche ass, sir," Ozzie said. "Guess what they're calling us now? The Harlem Hellfighters! And the Frenchies are telling the news hounds that we're the best soldiers they ever seen. You know what we yell every time we go over the top?"

Big Jim shook his head, fearing the regiment had lost all discipline during his absence.

"'Goddamn, let's go, boys!'" Sissle revealed, repeating the cry that Big Jim had yelped before making his first climb over the top. "It's become the regiment's motto."

Big Jim took off his glasses to brush the moisture from his eyes. "I guess old Black Jack wishes he had us over on the Marne now, huh?"

"That ain't all, Lieutenant," Ozzie said. "The Frenchies say they're gonna give Henry Johnson one of their Croix crosses."

Big Jim laughed between coughs. "Ol' Henry's come a long way from lugging trunks as a porter in Albany. Now you all know I taught him how to fight with a knife back at camp."

"Yeah, right," Sissle mocked. "You taught Johnson how to kill those twenty Germans single-handed, but you still can't teach Taylor here how to hit that high C note."

Big Jim shook his head in exaggerated despair. "Taylor, you oughta just take that damn oboe and turn it into a rocket launcher, for all the good it does us."

Ozzie acted hurt. "I'm getting there. The sergeant won't let me play it on the lines because he says the Boche send over the whizz-bangs to stop the noise."

Big Jim comforted his orderly with a hand to his shoulder. "Now that's the first thing you've said that I believe."

Sissle looked down at Big Jim's journal to catch a peek at the musical notes he was scribbling. "What you got cooking there, Jim?"

Big Jim winked at his old writing partner. "I think I got a hit on the hook, Sis. But I need a little help with the chorus."

"Let me hear what you got so far," Sissle said.

Big Jim coughed the phlegm from his clogged lungs, and sang:

> "What the time? Nine?
> Fall in line
> All right, boys, now take it slow
> Are you ready? Steady!
> Very good, Eddie.
> Over the top, let's go!"

Ozzie began dancing around the hospital beds, and Sissle started keeping time to the tune by tapping a bedpan against a windowsill. The nurses were swaying, and the patients in the other beds crouched up against their head-boards to listen as Big Jim started to find the strength in his voice again:

> "Quiet, lie it, else you'll start a riot
> Keep your proper distance, follow 'long
> Cover, brother, and when you see me hover
> Obey my orders and you won't go wrong
> There's a *Minenwerfer* coming — look out
> Hear that roar, there's one more
> Stand fast, there's a Very light
> Don't gasp or they'll find you all right
> Don't start to bombing with those hand grenades."

Big Jim stopped singing, frustrated, and dropped his head back into the pillow. "That's where I'm stuck. It needs something, but I don't know what."

Ozzie thought a moment. "Lieutenant, you need the sounds."

"Sounds? What are you talking about?"

"The sounds of the trenches," Ozzie said. "To make it like you is there. Machine gun fire. Grenades exploding."

Sissle huffed at Ozzie. "You can't have machine guns going off while people are dancing."

Big Jim broke a wide grin. "Wait, Sis, he's right. People back home are gonna to want to know what it was really like in no-man's land."

"Tat-a-tat-tat!" Ozzie teethed. "Bang! Boom!" He stole the bedpan from Sissle and clanged it against a metal chair, imitating the sound of bayonets clashing.

"Yeah, keep doing that, Taylor!" With difficulty, Big Jim stood from his bed, drawing the ire of the nurses. "Sis, give me some hisses."

"Hisses?"

Big Jim made an expanding gesture with his hands. "Gas explosions."

Now all the visitors in the ward were getting into the act, booming and sizzling and creating sound effects.

Big Jim twirled a thermometer for a baton and picked up the song again:

> "There's a machine gun, holy spades!
> Alert, gas! Put on your mask
> Adjust it correctly and hurry up fast
> Drop! There's a rocket from the Boche barrage
> Down, hug the ground, close as you can, don't stand
> Creep and crawl, follow me, that's all
> What do you hear? Nothing near
> Don't fear, all is clear
> That's the life of a stroll
> When you take a patrol
> Out in No Man's Land
> Ain't it grand?
> Out in No Man's Land"

Amid the applause from across the ward, Big Jim collapsed back to his bed and heaved for air. When he was finally able to speak again, he looked up at his unit buddies and gave them an order. "You boys get back out there and get this war over. I need to get home fast and record that hit."

Ozzie saluted him. "Yes, sir!" He turned to march out.

"Oh, and Taylor," Big Jim added. "You kill enough Boche out there for me, I might add an oboe to the score."

27

PICARDY, FRANCE
JUNE 1918

loyd Gibbons sped a military roadster north from Paris toward the city of Meaux, dodging caissons and the endless line of lorries that were carrying American soldiers and enough ammunition to blow up the entire Continent. He steered with his left hand while pecking at the keys of the typewriter at his side, a skill he had honed on the dirt roads of Mexico.

The nervous staff driver banished to the back seat pleaded with him. "Sir, I will be more than happy to drive while you craft your article."

Gibbons stripped the gears into fourth. "Not necessary, Private. You just sit back and enjoy the scenery."

The staff driver's eyes bugged as the roadster veered all over the road, drawing curses from the soldiers on foot who were forced to jump out of the way. "That clutch is a little tricky."

Satisfied finally with the wording of his dispatch, Gibbons pulled the sheet from the typewriter roller, folded it in half, and slipped it into his breast pocket. Earlier that morning, he had learned from one of his sources at Harry's Bar—where the AEF ambulance boys congregated to drown their sorrows—that Black Jack had finally agreed to send some regiments into the line around a town on the Marne River called Château-Thierry. After ditching Pegler, Runyon, and those other news sniffers to sleep off hangovers in the Montmarte, he had gained a forty-mile jump on what his gut told him would be an exclusive story on the first major battle fought by the doughboys.

But he still had one small problem, and it sat in the passenger seat next to him. He took a draw on his cigar and blew a puff of Cuban smoke into the snoring face of Lt. Oscar Hartzel, a former correspondent of *The New York Times* and now a censor for the Military Intelligence Division.

Hartzel awoke from his snorefest, choking and spitting phlegm. Waving a hole through the smoke in a desperate attempt to find air, he glared at Gibbons, as if trying to fathom how this overgrown brat he was ordered to babysit had managed to talk his way behind the wheel.

"Turncoat!" Gibbons harangued him. "You should be ashamed of yourself, Pretzel!"

Hartzel leaned over the door, trying to steady his champagne-scoured gut. "Not that again."

"Stifling the precious freedom of the press protected by the United States Constitution. And you, a former knight of the Fourth Estate. You know, they used to draw and quarter traitors over here."

Hartzel glanced at the ashen reflection of his own face in the rearview mirror. He had nearly embalmed himself with liquor from trying to keep up with Gibbons the night before. Now, he looked deader than the cadavers being driven past him on the French flatbed trucks. "Pull over at the next *tabac* you see. Let's grab some hair of the dog for the road."

"For shame, for shame." Gibbons glanced over his shoulder at the young private in the rear seat. "Shield your eyes, son. Here before you sits a once-proud newspaperman who has fallen enslaved unto the evils of alcohol." He shook a *tssking* finger at Hartzel. "No wonder old man Ochs fired your back-sliding ass."

Hartzel's liverish face flamed. "He didn't fire me. I quit."

"Ah, that's right. To join the dark side."

Hartzel slowly came back to life. "For the war, dammit. And, hey, we're all in this together, Gibbons. Or have you renounced your American citizenship? My job is to keep lunatics like you from blabbering the location of troop deployments all over the world so that the damn Kaiser doesn't read about it the next morning and aim his Big Berthas at us."

Rolling his eyes, Gibbons wheeled the right front tire into a pothole to jar Hartzel's headache in punishment. "The Germans don't have to worry about learning what Black Jack is doing. All they have to do is read the drivel that Creel and those lying toads on the Committee on Public Misinformation spit out. Then they can just assume we'll do the opposite."

Hartzel angled his chin to remind Gibbons they weren't alone in the car.

But Gibbons wouldn't be reined in. "Printing up posters of German soldiers raping women and killing babies. Have you seen any German soldiers raping women over here? Any Belgium babies being toasted like marshmallows on bayonets? I didn't think so."

"I had nothing to do with that."

"You're just a low-down government mouthpiece now."

Hartzel pressed his palm to his forehead, begging for relief from the throbbing in his temples. "You can muzzle the holier-than-thou horsecrap, Gib.

You're not over here to save the Constitution, either. The only oath of allegiance you ever took was to your own byline. If you hadn't pulled that little escape trick in Luneville, maybe Pershing would have given you some slack. You got no one to blame but yourself for me being assigned your babysitter."

"You ever been shot, Pretzel?"

Hartzel searched the floorboards of the roadster for live rounds, as if questioning whether Gibbons might be desperate enough for fame to put a bullet through a censor's head and blame it on stray German fire. "No, but at times likes these, I can understand the attraction."

"There's one question I want to answer for the folks back home."

"Yeah?"

"What's it feel like to be shot?"

"You should be in a straightjacket somewhere behind barred windows."

"That'd be the ultimate scoop!" Gibbons insisted with a pinching look indicating that he was damn serious. "I've been asking the boys in the hospitals what it felt like, but they don't have the descriptive wherewithal do the experience justice. Most of them just went into shock when they got the lead. They don't even remember being hit."

"How thoughtless of them."

"Let's make a pact, Pretzel. If either of us ever takes a bullet, we promise to stay conscious long enough to remember what it feels like. You in?"

"Yeah, sure. Getting shot can't be any worse than how I feel right now."

Gibbons rambled the roadster onto an old stone bridge that crossed the Marne. On the far side of the river, the road teed off in two directions. He cocked his ear and listened to the distant booms of the heavy guns. Trusting his instincts, he spun right and followed the sign for Montreuil. After another mile or so, the barrage from the German guns became heavier and closer. The road, or what was left of it, was so pocked with shell holes that the tires and axles threatened to fail.

"Uh, Gib." Hartzel ducked with each explosion overhead. "I think we took the wrong turn back there."

"I'm no von Clausewitz, but it's been my experience that the Germans usually fire their artillery in the direction where the enemy is coming."

Hartzel dipped his head below the dash for protection. "Brilliant deduction. You should have been a general."

"And with all of your loyalty, you should have been a press flack for the Spanish Inquisition."

After bouncing another mile across the pocked dirt road, Gibbons braked to a stop in a small village that looked as if it had just been shredded by a giant plow. Atop the crumbled *maison*, an American flag flapped next to a banner with a blue field with a laurel wreath. He grinned at the insignia he had last seen above the ramparts of Vera Cruz, four years ago. "The Marines."

Looking around, Hartzel scoffed at that claim. "Why the hell would Pershing send Marines out *here?* There's no water around larger than a puddle."

Gibbons jumped out of the roadster and surveyed the distance hills. A sentry guarding the entry into the village came running toward them with his rifle aimed. Gibbons raised his arms in peace and produced his credentials. "Who's in command here?"

"Colonel Neville."

"What's all the ruckus about?"

The soldier lowered his rifle, confirming they were Americans. "We're in a hell of a firefight with the Boche down there beyond those trees."

"Those trees have a name?"

"Belleau Wood is what the Frenchies call it."

Gibbons watched the black smoke of battle rising over the lush green ridges. "*Belleau…* that's French for beautiful. By God, it *is* a breathtaking place, isn't it?"

A Marine colonel, accompanied by three aides, came marching out of the *maison*, and he looked none too pleased. The officer's eyes narrowed with ire when he saw who was standing before him. "How in the hell did *you* make it up that road? The Boche have been hammering it all morning."

Gibbons reached out his hand in greeting, but it was refused. "Colonel Neville, the hero of Old Mexico. Take a good look, Pretzel. This old boy has a Medal of Honor stashed somewhere in his trunk."

The colonel looked like he could grind metal with his teeth. "Cut the bullshit, Gibbons."

Gibbons kept an eye trained on the smoking woods in the distance. "My press liaison here was just asking me what a bunch of brine-stinking leather-necks were doing in the middle of a cow pasture."

"That's none of your damn business," the colonel snarled. "Who gave you permission to approach my lines?"

Gibbons rolled his eyes toward Hartzel. "This sellout here will fill you in."

While Hartzel produced the GHQ authorization papers, Gibbons retreated to the roadster. Out of sight from the others, he slipped a folded paper from his breast pocket and inserted it into the typewriter. Muffling the keys as best he could, he quickly added a line to his report, then pulled the paper from the roller and refolded it.

He strolled back to the officers who were still looking over the credentials. "Don't you ladies have a war to fight? Or are you going to keep the bridge club meeting going until afternoon tea?"

Col. Neville threw the permission letter back at Hartzel. "There's an empty room upstairs. You two can set up there. Just stay out of my way."

"I've got a better idea," Gibbons said. "How about I go with your boys down to those beautiful woods. I'm somewhat of an amateur arboriculturalist."

The colonel glared at him with a mixture of disdain and grudging admiration. "Pershing warned me about that death wish of yours, Gibbons. I'm telling you, it's too damn hot down there. And it's going to get a lot hotter. The Germans are pounding us with their Seventy-Sevens."

Gibbons leaned down to tighten the strings on his boots. "We'd better get going, then, before the fun's over."

"Fine," the colonel said. "Maybe we'll finally get rid of you. Captain Hanson here will requisition a gun for you."

Gibbons slapped at the notebook and pencil in his back pocket. "I've got the most dangerous weapon known to man right here."

Shaking his head, Col. Neville walked back to his headquarters.

Gibbons started strolling down the hill toward the sounds of battle, but his chaperone called him back.

"Hold on, Gib," Hartzel said. "My orders are to stay with you."

"You don't want to die a government bureaucrat, do you, Pretzel? If I were you, I'd hand in your resignation right now and join the angelic realms while you still can."

While Hartzel, nerves flaring, was trying to keep his breakfast down, Gibbons reached into his own coat pocket and slipped his edited dispatch to the staff driver in the car. "Private, we won't be needing you from here. Do me a favor, will you? Take this cable back to Paris as fast as you can and tell the censor's office it must be sent overseas at once."

"Wait a minute, let me look at that." Hartzel intercepted the dispatch signed under Gibbons's byline and read it. The last line stated: *I am up at the front and entering Belleau Wood with the U.S. Marines.* Hartzel handed the dispatch back to Gibbons and shook his head. "You can't send this. It reveals the location of this operation."

"Come on, let it go, Pretzel. I don't have time to change it. Those vultures in the censor office will black it out anyway."

Hartzel debated the risk. Too gut-sick to shadow box with the irrepressible correspondent, he shrugged and motioned to driver off to deliver the dispatch, pushing the problem up the ladder.

ibbons led the green-faced Hartzel on a run across a wooded ridge toward the spitting of distant machine-gun fire. Jumping over dead *poilus* and U.S. Marines along the way, he stopped at a trail of paper

and knelt to gather the sheets up. Amid distant shouts of battle, he took a moment to examine his find: love letters and correspondence from home, discarded by the charging leathernecks in an effort to lighten their load.

He pushed on in his search for the advancing Marine lines, and soon he found bloodied bayonets and other grisly evidence of recent hand-to-hand fighting. Following a trail of empty shells, he came upon the edge of a wood, where two Marine crews had dug holes in a ditch. The landscape was not the thick forest that he had expected, but a patchwork of isolated copses separated by clearings planted in wheat and oats. As he gathered his bearings and motioned Hartzel up to him, he saw that the Marines had spread out in the open field to his left and right. The leathernecks were hovering low to the ground, constantly raked by murderous fire from German machine gunners hidden in the woods up ahead.

Across the field, a Marine officer spied the two new arrivals. But before he could protest their presence, his men stood from their dugouts and advanced toward the woods. Gibbons and Hartzel moved forward with the Marines, dropping to their bellies only when the Germans cut loose with fire. When the leathernecks reached the nearest brush, the Germans rose up from their holes and attacked, grappling and fighting knife to knife.

The heavy American guns behind Gibbons opened up, and the woods became hell on earth. The din was so loud that he had to signal Hartzel by hand to follow him into the next thicket. There they found a Marine major shouting orders to his ten runners who took turns dashing across the fields dodging German machine gun blasts to relay the next maneuver to the other officers.

Gibbons slid into a hole next to the officer. "Which idiot ordered this bird-brained cockfight?"

The major glared at him. "That'd be me, Ben Berry. And I presume you're the idiot who goes by the name of Floyd Gibbons."

"Reporting for duty."

"I won't waste a man trying to save your sorry ass out here."

"From the looks of things, you're doing a piss-poor job saving your own sorry asses. So I got no problem taking care of my own."

Sneering at the newsman, the major stood up and motioned for his Marines around him to move forward. Gibbons followed close on the officer's heels, with Hartzel straggling behind. Halfway across the field, the Germans opened up from the woods. Gibbons dropped his chin to the ground, and heard cries of wounded men all around.

Still standing tall, Major Berry turned to order his men to the ground for cover. Then, more quietly, he looked down at his bloodied sleeve and muttered, "My hand... gone."

From his belly, Gibbons risked looking up and saw the Marine officer clutching his bloodied left wrist in shock. "Get down!"

The enemy fire became more intense.

Major Berry crumpled, falling on his face. With bullets whizzing inches above his head, Gibbons crawled toward the wounded officer. He slid the officer's helmet to the right side of his face to shield against the hot German fire. He was almost within reach of the writhing officer when he felt a bolt of scalding heat just above his elbow.

Sonofabitch! What the hell was that?

He pressed his eyes closed, clenching his teeth. He'd never felt such pain. He opened his eyes again and looked down at his elbow. A bullet hole was soaked with blood.

I'm hit.

The next thought that came to his mind was not a prayer for survival, but a reminder to remember what being wounded felt like. A series of manic words cascaded through his fevered brain. *Molten lead poured into the marrow of one's bones. The sting of ice on skin, multiplied a thousandfold.* Don't lose consciousness, he commanded himself. Stay with the pain, every second of it. What was the lede? *The Marines entered Belleau Wood as boys and came out heroes...*

"Gib!" Hartzel shouted from twenty feet away. "You hurt?"

"Stay down! I got to get the Major—"

Something stabbed him in the left shoulder blade. "Christ!"

"Gib, you're bleeding in the back!"

He couldn't move his neck. He started bargaining with Fate. *Leave me my hands. Take my legs, but let me keep writing.* He finally managed to lever up on his right elbow, just enough to see Major Berry and Hartzel thrashing in the wheat. All around him, the Marines were bobbing up and down in the field, taking shots at the woods before ducking back to their guts. He pushed forward with his toes, inch by inch. His hands were now useless. Somehow he had to get a tourniquet on the major's arm or he would bleed—

He heard a *ping* against a rock—everything went white. *Glass crashing... Dunked in a barrel of whitewash... I can't see... Am I dead?... The lede, dammit ... One sinner in the trenches asked an Irish chaplain: Father, how will I know when I've reached Hell? The chaplain assured the man, if it's more bearable than the Front, then it's certain it's Hell you've found.*

Numb ... How could he describe numbness?

He pinched himself—he could feel his right hand. But he couldn't see. He felt something twitching next to him. He ran his fingers across the body in spasm and felt the buttons of a Marine uniform. Bullets snapped all around him. The Boche were shooting at anything that moved in this wheat.

"Quiet, soldier," he begged. "Lie still."

But the wounded Marine kept twitching and kicking, drawing more fire. Every minute or so, the poor leatherneck moaned like a stray calf lost from its mother. Finally, after several minutes, he became still, this time in death.

Gibbons groped the ground and found the dead Marine's gas mask. He had seen too many boys in the hospitals wheezing to their agonizing deaths with the gas gangrene. He knew he had to keep his head off the ground, away from the gas pools. But if he raised his head too far, the bullets would get him again. He decided he'd rather go fast. He propped his ear up from the blood-soaked wheat, hoping to hear what he couldn't see—a safe direction.

"Gib, you hit bad?"

"Stay put!" he ordered Hartzel, who lay cowering in a depression several yards away. "Don't try to come over! You'll draw fire!"

Hartzel ignored that command and snaked his way to Gibbons's side. He rolled his friend over and stared down at him in horror.

Gibbons recoiled, thinking it was a German jumping him. Dizzy from the loss of blood and suffering from a horrible thirst, he could only see out of one eye. But finally he managed to focus enough to find Hartzel's drained face blurring over him. "I guess it doesn't look pretty, huh?"

Hartzel didn't answer him—which was confirmation enough.

Hours later, darkness finally fell, and the Germans silenced their machine guns. Hartzel lifted Gibbons to his feet. Amid the cries of the wounded still lying in the fields, they staggered together toward the rear. Walking for two miles, they finally reached a field hospital, where a doctor unceremoniously pronounced that Gibbons's head wound was beyond anything he could repair.

The last thing Gibbons remembered was Hartzel flagging down a crowded ambulance and haggling for a spot in the front seat. In the rear lay three wounded Marines with horrible fractures.

The driver apologized for the bumpy ride. "We got ten miles to the hospital, fellas. If I go fast, you're going to suffer horrible. But if I go slow, your pal back there with the busted-up eye is likely gonna hemorrhage and croak."

One of the wounded Marines looked over at Gibbons's bloody face. Paled by what he saw, the soldier ordered the driver, "Go like hell!"

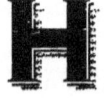artzel's staff driver arrived at the Army Intelligence headquarters in Paris around midnight. He ran up the stairs of the two-story gray-stone building across from the Invalides and found the captain in

charge of the twenty censors who sat at desks vetting pages of news copy before they were cabled to the United States. "Mr. Gibbons asked me to deliver this to you, sir."

The captain looked stunned. "Floyd Gibbons? From the *Chicago Tribune*?"

"Yes, sir."

The room fell silent, and the officer took the driver aside. "You've not heard."

"Heard what, sir?"

"Gibbons was mortally wounded," the captain said. "We received the wire from Second Division headquarters two hours ago. He won't make it through the night."

The driver dropped his chin, shaken to learn that the man he had come to admire was at death's door. The other censors abandoned their stations and came round the driver, eager to see what the famous correspondent had written for his last words. The captain read Gibbons's dispatch aloud to everyone: "'I am up at the front and entering Belleau Wood with the U.S. Marines.'"

"Floyd was with our boys," the driver confirmed, struggling to hold back his emotion. "He refused to take a rifle."

The typewriters stopped banging their rollers, and another lengthy silence extended across the room. Finally, one of the censors asked, "Captain, are we sending this cable over, or not?"

The senior officer studied the dispatch, trying to imagine what musings the great wordsmith had entertained when typing it out. He handed the dispatch to the censor and told him, "Let it go through as is. It'd be a hell of a crime to cut the last words Floyd Gibbons ever wrote."

The other censors nodded their approval, and they all stood at attention while the cable operator sent the dispatch across the ocean with a coda regretting to inform the nation that its intrepid author had died in the service of his noble profession.

Gibbons awoke in the American Base Hospital at Neuilly-sur-Seine with his arm in a sling. He looked around at the other beds through a narrowed vision and saw that all of the patients in the ward had bandages over their eyes. Even a rookie news hack could decipher from this circumstantial evidence what had happened. Sighing with resignation, he reached up with his free hand and found the expected gauze over his hollow left eye socket. Squinting to gain focus his remaining eye, he saw one of the medical bigwigs walking around the room in a white jacket.

A nurse carried two boxes filled with glass eyes, and the wounded cyclopes in the beds were all bartering over the selection of the iris colors available.

"Hey, doc!" Gibbons shouted. "Pass the grapes over here!"

The surgeon who had performed his surgery turned with a smile, grateful to find Gibbons conscious and with his famous bonhomie intact. The other one-eyed patients stood from the cots and gathered around the famous newsman, eager to hear his account of his exploits at Belleau Wood.

One of the mono-oglers asked him, "Gibbie, did you really take on an entire Boche machine-gun nest?"

"Nest? Hell, is that what they're calling a Kaiser's regiment these days?"

"You gave 'em a taste of Hades, eh, Gibbie!"

Another patient with his arm in a sling walked into the pavilion and strode down the aisle toward the gathering. Gibbons squinted at him with his good eye, and his memory fired up.

"I owe this man my life," Major Berry announced to the ward.

"Heck, all I did, Major, was tell you to get your fat ass down."

"You took several bullets for me. And for that, I would not miss this moment."

Gibbons looked around, wondering what the major was talking about. Berry nodded the surgeon to the task, and the doctor produced a special glass eye from the box—made with a green iris.

"Marine drab," the major said. "Let's see if it fits such a big head."

The men roared with laughter as Gibbons bowed to accept the acclaim. With dramatic aplomb, the correspondent lifted the shiny glass ball and, after the surgeon removed the bandages, inserted it into his empty socket. He stood, unsteadily, modeling his new accessory to applause.

The major produced a black patch with tie strings. "Finish the look."

Gibbons affixed the patch to his *faux* eye and winked with his good one.

"The Pirate of the Press," pronounced the major, as if knighting his new friend.

Gibbons struck a pose like Blackbeard. "Can I read with one eye, doc?"

"Let's find out." The surgeon motioned for a nurse to bring up a newspaper that she had been holding. He placed the front page of *The New York Times* in Gibbon's hands. "Give the column on the upper left a try."

Gibbons angled his head and brought the paper back and forth under his nose until the font came into focus. The date of its publication was nearly a week old. He read the first paragraph aloud: "'The United States Marines are engaged in a fierce battle with the Germans in a wooded region north of Paris known as Belleau Wood, according to a dispatch sent from the front lines by *Chicago Times* correspondent Floyd Gibbons.'"

"Woowee!" shouted one of the wounded leathernecks. "They know about us back home! Thanks, Floyd!"

Gibbons grinned and saluted the soldier. "How about that? Those bastards at *The New York Times* finally gave me credit for a scoop."

"Read on," the surgeon ordered.

"'Military censors permitted news of the battle and its location to be cabled across the nation in a rare homage to Mr. Gibbons, who was mortally wounded on the front lines with the Marines. Brigadier General James G. Harbord, commander of the Fifth and Sixth U.S. Marines, issued a statement saying that the Corps owes a debt of gratitude to the late Mr. Gibbons for shining a light on its unparalleled fighting prowess.'"

Gibbons faked staggering back into his bed. "Boys, the news of my death just reached me. As an old editor once told me, if a dozen men in a bar tell you you're drunk, fall down!"

The recuperating doughboys hung their heads in mock grief, and one of them offered a eulogy: "We gather here together to honor the passing of Floyd Gibbons, lady hound and first-class connoisseur of distilled Irish peat water. May he rest in peace in Hell, where all newspaper hacks eventually go."

Gibbons raised an imaginary toast to his own demise. "Friends, Romans, countrymen. Lend me your ear. I ask but one small favor in my memory. In centuries to come, whenever the United States Marines are spoken of in hallowed whispers, I would be humbly honored to have my name included in that roll of glory."

Saluting the man who had saved his life, Major Berry shouted, "From the Halls of Montezuma to the Keys of Gibbons's Typewriter!"

28

WASHINGTON, D.C.
SEPTEMBER 1918

Bert Hoover stared at his plate and poked his fork at the two round, padded cakes that looked to have been fried and dusted with cornmeal. Glancing up dubiously at the servant who had just delivered his dinner, he questioned why he was keeping two cooks and six attendants if the result was a cuisine one might expect to be served in a flophouse.

"Meatless Monday," explained his wife Lou, sitting across from him.

Reminded that it was that dour time of the week again, he waved the servant off to the kitchen. Weary from having put in another twelve-hour day, he sighed and tested the constituency of the new concoction, not oblivious to the irony. He had come up with the idea for Meatless Mondays and Wheatless Wednesdays, putting alliteration to work in the propaganda effort to win the war. Sometimes, he feared his life would be summed up in one word:

Food.

Or, perhaps, the lack of it. It seemed that no good deed went unpunished during these difficult times. He had performed so admirably in the Belgium hunger relief effort that President Wilson had called him home to head the new Food Administration agency. His was now the thankless job of trying to convince Americans to eat less so that more grains, milk, and meat could be sent overseas to the troops and the ravaged Europeans. Across the country, people were calling him the Food Czar, and the unpopular skimping and sacrifice was being dubbed "hooverizing." Half the world would remember him for keeping them from starving. But the other half—young Americans included—would no doubt forever associate his name with deprivation.

"What do you think, dear?" Lou asked gamely.

He looked around the dining room of the cold Rhode Island Avenue Victorian house that he had rented from Senator Harlan to serve as both a family home and his office. "I think it could use another fireplace."

"I mean the recipe. I came up with it myself."

He suffered a bite, rolling the dry dollop around in his mouth until he managed to swallow it. Transported back to those halcyon days in China, when he had acquired an appreciation for spicy, exotic flavors, he shrugged and muttered, "Tastes like peanut butter."

"I call it cottage cheese sausage," Lou said. "The peanut butter provides protein. I had it dissolved in soda and worked into the cheese. We added thyme, sage and chopped onion."

He pushed his plate away. "Maybe we should seal it into cans and drop it by air into the German trenches. Hope it explodes in their stomachs."

Lou ignored his sarcasm. "I've also come up with some other ideas. What if we encouraged housewives to carry cash at all times to purchase groceries when they are at they store? That way, they could save on gasoline."

"You mean women don't do that now?"

"Of course not. They have their purchases delivered."

"Heaven forbid an upstanding lady should be caught walking down the street carrying a parcel. The society pages would be outraged."

"I've saved my best for last." Lou stood, retreated to the kitchen, and returned wearing a drab tunic over her dress. "Look, it's cotton. Women can wear it over their better dresses so they don't have to launder so much. It will save on bills. We should call it the Hoover Apron."

His falsetto voice spiked. "Absolutely not! I don't want my name attached to every damn creation designed to incite ridicule!"

Lou glared at him. "You're not the only one who's had a long day. While you bounce around the city saving the world, I have to run the Girl Scouts of America and, by the way, raise two boys."

He noticed the empty chairs around the table. "Where are they?"

"They have debate practice this evening at Sidwell. It would nice if their father stopped by the school a least once this semester to encourage them."

"Where will they eat dinner?"

"They've recently taken an interest in invitations to eat away from home."

He couldn't blame them, given the menu. He raised his linen napkin from his lap and angrily tossed it onto the table. "Forgive me for being so neglectful, but I've been preoccupied putting out the fires you started with that Stanford mansion fiasco. I've got reporters calling me and asking why we need twenty-one rooms and why my wife is taking my sons to an ice cream parlor for sodas while I've been harping on people to cut back on everything."

"The house was not my fault! You've been promising me for twenty years that we'd settle in Palo Alto. Go ahead and start plans on the construction. That's what you told me."

"That was before the war."

"I dismissed the architect this morning, so you can stop worrying."

They sat stewing in silence, until Lou nodded away the servant who came in to see if they wished the servings removed. She gestured for the servant to shut the door behind her. Alone now with her husband, she confided, "I hate this city. I cannot wait until we can finally escape to California."

"You have your club. What is gnawing at you now?"

She walked over to a hutch and picked up from its counter a copy of that morning's *Washington Star*. She placed its front page in front of him. "The jury convicted Debs."

He shoved the paper aside, having already read the details of the trial of Eugene Debs, the Socialist union leader who had been arrested under the new Sedition Act. "The man is a rabble-rouser. He called for young men all across the country to resist the draft."

"When did speaking one's mind become a crime in the United States?"

He shifted uncomfortably in his chair, avoiding her judging glare. "It's war, Lou. We can't have an agitator like that poisoning the uneducated minds in the factories. Next thing you know, the anti-capitalist disease will spread and thousands will be on the streets protesting."

"They're already on the streets. Until they get thrown in jail."

"Lincoln suspended *habeas corpus* during the Civil War."

She was unmoved by his argument citing precedent. "Bert, you think I don't read? You think I don't know that Lincoln ignored the Constitution to stifle his political opposition?"

"I didn't mean—"

"What are we fighting for in France if we arrest people here who merely speak their opinion that the war is wrong? That mob in Montana was allowed to lynch that anti-war speaker from a railroad trestle. And the House won't even seat Victor Berger, even though the people of Wisconsin elected him to represent them. And the government won't accede to the will of the citizenry, just because he opposes the war?"

"The First Amendment must bend to dire circumstances."

Turning conciliatory for fear of raising his blood pressure, Lou sat in the chair next to her husband and took his hand. "Bert, our Quaker ancestors are watching us."

"Don't start that again."

"They came here because they were persecuted for refusing to fight for the English king. The government in England called *them* seditious, too. And here we are, sitting by as accomplices to these outrages while good men suffer for standing by their conscience."

"We've done more than most."

"But we haven't done enough."

"My dear, forgive me. But there are forces at work in the world that you don't understand. The Bolsheviks won't be satisfied with turning Russia into a godless nation. They are already over here spewing their venom in the trade unions. If the labor strikes become more violent, well…"

"Go ahead, say it."

"Our way of life will be over. All of this, these fineries, will be gone."

Hurt by his implication that she had become spoiled, Lou stood up and began collecting his plate and utensils.

"Leave that for the servants," he ordered.

She turned on him with an indicting glare. "If our way of life *is* going to change, I'd better get used to it."

He closed his eyes for a moment's respite from their quarreling. "I almost forgot. Two more will be joining us for the dinner party on Saturday night."

"Who?"

"The Assistant Secretary of the Navy and his wife."

A sour expression crossed Lou's face at the thought of that notorious political climber Franklin Roosevelt sitting at her table. "Does the man ever take a night off from his glad-handing and snorting around for patronage?"

"What did Roosevelt ever do to you?"

She fussed with the linens. "It's just… some of the ladies down at the club have been talking."

"About what?"

"The man's poor wife found some letters last week."

"Eleanor?"

"That cad has been carrying on an affair with Mrs. Roosevelt's social secretary for four years."

"Will she divorce him?"

"They say she offered Franklin his freedom. But the harlot he sleeps with is a Catholic. She's apparently too high and mighty to marry a divorced man."

He shook his head in commiseration, thankful at least that he did not have that problem. "We must not deal in rumor-mongering. We will show all due hospitality to the Assistant Secretary, whatever his sins may be."

Lou clanged her husband's plate onto the cleaning platter. "Yes, but he may find a dose of saltpeter in his giblet gravy."

29

LORRAINE, FRANCE
SEPTEMBER 1918

Walter Waters felt his toes burning as he slogged across yet another muddy field. It was the damn trench foot again, his unerring warning that all hell was about to break loose. That morning, he and his stretcher partner, Goins Gavin, had been drafted from their battalion in the 146th Field Artillery and sent up the line to an infantry regiment in I Corps desperate for medics. Now, here in the middle of the night, they were being marched single file down narrow duckboards with two hundred other doughboys. Up ahead lay a dim horizon rutted by splintered trees.

Their officers, as usual, were tight-lipped about the mission, but the Frogs back at camp had been grapevining for days about a big push into a salient a few miles ahead at a village called Saint-Mihiel. Quipsters had renamed the place 'Saint My Hell,' figuring that'd be what it eventually turned into. He didn't have much of a knack for translating fancy French words, but best as he could make out, a salient was kind of like a nasty hemorrhoid that stuck out and caused a lot of pain and trouble. The most effective way to deal with a German hemorrhoid, he'd been told, was to pinch it from both sides until the bloody Boche exploded in retreat. And that was about all he knew about the entire situation, except that Black Jack was bringing up the big guns and stacking them, axle to axle.

Never a good sign.

Two steps behind him, his buddy Goins, carrying the far end of their folded stretcher, reached over and tugged at his sleeve. "Dubya, I gotta piss like a racehorse."

"Wh-wh-what am I, your m-m-momma?"

"Tell the stripe we need to stop."

"Hell, I ain't t-t-telling him. He looks like he'd bite a m-m-man's head off."

"I can't hold it much longer."

"Let 'er fly on the run. Hell, we got so much mud on us nobody'd know."

"I ain't pissing myself like an old man. I got *some* dignity left."

"Suit yourself."

The trudging line came to a sudden halt, causing Waters to smack into the man in front of him.

"Watch it, jagoff," snarled the soldier he had just head-butted.

The captain leading the column snapped an order over his shoulder. "Shut up back there!"

Waters figured this was as good a time as any to plead Goins's case. "Captain, my orderly here needs to r-r-relieve hisself."

The captain turned and elbowed his way back to the end of the line. He pressed his nose against Waters's forehead and whispered through gritted teeth. "Listen up, you two Idaho spud heads. We run a tighter unit here in the infantry than you do in that tinkers outfit you call an artillery battery."

"Sir, Private G-g-Gavin has a balky bladder."

Goinsie was dancing in the mud, trying to hold it in.

The captain pulled his pistol. "I see that dick come out, soldier, I'll shoot it off."

That threat didn't help Goinsie's discomfort.

"I'm going to say this once," the captain warned them all. "And then we go silent for the rest of the night." He kept ramming his chin into the bridge of Water's brow. "Do you know what I mean by going silent?"

Waters nodded, then shook his head, confessing he didn't.

The captain holstered his pistol and drew a knife that would have made Jim Bowie jealous. "From this point on, no one speaks. *No* one. The Boche pickets are out there. If they hear us coming, we're ground meat for their big guns. You grab onto the pack of the man in front of you. There will be no light. Do not let go of that pack. One tug means 'yes.' Two tugs means 'no.'"

"S-s-sir," Waters said. "You m-m-mind telling us wh-where we're going?"

"Half a mile ahead, the front trenches. In five hours, at dawn, four of our corps will launch the largest American attack in history. Our job is to take a village called Thiaucourt. The Germans defend it with some Big Berthas. Most of the local Frogs there haven't been allowed outside in four years, but a few of them did us the kindness of risking their necks to come out here and lay this plank trail. Look around you. What do you see?"

Waters glanced up at the moonless sky. "I can't see nothing."

"Keep *that* revelation stuck in that thick skull of yours," the captain said. "The Boche have shelled this sector for two years. On each side of this duck-board, the ground drops into giant holes that are filled fifteen feet deep with mud. Now here's the part of my story that may pique your interest. The mud here is like quicksand. If you fall in, it takes ten men with three ropes to drag you out. Look around. You see anybody carrying ropes?"

Waters and Gavin swallowed hard and shook their heads.

The captain looked down at Waters's belt. "Where's your weapon?"

"I'm a m-m-medic, sir. We ain't s-s-supposed to wear one."

The captain demanded a pistol from one of his officers and drove its barrel into the crease of Waters's belt. "In my company, medics are armed." He turned to the other men. "Your lives depend on keeping hold of the backpack of the man in front of you. No talking. No gunfire. No lights. Any questions?"

The doughboys didn't dare ask, figuring that was a test. They stood aside on the board and allowed the captain to return to the head of the column.

As they resumed their silent approach to the Front, Waters felt Gavin grabbing at his pack. He wanted to tell him to lighten his grip, but he'd just been forbidden to speak. He wished Captain MacLeish were with them. That whip-smart fella had always been a calming influence on everyone, reciting his poetry whenever the boys had a bad day. But he had been sent back home to instruct artillery draftees after his brother, a fighter pilot, was shot down. He'd never forgotten the poem that the officer had written after receiving the news. To take his mind off the danger, he silently repeated the verses he had memorized:

> *And suddenly, and all at once, the rain!*
> *The living scatter, they run into houses, the wind*
> *Is trampled under the rain, shakes free, is again*
> *Trampled. The rain gathers, running in thinned*
> *Spurts of water that ravel in the dry sand,*
> *Seeping in the sand under the grass roots, seeping*
> *Between crack boards of the bones of a clenched hand:*
> *The earth relaxes, loosens; he is sleeping,*
> *He rests, he is quiet, he sleeps in a strange land.*

Several minutes into the nearly blind advance, a strange sensation thrust Waters back to the present. He realized that Goins wasn't holding onto his pack now. He tried to turn around to find out why, but he nearly lost his balance.

"Dubya!"

Still lurching forward, Waters turned and searched the darkness.

"Dubya! Help me!"

My God. Goins was somewhere below the duckboards, sucked down into one of those giant shell holes. He must have stopped to piss and fallen from the track boards. Waters kept his eyes fixed on the man in front of him. He was desperate to stop and save his buddy, but the captain was brandishing his knife above his head in a warning.

"Dubya! Don't let me go down!" Goins shouted, gurgling mud.

Waters felt his elbow brush against the pistol the captain had forced on him. He couldn't bear to hear Goinsie screaming. With each step closer to the Front, he heard his buddy's pleas fading into the night. He took his right hand off the pack of the man in front of him and reached for the pistol. He couldn't bring himself to draw it. That stripe would stockade him, or worse, if he fired.

"Give me a bullet, Dubya!"

Waters held tight to the pack under his chin and prayed Goinsie wouldn't suffer long. The last scream ended with a moiling gasp, and the darkness became silent again. Captain MacLeish's consoling voice came to his ear:

> *Between crack boards of the bones of a clenched hand:*
> *The earth relaxes, loosens; he is sleeping,*
> *He rests, he is quiet, he sleeps in a strange land.*

olonel Glassford raced his two-cylinder motorcycle ahead of the 26th Division's infantry column forming up behind the crest of a denuded ridge of hills. Reaching the highest point in the sector, he cut the motorcycle's chugging engine and pulled out his binoculars to study the moon-like terrain. Below him lay the Meuse valley, pitted with old trench systems and strewn in rusted barbed wire. The eerie stillness confirmed that here, on the north side of the St. Mihiel salient, the Germans had pulled back their suicide squads into secondary trenches, an ominous sign suggesting they knew what was about to hit them. The rain continued to come down hard, bringing with it a bank of morning fog that would obstruct the view of his 103rd Field Artillery gunners.

Glassford shook his head, frustrated by the weather. He had received orders to lay down a rolling barrage toward St. Hilaire to soften up the Boche for the assault. But the gray thickness was descending fast, and soon he wouldn't be able to see more than two hundred yards ahead, let alone locate the heavily defended village. He wiped the mud from his watch. Zero hour was in thirty minutes. If he couldn't get more precise coordinates, the bombardment would be a bloody mess; his howitzers would likely hit the advancing doughboys.

A gaggle of infantry officers, led by a dyspeptic colonel, came marching over the hill toward him. The colonel snorted and cut off a testy salute. "It seems, Colonel Glassford, your artillery sighters cannot read a map. They have rolled your guns right up behind my lines."

"Damn those boys," Glassford said. "Can't they understand orders?"

"Apparently not."

"I told them to set those howitzers *ahead* of your lines."

The infantry colonel reddened. "You were warned about these unorthodox tactics! How do you think it looks if your batteries cover more ground than my infantry?"

"I guess it doesn't shine too bright on your reputation."

"I noticed that your teamsters—"

"Gunners," Glassford corrected.

"They're wearing hand grenades. Why in God's name would an artilleryman need a trench explosive?"

Glassford glanced down at the fancy handled knife holstered on the officer's belt. "I guess for the same reason a colonel behind the lines would need an elephant gutter."

The officer bristled. "Your men are transporting their packs on the caissons. Regulations require all American soldiers to carry their packs."

"They have longer distances to cover. I need them at full strength."

"Get those guns back behind me! Standard rearage of artillery is forty-five hundred meters!"

"I prefer fifteen hundred."

The infantry officer glared at him harder. "How old are you, Colonel?"

"I'll be turning thirty-four soon, if I make it through this little scuffle. You can send my birthday card up the line with your messenger."

"Damn your insolence!" the striped relic shouted. "You're too green to be leading a brigade!"

Glassford got up nose to nose with him. "We're on the same side, in case you haven't noticed. I've got my gunners up here risking their lives trying to save as many of your men as possible. The closer I get to the Boche lines, the more precise I can direct the strikes that will determine if we win this fight. Now, thanks to your dicking around, I've got only twenty minutes to get down there and see what I'm going to be firing at."

"Down there? What the hell are you talking about?"

Glassford jumped on his motorcycle. "Hold your fire until I get back."

"I did *not* dismiss you!"

Glassford gunned his engine and raced the cycle down the ridge into the fog, dodging shell holes and zagging through the wire gaps cut by the scouts. At the bottom of the hill, he stopped and pulled out his compass. After gaining his bearing for St. Hilaire, he motored cautiously toward the old German defenses and searched for the first line of trenches.

Thwarted by an abandoned row of ditches, he rode up and down the obstacles, hoping to find a plank to cross, but they had all been smashed. He sped back toward the American lines and, fifty yards away, spun a wheelie. He drove his heel into the accelerator for a blind running start toward the German trench.

He launched into the fog.

He landed with a jarring thud, still on his wheels. On the German side now, he circled and scouted for a road or path. He checked his compass again. The mists swirled thicker, and he saw no identifiable landmark. He drove in deeper toward the east. The soup thinned a bit, and the fractured spire of St. Hilaire's church appeared, rising hazily in the distance. He pulled to a halt and confirmed the reading for the exact direction to give his gunners. All he had to do now was gain the range by counting the seconds it took him to race back toward his battery across—

The fog cleared over the ground ahead.

Twenty feet away, eight German soldiers sat around a mess bucket preparing breakfast. They looked up at him and went bug-eyed, as if visited by a ghost. Before they could jump for their rifles, Glassford pulled his pistol and peppered them with lead, dropping three. He slammed the motorcycle into gear and skidded off into the retreating mists, hoping to find the forward trench before the rising sun burned off the rest of the patchy fog.

German rifle fire rang out, popping the ground around his tires.

He didn't have time to take careful aim for the trench, so he lowered his head and gunned the throttle for the receding fog. He took flight again.

He landed on the Allied side. Flung from the cycle, he crawled and groped until he found its handles. He lifted the bike and jumped back on the seat.

Behind him, the Germans poured into the trench and fired.

Bullets buzzed his head as he drove the sputtering motorbike up the ridge and split the American lines behind the crest, nearly running over the toes of the ranting infantry colonel. Breathless, he leapt off the cycle and ran toward his waiting battery. He ordered Lt. Colonel Chaffee, his second-in-command, "Set the range for two thousand yards, Chaf. Creep up every three minutes and raise the elevation a degree with each roll."

"Where do we aim?" Chaffee asked.

"Ten degrees, north-northeast azimuth."

Chaffee wrote down the calculations and sent the order off with a runner. "We'd have a better angle at them if we dug in on the other side of this spine."

"Then get it done."

The infantry colonel could only look on in disbelief as Glassford's gunners rolled through his lines and began setting their sights. Noticing one of the howitzers with a bayonet taped to its barrel, the infantry colonel stopped the driver of its caisson. "What the hell is *that*, soldier?"

"Sir, it's a Glassford Trench Mortar," the gunner said. "We always arm our big boomers with these Boche ice picks. We tend to get a little close to the action at times, and they can come in handy, if you know what I mean. You and your boys give us a holler if you need any help down there on the playground."

The colonel stormed off.

Joe Angelo hunkered down in his rifle pit as a German artillery barrage crept closer. Looking to his rear, he saw their American tanks bogged down in the mud, grinding and groaning like dinosaurs struggling to escape some ancient bog. They were near a village called Essey, that much he knew, only because he had overheard the runners passing messages to Colonel Patton. The one benefit from being an orderly was having a decent idea of what the hell was going on all over the battlefield. Thanks to his eavesdropping, he could now estimate that their tank corps was somewhere aside the Rainbow Division on the southeast face of the St. Mihiel salient, driving toward the heavily fortified city of Metz.

But there were a lot *more* disadvantages, and the most worrisome was having to follow a lunatic officer determined to earn a monument to his death on this field. And there the Colonel was up and at it again now, marching from tank to tank and haranguing their drivers while daring the German snipers to take off his head. Angelo peered over his forearm. As the shells from the Boche heavy guns plowed the ground around him, he tried again to convince his superior officer to take cover. "Colonel! Please get down!"

The booms were getting louder, but Colonel Patton remained standing on a mound, surveying the field of carnage. "Angelo, go tell that sonofabitch Trammel to stop flooding that goddamn carburetor on that goddamn Renault!"

Angelo offered up a quick *Ave Maria* and took off on a dash for the nearest tank. He banged on the iron lid over the driver's compartment and yelled the order. Then, he scampered back across the field, weaving and skirting exploding shells like a rabbit on a shooting range. He dived back into the rifle pit below the Colonel's boots and pleaded with him again. "Sir, it ain't gonna do none of us any good if you get blown to bits."

"Goddamn," Patton muttered under his breath at something coming at him across the pocked terrain. "I'd rather see the goddamn Devil."

Angelo inched his head above the rim of the pit to discover what the Colonel had spotted. Walking toward them was a tall, slender brigadier general, newly pinned with his first star and sporting a barracks cap, plum silk scarf, and a muffler wrapped around his neck. The dandy held an ivory-handled pistol in one hand and a riding crop in the other. The doughboys around the lanky general kept falling and diving for cover, but he strolled coolly toward Patton as if on an afternoon jaunt in the park.

Arriving at their foxhole, the general saluted Patton and observed, "Your tanks are having a rough go of it, Colonel."

His face flaming with embarrassment, Patton straightened and returned the salute testily. "General MacArthur, I will have these tanks back in operation before your men hit Essey."

Hearing that name, Angelo risked raising his eyes a little higher to get a glimpse of the famous West Pointer the boys were calling the Beau Brummell of the AEF.

MacArthur tapped his thigh with his riding crop, as if keeping time with the gunfire. "We could use those tanks, if you manage to get them unstuck. But don't feel you've let us down if not. I'll take Essey regardless."

Patton turned another shade redder. "They'll reach that high ground if I have to drag them out of this muck myself."

MacArthur jutted out his chin and set his fists on his waist for the benefit of the men around him who were watching their exchange. "I suppose you heard about Belleau Wood."

Patton struggled to show no fear, but he couldn't help flinch with each *ping* of a bullet. "The goddamn Marines are getting all the credit for that firefight. Hell, I'd never seen such a botched operation. Our Army boys on the flanks had to go in and save their asses over there."

MacArthur gritted his pipe with clenched teeth, displaying his first sign of discomfiture. "That yarn-spinner Gibbons is to blame for that fiasco. Those incompetents in the censor office let his dispatch go across the wire. Next thing you know, the entire country will be laboring under the delusion that the Marines won the battle alone. Harbord's now pinning medals on the scoundrel and calling him an honorary leatherneck."

Patton nodded with a grimace. "I should have shot the bastard in Mexico when I had the chance."

MacArthur maintained a dashing pose, raising his crop in a salute to the doughboys hunkered down around him. "Well, all we can do now is win this fight and correct the record." He looked west, where the Allied artillery bombardment sounded the heaviest. "Our lads are doing some good work over there."

Trying to steady his hands, Patton pulled a paper from his back pocket and examined his order of battle. "New Englanders. Hundred and Third Field Artillery."

MacArthur nodded proudly. "Happy Glassford's outfit. Artillery was the right choice for him, I think. Let's hope he keeps his nickname today."

A German whizz-bang hissed down from the sky and exploded only a few feet away. Angelo saw Colonel Patton duck involuntarily, but General MacArthur, in a stunning feat of dramatic discipline, didn't even twitch.

Grinning, the general comforted Patton with some unsolicited advice. "Don't sweat over them, Colonel. It's the ones you don't hear that get you."

Angelo watched in disbelief as the two officers continued standing with their heads held high in the midst of the fusillade. Apparently neither wanted to be the one to break off the confrontation and allow the other to say for the rest of his life that he had not blinked under fire. Finally, he decided to risk a dressing down by coming to the rescue of his boss. "Colonel, Valerie in tank fourteen was asking to see you. Said it was urgent."

Having won the standoff, MacArthur smiled thinly and brought his riding crop to the bill of his tilted cap again. "Carry on, Colonel. Good luck with your armored horses."

As the general walked away, Patton dropped down into the foxhole and released a held breath. Motioning Angelo to follow him toward the protection of the nearest tank, he muttered angrily, "Armored horses my ass."

"Was he an old friend, sir?" Angelo asked on the run.

Patton spat a wad of dry bile ahead of him and drove it into the mud with the heel of his boot. "First time I ever met the sonofabitch. In this life, anyway. I think we squared off a few centuries ago at Thermopylae. I suspect he was a goddamn Persian."

Ozzie Taylor lugged a bag of stale baguettes over his shoulder as he darted from house to house while trying to time the German machine-gun fire. His buddies, at least those who had survived the onslaught, were pinned down in this smoke-choked village, and these loaves were the only food that Major Little back at regimental headquarters had managed to forage for them. Word was that Black Jack and the Frenchies were throwing everything they had at the Boche this night along the line that stretched from the Meuse River to the Argonne forest. The 369th's assault with the French Fourth Army up Bellevue Ridge here had taken three days. The Germans were putting up a fearsome last stand, fighting hand-to-hand in the streets and sniping from the windows.

Bullets cut the darkness, whizzing past his ears. He figured each miss raised the odds of the next one finding his skull. He was starting to regret volunteering as a runner between the white officers and what remained of the companies doing the fighting up front here. A week ago, he had reckoned that he'd be safer behind the lines, but the truth of the matter proved to be that a communications relayer drew the most fire. He was mostly delivering grim news anyway, a fact that made him unpopular with both the stripes and the enlisted men. Worst of all, while on his dashes, he had to ignore the many wounded who groaned for water and grabbed at his ankles as he skedaddled past them in the fields. He sure could use Big Jim with him right about now, telling him what to do and assuring him everything would be all right. But he was grateful to know that the Boss was safe in Paris, entertaining the Frogs on leave.

"Taylor!" a voice shouted from a blasted storefront window. "Get over here!"

Ozzie crawled over a cobblestone street strewn with shell casings and shards of wood beams. Halfway across, he heard several dull thuds, like a fist pounding a pillow. He realized to his horror that Germans on the rooftops were shooting at the bag of bread on his back, thinking he was carrying a wounded buddy. He doubled the pace on his knees and scurried into the open door.

Five men, their eyes ravenous, grabbed at the bag and scattered its contents— a few moldy baguettes and a couple of straight razors—across the floor.

Ulysses Tebbs, a private from St. Louis, picked through the scraps. "This is all they sent us? We ain't eaten in two days!"

Ozzie backed off into a corner, afraid they were going to tear him apart in retaliation. "I broughts what they told me."

Kid Hawk Hawkins picked up one of the rusty razors and examined its blunt edge. "What's this for? They expect us to cut the Boche throats when we run out of bullets?"

"Told us to shave," Ozzie said.

Kid Hawk threw the razor against the wall. "Why? To save them time back at the morgue?"

"Some of the boys shaved this morning before going over the top," Ozzie reported. "They was the only ones who's still alive. It's a portent."

"You don't even know what a portent is," Kid Hawk said.

"I think it's like a voodoo protective spell," Ozzie said.

A couple of the more superstitious men, not taking any chances, ran the dull blade across their chins.

Tebbs rifled through the bread shards until he found a piece that wouldn't crack his teeth. He tore into it, gulping it down before it was even half chewed. "What the hell is Little doing back there in his damn dugout? We've been holding these Boche sonsabitches off all night waiting for reinforcements?"

Ozzie tried to explain the lack of support. "The Major said Colonel Hayward is waiting for permission to send the last battalion down here."

"Hell, we been waiting long enough!" said Woney Williams. "Those white officers are just sitting dry while we're here doing their dirty work."

Eddie Washington peered nervously out the window, watching for the metallic flashes of a German Mauser. "The stripes are leaving us here to die."

Tibbs nodded bitterly. "Damn right they are."

"Yeah, I'm gettin' fed up with the white knights sending us to the slaughter pen," Washington said. "Fish, Hayward, Little. The whole batch'll go back to their mansions when this war is over and tell their smoking-club cronies how they led us with their swords in the air."

Ozzie had never seen the men so full of despair. "Major says to hang on."

Hawkins was pacing in agitation. "We got nothin' to hang on *to*. Half the regiment is shot up and punchin' their tickets at the Pearly Gates. Those damn rookies they sent us last week hightailed it off the first time we went over the top. We're out here on our own."

Ozzie tried to talk some sense into them. "If Big Jim were here—"

"Europe ain't here!" Williams shouted. "Anybody who's got any pull ain't here! He and his goddamn tune boys are in Paris sipping the vino and parlevousing with the dames. How'd you manage to get stuck back in this mess, Taylor? I thought you were assigned to wipe Reese Europe's fat expensive ass."

"They only transferred the band," Ozzie said. "I ain't made the cut yet."

Williams sneered. "So you're down in the bottom of the barrel with us again."

"They're using us for cannon fodder," Tebbs said. "I was talking to some of those Moroccans on our right flank last week. They said the Frenchies did the same thing to them on the Somme. Told 'em blackies can't fight, so they just threw them out there to draw the bullets."

"What's happening to those 368th boys?" Hawkins asked Ozzie.

Ozzie hesitated, not wanting to answer that question.

"You hear me, or your ears need swabbing?"

"Black Jack pulled them out of the line," Ozzie finally admitted. "Claimed they ran off scared."

The men froze, unable to comprehend how their fellow Negro regiment could have failed so shamefully under fire.

"They weren't trained proper," Hawkins insisted. "The Boche fight us to the death, but give up against the white boys. They won't surrender to us cause they think were the goddamn Sen'galese gonna cut their ears off and use their innards for drum twine."

"I can hear the whities spouting their jokes now," Williams said. "What'd a Negro soldier tell the Boche in the trenches? Shine or haircut?"

Tebbs spat a dry wad of phlegm in anger. "What're we fighting over here for anyway? We go back home, it'll be the same Jim Crow with his boot smashing ginst our heads. We're damn fools for not just pulling up stakes and stevedoring in Paris. At least we'd eat."

"Damn right," muttered Hawkins. "Those crackers won't fight aside us. Why should spill our guts over these fields for them?"

Washington kept looking out the window. "If we're gonna go, we gotta go now, before it gets light."

Hawkins and Tebbs picked up their rifles, and the other men followed them toward the door. They turned and saw Ozzie hanging back.

"You coming, boy?" Williams asked.

It took every ounce of his courage for Ozzie to shake his head. "I can't face Big Jim and tell him I ran."

Hawkins kicked an empty tin can across the floor. "Big Jim this, Big Jim that. I'm tired of that baton twirler taking all the credit for this regiment!"

"Go on, then," Ozzie said. "But while you're out there hightailing it to sunshine, just remember what they'll be saying back home. Every time a black man tries to take a step up the ladder, they'll be whispering behind his back that the Three-Sixty-Ninth couldn't stand the heat in France."

The men looked at their toes, shuffling and waiting for someone to make the first move.

Finally, Tebbs dropped to his haunches against the wall. "What's the name of this goddamn town anyway?"

"You authoring a gazetteer?" Hawkins asked as he and the other men reluctantly returned to their firing positions along the wall.

"I'd at least like to know the sonofabitchin' place they'll bury me."

Grinning grimly, Hawkins knelt aside the window and stole a glance out toward the sign on the battered *maison*. "Séchault."

"Custer's Last Stand at Sea Salt," Tebbs muttered. "I always thought the pale faces were the ones supposed to get massacred in that story." He aimed his rifle at the white village sign atop the commune headquarters and began peppering it with bullets.

"What you doing, Tebbs?" Ozzie asked. "We're short on ammunition."

"I'm gonna make that goddamn sign black as our faces. So every goddamn officer who comes through here remembers whose blood is soaking that ground out there."

It was still September, but Joe Angelo felt as if he'd been fighting nonstop for months. His tank brigade and the doughboys of the 35th Infantry Division were making a new push toward the Argonne Forest, and this time the brass had ordered them not to stop until they cracked the Hindenburg line and sent the damn Boche scampering back to Germany. Yet apparently Black Jack hadn't counted on a morning fog so thick that you couldn't see the man walking next to you. If the sonofabitching generals with their chevroned heads up their chevroned asses had bothered to check the weather forecast, maybe they would have thought better of ordering those artillery bastards a mile behind the trenches to launch their smoke bombs into no man's land and cut the visibility even worse.

He lugged the pigeon cage over his shoulder, wiping the bird shit from his shirt as he hurried to keep a step behind Patton. The Colonel was marching through the soup as if on parade, stabbing at the churned earth with his new shillelagh and barking orders in his high-pitched squeal at the tank drivers, even though they couldn't even hear their own thoughts above the grind of their engines. The rolling German artillery barrage was chewing up the ground in front of them, too close for comfort. He prayed for the Colonel to slow down before they all marched into one of those shells and got their heads splattered like watermelons on concrete.

He heard the crackling of machine-gun fire around him, which was not a welcome development, and soon the heavy mists were awhisper with the muffled pleas of lost doughboys trying to find their units. He turned to look over his shoulder and motioned up his fellow runners, five men chosen for the dangerous mission of sending communications and coordinates back to the rear line. "Colonel Patton!" he huffed, keeping his eyes down to avoid breaking an ankle in one of the pock holes. "We'd better hold up. I don't hear the tanks no more."

"They're ahead of us! Come on, Spartacus! Pick up the pace."

And that was another thing. He was getting damned tired of that nickname the Colonel had pinned on him because some Roman slave had made a bloody mess of things in the old country. He and the other runners pressed on, keeping their eyes fixed on the backpack of the man in front of them.

After twenty minutes of this ragged stumble into gray blindness, the Colonel became winded and sat down on a marking stone at a crossroads. While he studied his compass, the fog began to lift, revealing the rooftops of a village about five hundred yards to the north. "That must be Cheppy," the Colonel said with a self-congratulatory grin. "We'll be in Metz by nightfall, my stalwart legionnaires." He pulled his pipe from his breast pocket and lit up, then wrote a note in his order pad. He tore out the sheet and handed it to Angelo. "Send the pigeon to General Rockenbach. We'll give him the good news of our rapid advance."

Angelo questioned the wisdom of using their lone harbinger so soon, but he tied the note to the messenger bird's foot and released it with a prayer that its homing instincts wouldn't fail in this fog. He turned toward the ground that they had just crossed and watched the pigeon disappear into the gray wisps.

Moments later, the retreating fog gave way to streaks of sun, revealing the no-man's land for the first time. What he saw nearly two hundred yards behind him stole his breath. "Colonel, ain't those *our* tanks back *there?*"

Patton turned and nearly swallowed his pipe. Somehow, he had outraced his Renaults. He knifed up, desperate, and began pacing. Most of the forward tanks had become stuck in the mud, sitting ducks to be picked off. A German spotter plane buzzed the field, sending signals to the German artillery that sat dug in up the northern slopes. A second column of German tanks was now mashing into the halted Renaults, creating a snarled traffic jam, and the American infantrymen staggered between them, confused and panicked. Having lost their formations, many of the doughboys began retreating or hiding behind the disengaged machines. Patton tried to rally them, until dozens of German machine guns opened up from their entrenched positions in front of the village.

As bullets buzzed past like bees from an overturned hive, Angelo dived into a shallow railway with the other runners. He raised his eyes over his forearm and saw Patton standing several feet away, looking upward at the clearing sky and carrying on a conversation with the air as the gunfire zinged past him. "Colonel!" he yelled. "Get down!"

But Patton was mesmerized by something in the clouds. Suddenly, he ran across the field screaming at the retreating doughboys and making cutting hand signals at his tanks. "Come on, you sonsabitches! It's time for a Patton to die!"

Angelo swore under his breath. And then he swore again for taking the Lord's name in vain at such a dangerous moment. Ever since being attached to this cussing West Pointer, his own coarse talk had become so bad that twice he had gone to confession with the brigade chaplain just to clean the slate with the saints. Still, he had a damn good reason to be angry. Only a week ago, General Rockenbach had told Patton that under no circumstances should he walk into battle aside the tanks. He cursed again. It was just his black luck to get assigned as strikeman for the goddamnedest sonofabitching *pazzo* in the entire AEF, if you didn't count that scarf-sporting, crop-twirling MacArthur in the Rainbow Division.

"Angelo! Get over there to that tank and get that sonofabitch moving!"

Angelo froze in his crouch. *How does that sonofabitch expect me to move that sonofabitching tank?* Glared to the task by Patton, he whispered a bitter prayer, following it up with several more 'sonofabitches.' Then, he took off on a run across the field, weaving through a storm of machine-gun fire until, miraculously, he reached the tank whose nose was angled at a dangerous angle into a hidden water trench. He slid behind its rear drum for cover and kicked at its underside to get the attention of the two men inside.

"The Colonel says to move this sonofabitchin' tank!"

"The tracks are jammed with mud!" the driver yelled through his turret slit.

He was about to let loose with another torrent from Hell's dictionary when the Colonel came charging at the tank, driving a dozen frightened dough-boys in front of him with the end of his gnarled walking stick. As the bullets sprayed off the tank's plated armor, the Colonel pulled several shovels and picks from the side of the turret. He threw the tools at the cowering men and shouted, "Dig this sonofabitch out now!"

The frightened doughboys just stared at the tank, unable to bring themselves to pick up the shovels and expose themselves to the Boche fire. Patton grabbed a spade and hit one of the squatting men on the head, knocking him senseless.

Angelo feared the poor fella was dead. "Colonel, you gotta take cover!"

"To hell with the Boche! They can't hit me!"

The conscripted doughboys, convinced that this insane officer was even more of a threat to them than the Germans, scrambled for the tools and began digging wildly at the clogged tracks. Within minutes, the iron animal groaned like a monster being released from a bog and shot out from its muddy trap to resume its attack on the Boche lines.

Inspired anew, the Colonel ran across the field herding the fractured lines of the infantry into a pitiful gaggle. When he had gathered up a hundred men under the threat of his stick, he waved it over his head like a sword. "Let's go get 'em! Who's with me?"

The forlorn doughboys refused to follow Patton up the rise in the face of the machine-gun fire, but Angelo lowered his head in disgust and stayed within arm's length of his superior. Figuring he was destined to meet his Maker any moment now, he turned and saw that he and the Colonel were charging behind the tank with only four other soldiers. No sooner had he counted them, all four of his fellow volunteers went down, deader than Judas on the tree.

Yet the Colonel wasn't fazed. He soldiered on with his suicide charge, waving Angelo to his side and yelling again, "It's time for another Patton to die!"

Angelo pumped his short legs in a keeling effort to keep up. One of the Boche snipers must have heard the Colonel's prophecy, because seconds later Patton collapsed to his knees and fell face down. Several yards away, Angelo looked around and saw that he was now the only man left standing. He dropped to his belly and crawled like a crab toward the downed Colonel. "You hit, sir?"

The Colonel sounded delirious, thrashing across the ground while quoting Old Testament verses and conversing with ghosts. "To that copse, Uncle Taze-well! Hancock breaks! We got those sonsabitching Yankees on the run!"

Angelo finally reached the Colonel. He pawed at his writhing body to locate the wound. The Germans, not a hundred yards off, zeroed in on them with their sights. At last, he found the source of the gushing blood—a hole in the officer's upper left thigh. He sliced open the Colonel's pants and tied a bandage around the leg to slow the bleeding. The bullet had exited near the officer's rectum and left a jagged gape the size of a silver dollar in his left buttock.

Angelo swerved, light-headed, and caught himself before his head slammed the ground. He hadn't been this damn scared since a cave-in at the mine had nearly crushed him as a boy. He drove his head between his knees, trying to focus. If they stayed put out here in the open, it'd be just a matter of time before the Germans picked them off. Choosing the lesser of evils, he dragged the semi-conscious Colonel across the mud toward a small shell hole several yards away.

The snipers were reloading and shooting as fast as they could, desperate to notch their guns with the kill of an American colonel and his orderly. Near fainting, Angelo reached the gash of unturned sod and rolled Patton into its shallow impression. It wasn't deep enough to protect them both, so he hovered over his superior to shield him from the fire. Timing the shots, he looked over his exposed shoulder. The lead Renault tank sat like a guard dog yards away, helpless to come to their aid. But at least it wasn't retreating and abandoning them. He figured if the Colonel had any chance to make it, he'd have to keep him conscious and talking. "You in pain, sir?"

Patton was sweating and gasping. "Can't feel my legs."

"I think you're in shock, sir."

The officer flashed three fingers twice.

"Sir?"

"I'm thirty-three... my grandfather... thirty-three... when those Yankee bastards gunned him down at Winchester."

He pressed a shaking palm to the Colonel's forehead to calm him. "Yes, sir."

"Just saw him."

Dodging bullets, Angelo looked around. "Saw who, sir?"

The Colonel's shrill voice was slipping gears. "He's up there right now... in the sky with my kinsman... Hugh Mercer... All of my wounded progenitors... with me... I ever tell you how he fell at Princeton?"

"No sir, but—"

"Uncle Tazewell's up there, too.... Died a hero in Pickett's Charge. They're telling me... be brave." Patton tried to lurch his head up to ease his effort to speak. "You have any fighting men in your clan, Private?"

Angelo struggled to staunch the Colonel's bleeding. "Only if you're counting bar brawls, sir."

On his back, Patton arched his neck and gasped fractured ejaculations at the clouds passing overhead. "The spirits say... you come from fine fighting stock... One fought... against Napoleon... I knew you had pedigree when I... chose you... You saved my life once before ... Cannae... maybe Marathon."

Angelo levered all of his slight weight atop the Colonel, trying to keep him quiet to prevent the Boche from overhearing his delirious babbling and sending out a kill squad. "I think we're gonna be pinned down here awhile, sir, at least until dark. It's not safe to move you while those Boche have a clear line on us."

"Our ancestors are watching over us. Mine always watch me. They expect a hell... of a lot out of me."

"I know they do, Colonel. They ain't leaving you, and I ain't, either." Angelo's swollen tongue was burning. He searched for his canteen and saw it lying out of reach and riddled with holes. Blinking hard to keep from fainting, he stared up at the clouds as German lead whistled around his ears. Pressing so hard on the Colonel's wound that his hand threatened to cramp, he kept watching the clouds and trying to see what the officer had spied. If those damn spirits *were* up there in that sky, he wished they'd make themselves useful and come down here and help keep this sonofabitching hole plugged in their descendant's sonofabitching ass.

Anna always started her morning shift at Base Hospital 59 in Rimaucourt by walking down the aisle of the post-surgical recovery pavilion to check on the new American soldiers delivered to her care. She prayed this would be an uneventful day, or at least less hectic than the previous forty-eight hours when she had assisted the surgeons at the operating tables. Most of the men who reached this ward had survived the worst of their ordeals, first on the St. Mihiel salient, and more recently during what was being called the Meuse-Argonne Offensive. There was a good chance they'd recover if the infection and hemorrhage rates could be kept tolerable.

She weaved between the stretcher-bearers, replacing the transfusion bags and reading the scribbled charts. The dreaded transfer hour was near, when the patients were moved from one ward to another. Five different contingents of bearers were required to get the wounded from the ambulances to the triage stations. Four men stood waiting outside to unload the soldiers from the truck beds to the bathing tables; the mud mixed with blood was often so caked that rubbing it off threatened to remove the skin. Four more men were assigned to carry each soldier into the X-ray room, where a supervisor and four assistants often had to struggle to hold him down. Another supervisor and six bearers carried the men from the surgeries to the wards. In those rare moments when the cots were empty, another cadre of workers scurried about removing soiled linens and blankets. A five hundred-bed hospital employed enough bearers to fill an entire company of riflemen in the trenches.

Her nursing of these American boys brought back dark memories of her first days in the London hospital. There she had been thrust into service nearly two years after the start of the war, and by then, most of the men from the British Isles had known what grim business they were getting into. Yet Helen had once told her that, during the first bloody battles, the Brits had reacted with the same shock of discovery—that the world could descend to such brutality—now being experienced by these American troops. She kept her eyes trained down as she walked, looking for red stickers on the charts that indicated the patient was new. Their features were usually all the same now, drawn with that same ashen look of lost blood, their heads usually bandaged. She quickly scanned the physician's notes for one patient:

Colonel Pelham Glassford. Chin wound. Infection and fever.

Seeing two large feet dangling off the edge, she traced them to a handsome officer whose throat was wrapped in gauze. Immersed in his work on a drawing pad, he looked up from his etchings and greeted her with such a boyish grin that it threw her off-guard. She caught herself grinning back at him, just why she could not explain. But there was something about the twinkle in his blue eyes and the dash of his manner that she found almost surreal in such a melancholic setting.

"Are you the entertainment today?" he asked her.

"Entertainment?"

He widened his grin, a feat that didn't seem possible. "They told us some of the Paris film stars were coming down to give us a little show. I thought you might be one of them."

"Colonel, I grew up on a farm. I know what a load of manure smells like." She placed a palm to his forehead. "How are you feeling?"

"Should my heart be fluttering like this?"

She shook her head in mock disapproval, not wanting to let on that she was flattered by the compliment. "Let's change that bandage." While she carefully removed the gauze from under his chin, she looked down to see what he had been drawing. "You're quite good. Are you a professional artist?"

"It's just a hobby. I taught drawing at West Point."

After finishing with his new bandage, she took the drawing pad from him to examine what he had sketched: an old church surrounded by a graveyard. "A favorite place from home?"

His grin vanished. "No.… One of my captains was killed on the salient. We buried him at this church, not far from Vaulx. I'm not much at writing letters to grieving mothers. So, I try to draw the place where their sons are buried and send that to the families."

She finally regained her voice. "I'm sure they appreciate the kindness."

A bearded physician wearing thick spectacles and white coat came hovering over her shoulder. "Nurse! This chart is wrong!"

Startled, she resolved to instruct the physician, who was apparently new to the hospital, on the proper way to address a nurse. "Pardon me, but I did not fill out the chart. And may I ask who *you* are?"

"Doctor Chaffee. Specialist in rectums."

"There are no rectum wounds in this ward."

"I'll be the judge of that! Now roll this asshole over so I can have a look."

"I certainly will not!"

"Well, then. I will have to call for reinforcements." The physician turned and motioned toward the entry flap of the pavilion.

Twenty soldiers came marching down the aisle and filed in behind him, ready to arrest her at his command.

Anna stood her ground. "What is the meaning of this?"

"You will correct this man's chart at once, or I will have you shipped back to the States on the next steamer."

Anna yanked the chart from its hanger at the foot of the bed and studied it again. "What is wrong with it?"

"This man is identified as a colonel."

"So?"

"This morning he was promoted to brigadier general. And there is nothing here about his citation for gallantry against eight German boneheads who had the chance to shoot him but didn't, and now we have to keep putting up with his nonsense for the rest of the war."

Anna turned and found her patient trying to suppress a howl of laughter. She realized that she had been the butt of a joke. Red-faced, she came over him and more closely examined the new bandage on his chin. "I'm sorry, General, but it looks like I didn't get this on correctly." She yanked off the adhesive tape with one quick motion, causing him to cry out and brush away tears of pain. "Sorry. Sometimes we have to hurt you a little to help you." She put the bandage back on him in precisely the same spot. "There, that's much better."

"Atta girl." Lt. Colonel Chaffee removed his fake beard and shed the white-coat disguise. "But I still think I should perform the exam on this slacker, just to make sure he isn't smuggling any contraband into the ward."

Still smarting, Glassford saluted his men. "At ease, boys."

The men of the 103rd Field Artillery nearly crushed Anna as they crowded around their commander's bed, grasping his hand and expressing their gratitude that he had recovered from his shrapnel wound.

"Shouldn't you scoundrels be chasing the Boche right about now?" Glassford reached under his pillow and pulled out a hidden pack of cigarettes. He tried to pass it around for his men to enjoy some smokes, but Anna stole it, glancing at the oxygen tanks to remind him of the danger.

"They took us off the line for forty-eight hours, sir," one of the men said. "We sweet-talked our way down here to see the youngest brigadier in the AEF."

"Sweet talking seems to be the primary skill of this unit," Anna muttered under her breath.

"Nurse, you might want to warn your fellow angels of mercy about Happy here," Chaffee said. "He had quite a reputation as a ladies man at the Point."

"Yes, I've seen him in action." She caught her famous patient smirking at Chaffee. "How's that bandage feel, General? Does it need another try?"

Glassford, contrite, cowered into his pillow. "Just fine, ma'am."

"He was an accomplished thespian there, too," Chaffee said. "You must have him tell you how he dressed up as a geisha and drew a standing ovation for his rendition of the Mikado."

"Hey!" shouted one of the men. "That reminds me, General. You promised us a vaudeville show on your thirty-fourth birthday. You never got around to it. Interrupted by a little tussle with the Boche, as I recall."

Chaffee curled a roguish grin. "Yeah, Ferdie's right. We *do* owe the boys a performance." He scanned the ward. "What about right here?"

Worried that she was losing control of her station, Anna pushed her way to the fore of the bed again. "Absolutely not. This is a hospital, not a cabaret." She turned on Glassford with disapproval. "And you should consider your responsibilities, General. These men are of lesser rank than you."

Shamed, Glassford dropped his eyes to his chest. "She's right, Chaffee. Senior officers like us shouldn't be cavorting with the enlisted men."

Anna nodded in relief having finally restored some semblance of sanity.

Glassford flashed his teeth with a broad grin. "I'm declaring every man in this ward a civilian for one hour!"

"See, he *can* act." Chaffee strode down the aisle lobbying the other patients. "What about it, men? Would you like a little vaudeville show?"

Browbeaten by the applause, Anna glanced worriedly at the door, expecting her supervisor to walk in and find these men grubbing around the place like hogs. She looked down and saw Glassford shrug helplessly, as if he was at the mercy of the war gods. With a resigned sigh, she marched down the aisle, tied the entry ropes, and turned over the *No Admittance* sign outside. Then, she turned back to Glassford and warned, "You've got five minutes."

The men scrambled for what chairs were available, and those who lost out in the shuffle settled down on the floor. Anna helped the other patients to sit up against their headboards to watch the impromptu performance.

Glassford, looking like Lawrence of Arabia in his long nightshirt, arose from his bed and took center stage. "Chaffee and I need a fetching volunteer." He searched the tent. "Do we have a female in the audience?"

Before Anna could protest, several of the men herded her forward.

"All right, then." Glassford circled her, offering theatrical notes. "When I give the signal, you say one thing, and one thing only."

She glared at him with suspicion. "Which would be?"

"Niagara Falls."

She shrugged, seeing no harm in that small contribution. She nodded her readiness, eager to get this foolishness over.

Assuring that everyone was set, Glassford raised his arms for silence, and then he was off on his routine. He bent down on one knee and pleaded with Anna. "Madam, I am but a poor bum. Could you spare a coin for a meal?"

"Leave the lady alone!" demanded Chaffee, twirling an imaginary billy club.

"But Officer Chaffee," Glassford pined. "Mine is a sad tale. And I'd not have the lady here turn out to be a miserable hobo like me."

"Go on, then," Chaffee ordered. "Tell us your story of woe, poor man, so that we all might avoid your fate."

Glassford rose dramatically onto his toes and reached his hands toward the heavens as if lamenting to the Almighty. "I had me a fine family once. Beautiful wife, four children, all sweet-cheeked. I paid me bills on time, had money for Sunday dinner. And then, one day, I took me cherished ones on a trip into the lovely Lake region. As I sat there that day, enjoying a picnic of fried chicken, me wife decided to take a walk along the bluffs. And before I had me wing down me gullet, I hears me wife screaming for help. I rushed to her, but it was too late. She was disappearing down the rapids."

Chaffee cried, "Such a tragedy! Where did this horrid event occur?"

The patients watched in anticipation as Glassford cued Anna with a wink.

She coughed the nervousness from her throat. "Niagara Falls."

"Niagara Falls!" Glassford bellowed behind her ear.

His shout nearly startled Anna out of her shoes.

"My life was ruined at that place whose name brings nothing but pain upon me." Glassford lunged at Chaffee and wrestled his friend as if bent on strangling the Devil himself.

Struggling and fighting, Chaffee finally extricated himself from the grieving widower. "Get hold of yourself, man!"

That blasted admonition snapped Glassford back to sanity. Slowly he comprehended that something lost from his memory had sent him into a frenzy of possession. "What happened, Officer Chaffee?"

The patients and visitors howled with laughter.

Chaffee brushed himself off. "That lady said 'Niagara Falls' and you lost—"

"Wait!" Glassford froze, not certain of his hearing. He turned to Anna and, winking again to give the cue, asked, "Ma'am, what did the officer just say?"

Anna was now getting into the act. Fluttering her imaginary fluff collar, she revealed, "Why sir, I do recall him mentioning something about, let's see, what was it? Oh yes, Niagara Falls."

"Niagara Falls!" Glassford lunged at Chaffee again, driving him to his knees in a headlock. "Oh, the mere name sends me into convulsions! The place where I lost me dear wife!"

Chaffee crawled out from under Glassford's grip and backed away. "Get control of yourself, man! There appears to be a vicious demon lurking inside you! One that overtakes you at the utterance of those two words!"

The patients were now rollicking and laughing so loudly that Anna feared they might break their stitches.

Glassford dropped his hands to his knees, trying to regain control of his wits. "I'm so sorry, old chap. I've been told by a pretty nurse that at times I lose all control of me mind."

"Apologies accepted, sir," Chaffee said. "Now, if you will excuse me, I have to go downtown and pick up my new bride."

"New bride, you say?"

"Yes, we were married last Saturday."

Glassford reached for Chaffee's hand. "A thousand congratulations, sir. I do hope the two of you will be the happiest couple in the world. May I ask, do you plan a honeymoon?"

The doughboys edged up on their seats and beds.

"We do. A lavish honeymoon at that."

"If you don't mind me asking," Glassford said, "where will you be taking the little lady for your nuptial holiday?"

Wide-eyed with fear, Chaffee tried to avoid answering. "Sir, in all truth, the name of the place now escapes me."

Denied so rudely in his harmless inquiry, Glassford drooped his shoulders in a pose of sadness. Then, he glanced at Anna. "Madam, perhaps you might assist us. Did by chance the forgetful officer here happen to mention in your presence where he'd be taking his new bride on their honeymoon?"

She turned toward their audience and gestured with opened hands, silently asking the wounded men if she should answer him. They stood and pleaded for her to do it, stomping their feet to tell her in no uncertain terms that she of course knows where the cop and his bride will be taking their honeymoon, the only place in the entire world where an appropriate honeymoon *could* be taken. Bending to their pleas, she shrugged and replied, "Sir, please do not hold me to this, but I think I saw in Officer Chaffee's hospital chart that he intends to take his new bride to…"

"I beg of you, lady!" Chaffee cried. "Don't say it!"

Anna squeaked, "Niagara Falls."

Glassford let out a mighty roar of grief and fell upon Chaffee like a ravenous bear, pummeling him with pulled punches and chops. The other men formed a circle around the two wrestlers, egging them on and laughing so hard that the tent poles began shaking.

Surrounded by this theatrical chaos, Anna watched with tears in her eyes as a miracle unfolded. For these few precious minutes, this remarkable officer named Glassford had helped these scarred soldiers forget the war.

CHAUMONT, FRANCE
OCTOBER 1918

The Army often worked ass-backwards, Walter Waters had come to learn, and his temporary transfer here to the Chemical Warfare Service training school at Hanlon Field was just the latest confirmation of this unerring law of striped boneheadedry. He had already seen plenty of gas shelling up at the Front, but the brass, headquartered comfortably in that castle across the river, had decided in its infinite West Point wisdom that he and forty other doughboys should be pulled from their units for two days to be trained in the art of putting on a gas mask.

Not that he minded the rest, but the other stretcher-bearers in the 146th would have to do double time while he was away. Only a week ago, he had been promoted to sergeant, not due to any great leap of medical acumen or leadership on his part, but because most of the other veterans of the Mexico border duty had been killed or wing-clipped. If some desk colonel wanted to treat him to the first hot meal he'd had in a month in exchange for playing guinea pig with the new elephant-snout masks, who was he to complain?

That afternoon, he and the other men walked out of the mess hall rubbing their bellies and belching with satisfaction from a lunch of cornbread and peppered gravy. As they took a stroll, they heard a distant crack, one that seemed vaguely familiar. Another crack followed, and then another in the same interval, each reverberating with an echo through the crisp autumn sky.

They walked down the rows of barracks, stalking the tantalizing sound from their halcyon boyhood days. Turning a corner, they looked out over a flat, sheep-grazed pasture bordered by a meandering stream on one side and a long, tubular building on the other. In the middle of this emerald expanse, two dueling men stood facing each other. The tallest, blond and blessed with the predatory eyes of an eagle, wound up with his long right arm and threw a baseball toward a wiry, tobacco-spitting batsman. The hitter, gripping a thick limb as a substitute for a Louisville Slugger, whipsawed the ball over the pitcher's head.

"That's the Georgia P-P-Peach!" Waters shouted.

The other gas trainees froze in astonishment, unable to believe that they were watching the best hitter in baseball smack line drives across a Marne cow field. Ty Cobb, the Detroit Tigers's legendary centerfielder, acknowledged their shouting with a second spit of tobacco and then turned to wait for another pitch. The lanky hurler opposing him tracked down the lopsided baseball and returned to his mound, which consisted of a pile of fresh dirt recently raised by a gopher. The pitcher went into his windup and sent a tumbling curveball toward Cobb, who methodically slapped it into right field.

"Come on, Big Six!" Cobb shouted at the pitcher. "Cut loose with one!"

The doughboys traded another round of stunned looks.

Waters took a step closer to confirm the improbable sighting. "That's Mathewson d-d-dishing it up to him!"

"Give Peach the old backdoor, Christy!" shouted one of the men.

The doughboys ran to form a semicircle behind home plate, eager to see the famous manager of the New York Giants, Christy Mathewson, spin the seams on one of his unhittable screwballs.

Cobb slammed his bat against an imaginary plate and dared his buddy from the big leagues to try fooling him. "What's a matter, Big Six? You nervous? Ain't you ever had more than fifty people watching you?"

"Hell, he ain't thrown c-c-competitive in three years, Peach!" Waters shouted. "Let him g-g-get loose first!"

Cobb turned his bushwacker's glare on Waters. "Watch your mouth, boy!"

Waters and the other men retreated a step, aware of the Southerner's notorious temper and his penchant for cutting up opponents with sharpened spikes. Cobb had been known from time to time to go into the stands and fisticuff anyone who sounded like they'd had a daddy in Sherman's March. Everyone knew that the Peach had been brought into this world weaned on violence. When Ty was a lad, his father had come home one night suspecting the boy's mother of sleeping around. Armed with a pistol, the old man had staked out the roof waiting for the culprit, but his missus mistook him for a burglar and shot him dead, dropping him like a pigeon from the chimney.

Big Six cut loose a nasty screwgie, and Cobb just managed to foul it off.

"Pretty w-w-weak, Peach!" Waters taunted. "I saw Big Train s-s-strike you out twice."

Stalking the source of that slander, Cobb thumped his makeshift bat against the ground like a cop wielding a brains beater. "Who's got the smart lip?" When the men pushed Waters to the fore, Cobb pointed to the captain's bars on his collar and warned him, "Don't ever call me that again, or I'll crack your neck like a Sunday turkey!"

The gentle Mathewson hurried over to play peacemaker. "Take it easy, Ty. He was just tossing a few friendly gibes. Like at the ball game."

"I won't abide insolence! Not from some smart-assed Billy Yank!"

Waters saw Mathewson up close for the first time and was stunned by the thirty-eight-year old pitcher's sickly pallor. "Big S-s-six, you okay? You don't look so g-g-good."

Mathewson covered a nasty cough. "Been fighting the flu, is all."

Cobb walked over to a wagon and lifted the lid on one of the trunks on the flatbed. He began pulling out gas masks. "Form up! And get these on!"

The men fell into ranks and examined the twenty-pound contraptions that looked like football helmets with leather masks attached to a hose that filtered air through a canister of charcoal and soda lime.

"Hey, Captain, can we even breathe in these things?"

Cobb screwed his prunish face into a look that suggested he was going to bite the poor soldier's head off and spit it out for being too sour. "Hell, crackerhead, you think Captain Mathewson and I would have cut short our season and come over here as instructors to show you how to use these goddamn masks if they didn't work properly?"

"No, sir."

Cobb marched down the ranks as if addressing his team before the seventh game of the World Series. "Anybody else here have any doubts about the truthfulness of my word?"

Waters had some doubts, all right. For instance, if these gas masks were such an easy sell, how come those birds in Washington had to recruit two of the most famous baseball players in the world to promote them? He raised his hand and reminded Cobb, "It gets pretty t-t-tough out there in no-man's land, Captain. Breathing through that hose s-s-standing here is one thing. But when the f-f-firing starts and the smoke f-f-fills the air, there ain't much g-g-good air at all to be had."

Cobb blew into the front of a mask to prove that wind could pierce its filter. "There's plenty of goddam air in these."

"Then why does C-c-olonel MacArthur in the R-r-rainbow Division refuse to wear one?

The Peach turned redder than an overripe apple. "That stupid Yankee sonofabitch nearly went blind from a phosgene cloud, didn't he? They had to blindfold him for a week! Now shut your pie hole and grab that bat over there! We ain't got all day!"

Waters did as ordered and reluctantly picked up the shaved limb.

With a nasty sneer, Cobb walked down the line lecturing the confused men. "Captain Mathewson and I are going to exhibit for your education how easy it is to run and exert oneself while wearing these masks. We're all gonna play an at-bat wearing 'em. And this stuttering wisecracker here is going to lead off. You boys take positions out in the field. I'll ump."

"What's the rules?" asked one of the men, eager for a contest.

"Little game called Last Man in the Gas Barn," Cobb said. "You see that shed that looks like a giant stogie?" Receiving uncertain nods, the Peach explained what he had in mind. "Soon as Captain Mathewson records the out, you men are gonna remove your masks, keep them in hand, and hightail into that barn like you was going into the locker room at half-time of the Army-Navy game. The door will be shut behind you, and you'll be surrounded by a dim green light."

Waters pounded the bat on the ground, eager to show the Peach why he should have made the majors. He pointed out to the mound, imitating one of Cobb's upstart rivals, a combination outfielder-pitcher for the Red Sox named Babe Ruth. "Don't try that soft stuff on me, Christy! I'll eat that for breakfast!"

"Now listen up!" ordered Cobb, annoyed by the tomfoolery. "This is the critical instruction. Captain Mathewson and I will be in that barn there with you. When the officer at the valve gives us the thumbs up from a small window outside, we're going to signal you to put on your gas masks immediately. Don't dilly-dally in there. Ten seconds after the signal, the gas will enter the barn. The signal will be three raised fingers, followed by a tug of the front brim of his helmet."

One of the men in the rear piped up, "You never were much for following signals from the third-base coach, were you, Captain?"

Cobb glared the wag into a shiver. "This ain't a goddam game! We're using real mustard in there. You got the signal down in those thick skulls reportedly housing your brains?"

The men, sobered by the description of the dangers, nodded nervously. Finally, one of them blurted with preening bravado, "I reckon if Black Jack lets the two best players ever put on cleats go in that gas barn with us, we got nothing to fear."

Cobb pushed Waters toward home plate. "You got that right! Now batter up, fritter mouth!"

The next two minutes were a blur. Waters slammed on his gas mask, which pinched his neck and caused him to feel claustrophobic. A nose clip was supposed to prevent him from breathing through his nostrils, but it still felt loose. The Peach had promised him he'd be able to breath while running, but he could hardly wheeze enough air in to keep from passing out while standing in place. He managed to raise the bat from the ground, but before he could set it on his shoulders, he heard a swish around his knees. He looked down behind him through the two blurry oculars and saw that the catcher somehow had the ball in his hands. He squinted out at Mathewson, barely finding his silhouette.

This time, the pitcher lobbed the ball toward him on an easy arc.

Waters swung and felt a vibration in his hands, and next thing he heard was a distant baying of the command to run. He dropped the limb and took off on a staggering plunge toward what he remembered to be the direction of first base. He fell to his knees somewhere in the vicinity of the base, gagging and praying for air. He was about to rip off the mask when he made out, through the oculars, the demonic image of Cobb yelling a warning at him.

Now in an oxygen-deprived haze, Waters felt a sharp tug at his shoulder. Somebody removed his mask and slammed it into his hands. From his knees, he looked up and saw the other nine hurtling toward the barn, some vomiting, others passing out. How much time had passed?

He staggered to his feet and ran to catch up.

Cobb and Mathewson herded him and the other trainees into the long, narrow barn and flipped the lever to lock it airtight. Inside, he saw that a trench had been dug along the wall to imitate the terrain on the Front. After motioning them all into the defile, Cobb walked to the far end of the chamber and peered through the tiny glass window at the officers of the Chemical Service Corps manning the valves outside. The men inside clutched their masks while watching for the signal from the two baseball legends. Mathewson was distracted, rubbing his red eyes and hacking.

Seconds later, a low hiss came from somewhere around the foundations.

Waters grabbed at his seizing throat. A peppery stench suffocated him and singed his vocal cords. The men in the trench began heaving and gagging. Too choked to yell, Waters ran for the door and pounded on it.

Cobb and Mathewson signaled wildly and pointed for the men to put on their masks, but most were now thrashing on the floor and puking green vomit. Those who could still crawl piled on top of those in front. The iron panel covering the exit finally swung open, and the suffocating men scrambled to escape. Medics wearing gas masks rushed in and began dragging out the unconscious victims.

When Waters had finally managed to regain his breath, he looked up and saw Cobb berating the officer at the valve for failing to give the signal on time. Nearby, Mathewson was bent over in pain with his hands to his knees, blowing green snot from his nose.

And all around the field, men with burned lungs lay writhing in agony.

31

MINNEAPOLIS
OCTOBER 1918

Bert Hoover threaded his way across the crowded train platform, determined to find out what all the excitement was about. On a trip through the Midwest promoting his Food Administration's campaign to save grain for the troops, he had been informed that morning that his meeting with the local civic leaders would have to be rescheduled due to the fact that the entire city had decided to shut down in order to welcome home a native son returning from France. He was relieved to find that no one recognized him here, but he couldn't fathom which general or war hero was famous enough to supersede such a pressing national crisis as food conservation.

Right on time, the *Zephyr* from Chicago pulled into the station, causing people waiting on the platforms to become so jubilant that they threatened to push the stevedores into the track pits. The locomotive braked to a steaming halt and set the First Class car directly in front of a temporary grandstand filled with politicians and ward chairmen. Crouched below them hovered dozens of newspapermen and photographers. The door to the train stairwell opened, and a Marine Corps band marched out playing a rousing rendition of *Stars and Stripes Forever*. Next off came an impressive array of military officers, followed by an Irish piper who bellowed *Danny Boy* with such melancholy fervor that it brought tears to the eyes of the most hardened pols.

Hoover shook his head, bemused by the spectacle; he had witnessed traveling carnivals arrive with less fanfare. He half-expected Buffalo Bill to ride forth from the train car on his stallion.

Instead, a husky man in a khaki leatherneck uniform and campaign boots appeared at the door. Bundled with a black patch over his left eye and a sling holding his left arm, he swept his good hand across the crowd in a dramatic greeting worthy of a London thespian. Then, bringing to his side an elderly matron in a fur coat, he kissed her cheek and proclaimed, "Mother!"

The crowd applauded deliriously, and the Marine band struck up *Home, Sweet Home* as the man of the hour walked down the steps. Smothered with backslaps and kisses, he allowed himself to be escorted by an honor guard to a lectern waiting on the dais.

Hoover turned to a top-hatted spectator standing next to him and asked, "Is that fellow a movie actor?"

The man regarded him coldly, as if suspecting he might be a German spy. "Heavens, sir. Do you not read the papers? That is Floyd Gibbons. The hero of Belleau Wood."

Hoover narrowed his eyes with disapproval at the adulation. Of course he knew about the reporter who had made a name for himself in Mexico and France. But until now, he had never seen him in person. His opinion of the flamboyant risk-taker had never been very high, for he had always believed that newspapermen, like government officials, should remain hidden behind the story rather than become the center of it. Now that he saw Gibbons in the flesh, the war correspondent impressed him as being more P. T. Barnum than a humble Fourth Estate defender of the Constitution.

Reaching the podium, Gibbons thrust his fist into the sky and shouted, "I have returned to the most patriotic city in the great United States! The city that first welcomed me into the Order of the Knights of the Written Word so many years ago! Home, I tell you with all my heart! I am home at last!" As the crowds stomped and threw garlands at him, he swept his gaze over the vast assembly and fixed his eyes on three ranks of blue policemen on his flank. He pointed at them in a taunt. "I'm thinking it's rather funny, don't you, lads? Here I am with all these cops ahead of me. In the old days, they used to always be behind me, chasing my sources!"

The crowd roared again, drawing a grimace from police chief.

Gibbons next aimed his rapier smile at his fellow newshawks, who were scampering like rats along the railing below him. "Ladies and gentlemen, as I lay wounded for two hours in the mud of France on that hot June day, not knowing if I would ever again see the clarifying light of God's wondrous creation, one thought kept coursing through my fevered mind." He hesitated, turning his gaze inward in a studied pose of troubled contemplation.

"Tell us, Gib!" shouted an eager admirer.

Gibbons puffed out his chest to display his military ribbons. Then, slathering on a thick Scot-Irish brogue, he went on. "Aye, I kept athinking of me beloved editor from me formative years. There he is among us now. Stand up and take a bow, Bob Lee."

A crusty old desk editor, heartened at being singled out by his now-famous protege, stood to acknowledge the recognition.

"Why old man Lee?" asked a cad who worked at a competitor's newspaper. "He's never shot at anything but empty whisky bottles."

Gibbons delayed for effect, waiting for the crowd to quiet. Then, he wiped an imaginary tear from his eye. "I said to meself as I was lying amid those brave wounded Marines, many of whom were saying their Hail Marys for the last time, I said to meself—"

"Dammit, Gibbie," shouted one of the reporters who was tired of scribbling in his notebook and starting over again. "You gonna tell us what you were thinking when those Boche devils were about to gut you? Or are we gonna have to wring it out of you?"

Gibbons raised his good arm again, pleading for forbearance. He shielded his unpatched eye from the sun and insisted, "Bob, turn around so that the cameras can get you!"

Amid a blast of flashes, several reporters pushed the old editor to the fore.

"Look at those lines of experience in that adorable mug!" Gibbons shouted. "Now, I ask you folks, is that not a face that could hold a seven-day rain?"

The spectators howled their approval.

"Damn it, Gibbons!" The police chief shouted. "Get on with the story."

Gibbons placed his hand on his heart. "Where was I?'

"On the battlefield!" a hundred voices shouted.

"Ah yes. So, as I lay there wounded, I thought to meself, I can't die like this, not when Bob Lee still owes me four-fifty for that beer and sauerkraut sandwich I bought him ten years ago down at the Schnitzelbank diner!"

The roars of laughter were so thunderous that Hoover feared the crowd might threaten to collapse the grandstand. The craggy editor stood exposed to the ridicule of being a lunch poacher. Resigned to the indictment, he nodded to confess his guilt. He reached into his pocket, grabbed some coins, and paid Gibbons.

Gibbons stared at the pile of pennies just dropped into his hand. "What? After all these years, no interest?"

Hoover marveled at the performance worthy of a vaudeville stage, convinced that the rapscallion Gibbons was being wasted on the printed page. He counted charisma low on the qualities gifted to mortals by the Almighty, but he had to admit that the man possessed more syrupy charm than Douglas Fairbanks and more ambition than Henry Ford. He wouldn't be at all surprised if some enterprising political operative drafted the silver-tongued newspaperman to run for high office.

As the regimental band played *La Marseillaise*, a French consul stepped forward and pinned on Gibbons's chest the Croix de Guerre with Palm, a coveted award reserved by the government in Paris for recognition of heroic military deeds. When the adoring audience finally hushed again, the mayor stood and read a poem about Gibbons that had appeared earlier that week in the *Chicago Tribune*:

> "'The Teutons tattooed him with bullets,
> And cluttered him full of shell,
> But he didn't die and his good right eye
> Will yet see the Kaiser in Hell.
> And though he's a-bloomin' hero,
> A Croix de Guerre guy and all that,
> He walked right in with that same old grin
> And the same old size of hat!'"

Carried out of the station on the shoulders of the swarming crowd, Gibbons doffed his tri-fold Marine cap. When he passed Hoover, he winked.

Hoover couldn't be certain if the newspaperman had recognized him, or merely possessed that rare Mona Lisa talent for making everyone think he was looking only at him. He turned again to the gentleman aside him and remarked, "I don't know about the size of his hat, but his head appears to have swelled. What will he do for an encore, I wonder?"

"He is on a three-month lecture tour across the country. And rumor has it he is writing a book about his experiences in the war."

"Seems a bit crass, don't you think?" Hoover observed. "Cashing in while our soldiers are still fighting and dying?"

Offended by the remark, the man removed his top hat to emphasize his earnest feelings on the matter. "Mr. Gibbons has helped raise thousands of dollars in war bonds. I don't see *you*, sir, over in France sacrificing an eye for the cause. The Honorary Marine of Belleau Wood has given his pound of flesh. Now he is pursuing a hallowed American tradition."

"What tradition would that be?"

"Making a profit on a war started by the Yankee bankers and Wall Street tycoons. The robber barons cash in on the bloodletting every other decade. So why shouldn't the little fellow have his say and part of the pie?" With his diatribe finished, the man donned his top hat again and walked off.

Abandoned before he could defend the integrity of capitalism, Hoover was attacked by a hunger pang. Minneapolis was known for its superb steaks, he remembered. But then he saw, on the station wall, one of his agency's posters reminding Americans that today was Meatless Monday.

32

SEDAN, FRANCE
NOVEMBER 1918

As the scarred Belgian horizon slowly swallowed the sun, General Douglas MacArthur tightened the optics in his field glasses and peered across the shell-churned valley that funneled into the arc of the Meuse River. There, a half-mile away, the German survivors of the month-long Allied offensive had dug in, determined to make a last stand near a medieval château that had survived heavy fighting during the Thirty Years War. Every student of military history knew this to be hallowed ground. It was here, in 1870, where Napoleon III had surrendered to the Prussians, searing into the collective French memory a defeat whose ramifications were still being playing out. Three years later, that same French emperor, despondent on his deathbed, would turn to his doctor and mutter his haunting last words:

Were you at Sedan?

MacArthur prayed the same damning question would never be asked of him, at least not with the same implication of accusation and humiliation. He shook the blood back into his bluish hands and motioned for his aide to bring up the latest communication sent by that chickenhawk George Marshall, one of the many starched shirts at Chaumont who despised him for his courageous deeds in the field. Every time he thought of that cabal of GHQ sycophants, he couldn't help but glance down at his breast pocket, where a Medal of Honor and the stars of a major general should have been pinned. He smiled bitterly. At least he had won his brigadier promotion and six Silver Stars, the most recent after he had made good on his promise to take Châtillon or deliver a casualty list of five thousand American names with his own at the top. Even Pershing had not found a way to deny him those grudging honors.

The German strategy did not surprise him. With Ludendorff sacked and the Kaiser searching for asylum, the poor Boche who remained in those trenches ahead of him were waging a desperate rear-guard action, just as Robert E. Lee had done in the trenches of Petersburg. But he knew it would be only a matter of days before their guns were silenced. Then, the War Department would freeze all promotions and knock back most of the AEF officers to a lower rank when the Army was mustered out. He sighed with regret, certain that there would never be another war of this magnitude in his lifetime. He had only a few days left to make his mark for posterity and gain the lofty heights of distinction that he had promised his mother.

"General, the runners are waiting for your night order."

He nodded to the aide who held a lantern over his shoulder while he paced, studying the directive from Chaumont: *General Pershing desires that the honor of entering Sedan should fall to the American First Army.* He made a mental note that no duty officer would ever issue such unctuous and oblique sentences under his command. *Your attention is invited to favorable opportunity now existing for pressing our advance through the night.* That mealy-mouthed Marshall was better suited for penning invitations to cotillions. He, on the other hand, had suffered enough ass-covering language over the years to know when Pershing and his toadies were attempting transfer all the risk of failure on the ground officers. He drew a deep breath and reread the last worrisome sentence: *Boundaries will not be considered binding.*

"Sir, we promised the officers your orders an hour ago."

He saw from the heading of the GHQ directive that Pershing had sent the same order to the First Division, which now sat on the right flank of his Rainbow unit. "That club-footed dancer wants to beat the French to Sedan," he muttered through gritted teeth. "But he doesn't have the guts to come out and say it like a man."

"Which club-footed dancer, sir?"

He smiled grimly, not about to elaborate. "Did you play football, Collins?"

"Yes, sir. A bit in college."

"When is the most dangerous time of the game for suffering injuries?"

The aide thought a moment. "We used to get most of our busted knees and broken bones in the fourth quarter."

He slapped his riding crop against his thigh, his traditional sign of agreement. "Yes, when you and your squad were tired and overly anxious to end the thing. That is when the most egregious errors occur in any endeavor. When a team is worn out and doesn't think straight."

"Sir, I'm afraid I don't follow."

He folded Pershing's order and creased its corners with a finger snap in anger. "GHQ has commanded us to move on Sedan at midnight. Draft the order of battle for my signature and send them down the line with the runners. I will be in my tent. Wake me in four hours."

As his aide hurried off to relay the command, MacArthur walked back over the ridge where his Rainbow men lay bivouacked, exhausted from the weeks of pushing hard through the Argonne. He deemed it criminal to require them to get up and make a night assault, just to let Pershing steal Sedan from the French and become more of a darling to the press back home. Resigned to the inevitability of unnecessary casualties, he walked into his tent and fell into his cot. He was feeling oddly melancholic this night. Every muscle in his body ached, and since being gassed, he found it difficult at times to breathe. He had long ago learned to sleep lightly. Truth was, he had not enjoyed a full night of deep sleep since his plebe year at the Point.

But he was dog-tired now. His drowsy thoughts turned to his father, as they often did on nights in the field. As a boy, he had been sent to bed with stories of Captain MacArthur's experiences in the Civil War. One battle in particular had always captured his imagination. When the Confederate army of Braxton Bragg invaded Kentucky in 1862, the Union forces under Don Carlos Buell had stumbled into the rebels near a dusty hamlet called Perryville. The battle there had lasted only a few hours, but it was one of the fiercest of the entire conflict. His father had gained his first commendation of valor on those rolling hills. Yet what made that fight so memorable was the effect of the rundling Kentucky terrain. General Buell had situated his headquarters just a short ride from where the two armies were dueling in a thunderous cannonade. Due to a geographical quirk called acoustic shadow, Buell could not hear the guns, even though their firing was evident from fifty miles away in the other direction. As a result, Buell received news of the battle late and arrived on the field only when it was nearly fought out, thus missing a chance—

A volley of rifle fire, close range, rang in his ears.

Disoriented, and then wondering if he had been dreaming of Perryville, he staggered to his feet and lurched past his tent flaps into the darkness.

Ten American soldiers, led by a major, stood aiming their bayoneted weapons at him. "*Hände hoch!*" the major shouted.

There was barely enough ambient light to allow MacArthur to make out their shoulder patches. Was that a green pentagram surrounding a large red numeral One? He realized to his dismay that the American First Division—nicknamed the Big Red One—had quickly followed up on Pershing's dangerous order to ignore sector boundaries. In their haste to reach Sedan first, the advance companies of the First had swerved into his encampment thinking it was the German line. As he stared down the barrels and bayonets, he puffed his chest with all the poise of authority he could muster. "Major, tell your men to lower their guns."

The major answered that demand by cocking his pistol. "*Kapitulieren!*"

The soldiers ogled their captive's signature combat attire, which was devoid of any insignia of rank. MacArthur raised his hands, reluctantly obeying the German command for surrender that all doughboys were required to memorize. "Take it easy, men. How many German generals would know that the Red Sox won the World Series this year?"

One of the soldiers blurted, "Yeah, but only because the Cubs threw it."

"He speaks pretty good English, sir," another doughboy said.

The major wasn't impressed. "That's because they teach the Boche to fool us."

As the Big Red men closed in on their captive, one of them suggested, "Let's shoot him for lying like a spy."

The major ordered the prisoner, "Face away from us." Then, he warned his men, "If he makes one false move, let him taste some Bethlehem steel."

MacArthur turned his back slowly, praying silently that he would not be stabbed in the kidneys. He kept his hands in the air and said calmly in the most Southern drawl he could manage, "Major, check my tent. There you will find evidence of my identity as an American brigadier."

The First Division men chortled at his ham-fisted attempt to fool them, and the major got into MacArthur's face. "Hey, *Herr* Kraut, you think we're numbskulls? That's not an American uniform you're wearing. No general of ours would dress up like a vaudeville dandy."

"I got dibs on that *fräulein* scarf!" shouted one of the soldiers. "My wife's gonna be the only Irish gal in town wearing a genuine Boche neck strangler."

Another doughboy, also eager for a souvenir, stole the crop from MacArthur's grasp. "Where's your white horse, Kaiser? You whip prisoners with this, do you?"

In the nick of time, MacArthur's aide came running up the hill, followed by a dozen Rainbow privates. "General MacArthur! These Big Red thieves are rooting around in our grub!"

The soldiers of the First Division, jaws dropping, took a step back.

The major asked in a tremulous voice, "*You* are General MacArthur?"

MacArthur reclaimed his riding crop and readjusted his scarf over his shoulder in a gesture of contempt. "If you don't mind, gentlemen, my division and I have a show to perform for the Boche tonight. I'm confident we'll do better than this amateur comedy routine you just demonstrated with your map and compass. It would have been quite a blot on the Big Dead One's record to go down in history as the only American unit to capture and shoot an American general."

"Yes, sir," the shamed major sputtered.

"By the way, I encountered one of your tank officers at St. Mihiel a few weeks ago."

The shaken major nodded. "That would likely be Colonel Patton, sir."

"Ah, yes. As I recall, he also was finding the war a bit overwhelming for his talents. Did he ever get those rolling tin cans of his out of the mud?"

"He did, sir, but not before getting shot up pretty bad. His orderly kept him alive."

"I remember that boy," MacArthur said. "Nervous little runt of a rabbit." He threaded the soldiers who nearly shot him and brought his crop to the tip of his crushed cap in a lording salute. "Carry on, men."

The astonished doughboys bolted to attention and returned the salute.

A few steps away, MacArthur turned back to the humbled officer and added, "Oh, and Major, should you and your patrol ever again feel the urge to bag some big American striped game, do us all a favor and cull that herd of hyenas running amok in Chaumont, won't you?"

33

RIMAUCOURT, FRANCE
NOVEMBER 1918

Those dreaded hours of early morning were approaching, when the blood pressures of the dying men in the *salle de mort* spiked and plummeted, spiraling them into their final agonies of coughing blood and hemorrhaging from their volcanic wounds. In the ominous stillness that she knew to be the calm before the red storm, Anna sat next to "Thankee" Jan, a fair-headed boy from Minnesota who had gained his nickname because he always blessed the nurses with that Dutch expression of gratitude. Brought in from the Front two weeks ago with a ghastly stomach wound, he had been making good progress after the surgeons stitched him up with an intestinal bypass, even walking a few steps each day.

But now he lay just hours from death, consumed by gangrene.

She prayed he would fall asleep and pass peacefully, but he kept staring up at her with those sunken eyes and gripping her hand, afraid to let go.

"Miss Raber, is it Sunday still?"

She was embarrassed to admit she didn't know. The weeks and months were now lost in a haze, and she felt the passing of time not in the artificial divisions of the world at home, but in the growing coldness of the mornings and the disappearance of daylight. She flipped back a few pages of the copy of *Martyr's Mirror* that she was reading and found the year's calendar, torn from a newspaper for a bookmark. "It is now Monday. The eleventh of November."

Jan drew a long, wheezing gasp, and his eyes widened.

She felt his grip tighten. "Are you in more pain?"

His voice fell to a faint whisper. "Thou hast not kept my covenant and my statutes…. I will surely rend the kingdom from thee."

Remembering those fractured verses from the First Book of Kings, she leaned to his lips, trying to understand what he was trying to tell her. "The doctors have said no more morphine until another hour, but I will give you some if you need it."

He shook his head, desperate to be understood. "Eleventh of the eleventh book. God is speaking to me."

She cupped his desiccated hand between her palms to calm him.

"This is the day, He says... I will arise from my bed soon."

She had to turn away. When, finally, she managed to stanch her tears, she steeled herself and confirmed for him in a soothing, maternal voice, "The Lord blesses us all."

His fevered eyes lightened, and he arced his cracked lips into a weak smile. "Are you superstitious, Miss Raber?"

She never ceased to be astonished by the questions these men asked her with their last breaths. The Bible forbade all magic and superstitions, but she and her fellow nurses had a weakness for rituals and connections that might spare a life. If they administered the medicines at a certain hour and one of the men miraculously recovered, they would religiously follow the same schedule for the other patients. If a certain prayer sent a man into that final, blessed bliss of release, they would share that information and use it for the others. Yes, she had become superstitious—what mortal in such a war could avoid it? Yet she would not admit it to Thankee Jan, or anyone else. "I try to surrender only to the will of the Lord. Why do you ask?"

"Is it November?"

"Yes, it is."

He was trying to lift his head. "The eleventh day of the eleventh month. If I can make it to eleven o'clock, the Almighty will heal me. Pastor Jurgens always said the number eleven in the Good Book signified the coming of a miracle."

She slipped her fingers to his wrist. His pulse was weakening. She placed a palm to his forehead, trying to ease his agitation.

"Thankee," he whispered.

In her other hand, she brought the *Martyr's Mirror* to the bed and clutched it for strength.

Through his blurring eyes, Jan saw the leather-bound book. "Scripture?"

She shook her head, trying to find her voice. "It is an account of the martyrdoms of my Anabaptist forefathers. I find comfort in it."

"Will you read it to me?"

She hesitated, fearing that its stories of suffering would send him into a spiral of despair. But he implored her, struggling to lay his hand atop the book. At last, she nodded her assent to his request and opened the *Mirror* to the invocation, the passage that had always given her strength when her father read it from the pulpit: "'Yet to look upon all this will not cause real sadness, for though the aspect is dismal according to the body, the soul will nevertheless rejoice in it, seeing that not one of all those who were slain preferred life to death, since life often was proffered them on condition that they depart from the constancy of their faith. But this they did not desire; on the contrary, many of them went boldly onward to meet death; some even hastened to outstrip others, that they might be the first, who did not shrink from suffering anything the tyrants could devise, nay more than could be thought possible for a mortal man to endure.'"

She paused to steal a glance at Jan. For the first time in days, he looked serene. She read on, relating to him the many heroic sacrifices that her people had endured for their faith. Just as she used to do as a girl reading the book on a blanket in the fields while the men plowed, she lost all track of time as she merged her heart and mind with the saints of the Old Country.

Four hours later, a clamor in the next pavilion over startled Anna from her reading task. She looked down and saw that she had managed to finish nearly a third of the biography of the martyrs.

The light of day now filled the air slits.

One of the VAD aides came running into the *salle de morte* and popped the cork on a bottle of champagne. "It's over! They've signed the Armistice! The war is over!"

Anna, horrified by the insensitive intrusion, shouted at the girl, "Get out!"

As the church bells began ringing, the poor VAD, realizing what she had done, pressed a hand to her mouth and retreated from the death tent.

Anna stood and rushed to the flap to look outside. The villagers and soldiers were shouting and dancing, hugging each other and toasting to the peace. She glanced up at the clock on the old tower in the square. It was eleven in the morning. She gasped, and ran back into the tent.

Unable to move, Thankee Jan stared up at her in a panic. "You left me."

"Just for a moment. I'm sorry."

He was shaking furiously, trying to turn his head while pulling the trigger on an imaginary gun in his hand. The noise had transported him back to the trenches. "Attack! Let me at them!"

The stretcher-bearers began entering the tent and making their morning rounds to remove the corpses of those who had died during the night. One of the medics winked at Anna and reminded her, "I haven't forgotten that cup of tea you promised me, Miss Raber. I'll see you now, won't I, before we leave for the States?"

Anna turned back toward the bed in time to see Jan, lucid again, sink into his pillow. The boy suddenly understood what was happening. The Lord had not raised him from the bed, as his vision had promised. All hope now drained from his drawn face, and he closed his eyes for the last time. He managed to mouth a weak "thankee" to her, and turned aside.

He was dead.

Before she could recover from his passing, the head nurse burst into the pavilion. "Anna! We need you in surgery! Another transport of wounded is on its way."

"Wounded? But I thought the war was over."

The head nurse was livid with rage. "Pershing and his hotshots decided to take another run at some medals this morning. Apparently they didn't want to transport their ammunition back home, so they decided to empty their cartridges on the Germans and gain a few more stories of glory for their débutante balls back in Washington."

Anna couldn't believe what she was hearing. "Headquarters knew the cease-fire was only hours away? And they sent the regiments on assaults anyway?"

The head nurse took her aside, out of earshot of the patients. "The medics at the evacuation station just cabled us a warning. They said to expect at least two thousand more wounded delivered to the hospitals by tonight. Do the best you can to stifle any talk from the other nurses and VADs about the hour of the Armistice. When these poor men find out they were sent over the top for no good reason, they may riot."

Clenching her fists, Anna kicked a bedpan across the tent. "And I'll bet my ticket home there won't be any generals on *those* stretchers."

34

HAUTE-MARNE, FRANCE
DECEMBER 1918

Happy Glassford stood before a full-length mirror in the small château that had served as his headquarters after the Armistice. Attired in his full dress blues for the first time since the start of the war, he saw only a distant semblance to the youthful lieutenant colonel who had landed at Le Havre seventeen months earlier. He had lost twenty pounds and looked ten years older. His face was drawn and his eyes were bagged with exhaustion; the collar and sleeves of his tunic were so loose that his reflection brought to mind a dead Irishman laid out for a wake. He thought back to the last time he had worn this uniform, during the send-off ball for him and his fellow West Pointers at Fort Myer. It was now pinned with two new accessories: a general's star and a Distinguished Service Medal.

He reached down for his cap that he had packed away in his traveling trunk. Under it, he found a slender book, one of the few mementos he had brought overseas. A flood of memories swept over him. Six years ago, he had been an instructor of drawing at West Point when several second-year cadets were brought up on hazing charges. The superintendent, General Townsley, had convened a star chamber to intimidate them, hoping they would rat on their classmates. Appointed to the board of inquiry, he had incurred the superintendent's wrath by insisting that the military code did not require the cadets to incriminate themselves. Infuriated, Townsley had threatened him with a court martial. But in the end, he and the cadets had survived the general's blustering attempt to drum them out of the Army.

He paged through the furlough book that the Class of 1914 had presented to him on their graduation day, two years later. It was the only time in Academy history that a class book had been dedicated to a living officer. Tears filled his eyes as he studied the photographs. Many of those boys had been killed in the war.

"Hap." Ev Chaffee stood at the door. "We shouldn't keep the brass waiting."

Wiping his eyes, Glassford repacked the furlough book and nodded his readiness to be driven to Division headquarters at Montigny-le-Roi. There, in a few hours, President Wilson would hold a Christmas Eve review of the troops, followed by a reception for the senior officers. All of France was in a hullabaloo over the first American president to visit Europe while in office. The last thing he wanted to do right now was make pleasantries with politicians and fellow generals, but, resigned to the task, he set his cap on his head and walked toward the door with Chaffee. "Let's take the back roads. There have been some reports of German holdouts sniping in the hills above the Chaumont route."

Chaffee retrieved a rifle from the corner. "Then we'd better take our chaperone to the dance."

They walked outside into a square dusted with light snow. As they reached for the doors of their staff car, he remarked to Chaffee, "I forgot to tell you. I saw a strange thing on the last day of the fighting. Can't get it out of my mind."

"What happened?"

"A German grenadier stood manning his dugout until the very last minute before the Armistice. He stayed there even after his comrades had long since abandoned him. This Boche fellow saw me and looked at his watch, and I looked at mine. It was exactly eleven. He fired off his last clip in his machine gun into the air, stood up, and bowed to me. Then he walked off like a stage actor finishing a play."

"Hey, the play's the thing. And we but actors in a dream."

"More like a nightmare."

The two officers were about to step into the car when an elderly priest shuffled out of the small church of Vicq and hurried toward them, gesturing frantically. *"Pardonnez-messieurs! Un moment, s'il vous plaît!"*

"Merry Christmas, *padre*," Glassford said. "How might we make it merrier for you?"

The shriveled priest doffed his cap, unleashing his few thin strands of white hair as he bowed repeatedly. *"Général, pouvez-vous me dire à quelle heure le Président Wilson nous rendra visite?"*

"Here?" Glassford asked, laughing. "You thought the president was—" He stopped in mid-sentence.

Chaffee didn't understand a word of French. "What does he want?"

Glassford realized from the poor priest's stricken reaction that he had somehow fallen under the delusion that President Wilson would be paying his little hamlet the honor of a visit that night. He stepped over to the outer wall of the church and peered through the crack of a window. The pews were filled with villagers dressed in their finest suits and dresses. In the central aisle, a table sat filled with wrapped gifts, and over it hung a sign welcoming the American savior of the French people to Vicq. He shook his head in disbelief. This priest in his dotage had apparently told his congregation that Wilson would help them celebrate the birth of Christ, and these French had spent what little money they possessed to express their gratitude. The priest, he knew, would be shamed when the truth came out, and might even be forced to retire because of the embarrassing *faux pax.*

"Hap," Chaffee called over to him. "Pershing will have our hide if we don't get moving."

Seeing the priest shivering and confused, Glassford took off his overcoat to place it over the cleric's shoulders. He glanced toward the outskirts of town, where his men, billeted in barns and hastily constructed barracks, were singing carols. An aroma of lamb stew—their Christmas meal—wafted through the war-stricken village, and in the stable across the *rue,* the ring of an anvil echoed through the clear winter air. He wondered why Private Hadenworth, their blacksmith, would be shoeing the horses on Christmas Eve.

An idea struck him.

He wrapped an arm around the priest's shoulders and leaned down to whisper into his hairy ear. *"Père, vous êtes sur le point de commencer la messe pour votre congrégation."*

Informed that President Wilson would indeed be arriving soon, the smiling priest shuffled off toward the church give the good news to his congregation.

Chaffee glared at Glassford, suspecting one of his famous pranks. "What the hell did you just tell him?"

Glassford deflected that question. "What's Hadenworth's nickname?"

"The Schoolmaster. But why... no."

"Don't the boys call him that because he looks just like old Woodrow?"

"It won't work."

But Glassford thought it might. "Same height, six-three. Face like a droopy hound. Commandeer Private Jacob's spectacles and have the Schoolmaster report to meet on the double."

"You can't be serious."

"Who's our best seamstress?"

"Borger, but—"

"Tell him we need a pair of pin-striped pants and coat with tails on the quick. You should be able to rustle up a borrowed top hat from that hotel over at Langres."

"What about the presidential troop review?"

Glassford enjoyed his first boyish grin in months. "We had a flat tire. We'll get to Montigny-le-Roi in time for the reception."

While the French villagers knelt in their church singing their *chants de Noël* and practicing their speeches to the president, Glassford held court in his château headquarters next door. As he stood in the drawing room, an eye in the center of a storm, his doughboys scurried about him preparing for the greatest ruse of the war. He hurriedly wrote a speech and drilled Hadenworth until he had it down, then he watched approvingly as the men dressed the Schoolteacher in the hastily sewn suit and transformed him into a remarkable facsimile of the Virginian in the White House.

A corporal rushed in from the back door. "General, it cost us that case of whisky we finagled from the Rainbow boys, but we got the wheels you ordered."

Calling for silence, Glassford gathered his soldiers around him. "All right, men. You've got your marching orders. Don't screw it up." He turned to a nervous Hadenworth and smoothed the lapels of his black jacket. "If you pull this performance off, Schoolmaster, there's a promotion in it for you."

"That include a raise, sir?" Hadenworth asked.

"Ten bucks a month," Glassford said, neglecting to add that all pay increases would be countermanded after they were mustered out.

Hadenworth clapped his heels together to indicate his readiness, and Glassford hurried his presidential imposter out the rear alley to three GHQ limousines waiting with tiny American flags flying. The doughboys assigned to play the presidential honor guard formed ranks in front of the limousines, and on Glassford's nod, the entourage rolled out of the alley and into the main street of the village. The band marching behind the procession cut loose with *La Marseillais*. The rousing rendition brought the villagers running from their pews to the church door. The little priest threaded his way to the steps, determined to be the first to greet the American president.

The limousine pulled up, and Glassford got out first. He saluted the priest and turned to acknowledge the guest of honor. As Hadenworth stepped out of the sedan, the regimental band played *Hail to the Chief*. The French people applauded wildly, and one woman nearly fainted. They formed a congratulatory aisle and bowed to the president as he entered the small nave, doffing his top hat and adjusting the spectacles balancing perilously on his nose.

As the ecstatic townsfolk filed back into their pews, Glassford stepped in front of the altar and raised the hand of the diminutive priest into the air in triumph. *"Nous américaine rendre hommage au saint prêtre dans toute la France!"*

Just declared the holiest priest in all of France, the diminutive cleric wiped tears from his face, which was lit with an expression suggesting that Heaven would only be a close second to this proud moment.

The next ten minutes passed in a flurry of French exaltations and effusive professions of gratitude. When, at last, the Schoolmaster finished his canned speech in English, translated to French by Glassford, the American entourage turned to march out of the church before their charade was discovered.

Trailing Hadenworth with the honor guard, Glassford was stopped at the front door by the shout of *"Arrêter!"* He turned to find the chief military gendarme of the province standing at the sacristy. Glancing worriedly at Chaffee, who was looking over his shoulder for the quickest escape route, he began rehearsing in his mind the explanation he would have to give Pershing for this international incident, not to mention what the American newspapers would say about a general who gave orders to impersonate President Wilson.

The burly gendarme walked past the altar and down the aisle. Fixing his agate eyes hard on his captured prey, he bellowed, "General Glassford!"

Glassford heard a couple of his men behind him ratchet the bolts in their rifles. With his hands behind his back, he motioned for them to stay calm. "How can I help you, *monsieur*?"

"You can do me the favor of aborting your departure."

Glassford swallowed hard. "I am sorry, but I must return the president to Paris immediately."

The chief gendarme's stern frown gave way to a knowing smile. "*Oui*, of course you must. *Mais d'abord*, we have some business to attend." He turned and nodded at one of his police officers standing guard at the sacristy door.

Another French officer came strolling in from the vestry with a puppy bounding up on a leash. The chief gendarme took the wiggling puppy and placed it into Glassford's arms. "In gratitude for your kindness and sacrifice to France, the people of the Haute-Marne wish to make a gift to you." As the villagers applauded loudly, the officer elaborated. "He is bred from the finest military police dogs in our history."

The generous gesture struck Glassford mute. Finally, regaining his voice, he managed, "It has been our honor to come over and repay our debt to your nation for helping us gain our independence." The puppy licked his cheek, drawing laughter from the men. "Does he have a name?"

"Renauld de Chaubert. But now he should have an American name."

The puppy wiggled from Glassford's embrace, and to the horror of the villagers, ran at the president and clawed at his pant cuffs, as if sniffing out a crime. The Schoolteacher, still impersonating the president, reached down to pat its head, but the puppy snapped at his hand and barked him away.

"He'll have no problem becoming an American!" Glassford reassured the worried villagers. "We don't cotton much to authority, either."

"He's a scrapper, all right," the Schoolteacher said, forgetting his role as the fake Wilson. He quickly returned to a Virginia uppercrust accent. "A fine pedigree, indeed. Presidential in fact."

"Scrapper!" Glassford announced to the congregation, taking a cue from the Schoolteacher's observation. "I hereby dub him 'Scrapper' because he fights with all of the verve and *élan* of his French forefathers!"

With that valedictory drawing another frenzy of acclamation, Glassford seized the chance to hurry the top-hatted Schoolteacher out of the church and into the waiting sedan. The French children ran after the procession, fated to tell *their* children and grandchildren how the great American leader who fought the war to end all wars had once visited their village.

That evening, at the reception in Montigny-le-Roi honoring the generals of the American Expeditionary Force, Glassford was introduced to President Wilson in the greeting line.

"Mr. President," Glassford said. "I have a confession to make."

"I'm no priest," warned the president. "Although the Republicans certainly think I belong locked in a monastery."

"This is the first you've heard of it, sir, but this afternoon you made a speech in the village of Vicq, about fifty miles from here. I'm afraid the Almighty whispered a promise to the elderly monsignor there that his congregation would receive a special blessing from you."

Breaking a rare grin, the president raised his glass in a toast. "That is why we won this war, General Glassford. Americans refuse to wait for their commanders to tell them what must be done. In no other army could such a thing occur."

"Yes, sir. The boys did us proud."

Wilson savored another sip of his cognac. "We must enjoy these spirits while we can, General. The Prohibitionists have the votes in Congress to pass the Eighteenth Amendment. Our men may be coming home to a dry reward."

"Well, sir, the Lord managed to turn water into wine. I'm confident the veterans of the AEF will find a way to quench their thirst."

The president smiled. "You may have a career in politics. I could use another good speechwriter."

"I'm afraid I wouldn't last long in Washington, sir."

"And why is that?"

"I don't do well in crocodile swamps."

35

HOHR-GRENZHAUSEN, GERMANY
JANUARY 1919

Idaho winters could turn the Devil blue, but on this night Walter Waters was prepared to concede the prize for the coldest place on Earth to this desolate Hun city and its miserable stretch of cracked concrete pavement that he and Toddy Berks had been assigned to patrol. It was so damn frigid that he had to keep wiping the brim of his helmet to prevent the icicles from dropping like miniature spears through his nose. He couldn't even bend the soles of his frozen boots, a sorry state that now forced him to scoot warily along the glaze like a decrepit old ice skater.

Since landing over here a year ago, he had been laboring under the assumption that soldiers got to go home after winning a war. But Black Jack Pershing had decided to cross the Rhine and keep several regiments stationed at the bridgeheads to insure that the ghosts of the German army didn't somehow miraculously invade the Paris cafés and whorehouses. Last-in-last-out was the policy for this new occupation force, and it was just his daggum luck that the 146th Field Artillery Regiment had been one of the last units to cross the pond.

"You thinkin' what I'm thinkin'?" Berks asked him.

Waters huffed at the insufferable half-Injun shavetail who had arrived to join the regiment earlier that week from somewhere in the jungle of Appalachia. "How the hell would I k-k-know what you're th-th-thinking?"

"In the short time I've known you, Dubya, you've impressed me as the pondering type."

"Why don't you p-p-ponder the various and sundry ways you might shut your t-t-trap."

"Take it easy, for Christ's sake, I'm just trying to pass the time. What's gotten a burr under your saddle?"

"I'm not accustomed to p-p-partnering up with the town crier who goes rattling down the street like a t-t-tinker dragging his wares."

Berks lifted the small burlap sack tied to his belt. "This is gonna make my fortune, Dubya. People back in Wheeling were saying this is the last war ever gonna be fought. I'm telling you, these relics will be worth their weight in bullion some day."

"What the hell have you g-g-got in there?"

Berks peered into his stash and proudly rattled off the list of booty as if he were the lord high treasurer giving accountancy to the king. "Five Hun shoulder patches. Two belt buckles. Some letters in Bocheese. A bolo knife. And the crown jewel of the collection—a very hard-to-find trench grenade, certified as the genu-wine article from one of those Kraut prisoners we patted down on the train last week. This here pineapple would rearrange the heads and shoulders of an entire Berlin storm-trooping regiment."

"What the hell would you know about s-s-storm-trooping?"

"I went through training."

"Training? For what? How to p-p-piss into a latrine?"

"I don't have to take this abuse! Not from a goddamn medic who never fired—" Berks stopped himself, apparently remembering that his patrol companion was a sergeant, even if nobody in the regiment gave that rank much consideration.

"Never fired what?"

"You gonna bust me if I say it?"

Waters dropped the rifle from his shoulder and leaned it against the wall of an abandoned storefront. "I'm g-g-gonna bust you if you d-d-don't say, and real quick."

Berks took a step back to be safe. "The old-timers in the regiment said you wouldn't even put a bullet in your best buddy to save him a slow death."

"That ain't the way it h-h-happened!"

Berks raised his hands in a plea for Waters to calm down. "I ain't making any judgment, Dubya. I mighta done the same thing. It's just, I don't take kindly to gettin' my hide rode because I didn't get sent over here before the fighting stopped."

Waters started down their patrol route again, checking the locks on the doors and making sure there were no German deserters or Army grifters hiding out in the crevices. It was two hours past curfew, and this part of town, towered over by a giant ceramics factory that was abandoned during the war, looked pretty quiet. He kept his thoughts to himself as they walked in silence, except for the relics in Berks's sack rattling behind them on the sidewalk.

After several minutes, Berks risked another question, "They ever find him?"

"Find who?"

"Your friend who got devoured by the mud."

Waters felt one of his blinding migraines coming on. And his lungs were burning again, not helped by the cold air. He hadn't felt himself since that gassing fiasco with the baseball immortals, but he passed it off as just the effects of the grippe spreading around camp. When he managed to open his eyes from the pounding throbs, he found Berks still waiting for an answer. "You looking to d-d-dig him up and t-t-take him home for a souvenir, too?"

"No cause for that. I was just wondering, is all."

Tears began to freeze on his lids. "I never went b-b-back to look for him."

Berks shook his head. "Some farmer's gonna plow him up one day."

"Reckon."

"Tell me if I'm way out of the barn, here, Dubya, but I'd kick myself if I went back home not asking you.… What'd he look like just before he went under?"

"It was too d-d-damn d-d-dark to see."

Berks stared down at the pavement as if trying to see into the depths of Hades. "The farmer who digs him up is the only one who's ever gonna know. He'll be the lone witness to that poor fella's last expression of despair before he—"

A scream came from somewhere in the darkness, followed by a man's bark of what sounded like an order in German.

Waters grabbed his rifle and motioned for Berks to button his mouth. They stalked the source of the cry, angling from corner to corner. More shouts in German came from an alley to their left. Waters checked the shells in his rifle and clicked on the new mechanical flashlight he had been issued. The beam illuminated a bedraggled mob of boys and elderly women hovering over what appeared to be a bum sitting cornered in the alley. He motioned Berks up, and together they walked into the alley for a better look. There, caught by the light, was the German scum beating the poor homeless wretch and tearing buttons and swatches from his shirt and pants. He shouted at the thieving bastards, "S-s-stop!"

The gang of emaciated Germans in rags reacted like a pack of coyotes caught over the carcass of a wounded deer. One of the women turned and, flashing what was left of her teeth in a gesture of threat, snarled, "*Verräter!*"

Berks nervously fingered his rifle. "What's she saying?"

"I don't know."

The German boys in the stalk pack backed away, but the mother superior of the wretches stood her ground. She made a motion that appeared to mimic someone stabbing her in the back.

"This m-m-man attacked you?" Waters asked her.

The hag spat on the downed man who lay sitting against the brick wall. She and the others scrambled off into a warren, kicking him as they passed.

"Shit," Berks whispered. "The Kaiser shoulda put those *fräuleins* in his army."

They edged closer to see if the attacked man was injured.

Waters angled the flashlight and got a full glimpse. The fellow was in a German officer's uniform, and an Iron Cross, awarded for valor in battle, hung from his left breast. His face was bloodied and his frayed tunic with black stiff collar had been pecked at until it looked like the hide of a molted buck. He pulled out his canteen and offered the officer a drink of water. "Hey, pal. Why d-d-didn't you fight those horseflies off?"

The officer just stared at him with deadened eyes.

Waters dropped the beam of the flashlight to below the officer's belt to check for weapons. "Sonofabitch."

Berks backed away. "He only has one leg."

Enraged at how the crippled officer had been abused, Waters stood up fingering his rifle and searched the alley.

"Why'd they do this to him, Dubya?"

"Must have been some of them B-b-bolshevik bastards."

Berks helped the officer take another drink from the canteen. "Boys and women? They didn't look like Bolshies to me."

"They're all starving. Guess they g-g-gotta blame somebody for losing the war. The K-k-kaiser scampers off to hide, so the soldiers are all that's left to be s-s-scapegoats."

"Goddamn Hun!" Berks cursed. "We're lucky to be American, Dubya. Not that we'll ever lose a war, but the folks back home would never do this to us."

"The Lord has b-b-blessed us, all right."

When the officer was finished drinking, Berks screwed the cap back on the canteen. "What are we going to do with him?"

"Hell if I know. He needs a hot m-m-meal. We can try to r-r-rustle that up for him, I s'pose."

Berks untied the sack from his belt. He dropped its contents and began rummaging through them. "I think I got a can of Hun beans in here some-where. We can heat it up to tide him over."

The German officer enlivened at seeing the cache of souvenirs. Unable to speak English, he pointed at the pile.

"What's he want?" Berks asked.

Waters shrugged. "Not sure."

The German officer unpinned the Iron Cross from his breast and offered it to Berks.

"Holy Toledo!" Berks cried. "He's *giving* it to me? A German medal? You know how much that'll fetch, Dubya?"

Waters noticed the officer kept glancing at Berks's collection of war parapher-nalia. "He ain't giving it to you. I think he wants to t-t-trade it for something."

Berks rifled through his stash. "Ain't nothing in here worth an Iron Cross."

The officer struggled to reach the relic that he desperately wanted. Unable to crawl, he kept pointing.

Berks picked up several of the relics, until he found the one the German desired—the hand grenade.

"What's he want *that* for, Dubya?"

"Beats me, but you ain't g-g-giving it to him. I don't trust him."

"He ain't gonna blow us up. We're the only ones helping him."

"Forget it."

"I want that Iron Cross."

"I said it ain't happening. Th-th-that's an order."

Berks looked longingly at the medal just hanging like ripe fruit on the officer's uniform. "I got an idea. We'll keep our rifles trained on him as we back away. Then, when we're at the mouth of the alley, I'll roll the grenade to him. He can't do nothin' to us then."

Waters stomped his feet, his brain nearly frozen into a stupor. "I dunno."

"Look at him, Dubya. I think it has sentimental value for him."

"And the Iron Cross d-d-don't?"

"That medal was given to him by the very government elected by those assholes who just tried to beat him into sausage. No wonder he don't want it no more. It has more value to me than him. Come on, Dubya. It's the free market. That's why we fought this war, ain't it? To save the world for capitalism?"

Waters was just too damn cold to care anymore. "Maybe he wants it to f-f-fight off those wolves if they c-c-come back. Not a bad ending for 'em, I'd have to agree." He removed his overcoat and put it over the German officer. "Listen up, partner. We can't carry you out in your present state of health, so we're g-g-gonna let the MPs know you're here. Don't know if it'll do you any g-g-good, but maybe you'll get some grub, at least. Now, here's the plan." He pointed at the Iron Cross and told the officer, "You're g-g-gonna give that to Berksie here." He pointed at the end of the alley and made an underhand gesture, like bowling at pins. "We'll roll the memento of your service to you, understand?"

The officer took in enough of Waters's Injun signals to get his drift. He removed the Iron Cross, glanced at it one last time with tears in his eyes, and handed it to Berks.

"All right, then." Waters motioned Berks to back away with him. "You hang in there tonight, fella. K-k-keep the blood moving. If those harpies c-c-come at you again, you tell them the United States Army is on the hunt for them."

When they reached the far end of the alley, Waters checked the grenade to make sure the safety on the pin was set, then he nodded to Berks. "Give it a tumble."

Berks grinned with anticipation of his fortune as he took aim down the dark alley and underhanded the grenade like a Sicilian playing bocce ball. Waters flipped off the flashlight and listened to the thud of the rolling until it stopped. In the distance, he heard a weak voice rasp:

"*Danke.*"

As they walked away, Berks slapped Waters on the back and packed the Iron Cross in his pocket for safekeeping. "What'd I tell ya, Dubya. No sweat."

"Yeah, you're a regular Clemenceau with the peace negotiations. Quite a f-f-feat bartering down a gimp."

"I'm telling ya, I think I got a talent for the trading profession. Maybe I should look into joining one of those Wall Street brokers and—"

An explosion rocked the buildings behind them.

Ducking their heads under their arms, they turned and saw a cloud of debris settling over the alley they had just left. When the dust finally settled, Waters flipped on the flashlight again. He ran back down the narrow passage.

He turned and retched.

The limbs and organs of the dead German officer—who had just committed suicide—lay splattered along the bloody wall.

36

PICARDY, FRANCE
JANUARY 1919

Spotting a wooden observation tower rising high atop a snow-dusted slope, Colonel Patton banged his shillelagh against his orderly's foot on the accelerator. "Stop here."

Joe Angelo pulled their military staff car off the road and cut the engine. He protested weakly when his superior officer threw open the side door and removed the pillow that he had been sitting on to help ease the pressure on his rectal wound. "Sir, the doctors made me promise. I'm not supposed to let you out of the car."

Patton waved off Angelo's plea. Growling and grunting, he struggled to slide his feet to the ground. "The damn physics didn't do anything for me when I was bleeding to death out here. Now help me get out of this car and on that tower."

Angelo had figured this trip was a bad idea from the start. But the Colonel was such a pestering bore during his recuperation that the doctors at Bourg finally agreed to allow him a day's visit to the British battlefields on the Somme, just to get rid of him for a few hours. Now, Angelo realized, the Colonel somehow expected to get up the stairs of that rickety duck blind. He supported the officer with each painful step, until they finally staggered up to the highest level of the observation tower.

Breathing hard, Patton braced against the railing and swept his gaze across the panorama of small copses and rye fields. In the distance, the gray horizon reached toward the port of Calais and the English Channel. "This ground look familiar to you, Angelo?"

"No, sir."

"By god, it should."

Angelo was worried that the pain medication might be playing tricks with the Colonel's mind again. "Sir, I don't think we've ever been here before."

"I remember it like it was yesterday." The Colonel gritted his teeth, as if reliving a painful memory. "This is where the windmill stood."

Angelo wondered how he was going to drag the officer back down those stairs if the Colonel suffered one of his fainting spells. "Sir, I'm not sure these heights are good for your head."

"Edward the Third set his headquarters right here. He divided his outnumbered army into three divisions. That goddamn sonofabitch was a gambler, Angelo! Put his son in charge of one of those units. The Black Prince was only sixteen. Goddamn that sonofabitch Edward was a gambler!"

Angelo didn't have a clue what the Colonel was talking about, but he had learned from experience that when his superior got into one of his mystical moods, it was best to just play along. "Yes, sir. A gambler, for sure."

Patton swept his unsteady hand across the crest of the near hill. "Now, over there, that sonofabitch Edward built rows of ditches and pits and filled them with caltrops. Then, he set his Welsh longbowmen in a 'V' formation behind those hidden trenches."

Angelo shrugged. "Sir, what's the name of this place?"

The Colonel looked at him as if he were daft. "Angelo, get your goddam head out of your goddam ass and pay attention! It's Crécy, of course! Thirteen hundred and forty-six. A year that should be blazoned into the memory of every soldier."

Angelo hadn't heard of any battle on the Somme called Crécy, and certainly not one where the Brits shot arrows instead of bullets.

"This was where chivalry died, Angelo. This is where it all changed."

"Changed, sir?"

"War, goddamn it! Plate-piercing firepower was invented on this very ground. The French knights were cut to pieces in the thousands by the English arrows. By god, it was a sight to behold. When their armored horses gave out, they tried to charge up that high ground in the mud." Patton turned and shouted as if in the battle that very moment. "Mud, Angelo! That sound at all familiar to you? Goddamn mud up to our knees!"

The officer now seemed to be caroming back and forth between centuries. Angelo checked the bottle of medications in his pocket that the doctors had supplied. He feared he had given the Colonel too many pills.

Patton looked to the heavens as if greeting old departed friends. "Once again, I smell the heat sparks when my Flemish plate gave way. And the lance ripped through my entrails as on Crécy's field I lay."

"Sir?"

"A few verses of a poem I've been working on. Did I ever tell you about my first military maneuver, Angelo?"

"No, sir."

"I don't confide it to many people. Only the ones I trust. Most mortals think I'm just making it all up, but I swear to God it's true. When I was a small boy in California, I was playing war games with my cousins. I loaded all five of them in a small wagon and armed them with the bottoms of barrels to use for shields. Then I shoved that armored ramming vehicle down the hill. They pierced the turkey shed like a knife through butter and mangled a few poults in the process. But it was a hell of an assault, Angelo! Hell of an assault."

"Yes, sir."

"You know where I first witnessed that tactic?"

"Can't say I do, sir."

Patton pointed to the lowest point in the valley. "Down there in that hollow. King John of Bohemia fought alongside King Philip and the French that day. The sonofabitching Bohemian was blind, Angelo! Did you hear me? He joined the assault and he was *blind*. Now, here he tried the same tactic that had worked against the Turks years before. He set plates of iron along the sides of his wagons and pushed them into the breach. The sonofabitch invented the goddamn tank, Angelo! And because I was there to witness the marvel, I resurrected the tank to defeat the Hun in *our* war. You see how life comes full circle? The Bohemian sent his wagons against the Turks! And I sent my wagon against the turkeys!"

Angelo was about to laugh, but just in the nick he realized that the Colonel was dead serious. Baffled at how anyone could get a wagon plated with iron up that hill, he asked the Colonel, "If this King of Bohemia was blind, sir, how'd he know where to charge and swing his sword?"

Patton grinned and patted his orderly on the head, as if he had just stumbled upon a secret of the ages. "The King's squire led him by the hand across the battlefield. Never left his side. They both died at the hands of the English, arm in arm." He kept staring at Angelo, boring in on him as if there was something else deeper on his mind. "You sure this ground doesn't look familiar to you, son?"

"I'd be lying if I said it did, sir."

Patton sighed heavily. Slumping, he gazed across the grassy terrain and asked wistfully, "What are we going to do with ourselves, Angelo, now that it's all over?"

"I'll probably go back to my old job shoveling nitrate at the powder plant."

Patton firmed his jaw. "You're a lucky man. You have no aspirations. My life, on the other hand, is over. I'll probably die soon and reincarnate when the next war clouds gather in the heavens. I was trained to fight. There won't be another gathering of killer angels like this one. Not in my lifetime."

"It's been an honor serving you, sir."

Patton braced Angelo affectionately with a hand to his shoulder. "I didn't bring you all the way out here for another history lesson. I've got something to give you before you head home. Those asswipes at Chaumont usually deliver these by courier, but I pulled some strings to do it right." He reached into the inside of his breast pocket and pulled out a small, flat box.

Angelo accepted the box and opened it. Inside lay a medal that featured an eagle on a cross, hanging from a ribbon of blue and red. "What's this, sir?"

"The Distinguished Service Cross."

Angelo stared at the award in disbelief. "But I didn't do nothing."

"You saved my life. Just like that loyal squire who served King John of Bohemia to the end, you never left my side, not even when the firing got hotter than the arrows on this field. If you ever need anything, Angelo, you just let me know. Should we never meet again in this lifetime, we will join hands in the next to do battle with the forces of Evil."

Angelo stood at attention while Patton pinned the medal on his chest. "I don't know what to say, sir."

"For starters, you can say something to those birds at the War Department. Maybe tell them that your superior officer deserves a goddamn Medal of Honor for what *he* went through."

Angelo grinned. "Yes, sir. I can say that, all right."

Patton unpinned the DSC award from Angelo's shirt and put it back in its box. "I pulled a few strings to bring it out here and flash it to you early. The desk brass will do the official honors back at HQ."

"Yes, sir."

"Let's head back to Bourg, my brave squire. I've got another battlefield to show you on the way. You ever heard of Joan of Arc?"

"Who hasn't, sir?"

"One hell of a tough broad. I taught her how to use a sword." Patton closed his eyes to recall another stanza of his poem that he had penned about his many incarnations as a warrior. "'In the form of many people, in all panoplies of time. Have I seen the luring vision, of the Victory Maid, sublime.'"

37

BORDEAUX, FRANCE
JANUARY 1919

Anna stood alone on the upper deck of the steamship *La Lorraine* and watched the Aquitaine coast slowly recede from view. The other passengers, mostly American soldiers and Red Cross nurses bound for New York Harbor, were still in the dining room below, finishing their meals and discussing plans for their new lives in the States. But she'd had no appetite for either food or conversation for days, not since leaving those wounded men at Rimacourt. She burned into her memory the vanishing spires of France. So many nights she had lain awake dreaming of escaping the slaughter here. Yet now that the blessed release had finally arrived, she felt no elation or hope, only a deep loneliness. The idle chatting of strangers, particularly those who had not been at the Front, caused her to become so quick-tempered and sensitive that she was constantly driven to seek solitude. An unrelenting darkness stalked her now, and the only relief she could find was to pace the promenade, keeping her mind fixed on the next step. The crew thought her so odd that they called her the "Praying Ghost" behind her back.

Little did they know. She hadn't prayed in over a year.

She kept her head bowed as she made her way briskly past the rows of lifeboats and the rear boiler turret. A sentry walking the opposite direction nodded to her with a suspicious look, no doubt wondering why she was out in the wind on such a cold night. She kept walking, not wishing to explain herself to another sailor who had never stepped foot in a trench. The newly arrived recruits, sent after the Armistice to help transport the veterans back home, were the most insufferable, with their talk of disappointment at having missed—

She tripped on something in her path and stumbled to the deck.

"Oh, my Lord!" cried a woman's voice. "Are you hurt?"

She looked up from her hands and knees to find two identical faces staring down at her. She blinked several times, worried that a hit to the head had given her double vision. Two young women sat huddled together, arm in arm, on a tarpaulin roll occluded in a shadowed recess along the wheelhouse. The sun had fallen below the watery horizon, and what little light was available now came from a lantern near the stern. Climbing to her feet for a better angle, she discovered that the two women were both wearing the gray uniform of Red Cross volunteers. Were they twins? They were slender and had bagged eyes full of fatigue and sad, thin mouths. Her first impression was of two wet ducklings, lost and snuggling together to stay warm.

"We are so sorry," said one of the women, sounding nervous and distraught. "We always sit with our legs extended when we compose."

"Compose?"

The woman who had spoken hid a journal behind her back. "It is nothing. I am Gladys. This is my sister, Dorothea."

Anna introduced herself and shook their trembling hands. She noticed that Dorothea kept her gaze down, unwilling to make eye contact. At their feet lay several pieces of crumpled paper torn from the journal that Gladys held behind her back. As if sensing her curiosity, Gladys kicked the fragments of paper to the wind and tucked the journal into a crevice under the tarp roll. She thought about moving on, avoiding further conversation, but something caused her to feel protective over these two fragile spirits. "It's very cold out to be sitting and not moving."

Gladys drew closer to her twin; their movements were so mutually anticipated that they seemed almost joined in one body. "It's quiet here."

"I understand."

Gladys observed her uniform coat. "You are a nurse."

She nodded. "Where were you stationed?"

"We started as canteeners at Châlons," Gladys said. "After a few months, they transferred us to an evacuation hospital near Verdun."

"You saw some of the worst, then. Where is home?"

"Manhattan," Gladys revealed with no enthusiasm.

Dorothea spoke up for the first time. "Do you know how many knots the ship will be moving when we clear the harbor?"

Anna found that a very odd question, particularly from someone she had just met. "I don't, sorry. I suppose we could ask the captain."

"No!" Gladys insisted, squeezing her sister's hand to admonish her.

She was taken aback by the sudden forcefulness of the reply.

"We wouldn't want to bother him," Gladys explained, trying to allay Anna's confusion. "He is much too busy to answer the questions of stupid girls."

"You're hardly stupid girls. How old are you?"

"Twenty-two," said Gladys.

Anna smiled sadly. "I'm an old maid compared to the two of you."

Dorothea seemed to grow a bit more comfortable in her presence, and she scooted over to make space on the tarp roll. "Would you like to come out of the wind?"

Anna squeezed in next to the twins and buttoned up her collar. "It gets colder the farther we sail from port."

Dorothea watched the waves. "The water looks freezing."

"I came over in the summer," Anna said. "It was much more pleasant then."

The three of them sat the next several minutes in silence, listening to the lap of the white caps against the iron plating and watching the marine layer clouds slowly efface the stars overhead.

Anna could not explain why, but suddenly she felt the presence of death, a curse of intuition that she had developed from the many night shifts in the *morte de salle*. Her predictions about which patients would not make it through the night had become so accurate that she had gained a reputation for being somewhat of a soothsayer. During their off-duty hours, many of the nurses used to come to her begging to know about their loved ones back home. But she had refused to engage in any form of clairvoyance, knowing that it was condemned in the Bible. Still, she could not understand why the Almighty had burdened her with such a gift, if it was forbidden. She tried to shake off the black feeling, dismissing it as just weariness.

Out of the blue, Gladys asked her, "You have a *beau?*"

These two girls are certainly forthright, Anna thought. "Yes, but…"

"But what?"

Her throat gripped when she tried to explain. "I can't see his face. I don't know why, but I can't for the life of me remember what he looks like."

Gladys cupped a palm over Anna's hand. "There have been too many faces."

"I don't know… if I still love him. I don't know if I can feel at all."

Gladys stared off into the water. "That would be a blessing."

Stunned, Anna looked up at her through tears. "Not to love?"

"Not to feel…. It would be such a blessing not to feel." Gladys drew her sister closer and rested their heads together. "At the hospital in Verdun, there was this boy from Nebraska. We can't get *his* face out of our memory. He was the most beautiful and gentle soul we ever met. They brought him in with a stomach wound. One night, he hemorrhaged horribly. The doctors managed to bring him back. But after that night, he was terrified to be left alone. He got well enough to walk, and all day and night, he would follow us around, afraid that he would start bleeding again and die when no one was with him."

You must protect yourself, Anna.

Again she heard Helen's voice of warning, the one that always came to her in times of vulnerability. She wiped the tears from her eyes and whispered, "You both fell in love with him."

The twin sisters nodded, unable to speak of it further.

Anna hugged them, and at that moment—just why she could not explain—she accepted the painful truth that she had tried to deny these many months: She could never marry Micah. No man would ever be able to fill the void in her heart left by those soldiers she had nursed.

"How quickly can they turn the ship around?" Dorothea asked.

Anna was roused from her melancholy, astonished again by Dorothea's penchant for odd questions at the most inappropriate moments. "Did you forget something at the port?"

The twins kept staring at the horizon, as if not having heard her.

From their retreat into silence, Anna sensed that they now wished to be alone. She stood and took their hands in hers again. "Should you ever need anything, I live on a farm in Raglesville, Indiana. My father's name is Jacob Raber. I hope you'll write to me."

The twins would not release her hands. Finally, Gladys brought Anna's palm to her heart and pressed it against her overcoat. "Come walk with us."

You must protect yourself, Anna.

"Thank you, but I should go in now." She escaped their clutching hands and turned to make her way toward the stairwell door, about fifty yards down the promenade. Halfway there, she was nearly felled again by the same heavy feeling of doom. She managed to recover her sea legs and pressed on against the wind howling around her ears. She walked down the stairs to the lower forecastle deck and searched the numbers on the rooms.

Suddenly, she thought she heard a scream, faint but chilling. She stopped to listen. There was no echo, so she shrugged it off as just one of the crew giving orders for the drawing in of the riggings.

A half hour later, Anna, sitting near the hearth in the reading room for light, was startled from her study of the *Martyr's Mirror* by a sounding of the warning whistle from the stern.

The sentry she had passed earlier that night came running down the hall toward the dining lounge. "Overboard!" he shouted. "Overboard!

Her limbs went cold with fear.

She rushed back down the hall and up the stairwell, then hurried as fast as she could down the promenade deck toward the stern. The sailors were hovering over the rail with their telescope glasses, searching the foam being churned up by the propellers. The other passengers climbed up from the stairwells to see why the warning whistle had been blasted.

She hurried to a crewman. "What happened?"

"The two ladies jumped."

She ran to the railing and frantically searched the black waves. The ship was moving so fast that she could no longer see the lights from the port now. The deck was a pandemonium of panic as a crewman rushed to the forecastle to inform the captain of the overboards.

The captain came marching toward the stern. "Did anybody see them?"

"I spoke to them only twenty minutes ago," Anna said. "They said their names were Gladys and Dorothea."

A groan swept the huddled passengers, and the captain narrowed his gaze to search the ship's churning wake.

One of the crew asked him, "Should we turn it around, sir?"

The captain shook his head and kept staring off toward the east.

Anna finally managed to find her voice again. "Who were they?"

The captain seemed astonished by her question. "The Cromwell twins. I thought everybody on board knew them."

Before she could ask him why, he hurried off, shouting orders to his officers to keep on the westbound course, leaving the overboards to their fate.

A male passenger next to her lit a cigarette and offered it to her, but she refused it. Seeing her so shaken, he explained the captain's decision. "We've been running at eighteen knots. We're five miles away from the spot they'd be. Even if we went back, there's no way we could find them in time."

She pressed a fist to her mouth. Could she have prevented them from jumping? Why had she not detected the desperation in their voices? Had she become so familiar with death that it now seemed normal? Blind with grief, she whispered, "They seemed so gentle."

The man nodded. "Damn shame. They were the daughters of Fredrick Cromwell, the industrialist. They had a fortune waiting for them in New York." He took another puff from the cigarette and shrugged. "I suppose any one of us on this ship might have done the same thing. Hell of a world." He crushed the cigarette under his heel and walked back to the lounge.

Left alone on the stern, Anna collapsed, sobbing, to the tarp roll. As she leaned against the bridge, she looked down and saw Gladys's journal abandoned behind the tarp. Had the twin sister hidden it in the crease there? She pulled the notebook out. Opening it, she angled under the lantern's light, hoping to find some explanation for why the two sisters jumped. But only one page had been left in the journal. The other pages, she realized, had been torn out and ripped to shreds.

Had they contained attempts by Gladys to write suicide notes? She looked down at the last page. It contained a poem titled *The Mould*:

No doubt this active will,
So bravely steeped in sun,
This will has vanquished Death
And foiled oblivion
But this indifferent clay,
This fine experienced hand,
So quiet, and these thoughts
That all finished stand,
Feel Death as though it were
A shadowy caress;
And win and wear a frail
Archaic wistfulness.

She clutched what remained of the journal to her breast, feeling the shadowy caresses around her again.

You must protect yourself, Anna.

38

I WANT **YOU**
FOR U.S. ARMY

MANHATTAN, NEW YORK
FEBRUARY 1919

"Not this day, no sir."

As Ozzie waited for Big Jim to send him and the other Harlem Hellfighters up the Canyon of Champions, he kept whispering that vow of resistance at the Irish cop who was glaring vinegar at him from across the barricaded street. The morning was so bitterly cold that he figured not many would show up to see them returned home anyway. Behind him, he could hear the men in the regimental band cleaning their spit valves and blowing the stale out of their horns. He had the urge to rush back there and wish the tune boys good luck, but that cop looked downright pugilistic. Apparently the fuming paddy hadn't been given an adequate explanation for why the governor would allow three thousand uniformed Negroes armed with rifles to march past the department stores and homes of upstanding white folk.

Word back in France was that the Army brass had sent orders to the military police to get rough with the uppity Negroes and put them back in their place before they got home. The MPs had been ordered not to salute black officers, and some of the men had gotten the Jim Crow treatment at the train station in Brest. But when the white goons had tried to make them wait to go last on the gangway to the ship, Big Jim would have none of it. On their last day in France, the lieutenant had loomed over the white officer in charge, greeting him with a smile that wasn't a smile at all, but a warning that the regiment had one more battle left in it if required.

Not this day, no sir.

That's what Big Jim had told the troublemaking cracker.

The 369th had been the only regiment in the AEF not to get a sendoff parade before the war. Denied entry into the Forty-Second Division, they'd been told that black was not one of the colors of the Rainbow. To lift their spirits, Colonel Hayward had promised them a parade on their return home, even if they had to fight their way up Fifth Avenue. They had served the longest of any American unit and were the first to reach the Rhine. Throughout their ordeal, they had never given up an inch of ground. Hadn't lost a man captured, either. First into the trenches, first back home.

Nobody, not even the city's finest in blue, was going to deny them their due today.

There it was, Big Jim's whistle. And off they went, marching the seven miles up the most famous boulevard in the world, their hobnailed boots throwing off sparks and the glints from their bayonets calling down the shining angels to accompany them.

Moving in lockstep, Ozzie turned a conquering grin over his shoulder and shouted at the surly Irish cop still eyeing him, "Not this day! No, sir!"

Set in the French phalanx style, with sixteen men abreast and twelve deep, the regiment glided toward a pavilion of dignitaries just beyond Fifty-Ninth Street. Colonel Hayward, still favoring the broken leg that he had suffered in the Meuse-Argonne, limped ahead of them in the van. The standard-bearer at his side waved the blue regimental banner decorated with the Croix de Guerre. Next came Henry Johnson, who rode alone in an open touring car, an honor granted because he had won the Distinguished Service Cross. Behind them came a fleet of ambulances carrying two hundred wounded Hellfighters.

The regiment turned north at Twenty-Fifth Street, and Ozzie teared up on seeing the manifestation of a glorious miracle: Hundreds of thousands jammed both sides of the avenue as far as the eye could see. Black folk in the hundreds—some from the San Juan Hill District, others who had splurged on taxis from Harlem—ran alongside the motorcade to shout at their heroes. Here above these sidewalks where he had danced and played for coins as a boy, every balcony and window shimmered with the Stars and Strips. Negroes stood next to whites, and mothers held up their babies and broke through the barricades to kiss the men. Some women wore the black armbands with gold stars given to the relatives of those fifteen-hundred men who would remain forever underground in France.

He couldn't help but think back about how it all started with a ragtag militia practicing with broomsticks on their shoulders in the park. He stole another glance behind him. Big Jim, still coughing and weak from the pneumonia, was strutting and cutting the air with his drum major's mace.

A black lady tossed a bouquet of lilies into the lead car and swooned. "Oh, you wicked Henry Johnson! Oh, you handsome Black Death!"

"Looks like a funeral, Henry!" shouted a black businessman.

Grinning, Johnson stood in the car and pointed at his old friends. "Funeral for them Germans, Burton! Sure is a funeral for the Boche, all right!"

Ozzie thought nothing could heighten the delirium, but as they reached the Arch of Victory, Big Jim and his ninety tune boys broke into a rendition of the *Le Régiment de Sambre et Meuse*, the anthem that had launched millions of *poilus* into battle. The Boss was sending a message to these white folks in the richest part of the city: The French had welcomed them to their sides when the white American doughboys had refused to fight with them. Showered by wrapped candies and packs of cigarettes, Ozzie felt a lift in his step as the saxophones behind him put some hot sauce on the gumbo and the thirty percussion boys kicked in with the drums captured from the Germans in Alsace.

For another two hours, it was all a blur of cheers and blared notes and kisses and speeches. And then came a change in the air: collards were cooking in some kitchen somewhere up ahead. The band broke into *Here Comes My Daddy Now,* and Ozzie, having lost all track of time and place in the haze of memories and aged faces, looked up at the sign for the next cross street.

One-Hundred-and-Tenth.... They had reached the outskirts of Harlem.

A whistle blew, and the parade jolted to a stop. Big Jim walked up from his position at the rear of the procession and nodded to Colonel Hayward, who returned the gesture. As the Boss came towering over Ozzie, the crowds along the street, almost all black now, fell silent, wondering why the festivities had come to a halt.

"You don't look properly armed, Private Taylor."

Ozzie stole at glance down at the bolt of his rifle and tried to figure out what component he had failed to clean this time. "Sorry, sir."

"Private Hazard!" Big Jim shouted over his shoulder. "Step out."

Ben Hazard made a crisp right turn from the phalanx and came marching up to Big Jim.

"Trade arms with Taylor here."

Hazard snapped his weapon right front. He lowered it slowly to the asphalt, unzipped the canvas case it was stored in—and pulled out an oboe.

Big Jim circled Ozzie. "Did you leave your weapon in France?"

Ozzie was stunned. The Boss had remembered the oboe he abandoned before they hit the trenches with the Frogs. That scary night, he'd finally come to accept that the instrument was useless to him, miserable a player as he was. Besides, he was convinced there was no way it was going to survive all that mud and the fighting. Now, as he took the oboe from Private Hazard and examined it, he saw that the bore had been oiled and kept clean as a whistle. Somebody had taken care of it like a baby all these many months.

"Article Fifteen-Seven of the Army code of conduct!" Big Jim shouted. "Any soldier who leaves his gear unattended will be subject to reprimand! Am I right, Colonel Hayward?"

"Right as always, Lieutenant Europe. Carry on."

Ozzie was about to soil his pants at being called out in front of all these people. Then a thought came to him: If he was being mustered out, what the hell could the Army do to him now?

"You are now transferred to a unit more fitting to your level of competence."

Ozzie's voice cracked with shame. "Sir?"

There was a twinkle in Big Jim's eye. "To the Three Hundredth and Sixty-Ninth Regimental Band."

Ozzie blinked fast, not sure if he had heard correctly.

The men let out a deafening cheer as Big Jim took Ozzie's rifle and thrust the oboe into his hands instead. "Get back there with the woodwinds, Taylor. And if I hear one false note out of you, I'm going make you swim back to France."

Ozzie grinned from ear to ear. His dream had finally come true. He was now an official member of the most famous military band in the world. Protecting the oboe, he hurried off before the Boss could change his mind and, winking at Noble Sissle, squeezed in next to the clarinets.

Big Jim swept his famous wide glare across the crowds, until he found a little girl waving a flag at him. He strode up to the sidewalk, knelt down to her level, and asked her with solemn concern, "Hey, honey child, who's been here since I've been gone?"

On both sides of the street, the crowds hushed to hear the girl's answer.

She kissed Big Jim on the cheek and shouted, "A great big man with a derby on!"

Doffing his helmet, Big Jim arose from his knees and slammed his marching mace against the street like a black Zeus striking a thunderbolt to the earth. With that signal, the soldiers of the 369th changed formations, spreading out into wider lines so that their kinfolk could more easily see their faces. Cued to their grand moment, Ozzie and the band cut loose with the old Southern folk song, *Who's Been Here Since I've Been Gone?*

Unable to hold back their emotions any longer, thousands of family members and loved ones poured past the cops and mobbed their returned sons and husbands in the street. Ozzie and his uniformed buddies eased their military discipline and, with sweethearts and mommas on their arms, put the pepper back into the grinder as they swaggered singing and dancing toward the armory, where they would feast and dance the night away.

Home at last were the Hellfighters of Harlem, those great big men with the steel derbies on.

PARIS, FRANCE
MAY 1919

As Bert Hoover walked across the Place de la Concorde, he glanced up at the Hôtel de Coislin, the palatial edifice where Benjamin Franklin had signed the most important treaty in America's history to gain France's support for American colonial independence. He shook his head at the perverse irony of this location being chosen for his meeting with President Wilson: The two nations were now about to sign another treaty, one that threatened to doom millions of Europeans to starvation.

Earlier that night, he had learned that Clemenceau and the French were insisting the Germans accept new peace terms within seven days, or suffer a renewal of the war. So much for liberty, equality, and the brotherhood of man, he muttered to himself. Perhaps the motto on the pediment of the Pantheon should be changed to *Vengeance est à moi*.

Distraught over this last-minute insertion of more draconian demands, he had been pacing the streets for hours, trying to think of a way to stop the disaster. Once again, the allies had assigned him the thankless task of preventing a famine—this time in Germany and Russia. And once again, the French, goaded on by that rabid British skunk Winston Churchill, were making his job impossible. Woodrow Wilson had come to Europe demanding the Armistice be based on the end of secret alliances and the collective reduction of armaments. Yet in recent weeks, the president had capitulated to the embittered survivors of the Old World, who were setting their ravenous eyes again on the fledgling democratic republics.

He scanned the vast square and tried to imagine the guillotine doing its grisly work there during the French Revolution. Napolean had been the result of that bloodbath, as had every European war since. He turned away, resolved to make one last attempt to convince the president to stand firm on the Fourteen Points and the principles that had brought America into the conflict.

He entered the lobby of the adjacent Hotel Crillon and shook hands with Norman Davis, a fellow member of the American negotiating delegation. He had decided to bring Davis to the meeting for support, hoping the president would listen to the counsel of a seasoned diplomat. They took the elevator to the top floor. After twenty minutes spent waiting in the suite's large drawing room, they heard an adjacent bedroom door hinge open.

"There must be some crisis at hand," rasped a hoarse voice from the shadows. "For that is the only time, like Banquo's ghost, my friend Hoover visits me."

Hoover was alarmed by the president's gaunt appearance. This descendant of severe Scot Covenanters had never been a picture of health, but his white hair had thinned and his cheeks were hollow. Clearly, that political trench-fighter Clemenceau had worn the poor man down with his incessant harangues about French sacrifices. Dangling *pince-nez* glasses from his fleshless nose, the president shuffled with such bated steps that Hoover wondered if he had recently suffered a stroke.

Mrs. Wilson lingered at the bedroom door. "Not long, Mr. Hoover?"

Hoover nodded his acceptance of her request for brevity. He rushed forward to help the president to a waiting chair, and found him staring incomprehensibly at his colleague. "Sir, you remember Norman Davis. He is doing a fine job for us at State."

Wilson showed not a flicker of interest as he limply shook Davis's hand. He motioned his two guests toward the couch, and a servant arrived to pour tea. The president struggled to bring the tremoring cup to his lips. When the difficult task was finally accomplished with only a few drops spilled, he sank back into his chair, enervated from that simple effort.

Hoover started the meeting, knowing he had little time. "Mr. President, how are you feeling?"

"The grippe had its hand on my throat, Bert. But I am much stronger now, thank you."

Much stronger now? Hoover wondered what the man must have looked like when he had been in the highest throes of the influenza. A new strain was rampaging across the Continent, killing thousands whose immune systems had been weakened by malnourishment and despair. He counted it a blessing that he had left Lou and the boys back in the States for this trip over.

"Have you made progress on our food relief effort?" the president asked.

Hoover glanced at Davis, then moved to the edge of the couch, tensing for battle. "Sir, the blockade."

The president grimaced and looked annoyed as he fumbled for another sip of tea. "Yes, yes. The blockade. Clemenceau says we must keep it in place until the Germans sign the treaty."

"Mr. President, with all due respect, such a course of action is not only barbaric, but politically dangerous. The French and British have commandeered a fourth of the German homegrown produce. And they are preventing the Germans from exporting coal and other raw materials to pay for imported grain. This is nothing more than a mass death sentence."

The president seemed preoccupied, fidgeting with the cuffs on his draping shirt. "Convey your concerns to Lloyd George."

Davis, seeing the exasperation in Hoover's face, came to his colleague's assistance. "Sir, we did just as you suggested, weeks ago. The prime minister is sympathetic to the gravity of the matter, but he cannot bring the French to our side without your insistence."

The president kept glancing at the harsh light piercing the half-closed drapes. He raised his hand with difficulty to shield his sensitive blue-gray eyes. "The blockade will be moot in weeks. Clemenceau has promised me that the signing of the accord is being expedited."

"We don't have weeks," Hoover warned. "Our sources in Berlin report that every day food is unavailable in the markets there, the Bolsheviks and the Freikorps gangs of the unemployed army officers become stronger. There may not be a democratic republic left to implement the treaty by the time it is presented to the Weimar—"

"I am thoroughly informed on the situation in Germany!"

The room filled with a tense silence. Hoover realized, too late, that he had pushed too hard. Wilson, a former Princeton University president, was a testy scholar who rarely considered anyone else his equal in intelligence or philosophical understanding. Over these past months, he had become more impatient with advisors and resentful when anyone hinted at criticism. The once-jubilant French crowds now greeted him lukewarmly, and his proclivity for lecturing everyone on idealism had chafed the European leaders. In retaliation, Clemenceau, an indefatigable and stubborn martinet, had flogged Wilson with a thousand petty grievances and demands.

The president, seeing his old friend shaken by the rebuff, made a half-hearted attempt at an apology. "Bert, you have served the country loyally throughout this ordeal. You must take heart. Whatever we have failed to accomplish in the treaty will be remedied in the League of Nations. Germany will be admitted, and rehabilitated into democracy, it will soon thrive. This accord is merely a stepping stone to building the foundation for a permanent temple of peace."

Hoover drew a long breath to calibrate his next words, fearing they might be the last he would ever speak to this president. "The reparations are open-ended, sir. The Germans cannot possibly pay them. A nation hammered to its knees has only one path. Anarchy and revolution."

"It is a hard treaty," the president admitted, his vague gaze glazing over with the shroud of illness. "But a hard treaty was needed. My conscience is satisfied. We Americans have done all we can. We must go home now and see to the repair of our own hearths."

Mrs. Wilson reappeared at the door. She nodded at Hoover to indicate that her husband should now retire for rest. The president arose unsteadily and, with Hoover's assistance, shuffled off to her care. She led him from the room and toward his bed chamber.

Hoover felt a pang of despair as he watched the last hope for the West fade into the shadows. The champion of the new world order had become a broken old man, deluded in the belief that these ancient European enemies would resolve their animosities in some future parliament. The barn gate was being left open again, he feared, and the banished wolves of militarism and colonialism were already sneaking back into the chicken coop.

Herbert Hoover as a young engineer.

The President and First Lady Lou Hoover.

Cadet Douglas MacArthur at West Point.

MacArthur and Eisenhower during the attack on the Bonus marchers.

District Police Chief Pelham "Happy" Glassford.

Glassford patrolling the Anacostia camp on Blue Bessie.

Wilma Waters and Walter W. Waters.

BEF Commander Waters on the Capitol steps.

Floyd Gibbons after Belleau Wood.

The Headline Hunter at work.

Joe Angelo after testifying to Congress.

An unidentified Harlem Hellfighter at the Anacostia camp.

An unidentified American nurse
during World War I.

Helen Fairchild.

Hoover and MacArthur at the Waldorf Astoria Hotel in
Manhattan, where both lived during their last years.

Camp Camden, later renamed Camp Marks, in Anacostia.

The camp after the BEF expulsion on July 28, 1932.

PART TWO

OVER HERE
1931 – 1932

It was more of a war than was publicly admitted.
— General George Patton,
recalling the events of July 28, 1932.

40

WASHINGTON, D.C.
FEBRUARY 1931

As a blood-pressure cuff tightened around his arm, President Herbert Hoover thumbed through that morning's edition of the *Washington Star*. He paused at a cartoon lampooning him on a whimsical fishing expedition to catch enough trout to feed a nation of Hoovervilles. That distasteful epithet, coined by wags to describe the thousands of shantytowns sprouting up around the country, never failed to roil his stomach. Disgusted, he looked away from the editorial page, only to be assaulted by the same oppressive drab green that closed in on him here every day. He had wanted to repaint the walls of the Oval Office white after a fire destroyed the wing two years ago, but Lou, feeling the mood of the country was not right for such an innovation, had prevailed on him to restore the place exactly as Taft had first modeled it.

I cannot even govern my own household.

The gyrating hand on the blood-pressure gauge finally settled, and Admiral Joel T. Boone, his reedy, mustached White House physician, regarded the result as if he had just been dealt a bad poker hand. He adjusted the cuff for another attempt, but the president shook his head and ripped it off, refusing to be clamped again.

Hoover didn't need to be told the numbers were too high. The tightness in his chest and numbness in his hands were evidence enough. He glanced at his reflection in the glass of Lou's framed picture on the desk. His graying hair had thinned and his eyesight was so weak now that he had to squint even with the spectacles. Each day seemed to bring more bad news, sapping his vitality drip by drip. Born a year after the Panic of 1873, he had witnessed fourteen recessions come and go, but none had lasted as long as this latest downturn sparked by the stock market crash in October of 1929. The food riots in the cities were now becoming more frequent. Just last month, hundreds of women had been reported sleeping in Chicago's Grant Park.

Desperate for a respite from these burdens, he searched the mail, hoping for a letter from his son, Bert Junior. Instead, his gaze landed on the heel marks that his predecessor, Cal Coolidge, had left on the desk during his daily naps. He glared a silent curse at those infernal scratches. They had become his personal version of the Latin reminder whispered centuries ago by Roman servants to keep the emperors grounded in reality.

Memento mori… Remember, you are mortal.

This moribund economy was that snoozing New Englander's fault! How many times had he warned Coolidge against the evils of easy money and speculation? But the obstinate man had refused to listen to him, choosing instead to escape during his last year in office to the Black Hills, where he had spent more time watching rodeos than dealing with falling farm prices. Now he knew why Woodrow Wilson had deteriorated so rapidly during his second term. On mornings like this, he yearned to be back at Stanford, far away from politics and taking care of his neglected—

"Mr. President, I cannot get an accurate reading if you don't relax."

He returned to the newspaper and flipped its pages to a report of a speech given earlier that week by that Tammany Hall puppet, Franklin Roosevelt. His mouth soured as he read the New Yorker's vitriol glazed with sugary patrician eloquence. "Why is it, Joel, that when a man is on this job as I am, day and night, doing the best he can, that certain men seek to oppose everything he does just to be ornery?"

"Few people understand the stress of your job, sir."

He knew what the editors of the Washington papers would say to *that: At least he has a job.* He tossed aside the *Star* and, hoping for more empathy from the Midwest, picked up the *St. Louis Post-Dispatch.* Yet on page five, a two-paragraph notice below the fold sparked his ire again. He barked at the story, "Peel them for donations, why don't you!"

Mystified by the president's outburst, the admiral asked, "Sir?"

Hoover chastised himself for the indiscretion. More and more these days, he caught himself mumbling defenses at the cascade of criticism about his national stewardship. He ruffled the newspaper in frustration—as if the confounded stories might be shaken from the page—and displayed for the admiral's inspection the latest horror in print. It was an item tucked between accounts of the marriage of Amelia Earhart and the congressional push to have *The Star Spangled Banner* designated as the national anthem. "Look at this, Joel. They're building a church in St. Louis out of orange crates."

The physician felt his pulse. "How have you been feeling lately, sir?"

"As if I'm trapped in my own skin. Why is my face so puffy?"

"The swelling is edema. It's caused by lack of sleep. Let's try the other arm."

Hoover sighed. "This must be what a queen bee feels like. Being buzzed over in the hive all day, not allowed to move an inch."

"Now that you mention it, sir, honey as a substitute for—"

"You know what this country needs, Joel?"

"No, sir."

"A great poem."

The physician glanced at the door where Lou Hoover, unseen by her husband, had been eavesdropping. He humored the president by asking, "A poem?"

"Yes, something to lift people out of their fear and selfishness. Sometimes a great poem can do more than an entire session of legislation. You let me know if you find any great poems lying around."

"Yes, sir, I will."

Hoover's slurring right eye trailed to the stack of correspondence on his desk. He resisted the urge to throw the whole damn lot into the fireplace. On top sat an engraved letterhead that featured a bottle of Kentucky bourbon. He picked up the letter, sneered at its scratched signature, and tossed it aside. "Alben Barkley wants me to send homeless Americans to China. I'm surprised he didn't suggest indenturing them to shuck tobacco."

The admiral pressed his stethoscope to the president's chest. "Have you been cutting back on the salted ham and bacon, as we discussed?"

Hoover's voice shrilled with resentment. "This is the kind of inane advice I get from my vice president! And it doesn't get any better going down the list of my so-called experts. Pat Hurley over at the War Department suggested I order restaurants to package their leftovers and give them to the destitute. Can you believe that? And Mellon tells me to sit tight. He says the economy is just going through one of its periodic detoxifications. Liquidate labor, liquidate stocks, liquidate the farmers, and liquidate real estate. That's what my Secretary of the Treasury tells me will bring back prosperity." He looked at his watch. "How much more of this? I have a radio address to prepare."

"Not much longer, sir. … Do you get a thrill from speaking over the radio?"

Hoover huffed, aware that the physician was just trying to get his mind off the news. "The same thrill I get when I rehearse to a doorknob."

The admiral, helpless to calm him, shook his head at Mrs. Hoover.

"Bert," Lou said firmly, revealing her presence to her husband for the first time. "Allow Joel to finish his examination." Waved off, she closed the door to give the two men more privacy.

The admiral wrote out a new prescription. "Frankly, sir, Mrs. Hoover is worried about you, and so am I. She has told me there are times when you just sit and stare at the wall. The staff reports that you rarely interact with them."

"So now I have spies running around here like rats."

"There is a spiritual aspect to treating the body," the admiral said. "I know there aren't many people you can confide in here. Everything you tell me is strictly confidential, of course. Sometimes it helps to unburden one's soul."

Annoyed by the facile self-help suggestions, Hoover opened his desk drawer and pulled out a crumpled note written on the margin of a newspaper advertisement. He read the cursive plea aloud for the admiral's benefit. "'I am only a girl of twenty, but I know what it is to see starvation. People here are dying day by day. Young boys go wrong because their folks can't feed them. Girls take the wrong way too because they have to eat, so it is your duty to do something and do it mighty quick. Help us! Help us! Help us!'" He threw the letter back into the drawer. "Do you have any pills to cure *that*?"

Having overstayed his welcome, the admiral packed up his medical kit. "Sir, I tell all of my patients to try as best they can to find the positive in life."

Hoover stared down at his telephone attached to the bank of buzzers that he had ordered installed on his desk. The congressmen and bankers who came marching through here to pester him about bond interest rates always expressed horror at the innovation, felt it tainted the dignity of the office. But he didn't give a hoot about the empty trappings of power. What interested him was efficiency. And by his calculation, he was saving at least two hours a day by being able to beckon his five personal secretaries with the push of a button and speak to advisors over the phone instead of meeting them in person.

His eyes tracked over to the newspaper again, this time to a story about a veteran walking down from New Jersey to testify on the Hill that afternoon for the need of the annuity to be paid to the returned doughboys. He slapped the back of his hand at the photograph of the pitiful-looking ex-soldier. "That's all they clatter on about!"

At the door, the admiral turned back. "Sir?"

"This confounded Bonus handout for the veterans. Congress passed it over Coolidge's veto in 1924. It's not scheduled to be paid until 1945, but the VFW wants it distributed early. The nation is turning against itself, Joel. Cannibalizing its own flesh and blood like the Donner party crossing the Rockies."

"Yes, sir."

Hoover's billowy jowls flamed. "No one is starving in this country. I know a thing or two about starvation. I even had a report last week of one hobo who managed to find ten meals a day."

"I did hear another sad story yesterday," the admiral said. "One of my old classmates, a fine fellow who opened a solo practice in Buffalo, had to sell all of his furniture and equipment to feed his family."

"He must have been a damn poor businessman!" Hoover snapped. "The medical schools need to start offering courses on financial planning."

"You're probably right, sir."

Hoover grimaced at the incessant whir of the new air conditioner, the first ever installed in the White House. He closed his eyes in search of the Quaker gift of quietude that his mother had so praised when he was a boy. "What is that oath you doctors take?"

The admiral was thrown by the odd question. "First, do no harm?"

Hoover opened his red-rimmed lids to drive home a point. "Yes, first do no harm. Shouldn't the body politic be dealt with in that same cautious manner? The Democrats harangue me to print money and stimulate the economy with jobs programs and handouts. That would be like stuffing a sick child with sugar."

"Speaking of sugar," the admiral said gamely. "Mrs. Hoover has suggested to the kitchen staff that deserts be eliminated from the dinner menu. You've gained some weight this year. We need to seriously think about getting you on an exercise regimen. And I implore you to eat more slowly and cut back on these eighteen hour days."

"Of course," Hoover grumbled. "Just get rid of anything that has any taste. She has already destroyed our wine collection to appease the Prohibitionists." He hurried through the remaining pages of the paper until he came to the local District of Columbia stories. What he found did nothing to improve his mood. A column, headlined *The Nation's Capitol is a Yankee Doodle Dandy of a Speakeasy*, opined:

> *If you wanted a nice stiff drink in Washington, your best bet is to befriend a congressman. It doesn't much matter which particular congressman. Republican or Democrat, Bible-thumping son of the South or worldly big-city Yankee—nearly all have access to whiskey and gin. And for that you can thank a short, well-dressed former World War I tank crew member named George L. Cassiday, or, as he has become known across the country, the Man in the Green Hat, official bootlegger to the solons of Capitol Hill.*

Hoover tore off the clipping, determined to follow up on the matter. Only a few months ago, the Wickersham Commission had exposed an epidemic of brutal police practices and corruption in the highest offices of the nation's law enforcement departments. Now the entire country seemed to be backsliding into lawlessness. At a loss what to do about it, he asked the physician a question to which he already knew the answer. "What happens to the body when the heart is diseased?"

"Not a good prognosis, I'm afraid."

"Indeed! And how am I to govern effectively when my own backyard is rife with graft?" After staring at his in-box for several troubled moments, he rang his press secretary. When Ted Joslin arrived at the door, the president ordered the aide, "Call Herbert Crosby at the District Commissioner's office. I'd like a word with him."

The naked young beauty pulled back the bronze satin sheets on the bed and arched her back seductively. "Tatay, stay with me a little longer."

Lounging in his favorite green kimono, Douglas MacArthur lit the *Imperiale* perched at the end of his silver Mandarin extension, a gift from his benefactor, the president of the Philippines Senate. After several satisfying puffs, he put the cigarette out in a dragon-shaped ashtray and climbed from the bed to change back into his gray suit for the return walk of fourteen blocks to his War Department office. As he stood fixing his tie, he admired the petite curves of the seventeen-year-old Manila actress to whom he had just made love. These midday escapes to his secret Chastleton apartment on 16th Street were his only breaks from the pressures and boredom of civilian life. Truth was, he rather enjoyed playing out the fantasy of being an Asian potentate ensconced in his palace. During his three assignments in Manila, he had grown fond of Eastern culture and its devotion to authority and discipline. He often mused that if he could return to another era, he would choose to be a shogun.

"Tatay," purred the girl, who had been sheltered from the sun for so long that she could pass for a porcelain doll. "Why do you have to leave?"

It always brought a grin to his face when she called him the Filipino name for Daddy. "You know my schedule, Dimples. I have only an hour for lunch."

Dimples reprised her most accomplished role. Twisting her smooth cheeks into a pout, she batted her long lashes, crawled to the foot of the bed, and tugged playfully at his belt. "Say my name again. I like it when you announce me to the stage like Rudy Vallee."

Laughing at her childlike innocence, he humored her by rolling the 'r's in her middle name with dramatic effect. "Isabel R-r-osar-r-rio Cooper."

"Do you love me?"

"How many times must I tell you? Of course I do."

"Then take me to a show tonight."

That familiar grip of dread came over him again. *What am I doing with this child?* He was thirty-four years older than her, but he couldn't get her moonbeam delicacy and perfect pert breasts out of his constant thoughts, not since that day in the Manila theatre when he saw her make the country's first onscreen kiss. A month later, by a stroke of fate, he had been introduced to her at a diplomatic party, and it had been lust at first sight.

This is all Pershing's fault.

When that socialite bloodsucker Louise Brooks jilted the Black Jackass to marry him, the old warhorse, jealous of his heroism in France, had retaliated by ordering him transferred from his superintendent's post at West Point to the Philippines. Pershing had known damn well that Louise would never stay long in a foreign military outpost. After she demanded a divorce and fluttered off to find the next flower to sap, he had been left alone in Manila, lonely and despondent. Only then had Isabel been sent to him, an angel from heaven. And when he was called back to Washington to serve as Chief of Staff of the Army, he could not bear to leave her behind, despite the danger her presence in this city posed to his—

"Tatay! Did you hear me?"

He turned, distracted. "What did you say?"

"*Anna Christie* is playing at the Metro tonight. People say I remind them of Greta Garbo. I want to see her."

"You're not going out."

She bristled like a thorny *bougainvillea* flower. "Why not?"

"We've been over this. I cannot be seen with you. I've gone to a great deal of trouble to have your meals delivered here."

"Then I'll go alone."

He took a threatening step toward the bed. "No respectable lady frequents the city alone at night."

She grabbed a paperweight from the night table and threw it at him. "All I am is your prisoner!"

He ducked, narrowly avoiding being brained. "Calm down."

She kept jumping atop the mattress and flailing her arms. "I want to go out and have fun!"

He refused to give in to her childish outburst. The girl was half Scottish, and at times like this her Aberdeen father's stubborn Pict blood overwhelmed the submissive lineage of her Chinese *mestizzo* mother. He had learned how to abort her tantrums, at least temporarily. He opened the closet and brought out one of the gift-wrapped packages that he kept hidden in his trunk for such emergencies.

Dimples tore the bow off the box. "What is it?"

"Your favorite."

She pulled out a sheer *peignoir* nightgown. Disappointed, she threw it at the pile of lingerie that he had bought for her during the past month alone. "I want a fur coat!"

"Do you know how much I spent for this? Do you know how much I have to spend to keep you in this apartment?"

"Sable! I want a sable coat!"

"You don't need a coat. You are *not* going out."

She eyed the distance between them, like a cat about to pounce. "I'll go visit your mother. Maybe *she* will go to the theatre with me."

He lunged at her with a pointed finger. "If you *ever* come within a mile of my mother, I'll have you sent back to Manila on the next ship! She will *never* know of your existence! Do you understand?"

Frightened, Dimples dived back into the bed. She coiled into a ball and pulled the sheets over her head.

He escaped to the window and pushed open the pane for air. *What is happening to me?* He hadn't felt himself since France. He had been a failure as a husband, and now he was under the spell of this nubile extortionist. He couldn't decide if he really loved her, or if he was just a slave to her Oriental sexual charms.

There were rumors that Drew Pearson had been nosing around town, asking questions about his social activities in Manila. If that muckraking columnist or any of those other opium-sniffing hacks found out about Dimples, his military career would be over. He was no longer married, true, and even if he were, nobody gave a damn about a general taking a mistress. After all, Pershing had bedded so many conquests across France that the joke was half the *garçons* in Paris now sported mustaches and chewed tobacco. Frequent fornication was expected of an officer, but *only* with Caucasian women. He had violated an unwritten code by bringing an Asian concubine to Washington. And if his seventy-eight-year-old mother, who now lived with him in his official residence at Fort Myer, ever learned of these trysts, she would make the professional grief wailers of ancient Rome look frigid with indifference.

Dimples, repentant, emerged from under the sheets to try on her gift. "Did you get my size, Tatay?"

Distracted, he hadn't heard the question. He looked down on 16th Street and listened to the rain from a passing thunderstorm patter the pavement. In the small park across from the sidewalk, a ragged scrum of hobos sat huddled under a soaked tent. By the look of them, they'd been on the hoof for weeks. Disgusted, he shook his head. The bums in this city were becoming a damn serious problem. He couldn't even walk back to the White House now without getting accosted for change. One of them down there, a foreign-looking fellow dwarfed in a cheap black suit, was talking up a storm to the other gypsies. What was that hanging on his lapel?

No, it couldn't be.

But it was. He knew, because he possessed six of those same medals. Had that conniving grifter down there stolen the Distinguish Service Cross from a veteran? He had the mind to go down there and rough up the scoundrel. The shameful sight brought back a jarring memory from five years ago, when he lived in New York. One night, he had been leaving for West Point when a bum walked onto Riverside Drive and flagged down his limousine. Rolling down the window, he had found a gun pointed at his head. The slacker had ordered him to hand over all the money in his wallet, but he refused. Instead, he got out of the car and told the thief he'd have to fight him for it. The scofflaw turned pale, only then recognizing his victim.

General MacArthur… I was in the Rainbow Division with you.

Even after these many years, the memory of that confession still caused him to cringe. How could one of *his* soldiers have fallen so low in morals? That night, distraught, he had gotten back into the car and had ordered his chauffeur to drive off, leaving the grifter to suffer in ignominy and—

"Tatay, I adore the gown," Dimples peeped from the bed, still hiding under the sheets. "But can you get it in another color?"

He closed his eyes. He would give up everything just to be back in France, going over the top one more time. Nothing was more useless in this world than a soldier trained to win the war to end all wars. At the age of fifty-one, he had to accept the hard reality that he would never again experience the exhilaration of battle.

That afternoon, Rep. James Frear of Wisconsin gaveled to order a hearing of the House Ways and Means Committee. When the crowd in the expansive Capitol Hill room finally quieted, the chairman announced, "I understand there is a soldier here today who wishes to be heard on the pending legislation for payment of the adjusted compensation certificates."

The loose soles on the witness's shoes flapped loudly as he stood up from the rear seats and walked to the witness table. Halfway down the aisle, he stopped to look up in awe at the high inlaid ceiling of Italianate marble. He figured some of his Neapolitan relatives must have masoned those burnished stones, beautiful as they were. Behind him, he heard a few snickers and comments about the holes in his jacket.

Maybe these folks ain't seen a real soldier before.

Sure, he wasn't exactly tailored up in tails like those peacocks sitting up there on the high benches. But at least he had a suit on, the one and only left to him by his father, who had deemed it wasteful to be buried in it. The sleeves draped over his fingers, and the lining had been sewn and patched by the Italian ladies in Camden. But its thick Calabrian wool had held up pretty solid during his recent sojourn, all things considered.

"Please sit down and state your name," Rep. Frear said.

He dragged the microphone to his mouth. "Joe Angelo of New Jersey."

"You have a statement?"

"Yes, sir. I have a statement that I've been wanting to make for two years. My comrades and I hiked here from nine o'clock Sunday morning when we left Camden. I done it all by my feet, shoe leather. I was not picked up by any machine. I would not accept it. Why? I come to show you people that we need our Bonus. I represent eighteen hundred from Jersey like me. Men out of work. I have got a little home back there that I built with my own hands after I came home from France. Now, I expect to lose that little place. My taxes are not paid. I have not worked for two years and a half. Last week I went to our town committee, and they gave me four dollars for rations. That is to keep my wife and child and myself and clothe us. And also, I cannot put no coal in my cellar."

Angelo paused to lick his sun-cracked lips. As he poured water into the glass from the fancy pitcher, he noticed that the hearing room, lousy with conversations when he first entered, had turned silent. He stole a glance over his shoulder while he took a sip. In one of the rows behind him, a well-dressed woman, who looked vaguely familiar, was sitting with three children.

"Carry on, sir," the chairman said.

His thirst quenched, Angelo let out a satisfied lap with his tongue. "Now, I don't ask for the full Bonus. None of us do, as long as we can get enough that we can make ends meet. We don't want to ask for charity."

"What is that on your chest?"

Angelo lifted his lapel so that everyone in the room could see it. "This here is the Distinguished Service Cross. It was not put on me for laying in a dugout. It was not put on me for standing behind the lines. It was for saving Colonel Patton of the cavalry camp right across from Washington here. I was the only man left standing out of three hundred and five men. I didn't brag about it when I came back, for it is not worth the room it takes up to the outsiders, but to me, brothers, it is worth a million. I would never sell it even if I never got anything to eat. It was put there to stay, and that is where it will stay until my wife takes it off my dead body."

"Where did you sleep last night, soldier?"

"Me and the other boys stopped in the town here for a night's lodging, but they put us in the lock-up and they locked the door so that we could not get out. We are not crooks, but it is making us thieves."

The audience listened raptly as Angelo told how he had joined the Army and of the many battles he had fought. When he finished his ten-minute presentation, the people in the room stood and applauded.

A congressman whose nameplate read *Rainey* nodded proudly. "You have made the best speech we've heard yet."

"Thank you, sir."

"What's that on your wrist?" asked Rep. Frear.

Angelo removed his watch and passed it up to the bench.

The committee chairman read aloud the inscription engraved on the back of the watch: "Joseph Angelo, D.S.C. From Mrs. George S. Patton, Jr. In grateful remembrance of the Argonne, September 26, 1918."

Angelo pulled a spent bullet from his pocket and held it in the air. "Here is a little token, too. It doesn't mean much, I guess, only a stickpin. But this bullet was given to me by Colonel Patton's mother. She said, 'Joseph, I want you to wear that as long as you live and as long as it will stay with you. That is the bullet that went through my son's leg that day. That setting was bought from Woodrow Wilson's wife's jewelry store here in Washington, and as hard up as I am, that never goes in an uncle.'"

"Never goes to a what?"

"An uncle. That's what we call a pawn shop in Jersey."

"No one is willing to give you a job now?"

"No sir. I went to my old place at the Powder Works when I came home from France, but they'd gave my job away. So I tried the Fire Department. They said I was too small."

"How much do you weigh?"

"One hundred and seven pounds when I last ascended the scales for Uncle Sam. The doctor at the recruiting station wasn't gonna let me in, but I told him that Uncle Sam didn't go by weight, just by a man's interest in fighting. Danged if he didn't take hold of me and punch me hard. He said he couldn't find anything wrong with me, so he sent me down the line to another doctor. That feller said he'd let me in if I jumped six tables set in a row. I took a handspring and leaped over those six tables. So he put me in the Army."

When the laughter died down, another congressman on the panel observed, "I do not blame you the least for feeling aggrieved. I do not think you have been treated right. You say that watch was given to you by the Pattons?"

"Yes, sir. The Colonel's right over there at the cavalry stable in Fort Myer. Just pick up a telephone and ask him about Joe Angelo. See if he don't say that's the young man who saved me. I could go over there and ask him for money, but I ain't doing that. I ain't gonna have him pay for me."

"Have you ever applied for compensation?"

"Why do that? I would be stealing it."

"You got a certificate for your service, right?"

"Yes, sir. If I live twenty years, it will pay me one thousand, four hundred and forty-four dollars. But I don't think I will ever see twenty years."

"Have you borrowed on it?"

"Yes sir. By the time I get it, I won't have anything left."

"That is all the cash you've had in a year and a half?"

Ashamed, Angelo managed a reluctant nod. "I could make money under the table, if you know what I mean. But we have laws in the United States. No man should have to break the law to survive. Now, I could go bootlegging, but what am I doing? I could have went to France and I could have run out of my outfit and got in the dugout and hid away from the fires. But which is best, to be a live coward or a dead hero? I wanted to win battles. I wasn't worried about what I went through. I wasn't married, and I got a wonderful send-off when I went to France. My father throwed me out."

He waited for the chortles and guffaws to quiet.

"And when I came back I went home to my father and saw the big, fat woman sitting in my seat. I knowed her from the next door, so I said to myself, 'She is the last woman you want on Earth.' So when I came I looked at her, and I says to my father, 'Pop, what is *she* doing here?' He says, 'That's my wife.' I says, 'Oh, my God.' He says, 'Well.' She says, 'You get out of here! You get out of here!' And that was my welcome home, and I got out. So, folks, I tell you, all I will say to you is, help us through with the Bonus. That is the best answer for you folks to give the fellows at home. And don't forget me for a job. That is all I care for."

"God bless you for your service, Mr. Angelo," the chairman said.

The hearing was gaveled closed, and amid raucous applause, Angelo walked from the room swarmed by handshakes and backslaps. In the hallway, a security cop whispered to his ear that a lady would like to speak to him in the office of Senator Glass. He was escorted into a fancy lobby.

Waiting for him there stood the mother and children who had been listening to his testimony. The lady took a tentative step closer. "Mr. Angelo?"

"Yes, ma'am."

"I'm Beatrice Patton.... The colonel's wife."

The blood drained from Angelo's sunken cheeks. Yeah, that was where he had seen her before, in those newspaper photos. She had said some pretty awful things about him to the reporters, calling him a "catspaw" and a "pathetic type." Them were her words. What the hell did she want with him now? To slander him to his face?

She brought forward her three reluctant children. "This is Bea, Ruth Ellen, and George the Fourth."

The children looked up at him with fright in their faces.

"Would you tell them how brave their father was during the war?"

Sonofabitch, lady, he cursed to himself. *You drag my name through the mud and now you want me to sing lullabies to your babies?*

But he took a closer look. The boy had the same liverish complexion as his father. He knew it wasn't the Colonel's fault that his wife went off on him. He reckoned the tads shouldn't suffer because she understood nothing about what he and the other veterans were enduring. He swallowed his hurt and reached his hand out to shake little Georgie's tiny paw first. "Are you going to be a soldier?"

The Patton boy nodded with a quizzical look, as if to think otherwise would be absurd.

"Well, George," Angelo said, "if you're as good an officer as your daddy, the men will follow you anywhere."

The boy brightened, and his mother released a held breath of relief. "Mr. Angelo, would you tell my children about the day their father was wounded?"

Although he wasn't much taller than the youngsters, Angelo got down on one knee and brought them closer. "Your papa was leading the tanks into the enemy lines. He got hit pretty bad in the rump, but he didn't yell or nothing. He fell to the ground and was spouting blood. He kept giving orders to his men to keep fighting for our country here. I dragged him into a hole and stayed with him until we could get him to the hospital. We spent some pretty long hours together that day, your papa and me."

"Was that when he won his medal?" asked little George.

Angelo brought the boy's hand to his chest. "Yes, sonny, it was. He got one just like this. You be proud of your papa. All of you's."

Mrs. Patton pulled her son away. "Come, children, we've taken up enough of Mr. Angelo's time. You go on now into the hall and wait for me."

When the children had departed with the security guard, Mrs. Patton held back. She opened her purse and pulled out five dollars. "Please, Mr. Angelo, get yourself a meal tonight. And a train ticket back to New Jersey."

"I can't take that, ma'am."

She placed the money into his hand. "I insist."

He fought back tears, hoping his old boss would not hear of this. "How's the Colonel these days? I'd give anything to see him again."

Mrs. Patton was looking anxiously for the exit. "Well, you know, he's quite busy over at the War College."

"Yes, ma'am. He's an important man. If you get the chance, you tell him his old orderly said hello. Tell him Joe Angelo still remembers them ghosts at them battlefields where he and his knights fought."

MacArthur returned to his War Department office that afternoon and was handed a message that retired General Herbert Crosby had called. The former cavalryman, recently appointed District of Columbia commissioner by the president, wanted to see him at five o'clock near the restored Civil War defenses at Fort Stevens. No reason was given for the meeting, or for the remoteness of its location. Intrigued, MacArthur decided to bring along his assistant chief of staff, Major General George Van Horn Moseley, if only to be entertained by the Midwesterner's eccentric opinions and razor-sharp tongue.

After a half-hour drive north toward Maryland, MacArthur ordered Moseley to pull their staff car into a deserted parking lot. The two men got out and followed a wooded path that led to the spot where Jubal Early's Confederate troops had once made a half-hearted effort to capture the city more than sixty years ago. They found a saddled horse tied to a tree.

"Get down, you damn fool! Before you get shot!"

MacArthur turned a wry grin toward the source of that insolent command, which had first been shouted in 1864 by a Union major who hadn't realized the damn fool standing atop these breastworks was President Lincoln. Thrusting his riding crop under his arm, he strode over to greet the old colleague who had championed the armored mechanization of the cavalry. "Crosby, if I wanted a tour of a Union battlefield, I certainly wouldn't choose a secessionist Kansas Jayhawker to conduct it."

As Crosby shook MacArthur's hand, he eyed Moseley suspiciously. "I see you brought your batman, Doug. How often does George shine your shoes?"

"Fuck you, Crosby," Moseley snarled. "Don't you have better things to do in your waning years than bring us out here for one of your mushroom forages?"

Crosby swept the remote parking lot with wary eyes. Assured that no one else was around, he motioned for them to follow him down a rustic path. Notorious for always communicating through a haze of smoke, the new District commissioner stopped in a small clearing to light up another cigarette. He offered them a couple of Chesterfields from his silver case, and the three veterans of the Great War stood puffing and looking over the old fighting ground.

"Whatever it is you wanted to talk about," MacArthur said, "I assume the officer's club had too many ears."

Crosby's nod was barely perceptible. "The president called me this morning."

Moseley guffawed at the blatant name-dropping. "Did Hoover want you to fill that pothole across from the White House?"

Crosby took MacArthur aside while turning a cold shoulder on Moseley. "Doug, what I am about to discuss with you remains between us."

MacArthur shrugged. "Of course."

"The president wants a new police chief for the city. He's tired of reading about all the bullshit being shoveled around in that rotten department."

MacArthur glared at him as if dressing down a plebe. "You brought me all the way out here to tell me *that*? Hiring cops is a little under my pay grade."

"Oh, my apologies, Chief." Ten years older than MacArthur, Crosby was one of the few members of the tight-knit Army club who could talk so sarcastically to the hero of France. "I know how important it is for you to get back to the seventh floor and process those paint orders for the Fort Leavenworth latrines."

Trailing a step behind, Moseley rushed up to get into the old cavalryman's face. "You've ridden a horse's ass for so long, Crosby, you've turned into one."

Crosby brushed the crusty deputy aside to resume his conversation with MacArthur. "I've been going through the usual candidates, but none fit the president's criteria. The old guard here is so rife with corruption, we'll have to go outside the city to find our man."

MacArthur didn't really give a damn. He glanced over his shoulder at the car, eager to get back to the Chastleton and Dimples. "How can I help?"

"A few months ago, I ran into one of your old friends. Happy Glassford was back East helping the VFW prepare for the Armistice Day Jubilee."

MacArthur smiled from the memories of his school days with the fun-loving Glassford. "Hap's a good man. I wrote him a letter a while back after his father died unexpectedly. He took it pretty hard. He was a year behind me at the Point, you know. I took him under my wing. "

Crosby nodded. "I'm thinking of recommending him for the position."

MacArthur shook his head at the sorry fate that had befallen so many of his fellow West Point officers. "Is this what it has all come to? Years of training and fighting to end up as police chiefs and sewer commissioners?"

Crosby crushed his cigarette butt under his heel. "Doug, you knew Glassford better than I did. Is there anything more I should be told about him?"

MacArthur reflected a moment. He had never considered Happy Glassford the type of man to run a police force. But the more the thought about it, he realized that it might be a good idea to have one of his protégés as the law-enforcement chief in the nation's capital, especially if he ever decided to enter national politics. "He's as steady as they come."

"I need to be certain he'll toe the line."

"What line are we talking about?"

Crosby seemed miffed at having to spell it out. "I'm sure it hasn't passed your notice that the number of bums around here is growing at an alarming rate. Some of them are veterans."

That warning was a red flag waved in front of the bull-headed Moseley. "The Jews and Reds are causing this swarm of locusts!" the irascible deputy graveled. "I warned Pershing that allowing all those damn immigrants into the Army would come back to bite us. We're diluting our Anglo-Saxon blood that has won every war."

"George," MacArthur scolded. "I've cautioned you about such talk."

"Hell, Doug, you know as well as I do that we pay more attention to the breeding of our hogs and cattle than we do our populace!"

While Moseley ranted on about the dilution of American genetics and values, Crosby fixed a hard gaze on MacArthur. "We both saw what happened in Germany after the Armistice. I guess you read in the papers about Patton's orderly walking down here from New Jersey to beg Congress for a handout."

MacArthur's eyes narrowed. "What are you getting at?"

As if to underscore his point, Crosby stared off toward the ridge where desperate, ragged Confederates had once formed up in the hope of invading the capital. "Hurley told me the White House has received some disturbing reports. Veterans groups around the country are becoming more strident in their speeches and editorials."

MacArthur waved off the concern as just a temporary flare-up. "This damn Bonus fiasco has their feathers ruffled."

"What I need to know from *you*," Crosby said, "is whether Glassford will crack heads if necessary to clean up the mess around here."

MacArthur shrugged. "He distinguished himself in battle. I have no reason to believe he wouldn't do his duty to the highest degree of competency."

Despite the unqualified recommendation, Crosby seemed unconvinced. "I ordered his duty file at the Department sent over to my office for review. What's all this nonsense about painting? He seems to hang around a lot of left-wing bohemian types."

MacArthur kept one eye on the staff car. "Hap taught drawing at the Point. He's always had a creative bent. I'll vouch for him without question. Besides, it couldn't hurt to have a fellow West Pointer in charge of security in this city."

Crosby nodded. Then, he grinned and winked. "Now, if we could just get one of our own into the White House, eh, Doug?"

MacArthur offered no comment to that hope, but merely shook Crosby's hand and led Moseley back to the parking lot.

41

RAGLESVILLE, INDIANA
SEPTEMBER 1931

A nna felt the hard glares of the other mourners as the coffin was lowered into the grave. She knew what they were thinking: She hadn't shed a tear since her father passed away three days ago. It was against God's ways not to weep, they believed. The truth was, she considered him blessed to be finished with this cruel world.

Maybe her heart *had* become hardened. The last time she could remember crying was that night the Cromwell twins jumped to their watery deaths. Even when she had sat in her father's meeting house twelve years ago trying to explain to Micah why she no longer loved him, she had been incapable of dredging up any feeling of loss or grief. She had spent the time since the war in a fog of benumbed despair, having come home from tending gassed soldiers to nurse a father who had lingered on for years with a disease that slowly ate his nerves until he shook like the wind.

Yes, she could hear the thoughts of Micah and these men around her, just as she had heard the silent prayers of those soldiers dying in the field wards:

This farm lies fallow. There will be no harvest again this year. The woman is thirty-seven years old. In a time of want and hunger, it is indulging the wanton sin of pride against the Almighty not to take a husband and be productive.

Her father's dying request had been for Micah to take his place behind the pulpit. But Micah had already indicated his intent to remain at Bethel College, where he was now a professor of theology. Each Christmas for three years after her return home, he had made the long journey down to beg her hand in marriage, but she had always put him off.

When he finished the eulogy, the dirt was thrown into the hole and the mourners returned to the buggies without offering her condolences. Left alone in the small cemetery, she looked down at mound of fresh black loam and struggled to find comfort. *It is just a grave, like all the others. At least he lies here at home, unlike those who—*

"Anna."

Startled, she flinched.

Micah caught her before she stumbled and fell. "I'm sorry. I didn't mean to frighten you."

Recovering her balance, she brushed off his hand and set her face in stone. "It takes more than that now."

He frowned, not taking her meaning. "May I have a word with you?"

She couldn't look at him. "Don't do this. My feelings have not changed."

"No, I understand. Now is not the best time for this, I know, but I have to leave tonight. I have classes tomorrow."

"Time for what?"

Taking her gently by the elbow, he led her from the cemetery fence and toward the hill where they had once played as children. He was heavier now and wreathed in a thick beard, but he still had that unintended grin, even in sad moments like this. She took several deep breaths to chase the recurrent dizziness that had haunted her since returning from France. It was Indian summer, and a few stubborn horseflies still buzzed in the brown grass, but the turn of the leaves in the holler groves promised that winter was creeping in, finger by pale finger. She sensed the shift of his censorious attention to the fields that had not been planted that year for lack of help.

As they walked, he seemed to be struggling for the words to start. Finally, he said, "You remember that barn-raising feast we had up here?"

"That feels like a lifetime ago."

"You used to shoo those flies into my pie, Shoofly Raber."

"Don't do this, Micah. I know your tricks."

He stopped walking and forced her to meet his eyes. "Out of respect for your father's feelings, I waited to bring this up until he passed."

"I can take care of the farm myself."

"That's not what I want to talk about." He fidgeted with his pockets, just as he had years ago when he searched for the courage to invite her to bundle with him. "The elders of the congregation asked me to talk to you."

"About what?"

"They say you haven't been attending services."

"Hearts filled with such tolerance and unconditional love," she muttered with bitter sarcasm. "I cannot imagine why anyone would not want to bask in their presence."

"Anna, these people are your family."

She turned on him in hot anger. "They are *not* my family! I left my family in…" She stopped herself, knowing he would not understand.

He took her hands and pressed them together. "Will you pray with me?"

She escaped his importuning grasp. "I cannot."

"What has happened to you? You refuse to pray on the day your father goes to his heavenly reward?"

She turned away. "Does Scripture not say that God is like a loving father to us?"

"Matthew Six-Twenty-Five. 'Look at the birds of the air; they do not sow or reap or store away in barns, and yet your heavenly Father feeds them. Are you not much more valuable than they?'"

"What loving father would cause his children to endure so much pain and suffering? Not a Father I will worship."

"Anna, you are not the only one who has suffered. Look around you. In the English towns, people have no work. Children are going without meals."

Her fists were clenched so tight that she felt her nails digging into her palms. "I never said I was the only one!"

After a long silence, she looked up to find him bathed in tears of pain, gazing across the waving fields of golden rye on the farm down the road. His broad, expressive face had always been a flip-deck of emotions, and now his air of spiritual calm gave way to a haunted visage.

"When I was being held at that military camp in Kentucky, the officers stood us up against a wall one morning and told us we were going to be shot for refusing to fight. I prayed for the courage to endure the bullets. Yet God saved me. He saved me for His work in the fields of faith. He saved me for this very day, when I could bring you back from your loss of faith."

She stared at him with a slacked mouth. *He thinks God saved him?* She had never told him of the blackmailed bargain she had struck with the commandant of that camp to get him released. She felt the rage rising again in her throat. She was determined to puncture his delusion, but before she could utter the revelation, he reached into his coat pocket and brought out his copy of the *Martyrs' Mirror*, the venerated account of the Anabaptist heroes that they had studied together growing up.

"Do you remember Dirk Willems?" he asked.

She shook her head, though the name made her feel apprehensive.

He turned to a dog-eared page in the book. "Brother Willems was one of the first of the faithful who lived in the sixteenth century. The Spanish Catholics threw him into prison in the Netherlands. One night he escaped by climbing down a high window with a rope of knotted rags. The moat around the prison had turned to ice, and he was so light from having been starved that he managed to cross it. But the guard chasing him fell into the moat and cried for help. Brother Willems ran back to save his pursuer from drowning. Rather than thank him, the guard forced Brother Willems to return to the prison. A few days later, he was burned to death. He forgave the guard, for he knew that the Almighty would also forgive him."

She stepped away, feeling the need to be alone.

He reached for her and tried to bring her closer. "Anna, you must release this anger and pain in your heart. Forgive God for what you witnessed during the war, and He will forgive you."

Incensed that he could so easily dismiss the horrors as divine will, she shoved the book back into his hands, drawing a grunt from the force. "Now let me tell *you* a story. Have you ever heard of Lieutenant Tomas?"

"No, but—"

"He was a German soldier. Several hours after the armistice was signed, his commanding officer told him to go over to the Americans in a gesture of good will and give them the news that his German regiment would be vacating the house it defended. He was also ordered to tell the Americans that they were welcome to sleep in the house that night. As he walked to our lines, he was shot dead. God in His infinite wisdom chose not to convey the news of the surrender to that particular American regiment. Apparently, God wanted Brother Tomas to be the last man killed in the war, for no apparent reason other than the world needed one less kind man."

"Please—"

She came face to face with him, finishing with battened fury, "Why don't you go to Germany and find Lieutenant Tomas's mother! Tell *her* about the martyrs and bring *her* back to the faith!" She walked off before Micah, stunned by her outburst, could manage a response.

Floyd Gibbons floored the accelerator and sent his open-top Studebaker speeding down the country road while spitting gypsum rocks behind it like bullets from a Tommy gun. When the roadster hit its top range at sixty-five miles per hour, he reached over and punched a button on the new mechanical contraption those whiz boys at the NBC studios had rigged up under the dashboard for him. A thin metal cylinder began spinning in the wooden box that sat on the passenger floorboard, and his own voice began speaking back at him through a large round speaker bolted above the gearbox.

Clicking a stopwatch, he started counting the words in the recorded dispatch that he had filed ten years ago while covering the Russian famine:

"They were the backwash of the war—people who were uprooted from their homes and farms as early as 1914, and who since then had been walking from place to place with all their belongings on their backs and now they were dragging empty sacks, stomachs and pockets through this land of want."

His lone eye flitted back and forth from the road to the stopwatch:

"A boy of twelve, with a face of sixty, was carrying a six-month-old infant wrapped in a flighty bundle of furs. He deposited the baby under a freight car, crawled after him and drew from a pocket some dried fish heads, which he chewed ravenously and then, bringing the baby's lips to his, he transferred the sticky white paste of the half-masticated fish scales and bones to the infant's mouth as the mother bird feeds her young."

He clicked the stopwatch again as the last sentence of the recording whizzed to a finish. Two hundred and twenty-one words a minute. Not bad, but still twenty-five under his best. In radio, time was money, and the correspondent who could cram the most words into a minute of airtime would always be in high demand.

He leaned back in his leather seat and tried to stop worrying about the state of the world, a reflex that he had never come close to perfecting. During the twelve years since the war, he had rushed all over the globe, covering the Polish-Russian and Moroccan wars, crossing the Sahara desert to interview Arab sheiks, riding up the Niger River to Timbuktu, and island-hopping in the West Indies. This was his first real vacation in a decade, and he had decided to spend it taking a road trip to Yellowstone Park and visiting some of the country he had covered as a young newshawk.

He passed another farm truck groaning under a haul of stacked furniture. The farther out of Chicago he got, the more itinerant families he was encountering. Some sat stranded along the highway, clustering together in their misery in tents and shacks. Others insisted on traveling alone, clinging to what pathetic independence they could manage in a last gasp for dignity. He had never expected to see anything in America approaching the destitution in Russia, but the situation out here in the heartland was getting too damn familiar for comfort. He glanced at the rearview mirror and watched the rattling jalopy snort steam from its radiator. Unable to let it fade out of sight, he braked to a stop and shifted into reverse. He backtracked even again with the wheeled beast of burden and waved the driver down. Flicking away the dust, he pulled out his money clip, peeled off two bills, and reached the cash through his opened window.

The haggard-looking man behind the wheel shook his head. "I can't take your charity, mister."

"Not charity at all," Gibbons said. "I was admiring that chair you got strapped on your bumper. I've been looking for one like that for years."

"Why that old thing ain't worth the kindling."

"You fight in the war?"

"How'd you know?"

"I could tell by the way you roll that rig around the berms," Gibbons said. "Worst drivers I ever saw were in the Army."

In the rear bed of the truck, four freckle-faced boys raised their heads up like dragon's teeth through the mangle of strapped-down furniture. The oldest leaned over the side and yelled a discovery, "Pa, that's the Headline Hunter!"

The sharecropper and his wife, an emaciated sparrow who would have made Old Mother Hubbard appear youthful, took a closer inspection of the generous stranger. They looked as if they'd just been hit with frying pans.

Gibbons broke the grin of a gangster caught red-handed at the bank vault. He wagged a finger of warning at the star-struck boy who had pegged him, "Don't be too sure, son. A lot of people are running around this country posturing as the Headline Hunter. Why, last month they caught a fellow down in Florida wearing an eye patch and talking fast while claiming to be the radioman. Turned out he was just crazy."

The father reached his arm across to shake hands with fame. "We used to listen to you every Saturday night. Until…"

"We had to sell the radio," his wife explained.

Gibbons pulled another bill from his clip and gave it to her. "I can't be losing loyal listeners. You get yourself a new Zenith down at the Montgomery Ward."

The oldest son climbed atop cab's roof. "Mr. Gibbons, tell us that story again how you went walking that day with President Coolidge."

"Now Tom," the mother scolded. "Mr. Gibbons doesn't want to be bothered."

Gibbons removed his straw panama hat to rub his rugged scalp. "Let me see if I can remember it now. Oh, yeah. So, old Cal invited me over for one of his evening strolls down Pennsylvania Avenue before he turned in for bed at seven. Now, mind you, I'm the only newsman ever to be honored with such an invitation. Hoover doesn't even walk with his own advisors, let alone with ink-stained hacks."

Entertained, the boy slapped at his thigh as if pounding mites from a quilt. "Heck, Mr. Gibbons, you're more important to us than any of them politicians! You're the only one who tells us the truth!"

"Tom!" his mother admonished. "Have respect for our government leaders."

Gibbons gave a thumb's up to the woman's patriotism. "Old Cal wasn't much of a talker. We must have covered five blocks before he said, 'Nice crisp weather.' I tried to get the conversation stoked with a description of my excursions in Africa, but after ten minutes, all he asked me again was, 'You there, and when?'"

"What'dja tell him, Mr. Gibbons?" the son asked.

"At that very moment, I was about to cross the street when a taxicab came flying by on my blind side. Silent Cal yanked me back to the sidewalk, just in the nick."

"Praise Heaven!" the mother ejaculated.

Gibbons nodded at the sentiment. "I guess sometimes I get to spouting my ideas so fast, I forget my surroundings. If I hadn't been ambling with the president that day, I probably wouldn't be here conversing with you. Heck of a thing if I'd dodged all those bullets over the years just to be felled by a motor vehicle in the nation's capital."

The mother fanned her heated cheeks with her hand. "Lord, we could use Mr. Coolidge back there now."

Gibbons returned his hat to its perch and tipped its brim. "Here's hoping for an easier road up ahead for you good folks."

"Tom, pull that chair down for Mr. Gibbons," the mother ordered.

Gibbons held the boy at bay with a palm. "Where you all headed?

"Boise," the father said. "If the patch on this carburetor holds out."

"I'd be obliged if you could transport the heirloom up there for me." Gibbons pointed to his rear seat, which was filled with boxes of his books and fan letters. "I don't have much room left in this fancy tin can the sponsors make me drive. I'll catch up with you down the road."

"God bless you, Floyd Gibbons!" the mother cried, fighting back tears.

As the truck chugged off leaving a miasma of gas fumes and steam, young Tom, perched atop the cab, waved goodbye and hollered, "Signing off, Headline Hunter!"

Gibbons sat watching the dust from their bald tires spiral over the horizon like a twister. He didn't have the heart to tell those poor folks that they had heard the last of his Headline Hunter broadcasts, for NBC, at least. The sponsor of that show, the *Literary Digest* magazine, had canceled him after he turned up drunk at the home of the company's teetotaling president one night with a couple of speakeasy ladies on his arms. Seemed hilarious at the time, but in retrospect, it might not have been such a great career move.

He really didn't give a damn. Hell, he still had plenty of other radio shows and sponsors. His schedule was booked for two years with speaking engagements regaling crowds on his travels and exploits that led to his several books. Still, it burned him that he was the first newsman ever to be required to sign a morality clause in his contract. He had finally relented, but only after insisting on his own clause promising that he would never be forced to undergo facial surgery to beautify his war-worn looks.

And nobody, not even NBC and those Prohibition do-gooders, would *ever* take away the moniker by which he was known to millions.

No sir, he would always be the Headline Hunter.

He toasted that certainty with another swig of Four Roses bourbon from his flask, and then he headed back down the gypsum track. When he got up to cruising speed, he turned the dial on the dash radio until he found the voice of Lowell Thomas, the reporter that NBC had hired to replace him. That poor boy sounded downright nervous as he expounded on the pros and cons of Hoover's latest economic boondoggle.

He grinned, remembering his own first week on the air. He never had gotten over that sickly feeling right before a broadcast. His throat would go dry and his pulse would soar, and he'd be convinced that he was slipping into a hallucination, recreating in his mind's eyes the remarkable events he had witnessed. He was still just an old newspaperman at heart. Sure, he had made his big fame on the airwaves, but no print columnist was ever tossed out on his ass for keeping the bourbon business from going under. Radio sponsors were demanding too much power these days. It wouldn't be long before the suits on the top floors started censoring stories to avoid offending the mothers who bought their soap and soda water.

One upside of it was, if his lone eye ever gave out—and there'd been some recent scares—he'd still have the fastest voice in the business.

Another hour up the road, he spied a gathering of tents in an open field. A banner on poles invited motorists to Stop Here at Farley's Carnival Show. Like every author, he was incapable of passing up a chance to sell a few books. And like every man with a little kid inside him, he wouldn't be denied a circus. Besides, he hadn't had a good sausage dog since he had watched Walter Johnson throw flames out here years ago.

He pulled to the side and parked. Always prepared for such occasions, he unlocked the trunk and rifled through his tried-and-true array of disguises. He decided on the Red Baron this time: aviator goggles, soft-leather helmet, long red scarf, and a khaki pilot's jacket. After confirming his anonymity in the reflection of the windowpane, he walked into the fair as if one of the Wright brothers had just flown in for some cotton candy. He strolled *incognito* down the midway, guessing the fat lady's weight and throwing baseballs at milk bottles glued to shelves.

A few minutes into his tour of American low culture, he caught sight of a candy stand on the periphery of the fair grounds. There, standing on a block of wood, loomed a slim man about six-foot-four, clad in a silk top hat and black dress coat with tails. The fellow was barking at customers in a fervent effort to sucker them toward his array of delectable treats. Every so often, the prairie giant would lean out over the gawkers at such a severe angle that he seemed to defy the laws of nature.

Gibbons sauntered closer to this anti-gravity maestro and saw that passersby were being offered a chance to try their hand at winning a box of Choward's Violet Mints by guessing the digits drawn from a rotating basket of numbered cork balls. After observing the cork balls pop up for nearly a minute, he puzzled over the fact that the crowd seemed to be winning more than losing.

What kind of half-baked carny scam was this, anyway?

His journalistic instincts were firing. He walked closer, intent on discovering the trick behind this illusion. He circled the stand and caught a fleeting glimpse of the exposed back of the block elevating the barker. To his delight, he saw the answer to the mystery: the con man had rigged up a pair of shoes with metal plates that kept his cuff-covered heels attached to the block. Below the block, a pug hound lay guarding his master's secret.

A memory synapse in his brain fired.

He threw a pebble at the dog's hind leg, and when the hawker wasn't looking, whistled the dog over and whispered to it's ear: "Is that you, Scrapper?"

A lapping tongue to his cheek confirmed his suspicion.

With his eye patch hidden behind his goggles, he walked around the barker's stand and threaded the crowd that was watching this leaning tower of baloney's act. He rang up his loud radio voice and yelled, "I'll put twenty dollars on number twenty-six!"

The audience gasped at that princely sum.

The tilting barker nearly bit his lip. "That's a hefty wager, sir. We'd have to see evidence of your *bona fides*."

Gibbons pulled out a twenty-dollar bill and waved it for all to see.

"Any reason you'd pick *that* number?" the barker inquired.

Gibbons wiped two fingers across his goggles like windshield wipers. "My brother flew recon for the Forty-Second Division. He told me the worst damn fighting unit in the whole war was the Twenty-Sixth Yankee Division. Bunch of East Coast dandies, he called them. Couldn't aim a howitzer if the target was strapped to the mouth of the barrel. I figure that number's due to come up since it had such a poor run of luck in France."

The barker frowned as he peered down into the crowd, trying to place the head behind the goggles. "This is a free country, Lindbergh. Go ahead and bet your crop-dusting wages and lose them, if you're so inclined."

"On one condition."

The barker was fast becoming annoyed. "We don't let the customers set the conditions, sir."

"Not even for twenty bucks? That's more than most folks make in a week."

"What *is* your request, then?"

Gibbons held out the money at arm's length, as if dangling a dog biscuit. "You come down here and get it from me."

The barker appeared nonplussed by the challenge. "That's not necessary. Just hand the legal tender to my assistant over there."

"A hundred dollars! If you come shake my hand for it."

"Now, look, Wilbur. Why don't you run along back to your dirigible?"

The audience turned and eyed the barker suspiciously, questioning why he wouldn't descend from his perch to take the easy cash.

Gibbons removed his goggles and helmet.

The crowd squealed with sudden recognition. "It's the Headline Hunter!" shouted a dozen voices in the crowd. "The One-Eyed Knight of the Airwaves!"

Gibbons raised his arms like a ringleader as he strutted in front of the barker's block. "Ladies and gentlemen! Today I shall demonstrate a feat of magic never before seen in the Western Hemisphere. With one swipe of my mortal hand, I, a human Cyclops, shall produce before you the youngest general ever to have fought with the famous American Expeditionary Force."

He walked up to the barker and tore off the man's fake beard.

Happy Glassford stood exposed, his identity revealed to the astonished bumpkins. His ruse revealed, the West Pointer sheepishly stepped out of his bolted shoes. In his socks, he loped over with a wide grin and put the newsman's neck in a friendly arm lock in retaliation. "By God, Gibbons, what the hell are you doing here?"

Gibbons bowed to accept the accolades of his adoring public. "I was about to ask you the same thing, General."

"I'm a major now. The brass knocked me down a couple notches."

"Happened to the best of them after the war. Even MacArthur lost a star. I heard ol' Black Jack had to run him down and rip it from his shirt."

Swarmed by the fairgoers, Gibbons climbed atop the wooden block. "Folks, I'm going to renew an acquaintance with my old Army friend here. But if you'll all show up at those grandstands in an hour, I'll regale you with the story of how this tall drink of West Point water invented the Glassford Trench Mortar during the great Marne offensive!"

While the crowd applauded eagerly, Gibbons slipped an arm over Glassford's shoulder and whispered, "Any place a man can get a wee sampling of the local branch-water malt around here?"

"Sorry to say, but Iowa is a dry state. Like the rest of the country, in case you haven't heard."

Gibbons flashed the flask that he kept hidden in his pocket. "Then we'll have to temporarily secede from the Union." As they walked behind the tents sharing the flask, he asked his old friend, "I'm not against dishonest work, Hap, but seriously. What's this circus gig all about?"

Glassford shrugged. "I guess I've been a little at loose ends since the war. I tried ranching in Arizona, but that didn't work out. Then my father died. I was pretty down in the dumps for a while. There's not much call for an old soldier these days. I thought I'd pull up tracks and try the itinerant life for a few months."

"How's the painting going?"

"I've sold a few pieces."

"You let me know if you ever finish any good nudes."

They enjoyed a good laugh, and Gibbons waited for his friend to come clean with the reason for traveling with this circus. When the former officer refused to spill the beans, Gibbons edged closer. "Shouldn't you be in Washington right now?"

"Washington? Why would I want to go back to that cesspool?"

Gibbons looked at him quizzically. "You wouldn't be playing possum with an old newspaperman, would you?"

"I don't have a notion of what you're talking about."

"When was the last time you saw General Crosby?"

Glassford thought for a moment. "I ran into him a few months ago back East while I was helping put together the VFW Jubilee."

"You'd better get your bags packed and the cow manure scraped from your boots."

"Why?"

Gibbons looked around for prying ears. "You didn't hear it from me, but Crosby's going to offer you the police chief's job for the District of Columbia."

Glassford stopped in his tracks. "Some of those boys at Fort Myer put you up to this prank, didn't they?"

Gibbons raised his palm as if swearing an oath. "I'm as serious as Herbert Hoover in a church full of nuns."

"Off the record, you can take this to the bank. I'm no police chief. Never will be."

"You should think about it," Gibbons said. "Sometimes a man's destiny can come at him blind from the flank."

"Yeah?"

Gibbons nodded as he took another swig. "One night in Chicago a few years ago, I was feeling low about losing my mother. It was my first Christmas without her, and I was home on leave. The night editor at the WGN radio station asked me to fill in for a Christmas Eve cancellation. He interviewed me about my travels, and I guess I got a little misty-eyed about all the far-flung places I'd spent Christmas. Next thing I know, the station is getting inundated with fan mail, and NBC hires me. I was convinced that I was no radio commentator, but I took a chance. Maybe you should, too."

Glassford laughed and waved off the pep talk. "Police chief? Never gonna happen. But if it did, the first order I'd hand down would be to ban you from all press briefings."

Gibbons played hurt; then, he winked. "The only thing crazier than you taking that job is me covering City Hall in Washington."

43

WASHINGTON, D.C.
OCTOBER 1931

President Hoover made sure that all of the reporters had left the press room for the evening. Then, he pulled down his fedora to shadow his face and slipped out the rear doors of the White House. Bundled in the same camel hair coat that he always wore for his post-dinner constitutional, he headed across the lawn toward the corner of Seventeenth and E Streets, away from the Treasury Building, just to add another element of misdirection. At the curb, an unmarked car pulled up. After glancing down both ends of the dark street, he opened the back door and slid into the rear seat. "Take the Parkway," he ordered his senior press secretary. "In case we're being tailed."

As Walter Newton drove off and turned left on K Street, Hoover monitored the speedometer, making sure the aide stayed under the speed limit. The last thing he needed was a headline in the next day's newspapers: *Hoover Caught Breaking Law During Secret Escape from White House.*

"You sit back and relax, sir," Newton said. "I'll have you there in no time."

Hoover, exasperated, clenched his jaw. Why was everyone always telling him to relax? The world was falling apart around him, and he was supposed to *relax?* How much more of this humiliation could he endure? He prayed this hare-brained scheme didn't turn into another Valley Forge fiasco. Earlier that year, he had agreed to deliver the Memorial Day address at the site of the famous Revolutionary War encampment. Little good came of the gesture; the visit merely gave the quipsters and columnists the opportunity to suggest he was now taking credit for starvation a century and a half ago, too.

The bitter irony of this night's journey to his Canossa on Dupont Circle was not lost on him. Accused of being a puppet of Wall Street, here he was slinking out of the White House like a felon to meet with the nation's most powerful bankers at Andrew Mellon's mansion. He understood that a public summons of the top financial leaders to the Oval Office would have sent the markets into another panic. But did the summit have to be held in his own Treasury Secretary's opulent lair? No other secure choice could be found, he had been told. And he couldn't risk the press finding out about the meeting, especially with that gadfly Floyd Gibbons snooping around town again. Still, he couldn't fathom a less inviting place to deliver his plea for the bankers to help him save the country.

"Would you like to listen to the radio, sir? It's the Will Rogers hour."

Hoover shrugged with indifference. He knew the aide was merely asking for himself.

Newton turned the dial until he found the *Gulf Headliners,* the evening broadcast during which Rogers always rambled on about the events of the day. The cowboy philosopher was in the midst of a spiel about the economy:

"Worldwide depression, everywhere.

Herbert Hoover is to blame.

Disaster in the Earth and air,

Herb Hoover is to blame.

I find my eyes are getting dim,

Herb Hoover is to blame.

My bank account is very slim,

Herb Hoover is to blame.

My oldest boy is running booze,

And little Jennie smokes and chews,

I'm nearly dying of the Blues,

Herb Hoover is to blame."

Newton changed the frequency on the radio. "Old Will is getting pretty hard up for material these days."

Hoover wasn't listening. His mind was back in Belgium during those first months of the war. He still had nightmares about that miserable night when he had been forced to strip naked to pass through the German checkpoints. Yet that humiliation would pale compared to what he was about to endure. Never could he have imagined being forced to travel on the sly in his own country. He had warned Clemenceau and Wilson that the harsh Versailles treaty would come back to haunt the Allies. And now, just as he had feared, the European banks were crashing, hamstrung by German reparations. Earlier that year, he had convinced Congress to pass a moratorium on German loan payments to the United States. But that effort had proved no more effective than spitting into a tsunami. This night would be his last chance to buttress the Atlantic dam before it broke and drowned the American economy with another wave of deflation.

"Mr. President," said Newton, pulling the car to a stop. "We're here."

Hoover rolled down the window and stared up at a three-story Beaux-Arts building across the street. In one of the high windows of the penthouse, a dazzling chandelier reflected a shower of light across a massive guest hall, where smoke from several dozen cigars wafted like the vaporous murk of Hell.

"Would you like me to come in with you, sir?"

Hoover shook his head and ordered the car be parked where it wouldn't be noticed. Bracing for the ordeal, he got out and walked toward the entrance. A doorman allowed him entry and accompanied him up the elevator. When the mahogany doors to the top floor opened, he strode out into a marble hallway lined with paintings by the great masters. On his left hung Raphael's *Alba Madonna*, and across from that work hovered Jan van Eyck's *The Annunciation*. He had expected Mellon to greet him at the door, but the wealthy Treasury Secretary was holding court in the drawing room, chatting and smoking cigars with the heads of the largest financial institutions in New York.

Hoover flushed with pique. The insolent Scotsman wouldn't even give him the courtesy of a proper welcome. He was about to enter unannounced when a painting above the brass casing caught his eye. An engraved gold plate below it read: *St. Martin and the Beggar* by El Greco. A nobleman sitting on a magnificent white steed was shown stopping to drop a few coins into the hands of a half-naked beggar. Was this a warning sign from the Almighty? Or had Mellon strategically placed this painting above the entry to subtly remind his fellow financiers of Christ's pronouncement that the poor will always be with us?

Mellon finally turned and affected surprise, as if only then apprised of Hoover's arrival. "Mr. President, so honored to have you in my home."

A servant brought up a silver platter laden with caviar and oysters, but Hoover waved it away, repulsed by the thought of eating such delicacies while less fortunate Americans couldn't afford a cup of gizzard broth. As the other bankers gathered around him and hushed, he dismissed all small talk and said sternly, "Shall we commence, gentlemen?"

Mellon narrowed his cadaverous face into a glare of condescension at the rebuff of traditional pleasantries. Coldly, he led Hoover and the others into a large room furnished with a long conference table and a chandelier that lit the ceiling with a ghoulish, crystallized tint reminiscent of a funeral parlor. Without being offered it, Hoover took the head of the table, forcing Mellon to be satisfied with the position on his right. The president motioned for Ogden Mills, his assistant secretary of the Treasury, to sit on the other side of him.

When all were settled and restocked with cigars, Hoover got right to the point. "The banks in London, Antwerp, and Paris have ceased functioning. The Weimar Republic is on the verge of collapse. Mobs roam the streets in Germany and Austria. England has gone off the gold standard. Seventeen more nations have followed. There are rumors that mutinies have been suppressed in the Royal Navy. The world's financial system is suffering a heart attack. If we do not take remedial action at once, the economic damage will jump the Atlantic."

An uncomfortable silence settled around the table. The financiers looked at each other, clearly discomfited by what they perceived as hostile brevity and lack of nuance in Hoover's report.

At last, George Whitney of J.P. Morgan spoke. "Mr. President, we went along with your suggestion to suspend demands for payment of the German loans. That action did nothing to stop the money supply from shrinking."

Hoover, disgusted at being forced to come here hat in hand, could hardly bear to look at the greedy bankers. How many of them had sacrificed half their lives to serve the lesser fortunate of the world? He fixed his attention on the sheen of the mahogany table and, pressing his hands into its edge, insisted, "We must get credit flowing again here at home."

"Perhaps if you were a bit more upbeat in your public appearances," Whitney suggested. "You should talk to the country like a father who has optimism for his children."

Hoover stiffened. "I am not going to run around caterwauling like Billy Sunday! I have too much respect for the intelligence of the American people!"

William Potter, the chairman of the Guaranty Trust Bank, pursed his bloodless lips and lectured Hoover in a tone of condescension. "Depositors need to be reproached to keep their money in their accounts."

"No," Hoover said firmly. "Your banks, not the depositors, must lead the way. We cannot expect everyday folk to underwrite your timidity. You need to free up loans for the farmers and small businessmen. Millions have lost their savings because you keep your assets cloistered like pearls in clamped clamshells."

"We cannot make loans without collateral," warned Charles Mitchell of National City Bank. "And people don't have the collateral to offer."

Hoover was doing his utmost to remain calm, but the rage he had held in check for months was threatening to boil over. "They have no collateral, sir, because your banks have frozen their deposits. Can you not see that we are caught in a vicious cycle?"

Winthrop Aldrich of Chase National Bank drew another puff from his cigar. "How then do you propose to free up the money supply?"

Hoover heard clearly the nervy tone of challenge in that question. "By having your banks organize and attack the problem together. Capitalism in tandem with altruism has solved every problem this country has ever confronted. We businessmen fed a starving Europe during the war. We can certainly strengthen the foundations of our own house." He leaned forward to underscore the gravity of his plea. "I am one of you. I understand the calculus of risk. One bank alone cannot step out onto the ice unless all step out. I implore you to form a national credit association. Work as one voice to pump money back into the economy." When none of the financiers offered immediate support for the plan, the president sat for nearly a minute in vexed contemplation, his head down and his thoughts lost in his own misery.

Clearing his throat, Mellon added a coda to the president's proposal. "Purely voluntary, of course. We would not suggest any course of action that smacks of European or Russian socialist planning."

Hoover sat stunned, sabotaged by his own Treasury Secretary. He remembered a reporter once describing Mellon, quite accurately, as smoking like a man who recalculated the compound-per-annum interest on his tobacco with each puff. He knew very well what Mellon was attempting to do with his suggestion to take the White House proposal under advisement. By emphasizing the voluntary nature of the plan to ease credit, the prune-faced septuagenarian was sending his fellow barons a coded message that they need not worry about enforcement. Mellon seemed more concerned with enhancing his fame by building a national art gallery than resurrecting the nation's economy.

Hoover grimaced. His ulcer was flaring up again. In a moment of similar exasperation, he had once suggested to the White House press that the chief executive should have the right to execute two people a year without offering a reason. If armed with such a power this night, he wouldn't hesitate in choosing the victim.

Yet Mellon seemed not the least disconcerted by the presidential glare of indignation bearing down on him. Instead of yielding, the Treasury chief whispered his next observation with such a soft arrogance of authority that the bankers had to strain to hear him. "I think I can speak for all present. I recommend we consider what has been said this evening. Is that agreeable?"

These few men who held the nation's fate on their balance books nodded coldly in agreement.

Rebuffed in his call for immediate action, Hoover arose abruptly. He briskly shook their clammy hands and then made his way out the same way he had entered. He knew from their stony defiance what their answers to his request for voluntary sacrifice would be. Tomorrow morning, they would all rush to their offices and call in more loans, hoarding what assets they could salvage. Like Mellon, they were just biding their time, counting their bond coupons until their preferred brand of fascism could be installed in the government.

The only trouble with capitalism, he muttered bitterly as he slammed open Mellon's gilt doors and walked to the elevator, was the greedy capitalist.

44

PORTLAND, OREGON
NOVEMBER 1931

Flanked by his wife and two crying daughters, Walter Waters stood helpless as the tenement manager threw the last few pieces of their furniture out of their one-room flat that sat above the rail yards. Prodded by his wife, Waters tried to reason with the man. "I have money coming at the end of the m-m-month!"

The super kicked another chair down the stairwell. "Come back when you can lie without spitting."

"I got a lead on a j-j-job in Sellwood."

"Doing what?" the super scoffed. "Selling wood in Sellwood? Get the hell off this property. And don't come back."

Wilma Waters, scrawny as a heron and ten years younger than her husband, tried to plant a heel into the super's shin, but his forearm sent her staggering against the wall. "This ain't no way to treat a veteran and his family!"

The big tough just laughed at her. "The war's been over for thirteen years. This is Oregon, not Russia. Your 'hero' here ain't no Alvin York. And he has to pay rent like everybody else."

"He git a job, and then they keep laying him off!"

"Then why don't *you* get a job?" the super said.

"I've been working off and on down at Meier and Frank."

"Doing what?"

Wilma didn't want to answer, but she did. "I display myself in the street window."

The rent enforcer howled so loudly at her that he spawned another round of bawling from the frightened girls. "You stand in for them naked mannequins, do you? Or do they call you when they need to scare the pigeons off the sills?"

Wilma knelt down and tried to rub away the burning pangs in the bellies of her daughters. "Tell him, Dubya!"

Waters just stood there with his eyes cast down, a beaten man. "She brings in a d-d-dollar ten a day. B-b-but we got to eat."

The super snorted. "Not my problem."

"I got m-m-money coming from the government. The Bonus—"

The super pushed him aside with no more effort than if flicking a fly. "Yeah, Bonus! Bonus! That's the only word you can mutter clean. By the time nineteen and forty-five gets here, you can use that measly five hundred bucks to buy a nice granite stone that says, 'Here lies the Bonus of Wa-Wa-Waters.'"

The door slammed, and Waters was cast into the hallway's darkness. He staggered down the stairs and outside into a chilly fog that hung low over the harbor. His wife and daughters followed after him, fracturing the morning silence with their screams and crying. He circled aimlessly in the street, bereft of a direction. The marine soup that morning reminded him of those days on the Front when the smoke would linger over the trenches and nearly strangle you with its peppery stench of gunpowder. He sniffed the air and caught the scent of something burning down near the plaza. Above him, in one of the tenement windows, a radio was playing a Rudy Vallee song:

They used to tell me I was building a dream,
with peace and glory ahead.
Why should I be standing in line
just waiting for bread?

He started walking toward the aroma of charcoal, remembering fondly the beef barbecues of his youth in Idaho.

"Dubya!" Wilma cried. "Where you think you're going?"

"Aw, I just n-n-need to do some thinking."

"You ain't taking off on me again like you did in Idaho! Come on back here, Dubya! These girls gotta be fed!"

Waters disappeared into the mists as Rudy Vallee crooned on:

Once in cocky suits, gee we looked swell,
full of yankee doodle dum.
Half a million boots went sloggin' through mud,
I was the kid with the drum...
Brother, can you spare a dime?

od knows I've tried. Waters kept mumbling that protest as he limped down the crumbling sidewalk. How many hours had he been out here? Didn't matter. He had nowhere to go. What was a man supposed to do? Since coming back from the war, he had lost at least a dozen jobs. Sold cars in Weiser for a while, until nobody had any money left to buy one. How the hell was that his fault? Then he got hired on as a mechanic. But if people ain't got the money to buy a vehicle, it ain't long before they ain't got the money to fix one, either. After that, he had migrated west, picking asparagus and working in a bakery along the way. He'd thought he finally had the world licked when he arrived here in Portland two years ago. Made it all the way up the ladder to night boss at the cannery factory, but then that went under, too.

The mists thinned, and he came to an open concrete square dotted with abandoned oil barrels burning kindling fires. Hundreds of hollow-eyed men in threadbare jackets and trousers milled about aimlessly. One old codger slumping on his haunches offered him an apple for a penny.

He shrugged off the transaction by opening his empty pockets as proof of his poverty. The next block down, dozens of out-of-work fellows just like him stood in a bread line, waiting for a single ladling of that rotten vegetable stew they served with a piece of moldy bread. His stomach curdled at the thought of another day's meal of that gruel not fit for rats. Driven by a rush of anger and despair, he jumped on a cinder block and shouted, "F-f-fellas, I just got tossed outa my shanty by a vet! Wha-wha-t's it coming to if we turn on ourselves?"

The ghoulish faces below looked up at him languidly, as if pestered by a gnat. Most of the men ignored him, but one big-boned fellow had enough sap in his veins to quip, "What d'ya want, the Medal of Honor?"

"I say we go to Wa-Wa-Washington!" Waters cried. "Tell the president himself we need that mo-mo-money they promised us!"

"Yeah, you and Herbert would have a pretty talk," scoffed another veteran who tugged at the drab overcoat issued to him on mustering out in France.

"B-b-bonus for fighting!" Waters insisted. "That was the deal! Ever one of us is owed at least five hundred dollars! That was the d-d-deal!"

"That's three thousand miles to Washington," the hulking Irishman reminded him. "I could kick you farther than you can walk."

"What's your name?" Waters asked.

"Mickey Dolan."

"Let me t-t-tell you what, Mickey Dolan. I betcha we all w-w-walked three thousand miles in France. Hell, I remember w-w-walking three thousand miles in those d-d-damn trenches just to find the latrine."

Several of the men laughing bitterly, and a new voice from the retreating mists inquired, "How you figure to get us there? Hoover sending us an escort?"

Waters looked across the plaza. He saw that the questioner was a Negro sitting by himself and caressing a tube that resembled a grenade launcher.

Dolan walked over and hovered above the Negro. "Us? Where you think you're going, Sambo?"

The black man didn't back down. "I'ze just as much a veteran as you."

"Prove it. Or I'll put a knee in those flapping African gums."

The black hobo inserted one end of his grenade launcher in his mouth and, to the amazement of all, began playing a sad rendition of George M. Cohan's patriotic tune, *Over There*. After tooting the first stanza, he sang his own modified version of the lyrics:

> *Over here, over here,*
> *the Yanks are starving,*
> *the Yanks are starving,*
> *the Yanks are starving everywhere.*

While some of the men began clapping to the beat and singing along, Waters spotted a short, bald fireplug of a man perched on a crate under a lamppost. Possessed of dark, penetrating eyes and a proud Jesuit demeanor that seemed at war with his rags, that hobo sitting off by himself had been silently enjoying the oratorical performance like a customer in the back row of an outdoor theatre. The seated mime kicked his feet up and down against the asphalt as if mocking a marching routine, and Waters began to wonder if the fellow wasn't a little off in the head.

The mime imposter shifted his eyes toward the Negro, who was now singing and playing his instrument like a black angel of death summoning the multitudes to damnation.

Waters interpreted the odd fellow's gesture as a coded suggestion that he go over and befriend the black minstrel. He couldn't quite figure why this mute bum was trying to orchestrate his decisions, and he *really* couldn't figure why he was now feeling the impulse to humor him, but he did. He motioned the Negro over and shook his hand. "We c-c-could use a little entertainment on our way east. I'm Dubya Dubya Waters."

"Ozzie Taylor."

Dolan ambled over and circled the black hobo. "What unit?"

"Three Hundred and Sixty-Ninth."

Impressed by that pedigree, several of the white bums made a determined effort to rise from their stupor to more closely examine the claimant.

"You were with the Hellfighters?" Waters asked.

Taylor proudly displayed a frayed regimental patch that he had sewn on the inside of his jacket. "I was Big Jim Europe's orderly. This here's the oboe I played with him on our triumphal march home down Fifth Avenue."

One of the men whistled his admiration. "You don't say. Hell of a bandleader, that Reese Europe. What ever happened to the old boy?"

Taylor lowered his hangdog eyes. "He got stabbed."

"Was he f-f-fooling around with someone's wife?" Waters asked.

Taylor shook his head, as if not quite believing what he was about to report. "One of Big Jim's drummers didn't like the way he was being treated on the payroll. So he busted into the Boss's dressing room one night and gutted him in the neck with a pen knife."

Dolan kneaded up his cauliflower nose as if sniffing out a tall tale. "That's a whopper of a fish story, Oswald, or whatever the hell you claimed your name was. What exactly is a Harlem shoe shiner doing all the way out here."

"Looking for work. Just like you fellas."

Waters took a liking to the Negro veteran. "I say he c-c-comes with us."

Dolan bristled all six-foot-three of his imposing frame in protest. "First of all, I'm not traveling with no Ethiopian. Second of all, no soldiers ever marched on the Capitol. So it's not happening. None of it."

"Ain't no one never s-s-starved in this country before, too. And the man's a soldier, and he's welcome to c-c-come with us. What the hell difference does it make what c-c-color he is if he's down on his luck just like all of us?"

Dolan couldn't dredge up a rebuttal to that point.

Yet Taylor seemed a little skittish about the plan. "Now Mister Waters, I appreciate your way of thinking. But I reckon if the government sees a bunch of trained gunmen coming east, the G-men will have us in the stockade before we cross the Rockies. Especially with my ebony face in the regiment."

"We go peaceful," Waters insisted. "We got that right. Those Wall Street thieves go to Washington to lobby for their pockets to be filled. We ain't ever gonna get nothing done until we do the same. We go peaceful."

"Yeah," smirked Dolan. "Just like those boys in Dearborn went peaceful. They got their skulls peaceably knocked in for it, too."

"By God, I'm going!" Waters shouted. "You all c-c-can stand here and rot if you want, but I'm going! We'd never won the war if we stood around and q-q-quarreled!"

Most of the hobos laughed Waters off, and the sullen Irishman shot a jet of root juice at the unemployed canner's feet to chase him away.

"Take that to Washington with you," Dolan said.

The men walked off to return to their bivouacs around the barrel fires. Abandoned, Waters tried to step down from the concrete block, but his weakened legs buckled him, and he stumbled to his hands and knees. Chased by the catcalls and jeers, he arose and limped away discouraged, forced to find an empty corner.

Later that night, Waters walked the deserted streets trying to memorize a speech. He worked hard to smooth his stuttering, just as he used to do when he walked the rail spur as a boy. "It's in the Const-ti-tushun. Man's g-gotta *right* to assemble peaceful. Nah, man's gotta ri-right to ay-semble *peaceably.* Man's g-g-got—"

"Your dear voice is not clear, gentle and evening clear, as theirs whom none now hear."

Waters turned toward the silhouette of a bum sitting against the cannery wall. He came closer, angling for more light from the lamppost, and recognized the night warbler as the taciturn veteran who had traded nods with him in the plaza that afternoon.

The shadowy intruder gestured with his hands as if orchestrating music. "And though your hand be pale, paler are those which trail."

Waters looked around for a bottle. "Sounds like y-y-you been into some bad cognac, bub."

"*Au contraire,* my eloquent friend! I prefer the sweet nectar of the verse. Wilfred Owen, the troubadour of the trench. Until he became a small patch of England left in France. That almost rhymed, didn't it?"

"You a poet?"

"No, but I can spot one. I watched you on the stump this afternoon."

"Don't t-t-toy with me, fella. I've had enough of the needle for one day."

"Name's George Alford. Fifty-fifth Infantry."

"Mine's Waters."

"Yeah, I know all about you. You tried to push those privates off the dime with cold reasoning this afternoon. Men down on their luck don't navigate with their heads. You want them to chin the moon, you have to light a fire in their souls."

"Fat chance of that. I g-g-got this obvious problem with my t-t-talking."

"That's just the flame of inspiration in your throat burning those fine *mots* to cinders before they can reach the world's ears. All the great poets have that rush of the tongue. I think I may have a solution for your problem."

The squat veteran climbed to his ponderous feet. Tacking against the night winds with a crook-legged rodeo gait, he led Waters through the back alleys. When they came to the stockyards near the river, Alford signaled for him to stay silent and then led him past a couple of sleeping guards. This odd fellow had the route down so pat that Waters figured he must have made trespassing a regular habit. Together they threaded their way past a herd of cattle mooing sleepily, until they came to another section of the yards.

Thousands of turkeys sat huddled together behind a wire fence.

The birds watched suspiciously as Alford opened up a hole in the mesh and retied the strands of wire behind them. He stood up in the middle of the flock and, stretching his arms skyward as if to stretch his lungs, whispered to Waters, "Say hello to your troops."

Waters was beginning to wonder if he had put himself in the hands of a madman, but he had to admit the birds looked pretty succulent.

"Go ahead," Alford insisted. "Cajole these fine fellows into roosting with you on the Capitol dome."

Waters balled his fists; the prankster was obviously pulling a stunt so that he could tell the other fellows about it tomorrow. "You need some head d-d-doctoring."

"Maybe, but I'm not the one who can't spit out a full mouthful without tripping. Give it a try, like you did today."

Waters looked around the yard to make sure that Alford hadn't brought an audience of hobos to cackle at his gullibility. Assured that they were alone, he turned to the curious turkeys and said in a weak voice, "What I pro-propose is we take our gr-gr-grievances to the president."

The turkeys just stared at him.

"Hold on, Mother Goose, before you put these fowl to sleep. Dig deeper into the gut. Scream them like you are a man going over the top."

Waters was fed up with being jestered. "I got no job and no camp! But I ain't so low that I got to converse with poultry!"

The turkeys shook the night with gobbles that sounded like applause.

Alford grinned as if having conjured a magic trick. "Your first ovation. Give us some more of that high oratory."

Waters was amazed—these birds loved him. For the first time in his life, he felt free to say whatever the hell he wanted without fear of ridicule. He turned to his feathered constituency again and announced in the same confident voice, "Hoover and Mellon give loans to their high finance buddies! But not a dime to us vets! You beaks gonna sit here and take that?" He beamed from ear to ear as the turkeys gobbled their applause again.

"Yeah, you're a regular Teddy Rough-Riding Roosevelt," Alford said. "Now, here's the real test. Tell them something they'd rather not hear."

After thinking a moment, Waters shouted, "You're all looking at the basting pan tomorrow! Strung up and stuffed!"

To his amazement, the turkeys applauded with hearty gobbles again.

Alford wrapped an encouraging arm around the shoulder of his new protégé. "Those boys down at the plaza aren't much different than these clipped wingers. It's not *what* you tell them, but *how*. Give them the high notes, and they'll march to their own funerals."

The turkeys kept gobbling their ovations, and now Waters couldn't stop speechifying.

Alford spotted one of the hens that had gotten outside the fence. Her head was bloodied and drooping. He reached through the hole, picked her up, and grinned at dinner. "Turkeys all look the same to each other, till one gets a little red in the neck. Then the others will surround it and peck it until it bleeds to death. It's just their nature."

Waters didn't even hear him. Inspired by his newfound power of oratory, he stood gazing downriver toward the plaza, thinking about how, with this newfound power of his, he was going to change Mickey Dolan's mind about going to Washington.

Alford smiled with secret knowledge as he stroked the dying turkey's bloodied head. Watching Waters orate to the birds, he whispered another verse by the British poet Wilfred Owen: "The silver swan, who living had no voice, when death approached unlocked her silent throat."

45

WASHINGTON, D.C.
NOVEMBER 1931

With his suit jacket flapping over his shoulder, Happy Glassford rushed out the door of his newly leased Georgetown house, dubbed the "Borneo Embassy" by the society pages because so many *avant-garde* intellectuals, socialite grandees, homesick diplomats, and eccentric artists made pilgrimages there to admire his paintings and enjoy his dinner parties. Tucking in his shirt on the run, he hurdled Scrapper and hopped on Blue Bessie, his new two-cylinder motorcycle.

He shouted an order for the pug to stay and patrol the two-story brick colonial, but Scrapper had never gotten over his Gallic penchant for disobedience. With the dog chasing after him, he sped downtown, weaving in and out of lanes. He raced past several honking cabs on Pennsylvania Avenue and turned onto 14th Street NW, only to find that all of the parking spots at the District Building were filled. Already fifteen minutes late for his first day on the job, he decided to double-park behind a Studebaker.

Scrapper led him through the swinging doors. Waiting for him in the lobby was a crowd of cub reporters and the usual riff-raff of city officials and lowlifes appointed by their uncles and cousins. Herbert Crosby, accompanied by Douglas MacArthur and two fellow District commissioners, stood cooling their heels at a microphone. Behind them, uniformed cops, arrayed in a half circle, looked as if they'd rather be anywhere else.

"Sorry." Glassford straightened the knot on his tie as he rushed to the microphone. "Something has to be done about the traffic in this city."

The newsmen cackled at his quip, causing Scrapper to bark at the sudden noise, but the commissioners and police officers were not amused. Glassford looked around the lobby; sensing hostility from the cops, he was already starting to have second thoughts about taking this job. Crosby had put the hard sell on him, couching the offer in terms of duty to country. Only now, confronted by these crabby faces under blue caps, did he understand how difficult it was going to be to instill a new code of ethics and professionalism in the department.

Before his new hire could change his mind, Crosby grasped Glassford's hand and shook it with a half-hearted pump. "Glad you could make it, Major. Shall we proceed?"

As the cameras snapped away, Glassford waved to several acquaintances in the scrum of ambulance chasers, bootleggers, and pork-barrel stuffers, all who had come to find out what his hiring would mean for their illicit profits.

Crosby tapped the oval microphone. "Today, I am pleased to announce the hiring of a new police chief. Pelham Glassford is a decorated war hero, the youngest brigadier general to serve in the AEF. We feel he is exactly the kind of man we need to return the District metropolitan police force to its days of pride and glory." The ranks arrayed behind Crosby didn't appear to agree with that sentiment, but he didn't let their muted reaction deter his bombast. "In a testament to the high esteem held for Chief Glassford, General MacArthur has taken time from his busy schedule at the War Department to come by and show his support to his old West Point classmate."

MacArthur raised a patrician hand to acknowledge the applause, performing his best imitation of Caesar accepting homage from the plebeians.

Crosby cast a bemused eye at MacArthur's over-the-top performance as he held forth a Bible to Glassford. "He has a lot of work waiting for him, so we should let him get on with the task at hand. Do you, Pelham D. Glassford, swear to uphold the laws of the District of Columbia?"

"I do."

More camera bulbs flashed, and behind the blinding phosphorescence, someone in the news pool shouted, "We'd like to ask the Chief some questions!"

Crosby hustled Glassford off toward his new office upstairs. "That's not the way we do things around here. The police chief puts the questions *to* the criminals, not the other way around. I'm sure Chief Glassford will announce a press conference in a few weeks, once he gets his feet on the ground and has a chance to review his department."

The press began obediently departing like sheep to their pens when the same voice from the shadows demanded, "What are you hiding, Chief?"

On the staircase, Crosby spun back and squinted his mandarin eyes into the gang of pencil pushers to find the scoundrel. The beat reporters, confounded, glanced at each other, wondering who would lose their City Hall access for asking the impertinent question.

"Just how *does* Chief Glassford plan to weed out corruption in the force?"

The clatter of confusion heightened as the crowd searched for the source of the discarnate interrogation. Crosby and his fellow commissioners grew irritated, and the reporters began accusing one another of being the ventriloquist who was shooting his voice around the lobby.

"That's why we appointed a man who is not beholden to the Department," Crosby told the hidden inquisitor. "It demonstrates our commitment to a clean system."

"He's never done a day of law work in his life! What are his qualifications?"

Seeing the cops in the ranks nod in agreement with that protest, Crosby became even more incensed. "Come out and show your face, young fellow!"

"Will you settle for half a face? And I'm not that young."

Glassford circled back down to the microphone to defend himself. "I've commanded men in battle. Leadership demands the same qualities, whether it's on a bayonet charge or on a speakeasy raid. I've been promised a free hand to reform this department, and I intend to do just that. And as for qualifications, why, I've received a few speeding tickets in my time."

The reporters hee-hawed and exchanged elbows to ribs, convinced that covering this new chief *cum* comedian was going to be high adventure.

"Any more questions?" Glassford asked. "My office will always be open."

Scrapper sniffed under the stairwell recess until he ferreted out his prey. Driven forward by the hound, Floyd Gibbons, grinning drolly, emerged from behind a column and patted the dog's head. "I do have one more."

The reporters caterwauled yelps of adoration, swarming him as if he were Douglas Fairbanks, Jr., walking onstage.

MacArthur sneered at the former war correspondent who had long been a thorn in the side of the Army brass. "Who allowed *him* into the building?"

Two cops moved in to escort Gibbons out the doors for not having the requisite District press credentials, but Glassford motioned his new charges to stand down, honored that the famous radioman had stopped by on his first day in office. "Mr. Gibbons, you go ahead and ask away. I'm a firm believer in open and transparent government."

A match blazed, and Gibbons lit up a cigarette. After lobbing a lording smirk at MacArthur and Crosby, the radio celebrity turned and asked the man of the hour, "How do you feel about whorehouses, Chief?"

The confident smile on Glassford's face froze. Seconds passed as he tried to figure the best way out of this ambush. Finally, he said, "Last time I checked, prostitution is against the law in the District of Columbia. And I've just taken an oath to uphold that law."

Relieved by the answer, Crosby whisked Glassford from the microphone.

"Yeah," Gibbons said. "But do you think it *should* be against the law?"

The lobby came to a hushed standstill again.

Two steps up the stairs, Glassford stopped climbing. He figured the Texans at the Alamo had stood a better chance of escape. If he tried to dodge the issue, his tenure would likely start with a nationwide radio broadcast decrying the same old hypocrisy in the District police force. Maybe it hadn't been such a wise idea to confide to Gibbons back in France about his theory on how to stop venereal disease in the Army. Feeling the heated gazes of the commissioners and cops waiting for his answer, he knew the best defense was a good offense. "Not all of us enjoy the services of a harem compliments the King of Morocco, Mr. Gibbons."

Gibbons didn't miss a beat. "Came with the medal. It would have been a diplomatic insult for an international figure like myself to decline the gift." He turned to MacArthur with a taunting grin. "Don't you agree, General?"

MacArthur was no longer pretending to smile. "You're off your usual turf, aren't you, Gibbons? Shouldn't you be in Russia helping Stalin shoot peasants and harvest this year's caviar crop?"

Gibbons cut a dashing pose for the photographers, flipping the front brim of his panama hat back to better reveal the famous face that had been weathered by the sands of the Sahara. "I came home to claim my fortune. I heard a rumor the government was finally going to pay the money it owes us doughboys for fighting in France."

"*You* are not a soldier," MacArthur reminded him.

"I've got one more wound than you do, General." Gibbons snapped the elastic of his eye patch and pulled out the *Croix de Guerre* medal from his breast pocket. "In France, this says I *am* a soldier. And as I recently told some of my AEF comrades who are still living in tents and pissing in latrines because they can't afford running water, before you know it, Hoover is liable to do something really Bolshevistic like give food to starving folk."

The reporters roared their delight at that crack.

MacArthur set his arms akimbo. "You heard wrong."

Gibbons fastened his luminous lone eye on his prey like a searchlight. "So, the President is *not* giving food to starving folk?"

MacArthur was not about to let this silver-tongued devil twist him into one of his headlines. "The Bonus! I'm talking about the Bonus! The President has made it clear that veterans will not be put on the dole. Communist elements are stirring up these boys, putting evil ideas in their heads."

"Well, if they can't eat, then there's only one thing left to do." Gibbons swiveled on his heels toward Glassford again. "Now, what about those whorehouses, Chief?"

The younger reporters waited to see how Glassford would jump this lasso.

Glassford couldn't find a slipknot, so he figured he might as well get on with it. "In many cities, the police have technically accepted prostitution in red-light districts for decades. The women get the worst of the deal, while the criminal syndicates get rich. In my opinion, we'd go a long way to solving a health problem by having the government license the practice. Give the money to the young ladies and the taxpayers, and take it from the felons."

Crosby turned and glared at MacArthur for failing to warn him of *that* skeleton in the closet.

Feigning moral outrage, Gibbons poured more syrup on the folksy drawl that he had perfected during his book tours through the Midwest. "Are you speaking from personal experience, Chief? I don't know about Arizona, but that's not the custom here in the District. Are you only going to enforce the laws you like?"

Glassford admired his old friend's shrewd interviewing style; he parried Gibbons with a dig of his own. "If you want to see how I'm going to enforce the laws, Headline Hunter, just stick around. But from what I hear, we might have to frisk you first for hidden vials of illegal liquor."

Crosby commanded the microphone again. "That's it! Back to work!"

But Gibbons wouldn't be denied the last word. "Hey, Chief! I heard you say you'd received a few speeding tickets in your day. How's your record on parking fines?"

This time, Glassford laughed as he circled back once again to the microphone. He had expected Gibbons to throw something more hard-hitting for his last punch. "I'm pretty clean on those, glad to say."

Behind its patch, Gibbon's nonexistent eye was twinkling with mischief. "You might need to update your *curriculum vitae*."

"Why's that?"

"There's a blue Harley parked illegally behind my Studebaker outside. Being the concerned citizen I am, I pointed out the infraction to one of your shoe leathers. He's writing up a ticket as we speak."

The reporters bayed like cattle at fresh winter hay in a stampede toward the doors to be the first to snap a photograph of the offending motorcycle. Scrapper barked after them, champing to defend his master's property.

In the bustle, MacArthur tried to escape through the back entrance before his reputation could be further besmirched by this city-hall hog auction. Marching past the grinning Gibbons, he snarled, "I didn't think the Marines let you to go anywhere without two leathernecks rolling a red carpet in front of you."

"You aren't still sore about that Belleau Wood dispatch, are you, General?"

MacArthur captured the radioman's elbow and forced him into an alcove. "The Army never got the credit it deserved for that battle. And you're to blame."

"Now that I've finally got you alone." Gibbons blew a puff of cigar smoke into MacArthur's face. "I was hoping you could recommend some movies for me to catch up on in my free time."

"What the hell are you talking about?"

"I'm becoming a real fan of Filipino actresses."

MacArthur looked as if he might launch a fist to Gibbons's remaining eye. "You and that alley scrounger Pearson might want to review the laws on libel."

"Oh, I did that already. The NBC barristers told me that truth is a defense. And thanks to your own indefatigable efforts, you happen to be a public figure. I wonder how the toast of the Manila screen would do giving a performance in a witness chair?"

As MacArthur huffed off, Gibbons serenaded him with the Marine Corps anthem: "From the halls of Montezuma to the shores of Tripoli ..."

Two weeks later, summoned to the White House to discuss the congressional debate on military budget cuts, MacArthur and his War Department colleagues were escorted into the Oval Office. They found the president standing at a crack in the drapes, watching two thousand Communist protestors yell at him from across Lafayette Park. The mob behind the iron fence shouted slogans through megaphones.

"We're gonna hang Herbie Hoover from a sour apple tree!" the protesters shouted. "Down with Hoover and his beans!"

MacArthur took careful note of how the president reacted to the derision. The old Hoover would have stiffened his neck and gone right back to work, but the poor man just stood there in the corner, intermittently staring blankly across the grounds and then looking down at his shoes, as if an answer to his woes might be found written in the nap of the rug.

The office smelled of medicine, and several prescription bottles sat in a drawer left open. In recent months, Administration advisors had been whispering concerns about the president's mental state. Hoover now met visitors with a tepid handshake and the lugubrious enthusiasm of a funeral home director displaying his array of casket choices to a mourning family. His gait had become ponderous, and his swollen face, set atop stiff high collars reminiscent of the last century, was so pale from lack of sun that H.L. Mencken had described it as possessing a "curiously lunar terrain." When visitors were ushered into his presence, the president would answer a few questions in a clipped monotone and wait for them to become so uncomfortable that they would excuse themselves.

Servants had even reported that he never acknowledged them, causing them to wonder if he knew they were present.

MacArthur glanced at the coffee table to see what the president had been reading that morning. The early edition of *The Chicago Tribune* lay open to an editorial condemning the government's coddling of the leaders of this so-called Communist Hunger March. The Secret Service was on high alert; a heavy guard had been stationed around the White House. Death threats were circulating across the city, and some congressional leaders had asked for armed protection. Just last month, while attending the World Series in Philadelphia, Hoover had been jeered by truculent crowds demanding he give them back their beer. With each passing day, Washington felt like a powder keg about to explode.

MacArthur strode over to the president and, standing next to him, studied the angry faces of the protesters across the grounds. Happy Glassford, riding his blue motorcycle at the head of the Red procession, had cleared all traffic from Constitution Avenue. The new chief had even provided the Communists with trucks to ride in while they sang the *Internationale* and hurled curses at storefront businesses. The rabble looked to be mostly Jews, bums, and Negroes, shivering pitifully in the bitter cold, but he knew better. Lurking in those ranks were devious instigators taking orders from the Russian Comintern.

His old classmate had been on the job for just a month, but MacArthur was starting to have doubts if Glassford was up to its demands. Ol' Hap was being too damn sympathetic to the agitators. He had even suggested to the White House that the Reds be treated as tourists and fed meals cooked up by the chef at the Mayflower Hotel. More worrisome was the fact that the president had submitted to this non-confrontational approach, authorizing bedding and cots to be issued from the military's armory for use by the Reds. The newspapers that morning had reported that Glassford attended a Red rally at the Auditorium on the night prior, sitting there puffing satisfied on his pipe while listening to harangues against the capitalist system. MacArthur shook his head. Never in his wildest dreams could he have imagined that a West Pointer placed in charge of law enforcement for the nation's capital would be escorting a gang of Bolsheviks through Washington like a tour guide.

"Moran suggested that I escape to Camp Rapidan for a week," Hoover remarked to no one in particular. "But I refused."

"I think you made the right choice, sir," MacArthur said. "It would not have looked good to be seen running from these troublemakers."

Hoover turned a prickly glare on him, as if detecting criticism embedded in that remark. "What good would it do? The last time I went fishing down there, the press reported that I caught eighteen trout in a rainstorm."

"I do remember, sir."

"Those infernal reporters can't even get the weather right. It didn't rain a drop. And then they go and accuse me of exaggerating my catch."

"The worst of the lot is that provocateur Gibbons."

Hoover's vocal chords sounded constricted from the months of stress and internalized anger. "That traveling showman wants another interview with me. He must be hard up for more frogs to skewer."

MacArthur set his jaw. "I would not accommodate Gibbons, sir. He twists and distorts even the most unassailable facts for his radio diatribes."

Hoover walked back to a chair that faced two sofas and motioned for the others to sit. MacArthur obeyed, along with Secretary of War Patrick Hurley and General Moseley.

As they waited for the president to open the meeting, MacArthur realized that Hoover had forgotten why he had called them there. "Sir, we have serious concerns about the World Disarmament Conference in Geneva next month."

Hoover slumped with annoyance, reminded of that nettlesome issue on the agenda. "Of course you do. You wish to defend your appropriations."

Patrick Hurley had come prepared to fight for his War Department turf. "Sir, we accept the necessity of cutting the military budget during these times of economic constriction. I asked General MacArthur here to prioritize the needs of our nation's defense for the coming decades."

"We could start by cutting officer pay increases," said Hoover testily.

Alarmed by that petty shot across the bow, MacArthur straightened his back. "Sir, with all due respect, I think we need to think in broader strokes. The Prussian strategy during the war turned it into an all-out struggle between the populations of nations, not just a conflict between professional armies, as it had been for centuries. This evolution to expensive aeronautic machines is now threatening to bankrupt the economies of the world."

"And just how can we prevent such a catastrophe?" asked Hoover.

"Thirty-five percent of our Army budget is now devoted to aviation," MacArthur said. "The most efficient path to economic sanity would be for you to propose in Geneva that all nations give up naval and military aviation in their entirety and not to subsidize civilian aviation."

Hoover glared at the military men. "Have any of you even piloted a plane?"

MacArthur shifted on his cushion. "No, sir, but—"

Hoover cut him off. "I remember a conversation I had once with Douglas Haig in London. I asked him why the British spent so much to maintain their military horses. He told me with great confidence that the cavalry was the one unit in the British arsenal that would never be compromised."

Moseley snorted. "Doug Haig didn't know which end was the horse's ass. He never made it within thirty miles of the Front."

"George," MacArthur cautioned his deputy sternly. "I think the President is suggesting that we carefully evaluate our recommendations."

Hoover reddened. "I don't mince words. Nor do I make suggestions. What I am asserting, unequivocally, is that I do not intend to sacrifice this nation's air defense to subsidize officer housing. Now, is there anything else?"

MacArthur glanced at Hurley, now questioning if this was the appropriate time to bring up another pressing matter, but he feared not being presented with another chance. He told the president, "Sir, we have some concerns about another development."

"Yes?"

"There has been a disturbing spread of these pacifist movements in recent months. With all due respect to your faith—"

"My Quaker upbringing has nothing to do with how I govern. I have demonstrated my firm commitment to defending the nation."

"*Bon, bon.*"

Hoover scowled at him. "What did you say?"

MacArthur realized what he had just unconsciously uttered. "Sorry, sir. And old speech habit from France."

Hoover stared blankly at the general, as if not quite knowing what to think of him.

Hurley cleared his throat to bring the discussion back to the budget. "What General MacArthur means, sir, is that we've been getting blowback by these ministers who oppose military training in high schools and colleges."

MacArthur became animated, as he always did when the subject of pacifism was broached. "This Fosdick radical in New York has been preaching that Christ would approve of those who refused to take up arms in defense of the country. Such an attempt to separate religion from patriotism is dangerous and must be countered. It leads to the anarchy we are witnessing out there this afternoon."

Hoover blinked hard. "Anarchy?"

Moseley catapulted to his feet. "Mr. President, I propose we gather up these Reds around the country and segregate them in island camps. We have military transport at the ready in San Francisco to ship them to Hawaii."

MacArthur tried to bridle his opinionated subordinate. "George, we needn't go into specifics—"

"The roundup would have a beneficial effect on the crime wave," insisted Moseley, enraptured by his own exhortations. "It would prevent the classes from mixing. We could do the same to felons and scofflaws, too."

Hoover stood abruptly. "Thank you, gentlemen."

Moseley bit off a couple more portents of doom before sputtering to a fractured silence. Stung by the cold abruptness of their dismissal, MacArthur and Hurley came slowly to their feet. They waited to be asked to stay, but when that request did not come, the two War Department officials traded icy handshakes with the president and led the baffled Moseley through the antechamber of the secretaries.

When the military men emerged from the White House, the Communist protestors beyond the fence showered them with curses. MacArthur, moving fast, was the first to reach the sidewalk. Passing construction crews at work rebuilding the West Wing, he led Hurley and Moseley through the guard station at the fence and headed for their refuge in the War and Navy Building next door.

Out of view at last of the demonstrators in Lafayette Park, Hurley looked back over his shoulder at the White House and whispered with suppressed anger, "That man is turning to jelly."

MacArthur was still smarting from the president's sharp rebuke of his plan to limit the budgetary cutbacks. "He does not seem well."

Hurley made certain the White House guards were out of earshot. "Your undercover agent... Have you received your daily report?"

MacArthur nodded, keeping his eyes trained ahead.

"Do any names of those Reds out there match up with the ones on file?"

"A couple of minor operatives. Timons says most of the marchers claim to be just homeless and hungry."

"Do you believe it?"

MacArthur barely shook his head as he monitored the police officers and Secret Service agents posted around the grounds. He covered his mouth discretely. "The German Bolsheviks spent months infiltrating the disenchanted elements of the Weimar Republic to win over their trust. The Communists here are using the same devious methods, living in the shantytowns and creating new identities among these uneducated veterans. The Reds will bide their time until the opportune moment to light the match."

As Hurley climbed the steps to the War and Navy Building, he angled his hawkish eyes toward the equestrian statue of Lafayette across Pennsylvania Avenue. His face darkened as he watched Glassford escort the Communist protestors to waiting trucks to be fed sandwiches and warmed with coffee. "That subject you brought up this morning."

"The White Plan?"

Hurley nodded. "Have it reviewed for updating. Your eyes only, and those you trust."

46

PORTLAND, OREGON
MARCH 1932

Floyd Gibbons threaded his way through the packed Portland armory with the newest invention in radio technology strapped to his chest: a portable short-wave transmitter connected to a wired microphone, which he had first used to broadcast the transatlantic landing of the *Graf Zeppelin* dirigible in New Jersey. He received dozens of news tips every day, but one from his West Coast runner earlier that month had caught his attention. Hundreds of homeless Oregon veterans had decided to hold a meeting to protest the government's refusal to pay their bonus compensation early.

On his recent reporting trips, he had sensed that the economic despair in the country was slowly curdling into rage. And though the Communist Hunger March in Washington had fizzled—thanks to Happy Glassford's clever strategy of treating the Reds like dignitaries to steal their thunder—he was starting to encounter the same furrowed glares of nothing to lose that he had witnessed years ago in Germany and Russia. Portland had a long history of labor unrest, and he suspected the unemployed soldiers in this city would make a volatile mash with the local union organizers and grizzled dockworkers. So, with his old crime-beat instincts sparked, he had taken the train across country to check out the lead, stopping along the way in Chicago and Minneapolis to give speeches and make his Saturday night broadcasts.

Now, as he prepared to broadcast his interviews live that wintry night, he shook hands with hundreds of the homeless veterans, many of whom had walked in from as far away as Seattle, Vancouver, Spokane, and Boise. He hadn't felt such tension since the beer halls of Germany, where the *Landesjaeger* regiments had banded together to fight the Bolsheviks with the machine guns and rifles they had hidden in cellars after the war. With his voice warmed up, he pressed the microphone to his lips and began painting a picture for his radio listeners with his famous staccato delivery:

"Ladies and gentlemen, this is Floyd Gibbons, your intrepid reporter, brought to you by the Blue Network. Tonight, by means of a revolution in technology, a step for mankind, a marvel of science, tonight you are experiencing firsthand history as it happens...."

A thunderous cheer went up as he walked the hall rattling off his report:

"... I come to you this evening from Portland, Oregon, where all around me, veterans of the war to end all wars have gathered to ask a simple question: Why are those who manned the trenches for liberty now forced to suffer the ravages of hunger, humiliation, and homelessness? Yes, I am roaming this hall of heroes and talking to the doughboys who, like many of you on this cold, unyielding night, are feeling a hole in their stomachs. But unlike you, some of these men took a hole in their stomachs in France. And now all they want is to understand why the government they once defended shows so little interest in their oblivion and despair. The word on every lip here tonight is the same: Bonus... Bonus... Bonus... Let's listen in."

He aimed his microphone up at the podium, where an American Legion lobbyist was trying to talk down the restive veterans. "The Legion's got your best interests at heart, men," the lobbyist bawled across the hall. "If we push for the Bonus now, we'll give up political clout for other needs, like disability and pensions!"

One of the veterans, a rail-thin man with shocks of blond curls and manic blue eyes, elbowed his way to the base of the stage and shouted up at the portly lobbyist, who clearly hadn't missed any meals. "Ain't you late f-f-for your lunch with Andy Mellon?"

On the auditorium floor, another veteran in the crowd turned to a buddy and scoffed, "Moses is at it again."

Overhearing the putdown, the blond heckler whirled and pointed a bony finger at Chester Hazen, a homeless ex-sergeant who suffered so badly from asthma that he had to have two of his former privates walk at his side at all times and fan air to his nose. "Yeah, you're good at cracking jokes, Hazen! But you ever seen a rod turned into a s-s-snake?"

"You turning biblical on us now, are you, Waters?" asked Mickey Dolan, the Irishman who ruled the fire barrels down in the plaza.

"You ever s-s-seen the waters part?"

Dolan displayed a raised fist to him. "I could part a Waters right now, all right! All the way down your scalp to that gizzard neck of yours!"

Hazen slapped Dolan on the back, enjoying the quip. The former sergeant came face to face with the brash blond agitator who was trying to steal the show. "You gonna give us a miracle demonstration, Dubya?"

Pushing his tormentors aside, the wispy blond veteran jumped onto the dais. "I'll d-d-do that and more if you show me one s-s-starved vet who was ever brought back from the dead by a pension!"

That comeback left Dolan and his wheezing buddy red-faced and speechless. At the podium, in the midst of all the hectoring, the Legion lobbyist was still trying to regain the attention of the crowd.

But another veteran, this one short and bald with a barked stump for a face, climbed to the platform and came aside the blond agitator for support. "I say we give Moses here a hearing, boys!"

Gibbons couldn't take his eyes off the stuttering blond Quixote and his bullet-headed Panza. Something about this stammering veteran called "Dubya" by the other men seemed vaguely familiar, but he couldn't place why. The agitator was barely able to utter three words without losing his way, but he possessed a cryptic magnetism that made you want to hear what he had to say, even if the sentences came out sawed. Gibbons pushed forward to get his microphone closer to the Bonus evangelist, who was now stomping and gesticulating across the stage like a copperhead charmer in an Appalachian church.

"The Legion gets cozy with the highfalutins in Washington!" the vet yelled. "They tell us to write letters! You ever gotten a letter from a congressman?"

"Hell, who can afford a stamp?" shouted his partner, on cue.

The veterans quieted their braying to hear more of what this self-proclaimed prophet from the gutters had to offer in homespun wisdom.

"Damned right! But we got feet, don't we? And we got the time, or do you boys need to be somewhere tomorrow? Those rich cats in Congress ain't gonna budge until they see our stubbled mugs up close!"

Gibbons marveled at how the tall, slip-mouthed malcontent was becoming more comfortable under the stage lights with each bellowed blast of anger. As the applause grew louder, even his stuttering seemed to fade.

"Hoofing off is fine for you sourdoughs!" shouted another veteran. "But some of us got wives and offspring. We just gonna up and leave them?"

The soapbox orator seemed to have thought up an answer for every objection. "You any help to them on the bread line? You don't want charity! Hell, neither do I! You want a job!" The lanky testifier winked at his short partner next to him, as if the two were sharing an inside joke. Then, he looked down at another vet and pointed him out. "You there, Tom! Once you get your Bonus, what you gonna do with it?"

Thrust into the spotlight, the scoffing veteran named Tom was forced to ponder that question, as if the possibility had never dawned on him. "Reckon I'd buy a truck, do some hauling."

"Damn right you would!" shouted the blond hothead. "Hoover calls that Bolshevikism! You a Bolshevik, Tom?"

Tom the veteran was now coming around to seeing things differently. "I ain't never seen a Red hauling rock for two cents a ton!"

The blond tilter at windmills was on a roll, strutting across the stage while pointing at various upturned faces below him. He peered into the crowd, and finding what he was looking for, pointed at the big Irishman who had ridiculed him from the start. "What about you, Mickey Dolan?"

"I'd buy my young'uns some clothes," Dolan admitted. "I'd also pay the rent and the grocery bill. And by God, we'd have at least one Sunday dinner!"

"Hell's bells!" cried the blond Quixote. "Me and the missus boiled a pig knuckle in water for our Christmas feast this year!"

Gibbons shook his head in admiration. The fellow was a natural tent revivalist, isolating the heretics with shame and giving the rest of the congregation dreams to ponder in the great beyond. Somebody ought to tell him he could make a good living selling the Lord for donations. While the veterans hooted and hollered, Gibbons searched the floor for a pair of shiny shoes and spied a plainclothes cop standing near the door, surveying the scene. He sauntered up to the undercover operative and slipped him a dollar bill. Going off air for a commercial, he stuck his microphone in his belt and, feigning contempt for the veterans, whispered, "Who's the crackpot up there?"

"Name's Walter Waters."

"Has he ever done any preaching?"

The cop shook his head. "Garage mechanic, farmhand, baker. His last job was an assistant super at the cannery on James Street. The only thing that got canned was his ass."

"He's got a gift for channeling the Holy Ghost, all right. And the straight man with him?"

"A lumberjack named Alford."

"They make quite a team."

"Yeah, a regular George and Gracie."

"Maybe this Waters character will pied-piper these rats out of your hair."

The cop spat a big shot of chaw juice at the floorboards to deny that hope. "Fat chance. He doesn't have the brains to lead a horsefly to cow shit."

On the stage, Waters was reaching a crescendo with his clamor for action. "I say we take the ankle express over to the station! Catch the boxcars east! I got my trunks p-p-packed!" He pulled out the linings of his empty pockets. "How about you b-b-boys?"

The entire hall was roaring with laughter.

But then a little Italian fellow, tented in a voluminous black suit, squirmed his way up to the boards like a muskrat in a river dam. The gnomish intruder poked his head up through the forest of smelly torsos and shouted at Waters, "Saying we vets were to go to Washington, what makes you think *you're* coming along, pal?"

Confused by that challenge, the veterans fell silent.

Alford peered down into the sea of shadowed faces to uproot the culprit. "Who the hell are you, Guippo?"

Dolan lifted the little Italian veteran up to the stage.

"That's Joey Angelo!" shouted a gravely voice from the rear of the crowd. "I saw his mug in the fish wrap last year!"

While the veterans on the floor craned their necks in awe, Dolan circled the chirping cricket. "You're the Joe Angelo who saved Patton?"

Angelo pulled his Distinguished Service Cross out of his coat pocket. As if blinded by a powerful talisman, Waters stepped back, deflated at being over-shadowed by a genuine war hero.

Alford wasn't so impressed. "What the hell is a Jersey dago doing out this way? You run out of fish in the Hudson?"

Angelo closed in on the lumberjack. "If it's any business of yours, Buckweat, I figured if I was gonna starve, I might as well see the country doing it."

Waters got between the two men to break them apart. "Why don't you go on b-b-back East. We got our own p-p-p-problems out here."

"Sounds like you got more problems than finding a square meal, machine-gun mouth." Waging a staring contest with Waters, Angelo tested him with a question. "Which side of a French Lebel does the bolt sit on?"

Waters waved off the challenge as a trick. "Left, of course."

Angelo raised his pygmy arms in triumph. "There's your proof, boys! This blowtorch never shouldered a rifle in his life!"

Stunned by Waters's ignorance of armaments, the angry veterans surged toward him. Dolan reached the agitator first and snarled into his face, "That so, Moses? You been lying all this time to us about your gallantry? Maybe we ought to put you on a boxcar out of town, free of charge."

Waters bent over, clutching his chest. He couldn't form the words.

Alford rushed to his side. "I was with this man during a night reconnaissance on the Meuse! He fought as hard as any man here!"

Gibbons hoisted his microphone higher to catch the exchange. "That right, Waters? Were you in the trenches?"

Waters rolled his cold cobalt eyes shiftily across the hall. "Well, I ain't one to trumpet my exploits. But there was that time I squared off against two officers with only my gas mask for protection."

"And?" Hazen demanded.

Waters coughed from the memories of his botched gas training. "You see me standing here today, don't you?"

Before Angelo could lodge another protest, Alford shouted over his head, "Hell, boys, any man that can fight off a couple of Jerry stripes with nothing but a piece of leather ought to be able to get us to the White House! I say we jump the eleven oh five tonight!"

Convinced by Alford's fiery testimonial, the veterans shook the stanchions with their whistles and applause.

"I'm for it!" cried Dolan. "Let's go!"

With the big Irishman blessing the plan, the veterans headed for the exits.

"I done walked to Washington once already!" Angelo shouted.

The veterans stopped their rush for the doors.

Dolan asked Angelo, "What happened when you got there?"

"Those flapping birds in Congress told me I was the greatest thing they'd seen since the invention of pepperoni. Then they sat on their fat *asinos* and did nuthin' to help me."

"What are you saying, exactly?" asked Hazen. "We speak American around here."

Angelo mimicked a march across the stage. "Lemme do a show and tell, then, for you lamebrains that got loose seeds rattling in your empty heads. I'm saying I done made that damn journey, and it's too damn far to walk or ride the rails. Besides, before I left Camden, I heard tell that Hoover just hired a new police chief in Washington. The feds probably got themselves a real ball-buster with the billy club."

Slammed back to reality, the veterans hung their heads and cast their gazes toward the floor. After a long silence, during which nobody offered a word of encouragement, they began filing silently from the hall with their chins slung low, resigned to returning to their bedrolls in the parks and alleys.

Gibbons was astounded by what he was witnessing. In the span of only a few steaming breaths, these veterans had slid back into their familiar ennui and despair, the hope of a new beginning yanked from their hands by cold reality. Could these forlorn men truly be the proud doughboys who had pounded the Germans in 1918? As the hall began to empty, he saw Waters standing off in a corner, rehearsing the words of his speech that had just failed him. The lumber-jack Alford nuzzled up aside his friend and consoled him with a hand to his slumped shoulder. After watching two veterans commiserate over their failure,

Gibbons looked across the hall and nodded to the undercover cop, conceding the agent's observation that this tree hacker might be pulling the strings for the stammering Bonus barker.

Maybe this Alford fellow wasn't Sancho Panza, after all. Maybe he was really playing the role of Cyrano de Bergerac. Shrugging at the mystery, Gibbons signed off his broadcast for the night and walked out of the armory into an icy wind. Up the street, he heard an Appalachian blues tune blaring down from the top floor of one of the brownstone tenements. A scratchy phonograph spat out the melancholic voice of Dock Boggs clawhammering above the up-picked strings of a West Virginia banjo:

> *Oh Death's Little Black Train is coming,*
> *Get all your business right.*
> *You better set your house in order,*
> *For that train may be here tonight.*
> *God spoke to Hezekiah,*
> *On a mountain set on high,*
> *You better set your house in order, he said,*
> *Or that train will be here tonight.*

Gibbons looked around the bleak streets. Finding no cops lurking, he pulled out his flask and took an illegal drink to warm his blood. As the whiskey trickled down his throat, he stole a glance over his shoulder and saw Walter Waters limping alone toward the cannery district. Something deep in his reporter's gut told him that the country hadn't heard the last of that Bonus agitator and his pipe dream to ride the rails to Washington.

47

POCATELLO, IDAHO
MAY 1932

The locomotive hissed and screeched to a jarring stop, waking Ozzie Taylor from a fitful sleep in a dark corner of one of the livestock cars. Grasping his oboe to his chest, he shot up to fight off a shadow and yelled a warning, "Steve's got a knife, Boss!"

Several slumbering veterans stacked like corpses all around him erupted and dived out of the sliding door, convinced that the Union Pacific bulls were ambushing them again. Finally freed from the mangle of arms and legs, Ozzie staggered up from the dewy wheat grass and balled his fists to confront the railroad toughs, but all he saw were endless folds of tawny humpbacked hills rushing toward the snow-capped Rockies in the distance. He heard a banging sound behind him. A sign pocked with buckshot rattled alongside the tracks, promising that Pocatello, population 16,471, was two miles away.

He rubbed the sleep from his eyes and tried to quiet the burning rumblings in his stomach. Slowly it dawned on him that he had been in the throes of the same nightmare that attacked him every night, the one in which he saw that murdering drummer coming to slice Big Jim in the jugular. As he looked around, it also occurred to him that the place was awfully barren, especially for a black man from Harlem.

Sprawled on the ground, Waters pushed Angelo's head off his ankle and climbed to his feet to assess the situation. He searched for the promised caravan of trucks, but there wasn't a vehicle in sight. "Where the hell is Hazen?"

The rest of their three hundred volunteers from Oregon slowly tumbled out from the boxcars and huddled together for warmth. They performed their usual morning ritual, asking each other for nonexistent smokes, as if the mere wishing could make a whole pack of Lucky Strikes appear overnight by magic.

Mickey Dolan walked over to a prairie bush to take a leak. "That sonofabitch Hazen was supposed to meet us here with the donation money."

Most of the men were weak from hunger, and several were coughing and hacking from the consumption spreading through their ranks. They began dropping to their haunches like the wounded on the Marne, and Ozzie was starting to think that maybe the idea of jumping the cars in Portland hadn't been such a good idea, after all. But Waters had kept at them, week after week, insisting that a man could be jobless just as easily in Washington, until finally one night the boys had gotten so riled up that they'd all decided to hightail it over to the station just to shut him up.

After getting wind of the plan to catch a free ride, the Portland railroad agents had ordered the next train out to speed through the city at fifty miles an hour, too fast to jump. But that tactic didn't stop ol' Dubya-Dubya. No sir. He convinced the boys to stand on the rails and slow the next locomotive coming in, then scramble atop the locked cars. The security thugs had warned them they'd all be shot, but Dubya-Dubya just told them to bring it on, that they'd all rather die fast than slow. That did the trick, all right, and one of the rail crew had loaded all the veterans onto two empty cars and had hooked them to the end of this procession. Yes, sir. Ol' Dubya-Dubya had gained some newfound respect from the boys after that showdown.

Still, that short-lived triumph didn't change the hard fact that they hadn't enjoyed a square meal since crossing the Oregon state line.

George Alford bowlegged it over to the locomotive cabin and kicked at the grille. "How come we're stopping here?"

The engineer risked poking his head through the cabin window. "Those are my orders. I can't take you fellas into Pocatello. We're sitting here for the night."

Disgusted, Angelo perched on a fence rail to wipe the cow manure from his pant cuffs. "Three days in a stinking cattle car. Congress oughta pass a law putting water troughs in them. It's not humane for the animals."

Ozzie didn't exactly share that sympathy. "At least the livestock get fed."

"I'll wring Hazen's neck!" Dolan growled. "He promised us breakfast today!"

Angelo kicked at the rotting fence rail under his feet. "I warned you geese that Hazen was gonna steal the damn money!" Tired of listening to everyone bitch, he sprang from his perch and walked over to a group of veterans from Seattle. Gathering them around, the little Italian-American veteran whispered something, and they all began following him down the tracks on foot.

Waters came shambling up to confront them. "Where you think you f-f-fellas are headed?"

Angelo shot him the finger. "Feed on your own range, Moses."

Waters was on Angelo's heels. "We gotta s-s-stay together."

Angelo mocked his stammer. "You th-th-think so? You af-af-afraid the Hun are gonna attack us out here, Sergeant York?"

Alford came up aside Waters to double-team Angelo. "You're aching for a bruising, you greasy olive pit!"

Angelo had to be restrained from jumping the plug lumberjack. "And who's gonna do it? You gonna rev up your mouthpiece here to do it for you?"

Dolan dragged Angelo off Alford. "You got so much vinegar in your veins, Wop! Go on ahead into town and tell those cowboys how you want to take a loan on Patton's watch."

Horrified by that suggestion, Angelo lifted his wrist to display his most prized possession. "This watch ain't going nowhere! And if I die and one of you'ze try to take it off me, I'll rise up from the dead and haunt you to the grave. You hear me?"

Alford snorted. "Hell, I think even Custer's bones heard you!"

Irate at the whole lot of them, Angelo stormed off and led his little band of dissidents toward the distant cluster of spires and houses. Left with the choice of starvation or walking into town, the other veterans groaned and levered to their feet to follow him.

Two hours later, the wretched procession of famished veterans reached the main street of Pocatello, an old mining town choked by a great dark cloud of loess soil and coal cinders stirred up by wagons and automobiles. The sleepy burg was bounded on one side by the round purple mounds of the Bannock Range and on the other by an impenetrable helix of bin chutes, sluice viaducts, and rickety water towers. The unpaved streets had been platted in the form of a cross, with a brick courthouse situated at the spot where Christ's feet would have been nailed. The few townspeople out navigating the pounded hardpan that passed for sidewalks that morning slowly became aware of a foreign stench mingling with the usual aromas of horse manure and petrol fumes. They peered beyond the rail-crossing grade and saw a trickle of shabby invaders.

Angelo approached an unescorted lady who had taken refuge under the awning of the Fargo-Wilson-Wells department store. He offered his upturned hat for a donation. "Missus, spare some change for a veteran of the Argonne?"

Frightened, the woman dipped into her purse for a couple of coins.

Angelo bowed to her and reached into the felt bowler to grab the change, but the hat and coins went flying into the air. Blowing steam from his round ears, he spun to find the culprit who had knocked it out of his hands.

Waters picked up the coins and, rubbing them clean, handed them back to the woman. "I apologize for the r-r-rudeness of my private here, ma'am."

The lady looked shocked by his act of chivalry. "Well, if the man is in need."

"We're all in need," Waters said. "That don't make it right to pester a lady."

Angelo hopped around in a circle dance, hankering to pummel Waters into oatmeal. "Who the hell appointed you Black Jack Pershing?"

When Waters just glared at him, Angelo knocked him flat to the ground. The dozen or so townspeople backed away from the fracas, but the other vets hurried up to witness the fight.

Angelo wailed away on Waters. "You ever crawl my hump like that again and—"

Dolan restrained Angelo's arm on the recoil. "Drop him."

Angelo fought and bit at Dolan like a trapped leprechaun. "This ain't your concern, Paddy!"

Another veteran who had joined up with the rail riders a few days ago in La Grande circled Dolan, sizing him up close for the first time. "Wait a minute. I've seen those hands before."

Dolan glared a demand at the rookie rail rider to mind his own business. "Go find yourself a cup of coffee, Rowlands."

The grinning Idaho veteran wouldn't be chased. "Ain't you Mickey Dolan, the prize fighter? Yeah, I seen you bounce Frenchies off the boards in Paris."

The crowed stood marveling at Dolan's massive gnarled hands.

Ozzie muttered what the others were thinking. "Mortars with knuckles."

The proprietor of the local general store suddenly realized that a black man was traveling with this pack of hobos. He lifted Waters to his feet and produced a handkerchief for him to clean himself up. "You the leader of these fellas?"

Waters wiped a seep of blood from the corner of his mouth. "Nah, we're all equal in rank."

"Not all of you." The storeowner angled his head toward Ozzie. "This nigrah here can't be accompanying you into our stores."

"He's a vet, just like the rest of us."

The storeowner studied Waters as if trying to judge how far the hobo would go in enforcing his ban against segregation. Seeing how the man had just taken a bruised jaw to defend his principles, he decided not to press the objection.

Angered that Waters had been given a reprieve, Angelo shook off Dolan's grasp and headed off toward the saloon with his companions.

"H-h-hold it, Angelo," Waters demanded. "We settle this now."

The other veterans formed a circle around them, eager for another fist show. Angelo thrust out his chin, begging Waters to make a play for it.

Instead of throwing a punch, Waters turned to offer a warning to the other vets. "Boys, a full house d-d-divided don't win no pots. We're all enlisted m-m-men here. I know that. And I know no enlisted m-m-man worth his salt is gonna take orders from another enlisted m-m-man."

"Spit it out," Angelo taunted. "Me and the boys are thirsty for some brews."

"What I'm saying is, If we d-d-don't get some military discipline purty d-d-damn quick, the only White House we're g-g-gonna see is some whitewashed local pokie."

Alford seized the promise of the moment. "What about it, boys? Waters is talking some sense. I say we elect a commander, and what he says goes."

Angelo, feeling all eyes angling toward him, shot a wad of dry bile to the dusty street. "I suppose you got someone in mind, Alford. Like your little puppet here."

Waters stepped in front of Alford to put a stop to his nomination. "I'll solve your d-d-dilemma real quick, Angelo. I d-d-don't want the job. Fact, I think you'd be the perfect c-c-candidate. You always got a suggestion ready."

Thrown on his heels by that offer, Angelo checked the reactions of the other men. "Nah, you ain't trickin' me into that. I ain't taking charge of these losers."

"Then shut your trap, Angelo." Dolan turned to the other veterans. "You lads know I ain't got no love for Waters here, never have. But the way I see it, he stuck his neck out to get us a thousand miles already. Hazen spit the bit on us. I say we give Waters the reins for awhile and see how he drives the wagon."

The men haggled among themselves for nearly a minute, then Ozzie stepped up to announce their decision. "We done taken a vote. We're willing follow Dubya-Dubya."

Waters looked to Angelo for his reaction. "That square with you?"

Angelo pawed at the ground, then nodded.

After receiving a voice approval from the other men, Waters paced in front of the them. "All right, then! Get in ranks!"

Ozzie was stunned. Heck, they hadn't drilled in over a decade. Looking at each other skeptically, as if wondering what nonsense they had just spawned, he and the veterans stumbled into position, forming up five ragged rows.

"Here's my regulations!" Waters shouted. "No begging! No bug juice! No airing the lungs! No talk against the government! And any man who wants to join this unit has got to show me his discharge papers!" He turned to Alford and ordered, "Sound the bugle."

Alford whispered to his ear, "We don't have a bugle."

"What happened to it?"

"Hazen took that, too. Probably sold it for booze."

Confronted with his first conundrum of command, Waters pondered the dilemma. Finally, he shouted, "Taylor!"

Ozzie hustled up. "Yes, sir?"

"Can you play *Reveille* on that grenade launcher you carry?"

Ozzie's eyes widened in protest. "I ain't never tried."

"Give it a shot."

Ozzie feared the reaction of the white folks who were glaring venom at him, but he brought the reed to his lips and blasted out the strangest call to morning muster that an army on this Earth had ever heard. The tune did the job, though, and the veterans came to a haphazard attention.

Waters walked down their ragged ranks. "Anybody got railroad experience?" When six veterans stepped forward, he handed out his first commission. "You're the transportation committee. Make sure we got boxcars each morning. We'll also need some military police. Angelo, you pick a half-dozen of the best knucklers and head 'em up."

Angelo slacked his jaw at being chosen by the man who just moments ago had been his wrestling enemy.

Standing three rows away, out of their earshot, Alford smiled and shot an elbow into Dolan's side. "Our new stripe is a fast learner."

"How you figure that?" Dolan asked.

"You have to let a bull's horns grow before you saw them off."

Waters was now strutting like Black Jack himself. "Foley!"

"Yes, sir?"

"You were a supply sergeant during the war, right?"

"Yeah, why?"

"What's our situation regarding breakfast? Army marches on its stomach."

Foley shot a confused glance at his comrades. "Hell, Dubya, you know damn well what the situation is. We ain't got a wild onion among us."

"Do I have to th-th-think of everything? Send the men in p-p-parade formation down the street. Determine if any of the good people of this fine town would care to help the cause. No panhandling, just d-d-donations."

"What cause would that be, sir?" Foley asked.

"That's a damn g-g-good point. We need a name for our unit."

"How about Veterans Near Starvation?" Angelo suggested.

"Nah, that won't do," Waters said. "We n-n-need a more uplifting title."

The woman who had made the donation to Angelo suggested, "How about the Bonus Expeditionary Force?"

The men grinned and nodded their approval.

"The BEF from the old AEF," said Dolan. "I like the ring of it."

Waters saluted the lady for her contribution to the cause, and on his signal, Foley took his position at the front of the haggard square of veterans. "All right boys! You heard him! Let's give 'em a taste of the Saint My Hell Two-Step!"

With hats upturned, the veterans shuffled down the street with all of the aplomb they could muster, as if heading for the Arch de Triumph in Paris.

Wheezing and breathing hard from the mountain elevation, they soon began to labor and slowed to stop for rest after only two blocks. Foley unfolded a ragged American flag from his knapsack and ordered three of his fellow veterans to hold one of the corners horizontal so that people could throw coins into it. A few of the local residents stepped up to donate.

Alford, bringing up the rear of the column, whispered to Dolan, "Dubya's likely to be the target of some crazies down the road. He's going to need a loyal bodyguard."

Dolan backed off, shaking his head. "You don't want me."

Alford stared down at the Irishman's hands. "You're exactly who I want."

Dolan held a pained expression. "There's something you oughta know first."

"It'll have to wait." Alford kept a watch on Waters while he glad-handed the townsfolk. "Right now, we've got an army to feed. Just stay close to the commander and keep cat eyes out for government assassins."

F our days later, the resolute three hundred of the Bonus Expeditionary Force—give or take fifty, depending on the daily fluctuations in desertions and recruits—sat around a bonfire in a rye field on the outskirts of Council Bluffs, Iowa. Fate had continued to smile on them: Word of their trek for economic justice was being spread all across the Midwest, and at the train stations in Green River and Cheyenne, appreciative Wyoming crowds of several thousands had fed them hot meals and ice cream and had given them keys to the cities in honor of their service. Many of the men—a grudging Joe Angelo included—now attributed this turn of fortune to their choice of the stuttering blond Bonus evangelist as their new commander.

This morning, even the weather had turned pleasant, and Waters took the opportunity to lounge on the grassy banks in his shirtsleeves while the other men washed up in the Missouri River. A widow of a deceased veteran in the last town down the tracks had gifted the unit with a copy of *The Daily Nonpareil*, the local county's newspaper. He hadn't had a chance to catch up on the events of the week since leaving Portland, so he rested against a tree and flipped the paper open to the front page to see what was going on in the world. The bold headline of the lead story nearly stole his breath.

Alford, clad in his long johns to let his washed overalls dry on a limb, looked over at him. "What's wrong, Dubya?"

Waters had trouble getting the words out, and this time not only because of his stutter. "They f-f-found the Lindbergh baby."

Hearing the report, the men splashing along the banks came running to find out more. Alford hesitated before asking, "Alive?"

Water shook his head. "The bastards buried it five miles from its home." As the men stood silent around him, unable to comprehend the heinous murder, he kicked at the ground in anger. "The world's going to hell."

"I reckon the rest of the news don't get no better, either," said Dolan.

Waters scanned down the columns for the political items from Washington. "Looks like Patman's bill for the Bonus is stuck in committee."

Ozzie shrugged. "Whatever that there means."

"What it means," Alford said, "is that Hoover and those Wall Street mouthpieces in Congress are blocking it from being voted on."

"How much longer till we get to Washington, Dubya?" Angelo asked.

Ciphering in his head, Waters divided the miles into days. "Depends on the railroad suits. I'd say another week, if we don't hit headwinds."

Crestfallen from the Lindbergh news and the vote against the Bonus bill, the men retreated to their spots on the riverbank to contemplate the ordeal ahead. Trying to get his mind off the tragedy, Waters turned to the back pages of the newspaper and glanced over the community items for Council Bluffs, the next town on their itinerary. One brief note stated that a local girl, age twelve, lay near death in the hospital there. He stared at her photograph. It could have been taken of an angel. He couldn't understand why men like Andrew Mellon were allowed to live to a ripe old age while poor innocent girls like this were—

"She won't suffer much longer."

Waters looked up to find hovering over him what appeared to be two castoffs from a traveling circus. The one who had spoken that assurance was a munchkin who wore an outrageous stovepipe hat and sported a black beard with no mustache. The man resembled what Abe Lincoln might have looked like if the Civil War president had been compressed a foot by a pile driver and clipped of his upper lip hair. Next to this walking oddity stood an Indian in full-feathered regalia and armed with a bow and arrow.

Down at the river, Angelo spotted the two strangers. "Mama Maria! I don't know if I'm supposed to surrender to General Grant or Sitting Bull!"

The little Lincoln impersonator offered his hand to Waters in greeting. "Is this where a man can hook up for the Washington roundup?"

Coming up with the other men to see who had arrived, Angelo doubled over with laughter. "We're a military unit, bub, not the Buffalo Bill show."

Pelted by guffaws, the stove-piped newcomer calmly announced, "You boys don't look too bright, so let me paint you a picture. My name's Charlie Lincoln. I'm a survivor of Chateau Thierry and battles hence. Most folks in Iowa can tell right off that I'm a descendant of Abe hisself. Sixth cousin."

Angelo circled the outlandish prairie itinerant. "Now that you mention it, I can see the resemblance. From the knees down, anyway."

"About time."

Angelo kept a straight face. "Yeah, I heard tell that old Abe dressed up like a woman so's he wouldn't get shot. Look at them pretty little legs, boys. Don't Charlie the side-splitter here look like Missus Abe going to Washington?"

Waters was enjoying the idea of someone else being the brunt of the jokes for once. "Who's your scout?"

Lincoln brought forward the inscrutable Indian at his side. "This here is Chief Running Wolf."

Alford reached out his hand, but the Chief didn't reciprocate the gesture. "He don't talk much, does he?"

"He's Apache," Lincoln said. "Uses his fingers for signing and his bow for punctuation. He fought in the Spanish-American War with T.R. and the Rough Riders. He also revealed to Wild Bill Cody the great secret of Geronimo."

"What secret was that?" asked Waters.

"How to take a piss while galloping bareback."

"I did not know that was an Injun skill," Alford said.

Lincoln nodded. "The Chief is also a member of the Masonic Order."

Waters sized up the Apache. "A redskin Freemason. Now that's a conversation piece, if nothing else. Can he do anything b-b-besides hold cigars?"

Lincoln cued his sardonic companion to the task. Running Wolf walked off a few steps, pulling three tin cans out of his rawhide knapsack, and set them up in a row on a fallen tree limb about thirty yards away. Returning to his perplexed audience, he drew out one of the arrows in his quiver and notched it on his bowstring.

Lincoln challenged the lounging veterans. "Any of you codgers got enough eyesight left to see the names on those cans?"

They all squinted at the distant targets, until Angelo yelped the answer first. "Them are Hoover, Mellon, and Hamilton Fish's faces painted on those tins!"

Lincoln puffed out his chest and pulled at his lapels, as if walking the ring like a barker. "The Chief here shoots 'em for donations."

Waters wondered if there might be a capitalist future for this Indian Freemason. "Let's see a demonstration."

Running Wolf pulled the bow taut and let fly. His arrow got Herbert right in between the brows. The men slapped the Apache on the back, impressed.

Angelo thumped Lincoln's hat with his forefinger. "I can see maybe the value of letting the Chief here join up with us. But what skills do *you* employ besides scaring young'uns on Halloween?"

"Glad you asked. So happens, I'm an inventor."

Ozzie sat nervously fingering the keys on his oboe. "An inventor of *what*?"

"I roam the state testing out the newfangled. You see that fence over there?"

The veterans peered into the distance at three barbed wire strands held aloft on posts by white porcelain knobs. Several of them walked over to inspect the enclosure.

Angelo looked it up and down. "It's a fence. So what?"

"This here's a new model they're using out in farm country these days," Lincoln said. "It's a miracle of modern science. They run a juice through those filaments, so when it rains at night, the coils glow. H2O does the trick. Helps keep the cows from blinding into it."

Angelo wasn't buying it. "Boys, I think this gypsy is building us a high line."

"You Paul Bunyans suit yourselves. But there's one way to find out."

"How's that, exactly?" asked Dolan.

"Take a whiz on it. If it don't sparkle like the French Quarter, I'll eat my most prized family heirloom here." Lincoln pointed to his top hat.

Angelo and a dozen other veterans—except for Waters, who sat watching the experiment from afar—couldn't wait to send this blowhard off in shame. They lined up along the wire and unzipped. Dozens of streams of urine hit the fence and—*ZZZZZZZZIPPPPP*—the electricity crackled. They jumped across the field like rabbits holding their aching crotches.

"I think I burned it off!" Angelo cried as he chased Lincoln across the prairie grass. "That hoosier tried to turn us into geldings!"

Perched on the nearest hill, Waters laughed until he cried. "You men sh-sh-should know better than to leave your weapons unattended."

Lincoln scurried back up the ridge and sidled next to the BEF leader, figuring he was the only one in this roving band of rejects who would protect him from being thrashed for the prank. He thrust his hand out in greeting again. "By the cut of your jib, I'd say you're Walter Waters of the Sixty-Sixth Field Artillery."

"How'd you kn-kn-know that?"

"Vets all over these parts know about you. The Chief and I came to muster in."

Waters debated their offer of enlistment. Finally, he turned toward Angelo and ordered, "Process their papers."

Exasperated at that decision, Angelo put out his hand, alternately opening and closing his fist in threat. Lincoln reluctantly pulled his discharge documents out of the hollow of his stovepipe and surrendered them for inspection.

Waters asked Lincoln, "So, we're g-g-getting famous, huh?"

"In a manner of speaking. Every town east from here to St. Louie is boarding up and passing out guns. The politicians in these parts have their constituents believing you boys are the second coming of the Jesse James gang."

Waters was outraged. "What? Why, I gotta half a mind to—"

"Well, lookee here." Angelo fingered through Lincoln's documents.

Lincoln kept his eyes pinned on the ground.

"You f-f-find something of interest, Angelo?" Waters asked. "Or are you planning to use those for the outhouse?"

Angelo circled Lincoln. "Seems Abe Junior here is a fence expert, after all."

Alford shrugged. "Well, then, he was giving it to us straight."

Shaking his head to negate that suggestion, Angelo thumped Lincoln's hat again. "Awarded the barbed-wire garters."

Stunned, the veterans closed in on Lincoln with threat.

Waters confronted him. "You were d-d-dishonorably d-d-discharged?"

Lincoln shuffled from heel to heel. "I came up with some shell shock."

Angelo shoved a hand against Lincoln's chest, knocking him off balance. "Shell shock my ass. Says here you were blued for refusing to go over the top. Get outa here before we tar and feather you."

Lincoln and the Apache chief gathered up their haversacks and prepared to hightail it before they suffered a beating.

"They stay," Waters ordered.

Lincoln halted his retreat, shocked as the others by the reprieve.

Now Angelo was the one sputtering. "Whatd'ya mean? We agreed—"

"We agreed everyone who joins has to have p-p-papers. He's got p-p-papers."

"He's a yellow-bellied sloper," Dolan protested.

"Maybe so," Waters said. "But the government says you're a bum and a Bolshevik. We're all runts to be tossed off. Anyways, I got a use for him." He turned to Lincoln. "You from Council Bluffs?"

Lincoln nodded uncertainly. "I wouldn't go in there, if that's what you're thinking. They got a sheriff aching to crack your beans."

"That so? Well, I'm not about to be treated like bologna bulls in the very country I fought to save. You boys still got your Army tags?"

The veterans, now even more confused, traded worried nods.

"Hand 'em over."

The men wondered what their eccentric commander was thinking up now. Shrugging, they pulled the chains off their necks and gave them up.

Waters stuffed the tags into his shoulder bag.

The sign on the rail station said *Welcome to Council Bluffs*, but Waters didn't see much to confirm the sentiment, given that the platform was filled with armed men who looked none too happy. His veterans opened the doors to their cattle cars and waited to find out if their leader would order them to disembark or head on down the line to friendlier confines.

"The pup there with the holster," Lincoln whispered to his ear.

Waters studied the uniformed man heading the posse. "He's the sheriff?"

"Nah, that's his deputy. Sheriff Briggs don't stray much from the jail."

Waters looked down the line of cars at his jittery men and saw that they were none too eager to step off the train. He saluted the deputy with a grin and aimed one foot toward the platform. "You can cancel the twenty-one gun salute."

The deputy inched a hand toward his pistol. "Just hold it right there."

Waters studied the riflemen and the frightened townspeople who stood behind them. "You got some kind a typhoid epidemic here, or what?"

"You tumbleweeds just take your trouble on down the road."

Waters saw that the deputy's hand was shaking; the fellow looked more scared than his veterans. There was no turning back now, so Waters stepped off the car and planted himself in front of the astonished lawman. He shouted over his shoulder, "Angelo, line 'em up!"

The posse raised their guns, expecting a scuffle. The other veterans hesitated, but Alford jumped out and came up to stand next to Waters. One by one, the men followed his example, until they were in the formation that they had drilled.

Smiling with pride at their discipline, Waters turned back to the deputy and asked, "You got a hospital in this town?"

The deputy appeared fidgety, not certain what to do next. "Up Main Street, next to the courthouse. You floaters take another step, you'll get a free visit."

Waters walked to the head of his ranks, worried that any moment now he might get a bullet to the back of the head. As he passed Dolan, he whispered, "Listen for the hammers." With the Irishman at his side keeping a lookout for weapons, Waters shouted to his men, "Eyes front and center! March!"

The other veterans, despite suffering from a bad case of the nerves, followed him through the station and up the slope toward the town's main street.

The riflemen looked to their deputy for orders, but the exasperated deputy couldn't bring himself to give the command to fire. "Damn it! Briggs is gonna have my hide! Get up to the courthouse before those bums do!"

Waters signaled for marching music, and Ozzie wailed away at *Pack Up Your Troubles In Your Old Kit Bag* on his oboe. Meanwhile, Lincoln, resplendently bizarre in his stovepipe hat, pounded on an old drum that he had found in a garbage dump a few days back. The locals who came down to the station expecting to see a violent confrontation followed this queer procession into town. As the veterans shuffled along, Alford unfolded a blanket and ordered his treasury committee of three men to carry it from sidewalk to sidewalk to catch coins for donations. When the veterans reached the courthouse on the square, they found more residents gathered there in nettled silence.

Waters scanned the streets until his eyes alighted on a two-story building across the way. The sign above the entrance identified it as the county hospital. He led his column up to its doors and brought the vets to a halt.

Ozzie turned a glance over his shoulder. Lincoln was lingering a few steps behind, intrigued by a historical marker about the local Pottawattamie County Jail across the street. Ozzie backtracked and whispered, "You coming, Charlie? I wouldn't straggle from the pack. You might get clipped."

"Oz, come here and look at this. Says here the pokie in this town is a one-of-a-kind structure. They call it a human rotary. Eighteen squirrel cages with pie-shaped cells turn like a lazy Susan."

Ozzie walked over to check out what he had found. "Why'd they do that?"

Lincoln squinted at the small lettering on the plaque and read it aloud for Taylor: "'The object of our invention is to produce a jail in which prisoners can be controlled without the necessity of personal contact between them and the jailer. It provides maximum security with minimum jailer attention. If a jailer can count, and he has a trusty he can trust, he could control the jail.'"

"Damn," Ozzie muttered. "What's this world coming to? Purty soon they'll be using a machine to hang the criminals, too."

Up ahead on the steps of the courthouse, a big-bellied brute in a butternut uniform and Texas Ranger's hat stepped through the doors. The townspeople hushed and parted to make a path as the lawman walked across the street toward the hospital. Surveying the cowering ranks of veterans, he quipped an aside to his deputy, "What a sorry-looking bunch you've allowed into our midst, Gullip. I thought you said we had a band of marauders invading us. These old-timers couldn't peel the bark off a spud if it was soaked in linseed."

Angelo and several other veterans took a menacing step forward, itching to trade fists with the sheriff, but Waters glared them back into line.

The sheriff walked down the ragged column, drawing flinches from the apprehensive veterans as he passed. After making another ominous circuit, he ordered Waters, "Now you freeloading vagabonds just do an about-face and take your circus back down to the station."

Waters was shaking inside, but he stiffened his backbone. "Angelo! Lincoln! Alford! Roll up your s-s-sleeves and get up here!"

The three summoned veterans reluctantly stepped to the front. They curled their cuffs to their biceps, preparing for the fracas.

Waters bared his arm right under the nose of the lawman. "You gonna shoot unarmed v-v-vets, Sheriff?"

The sheriff grinned evil through his yellow teeth as he unbuckled his gun belt, champing to deal a bruising lesson to the windbag hobo. "Your mouth is about to meet its shadow."

Waters stepped forward, close enough to smell the talcum on the sheriff's neck. Just when the sheriff was about to land a fist into his skull, Waters moved past him and walked into the hospital. The sheriff and his deputy shared baffled glances, wondering if this head bum was conceding defeat and heading toward the hospital bed where he'd eventually end up.

Waters stuck his head back out the hospital doors and called over the sheriff to the three veterans he had picked, "You coming or not?"

While the other veterans remained outside, Angelo, Dolan, and Alford shrugged and followed him into the hospital. In the lobby, a doctor, expecting trouble, confronted them and blocked their entry to the rooms.

"Are you the head bone-sawer here?" Waters asked the doctor.

"What if I am?"

"I understand you've got a little girl desperate for some strange-type blood." Waters handed the doctor the army tags that he had collected the day before after reading about the sick girl in the newspaper. "I was told during the war that mine's a peculiar kind. These boys are also willing to give if you drain me dry."

The doctor examined the tags and saw that they listed blood types. The look on his face transformed from disgust to grateful relief.

Twenty minutes later, Waters and his three volunteers walked back out of the hospital. The townspeople, having heard what they had just done, swarmed them with thanks and offerings of food and clothing. As Waters marched his men back to the train station, he winked at the embarrassed sheriff, who stood with his deputies, their shirtsleeves still rolled up, looking like the hogs that had just missed the morning feed.

Two nights later, hundreds of curious St. Louis residents stood on the bluffs overlooking the Mississippi River and watched as Waters led his three hundred men on foot toward the toll bridge that spanned the Big Muddy. The veterans didn't have more than five dollars among them, not enough to buy a decent breakfast let alone get the entire regiment to the other side. But Waters was determined to reach Illinois if he had to drown trying. As he walked, limping from his sore feet, he didn't dare look over his shoulder for fear of it being taken as a sign of cowardice. He could hear the clomping of the feet to his rear slow down in hesitation.

Staying ten feet behind the BEF leader, Ozzie whispered, "Dubya, what if that fella in the booth demands remuneration?"

"Just keep moving and keep your eyes on the road," Waters ordered over his shoulder. "Pass the order down the line."

Waters knew the men couldn't figure what he had in mind, but they did as he commanded, marching two abreast and making as if they were overtaking the bridge at Château-Thierry. When they reached the tollbooth, the collector stepped out with a pistol in hand and stared at the strange procession. Waters picked up his pace, as best as a hungry man could, and walked right past the booth. The astonished toll collector just stared at them passing by, as if he were watching a battalion of ghosts crossing the River Styx on its way to the afterlife.

Waters listened for a shout or the crack of warning gunfire. If it took a bullet to the back of his head, so be it. He was fed up with the shenanigans being pulled to prevent him and his men from reaching their destinations. Those B&O thugs had stopped him on the outskirts of St. Louis, forcing him to get off the boxcars. In retaliation, he had lined up Dolan, Angelo, and the others along the tracks, daring the railroad suits to make the first move, but the thugs had finally backed down. On orders—probably from Washington— the trainmaster wouldn't take the locomotives across the river. So, he had decided to march his BEF boys the twelve miles over this bridge and through East St. Louis to the B&O switching yard, where all the trains from this side of the Mississippi were sent east.

When their column was finally a safe distance onto Illinois territory, he risked turning around. The toll operator had taken refuge again in his tiny castle—and his veterans were all grinning, astonished that his bold strategy had worked.

Ozzie played his oboe while the veterans behind him trudged east singing melancholic verses from *I Surrender Dear*, a soothing melody made famous by Red Norvo and his Swing Septet. When their song was finished, they kept moving in a slow, watchful silence, sensing that this miraculous crossing now marked a turning point in their dream of a new life.

But Waters knew the worst wasn't over. He hadn't told them that another dangerous stage of their journey was waiting just down the road.

As dawn broke over the smokestacks and hardscrabble skyline of East St. Louis, Waters and his men caught their first sight of the round switching barn in the B&O rail yards. Their celebration was cut short, however, when hundreds of blue-clad railroad security men, armed with shotguns, appeared from behind the sheds and empty cars.

The superintendent of the B&O security force walked up and drove a finger into Waters's chest. "I thought I told you not to step foot here."

Waters looked at the name on the railroad man's badge. "John Young. And I thought I t-t-told *you* that no train is going east from here without us on it."

"You and your bums are trespassing on private property."

"We're a duly mustered regiment. Ain't you been reading the papers?"

The agent, who had first accosted the veterans the day before on the western side of the river, shoved Waters back. "You take one step into these yards, you'll have blood on your hands."

"You ain't got j-j-jurisdiction!"

Young knocked him to the ground. "Big word for a puny hobo. I got jurisdiction in *these* yards. And we got a little barracks set up for you soldier boys over there in that vacant field. You're used to sleeping in barracks, aren't you?"

Alford turned and saw their comrades being roughed up and herded toward an open space in a garbage dump that had been fenced off from the main rail yard. He shouted for his chief of military police, "Dolan!"

Young and his armed agents closed ranks, waiting for the tough Irishman to make the first move.

Dolan stood frozen.

"Mickey!" Alford pleaded. "We gotta fight back!"

Dolan kept his eyes on the ground. "I tried to explain."

"You're the captain of the bodyguard!" Lincoln reminded him.

Dolan shook his head. "I don't raise my hand against any man no more."

"What the hell are you talking about?" Alford asked.

"I swore not to use my fists again," said Dolan.

Alford was flummoxed. "You been talking a good enough game of the rough stuff for months. Hell of a time to tell us this now."

The railroad thugs laughed at the scrapping hobos. "Soldiers without guns," quipped Young. "And a bodyguard who doesn't fight. I'll bet they've got a cook who doesn't fry and a bugler who doesn't toot."

Burned by glares accusing him of betrayal, Dolan suffered in silence as he and the other veterans were prodded into their new confines. The railroad guards patrolled the fence, making sure none of the veterans tried to return to the cars in the yard.

"How long you g-g-gonna keep us here?" Waters demanded of the agent.

Young raised his middle finger as he walked back down the ridge toward the giant round switchyard barn, where dozens of tracks entered like spokes of a wheel to permit different trains to be shifted to alternate routes. "Until you boys get homesick. And until we get all these trains refueled with coal and out of this yard heading east without your scrawny carcasses on them."

The veterans sank to the ground, hungry and dejected.

Out of earshot of his prisoners, Young motioned over one of his officers. "These whipped mutts won't give us any trouble. Leave a couple of the men to watch them and send the rest home. I'll see you in the morning."

H ours later, deep into the night, Waters was awakened by jostling on his arm. He stirred to his elbows and rubbed his eyes. Staring down at him were ten strangers.

The tallest newcomer whispered, "Those thugs are trying to hustle you."

Waters rose to his knees. "What do you mean, hustle?"

"They're running the shift locomotives up and down the tracks and trading off cars to confuse you."

Waters bounded up and ran to the pen fence. In the yards below, dozens of cars were being moved in and out of the shifting barn like the old Army game of three shells and a pea. The train that he and his veterans had ridden into St. Louis was already across the river, waiting to be reloaded with coal when the colliers reported to work in a couple of hours. Ten other locomotives sat aimed in different directions, ready to be hitched to any of the cars. He turned back to the man who had just warned him of the subterfuge and asked his name.

"William Hruska. I bring more veterans. We read about you in papers."

Awakened by the whispered conversation, Alford came over and sized the newcomer up. "You talk like a Russkie."

"Lithuania. But am no Red. Come from Chicago."

"You were in the AEF?" Alford asked.

Hruska nodded. "My father and mother killed by Bolsheviks."

Waters searched the vacant lot beyond the fence. "Where're the guards?"

Hruska curled a grim smile and made a pummeling gesture against his head. "I remind them what happen to those who massacre workers in Dearborn."

Waters shook the Slav's hand in gratitude. "I don't care if you're Stalin himself. You showed up just in the nick. Glad to have you with us."

"What are we gonna do, Dubya?" asked Angelo.

"We need a plan."

"Yeah, well, you're the commander," said Lincoln. "Come up with one."

Illuminated dimly by a few security gas lamps, Waters stood behind the fence and studied the tracks that radiated out from the shifting barn in the yard. He asked Hruska, "You know where we can get soap around here?"

Hruska pointed to a maintenance shed.

"Go round us up some buckets and suds."

While the Lithuanian veteran and his small band of veterans took off on their foraging sortie, Waters motioned Alford over for a private talk. After they had finished strategizing, he roused the men from their slumber. "As of this moment, I am resigning my post as leader, until I say otherwise."

The veterans reacted as if he had just committed treason. "The hell you are!" Angelo griped. "You got us into this mess! Now you're walking out?"

"Go with Alford," Waters insisted. "He'll tell you what to do."

The next morning, Agent Young and a hundred officers of his armed security force strolled into the East St. Louis rail yard, assigned there to send off that day's schedule of trains. As the sun broke over the horizon, they looked up and found three hundred hobo veterans sitting atop the entire rolling stock. Incensed, Young spun toward the fenced vacant lot and saw that the wire pen had been cut.

The door to the railroad storage barn hinged open, and Waters walked out. "Morning, boys. We made some changes to our accommodations."

Young could have lit a match with the heat sizzling from his face. "You Oregon pissant!" He thrust a paper into Waters's hand. "I've got a warrant for your arrest. Let's see if you can pull your escape stunt from jail."

Waters examined the document. "Looks like you made a mistake."

Young laughed gruffly. "You stew tomatoes *and* practice law now, do you?"

"A man don't need to be a lawyer to see that this paper don't apply to me."

"What the hell are you talking about?"

"This warrant is for the arrest of the leader of these men."

"You can read. Good for you. Let's go."

"Sorry, but you got the wrong man. This unit ain't got a leader."

Alford yelled down from his perch atop one of the cattle-car roofs. "That's right, Johnny boy! We believe in democracy!"

Waters enjoyed the superintendent's slack-jawed reaction. "No train's gonna move out of these yards unless we're on it."

"We'll see about that." Young motioned for one of his B&O engineers to fire up a locomotive and hook on a couple of empty cars to head them out.

The engineer pushed the throttle, but the wheels just spun in place. He looked down from the engine window and shook his head at the agent.

"What the hell's wrong?" Young demanded.

The engineer climbed down and ran his hand along the rails. He raised his greasy finger for the agent's inspection. "They soaped the tracks."

Young looked like he'd just been trumped with four aces. "The entire Eastern seaboard depends on this rail yard! You bums will bottle up half the country!"

Waters casually examined his dirty fingernails. "I reckon the country will jest have to be bottled up for a spell. Might do them some good to see what it feels like to go for a few months in deprivation."

Young spun on his heels and started to walk away.

"Oh, and I wouldn't try any gunplay, if I was you," Waters warned. "That would be awfully bad publicity for the B&O." He pointed to the bluffs overlooking the yard. "Besides, you might hit some innocent bystanders."

As the dawn light became stronger, Young looked up at the heights and saw hundreds of spectators. Drawn by word of mouth during the night, they sat watching the standoff and yelling support for the veterans. A member of the local VFW chapter turned on the radio of his parked his Model T Ford to offer the men some entertainment while they suffered the rising heat. The program being broadcast that hour featured Father Charles Coughlin, the famous radio priest listened to by millions of Americans.

Waters grinned at Young. "Looks like we're the new show in town."

Before Young could grouse another threat at the hobos, the radio blasted Father Coughlin's strident tirade for radical populism across the rail yard:

> "Oh the world of politics is plagued with Pontius Pilates whose voices echo in the halls of parliaments and congresses, sounding the release of a new Barabbas and everlasting condemning the innocent brothers of Christ to walk the highway to Calvary. Gentlemen of industry and finance, the finger of history will point to you and to your servants in Washington for stoking the class hatred which soon will burst forth to destroy your property...."

The guards patrolling the locomotives also stopped to listen to the radio priest's mesmerizing diatribe:

> "... On Christ's triumphant march to the City on the Hill, He paused along the way and wept, exclaiming 'Oh Jerusalem, Jerusalem, if thou also hadst known the things that are necessary to thy peace.' But now they are hidden, for the days of conflagration are upon thee...."

While Young marched huffing out of the yards, Waters climbed atop one of the trains and walked along the roofs to offer encouragement to his men and to distribute what donations of coffee and smokes he had been able to forage from the bystanders. As he pondered Father's Coughlin's radical sermon, he thought about how Jesus must have felt on His march with the Apostles toward the great City on the Hill. He had sensed from the start that the Good Lord was with him on this quest to confront the moneychangers and Pharisees of the Temple in Washington. Yet Christ, he also remembered from his Sunday school days, had first endured some time alone from His disciples before meeting His fate.

Word was that the temperature would reach the nineties. Wiping his brow with a dirty oil rag, Waters called Alford over atop one of the cars and put an arm over his friend's shoulder. With a grin, he said, "It's gonna get hotter soon."

Alford nodded. "Humidity's bad, too."

"Nah, I'm talking about the political heat."

Alford blew air into Waters's face, mimicking a fan. "Nothing we can't handle, General."

Waters studied his friend. "Are you my John the Baptist, Georgie?"

"Did you happen to stumble on a hooch still around here, Dubya?"

Waters grinned like a prophet just handed a revelation. "I'm gonna walk on ahead to Caseyville while you boys keep staring down the law here."

"Why the hell are you doing that?"

"I need to do some thinking alone. You know the Good Shepherd had to get away to Hisself for awhile before he entered Jerusalem."

"Not to be a quibbler, Dubya, but you aren't exactly the Good Shepherd, not by a long shot. And we aren't going to Jerusalem."

"Maybe not, but it sure f-f-feels like the welcome mat is getting more slippery the farther east we get. Same thing happened to Christ."

"Hoover and the feds are probably paying off the local pols to stop us."

Waters had already figured that out. "Once we get free of this muskrat trap, we're gonna need more provisions and permissions to t-t-transport across Illinois and Indiana. I need to go up the road to plead our c-c-case with the powers that be. Convince them that it's in their best interest to speed us along. You keep the lid t-t-tight on the teapot here, and I'll be back in a couple of days."

Alford gave him an uncertain nod. "I'm not sure how the other boys will feel about that. Some think you tend to disappear when the going gets rough."

"You'll handle them just fine." Waters threw his knapsack over his back. "You always do." While the men slumbered atop the rail cars, he slipped out of the yard to hitchhike a ride east. Hoofing it down the deserted streets, he listened to the fading voice of Father Coughlin preaching how Christ had suffered His Judas. He was convinced that the radio priest had been talking directly to him during these past two days. Taking heed of the sermon, he vowed to remain on guard against the insidious approach of Evil, for the Devil never rested in his determination to thwart the great cosmic battle for economic justice.

48

WASHINGTON, D.C.
MAY 1932

The president hurled a medicine ball into Patrick Hurley's gut.

Staggered but still upright, the War Department chief gripped the seams of the leather spheroid and eyed the six other Administration advisors in suits who formed a circle with the president on the White House lawn. The tall New Mexican had to take another moment to regain his breath while he chose which of his smirking rivals to punish next.

"Are you injured, Patrick?" the president asked.

Hurley gulped for air. "No, sir. Fine toss."

Impatient with the pace of the throws, Hoover angled the brim of his fedora down to shade his eyes from the harsh sun and silently cursed his physician for ordering him to endure this torture to strengthen his heart. In a fit of spite, he had decided that if he were to be condemned to such a humiliating exertion, his advisors would suffer with him. This fifteen-minute ordeal of strength-building each morning did, however, provide him with one unexpected benefit. By observing the choice and ferocity of the throws, he was able to ferret out the animosities simmering inside his Cabinet. Problem was, he wasn't getting much exercise at it. These cowards in the circle around him were reluctant to put any force behind the ball for fear that their careers would be ruined with a headline announcing that they had maimed the leader of the free world.

"Sir, I'm coming back your way," Hurley warned.

Hoover rolled his eyes. "How many times do I have to tell you? You don't have to announce your intention like Grantland Rice calling a play!"

"Yes, sir." Hurley hovered the heavy ball between his knees, as if shooting a basketball free throw underhand, and lofted it as gently as possible.

Hoover wrangled the ball into submission and scanned his potential targets. For the first time in his life, he wished Andrew Mellon were still around. What he wouldn't give to lob a cannon shot into the bowels of that decomposing bag of haggis. But the bilious Scotsman had escaped impeachment for tax fraud by resigning four months ago to accept an ambassadorial appointment to the Court of St. James in London. The remaining choices for a punishing heave were less satisfying. His old friend at Treasury, Ogden Mills, stood in Mellon's stead, and next to him was Bill Moran, the head of his Secret Service, who always kept him informed on the whispers in the outside offices. His personal aide, Walter Newton, was eager to receive the toss, but he was too valuable to risk breaking a hand.

His cold eye finally settled on the miasma of smoking across from him. There stood MacArthur, striking a ridiculous pose while chewing on that insufferable pipe. The Army Chief of Staff waited insouciantly with one hand on his hip, as if daring a test of his quickness. Sure, the man had been a base-ball player at West Point. Just ask him, and he'd tell you *ad nauseam* about his exploits on the diamond. Yes, he would send Dauntless Doug reeling. He took aim at MacArthur's pipe and let fly.

MacArthur caught the pass easily, not missing a puff. He held the ball aloft like Atlas supporting the globe and announced from the corner of his thin lips, "Very nice heave, sir. This feels like a ten-pounder. We used twenties at the Point."

"Did you now?" Hoover retorted, not giving a rat's posterior. "I was working three jobs at age ten. My stepfather did not favor the frivolities of sport."

"We'll just have to agree to disagree on that, Mr. President. When I ran the Military Academy, I felt so strongly about the importance of athletics for the development of a young man's character that I instituted a rule requiring every cadet to participate."

"It didn't seem to do much for your classmate Glassford's sense of judgment. What sport did *he* play? Chess?" Hoover could see from the nodding reactions that his advisors had taken his barbed reference to the popularity of that board game in Russia as a dig at Glassford's penchant for coddling protesting Communists. Amid a fraught silence, the ball went thumping around the circle for several more turns, until it came back to him. He flung the spheroid at Hurley again, this time accompanied by a complaint. "That police chief came here this morning wanting to talk to me about these veterans holding up the trains in St. Louis."

Hurley was flabbergasted. "What did Glassford want *you* to do about it?"

Hoover gritted his teeth as he heaved the ball across the circle at Newton. "The man expects me to support the Bonus legislation. He said that it would defuse the situation."

"And what did you tell him?" Hurley asked.

"I refused to see him. I am not some small-town mayor! Since when does a local cop think he can call on the White House as if it were city hall? I had Newton here listen to his distasteful solicitation and then send him off."

Newton nodded his approval of that decision as he relayed the ball down the line. "Glassford has a tin ear when it comes to politics. After we rebuffed him, he had the temerity to go up to the Hill and lobby Watson and Rainey for that budget-busting bill."

Hoover fumed. "I'm surprised Wright Patman didn't offer him a staff job."

Newton put some extra force into his next throw. "When I heard about Glassford's end run, I called him and advised in no uncertain terms that he had publicly embarrassed the Administration by going over the head of the commissioners and speaking to the newspapers about this."

Hurley looked pleased with the report of Glassford's woodshedding. "Well, that certainly put him on notice that he treads on thin ice."

"I wouldn't be so sure," Newton warned the War Department chief. "Word around town is he's been meeting with local veterans clubs and social agencies, asking them to help feed the bums in the city."

The president turned an icy glare on MacArthur, waiting for his explanation of his West Point classmate's refusal to play by Washington rules.

Between pipe puffs, MacArthur offered a suggestion. "Sir, it might be beneficial for Secretary Hurley and Commissioner Crosby to have a heart-to-heart talk with him. Hap Glassford understands the importance of chain of command. He'll get the message."

"What about you?" Hoover asked pointedly. "Don't you want to be part of this conversation, given your history with the man?"

MacArthur shook his head and leaned back, as if attacked by a foul odor. "I think it would be unproductive for me to become involved. It's a local District matter."

Galled by the general's blatant attempt to gain distance from the problem, Hoover caught the ball and dropped it angrily to the ground. He stared at its seams for several seconds, and then shook his head with an air of apocalyptic dread. "If those rail riders from Oregon break loose from St. Louis and head this way—"

"They're not going to break loose," Newton promised.

Hoover shot a suspicious glance at the aide. "Do I need to know why you're so certain of that?"

Newton warned off the president's inquiry with a stern shake of his head. "On another matter, sir, the B&O requested a loan from the Reconstruction Finance Corporation a few weeks ago."

Hoover was baffled as to what possible significance that minor development could hold. "What does that have to do with—"

"The loan went through without delay," Newton advised him, shooting a knowing glance at Hurley. The aide then turned back to the president and added with affected nonchalance, "The B&O executives were very appreciative."

Hoover frowned, finally taking the import of the report. The crassness of politics revolted him, always had. With a sigh of disgust that was closer to a groan, he kicked the medicine ball across the lawn and, with his foot now aching, limped back to the White House.

That night, sitting alone at his desk in the District Building, Happy Glassford stared at one of his unfinished paintings on the easel in the corner of his office. Since taking this job, he hadn't found the time to finish the watercolor landscape of the Chesapeake Bay. Scrapper, sprawled at his feet, looked up at him with hooded eyes, as if chastising him for neglecting his true love, the brush and textured paper. He took a long draw on his pipe and reminded the dog, "I don't see you producing any masterpieces lately either, old boy."

Scrapper wagged his tail a couple of times, then walked off a few steps and plopped down for a nap.

"Sure, abandon me. Everyone else in this damn town has."

He envied the dog's ability to shed all cares. He, on the other hand, hadn't enjoyed a decent night's sleep since receiving the report about those Oregon veterans who were vowing to march on Washington. He couldn't get out of his mind the memory of the thousands of ragged German soldiers straggling back across the Rhine after the surrender. Most of those congressmen on the Hill hadn't fought in the war. They didn't understand the potential danger of this gathering storm. All that morning, he had made the rounds in the Capitol, pleading support for the Bonus bill to stave off the invasion of homeless veterans. But except for Wright Patman, the politicians had mostly belittled his warning, declaring their confidence that the "bums," as the representatives called them, would never get out of St. Louis.

He opened one of his desk drawers and glanced at a bottle of bourbon that he had confiscated in a raid earlier that week. He closed the drawer without touching the liquor. Thanks to the temperance vigilantes, he couldn't even unwind with a drink in the evenings now. He didn't dare sneak even a dram. Although the hour was late, he couldn't be sure that one of his many disgruntled officers wasn't watching through the door cracks, looking for any excuse to run to the newspapers with a scoop that the city's new cop boss was flouting the dry laws he was sworn to uphold.

He smiled wearily at the dog. "You feel like some music, Scrapper?" The dog didn't move, but he turned on the Philco anyway. He twirled the dials looking for some Charlie Patton on his favorite blues station. He stopped at a shrill voice in the midst of a rant:

> "Gentlemen of industry and finance, the finger of history will point
> to you and to your servants in Washington for stoking the class
> hatred which soon will burst forth to destroy your property.... "

He spun the dial again. The last thing he needed to hear right now was that damn radio priest blustering his venom. Unable to find a clear station, he landed on another familiar voice, one so rapid in its delivery that even Scrapper was roused:

> "It seems, ladies and gentlemen, that this train full of men from
> Oregon has become a symbol for every despair this country
> knows. Tonight, in a dark, damp rail yard in the heart of this
> great country, two battles are being waged. One is for control
> of the economic crossroads of America. But a more desperate
> battle is for the souls of men and women who could be forgiven
> for believing that God is right behind our government in aban-
> doning them.... "

He opened a bottle of aspirin and swallowed down a couple. His head always hurt from the way Gibbons rattled on like a machine gun. Desperate for some soothing musical relief, he twirled the dial again, but accidentally landed back on Father Coughlin:

> "You preach the sophistry of free contract and hold Christ, in
> the person of the working man, a captive in Pilate's dungeon,
> flogging his back with the lashes of greed while preaching the
> sanctity of capitalism and the Constitution...."

He checked his watch. His old friend Gib was broadcasting at a different time than usual. That one-eyed news buzzard must have modified his schedule to go head to head with Coughlin. The Battle of East St. Louis, as the papers were now calling this standoff between the homeless veterans and the railroad cops, had become such a lightening rod for emotion and anger that the two most famous radio voices in the country were waging a duel over it. He quickly flipped the dial back to Gibbons:

> "The self-proclaimed radio priest sells his bitter brand of anti-
> Semitism and radical Christianity to prey on the fears and pain
> of good folk. Ladies and gentlemen, your Headline Hunter has
> manned the trenches of Flanders. He has walked the desolate

streets of Germany. He has stridden the very steps of Christ in Palestine, where two thousand years ago rival prophets of doom and despair preached the same message. Things have changed very little, I'm afraid. This, ladies and gentlemen, is how it always starts.... "

He shook his head wearily. Maybe he should have dragged Gibbons with him to the District Commission office that afternoon. Crosby had dressed him down severely, accusing him of embarrassing the president by going around town sounding like Cassandra with these warnings of an imminent crisis. Their exchange had been so heated that he had written it down afterwards, in case he ever required a record of it:

> *Crosby: If you feed and house these rail riders, others will come by the thousands.*
>
> *HG: It would be far better to have ten thousand orderly veterans under control than five thousand hungry, desperate men breaking into stores and committing other depredations.*
>
> *Crosby: What is the police force for?*
>
> *HG: Are you making a suggestion or issuing an order?*
>
> *Crosby: In the Army, it has been my experience that a suggestion is obeyed the same as an order.*
>
> *HP: We're not in the Army now. This emergency places a tremendous responsibility for preserving law and order, perhaps protecting life and property, squarely on my shoulders. I cannot follow suggestions. If you desire to take the responsibility yourself for such a policy, all you have to do is to issue written orders, and they will be carried out. In the absence of such orders, I shall take what I consider the correct course.*

He didn't need to be told his job was in jeopardy. Crosby had backed down from the threats for now, but he wasn't naïve about how politicians operated in the dark. He thought back to his plebe year at the Point and the demerits that he had piled up for bucking the system. Those hadn't exactly been a good career move, either. Sure, he had risen up the ranks anyway, but he knew what some of the senior brass thought about him: the painting, the bohemian lifestyle, the failure to hold down a steady profession since the war. Except for MacArthur, those War Department chickenhawks considered him a loose cannon. Tired of being aimless and never setting roots, he really wanted to keep this job. Maybe he *should* give in to Crosby's demands and run the police force in the traditional way, cracking heads and playing the system under the table. Sure, why not. He resolved to try their way for once, become part of the team and show a little force.

He propped his feet up on his desk and opened the surveillance file delivered that afternoon. At his request, the Portland police had forwarded their agent reports compiled about this fellow who had been stirring up the veterans in Oregon. Walter W. Waters was his name, a former medic in the 146th Field Artillery. Promoted to sergeant and honorably discharged during the war. He read down a paragraph: *Can't hold down a job for more than six months.*

He smiled at the irony. "Sounds like someone we know, eh, Scrapper?"

The dog ambled over as if to see what his master was looking at. On one photograph, a pair of mesmerizing eyes stared up from the glossy print. Glassford studied the narrow, blond face. The Portland police report said the man had gone by several aliases after the war, including the name Billy Kincaid. He angled the photograph into the light, wondering aloud, "Who are you *really*, Walter Waters?"

He scanned down the page and read the police analysis of his mental state: *Unstable and moody, but possesses charismatic tendencies.*

He closed the file and patted the dog on the head. "The fellow may have a future in politics, what do you think, Scrapper?"

49

EAST ST. LOUIS, ILLINOIS
MAY 1932

On the third evening of its standoff with the B&O authorities, the Bonus Expeditionary Force, now at nearly four hundred men in strength, lay scattered across the roofs of every car in the rail yards, still patrolled by armed guards. More spectators had come to offer their support for the veterans, filling the surrounding heights, and the radio in the car parked on the hillside was still blaring its daily dose of Father Coughlin's evangelism:

> "When Judas betrayed Christ, Pilate said: 'Behold this man! Shall not the hearts of the angry mob be softened?' And then Pilate asked, "Who shall I release unto you, Christ or Barabbas? And they asked for Barabbas. 'Oh Woe to you, you Judases, because you devour the house of widows. For this you shall receive the greater judgment.... '"

As the sermon hour crescendoed to a finish, most of the local folks who sat perched on the ridges stood to go home for the night. Once again, a despairing silence fell with dusk over the yards.

Lincoln bedded down next to Angelo atop the hard metal of a boxcar. Setting his top hat on his stomach and resting his hands behind his head, he mused nostalgic. "Joey, that radio converter reminds me how my daddy used to talk. We'd walk back from Sunday service, and Pa would be telling Ma bout how Jesus was being crucified on a cross of gold. I couldn't figure how they hammered those nails into gold."

Angelo tossed and turned, but he couldn't get comfortable. Frustrated with the rivet bolts poking his back, he climbed down from the car and found a soft spot on some grass several yards away. "Damn those tins! I'm hitting the soft stuff down here. You boys are welcome to join me."

"Dubya said we all had to stay put."

Angelo tormented Lincoln by sighing heavily as he luxuriated in the soft grass. "Don't I recollect that Waters resigned as leader? We shoulda grabbed a locomotive while we had the chance. Now we're stuck here while those birds in Washington have time to build up their trenches. I need to get some winks."

Through the dimming light, Lincoln searched the rows of cars behind them. "Where the hell *is* Dubya, anyway?"

"Apparently he's too high in rank to sleep with us. He had to head on down to Caseyville to find a flophouse. Left us to do his dirty work."

"I'm sure that ain't the way it was."

"No? Then how was it?"

"Come on, now, Joey. He's probably reconnoitering the enemy ground up ahead before sending us into the breach."

"The only breach I've seen around here is your yapping mouth. Now shut up and let me get some shut-eye." Angelo stretched his arms and yawned for the benefit of Lincoln and the other veterans, who looked down at him with envy. "Aahhhh, this Illinois prairie grass is better than duck down."

The other men on that line of cars traded daring glances. Shrugging, they climbed down to find sleeping spots near him.

Lincoln refused to join the mutiny against orders. Instead, he walked down the line of cars and found one out of hearing distance of the deserters. *Tenderfoots. A real soldier can sleep anywhere.* Using his jacket for a pillow, he began thinking about the hot breakfast that Dubya was likely negotiating for them down the road. His eyes soon fluttered, and finally he drifted off as the breeze from the Mississippi River gently brushed his face.

By golly, before he knew it, he was on a riverboat. Not only that. He was in full gambler's regalia and stationed at the high-stakes table. There were pretty bar girls dancing and kissing him each time a big pot came his way. He was in fine form, all right, winning enough to set himself up for life. The riverboat, which had started off from the port with a smooth gait, suddenly began picking up speed. Jolts from the waves shook the casino, and the table with the chips rocked violently, scattering his precious fortune. He scrambled to claw the chips back to him, but the more he tried, the faster the boat lurched and pitched.

"They're running Number Five!" somebody shouted.

He knifed up, startled from a dream. He was moving, for sure, but he wasn't on a riverboat. The spin of metal wheels and the screech of steam blasted at his ears. He climbed to his hands and knees, and looked down. In the darkness, the train was heading out—and he was the only man atop the cars on this line.

Hearing the steam hiss, those veterans sprawled on the boxcars of the other lines woke up. They stood, rubbing their eyes, and looked across the yard.

Hruska and Alford hurried down from their roof and tried to catch the moving caboose, but they were losing ground fast.

"Charlie!" Alford shouted. "Get off!"

Lincoln was afraid to jump. Hanging onto the rivet ribs, he angled his head over the side of the car and saw the engineer in the locomotive cab cranking the engine to full speed. Agent Young and one of his armed thugs were also in the cab. Lincoln ducked back out of sight, afraid the agent would shoot him if he discovered him still on board. He heard the smirking agent tell his guard:

"Looks like we finally got rid of those tree monkeys."

Terrified, Lincoln lay on his stomach praying. *I ain't running no more, Lord!*

T he veterans in the yard watched the escaping train disappear across the eastern horizon. Alford searched the grounds and saw that Angelo had bedded in the grass. "You stupid Wop! I told you to stay on those cars!"

Angelo was itching to throw down. "Yeah, you and Waters also said we'd be in Washington by now! Why should we be sitting here, meals for the mosquitoes at night, while Waters is warming his ass in some hotel down the road?"

Alford reared back with a fist. "I oughta—"

Hruska broke them apart. "Must get Lincoln off!"

Angelo brushed off Hruska's grasp. "What's the hurry? He'll just get to Washington a couple days before us."

Hruska made an arch with his arms. "Underpass before Caseyville."

Dolan's jaw dropped. "What's the clearance?"

Hruska spread his hands to measure off about two feet.

Still, Angelo refused to budge. "If we leave these yards, those B&O boys will just whip out the other trains. We'd be stuck here for another month."

Alford paced down the tracks, trying to come up with a plan.

"What would Waters do?" asked Dolan.

"Hell, I'll tell you what'd he do!" Angelo shouted. "He'd do what he always does! He'd get out of Dodge just before the shooting starts!"

Alford hung his head, defeated. "He's right. If we take off and try to save Charlie, we'll just play into their hands. That's what they're hoping."

"Yeah," Dolan said. "But if we don't get that train stopped, every vet in the country will be hearing how we were conned."

"I'm not risking another man's life," Alford said. "Say goodbye to him, boys. He's a casualty of war."

Distraught over the terrors that awaited poor Lincoln down the line, the veterans were about to return to their sleeping stations atop the cars when an old man in denim overalls climbed over the fence, walked up, and told them, "My son was killed in France. If it's any help to you fellas, take my truck over there."

Alford checked out the man's flatbed jalopy. "How far is it to Caseyville?"

"About thirty miles."

Alford jumped into the passenger seat of the truck. "Billy, get ten men! Let's go! The rest of you birds get back on your roosts!"

As the flat Illinois farm country rushed past him in a blur, Lincoln snuck a look at the ground. He was starting to feel dizzy sick. The grading was racing by way too fast, and he figured he'd likely break his neck if he tried to jump now. He risked another glance over the side.

Laughing at the success of his ruse, Agent Young stuck his head out of the locomotive window and turned toward the rear. His eyes bugged at seeing Lincoln's arm hanging over one of the boxcars. "Son of a bitch! Henderson! I thought you said all the hobos were off?"

The engineer peered out the cabin toward the rear. "That fella'll be sliced like a watermelon at Caseyville. We best crank it down while we can."

"No one stops this train."

"I'm the engineer—"

Young pulled a pistol. "If you cherish your job in these times of economic woes, you'd best keep your hand off that throttle."

Back at the rail yards, Angelo circled his bedroll nervously, feeling guilty about having abandoned Lincoln on the roof.

A security guard walking by him muttered, "Nice job, Guido. Maybe you should think about railroad security work. You're a natural."

Angelo had to be restrained from charging the smart-mouthed thug.

The guard just laughed at him. "Haven't you caused enough trouble for one day, you sawed-off pepperoni grinder?"

"Dollar says we see that train back here by nightfall!"

The guard debated Angelo's wager. "You floaters don't have a buck among you. But just to be sporting, I'll take that bet, and squeeze payment out of your olive-oozing hide."

Alford and his ten volunteers sped their borrowed open-bed truck down the Illinois highway. Twenty miles out of East St. Louis, they spotted the train on the tracks that ran alongside the road. Alford stuck his head out from behind the wheel. Turning toward the back of the truck, he ordered his posse of veterans, "You boys get down!" Then, he checked again with Hruska in the seat next to him. "How far, Billy?"

The Slav veteran raised three fingers to indicate the number of miles before they reached the underpass.

The men in the truck bed dropped to their knees, and Alford pulled his hat down over his eyes to shadow his face. When they pulled even with the locomotive, he looked up at Lincoln, who was holding on for dear life. Alford tried to get his attention, but little Abe didn't recognize him. Alford sped up next to the locomotive cab and waved like a yokel, but the engineer, preoccupied with the tunnel fast approaching, just nodded at him without changing his determined grimace. Alford shifted gears and drove out of sight around a bend up ahead.

The engineer kept his eyes pinned on the curving tracks. "Caseyville's round the next bend. I ain't taking responsibility."

Young fingered his trigger. "He sees that hole, he'll jump. Bums get banged up riding rails all the time." The agent began singing a tune, "She'll be coming 'round the mountain when she—" The locomotive jolted, and an explosion of brake steam sent him and his armed guard bouncing off the cab wall. The train screeched to a grinding halt. Recovering his balance, Young raised his pistol to the engineer's temple. "I guess I need to clean your ears."

The engineer stood frozen with his hand on the brake lever. Young turned toward the low underpass a hundred yards away. A truck sat stranded, straddling the tracks, and its driver stood hovering over the truck's engine with its hood up. The agent stepped out of the cab to chase the hayseed off.

"I was sure this old Ford could fit through," the truck's owner said. "But darned if I don't believe I miscalculated."

"Get that rig off these tracks before we turn it to kindling!" Young ordered.

Alford turned with a grin. "Now, is that any way to talk to a veteran?"

Young's jaw dropped. Realizing he'd been tricked, he marched toward Alford, hankering to hammer the insolent bum. Hruska and the other veterans—armed with clubs and farm implements—stood up in the truck bed.

Alford walked up and thumped the stunned agent on the shoulder. "You don't mind if we catch a ride back to St. Louie, do you, Johnny boy?"

Outnumbered, Young holstered his pistol and backed off. On the train roof, a wobbly Lincoln arose from his hands and knees to test his shaking legs.

Alford wagged a finger at his order-abiding comrade. "Lincoln, ain't I warned you time and again about the dangers of riding boxcars?"

The spectators and veterans waiting back at the rail yard kept watching the tracks heading east, but with each passing minute, they began to despair of ever seeing Lincoln again. Then, when all hope seemed lost, the caboose came chugging toward them through the grimy clouds.

The bluffs erupted with wild cheers. As the train rolled back into the yards, Lincoln stood atop his boxcar like a conquering hero and waved at his joyous comrades. Forced to ride in the caboose, Agent Young and his guard, steaming hotter than the engine pipes, stood red-faced at the railing. Alford and his fellow rescuers leapt off their arriving cars and lifted Lincoln into the grateful arms of their buddies. The BEF men paraded Lincoln around the yards on their shoulders while the crowds of onlookers applauded.

The locomotive's engineer saluted the veterans. "When you boys get ready to head on to Washington, I'd be honored to run you there."

A man in a dark suit broke through the celebrating throngs. Accompanied by an armed escort of state troopers, he approached Alford with a document in his grasp. "I'm John Carver, an aide to Illinois Governor Emmerson."

The veterans hushed, expecting a fight.

Alford stepped up to square off with the state official. "You can tell the governor that if Hoover himself can't stop us, he don't have a chance, either."

Carver handed Alford the letter in his possession and reached out his hand in welcome. "The governor doesn't want to stop you from going to Washington. In fact, he has arranged transport to take you and your men to the Indiana state line. Your friend Walter Waters is quite persuasive."

Alford was suspicious of that offer. "How much is that going to cost us?"

"Free of charge."

Alford raised his arms in triumph. "You hear that, boys? Didn't I tell you old Dubya would make it happen! First the government tries to bottle us up! Now they're sending limousines to take us to see ol' Herbert!"

Renewing their celebration, the singing veterans carried Lincoln around the yards on their shoulders, until coming to Angelo. They stopped their circling procession long enough to let the two bunkmates confront each other.

Lincoln clutched at his stovepipe hat, afraid Angelo would knock him upside the head for not jumping when he had the chance. "But I didn't run, Joey."

"No, you didn't, my little rail splitter. No, you didn't. And tonight, you're gonna have a presidential feast fit for Ol' Abe hisself." Angelo scanned the crowd until he spotted the mouthy security guard.

The guard tried to slip away, but the veterans blocked his path.

Bringing Lincoln with him, arm in arm, Angelo walked up to the guard and opened his palm. "Hey, Jerry! How about a donation for the returned victor here?"

Surrounded, the guard slapped a dollar bill into Lincoln's hand to pay off his wager, and then stormed off.

50

WASHINGTON, D.C.
MAY 1932

MacArthur glanced up from his desk and found George Moseley at his door, brandishing a rolled newspaper like a mace. "How long have you been standing there?"

"Long enough for another hundred bums to invade the city," Moseley said. "Have you thought about what we talked about yesterday?"

Miffed that an intruder had been allowed to trespass his office's picket line, MacArthur barked at the lobby, "Eisenhower!"

His adjutant, Major Dwight D. Eisenhower, rushed in from his station just outside the door on the upper floor of the old War Department building. "Yes, sir."

"What did I tell you about announcing visitors?"

"Sir, General Moseley ordered me to allow him in without warning you."

Rolling his eyes, MacArthur shot a sneer at Moseley and waved the aide out. "Shut the door behind you."

Alone now with his superior, Moseley grinned at having captured the hero of the Marne undefended. "That desk stripe of yours is useless, Doug. Hell, at least get an officer in here who has had some combat experience."

MacArthur brushed off the suggestion. "He may not be much of a guard dog, but I see something in him. He's going to be a fine soldier, mark my word."

"How long are we going to wait before we move on the White Plan?"

MacArthur stood and, lighting his pipe, walked toward the far window to draw Moseley away from the door, out of earshot of anyone who might be lurking in the lobby. With a heavy sigh suggesting that he had given the matter much thought, he warned, "We must be absolutely circumspect."

Moseley unrolled the newspaper to display the headline in that morning's *Washington Post*. "Those rail hobos broke through from St. Louis last night.

This codger crusade is now on every front page in the country. Damn it, Doug! If they catch the trains right, they'll be here in less than a week!"

"There are only four hundred of them. We've got that many in the city now."

Moseley stood gape-mouthed, incredulous at MacArthur's lack of alarm. "Haven't you been reading the reports? These Oregon hobos are just the vanguard. The Intelligence Division says there could be thousands more on the way. This agitator Waters is becoming a goddamn pied piper hero to every drifter from California to New York. The Reds have infiltrated them. You know how those bastards operate."

"Has Governor Emmerson called out the National Guard?"

Moseley snorted. "Hell, Emmerson is giving those freeloaders a parade across Illinois. The damn politicians are just hurrying the scum to us now."

"It's Glassford's problem."

"If we leave it to Glassford, we're all going to end up shoveling shit in the gulags. Did you hear what that sonofabitch asked Hurley yesterday?'

"I really don't want to know."

"Glassford wants the Army to authorize funds for shelter and bedding for this Oregon plague of locusts coming at us. Can you believe that?"

"And?"

"Hurley sent him off with his tail between his legs. Said the federal government wouldn't recognize the invasion. But your old pal is one stubborn sonofabitch. He went behind Hurley's back and begged the brass at the Navy Yard and the Marines for help."

For the first time, MacArthur expressed concern. "Marines?"

"They all turned him down, thank God."

MacArthur paced the office, puffing furiously on his pipe. "I wouldn't be surprised if Floyd Gibbons was behind this appeal to Quantico. We need to keep a close eye on the leathernecks. Smedley Butler has been going around the country giving speeches on behalf of the Bonus."

Moseley made a strange gurgling sound of disdain in his throat. "A Quaker Marine running for the Senate. What the hell's the world coming to? If Butler gets elected, we'll have to circle the wagons around our appropriations."

MacArthur debated the possible consequences of implementing the first steps of the secret military plan to defend the city against a civilian invasion. "We'll need to manage this on the highest security level."

"The president gave his approval?"

MacArthur's eyes darted off. "Hurley managed to extract a mealy-mouthed general directive about national security. But the president has yet to be briefed on the details."

Moseley pounded the desk with his fist. "Let's put the damn thing in motion, then."

MacArthur picked up his old riding crop from the bookcase behind him and gently slapped his thigh. "Our arrangements should not be revealed, even to the senior brass at Fort Myer. Not until we are ready. There are too many sympathizers over there."

"Sympathizers? Hell, come out with it, Doug. You mean Communists."

"We can't be too careful. Yesterday I saw something that struck me as a warning sign. Several dozen of these dole-clamoring veterans have camped outside the barracks across the river. Some of the enlisted men were giving them handouts and money."

"You think there's a conspiracy brewing in the ranks?"

MacArthur deflected the question. "How many tanks do we have at Fort Meade?"

"Twenty."

"Transfer five of them to Fort Myer at night. If anyone asks the reason, tell them the tanks are being used for training."

Moseley walked over to a wall map of the city's ring of defenses. "We'll need transport at Fort Washington to bring troops down into the city on the quick."

MacArthur nodded. "Send Perry Miles a fleet of trucks. If he asks the reason for the transfer, tell him it's an appropriations issue. Then bring in more troops from Fort Meade and Fort Holabird. Coordinate with Moran to draw up plans to defend the White House and Treasury Building. One of the first targets of any attempted coup will be the Bureau of Printing and Engraving. If the Reds get their hands on the currency plates, all hell will break lose."

"We should find some good undercover agents to infiltrate this hobo army."

MacArthur gaveled the contents of his pipe into an ashtray. "I'll speak to Al Smith over at Intelligence. He has a stable of trustworthy operatives."

Moseley rapped his knuckles on the desk in approval. "Crissakes, Doug. Now *that's* what I call a command decision. I wish you were sitting in the White House instead of—"

"George!"

"Hell, it's my opinion! And I don't give a damn who knows it! We need somebody running this country who'll show some spine against these insurrectionists."

"That will be all."

Moseley saluted with a knowing smile, and walked out.

MacArthur waited until the lobby was clear, then called for Eisenhower again. Motioning for the door to be closed, the general pulled a gift box from the lower drawer of his desk and handed it to his aide.

Eisenhower stared at the wrapped bow. "Sir, I don't know what to say."

MacArthur glared at the presumption. "It's not for you, Major."

Eisenhower reddened with embarrassment. "No, of course. Sorry, sir."

"I need you to make another delivery. And tell Miss Cooper that I won't be home for lunch today."

"Yes, sir."

MacArthur studied his aide's reaction. "How is Mamie?"

"She's fine, sir. She complains about the long hours, but what Army wife doesn't?"

"I've no doubt she takes my name in vain every night."

"Right after mine, sir."

"And young John? Is the boy going to be a soldier?"

"He enjoys walking Civil War battlefields with me, so there's hope."

MacArthur felt a pang of regret. "I wish I had a son to do that with."

"Still time, sir."

MacArthur leaned back in his chair. "Major, I know you disapprove of my arrangement at the Chastleton."

"Sir, I—"

"You needn't defend your beliefs. Perhaps someday you will understand. There comes a time in a man's life when ..." MacArthur's voice trailed off, and he coughed down the emotion in his throat. Straightening his back, he returned to form. "Tell Dimples how beautiful she looks, will you? That will make her feel better. She's been restless lately."

Eisenhower saluted and turned for the door.

"Oh, and Major."

"Yes, sir?"

"Take Mamie out this weekend. Maybe a nice dinner at the Officer's Club."

"Any particular reason, sir?"

MacArthur walked to the window and looked toward the White House. "She may be seeing even less of you during the next few months."

51

WASHINGTON, INDIANA
MAY 1932

Anna fidgeted with the hem of her sleeve while waiting for the vice-president of the local bank to scroll through a thick plat book that sat perched on a stand behind his expansive desk. Beyond the large glass window, in the main lobby, several English customers at the teller grille stood staring at her. To keep from being distracted by their whispered gossip, she fixed her gaze on the molding along the desk's undercarriage. The workmanship was shoddy and crude. She could hear her father's gentle voice admonishing her to avoid dealing with any person, particularly an English businessman, who paid so little attention to craftsmanship. *God dwells in the details*, he had always reminded her.

"Ah, here we are," Mr. Redding said. "Twenty-seven degrees north. Forty-two east. About a mile east of Raglesville?"

"Yes, that would be mine."

The banker adjusted the spectacles perched on his nose. "Looks to be about a hundred and ninety acres."

"My father always said it produced like three hundred."

The banker smiled at her clumsy attempt to negotiate. "I remember your father. He used to drive his buggy in to town every other Friday. You must have been the little girl who rode with him. Were you his only child?"

She glared at him, seeing through his question. "You want to know if I have any brothers to take over the farm."

The banker flinched from her directness. "I didn't mean—"

"You needn't apologize. I get the same treatment from my own people. I'll make this easy for you. You're wondering why I haven't taken a husband."

"That's none of my business, of course, except—"

"I've managed on my own."

"I'm sure you have. But you're asking about a loan."

"Just inquiring," she corrected. "I'd like to know my options."

The banker closed the plat book and returned it to the shelf. "I'm going to be frank with you, Miss Raber. You seem to be a woman who takes life head on, as it comes. You've got every right to conduct your business as you see fit. But when you borrow money from a bank, that business also becomes *our* business. If we were to grant you a loan, your farm would stand as collateral. If there is a risk that the crops won't be brought in or the land might go to waste—"

"You're welcome to come out there to take a look," she said. "See for yourself that it's not going fallow."

He studied her. "May I ask why you need the loan?"

"There are the horses and seed grain to purchase. And I have to pay laborers to help me work the fields."

"I don't think we've ever had anyone from the Mennonite community come in here to do business with us. I thought your folk helped out each other in need."

She turned aside to hide the flush in her cheeks. "Not in my case."

The banker rested his chin on his interlocked hands. "I had a brother in the war. I know what you did for our boys."

"I'm not asking for charity, Mr. Redding. Do you have a number in mind?"

The banker eased back into his plush swivel chair and studied an imaginary number floating somewhere in the air. "I suppose we could manage five hundred dollars."

Anna rose up, insulted. "Five hundred. For the whole farm as collateral? That wouldn't buy a decent pair of matched plow horses."

"Times are tough, Miss Raber. People keep pulling out their deposits. As a result, there's not that much money to lend. And if, God forbid, we had to take over your farm, there's nobody around with enough money to take it off our hands."

Anna gathered her bonnet and said testily, "Thank you for your time."

"I'm sorry."

She hurried from his office, whisking past the oglers at the teller windows. When one of the English customers nodded to her, she turned back and told him, "You're wasting your time here. That man in there who keeps the key to the vault just told me he doesn't have any money."

Before the astonished people in line could make sense of that alarming indictment, she marched out of the bank in a huff. She stood on the sidewalk, trying to calm down and wondering what pile of manure life would throw at her next. She turned toward the movie theater and saw a column of bedraggled men walking toward her down the middle of Main Street. The residents backed away as if the Devil himself was leading a ghostly procession of the damned to the cleft of Hell. Four of these men held the corners of a blanket while angling from one sidewalk to the next, begging for alms. She asked a woman hurrying to escape into the bank, "Who are they?"

"Them's the veterans."

"Veterans? What are they doing here?"

The woman looked at her as if she were daft. "Ain't you listened to the radio?" Then, she took in her plain Mennonite dress, and suddenly she understood. "No, I reckon not. Those bums broke through St. Louis. They rode the rails all the way from Oregon."

As Anna watched the shoddy veterans stagger past, she became outraged. Some of them looked in worse shape than the doughboys she had treated for exhaustion in France. She walked alongside the pitiful procession and called out to the closest of the veterans, a short, dark-haired man. "What's your name, sir?"

"Angelo, ma'am. Joe Angelo."

"Where are you all going?"

Angelo limped down the street, wincing from the bunions on his heels. "To Washington to get the money the government owes us."

"How many are you?"

"We got about four hundred. But there are more of us heading east from other parts of the country, so they tell us."

"Lord, you'll be fortunate to make it a mile out of town in the sorry shape you're in." She stopped him and felt his wrist to test his pulse. "Where have you been sleeping?"

Angelo drew his hand away, ashamed of his lack of strength. "They camped us outside in that field over there. On the outskirts of town."

"Did you eat this morning?"

"They fed us some slumgullion." Angelo pointed to some of the men walking behind him. "Charlie Lincoln there is one of our quartermasters. He saved some in that bucket he's carrying, in case we need it."

Anna held her hand out to halt Lincoln. She peered into the rusty milk pail and brought a hand to her mouth. The stew of meat bits and rotten vegetables was so putrid that she wouldn't think of feeding it to her livestock. Without stopping to consider, she rushed to the sidewalk and hurried down the block to Kramer's sundries store. She pulled a newspaper from the stand and scanned the headline: *Nation's Capital Braces for Invasion of Homeless Veterans.* She read down the paragraphs, until one line stopped her:

District Police Chief Pelham Glassford, the youngest brigadier general during the war, has petitioned Congress and the White House for assistance in meeting the expected onslaught of Bonus marchers, but he has been repeatedly turned down in his efforts.

That name pricked her memory. Glassford… Wasn't he that wounded officer who had performed the vaudeville skit for her patients in the hospital? She hurried across the street to the butcher shop. She walked in and asked the clerk behind the counter, "How much for a bologna sandwich?"

"Ten cents."

She opened her change purse and counted only five dollars. "Will you let me run an account?"

The clerk's eyes narrowed. "How many sandwiches do you need?"

"Four hundred."

Astonished, the clerk peered beyond her shoulder through the window. Suddenly he realized what she was planning. "Sorry, but we can't do that."

"I'll work it off. I promise I'll be good for it."

The clerk debated her plea, then caved. "It's going to take me a while."

She smiled through tears. "Bless you. Can you have someone deliver them to those men before they leave town?"

"Yeah, but where are you—"

She dashed out of the market and marched back down the street to the bank. She walked up to the teller lobby, passed the same customers in line, and without being announced, invaded Mr. Redding's office again.

He looked up from his desk. "Well, that was quick. Have you reconsidered?"

"Ten thousand."

The banker nearly swallowed his waxed mustache. "Look, Miss Raber, I'm stretching my books just to offer the five hundred. There's no way—"

"I don't want a loan. I'm selling the farm."

"That's a mighty hasty decision. You should take some time first."

"I've taken all the time I need. I'd like you to sell it for me. Take whatever fee you feel is fair."

The banker began fussing with his pocket watch. "As a bank, we don't sell property. You have to find a land agent to do that."

She leaned over his desk to press her plea. "Mr. Redding, you're one of the most important men in this town. I know anything can get done if *you* want it done."

"Well—"

"I've never asked anyone for help before. But I'm asking you now. I need for you to sell my farm for me, and I need an advance of two hundred dollars."

After pondering her plea, the banker walked out of the office and disappeared behind the brass prongs of the teller's window. Out of earshot of the customers still in line, he whispered something to a female employee. The teller opened her register and counted out several bills into his hand. The banker hid them in his vest pocket and strolled casually back toward his office, waving and chatting casually with his customers. He closed the office door behind him and delivered the two hundred dollars to Anna. "Please do not mention this to anyone," he said. "Every man and woman down on his luck from here to Loogootee would be at my doorstep."

"Thank you."

"There'll be paperwork to fill out."

"I'll be back in half an hour. Oh, and one other thing. Send forty dollars from the proceeds to Kramer's market. Put the rest in an account for me."

Before the banker could ask where she was headed, Anna hurried through the lobby and out the door. She looked up Main Street and saw that the parade of veterans was now on the outskirts of the city. A fleet of Indiana National Guard trucks waited there to take the veterans across the Indiana border to Ohio. She hurried to the railroad station a few block away and came to the ticket window. "When's the next train to Washington, D. C.?"

The ticket clerk hesitated. "I'm not supposed to let anyone know about that until those bums get out of town."

Anna's face reddened. "Those men that you call bums risked their lives in France so you could stand here and make a fool out of yourself! Now tell me when the train leaves, or I'll bring them all down here to ride with me!"

The clerk needed a moment to recover, having apparently never heard a Mennonite lady talk so forcefully. Driven by her fierce glare, he finally surrendered the information. "The one from Vincennes going through Cincinnati will be here in an hour fifteen."

She slapped down a couple of bills. "One ticket."

"Return trip?"

She hadn't felt so certain about anything in her life. "One way."

52

WASHINGTON, D.C.
MAY 1932

The doors to the swank Mayflower Club flew open. Glassford, in street clothes, burst inside followed by a phalanx of his cops. He moved quickly past the yellow-draped tables and cornered the owner of the speakeasy behind the bar. While his officers herded up customers swigging their last gulps of illegal booze, he walked the length of the bar, half-expecting to find a couple of congressmen in his roundup.

Zebbie Goldsmith, the owner of the Dupont Circle speakeasy, fought against the cuffs clapped onto his wrists. "What the hell's going on? I paid on time!"

"You did, did you?" Glassford checked his own reflection in a bar-length mirror crowned by rows of bottles. "We'll have to see about a refund. Whose palm did you grease?" He caught Goldsmith trading a knowing glance with Lt. John Edwards, a holdover from the previous department regime. He walked behind the bar and brought down a bottle of champagne to read the label. "How much for this one?"

"Two bucks a quart," Goldsmith said. "You show me a little leniency, Chief, and I can get you a deal."

Glassford opened the bottle and smelled the cork. "That's some expensive hooch, Zeb. With an investment like that, you should keep your inventory where it can't fall."

"That's why I got them up there where—"

Glassford hammered his nightstick across the row of exquisite bottles, sending shards of glass cascading to the floor. "There must be a breeze in here."

Goldsmith glared revenge at him. "I thought the feds were the ones who were supposed to invade a man's sanctuary and bust up his property."

"They don't seem to be doing a real thorough job, do they?"

"I know what's going on here!"

"I'm not surprised," Glassford said. "You're a bright fellow."

"Crosby's been pounding you like hamburger over those Reds you been letting run loose all over the city. So, you come in here to show them how tough you can be." The owner stole another glance at Lt. Edwards, but the veteran cop acted as if he wasn't listening. Seeing that his protection plan had been disrupted by the new regime, Goldsmith snarled, "Harassing good, hard-working Americans. Why don't you go down the street and bust a couple of those whorehouses those congressmen frequent? Oh, that's right, I forgot. You're the forward-minded police chief who thinks prostitution should be legal."

"Does the oratory come free like the peanuts?" Glassford asked. "Maybe you should run for Congress with a mouth that golden. Then you could save yourself a bundle and serve that high-grade gin mash to yourself."

"Powerful people come in here! You're making enemies in high places!"

Glassford laughed. "You think I don't have enemies in high places already?"

Hauled out, the owner shouted, "A man can get a poke, but he can't have a drink at the end of a hard day! Hell of a country this is turning into!"

One of Glassford's officers pointed to a painting of a lounging nude woman that hung above the bar. "What about the pornography, Chief? You want that confiscated, too?"

The cops and their handcuffed prisoners turned to hear Glassford's answer.

Glassford glanced up at the wall, seeing the painting for the first time. "Well now, Jensen, there's a fine line between pornography and high art."

"Looks like smut to me, sir," said the rookie officer.

"Check the name of the artist on the lower corner!" shouted the struggling owner from the door. "Maybe Chief Clean Ass here can apprehend that scoundrel who has been dirtying up people's morals!"

The young cop hopped over the bar to get a closer look at the signature below the nude lady's feet. "Says here it was done by some jackass named 'Happy something.'" The officer did a double-take and turned ashen.

With his eyes glinting amusement, Glassford slapped the handcuffed owner on the back as they all walked out together. "You have superb taste, Zeb. Remind me to tell the judge at your bail hearing."

While his officers loaded the first of two paddy wagons and sped the arrested patrons off to the jail, Glassford walked alone down Connecticut Avenue, enjoying a well-deserved pipe smoke to celebrate his first bust. He'd already made sure the newspapers got word of the crackdown, and the morning editions were sure to send ripples of nervousness across the underbelly of the city, all part of his plan. That should get Crosby and Hoover off his back for a while, at least. And maybe some of those hypocrites up on the Hill would finally take notice and give him more of a hearing next time he lobbied them for the Bonus bill. Yeah, it felt pretty good to flex a little muscle. Truth was, he hadn't felt this good since that morning he first stumbled into the German lines on the Meuse. This job might turn out to be fun after all.

"Spare a dime, buddy?"

Glassford turned and found a hobo curled up in the shadows of an alley. "A dime?"

"I could really use a meal."

"Yeah? Got any particular entrée in mind? Like maybe of the Kentucky liquid variety?"

"I don't need your smart talk, pal. You don't want to give, just walk on."

"What's your name?"

"Shipley."

Glassford jingled the change in his pockets. "Come along. I'll see what I got."

The hobo struggled to his feet and followed Glassford around the corner, only to discover a second paddy wagon waiting.

"Edwards, I got another customer for you. Not bad for a new chief, eh?"

Discovering that he had been double-crossed, the panhandler glared an accusation of unfairness at Glassford as he was pushed into the police truck with the booze violators. As the second paddy wagon sped away, Glassford relit his pipe, determined to enjoy his smoke. Hell of a situation when a man couldn't get through a good plug of tobacco without getting hit up for a donation.

Through the aromatic haze, he saw a slender shadow standing near a lamp-light whose bulb had burned out. His hand reflexively edged toward his side, but he remembered that he hadn't brought his pistol. During the war, he had been taught to elicit a verbal response in such dangerous situations, so he called out, "Are you waiting for someone?"

The lurker refused to answer him.

He squinted harder to make out the occulted figure. His pulse was racing; the last thing he needed was a headline telling how he got himself mugged after a raid. He reached into his vest pocket and pulled out his badge, hoping its flash would be enough. "I'm a police officer. Did you hear me?"

A woman draped in a dark-blue Salvation Army cloak walked into the dim moonlight. "Are you going to arrest *me* for vagrancy, too?"

He was confused, thrown off his stride. He strained to get a better look through the descending night fog. "Now, why would I do that, ma'am?"

She came a step closer. "Why not? It would be another notch in your gun. Or do you only pick on poor, helpless men?"

Something in his submerged memory caused him to cough. "That fellow was breaking the law. If I start making exceptions, they'll overrun the city."

"Did it ever occur to you that the man might have been hungry, just like he said?"

"These slackers see passing the cup as easier than getting a job. He knows he'll be back on the street before the next business day."

The woman glared disgust at him, then turned and walked away.

"It's not safe for a lady to be on these streets alone at night." When she just kept walking, he tried again. "Ma'am, I don't believe I caught your name."

She pirouetted on her heels. "That must be very upsetting to you, Chief Glassford, considering your talent for catching everything that crosses your path." She whipped her cloak's cape over her shoulder and marched off.

Baffled by the odd confrontation, he stood motionless, until the ashes from his forgotten pipe spilled and singed the hairs on the back of his hand.

The next morning, the District courtroom was packed with city residents who had read about the Mayflower Club raid in the early editions. As the arrested speakeasy patrons sat in the jury box waiting to be arraigned, Judge John Gallagher waved Glassford up to the witness box. "We don't often have the pleasure of the head honcho down here testifying."

Glassford, in full uniform, took his seat next to the bench. "Just sending a message, Judge, on how serious I am about cleaning up this city."

"Well, then, we can all take heart." The judge scanned the rows of hooch violators to determine if any merited the special accommodation traditionally afforded to congressmen and senior government officials. Seeing none of any prominence, he motioned them all forward. "I think we can dispense with these malfeasants quickly enough."

"Yes, sir," Glassford said.

The judge lectured the forlorn customers being arraigned. "You gentlemen are fortunate to find me in a pleasant demeanor this morning. If Chief Glassford here has no objection, I'm going to assume that the night you spent in our local lockup, along with a five-dollar fine, will cause you to repent the error of your ways."

Glassford nodded. "I think it's a fair sentence, Judge."

The judge looked down at the scofflaws for a response. "Are you willing to plead guilty under those terms?"

The boozehounds reluctantly nodded their agreement.

The judge slammed his gavel. "Pleas entered and accepted. See the clerk about payment of your fines." He stood up and was about to retire to chambers when the prosecutor, who had not been able to get a word in edgewise, cleared his throat. "Your Honor, we have one more case."

The judge peered across the bay of arrestees and found a haggard man in a stained suit sitting in the corner. Sniffing the air as if picking up a stench, the judge looked down at Glassford for an explanation of this arrest.

"Mr. Shipley over there accosted me for money last night."

The bailiff prodded the homeless man to his feet, and the judge shook his head. "What's this world coming to when a man tries to panhandle a cop?"

Glassford agreed with that sentiment. "I just want to reacquaint the fellow to the discipline I'm sure his daddy taught him."

The judge motioned the homeless man forward to get a better look at him. "How long have you been begging?"

"About three days, sir."

"About three days?" the judge mocked. "You've honed the act quickly." He turned to Glassford. "Does he seem pretty polished to you, Chief?"

"Like he's been taking the show on the road."

Shipley tried to straighten his arthritic back in protest. "I ain't no bum, Your Honor. I'm an ex-Marine. I come to the capital to see about some compensation owed me by the Veterans Bureau. I ran out of money, is all."

"A Marine. You're a bright fellow, then. You knew loitering and beggary was against the law here in the District, didn't you?"

"A man's got to eat."

The judge pondered the appropriate punishment. "I can give you thirty days. But considering your service to your country, I'll let you off with an afternoon in the wood yard. A country fellow like you should be skilled with an ax."

Someone in the back of the courtroom asked to be heard. Glassford peered across the rows to find the source of that request. The Salvation Army nurse who had watched him make the arrest rose from her seat on the rear benches.

"I know Mr. Shipley," she told the judge. "I helped him find a pair of shoes down at the donation center yesterday."

The judge tapped his fingers in annoyance. "This is highly irregular, Miss...?"

"Raber.... Anna Raber."

Glassford tried to place that name as the judge waved the nurse up to the bench. Now that he thought about it, her face, seen for the first time in the full light, was beginning to look more familiar.

Anna walked through the swing gate and into the area reserved for the lawyers. "Mr. Shipley has no one to represent him."

The judge rolled his eyes in exasperation. "Ma'am, if the city hired a lawyer for every vagrant that came through those doors, we'd all be broke."

"I'll plead his case, then."

The crowd in the courtroom began buzzing about the woman's *chutzpah*.

Trumped, the judge slumped back in his chair and glanced testily at his watch. "You've got two minutes. Let's hear your defense."

Anna turned toward her witness. "Chief Glassford, did you ever violate an Army regulation during the war?"

Glassford looked up to the bench in protest. "Now, wait a minute, Judge. I'm not the one on trial here."

She kept him pinned down. "I'm just trying to demonstrate that Chief Glassford talks out of both sides of his mouth when it comes to following the law."

The judge was intrigued. "I guess you'd better answer the lady, Chief."

Glassford squirmed. "Sometimes a soldier has to bend the rules in the heat of battle."

Anna leaned in closer. "Did you ever pull rank and conduct unauthorized theatricals for wounded American soldiers against Army medical regulations?"

Glassford's eyes widened. Now he remembered: She was the nurse at the hospital in Rimaucourt. "I don't see how any of that has anything to do—"

She cut him off. "Your Honor, I extracted this admission to establish that Chief Glassford has a penchant for going around in theatrical disguises."

Cringing at the crowd's laughter, the judge saw that he was about to lose control of his courtroom. "I'm waiting, Miss Raber, to hear how this revelation bears upon Mr. Shipley's case."

Anna turned back to interrogate Glassford further. "What were you wearing last night when you arrested Mr. Shipley?"

"Why, I was in a suit, but —"

Anna appealed to the audience. "A civilian's suit? Not your uniform?"

"Yes, but—"

"Are you ashamed of your police uniform?"

"Of course not."

"Then there could be only one other reason you chose not to wear it." She leaned in to him again. "You were trying to entrap Mr. Shipley into asking you for a donation."

Glassford was so flabbergasted that he couldn't find a word in response.

Anna appealed to the judge. "Your Honor, isn't there a law that requires a policeman to be in uniform so that citizens can know they are dealing with an officer?"

The judge glared down at Glassford. "I believe there is."

Anna paced at the railing. "Poor Mr. Shipley there would *never* have asked the Chief of Police for a dime if he had been in proper uniform."

The courtroom denizens burst out with applause for her summation.

Shipley stood swaying like a rotted post in a storm, trying to follow this inexplicable turn of events.

The judge tapped his gavel to regain silence. "I'm afraid Miss Raber has a point, Chief. I'm going to have to let Mr. Shipley go free and—"

"Your Honor," Shipley said. "I'll take the thirty days."

The astonished courtroom fell silent.

The judge leaned over his bench. "What did you say?"

Shipley kept his head bowed. "I appreciate the nurse here standing up for me and all. But if I got a choice, I'll take the jail time."

Glassford, indignant, arose from the witness chair and came hovering over Shipley. "Don't smart talk the judge, or you'll get it."

Shipley fixed a glum gaze on Anna. "They got meals in jail, don't they?"

Glassford, stunned, settled back into his seat. He saw tears in Anna's eyes.

The judge was nearly apoplectic. "You mean to say you'd give up freedom for a bowl of soup? What'd you fight for over there in France, anyway?"

"I didn't fight to come back to starve. And be called a hobo on top of it."

The judge slammed his gavel so hard that he nearly cracked its handle. "Get him out of here! Thirty days!" He stormed off the bench and marched into chambers as the courtroom erupted in jeers and shouts of contempt at Shipley being escorted out.

His confidence shaken, Glassford arose unsteadily and, with head lowered, walked from the courtroom. In the lobby, reporters rushed at him for quotes about the speakeasy raid, but he brushed them aside and hurried away, seeking refuge on his motorcycle.

Anna, cradling two books under her arm, stood waiting for him aside Blue Bessie. She had a look of equal parts satisfaction and contrition. "I'm sorry."

"No, you're not."

"I don't expect you to believe me, but I didn't come here to ruin your day. I wanted to give you something." She handed him the books.

Glassford read the author names on the spines. "Steffens and Dreiser." He shook his head at the implication of the gift. "I see you've still got that same gentle bedside manner."

"You're just suffering from a little cognitive dissonance. You'll recover."

He thumbed through one of the books. "Big words for a country girl. I suppose they're in *here* somewhere."

"Just because I was raised Mennonite doesn't mean I don't read. There wasn't much else to do in France at night while I was waiting for the hemorrhages."

"'Cognitive distance,' you said? What is that?"

"'Dissonance.' I learned about it from a French psychologist who treated the *poilus* for shell shock. It means your mind is straddling a fence. Caught between the world that was and the world that's coming. We saw a glimpse of the world that's coming in that courtroom. And it's coming faster than you think."

"You seem to have all the answers. What do you suggest I do about it?"

"Get ready."

"I've been trying to get ready ever since those men left Oregon. But the powers that be around here don't exactly cotton to the way I do things."

"I know that feeling. At least they still talk to you."

"If you're so gung ho, why don't you help me out?"

"Doing what?"

"Those West Coast veterans are going to be here any day now," he said. "Just between you and me, we've received reports that thousands more are following them. I've got my eye on a spot for an encampment down at Anacostia Flats. It's in the southeastern part of the city, down across the east branch of the river."

"*Across* the river." Her tone suggested she was skeptical of his intentions. "In the working poor section, away from the mansions on Massachusetts and Connecticut. I haven't been here that long, but even I know that area is bordered by a lunatic asylum on one side and the Negro streets on the other."

"They'll have water down there for their washing."

"Those river flats can only be accessed by a drawbridge. The Navy Yard is nearby. You'll be able to keep them penned in and guarded."

The depth of her cynicism—and Machiavellian perceptiveness—left Glassford shaking his head. True, Anacostia was not the most appealing of District locations, having been ignored by the French architect L'Enfant in his grand plan for Washington and left undeveloped for decades. But he had few options in the city for a large encampment, and the lowlands had the advantage of being within walking distance of the Capitol for the men to present their petitions. "They're going to need soup kitchens and shelter. If I spread them out all over the city, it will be a logistical disaster."

Anna softened her suspicious stare. "I'll help out with the cooking."

As magnanimous as that offer was, Glassford waved it off. "Stirring soup is not what I have in mind for you. There's a more serious problem I need to head off, and fast. With thousands of malnourished men and their families living in such close confines, their resistance to disease is going to be weakened. We both saw that in France. I'm going to set up a medical station inside the camp. I need someone I can rely on to oversee the clinic. Someone who's had experience with trauma and mud."

Anna hesitated. Then, she said, "I'll do it, on one condition."

"Name it."

"Promise me you'll never betray them."

He was coming around to the notion that this was a woman not to be crossed. He shook her hand to seal the vow, holding it a bit longer than necessary. "Get me a list of the medical supplies you'll need. I'll see what I can do about pestering the local hospitals for donations." When she nodded in gratitude, his smile widened into the boyish grin that had become so famous years ago at the Point. "And thanks for the books."

53

CUMBERLAND, MARYLAND
MAY 1932

Bivouacking for the night, Ozzie Taylor and the other BEF men sank to their haunches along a corrugated tin wall in an abandoned skating rink where the Maryland National Guard had dropped them off after the long haul across Ohio and West Virginia. Having found a passable sleeping spot near a fire that raged in a greasy oil barrel for heat, Ozzie looked up and saw rattling above his head a rusted sign welcoming all to *Skate Your Cares Away*. Wishing it were just that easy, he leaned his oboe against a post and rested a gunnysack filled with sand under his head for a pillow. After whittling a point on the nub left from his pencil, he pulled out an old racing form from his rear pocket to add a new notation to the column of figures he'd been compiling.

Lincoln sidled up next to him to see what he was scribbling. "You planning on putting a sawbuck down on Burgoo King at the Belmont there, Oz?"

"Nah, I'm just keeping a record."

"A record of what?"

"How far we've traveled. What's your guess, Charlie?"

Lincoln removed his stovepipe to scratch his head. "A far piece. That's about as close as I can come."

"Three thousand miles in eighteen days. Who woulda thought that?"

Resting a few feet away, Mickey Dolan tossed an old board into the fire can. "Not Herbie Hoover, that's for sure. How much more we got to go?"

The men turned to Alford for the answer to that question, now that Waters, as usual, had gone on ahead to scout the enemy territory.

"Little over a hundred miles before we cross into Washington."

Lincoln stared into the darkness. "Are we just gonna walk on in to town?"

"Waters cut a deal with the Maryland governor," Alford said. "The National Guard has agreed to drive us to the District. Once Dubya gives us the signal, we'll haul ass up to the Hill and show those birds some real lobbying. You boys get yourselves shaved up in the morning. I figure we'll be shading under the Washington Monument by day after tomorrow."

The men traded sullen glances; now that the reality of their dream seemed within reach, a worried silence came over them.

Alford walked down the abandoned rink handing out cough drops. "Donation from the local drugstore. Keep your lungs in good working order. We got some hollering to do in the chambers of Congress." After dispensing their substitute for hard candy, he lingered a few steps away, under a hole in the roof, and stared up at the clear sky.

Lincoln couldn't sleep, so he sat back up. "Georgie, what are we gonna be facing in Washington?"

The men stopped crunching their cough drops long enough to hear the answer to the question that had been weighing on all their minds.

Usually Alford was upbeat, but on this night he sounded fatalistic. "The papers say the District commissioners gave the police chief an order to have us out of the city in forty-eight hours. This fella they hired is a shavetail. I guess we all know what that means."

"New stripe always has to prove himself," Angelo muttered. "Fresh meat in the trench itching to go over the top."

Dolan nodded with a look of grim determination. "The police have cracked heads everywhere else. Don't expect Washington to be much different."

Alford kept staring up at the stars. "We're going to the land of Uz."

Lincoln craned his neck, trying to see what Alford was gawking at. "The land of what?"

"Uz was the place where Yahweh persecuted Job. You've read the biblical story of Job, haven't you, Charlie?"

Lincoln wouldn't look at him straight away. "I ain't never had much formal learning."

Alford *tssked* him for having neglected his education. "And you being a descendant of the Great Reader himself. You see, Job was an upstanding and righteous man, but God put him in a breadline anyway."

"How come God did that?"

"That's just what Job wondered. So, he went searching for God to demand an answer. And all of the rich folks in Uz told him he was being punished." As Alford regaled the men with the biblical parable, he saw Dolan dip his head in private despair. He wondered what the big Irishman was distressed about, but he went on to finish his story. "After riding the rails for weeks, Job finally finds the Big Boss Upstairs."

"What'd God tell him?" asked Ozzie.

Alford kicked at the cracked concrete floor. "God pointed to his big house in the sky and his fancy white robes and said, 'Who the hell are you, you lowlife, to be questioning a man of authority such as Myself? So shut up!'"

Lincoln was appalled. "What'd Job do about that?"

"He just shut up like he was told and walked away."

Angelo jumped to his feet. "You mean God didn't have no reason to put Job through the wringer? He just did it for spite?"

"All according to the Good Book itself," Alford confirmed. "God admitted that He was just playing a friendly game of poker with the Devil. Like them politicians in Washington have been using us as chips in their big Wall Street craps game."

Angelo circled with his fists balled, looking for something to smash.

Hruska had been listening from the corner. "You always badmouthing this country, Alford. In Russia, Bolsheviks have us strung up by now."

Alford snorted. "You're quite the expert on what Bolsheviks do, Vilhelm."

"I should be. I see them put bullet in my papa's head."

The men gathered around him to hear more.

"How did *you* get away?" Lincoln asked.

"My nana hid me in well. Then sent me here to America. Fifteen years ago. When I get Bonus, I send for her." He coughed down the swell of emotion. "This is still the best country in world."

Angelo was pacing faster now, his anger building. "The way I see it, that feller Job and all the rest of you just need some inside pull with the Man, like those Wall Street plutocrats pay to get!"

Alford gave up a cynical toot of a laugh. "And I suppose you've got some pull with the Man in the White House."

"I just might."

Lincoln came to his knees. "Who, Joey?"

"Colonel Patton."

Ozzie rustled with surprise. "That stripe you saved in France?"

Angelo nodded with pride. "He told me that if I ever needed anything, just let him know. He's a big shot in the cavalry now. He'll help me get my Bonus."

The other men brightened with that prospect, but Alford saw that Dolan remained somber. "What about it, Mickey? Everybody seems to have a plan except you. You got anybody waiting for *you* in Washington?"

Dolan glared at Alford, then picked up his blanket and walked to the other end of the rink to sleep alone.

54

WASHINGTON, D.C.
MAY 1932

On the grassy flats of Anacostia, across the river from the Navy Yard and the Marine Corps barracks, Lt. Edwards walked down a line of junior police officers while instructing them on the use of riot gear. "Never fire over the heads of rioters. Aim low with full-charge ammunition. Most rifles are sighted too high for the average riot distance and are likely to wound innocent persons."

The men in the ranks stole distracted glances toward the bluffs behind the lieutenant, where Chief Glassford, accompanied by two men, stood listening.

Edwards remained unaware that his commander was watching. "Negotiating with a mob is a sign of weakness. By their inferior nature, rioters and trouble-makers are peculiarly prone to dejection or elation. They will sneak into their hiding places or swarm into the streets at the smallest instigation."

Glassford had heard enough. He walked down the path to the drill ground with Harry Shipley, the homeless veteran arrested for panhandling, and a third man dressed in U.S. Army fatigues.

Lt. Edwards, not seeing their approach, continued his lecture. "If you start to execute a duty, finish it. Retreating will only—"

"Thank you, Lieutenant," Glassford said. "That will be enough."

Edwards flushed, incensed at being secretly observed. "I was just instructing the men on riot procedure. With these vagabonds pouring in—"

"I'll let you know when and what instruction will be given. And it won't be prisoner-of-war tactics."

Edwards chafed at the putdown. "These are standard procedures."

"Procedures responsible for the massacre at Dearborn."

Grumbling a curse under his breath, Edwards traded insubordinate glances with several cronies in the ranks.

Glassford pulled the officer aside. "I know you're raw over being passed over for my job, Edwards. But if you can't follow my way of doing things, I suggest you look for other employment." He motioned Shipley up to his side. "See to it that this man gets a uniform."

Edwards set his jaw. "You're giving jobs to these hobos now?"

Glassford took a billy club from one of his cops. "This is used to direct traffic, not to beat heads. Understand?"

The cop glanced at Edwards, then said frostily, "Yes, sir."

Glassford brought forward his companion in the Army uniform. "This is Captain John Hucks from Fort Myer. He will be instructing you in the martial art of jiu-jitsu."

Edwards and several cops held looks of disbelief.

"You will learn to bend to force," Glassford said. "Not give it."

One of the officers in the line, a brawny man named Shinault, smirked and muttered to the cop next to him, "We'll see how Chief Watercolor bends when he takes a punch in the gut."

Hearing the remark, Glassford wheeled on Shinault. "Front and center!"

Shinault stepped up slowly, spoiling for a fight.

"I take it you don't particularly care for my approach."

"There's nothing wrong with the old way."

Glassford removed his hat. "Give me your best shot. That's an order."

Shinault held back, but his defiant eyes betrayed his eagerness to teach this appeaser a lesson. Edwards and the other men nodded him on. When Glassford motioned him forward, Shinault raised his fists and stalked the police chief. Infuriated by Glassford's dancing footwork, the officer took a wild swing at his chin, but Glassford easily deflected the blow. Confused by the defensive tactic, Shinault swung again. Glassford intercepted the punch and took the officer down to his knees from the force of his own momentum. With his arm locked behind his back, Shinault could only look up at Edwards and beg for help.

Glassford released the pinned cop and shouted an order to the ranks. "Every man who is a veteran, step forward."

A third of the men—including Edwards and Shinault—came up.

Glassford took a large rolled map of the United States from Shipley and hung it on a notice board. He pulled a stack of note cards from his pocket and began tacking them over many of the states, until he had nearly half the country covered. "The veterans from Oregon will arrive in the city tomorrow. More are following them. Eight hundred left Chicago two days ago. Two hundred more from Utah. Another two hundred from Tennessee. Four hundred from New Jersey. And these are just the ones we know about."

"How many you figure in total, Chief?" asked one of the younger cops.

"Truthfully, I don't know. But those of you who served in the military, and you *only*, will keep watch over these veterans when they get here. No other officers will have contact with these groups. And no live ammunition will be carried. Is that understood?"

The chosen officers nodded, though some could not hide their skepticism.

"Now, we've got some Communists in town trying to stir up trouble," Glassford said. "These instigators will likely try to mix in with the veterans and create havoc. You may not like Communists, and that's your prerogative. But I don't read anything in the Constitution that says they don't have the same rights to assemble and express their views like everyone else." He reached into Shipley's knapsack and pulled out the two books that Anna Raber had given him. "Every officer in this force will read Lincoln Steffens and Upton Sinclair. You'll be required to prove it on a written test."

Shinault and Edwards were forced to swallow their bile in silence.

Captain Sid Marks, Glassford's most loyal officer, drove Blue Bessie down the bluffs to the parade ground and offered the motorcycle to him. "Chief, he's here. I got him waiting for you in the Kaufman Building down on Eighth Street, just like you said."

"Do I need to go in there armed?"

Marks shook his head. "He looks pretty harmless."

Glassford signaled for Captain Hucks to continue with the new training.

"One more thing." Marks angled his shoulder to prevent the ranks from hearing him. "The Worker's Ex-Servicemen League is back in our hair again."

"I thought we got rid of them two months ago?"

"The Detroit police cabled us this morning. A Communist rabble-rouser named John Pace left Michigan yesterday. He's heading our way."

"What's his background?"

"Ex-Marine, and tough as coal. He turned Red after he lost his contracting job. Word is he's bringing in some firebrands with him. The Detroit department says he's been blowing off steam about infiltrating the veterans and storming the White House."

Glassford nodded and sighed as he mounted the motorcycle. Why, he wondered, did trouble in this job always seem to come at him in battalions?

Waters paced the peeling linoleum floor of the abandoned apartment store near the old Navy Yard. The cop who had picked him up in Cumberland that morning had ordered him to wait here, but that had been five hours ago. As the afternoon shadows grew longer, he began to suspect that he'd been conned. Was this Dearborn all over again? Had these Washington stripes ordered him here alone to deliver a message with their batons? He stole a nervous look through a wall crack toward the Potomac and the cranes that hovered over the ship docks. He'd been driven into the city through the back door, the Negro neighborhoods. Grimed with tenement shacks, this part of the city was not what he had expected. He was starting to wonder if maybe things weren't any better here than in the rest of the country.

A distant door squealed open. He heard footsteps. His heart raced.

A tall police officer, hiding his hands behind his back, walked into the diffused light. When the officer came within striking distance, he brought forth his right hand. Waters flinched and covered his face, expecting a blow.

"Sorry, it's only lukewarm," the cop said. "Took me a while to find this place."

Waters risked opening his eyes. He blinked in surprise. The cop was offering him a cup of coffee. He looked beyond the cop's shoulder, expecting to see his toughs, but the cop had apparently come alone. He gratefully accepted the offer and sipped the brew, the first nourishment he'd had since that gruel they'd been served up in Cumberland.

"Hundred Forty-Sixth," the cop said. "You boys weren't more than a mile from my unit at the Marne."

Was he dreaming? The head cheese had come down here himself?

The police chief extended his hand in welcome. "Happy Glassford."

"G-g-general, I didn't expect to t-t-talk to you."

Glassford laughed. "Who'd you expect? The President?"

Waters released a breath of relief. "I'm glad to kn-kn-know an Army man's in charge down here. Tell you the truth, I didn't kn-kn-know what to expect."

Glassford found a couple empty paint buckets and turned them upside down to sit on. He motioned Waters over to take a load off with him. "Tell me what you've been up to since the war."

Waters got the feeling that he was being sized up. "You r-r-really care? Or you just trying to t-t-trick me to let my guard down?"

Glassford took off his boots to give his feet a breather. "These damn police shoes are worse than those shitkickers they issued us in France."

"I still use mine to c-c-carry kerosene."

Glassford nodded as he rubbed his sore toes. "I understand you haven't exactly had it easy since the war."

"I ain't had it no different than most."

"I hear you. I'll bet I've lost more jobs in the last ten years than any vet in the country."

Waters gave him a suspicious glance. "I'd take that bet, if I had any dough."

"Carnival barker. Rancher. Newspaperman. I've lost count."

"Try c-c-canning tomatoes at ten cents a day."

Glassford smiled sadly. "I guess that would be pretty close to the bottom of the barrel." He pulled out a chaw of jerky and offered Waters a pull. "What condition are your men in, Sergeant?"

Addressed by his old military rank, Waters came to his feet and stiffened to attention. "They look about as thin and forlorn as those B-b-boche we sent back over the Rhine in Eighteen. We've been between hay and grass for more than a few months now. And not to be c-c-contrary or nothing, General, but they ain't my men."

Glassford motioned him back down to his seat on the bucket. "I must have heard wrong, then. I was under the impression that you were the Black Jack Pershing of the BEF."

Waters couldn't suppress a grin at the discovery that his reputation had made it all the way to the nation's capital. "The boys just look to me for orders from time to time. But we're a d-d-democracy."

"Well, we're going to have to change that. These veterans coming in from all over the country are going to expect discipline and drilling, just like in the old days. An army doesn't run like a democracy. There has to be a chain of command. And I'm hereby officially recognizing you as Commander of the Bonus Expeditionary Force here in Washington. You'll report directly to me. And I'll convey my directives through you. Is that agreeable?"

Buoyed by the recognition, Waters saluted. "Yes, sir. You can c-c-count on me."

"Good. Now, here's our current situation. I've been handed a forty-eight hour ultimatum by the commissioners to get you and your men into the city, let you have your say to Congress, and then escort you back out."

Waters paled on hearing of the short deadline. "General, no disrespect intended, but we ain't leaving until we get the m-m-money owed us."

Glassford studied him. "Let's take one day at a time. You know the old saying: A military plan gets ditched the first day of battle."

"Yeah, we s-s-saw that on the Meuse, didn't we?"

Glassford put his boots back on and stood up, preparing to leave. When Waters rose to his feet with him, the police chief patted the veteran on the back. "I'm going to let you in on some classified intelligence. I need you to keep it from trickling down to the ranks."

"Yes, sir."

"We've got some Communists roaming the city. And more are on their way. Unfortunately, some of them are veterans."

"There ain't no Reds in my unit, General! I'll go down to the Supreme Court and swear to that on George Washington's Bible! We're all loyal American soldiers, through and through."

"I never doubted it. But I need you to keep a sharp eye out for anyone who starts talking treason against the government."

"There won't be any of that radical winding. You got my word. And I already b-b-banned all panhandling and liquor consumption. If any of those Reds c-c-come trying to horn in, we'll reason with them with the logic of knuckles."

Glassford walked him toward the door. "What do you think of this place?"

Waters looked around the vast empty store. "I've taken shelter in worse."

"We'll be quartering you and your Oregon men in here tomorrow."

"We were hoping to be a little c-c-closer to the Capitol. Maybe on that street where the Wall Street lobbyists b-b-bed down."

"I'll keep looking for better accommodations. One of my officers will drive you back to Cumberland tonight." Glassford shook hands with Waters and turned to walk out. At the door, he turned back. "Walter?"

"Call me Dubya, sir. Everyone else does."

"All right, then. Dubya, how many vets do you figure will be coming to Washington?"

"I'd take the over on twenty thousand."

Glassford's smile vanished. He looked shaken, but quickly recovered. He reached into his pocket and handed Waters a wad of bills. "Get your men a good breakfast and some smokes. I want them walking on full stomachs when they come into town tomorrow."

Waters counted out fifty dollars. "General, where'd you g-g-get this kind of payroll?"

Glassford turned and, without answering, walked out.

Waters was stunned. The police chief, he realized, was paying for the BEF's first meal here out of his own pocket.

55

ANACOSTIA FLATS
JUNE 6, 1932

Floyd Gibbons drove his Studebaker out the gates of the Marine Corps barracks and headed south past the Navy Yard. He was in a wistful mood that afternoon, having just met with his old leatherneck buddies to help them plan the anniversary remembrance of Belleau Wood. He glanced at his wristwatch and swallowed hard. It was at this very hour, fourteen years ago to the day, that he had lost his eye to that ricocheting German bullet.

He parked the car on the banks overlooking Anacostia and got out to survey the surreal scene across the river. This swampy backyard, first home to the Nacotchtank Indians and later to freed slaves, had been transformed into the largest Hooverville in the nation. In just one week, twenty-three thousand veterans had swarmed into the city, and the newspapers were warning that a million more might be on the way, drawn by reports that an unemployed former medic named Walter Waters was determined to get the money owed him by the government.

Summer in this drained marshland always frayed the nerves, and he figured this June would be no different, given that it was already on track to become one of the hottest months on record. The residents here were growing edgier as each day brought new and alarming rumors. The latest gossip was that MacArthur, fearful the veterans would storm government buildings, had ordered the hammers unscrewed from all the Enfields stored in the local armories.

He swatted at a cloud of mosquitoes as he walked toward the Anacostia Bridge. Framed by the Capitol dome to the north, the mud slicks of Camp Camden—named after the New Jersey veterans who first plotted lots there—were blanketed by a shimmering haze. Smoke trails rose from the pipe chimneys of the squat shanties, and hundreds of frayed American flags flapped from the roofs in the desultory breeze. As far as his lone eye could see, rows of tents and shacks had sprung up along unpaved streets platted in the Army style, with designated companies housed together. The trees along the river were hung with scales of washed garments, and on one corner of the encampment, gangs of veterans searched for construction materiel in a refuse dump. At the entrance, a sign had been posted: *Welcome to the Bonus Expeditionary Force, the Army of No Occupation.* This dense enclave of the forlorn—created piecemeal from cardboard boxes, egg crates, abandoned box springs, wrecked Model T Fords, oil drums, and mesh wire—reminded him of an American wood-and-tin version of Cairo's City of the Dead.

And Anacostia was just the largest of the twenty homeless camps scattered throughout the District.

He shook his head at the cruelty of God's abandonment. Many of those men down there had walked behind the Unknown Soldier's caisson in 1921. Now they were gaunt and sickly, their leathery faces etched with despair, most appearing much older than they should. In recent months, the country's mood had spiraled even deeper into anger. Just last weekend, during a doubleheader in Chicago, the Tigers and White Sox had cleared the dugouts with a vicious fracas that had become known as the Memorial Day Brawl. Baseball fisticuffs were commonplace, but an air of national desperation, not helped by a home plate umpire who wanted to fight the entire White Sox team, had ignited that riot. On a day reserved for enjoyment and honoring deceased ones, fans champing to lash out at Fate had tried to pour out onto the field. Reports from other ballparks confirmed that this season was marked by an uncharacteristic ugliness, on and off the diamonds. He held to the theory that baseball was the canary in the coal mine for America. After all, it hadn't been that long after the Black Sox gambling scandal when the Wall Street shenanigans that led to the Stock Market Crash had come to light.

Yes, there was something different about this summer. He could feel it in the ache of his empty eye socket. Those priests of demagoguery, Coughlin and Cox, could feel it, too, and they were circling the rancid byways of capitalism like hawks, eager to pounce on rotting road kill everywhere.

As he walked across the drawbridge, the languorous thrum of pots swinging over fires gave way to a sudden clattering of excitement. Word was shouted down the muddy thoroughfares that the Headline Hunter had come to give witness to their plight, and the veterans lazing all around him under the shade of tents were up on their feet and buzzing like bees in a kicked hive.

"Floyd Gibbons!" cried the wife of a veteran. "Why, I'll be! I'd sooner see you down here than St. Michael the Archangel hisself!"

Finally released from the woman's embrace, Gibbons shook the hundreds of hands being thrust at him from the weary but hopeful veterans. "How long you folks planning on stay in our fine city?"

The men, decked out in their ratty fedoras and suit vests in a pitiful grasp for dignity, circled round to greet him. "The commissioners are giving us forty-eight hours to get out, Floyd," said one. "We've been here a week already, but they keep pushing back the deadline."

"We ain't going nowhere!" insisted another veteran. "Hell, the Kaiser didn't uproot us after eighteen months. Sure as hell a bunch of politicians aren't gonna do it in two days!"

"You see that gallows over there?" asked the bear-hugging wife.

Gibbons squinted at a raised wooden platform in the center of the camp. "You hold many executions, do you?"

The woman slapped at her thigh, entertained by his wit. "Floyd, I'll be! You are a corker! No, that's there's where those Hill fat cats come to stand with their hands in their fancy silk shirts while they try to snooker us with their lies. You ever find yourself unable to sleep, just come on down here and listen to those birds chirp. They're here night and day to offer us their wisdom in return for votes."

"They bring the flies with them, too," the woman's husband added.

Gibbons sniffed the air. "I haven't smelled a fragrance like that since the Marne. Could those be Army beans on the fire?"

A codger in a crenellated straw hat came staggering at him with a steaming pot in his gloved hands. "Try some of my mulligan stew, Floyd! This here's the recipe that sent the Hun crawling back to Berlin!"

"He ain't lying, Floyd! The gas that emits from Henry's legumes made the Boche nostalgic for some good old-fashioned mustard clouds!"

Gibbons brought the ladle to his lips. Stifling a cough from the bitter taste of the gruel, he faked approval with a wide smile. "By God, that *is* tasty! But I think it might use a dash more leather and saltpeter!"

"Maybe Hoover's got some salt shakers over at the White House he could loan us!" shouted a veteran. "You ask him for us next time you're over there, will you, Floyd?"

"I'll do more than ask." Gibbons turned serious as he studied the veterans and their families congregated around him. "How are you folks holding up?"

The crowd grew silent, and most of the residents hung their heads in shame. A young boy in overalls lifted up his pet rabbit to him and stroked its head. "He ain't gettin' enough to eat, Mr. Gibbons. The nurse said he won't make it much longer."

Nearly undone by their plight, Gibbons needed a moment to recover his composure. "Now, listen here, folks! When some overstuffed spit hog like me comes down here and asks you good people how you're faring, you look them straight in the eye and tell them you're doing as well as any good American who's got his head under the damn boot heel of those Wall Street robber barons!" When his words of encouragement brought a rousing cheer, he asked them, "You all got a tin over your head, at least?"

"Lot of us slept in the rain last night," a veteran said. "There ain't enough lumber and pine boards in the garbage pile to go around."

Angered at the government's neglect, Gibbons reached into his pocket and passed out what few bills he had on him. "Folks, that's all I got."

"You got a lot more than that!" shouted a voice from behind the scrum.

The crowed parted to allow a thin, blond man to approach the radioman. Several moments passed before Gibbons recognized him as the stuttering Bonus evangelist from the Portland meeting. Accompanying the BEF leader was an entourage of junior officers led by George Alford and a bodyguard that included Mickey Dolan and William Hruska. Gibbons relaxed and grinned when Waters came up to offer his hand in welcome.

"Your words are heard by millions, Mr. Gibbons," Waters said. "Those are worth more to us than all the gold in Fort Knox."

Gibbons was impressed by the unemployed canner's newfound eloquence and the deference he now commanded from these veterans. "Looks like you got yourself a disciplined army here. Your militia on the bluffs up there almost arrested me for a Boche infiltrator."

"We do what we can with what we got." Waters eyed him with a knowing grin. "I don't reckon you remember me."

"Oh, I remember you, all right. You had those boys in the Portland armory stirred up like a Kansas twister trapped in a barn."

Waters's grin curled wider. "Nah, I mean earlier." Seeing the radioman scratching his head in confusion, he let him in on the secret. "I've sealed my lips on the matter. But if that cop in Weiser ever finds that ax, you may be looking at some jail time for cutting the town's telephone wire."

Gibbons's lone eye rounded. "Master Pip of the Prairie!"

Waters nodded. "The way I figure it, you're to blame for all this. If you hadn't filled my head with all those highfalutin ideas about seeing the world, I wouldn't have run off to join the National Guard."

"You've become quite the orator since those days walking the Idaho tracks."

"I have my moments. How about we give you a tour of the camp?"

"I'd like that."

"First, I hope you'll join us in our daily playing of the National Anthem."

The veterans removed their hats and placed their hands to their hearts as a Negro veteran armed with an oboe came to the fore. Gibbons looked around and saw to his surprise that several black veterans and their families were intermingled with the whites here.

The little black man with the oboe saluted him. "Mr. Gibbons, my name's Ozzie Taylor. I fought with the Hellfighters. It's an honor to play for you."

Gibbons returned the salute. "Honor's all mine, Taylor. Looks like the first casualty inflicted by the Bonus Expeditionary Force was ol' Jim Crow. I'm mighty glad to see he's been cashiered and given the boot."

"We're all the same down here in the country's trash heap," Waters said. "The whites are hungry and poor. The blacks are poor and hungry."

Not to be outdone in the introductions, a pint-sized fellow in a stovepipe hat and speechifying tails elbowed his way to the front and bowed. "Sir, I'm Charlie Lincoln, the sixth cousin of the Great Emancipator. And I *am* available for radio interviews at your convenience."

"Can you recite the Gettysburg Address backwards?"

"No, sir, but I can recount from memory every speech Herbert Hoover ever gave supporting us vets. You wanna hear a recitation?"

"I may regret saying so, but sure."

Lincoln adopted his famous rail-splitting pose, and after a minute had passed in this pantomimed silence, he doffed his stovepipe. "Now, for an encore, I'd like to sing my new radio hit song." He cleared his throat and crooned:

> "My Bonus lies over the ocean.
> My Bonus lies over the sea.
> My Bonus lies over the ocean.
> Oh bring back my Bonus to me."

The crowd, evidently practiced at this routine, chimed in with the chorus:

> "Bring back, bring back
> Bring back my Bonus to me, to me
> Bring back, bring back
> Bring back my Bonus to me."

The veterans cheered as Chief Running Wolf pulled an arrow from his quiver and set it on the string of his bow. The Apache Freemason drew the bow back and let fly with the arrow, hitting a bullseye drawn over an image of President Hoover that had been painted on the side of a shack.

Bent with laughter, Gibbons clicked his fingers at Ozzie for a beat. "Private Taylor, give me a little Reese Europe with that note launcher of yours."

Ozzie wetted his lips in preparation for strumming the reed. "Yes, sir, and let's make the angels take observance while the Devil dances for his sins."

"Just make sure Herbert up there in the White House can hear it, too."

Ozzie brought the oboe to his mouth, and the men came to attention, solemn and proper. He played a soulful rendition of the National Anthem that brought dampness to the eyes of all around.

Gibbons was nearly moved to tears. Recovering his voice, he said, "You folks might be a tad shy on edibles, but you're blessed in spirit."

As Waters escorted the radioman through the camp, the crowds surged behind them like the multitudes at the Sermon on the Mount. One veteran led a burro by the reins with a sign hanging from its neck that said: *Ask me about Hoover.* When passersby posed the popular question, the burro dutifully shook its head. After walking a hundred yards or so, Gibbons stopped at an intersection of four streets where a circle of planted geraniums surrounded an iron pipe that stuck up out of a mound of freshly dug ground. A cup for donations lay nearby. Alarmed, he asked the veterans, "Somebody's grave?"

The men lowered their heads in grief, and Waters led him to the pipe in solemn ceremony. "Mr. Gibbons, say hello to Private Angelo."

Gibbons had on occasion in his life been known to say a few words to a gravestone, but he felt foolish speaking to a pipe that was being used for a marker. Yet the veterans seemed to hang expectantly on the ritual, so he complied with the request. "Soldier, we pray you have received your heavenly reward so due you."

"Hell, I'm still waiting for my earthly reward so due me!"

Startled, Gibbons staggered back from the voice bellowing up from the pipe. He clutched his chest, as if nearly killed by the shock of the resurrection. The veterans and their families howled with laughter at his expense.

Waters threw open a pine door to reveal a glass coffin underneath. "This here's the submerged voice of Joe Angelo from Camden, New Jersey. He had himself buried alive to protest the refusal of the president to give us our Bonus." Waters leaned over the pipe and shouted, "How you doing in there, Joey?"

"Hoover given me my Bonus yet?"

"Not yet!" the veterans all shouted.

"Then I ain't coming up!"

"Joey! Say hello to the Headline Hunter!"

"Hallooo, Floyd!" Angelo shouted up. "Make sure you put in your headline that I saved Colonel Patton's life. I got the medal in here to prove it!"

Gibbons hovered his good eye over the mouth of the pipe and saw a drawn Italian face staring back up at him. "You need anything down there, soldier?"

"You got any smokes?"

Gibbons pulled a pack from his pocket and drew a couple of cigarettes out. He dropped them down the pipe, one by one. "You sure it's wise to light up down there, considering the paucity of air?"

"I'll save 'em for later! Thanks, Floyd!"

The entourage next led Gibbons toward a large square stall crowned by a billowing roof of green sailcloth. There, behind low rows of shelves, female volunteers passed out donated books to the veterans and held reading and writing classes for the youngsters. Adjacent to this makeshift library stood an open-air medical clinic staffed by three women.

"Floyd!"

Gibbons did a double take to make certain his one eye was still operating properly. Behind the counter, passing out bandages and aspirin tablets, stood Evalyn Walsh McLean, one of the wealthiest socialites in the city. He had attended many a party at her mansion on Massachusetts Avenue, where she enjoyed displaying her most prized possession, the Hope Diamond. "Shouldn't you be planning the next débutante ball, Evalyn?"

"Floyd, it's horrible what's happening to these people. Can't you pester that uncaring man in the White House to do something about this?"

"Herbert doesn't seem to listen to me."

"Pray for him," suggested another woman, who was clad in a blue-and-white nurse's uniform. Coming up next to Mrs. Walsh, the nurse testified, "Prayer is much more powerful than argument, don't you agree, sir?"

Mrs. Walsh introduced her fellow volunteer. "This is Lauretta D'Arsanis from New York. The men call her the Little Flower of St. Theresa. But watch your extremities. She likes to bite the Devil wherever she finds him."

The Little Flower sized him up. "Do you pray, Mr. Gibbons?"

He turned away as if he hadn't heard her, but he slipped his hands into his pockets on the off chance that Mrs. Walsh's warning about the biting was not figurative. He noticed another nurse on the far side of the clinic, huffing in disgust at the suggestion of spiritual intervention.

Mrs. Walsh detected his distraction. "Oh, yes, and this is Anna Raber. She has come all the way from Indiana."

He lingered on her familiar features. "Did you nurse in the war, ma'am?"

Anna continued checking the pulse of her patient in the clinic chair. "I was assigned to the hospital at Neuilly-sur-Seine when you were brought in with the wounded from Belleau Wood. You were quite a handful."

"I don't remember much about those hours. The ether was pretty heavy."

"I remember enough of it for the both of us," Anna said. "You fought off the surgeon and demanded to smoke a cigar before going under the knife."

"I've built up some down time in Purgatory, I fear."

Anna tapped her patient on the shoulder in a signal that she was finished with his examination. She drew the radioman out of earshot of the others in the clinic. "What do you intend to report about these men?"

"That they are hungry, for one thing. That looks pretty evident."

"There are forces of malice at work in this city, Mr. Gibbons."

"From your sour reaction to that nurse's suggestion to pray, I wouldn't have taken you for the Bible-thumping type."

"Forces don't have to be spiritual to be evil," she said. "These men and their families cling desperately to what little hope is offered. They see only what they want to see. But I have seen the looks of disdain on the faces of this city's residents when these men have their backs turned to them. The more fortunate view this camp as a zoo. They come down here on weekends to ogle the strange animals. But they're afraid that the beast might get loose and soil their lawns."

He nodded grimly. "The real zoo is up on Capitol Hill."

"People around here say you have influence in high places."

"I tell the truth as I see it. What little influence I have comes from that paramount rule of my life."

She looked hard into his unpatched eye. "You have the gift of seeing what others cannot, Mr. Gibbons. I beg you, before it is too late. Help us protect these men and their families from—"

A great roar interrupted her plea, and Gibbons, hidden behind the scrum of men, turned in time to see the throngs abandon him to rush toward a rider entering the camp on a coughing motorcycle. The men swarmed Chief Glassford as he dismounted Blue Bessie and stood observing the shanty-town that was growing by the hour. A dirty-faced girl in a calico dress came running up and read a poem to Glassford that she had written in a class being conducted by the Salvation Army:

> "A Modern General Washington.
> Build him a monument thousands feet high,
> Let it tower toward the pale blue sky,
> In years to come and generations too,
> The story will be told as if it was new,
> Of the heroic part that General Glassford played,
> As treating all men as humans in the Bonus parade."

Embarrassed by the clinging adulation, Glassford patted the girl on the head as he walked to the small, outdoor BEF library, which was nothing more than a few planks set up in a hollow square and shaded by tins. Catching sight of the Indiana nurse, he reached into his coat pocket and, withdrawing two books, handed them to her. "I'm afraid these are overdue."

Anna tested him with a sideways smile. "That side of beef brought to us this morning. You wouldn't have had anything to do with that, would you?"

Glassford affected surprise. "Was there a delivery? I wasn't informed."

Her eyes narrowed to belie that fib. "There's a rumor around the camp that you paid for it out of your own pocket. I guess we can overlook the library fine this one time." She found another book in the stacks. "Here, you might try Thucydides for your next reading, General …Washington, is it?"

"Thucydides. Didn't he write about bullies trying to beat up on poor helpless men?"

"I find his first lesson of history quite instructive."

"And what might that be?"

"Those whom the gods would destroy, they first make mad with power."

Glassford glanced over his shoulder at the crowd's adoration, taking in her veiled implication. He stared at her, a bit too long for courtesy. Then, to change the subject, he asked her, "Have you ever been painted?"

"Only by the Dutch masters," she said sarcastically.

"I wonder if you might allow me to repay the kindness of the loan?"

"I'd rather not adorn the walls of speakeasies."

Thrown on his heels, Glassford was about to ask how she had come by that piece of surveillance when a man behind him tapped an admonishing finger on the overdue books.

"You start letting people get by with flouting the law, pretty soon everybody is doing it," Gibbons said. "At least, that's what I read in the papers."

Unaware that his old reporter friend was in the camp, let alone eavesdropping on his conversation, Glassford called out, "Waters!"

The long-legged BEF commander came bounding up. "Yes, sir."

Glassford angled his head toward Gibbons. "What'd I tell you about letting lowlifes invade your perimeter?"

"To be honest, General," Waters admitted, "sometimes it's kind of hard to tell the lowlifes from the residents."

Glassford, laughing, turned from the crude library counter and raised his hands for silence. He quizzed the veterans, "What are the regulations here?"

"No panhandling!" responded hundreds of gravelly voices in military unison. "No liquor! No radical talk!"

Praising their memory with a sharp salute, Glassford walked through the camp on inspection with Waters and Gibbons. He firmed an affectionate grip on the BEF commander's shoulder. "There's another load of lumber heading down from Annapolis this afternoon. Why don't you make sure there's a team to unload it at the entrance while I deal with this pestering news hawker here."

"I'm on it, General." Waters lingered, grinning and casting significant looks back at the small library, where Anna was still watching them.

"You got something else on your mind?" Glassford asked him.

Waters smirked. "You ain't contracted the calico fever for our Anna, now have you, General? If you have, your courting manner is about as successful as a man scratching his ear with his elbow."

"There's an old saying in Arizona, Waters. Tossing your rope before tying a loop won't catch a calf." He waved the BEF leader off to his assigned task.

Alone now with Gibbons, Glassford glanced back and caught Anna looking away quickly. He winked at Gibbons and, with Scrapper following them, led the radioman toward a quiet, shady spot near the river.

"You've got quite a military operation going here," Gibbons said sarcastically. "I haven't seen such an impressive display of discipline since Pershing and Patton lost half their horses chasing Villa in Mexico."

Glassford's grin evaporated. "Off the record?"

Gibbons nodded his agreement to the condition for the interview.

"I'm sitting on a powder keg here," Glassford said. "I've managed to scrounge up enough food to keep the vets content so far. But each day, more of them arrive, and that means less rations to go around. I'm running out of donations. If these men and their families are forced to go more than a day without a meal, I don't know what will happen."

"Your old classmate Mac has plenty of field kitchens and cans of stewed tomatoes rusting away in the Army storehouses. Why don't you ask him to help you out?"

"I have. He won't do it."

"Has he even been down here to visit these men?" Receiving a shake of the head, Gibbons bit his lower lip in anger. "That rank-climbing sonofabitch won't stand up for those who put him where he is today."

"I'm sure the General has a good reason."

"What about Hoover and Congress?"

Glassford shrugged. "I haven't got a clue what the President is thinking. Hurley won't let me in the White House to speak to him. I finally managed to convince the Senate to appropriate an emergency bill for seventy-five thousand dollars, but the commissioners refused to accept the money."

"Politicians turning down free money? The End Times must be near."

"Crosby told the Appropriations Committee that it would only bring more homeless vets to the city."

"Be careful, Hap. I've seen how these fluttering peacocks operate in a clench. They'd hang their own mothers to save their hides."

"It'll all blow over soon. Once these boys get to make their point on the Hill, they'll go back home."

Gibbons looked skeptical about that expressed hope. "I don't know. They seem pretty staked in for the long haul. What happens if those congressional blowhards don't pass the Bonus bill?"

Glassford listened to distant accordion playing a melancholic rendition of *Misere*. "I'll deal with that when the time comes. Right now, I've got more pressing problems."

"Anything I can do to help?"

Glassford pinned him with a calculating eye. "I need to raise money for camp food, and quickly. This fellow Pace and his Weasel Communists from Detroit are trying to stir the pot and cause trouble about the lack of rations."

"One thing's for certain. You've got those starched shirts in the White House circling the wagons. They've turned the grounds over there into an armed fortress. Hoover won't even risk stepping outside to escape to Camp Rapidan. They all think the city is rife with assassins."

"We both saw what happened in Germany when a man is forced to go more than a couple of days on an empty stomach. Bolshevism and fascism start to look a lot more inviting than capitalism."

"I could give a few speeches," Gibbons said. "But that won't rake in much."

"You know Jimmy Lake over at the Gayety Theatre?"

"Carnation Jimmy? Yeah, he's an old Marine major."

"I hear he's the man in town to stage a big promotion."

Gibbons nodded. "Jimmy knows the right people, all right. What do you have in mind?"

"A fifteen-bout card for a fight night. We'll sell tickets and bring in the best boxers in the Army and Marines, along with some of the men here in this camp."

"I always figured your carny-barking would come in handy one day. But are you sure a boxing match is such good idea?"

Glassford took a long draw on his pipe. "Waters has been hankering to hold a parade past the White House. I'm going to let him do it to blow off some steam. I was thinking a boxing benefit on the night after might bond the regular Army boys and the vets, bring them a little closer."

Gibbons playfully tapped Glassford's boot heel with his cane. "Then again, it might start a war. Of course, on the positive side of the ledger, old Mac will have a fit when he finds out the Marines are helping sponsor it."

Glassford shook his old friend's hand in gratitude. "Grease the wheels over at the barracks on this, will you, Gib? Do that for me, and I might overlook that Studebaker parked next to the fire hydrant up there."

56

WASHINGTON, D.C.
JUNE 7, 1932

eave it alone.

That cold Caledonian specter had been gone from Washington for six months, but Hoover could still hear Mellon with that thick brogue whispering his favorite Darwinian admonishments about the necessity of culling the weak from society.

Leave the economy alone.

Former soldiers sat not two blocks away, cooking beans on the sidewalks.

Damn it, Mellon. The entire city now looks to be inhabited by stick men.

As the long days of summer became longer, he found himself arguing more and more with the irksome memory of his former Treasury secretary. This morning, as he stood at his bedroom window, he looked across the Ellipse toward Constitution Avenue, where ten thousand District residents had crowded along the traditional ceremonial route to witness the most woebegone parade in American history. This self-styled Bonus Expeditionary Force—the very sound of it curdled his gut—was marching down from the Capitol to demand a handout. The dawn surveillance reports confirmed that the procession was being led by that Oregon loudmouth Waters, who now strode around the city accompanied by a gaggle of misfits claiming to be his bodyguard and adjutants. Behind Waters limped decorated heroes of the AEF, disabled veterans on stretchers, and the rest of the pathetic horde with their families and animals.

And with them were hundreds, maybe thousands, of secret Communists.

The nation will recover by its own inherent strength.

Easy enough advice for Mellon to dispense. The man was no doubt sitting in some Regent's Park tearoom that moment grumbling about the framing of one of his new acquisitions for that art boondoggle he was scheming. Soon the hobos would be able to camp out on marble floors under the brush strokes of Raphael and van Eyck. And that Texas windbag Wright Patman was making political hay on the floor of the House by claiming that allowing Mellon to escape to London during his impeachment hearings for tax fraud was like handing down a verdict of innocence while the jury was still in deliberations.

The criticism about the appointment was unfair, but he counted it worth the blistering he was taking in the press just to be rid of that coin-jingling corpse and the curse of his Highland gloom. A National Gallery of Art for a city of a million destitute Americans. *Brilliant idea, Mellon.* His face reddened as he heard a tune being sung by the parading veterans:

> "Oh the strangest Prisoner in the land
> Lives in a big white house.
> In a cage that is fit for a lion,
> He moves with the soul of a mouse.
> And alert at the gate and portal,
> Door and chamber and hall,
> Are a swarm of secret servants,
> On guard lest Vengeance call.
> The Prisoner may not stroll abroad
> In the comradeship of the street,
> Lest suddenly the accusing eyes
> Of Hunger he should meet
> He may not know the common touch
> Nor walk in the common ways,
> Lest he feel suddenly face to face
> Stern Retribution's gaze."

His wife Lou, sitting across the bedroom in front of her vanity mirror, fussed with her earrings. "Bert, please come away from the window."

He wouldn't budge from his lookout post. "There is one great advantage to holding to orthodox religion."

"What would that be, dear?"

"It includes a hot Hell."

"You must lift your mood," she begged.

"No doubt that scalawag Gibbons is down there in the middle of the protest pouring gas on the flames. I hope he finds special facilities in the world to come."

"Bert! That is not a Christian thing to say."

Weary of it all, he pressed his forehead against the pane. "Look at this, Lou! There Glassford is, on that damn motorcycle again, preening like he's running for office. He's turning the entire city into a flophouse."

"You're getting agitated again. Joel warned you not—"

"I've got plenty to be agitated about!" He lifted a letter from the nightstand and waved it at her. "Have you seen this?"

Lou refused to look at the letter. "If I read ever piece of hysterical diatribe that came through here, I wouldn't be able to sleep at night."

"This isn't from some housewife in Topeka complaining she doesn't have enough sugar for her Sunday cakes. The president of the National Geographic Society wrote it!"

"Bert, enough. Let's go downstairs for breakfast."

Despite her protest, he insisted on sharing the letter. "The head of the Society expresses his grave concern that I may not be able to go to Constitution Hall next week to present the medal to Amelia Earhart."

"That's only a couple blocks from here," Lou said. "Why on Earth would he think you couldn't make such a short journey?"

"Because it is *his* belief that most of these so-called veterans out there are Communists! He's warning me that Reds disguised as veterans have overrun the city! He thinks there's going to be a *coup*."

"What do Hurley and MacArthur say about this?"

The president paced back and forth past the window, every so often glancing down at the growing crowds. "I can never get a straight answer from them. They talk in that damn Army code to cover their rears."

She came to his side. "Do you trust them?"

He looked at her quizzically. "Why do you ask that?"

"It's just … you've never been in the military. From what I've been told, those West Pointers always take care of their own."

"You're suggesting I'm not getting good advice."

"All I'm saying is, be careful. If there were only someone else you could confide in. What about that young Marine you befriended in China?"

"Smedley Butler?"

"He's a fellow Quaker. And isn't he retired from the service?"

The president waved off that suggestion. "The man is a spent firecracker. Don't you remember how he ran off at the mouth about Mussolini. I had to order him court-martialed until he apologized to the Italian government. He despises me, and the feeling is mutual."

"Have you thought about …" She stopped.

He always hated it when she cut short her thoughts. "About what?"

"Maybe it would be helpful if we visited one of the soup kitchens in the city. To show that we care about these poor souls."

"I *do* care about them!" he snapped. "I don't need to go out and put on a show of it, just for the cameras. I will not turn myself into a pandering hypocrite."

"Bert, the little things. At least, when we pass them on the street in the car, look at them and nod. You just stare ahead as if they're not even there."

"I am not a vaudeville actor!"

She sat on the bed, drained by their arguing. "Have you seen the photos in the newspapers? That camp in Anacostia looks frightful. Evalyn McLean—"

"McLean? Why are you talking to *that* woman? She's only making things worse, traipsing around dispensing donations from her fortune like some saint. If that gets out in the press, every deadbeat in the country will come here."

"Evalyn said the heat is unbearable down near the river. The dust and foul smells. And the flies, oh, the flies. They hover in clouds over open latrines. There are children, entire families, living in boxes the size of an outhouse."

"It will all be over when the House votes down that Bonus fiasco."

"And when will that be?"

"Thanks to the wisdom of the voters, Jack Garner is now in charge of those stockyards up there. So, we can be sure of one thing. He and his fellow Texas claim jumpers will drag this out as long as it's to their political advantage."

Lou pressed a palm to her heated forehead. "I can't take another day cooped up in this place. I think I'll ask Lawrence to take me on a drive around the Mall tomorrow."

"Not tomorrow."

"Why?"

"Glassford is holding his mooch-stew boxing show at Griffith Stadium."

"Why should that change *my* plans?"

"Twenty thousand ex-soldiers will be all worked up after throwing punches and drinking cheap illegal beer. I don't trust that pacifying police chief to keep the situation in check."

"You think there could be violence?"

"Just stay in, to be safe."

Tired but exhilarated from their parading that morning, Waters and his BEF veterans fanned out on both sides of Eleventh Street to search every alley and garbage can for a lost comrade. While Glassford had been leading their procession back up Pennsylvania Avenue to the Capitol, his dog Scrapper, a favorite of the Anacostia camp, had run off on an adventure of his own. Seeing the distress in the chief's eyes, Waters had ordered his troops to canvass the city on a hunt for the pug. Despite having eaten nothing since the hard biscuits passed out for breakfast, the Oregon men had readily accepted the assignment, eager to repay the many kindnesses that Glassford had shown them.

Lincoln asked Waters, "Scrapper decide to ride the rails, Dubya?"

"You're the blind ones," Pace said. "Glassford and his bought cops are playing you for patsies. He's keeping you placated for the Wall Street fat cats. If they ever give us our Bonus, which they won't, how long you think that money's gonna last you? A year maybe? Whatdya gonna do then? We got to change the way the game is played."

"You're the one t-t-trying to play *us*," Waters said. "You been stirring up trouble around town and hoping Glassford will crack our heads for it."

Pace ignored his rival leader and kept talking to the other veterans. "Don't you see what's been happening here? This so-called commander of yours here gallivants around rubbing elbows with the high and mighty up on Dupont Circle while you boys sleep under the tins down at the sewers. Hell, the papers this morning said you even had tea with that capitalist socialite McLean woman. You had any high tea recently with the rich and mighty?"

Waters felt the questioning glances from his own men. "I have to meet with wealthy people. I'm out there day and night trying to raise money for us. You think I can raise money down in the ghettos?"

"Where *is* all this money I hear you've been collecting?"

Waters shifted his eyes. "Glassford's our treasurer."

Pace gave up a raw laugh. "Glassford again! So, the cops who work for the bankers control the money of the Bonus babies! No wonder you're down here sleeping in the mud." He turned and motioned for his men to follow him into the camp across the bridge.

"You take another step," warned Lenny Currans, the BEF boxer on that night's Griffith Stadium card, "and I'll start the matches a little early."

"You better save those fists for the Army toughs, Currans."

Without warning, Pace rushed for the bridge, followed by his Communist veterans. Waters pointed his men on a run to catch the invaders. Currans grabbed Pace and swung him around while the other veterans split off into scuffling bouts. Angelo drove a fist into Pace's face and staggered him, but the Communist leader stayed on his feet and flashed his knuckles. He pawed at the concrete with his heel and was about to charge the Irishman when the blare of a police horn froze them all.

Glassford sped down Eleventh Street on his motorcycle, followed by four cars filled with cops. The officers bolted out, brandishing clubs. The chief, dismounting, motioned for his men to hold their positions. He looked at his watch as he walked up to Waters. "I didn't think the matches started until seven. It's not fair to those Army opponents for you fellows to be getting in some early practice, now is it?"

"General, these Reds were t-t-trying to infiltrate our camp."

"Is that right, Pace?"

"That ground is open to the public," Pace said. "There's nothing in the Constitution says me and my men can't walk around in this city."

"Just like you walked around in Dearborn during the riots there?"

"I had nothing to do with that."

Glassford circled the Communist ex-Marine. "There's a rumor you were arrested in Detroit for trying to chloroform an alderman."

"You're damn right I did. That alderman deserved to be chloroformed."

"You need a billet tonight? Maybe some hot food, too?"

Pace, expecting rough handling, looked confused. "Well, yeah. That's why me and my comrades were heading into the camp."

Angelo was incredulous. "You ain't gonna feed and house this Red scum, are you, General?"

Glassford motioned up a half dozen of his cops to take Pace and his Communists into their protection. The BEF men glared at him with disbelief as the agitators were led to the waiting police cars for an escort. When the Communists had finally been hauled off, Glassford put an arm around Waters's shoulder and led him and the BEF men across the bridge to talk to them privately. "We found the bodies of a couple of Pace's men in the river yesterday. You fellas wouldn't know anything about that, would you?"

"We're not murderers, General," Waters said. "If these instigators sneak into my camp, I can't be accountable if some patriot decides to choose them the quickest way out."

"You been holding kangaroo courts on them? Giving out whippings like in the old days?"

"They say they're veterans," Angelo reminded the chief. "If they're veterans, they should get an Army punishment."

Glassford removed his cap and wiped the perspiration from his brow. "You men are going to have to help me out and show some restraint when Pace and his boys start baiting you. They're trying to force my hand. I can't have violence and vigilantism on the streets. The papers will report it, and those congressmen on the Hill who want you out of here will have their reason."

"We're d-d-damned if we do and d-d-damned if we don't," Waters said. "Hoover says we're Reds. The only way to show him we're not is to get t-t-tough with them. But if we get t-t-tough with them, then they say we're breaking the law."

Glassford didn't have a good answer to that complaint. "Let's take it one day at a time. First order of business is to get some money raised tonight so you'll have food. Then we get those congressman to vote on your Bonus so that you can go back home by next week." He walked off toward his parked cycle, and then turned back. "Currans!"

Currans stepped forward, expecting to be cuffed for some infraction.

Glassford reached into his pocket and threw him a wrapped liverwurst sandwich. "Eat up, champ. I managed to get a scouting report on the fellow you'll be squaring off against tonight. He's got a nasty left hook, but he leaves his right side open."

Waters and the veterans grinned, grateful for the scouting report.

Douglas MacArthur stood at the open window of his second floor office in Fort Myer and looked down at the long rows of white headstones in Arlington National Cemetery. There, in Section Two, his father and brother lay buried under the shadows of Robert E. Lee's old mansion. He often stood here in the morning, admiring the vista and savoring his pipe while thinking of the many comrades who lay across the way in that hallowed ground. On the first Sunday of every month, he drove his mother there to place flowers on the gravesites. She had already designated her resting spot, next to the Captain, and insisted that her sons join them there for all eternity.

Once he had hoped for something more fitting, perhaps an equestrian monument, but that possibility had died with his survival of the war. The modern soldier, he had come to accept, endures not only the loss of chivalry as an inspiration for courage, but he must go to battle knowing that his deeds will never be lionized in stone with such past grandeur.

His eyes trailed beyond Hatfield Gate, across from the Potomac, where the usual riffraff of hobo veterans was trying to mooch food and cigarettes from the troops. Fearing that the Communist veterans would sway them with their lies, he had ordered the regulars sequestered to the post, but that hadn't stopped the flood of Red propaganda from seeping into the barracks. Only yesterday, he had been brought a collection of secreted handbills inflaming the soldiers to action on behalf of those vagrants down at that mud pit in Anacostia. The atmosphere of suspicion had even reached the Officers Club. He couldn't be certain whom these insidious tactics might have turned.

He checked his watch. His train would be leaving in six hours. Moving to his desk, he looked over his notes again for the commencement speech that he would be delivering tomorrow at the University of Pittsburgh. His theme was timely: the dangers of pacifism and its cankerous bedfellow, Communism. He had briefly considered canceling the speech because of the threat of violence during the boxing match that Glassford had arranged in Griffith Stadium that evening. But Moseley and the other officers had assured him that they could handle the situation in his absence.

Distracted by shouts of battle, he returned to the window. Under his orders of secrecy, the troops had begun practicing the new civilian riot drills on Summerhall Field. Half of the men, assigned to play the role of Red instigators, stood behind a picket fence and hurled curses and rocks at the other half, who played the police. From their rear, across Jackson Lane, a squadron of senior cavalrymen charged at the rioters to train their mounts not to spook from the clamor. Leading them was a helmeted rider who laughed wildly as he wielded a polo stick around his head like a mace.

He watched with rising dismay as the officer in the van stampeded through the lines like a French knight at Agincourt, nearly braining several of the bareheaded thespian rioters. "Damn it!" he shouted at the hallway outside his door. "Who the hell is that lunatic? Get somebody down there to rein him in before he fills the infirmary!"

General Moseley hurried in from his adjacent office and peered down at the melee. He grinned. "Why, Doug, that's your favorite tank commander."

"When did he get reassigned from the War College?"

"Couple of days ago."

MacArthur watched from on high as Major George Patton charged across the narrow strip of no-man's land that separated the riot soldiers from the pretend row of frothing rioters.

"When you fire at the bastards, don't hold back!" Patton shouted at the riot trainees. "A few casualties will go a long way to saving others! Do you hear me?"

The soldiers, dodging his polo stick, stood at attention. "Yes, sir!"

"And when a mob starts to move, keep it on the run! Move them with the bayonet! Once they're on the run, a few good wounds in the buttocks will encourage them!"

"Sir, what if they resist?"

Patton glared at the soldier in utter disbelief. "What kind of bone-headed question is that? If the enemy resists, *you kill the enemy!*"

The opposing lines traded confused glances, uncertain if Patton was joking.

In his office overlooking the drill, MacArthur drew down the shade. He could sense a growing disaffection in the ranks. It was an intuition he had developed in the trenches of France. In recent days, he had become increasingly alarmed that some of the regulars might disobey orders and go over to the side of the Bonus marchers. He had taken steps to secure the armories, but if whole regiments decided to turn against the government, there'd be nothing a few loyal guards could do to stop them.

Moseley detected his concern. "I can have Patton remanded.

MacArthur shook his head. "He'd just raise hell about it on the Hill."

Moseley shut the door. "That intelligence project ordered by Hurley."

"Yes."

"The first reports came in this morning."

"How many veterans have been confirmed as Communists?"

Moseley's bagged eyes tightened with disdain. "That con man Waters and his rail-riding gang are a wily bunch. So far, they've been saying all the right things. Looks like only one of them has been meeting secretly with Pace."

"What's *he* been saying to the Reds?"

"We don't know."

"Anything else of interest?"

After a hesitation, Moseley revealed, "One of the agitators reportedly called for hanging you from the Capitol."

The only reaction evident in MacArthur's face was a slight twitch at the corner of his mouth. "Tell the MID operatives that we need more proof. Whatever they have to do to get it."

Moseley nodded. "I spoke to Crosby last night. The President is mad as hell about Glassford feeding and lodging those hobos. The White House may order him fired."

"It won't happen. The press adores Glassford. Hoover doesn't have the spine to risk such a move so close to the election."

"What are we going to do about him, then?"

MacArthur bored a plunger into his pipe while debating his next move. "Ask him to come by and see me before I leave for Pittsburgh this afternoon. Suspend the riot drilling while he's on the post."

Moseley grinned. "You gonna talk some sense into him?"

MacArthur stared at a lithograph of the Battle of Shiloh on his wall. "Do you think Grant was drunk at Pittsburgh Landing, George?"

"Probably no drunker than Sherman was crazy."

"I've often thought that if Grant had endured the bad luck of suffering his first defeat in Virginia with the Army of the Potomac, Lincoln would have fired him. And he would have been cast to the dustbin of history with McDowell, McClellan, Burnside, and Hooker. Out West, in Tennessee, nobody cared if he lost a couple of battles."

"You trying to make a point, Doug, or just off on one of your rambles?"

MacArthur tapped his pipe against the ashtray to clean it. "Sometimes a man has to be shamed before he can rise to his true destiny."

A parade of cold glares greeted Glassford as he walked across the Fort Myer grounds. From the way the officers edged away when he approached, the message was clear: He wasn't the most popular man around Army circles right now. That was probably why his old classmate MacArthur hadn't invited him for drinks at the Officers Club. A venue that public for their meeting might get the tongues wagging to the press.

He climbed the steps to the second floor of the fort's library. The duty officer at the information desk saluted stiffly and led him in silence to a small room that held the post's collection of regimental histories. The officer closed the door and left him alone with MacArthur, who stood perusing the dusty volumes in the stacks. He cleared his throat to reveal his presence.

Turning with that famous patrician smile of his, MacArthur reached for Glassford's hand and, as if by habit from their years together at the Point, stole a judging glance down at his old friend's scuffed wing tips. "Hap! You look well. The new job suits you."

"It's keeping me out of debtor's prison."

MacArthur picked out a biography of Robert E. Lee from the shelved books and thumbed through it. "I wish I had taken more time to build a private library. It's one of the luxuries a soldier must forgo, I suppose."

Glassford studied the impressive array of yellowed military maps hanging on the oak walls. "Do you spend much time in here?"

"More and more, as I grow older. Alexander the Great employed ten historians on his marches through Asia. The scholars could pontificate to him on any question of military fact or strategy from the past thousand years. That wouldn't be a bad innovation for the Army, don't you think?"

Glassford laughed softly. "I doubt the Army could find anyone with more knowledge of history than you."

MacArthur held a skeptical eye on him, as if suspecting he was being stroked. "If you had practiced more of that flattery over the years, Hap, you might have an office over at the War Department by now."

"We both know I don't possess that talent."

MacArthur sat on the corner of a conference table, letting the silence extend.

Still uncertain why he had been summoned, Glassford resolved not to let the opportunity pass. "General, I know my requests for food and bedding were probably intercepted before they got to you, but—"

"I received them."

He was thrown by the sudden shift to a cold, formal tone. "I need help with these veterans. I finally convinced Congress to authorize seventy-five thousand dollars in emergency funds, but the commissioners turned it down. They said it would only draw more vagrants to the city. Now I'm running out of time. Crosby has blocked every attempt I've made to get those men decent shelter. Those field cots and canned stores in the local armories are so old, they won't ever be used."

"I'm afraid I can't be of much assistance to you."

"Could you at least come down and speak to the men? It would do a world of good for their morale."

MacArthur thumbed through the Lee biography until he came to the chapter on the Peninsula Campaign. "Do you know McClellan's fatal flaw?"

Glassford couldn't fathom what that question had to do with the crisis at hand. "A reluctance to fight."

MacArthur placed the book back on the shelf. "A reluctance to fight, caused by his getting too close to his soldiers.... You're playing with fire, Hap. Those malcontents you've befriended will turn on you. You must reestablish the emotional distance of command."

"They're good fellows at heart. Just down on their luck."

"In the annals of military history, one rule above all has always proven true. The officer corps must not lower itself to the level of the common soldier in the ranks. Wellington and Napoleon swore by that maxim."

"American soldiers are different."

"Not really." MacArthur grasped Glassford's shoulder to drive home his point. "You always wanted to be liked, Hap. That year when you were drawing instructor at the Point. What class was it?"

"The 'Fourteen."

"Yes, they dedicated their class book to you, if I recall. That must have been one of your most cherished moments."

He felt his throat tighten from the memory. "It was."

"How did your men feel about you during the war?"

"We got along splendidly."

MacArthur walked along the shelves until he came to another volume. He pulled it out and read the title on the spine: *The War Story of C Battery, One Hundred and Third Field U.S. Artillery.*

Glassford was intrigued, until that moment uninformed that a history of his old battery had been compiled. "Who wrote that?"

"Lt. John Russell. You've never read it?"

He shook his head. "I wonder why Russell never sent me a copy?"

MacArthur opened it to page 167, which had been bookmarked. "You were transferred from this unit, as I recall."

"Promoted to command of the Sixty-Sixth Brigade."

"Who took over for you in the Hundred and Third?"

"John Twachtman."

"Of course. It says it right here in the account." Without waiting for a request, MacArthur read the paragraph aloud: "'When Lieutenant Colonel Twachtman stepped into the office vacated by Colonel Glassford, and assumed command of the regiment, the men were happy, for they knew that they were now to serve under an officer who was with them in action and spirit.'"

Glassford blinked back tears. This betrayal by his old comrades had blindsided him. How many regimental and brigade reunions over the years had he attended with them, and they had said nothing? Had his enlisted men and junior officers been smirking and laughing behind his back all those many months? Why had none of them brought this memoir to his attention?

MacArthur drew a cup of water from the cooler in the corner and offered it to him. "I didn't show you this to be cruel. I've had much worse written about me. You must understand that noncommissioned soldiers cannot be led with love or affection. The dynamic inherent in command breeds resentment in the common ranks."

Glassford was too ashamed to look up at the man he so admired.

"Do you remember what I told you that day of your plebe year, when I was forced to testify about the hazing?"

Glassford knew that MacArthur was attempting to conflate loyalty to the Point with adherence to the War Department's hard-line policy on the homeless veterans. He coughed back the emotion and, barely above a whisper, gave the time-honored answer. "Never betray the Corps."

MacArthur gathered up his briefcase and hat. "Stay as long as you wish, Hap. Have a drink at the club and put it on my account. I'm afraid I have to catch a train."

Glassford, his spirit crushed, could only manage a weak salute.

At the door, MacArthur turned back. "For the good of the country, Hap, I hope to find these"—he chose the next word carefully—"*men* out of the city on my return."

That night, Anna patrolled the central square of the Anacostia camp, disgusted by the marathon dance contest that she was witnessing. The speaker's stand had been temporarily removed to make room for a patchwork of mud-oozing duckboards, laid on the puddled ground to form an uneven dance floor. Flickering lanterns hoisted on poles ghoulishly illuminated the twenty surviving couples, mostly barefoot veterans wrapped arm-in-arm with comrades. Some of the dancers had slicked their hair back with cheap brilliantine in a woebegone attempt to appear dapper. They staggered and swayed with fatigue, desperate to get the five dollars put up by a local butcher for the winner of the first annual BEF Charity Bunion Derby, which was being held on the evening before the big boxing match at Griffith Stadium.

The lugubrious music leading their plodding steps was being supplied by the Hoover Blowhards, a band that Ozzie Taylor had recruited from the hardscrabble collection of banjo strummers, fiddlers, and mouth harpists who populated the shack city. As Ozzie led them with his oboe in a slurring rendition of *Shuffle Along*, the other veterans lazed around on the ground, cheering the contestants on whom they had placed private wagers for buttons or the next day's helping of the mulligan stew.

As Anna checked the weakening pulse of one slumped contestant, she looked toward the riverbank and glared shame at the hundreds of Washington residents who had paid the twenty-five cent donation to gawk at this spectacle of misery. Having reached her fill of this nonsense, she marched over to confront Waters, who was officiating the event. She pointed to the poor veteran whom she had just tended to, and insisted, "That man needs rest!"

Waters shrugged. "There's nothing I can do about it, Anna. Rules are rules."

Across from her, on the floor, Charlie Lincoln was leaning against Chief Running Wolf, barely moving his swollen feet. Overhearing her plea for mercy, he shouted, "Them's the rules, Miss Raber! He goes to his knees, he's out!"

In a huff, Anna walked onto the floor and checked the pupils of the other stubborn dancers. Over her shoulder, she demanded, "Who makes the rules?"

Waters angled his head toward a betting stand, where the butcher who had put up the prize money was doing a fine business collecting side wagers.

Anna shouted at the butcher, "You let this man take a break! Or I'm calling the police chief and have him stop this!"

The butcher laughed. "You don't have to call him. He's right over there!"

Anna spun on her heels, and the veterans packed around the dance floor parted to reveal Glassford perched on Blue Bessie. Anna flushed with anger. Had he been in the crowd all along, allowing this travesty to proceed? She threaded her way across the duckboards and met him with such a countenance of vehemence that the veterans surrounding the chief backed away with grins of anticipation. "*You* sanctioned this?"

Before Glassford could defend himself, the butcher holding court behind the betting stand piped, "Sanctioned? Hell, he's got a dollar on Old Abe's cousin!"

Anna turned a shade redder. "Why don't you just line them up and let the locals pay to shoot at them like a turkey hunt?" She expected one of Glassford's usual quips in reply, but he just sat on his cycle with a shaken, red-eyed look. She had never seen him appear so unnerved. "Are you not feeling well?"

"Long day."

"Then maybe you can empathize with those poor souls who are debasing themselves for a meal. Is there no dignity left in this city?"

"Not much, from what I can find."

Finding his spirits so low and uncharacteristic of him, she eased her strident tone. "I'm sorry if I spoke harshly, but something must be done about this."

Glassford reported her demand to the sponsoring butcher. "Jake, the lady says something must be done."

Ozzie and the Hoover Blowhards softened their music so that all could hear the decision. The butcher rubbed his chin while assessing the situation. "It has been known, in the annals of corn and callus carnivals, to allow a ten-minute substitution for contestants who demonstrate a medical necessity. I'm willing to bend the rules just once." He looked harder at Anna and finally offered her a concession. "You can choose one couple to give a ten-minute break."

She studied the twenty couples pleading with hangdog eyes for rest. She knew the man she had just checked was in danger of passing out if he didn't get off his feet soon. At last, forced to decide, she chose the lesser of evils. "Hoagie Jackson and Merle Compton."

"That ain't right!" shouted Lincoln.

The veterans buzzed around the betting stand, reassessing their wagers in light of this alteration in the competition. The butcher motioned the chosen couple off the floor, and they immediately collapsed. Several veterans helped drag them to chairs. Having accomplished all that she could for the pitiful contestants, Anna began walking the path up the ridge to retire to her spare apartment on the third floor of the Salvation Army building.

"Whoa, there, little lady," the butcher said.

She turned. "Yes?"

"You didn't give me a chance to explain all of the rules."

She narrowed her glare, suspecting a ruse. "What else?"

"There has to be a substitute couple for those chosen to rest. We're holding a dance marathon here, not a cotillion."

"I'm sure there are plenty of volunteers."

The butcher turned to Glassford, "My choice?"

Glassford shrugged. "You bent the rules for Miss Raber here. I don't see why it shouldn't be your choice." He turned to Anna. "Do you?"

"There are twenty-five thousand men to choose from, so have at it." She resumed her walk home.

"I think the crowd would love to see the Chief here show us a few steps," said the butcher. "Am I right, boys?"

"Now, hold on." Glassford was about to crank up Blue Bessie for an escape.

The veterans cheered the choice, and Anna smiled with revenge as she strode off, pleased that she had not only helped the sickly veteran Hoagie, but had put the publicity-hounding chief of police in a pickle, too.

"We've heard the stories, General!" shouted Waters. "You used to cut a mean rug at the Point."

"Those are slanderous rumors."

The butcher surveyed the crush of veterans. "You're gonna need a partner."

"Hey, General!" Ozzie shouted. "Maybe Hoover'll come down from Fortress White House and do the old two-step with you!"

Several wives of the veterans pushed to the fore, eager to dance with the popular police chief. The butcher looked them over, rubbing his chin in debate. Slowly he turned toward the bluffs. "I'm thinking more along the lines of a Clara Barton waltz."

The camp hushed, stunned by the unexpected choice. Only Anna remained in motion, now out of earshot of the negotiations. She had nearly reached the camp's gate when Mickey Dolan and his men, seeing the butcher's signal, stopped her with outstretched palms and wide grins. Before she could question why she had been delayed, the BEF guards threaded their arms through her elbows and squired her back to the dance floor.

Glassford, in no mood for dancing, looked over his shoulder for an escape route back to his motorcycle.

Delivered to the smirking butcher like Queen Boadicea to Caesar, Anna demanded to know the reason for the summons. "What is it now?"

"The Chief here would like the honor," said the butcher.

Anna suddenly saw the trap that she had unwittingly helped set. After a quick glance at Glassford, who was trying to make an escape for his motorcycle, she insisted, "Dancing is against my religious beliefs."

The butcher nodded in mock empathy. "Of course, ma'am. I understand." He motioned for Hoagie and his partner to be dragged back to the floor. "Get 'em started again."

Anna watched, incredulous, as the two veterans, dead asleep, were roused and dragged back to the boards. Appalled, she finally relented and signaled for the dance referees to hold up. As the butcher and the veterans leaned toward her for a reaction, she stole another glance at Glassford, who looked as green as a schoolboy at his first hoedown. She didn't know what annoyed her more: being conned into this charade, or the fact that Glassford seemed so eager not to dance with her.

The butcher nodded for Taylor to ratchet up the music, a tactic that drew a few more twitches and shakes of life from the slumping couples. Pushed toward the floor, Glassford took Anna with him and faced off with her, his right hand at her lower back and his left hand intertwined with her hand in the air. With every eye in the camp riveted on them, he took the first step and rammed his knee into her immovable thigh.

Anna hadn't been this close to a man, at least one not wounded, since the night of her bundling with Micah. She whispered to him, "I don't know what I'm doing."

"Evidently."

She planted her heel into his arch. "I *do* know how to shoe a mule."

He whirled her and then whispered to her ear, "Just follow my lead."

"Everyone in this camp seems to follow your lead," she said. "I don't see it getting them anywhere."

"Maybe you should just concentrate on the steps."

She sensed a bruised hurt in his voice. "What has happened?"

His gaze shifted off to avoid her hard inspection. "Nothing you need to be concerned about."

He dipped her abruptly, nearly costing her a breath. When she was brought back upright, she clung tighter to his arms and gasped, "You seem adept at keeping lots of things spinning at the same time."

"I used to do a little carnival juggling."

"I would have guessed an illusionist."

Burned by the veiled reference to his tactics with the veterans, Glassford glanced at the watchful eyes crowded around the dance floor. "I've pretty much had my fill of critiques on my policing style for one day."

"What are you doing with these men?"

"I want to see them stay safe."

"But go home."

"You may not believe me, but I understand what they're going through. I was also lost after the war. Couldn't find a reason to live. So I came here, too."

"And have you found it here? Your reason to live?"

His bleary eyes filmed over. "Nothing replaces the bonds of men thrown together to accomplish some great task. It's not really about the Bonus."

"What's it about, then?"

"Recapturing that time in their lives when they had a great purpose."

They both fell silent, and she moved slightly closer to him.

"So," he said. "What's your secret?"

"Me? Anger, I guess."

"No!" he said sarcastically. "You're such a wilting flower."

She smiled ruefully at the dig. "I think it was after about the thousandth gassed soldier I watched gag his last breath. …" She looked away.

"And?"

She turned back and studied his expectant eyes, wondering if she could trust him. Finally, she revealed, "I became a subversive."

He backed away a step. "You don't mean … "

She nodded. "You probably shouldn't be touching me. I hear it's contagious."

"But, I've never—"

"Never seen me pass out leaflets? Never had your undercover agents hear me give speeches or call for riots? There are subversives of the head and subversives of the heart." She waited for his reaction, but found him staring off into the distance, preoccupied with some unspoken burden. "Don't worry, General. I don't start fires."

The butcher gave the signal that the ten minutes were up, and Hoagie and Merle, recovered sufficiently to resume their quest, took to the boards again.

Glassford led Anna off the floor and toward his motorcycle. "I'll escort you home."

"That's not necessary. But thank you, anyway."

As Anna walked alone toward the bridge, Waters strolled up to Glassford and reported, "Good haul, tonight, General. We collected fifty bucks."

Glassford had other things on his mind. "They got elk in Oregon, Waters?"

"Big as elephants."

"In Arizona, ours scared off the dinosaurs. What I wouldn't give to be back on a horse, tracking some right now."

Waters sized him up. "You wouldn't be trying to make me homesick, now would you, General?"

Glassford acknowledged the BEF commander's caginess with a punchy nod of concession. "You ever have a problem earning the respect of your men?"

"Only about every day."

"How do you handle it?"

"From time to time, I disappear and put somebody in charge who don't know hills from beans. Soon enough, the boys start appreciating me again."

Glassford was half-listening as he watched Anna hurry past through the camp gate and walk across the Anacostia Bridge.

Detecting his distraction, Waters cranked the handle gas on Glassford's motorcycle for him and sent the police chief off with some advice. "General, you *really* need to paint her."

57

WASHINGTON, D.C.
JUNE 8, 1932

Surrounded by fifteen thousand cheering spectators, Ozzie ducked and jabbed at Billy Hruska in the seat next to him. He couldn't help parroting the moves of their BEF buddy, Lennie Currans, who was fighting the Fort Meade Army champ in the elevated ring set atop the Griffith Stadium infield. Ozzie swigged another drink of the sour nickel beer, pacing himself for the fifty charity bouts scheduled that night to raise money for the camp. He handed the bottle to Hruska for a hit. "I bet you never saw nothing like this in Littlevania, Billy boy!"

"Lithuania!"

"All right. Take it easy. I ain't memorized every country on the globe."

Hruska nervously tapped his shoe against the concrete stands, grimacing and groaning every time Currans took a hard punch to the gut. "I told him eat all of sandwich! Look at him! No strength!"

"He's holding his own." Ozzie squinted down at Waters and Angelo passing the hat ringside for donations. "Maybe Dubya and Joey will get enough dough tonight to quartermaster us some decent coffee tomorrow. That slime they been serving in the camp would gag a cow."

Hruska vaulted to his feet to cheer Currans on. "Give him hook left!"

Ozzie nearly rolled out of his seat laughing. "You're gonna fracture my ribs, Billy! You mean left hook!"

"I mean what I say!"

An Army regular sitting several rows behind them threw a bottle at their heads and shouted, "Sit down, you stinking Russkie!"

Hruska spun to find the culprit. "Am no Russian!"

Sinking down to avoid being recognized, Ozzie pulled Hruska back to the seat. "Take it easy, Billy."

"How you like it if someone call you Nigerian?"

"All right, you got a point."

In the ring, Currans was getting the worst of it from the Army tough, who kept head-butting and bulling him into the corners. Glassford, refereeing the fight, broke up their clench and pointed a warning at Curran's opponent to refrain from using the sharp tactics.

Ozzie scanned the stands on the far side of the ring. The rows over there were filled with burly troops from the nearby bases who had been given leave to attend. "They must be feeding those boys better than they did us. Steaks and potatoes, looks like to me. None of that stinking corn beef and lice crackers in the trenches."

"Yah, they eat better, for sure."

Across the way, Ozzie spotted Alford talking to a couple of strangers on the second-level concourse. "Hey, there's Georgie. He's back in town."

"Where he go?"

Ozzie shrugged. "Georgie goes where Dubya tells him to go. Dubya gives him lots of important diplomatic assignments."

"You mean like finding Dubya lunch?"

"Now don't be that way, Billy. Dubya's got a lot on his agenda, always meeting with Chief Glassford, and all. Hoover gets his meal served to him. Why shouldn't the commander of the BEF?" He stood up and waved at Alford, trying to get his attention. "Hey, Georgie! Where you been?"

Hearing his name shouted, Alford looked up at the bleachers and saw Ozzie waving at him. Instead of waving back, Alford frowned and hurried away through the concourse exit.

"He looks happy to see you," said Hruska sarcastically.

Ozzie slumped into his seat. "Georgie's got things on his mind."

"Yah, deep philosopher."

Ozzie started humming a tune to take his mind off the burn in his gut. "Aw, that moon has gone down, baby, North Star 'bout to shine."

Hruska turned a glare on him. "Why you sing while comrade Currans gets teeth knocked in?"

"Nervous habit, I guess."

"What is?"

"What is what?"

"Dat canticle, you crazy Nigerian!"

Ozzie had to think a moment. "You mean the tune? Why, that's ol' Charley Patton. That Mississippi boy can make the wolves whimper. I saw him play once on my sojourn out West. It was in Detroit, I think. Yeah, I remember now. You shoulda heard him play that slide guitar, Billy. Dang, I wish Boss Jim coulda lived long enough to see him. The man has honey in his veins. Now that you've got my memory gusher bubbling up, come to think of it, I saw something else that week in Detroit that made me sit up and take note."

"Shut up so I can watch fight."

Ozzie was on a testifying roll. "This boy I saw box at the Kronk had wizard hands. I tell ya, that poor sucker fighting him couldn't see them coming."

Hruska sprang up again and shouted at Glassford, "Army man cheats!"

Glassford, hearing the heavily accented hollering, looked into the stands and pointed a finger at Hruska in a good-natured warning to mind his manners.

"Now here's the part of the story you won't believe," said Ozzie. "I went up after the bout to shake the boy's paw, but he couldn't get two words out sideways. Just like ol' Dubya down there. So I told him to just write his name on a page of newsprint for me."

Hruska wasn't listening. "His ears! Punish ears!"

"He wrote his name so big that he only had room for his first and second."

"Blood him!"

"Joe Louis. Can you believe that? That boy was going around identifying himself with two first names. I told him, son, you ain't gonna get nowhere in life unless you get yerself an important-sounding last name. People just won't give you no respect. Take me, for instance. You think Big Jim woulda put me in his band if I had told him my full name was Oswald Henry—"

Suddenly, the crowd on the BEF side surged to its feet with a collective groan.

Ozzie looked down at the ring. Currans was sprawled across the mat. The only part of his anatomy moving was a twitching foot. The Fort Meade champ had knocked him out cold.

As the BEF men sat disheartened, the Army regulars on leave across the way raised their beers in a taunting toast and sang "Over There" to rub in their victory. The BEF's corner man revived Currans with some salts to the nostrils, and Glassford helped him stagger off the mat.

"Why don't you codgers go back to the old soldiers' home!" shouted one of the celebrating Army men. "Fighting German scum is one thing! You best never take on Americans!"

Waters had to restrain Angelo from rushing the soldier. While several Army officers smiled smugly and enjoyed cigars from their ringside seats, Waters and his entourage mulled about in the aisles, dejected. Hundreds of veterans headed for the exits, too angry and humiliated to stay for the other fights.

While Currans, still groggy, was being helped from the ring, Mickey Dolan stood up from his seat in the bleachers. The big Irishman walked down the ramp steps toward the ring where the Fort Meade champ was parading around the ropes with his hands held aloft. As the crowd hushed, Dolan looked up at the winner and asked, "When's the main fight?"

Waters and the other veterans turned, surprised to hear Dolan, the quiet one, taunting the Army champ. They were even more astonished when Dolan climbed into the ring and removed his shirt.

The Army boxer spat at the canvas and rubbed his spittle into the mat with his heel. "Yeah, I heard about you. The mick who won't fight. You gonna throw punches or try to choke me to death?"

Dolan didn't take the bait. Waters and the vets came back to life, appreciative of the sacrifice that Dolan was willing to make to defend their honor.

Glassford questioned the wisdom of allowing the late change to the card. But seeing the BEF veterans clamoring for the challenge, he finally agreed to it. "Same rules, men? Winner takes twenty-five bucks?"

"No."

The crowd, confused, leaned forward to hear what Dolan wanted.

The Army champ laughed at him. "You giving up before we even start?"

"If I win," Dolan said, "we get Army cots."

The Fort Meade fighter looked over at his commanding officer in the VIP section. The officer nodded.

When the fighters were gloved up and ready, Glassford signaled for the bell to start the first round. The Army man charged before Dolan could even get his hands up, hammering him with shots to the head and body.

"Make kidney pie outa him, Mick!" Ozzie shouted.

Despite the raucous cheering from the BEF side, the Army champ shoved Dolan around the ring like a slab of hanging beef. Dolan tried to take the offensive, but he couldn't get inside the man's reach, where his massive hands could do their damage.

In the stands, Hruska turned away, unable to watch. "Let's get out of here."

Ozzie couldn't believe his ears. "But it just started, Billy."

"I need air. And a smoke."

"Where you gonna find a smoke?"

"I got a pack hidden down at camp."

Ozzie didn't want to break away from the fight, but he hadn't enjoyed a cigarette in a week. He figured he could hightail it down across the bridge, light up for a couple of minutes, and be back in time for Mickey to finish the guy off. "All right, but I get one tonight, and one for my stash."

Hruska, green in the gills, nodded. While the fans pounded their feet and shouted at the mayhem in the ring, he and Ozzie hurried up the steps and made fast for the turnstiles abandoned by the ticket collectors.

"You feeling all right, Billy?"

Hruska held his stomach. "Beer skunked."

"You think old man Griffith is pawning off some of his spoilage on us?"

"He is businessman. All crooks."

Ozzie started hoofing it over toward New Jersey Avenue, the main drag back toward the Capitol and Anacostia beyond it to the south. But he saw Hruska angle off toward a side street, taking a short cut. "Billy, you know Glassford's orders! We gotta walk New Jersey back to the camp."

Hruska was looking for a spot to vomit. "I am American. I can walk where I wish, like everyone else." He hurried off and disappeared around a corner.

"Hold on. I'm coming." Ozzie stopped a moment, distracted by a distant grind of metal against metal to the north. Where had he heard that sound before? Wait, yeah, it sounded a lot like the rolling teethed tracks on those Renault tanks that the French used during the war. He drove a finger into his ear, trying to chase the hallucination. Damn crazy what hunger could do to a man. If he didn't get some grub soon, he'd likely soon be hearing the pings from French Lebels and Hun pleas to surrender. He ran to catch up and find Hruska. "Don't spill your guts, Billy! You'll be twice as hungry. You better keep it down and—"

Turning the corner, he saw two white men in dark suits and fedoras pulled down over their faces. They had Hruska braced up against a brick wall. Hruska looked at him with a silent plea for help.

"You with this Red, nigger?"

Ozzie fought the urge to run. "He's no Communist, sir. Billy here's with us down at the camp."

"He doesn't seem to have the stomach for boxing, now does he?" One of the thugs drove a fist into Hruska's gut, causing him to puke blood. "How about that? He looks pretty damn Red to me."

The second tough took a step toward Ozzie. "You one of Pace's spies?"

"No sir."

"A lot of you colored boys seem to be taking a shining to Pace."

"We ain't got nothin' to do with that man, sir."

"No? We've been noticing how you spend a lot of time chewing the fat with this Russkie here."

"He's a vet. One of us."

"We're thinking more like he was sent over the tundra to train Weasel rats. We're going to beat some more of that vodka twang out of him to make sure."

Ozzie tried to quell his shaking. He hadn't been so scared since the first time he went over the top with Big Jim and the *poilus* in France. He could hear Big Jim whispering into his ear: *You didn't beat the Boche just to stand down to a bunch of head crackers in your own country.* He braced his shoulders and said in the firmest voice he could manage, "Let that man go. He earned the right to walk these streets."

The two thugs laughed, and the taller one came hovering over him like the Devil's shadow. "Those Frogs put some crazy ideas in that nappy head of yours over in France, didn't they, nigger? You better get something straight. You and your kind need to reacquaint yourselves with the laws of the United States."

Ozzie refused to back down. "I took down a dozen Hun bigger than you. I can do it again, if I have to."

The brute stared at him, debating how far the Negro veteran would go to defend his friend. He turned and threw another punch into Hruska's ribs. "This is your lucky night. We're gonna let you two tramps go on down to the river, free of charge. But if you or your Bolshevik comrade here breathe a word of this little encounter to Glassford, we know where to find your shack."

The other thug grinned more threat at Ozzie. "That Anacostia dump is a dangerous fire hazard. Somebody really needs to do something about it before an accident happens."

The taller attacker threw Hruska to the ground and whispered a warning to Ozzie as he walked past. "Take a message back to that stuttering toothpick. Tell Waters to get the hell out of this city before he can't talk at all."

As Ozzie helped Hruska stagger away, he heard a roar from the BEF section of the stadium.

58

WASHINGTON, D.C.
JUNE 14, 1932

Joe Angelo hurried up the Capitol steps, bound and determined not to miss the historic event that he and his fellow BEF marchers had fought so hard to make happen: Speaker Garner was finally bringing the Bonus bill up for a full vote on the House floor.

That morning, the city's residents were more nervous than usual, fearful of what might happen if the tally went against the veterans. Although Waters had ordered the men to stay out of the House galleries to avoid the appearance that they were trying to pressure the congressmen, word had spread across the camps that several hundred of the fellows were going up there anyway.

With Charlie Lincoln trailing behind him, Angelo weaved through the crowded rotunda. Having learned the his way around the Capitol during his testimony a year ago, he led his buddy past two stairways lined with spectators waiting for a chance to find a seat. They slithered into an empty corridor that looked as if it hadn't been used since George Washington cut the cherry tree down and, after navigating a maze of corners, came to an elevator marked with a lacquered sign that warned *Members Only*.

Angelo pressed the button.

"Joey, what are you doing?"

"Stand up straight and act like you own the place."

"But I don't own the place. And neither do you."

"If this vote goes right, we'll both have a mortgage on it." As the elevator groaned toward them from the floor above, Angelo checked the ashtray for salvageable cigarette butts. "We paid taxes to build this Taj Mahal. For the people and by the people. That's what the document said, last time I read it."

"Dubya will throw a fit if he finds out we didn't stay in camp."

Angelo paced in front of the doors, impatient for the elevator cab to arrive. "Sometimes Dubya walks around with that Oregon noggin of his up his Oregon ass. I'm an old hand at this congressional game. I ever tell you how I testified to a standing ovation?"

"Only about a thousand times."

"Those polecats nearly climbed over the hearing bench to shake my hand."

"If you were such a great lobbyist, how come we don't have the Bonus?"

Angelo conked him up the side of the head. "Take off that stovepipe! You don't wear a hat in the halls of Congress. Were you raised in a barn?"

The elevator cab thumped to a halt, and the doors opened. Inside, a young page in a suit and tie stared wide-eyed at the two veterans. He tried to push the button to shut the entry grille, but Angelo thrust his forearm into the breach and ambled into the cabin, motioning Lincoln to follow him.

"This is for congressmen only," the frightened page squeaked.

"You forget something, sonny?"

The page didn't have a clue what Angelo was talking about.

"For starters, you can call me 'sir.' Angelo thrust out his chest for the boy's inspection. "You know what this is? The Distinguished Service Cross. I dragged a colonel's bloody ass halfway across France to earn this." He slipped the metal over. "Says here in the fine print that, as a reward, I and a guest of my choosing are entitled to ride any elevator in the United States free of charge."

"I'll get fired."

Angelo hit the lever to take them skyward. "Then you'll be in the same boat with us."

The page kept his distance from the two veterans. "Which floor... sirs?"

"Take us up to that big room where those roosters are debating the Bonus."

"You mean the House chamber?"

"Yeah. That'll do."

The page fingered the lever nervously.

"Whatdya hear?" Angelo asked him.

"Hear?"

"About the vote. You've been driving these politicians up and down this shaft all day. You get the gossip. What are the chances we get our money?"

The page stole a begging glance up at the revolving floor numbers. "It's going to be close. But even if it wins the House, the Senate has to pass it, too."

Lincoln inspected his blurred reflection in the brass panel to smooth out his greased hair. Thumping the top of his stovepipe with an anxious thrum, he asked the page, "Whose bread needs to be buttered?"

"Well, Representative Vinson is for you. And Patman, of course."

"Vinson's that Kentucky colonel, right?" Angelo said. "We seen him out at the camp. Good man. I like the cut of his gibe."

"You mean jib," the boy said.

Angelo didn't take kindly to having his diction corrected. "I meant what I said, you snot-nosed tadpole!"

"He's right, Joey. It's jib."

"Hell, I heard the old fart tell a joke down at the flats one day that nearly had everyone flapping in the mud. I said 'gibe,' and I meant 'gibe'!"

"Calm down, Joey," Lincoln pleaded. "It's no big deal."

Angelo bent back the curling lapels on his frayed jacket. "Sorry, Emancipator. This vote's got me a little on the knife's edge."

"We're all walking the tightrope. No need to apologize."

The page leaned in toward the two veterans and whispered a secret. "The President's people have been up here trying to strong-arm the Republicans to vote against your bill. Frear and Crisp are talking it down hard."

Angelo turned crimson. "Any of those birds gonna champion our cause?"

"Congressman Eslick."

Angelo nodded. "You may have a future in politics, sonny." He confided to Lincoln, "Dubya didn't have Eslick on our racing form. That's one more for us in the plus column."

"I just took Mr. Eslick and his wife up ten minutes ago," the page said.

"How'd he look?" Angelo asked. "Ready for a fight?"

"He was complaining of indigestion. The missus was lecturing him on eating that extra helping of grits this morning."

Angelo held is stomach in mock agony. "Oh, Charlie, the poor congressman had to force down a second serving of grits. The misery of it all!"

Lincoln felt his own protruding ribs. "I'd like to see him try some mulligan stew once a day for a month. See how *that* helps his digestion."

"Yeah, he probably bit into some spoilt Tennessee ham."

The elevator thudded to a stop, and the page cranked the door open. "Good luck, sirs."

Walking out, Angelo stole a glance over his shoulder and noticed the page waiting, holding the door open. He prodded Lincoln with an elbow. "Where's your manners? Tip the lad."

Lincoln stared at Angelo as if he had gone over the bend. "You know we don't have a nickel between us."

Huffing at Lincoln's cheapness, Angelo palmed the boy's hand. The page looked down at his fingers, expecting to find a coin. Instead, he stood staring at his empty digits.

Angelo patted him on the head. "You're one lucky sonofagun, sonny. Now you can tell everyone you touched the hand of a decorated veteran."

The two veterans bulled their way through the second-floor throngs and descended into the packed gallery balcony overlooking the House chamber, where the debate on the bill was already in progress. Nodding to several BEF comrades who had gotten there early for seats, Angelo scanned the front row and saw a mother and her daughter, both in tall feather hats, fanning their rouged cheeks. Winking at Lincoln, he kneed his way down the row until he came to the women. "Sorry, ladies. I'm afraid you'll have to move."

The mother looked up at him and squinched her nose in disgust. "What is that horrid odor?"

"Must be that joint balm you rub on those bony knees of yours. That stuff would gag a dead buffalo."

The lady was outraged. "The nerve! Where is the attendant?"

"Oh, he sent me over. There've been a hell of a lot of complaints about your two's Egyptian turbans blocking the view."

"Turbans?"

Angelo brushed aside the feathers on the ladies' hats. "You'll have to move to the back row."

"How dare—"

Angelo put a finger to his lips in a signal for her to pipe down. He angled her attention toward several congressmen on the floor who were staring up at the commotion. "You'd better move before your names get in the papers."

Petrified at the prospect of being called out in the society pages, the two ladies stood and hurried for the exit. Angelo and Lincoln took their seats at the railing, bowing to the applause of their fellow BEF members.

On the floor, Charles Crisp of Georgia, who had inherited his theatrical way of speaking from his British-actor grandparents, was at the podium railing against the Bonus as a handout. "If we give in to this attempt at extortion, the masses of the American people will have to pay the bill!"

The BEF men in the galleries booed the Republican congressman. Angelo rained down insults on him. "I'll tell you who paid the bill! Those boys serving as fertilizer for the poppies in France, that's who!"

Republican John Nelson of Maine stood to deny those charges. "We are at the crucial period of an economic depression without parallel! Without precedent in the history of this country! For six months we have labored here to put forces at work to arrest deflation! The money necessary to pay this Bonus means the wrecking of all the good we have done. It is the road to ruin. This is our zero hour!"

Dozens of his fellow GOP congressmen erupted with cheers.

"What's happening?" asked Lincoln, trying to see over the railing.

Angelo angled over the banister. "That chattering chipmunk Fish is taking the floor now."

"Hell, that rich bastard will take anything he can get his hands on."

Republican Hamilton Fish of New York sneered up at the veterans in the galleries. "I will not be intimated by a mob!"

"No!" charged a Democrat from across the aisle. "But you'll be intimidated by the Fords and Mellons and their lucre!"

Charles Martin of Oregon, a retired major general, surged to his feet to agree with Fish. "Veterans don't have a right to hold the government hostage!"

Thomas Blanton, one of Wright Patman's Democratic colleagues from Texas, refused to let that insult pass. "Those men up there have the same right to come here as the lobbyists in their silk-hats and velvet spats! General Martin and General Harbord criticize these hungry veterans who carried that flag yonder to victory in France. It is hard for these generals to take orders instead of give them!"

"Damn right!" Angelo shouted.

"Point of order!" bellowed several congressmen. "Point of order!"

Rep. Blanton refused to yield the floor. "These soldiers have as much right to stay here as the generals! As much a right as any rich, pot-bellied lobbyist! They went through hell during the war. I say for them to stay here as long as they damn please!"

"The President will veto this travesty!"

"Then let him reap the shame!"

The galleries hushed as Rep. Edward Eslick, a Democrat and long a supporter of the veterans, walked slowly to the podium.

"Here comes the thunder," Angelo whispered.

Lincoln wiped the sweat from his brow. "Damn, it's hot in here."

"And it's about to get hotter." Angelo bumped Lincoln's elbow to draw his attention to a lady sitting a few seats away. "That's his wife, Willa. I saw her helping out at the soup line."

"Good for her. She came to see his big moment."

Angelo clapped wildly for their champion. "Some of the Tennessee boys in camp have been calling him Davy Crockett, seeing how he's been taking up for the common man and all. I'd put down a wager that if Eslick pulls this off, there'll be some talk of him running for president."

"He cuts a fine figure. If he does make a bid for the White House, I wouldn't at all be surprised if he asks me to campaign with him, being Old Abe's sixth cousin and all."

"I'm sure you can count on a Cabinet post. Probably Secretary of Bullshit."

"Put a cork in it. I want to hear what he has to say."

Eslick gripped the podium, his face so gaunt and pale with rage at the slanderers of his beloved veterans that he looked about ready to snap his suspenders at the clips. He looked up at BEF men, and his genteel Tennessee twang boomed across the chamber with a funereal resonance. "Uncle Sam, the richest government in the world, gave sixty dollars and an IOU that will pay you twenty-seven years after the armistice! But Mr. Chairman, I want to divert you from the sordid! We hear nothing but dollars here! I want to go from the sordid side—"

The congressman staggered and fell.

Several of his colleagues ran up to the podium and tried to revive him. Gasping, his wife, Willa, hurried from the galleries, nearly stumbling down the stairs. Her husband's limp body was carried to the lobby, and she knelt at his side while the House physician worked feverishly over him. After several minutes of frantic exertion, the physician stopped his ministrations and shook his head.

The widow's shriek of despair chilled the packed galleries.

Rep. Patman returned to the floor. With voice cracking, he announced to the gallery spectators, "My good friend—*our* good friend—is dead!"

The next day, while most of Washington remained riveted on the Bonus debate that had resumed in the House, Floyd Gibbons walked past the rows of white military headstones in Arlington National Cemetery. The grounds were nearly deserted that afternoon. From his high vantage, he looked out over the city and marveled at how much it had changed since he was a boy. The swampy marshes south of the Washington Monument had been drained, and an open parkland, bordered now by new federal edifices, was being created atop the reclaimed mosquito haunt. On Pennsylvania Avenue, the main artery, many of the old historic hotels and pubs had been razed to make way for new office buildings. Where General Grant had once checked in unrecognized to the musky Willard Hotel, a new twelve-story Beaux Arts monstrosity was rising in its place.

He was grateful, at least, that this cemetery remained the same, except for the number of headstones. Many of his dead AEF friends were still buried in France, so this was as close as he could get to them now. Whenever he returned to Washington, he made it a point to make a pilgrimage out here to the Tomb of the Unknown Soldier.

Oddly, what he remembered most about that chilly November day in 1921, when the remains of that chosen anonymous doughboy had been brought back and interred in that marble sarcophagus, was not the pomp of the solemn parade behind the caisson with President Harding marching alongside Black Jack Pershing. No, it was the thousands of American soldiers, commissioned and discharged, who had lined the Capitol to escort the casket from its temporary place of honor.

The country had never suffered a military coup. But he remembered thinking that day how easy it would be for the regular troops posted around the city to storm the Capitol. The ancient Romans, constantly on guard against the volatile fusing of political and military power, had forbidden their legions from entering Rome on penalty of death. When the Unknown Soldier Tomb was sealed on that morning eleven years ago, these rolling greens of Robert E. Lee's old home had been filled with thousands of former doughboys, their backs bent and their hats doffed in respect. He had never seen so many American veterans in the nation's capital.

Until this summer.

As he climbed the summit toward the Tomb, he recognized a veteran from the Anacostia camp kneeling alone in front of it. The man's face was contorted in grief. He stood back to respect the veteran's privacy until, after nearly a minute of this agonizing prostration, the man stood up with a wilted lilac in his hands and made a move to lay the remembrance on the lid of the Tomb.

The guard snapped his bayoneted rifle to attention in a warning for the veteran not to come closer. Startled, the veteran hesitated, as if debating whether to defy the challenge. Finally, he thought better of pushing the confrontation, and walked away, aimlessly tossing the lilac onto a hilly knoll where no graves existed.

Gibbons knew at once what had happened. He rushed down the hill to catch up with the veteran who had been turned away. Out of breath, he finally reached him and grasped his arm to delay him.

The veteran turned with fists clenched, ready for a fight. His face, screwed in anger and pain, melted into surprise. "Mr. Gibbons."

"You're that Irish boxer. The one who fought the Fort Meade champ the other night at Griffith."

Mickey Dolan, the tough enforcer for the BEF military police, dropped his moist eyes toward the ground. "If you bet on me, that's your mistake."

"You put up a hell of a battle. Damn fine effort."

"I lost."

"Not the way I saw it. Your buddies down at Anacostia had a little more spring in their step after you drew blood." When the vet still wouldn't look at him straight, Gibbons pressed him by sharing a suspicion. "I've covered more than my share of matches over the years. I know when a fighter is pulling his punches. You weren't all in on that match. How come?"

Dolan looked angry enough to go all in on him right there. "I don't want to be in one of your radio stories."

Gibbons noticed that Dolan's attention kept trailing back to the Tomb. "You didn't come to Washington for the Bonus, did you?"

"I'm done talking."

"You'd be up at the Capitol right now if that was the reason." When the vet wouldn't deny that charge, Gibbons pulled out his silver flask, took a swig, and offered it.

Dolan looked around, revolted by the sacrilege.

"We're Irish. This is Kilkenny holy water. You and I have earned the right to have a drink with these boys under sod here."

Dolan finally relented and downed a swig to toast his fallen comrades.

"What unit were you in?"

"Rainbow Division."

"One of Mac's boys. You took some hell on the Meuse."

Dolan accepted another hit from the flask.

"You know," Gibbons said, "I visit that Tomb every time I'm in town. You'll think I'm crazy, but ever since the war, I keep having these nightmares. That day I was shot at Belleau, I fell next to a leatherneck boy who'd been hit bad in the chest. He kept groaning and trying to roll on his back. Thing was, he was still wearing his knapsack. Every time he moved, the Germans would spray us with bullets. I think he knew he was going to die, but he kept trying to shield me."

A shouted command above them was followed by the blast of the rifle salute, confirming the changing of the honor guard at the Tomb.

Gibbons forced down the lump in his throat. "The ghost of that leatherneck keeps coming to me at night.... I can't shake the feeling that he's the one buried in that Tomb."

For the first time, Dolan looked up at him. "Where did they…" He couldn't finish the question.

"Find the body?"

Dolan nodded.

"In 1921, the War Department ordered the Quartermaster Corps to exhume four corpses from the American cemeteries at Aisne-Marne, the Somme, St. Mihiel, and—"

"The Meuse-Argonne?" Dolan said, hopefully.

Gibbons confirmed that the place where Dolan had lost his friend was one of the chosen locations. "All four were inspected for combat wounds. When no evidence of identity was found, they were placed in identical caskets and taken to Châlons-sur-Marne. On the morning before the final choice was made, the caskets were rearranged on the shipping cases to insure anonymity. A sergeant from the Fiftieth Infantry was designated to make the selection."

"How long did it take him?"

"I was told the sergeant walked around the caskets several times before placing a spray of roses on one of the caskets."

Dolan kept looking over his shoulder at the hill behind them. "My buddy's in that Tomb. I know he is."

Gibbons adjusted the patch over his missing eye, sensing phantom tears. "You know what Chesterton said about us?"

"Can't say I've ever met the fella."

"'We Gaels are men that God made mad. For all our wars are merry, and all our songs are sad.'" Gibbons allowed the silence to grow, then confided to Dolan, "My grandpap in Ireland once told me of an old ritual that his fore-fathers performed when their comrades-in-arms were buried. One of them would be designated the sin-eater."

"Sin-eater?"

Gibbons put his hand over his heart to confirm the truth of it. "They didn't have a potato among them to share, so they changed the honorary role to sin-drinker. They would beg the local barkeep for a pint of ale, and after recounting the various sins of the deceased over the coffin, the chosen martyr would drink down those sins, taking them into his flesh and absolve the departing soul from their punishment." He grasped the veteran's chiseled biceps to drive home his point. "What say you and I put our comrades to rest, Mickey Dolan. Will you drink down their sins with me?"

Dolan accepted the flask again and sent the scotch burning down his throat. He returned the flask and cried out in pain, *"Faugh a Ballagh!"*

Gibbons joined him in repeating the old war call in the language of their eternal enemies, the English. "Clear the way!"

Dolan licked whisky and salty tears from his lips. "Who's going to drink our sins when *we're* gone?"

Gibbons raised the flask in a silent pact to perform the task for each other. "I'm warning you, Dolan. You'd better start stocking up the stout. Considering the trail of depravity I've left behind, you'll be getting the worst of the bargain."

T here was an hour of daylight left, and Anna, weary from the long day at the camp's medical clinic, decided to climb the heights overlooking the Anacostia River to enjoy a moment alone in one of her favorite spots. To catch up on her reading or just sit with her thoughts, she often retreated to this secluded corner of the old Congressional Cemetery that sat nestled under weeping willows. The encampment across the water was now tranquil; most of the veterans had walked to Union Station to pay their final respects to Rep. Eslick as his coffin was escorted to a waiting train.

She feared this was merely the calm before the storm. The House, shaken by the congressman's death during his fervent plea for the Bonus, had passed the bill by a vote of 211 to 176. But the Senate vote, scheduled in three days, promised to be more difficult. If the senators denied the veterans and their families the only hope they still held, she didn't want to think about what might happen.

She brushed aside a few branches and walked down the bucolic path. Turning a corner to the open vantage, she came upon Glassford sitting on a stool in front of a canvas hoisted on an easel. He was painting a panorama of the river. She didn't know what disconcerted her more: that she had intruded upon his private moment, or that he had stolen her favorite retreat.

Hearing her footsteps crackle the leaves, Glassford looked over his shoulder and grinned at seeing her—and finding her so discomfited. "I could put you in the picture. But I don't know if I brought enough red pigment to do your blush justice."

Refusing to be chased from *her* spot, Anna examined what he had stroked on the canvas so far. "I thought you took pride in realism."

"I do."

"You've failed to include the drawbridge and all the cops you've stationed on the perimeters to guard them."

Glassford let her taunt pass. He stood and offered her the stool. When she accepted and sat down, he found a loose tree stump and pulled it over to the easel for a new seat. "Have I poached your hideout?"

"You have, but then most of this city now seems to be under martial law."

"I take it you don't approve of the way I've been handling the situation?"

"Could you do something about the noise at night?"

"Noise?"

"I keep hearing the rumbling of tanks."

He laughed to dismiss such an absurd worry. "Let me know when you start hearing howitzers. Have you always suffered from nightmares?"

"Only the real ones."

He lost his grin. "What are you suggesting, exactly?"

She deflected the question. "How's your reading going?"

"That last book you loaned me, the one about the meat-packing industry. That one set me off my lunch for a week."

"Sinclair … He can do that to you."

"You got anything in that library down there a little merrier?"

"We received a box of donations in this morning. As I recall, there was one volume that might do you some good."

He dipped his brush in the blue oils and stroked the sky on the canvass. "What is it?"

"A story about ancient Greece. It's called the *Anabasis*. Written by a soldier."

"Give me the synopsis."

"The author, Xenophon, volunteered to go overseas with an army of poor Greeks. They were hired to fight another king's war."

"I don't remember encountering that book at the Academy."

"I doubt the Army teaches it."

"Why?"

"The Greek soldiers find themselves abandoned in a strange land. They have to find their way home before they starve. Along the way, nobody cares about their survival."

"And why is that?"

"They're no longer useful to anyone."

Taking her inference, he dropped his brush to the palette. "Look, I've got everybody from the President down to the newspaper delivery boy telling me what a lousy job I'm doing. I don't need to hear it from you, too."

"The donations are drying up."

He kicked at the ground in anger. "You think I don't know that?"

"Do you have plans to use force against these men and their families?"

He acted stunned by her temerity. "Off the record?" When she nodded, he confided, "That all depends."

"On what?"

"If they turn violent."

She kept him pinned with a knowing glare. "You are playing these men like chess pieces, manipulating their every move. You think I don't see it?"

"You call it manipulation. Others would call it leadership."

"Did it ever occur to you that *you* might be the one being played?"

"What are you talking about?"

"You're not a politician. Everyone can see that, Chief Glassford."

"If you're going to cut me down to size, you might as well enjoy the irony in the exercise. Call me Happy."

"I'm not cutting you down to size. I'm trying to get you to open your eyes. Those politicians in the White House are ruthless. They don't care about these veterans. All they care about is their own careers and fortunes."

"They're good men, Anna. I've known most of them since West Point."

She scooted her stool closer to demand his full attention. "These veterans haven't done anything to suggest they want violence."

"No, but they need to go home. I've got the Administration riding me day and night on this. Between you and me, I may not be long for this job. I wake up every morning expecting to find a termination order slid under my door. If the commissioners replace me with someone from the old guard, you'll remember me as a pacifist."

"The veterans and their families will go home when they get the money due them," she said.

"And if the vote in the Senate goes the other way?"

She looked out across the camp, preferring not to think of that possibility. "Why aren't you home tonight with your wife?"

Stunned by her intrusion into his private life, he snapped back at her. "Why aren't you back in Indiana on a farm with a husband?"

She hadn't expected such a sharp riposte, but she had opened herself to it. "I see your surveillance extends beyond the District borders."

"Better be careful with all that talk about sharing resources with the poor."

"I was taught those values as a child. It tells a lot about where this country is going when a Mennonite can be mistaken for a Communist."

"I wasn't suggesting that." He tapped his brush aimlessly against the easel in troubled debate. Finally, he admitted, "Being married to a soldier returned from a war is no picnic. I haven't been much of a husband since coming home from France. Something changed over there. I've never quite been able to put my finger on it. I can't shake this restlessness."

"What's your wife's name?"

"Cora."

"Do you still love her?"

Glassford didn't answer her. After several moments passed, he asked, "Do you think one kind of love"—he hesitated, for what he was thinking was not easy to articulate—"can drive out another love, one less intense?"

She understood at once what he meant. But she had buried that wound long ago, and didn't want to reopen it.

"Those boys in France," he said. "The ones you held hands with while they died. The ones you watched being cut open. Did your love for them overwhelm all other loves?"

She closed her eyes, trying to chase the memories. "I should go."

She stood and was about to leave when she saw him slump over his knees, silently sobbing in pain. She was taken aback. This sudden rush of emotion was so uncharacteristic of him. Had she misjudged him all along, thinking him just one of the many military men in this town who had been turned to stone? As she watched him break down, ashamed and seemingly burdened by cares that she did not comprehend, she realized that he was not like the other cops and military officers. His was the soul of an artist trapped in a uniform. She reached to comfort him, but then, remembering that he was married, thought it best not to make the attempt, and hurried away.

59

WASHINGTON, D.C.
JUNE 17, 1932

Glassford countersteered Blue Bessie down First Street on his morning inspection of the Capitol grounds. He rode past the Supreme Court building and turned left on Constitution Avenue, which, after three straight days of thunderstorms, was now a river of cascading rainwater. Puffing cheerfully on his pipe, he waved to the worried Hill staffers who were sloshing hurriedly to their offices while trying their best to avoid a confrontation with the five thousand veterans who had converged at dawn on the puddle-slicked Capitol steps.

He tried to put on a confident front, but he knew he wasn't fooling anyone. He hadn't slept for two nights, and the deep lines in his face betrayed the tension of a city trapped in the last days of a long and bitter siege. He figured the president hadn't gotten much sleep, either, and for good reason. By now, the senators had boarded their wicker monorail coaches in the tunnel leading from their offices across the street, and within minutes they would be voting on the Bonus. If they failed to follow the House's example and pass the bill, all hell could break lose. It was Friday, the day of the week when distasteful congressional business was always scheduled so that the rats could scamper out of the city before the papers carried the bad news the next morning.

And he would be left to deal with the consequences.

He never gave much credence to omens, but in times past, the sacrifices would have been doubled in the temples to expiate such a pervasive sense of doom. The camp at Anacostia was now a quagmire of misery and pestilence, and the soaked BEF men, irritable and hungry, scrapped more frequently with Pace's Communists. Several of the veterans had contracted pneumonia, and those who could still walk up from the river flats were in a sullen, rancorous mood, chafed at having been forced to wait so long for Congress to act. The fatalists among them saw Rep. Eslick's death in the midst of his plea for the

Bonus as evidence that even God had turned against them. Others walked the streets like Old Testament prophets, reminding citizens that five congressmen in this session had died in retribution for their hardened hearts. The night before last, the BEF had suffered its first casualty when a Kentucky veteran, worked up about the Senate vote, had dropped dead from a heart attack. And there was his own personal loss, one that struck him hard: Scrapper had never been found.

The entire city, demoralized and rancid from the rains, seemed on the verge of sinking into the Slough of Despond.

As he turned back up Pennsylvania Avenue toward the rotunda, he stole a glance over his shoulder to make sure the officers he had stationed around the Capitol were carrying out his order that only two of them be seen together. More and more these days, he had been watching his back for an attack. The worst of the threats now came not from the veterans, but from those meddling saber rattlers in the Administration. The streets were rife with rumors that the Army was practicing riot maneuvers on Long Island. Intelligence like that never leaked out casually, he knew. Someone at Fort Myer had planted the leak with the veterans to serve as a veiled threat.

A week ago, when he had proposed that Congress follow the example of ancient Rome and give state and federal land to the veterans to farm, Vice-President Charles Curtis and the District commissioners had ordered him, on threat of termination, to abstain from making any more recommendations about policy. Just that morning, Waters and the other BEF officers had complained to him that undercover government agents had taken some of their veterans out of Anacostia to get them drunk and foment dissension. He had seen the same subversive tactics used in Germany. This was all the handiwork of seasoned operatives. He knew, because he had been the victim of it himself. More than once he had thought about submitting his resignation and heading back West, where the only assholes he'd have to deal with dragged tails behind them. But he couldn't abandon these men, not after the country had forsaken them.

He circled around the north wing of the Capitol and made a quick estimate of the number of veterans who had come up from Anacostia within the last hour. Several were giving rousing speeches on the west steps, and others had found spaces inside on the marble floor of the rotunda to sleep. Strange, he thought. Not many more had moved up here from the flats. The plan he had approved called for Waters to bring up all of his veterans before noon, keeping them in ranks by regiments and companies. That way they would be in one place, where he could keep watch over them. He had also allowed a field kitchen be set up beyond the plaza, and dozens of the veterans were now lining up for a breakfast serving of stew and donated bread.

On the Capitol lawn, a couple of news photographers snapped away at some veterans wolfing down the gruel, pestering them to lay on the wet ground and exaggerate their misery to enhance the poignancy of the shots. Outraged, he gunned the cycle toward this flock of clicking geese and sent the news culprits scattering.

"What the hell?" cried one of the photographers sprawled across the mud. "You trying to kill us, Chief?"

"Now you know what it feels like to be down there with them."

"We're just getting a story."

"By forcing those men to suffer more indignities?"

"Now hold on there. You feed the Reds but then you rough up hardworking journalists?"

"The only hard work I've ever see you do, Hanson, is lifting those heavy shot glasses down at Hannity's. You keep your distance from these veterans. I'll haul you in if I see you agitating them again."

"Biting the hand that feeds you," remarked a female voice behind him. "Not a good career move, antagonizing the press."

He turned to find Anna helping the hassled old veteran to his feet.

The downed veteran wiped the mud from his pant cuffs and nodded to her appreciatively. "Now don't go too hard on the General there, Miss Anna. He's got a lot on his shoulders these days."

Anna studied Glassford, still concerned about his emotional collapse last evening on the bluffs. She softened her usual stern manner with the police chief and, in almost an affectionate tone, assured the veteran whom she had just lifted to his feet, "The Chief gets three square meals a day. He should be able to handle a little Washington heat."

Glassford was in no mood for another round of criticism from the Avenging Angel of Mercy, even if this time it came coated in sugar. He asked her, "Come up to watch the show, did you?"

"How long is it scheduled to be in town? Maybe I'll just wait and catch the performance next year." She saw that he had taken her verbal jab with less humor than usual. "Is something wrong?"

Glassford checked his watch, knowing the Senate vote could come at any moment. "How come there aren't more men up here from the camps?"

Anna shook her head, exasperated. "First you scheme to keep them away from here. Now you want them around. Maybe they're just confused."

"You don't find it odd that thirteen thousand men whose lives depend on what happens this morning aren't gathering to rally for the vote?"

"Most of them too hungry to make it up here. You try climbing this hill from that camp on an empty stomach."

Glassford searched the mass of veterans crowded on the Capitol steps. "Have you seen Waters?"

"He's in the Senate cloakroom with Angelo. Last I heard, they were trying to buttonhole a few more votes."

Glassford studied one of his officers near the steps, a holdover from the old regime, whom he had assigned to guard the Capitol doors. For the first time since he had taken the chief's job, the disgruntled officer smiled back at him. That cunning glance sent a shiver of foreboding down his spine.

Sensing his distraction, Anna asked him, "You sure you're okay?"

Pale with alarm, Glassford hurried toward the steps to find Waters.

Ducking the rain under his Anacostia tent, Ozzie stretched his arms across his soaked bedding and yawned until his false teeth hurt. "Is it still coming down, Charlie?"

Lincoln lifted the flap, and a wave of water that had collected in the crease of the canvas doused him. "Dammit! I didn't need that, first thing in the morning."

Ozzie stretched his limbs. "What time is it?"

"Let me check my new gold timepiece here." Lincoln pulled out an imaginary pocket watch and flipped it open. "Says half past who gives a damn."

Ozzie jumped to his feet. "We'd better get up to the Capitol. Dubya wants all the regiments mustered by noon."

Lincoln placed his stovepipe hat over his nose to block a leak in the tent. "You think those fat Senate ducks are gonna change their vote just because we show up?"

"We're in an army, in case you forgot."

"I thought in an army, they paid you. You seen a paycheck recently?"

Ozzie staggered. "I'm so dang spent, I can't move my legs."

"We need to get some grub."

"You want breakfast, you'll have to go lobby for it."

Lincoln climbed groaning to his feet. "What are you talking about?"

Ozzie reached to the shelf above his head and checked on his oboe case, making sure it was still watertight. "Glassford moved the field kitchen up to the Hill."

Lincoln plopped back down. "So now I gotta choose between starving or walking to death?"

"No use putting it off. You know what Dubya says. Work if you wanna eat."

"That was James Smith said that. Dubya woulda put a few more stutters in it."

"James Smith. Is he new around here?"

"No, you harebrain. He was that Redcoat homesteader in Jamestown."

Ozzie shrugged, didn't have a clue what Lincoln was babbling about. "Let's go get Billy. He'll carry us over the Jordan waters on his back."

The two veterans staggered out of their tent and looked around the camp. Rubbing the sleep from their eyes, they found the muddy streets deserted. They stumbled past several huts, searching for mates, but everyone was gone. The fog from the night rain was so thick, they couldn't see more than fifty feet around.

Lincoln shouted, "Billy! Where in God's name are you?"

A voice replied from an indeterminate distance. "The river!"

The two vets moved warily toward the heavily accented Lithuanian voice. The fog thinned as they approached the banks of the Anacostia, and they saw thousands of their fellow veterans standing at the bridge, shouting and circling their fists in hot anger.

Lincoln couldn't figure what all the ruckus was about. "Hey, Billy boy!" he shouted at Hruska again. "What's going on over there?"

Hruska elbowed a path back through the raging veterans and pointed his two friends toward the bluffs on the far side of the river. "Cops raise drawbridge! They trap us!"

Lincoln and Ozzie ran along the river trying to find a vantage through the mists. On the far abutment of the drawbridge, they saw Lt. Edwards and Officer Shinault, accompanied by a hundred police officers standing shoulder to shoulder and armed with machine guns. The cops were laughing at the trapped veterans. The river was too deep to ford, and none of them had the strength to swim it.

"We're done for!" cried Ozzie. "Glassford double-crossed us!"

"This ain't Glassford's doing! That bastard Edwards schemed this!"

Ozzie looked around for Alford, who was always put in charge when Waters was preoccupied with negotiations or away from camp. "Where's Georgie?"

Several veterans rolled their eyes, and one observed bitterly, "As usual, no one's seen him."

Edwards shouted at them from across the river. "You boys might as well go back to your beauty sleep! If you get hungry, we'll shoo some carp downstream towards you."

The veterans stood in slumped silence, defeated. Denied in their right to lobby the Senate, several began walking back to their shacks, too humiliated to put up more protest.

Lincoln watched the defections with disbelief. "You birds are deserting?"

One of the retreating men waved him off. "It's no use. We never had a chance."

Lincoln refused to give up. "We're getting over that damn river!"

"Yeah?" scoffed another vet. "You gonna shoot us over in a cannon, Li'l Abe?"

Lincoln paced in an ever-tightening circle, his anger rising with each circuit and his stovepipe hat thrumming on his oversized head. Finally, he halted his agitated perambulation to glare damnation up at Lt. Edwards. With a fierce look of quiet determination, he motioned Ozzie over to him and whispered into his buddy's ear. Ozzie gave his shack mate a look suggesting the onset of insanity, but finally, driven by Lincoln's insistent glare, took off on a run toward the commissary.

Lincoln searched the camp until he found what he sought. He walked over to Sol Berkowitz, one of Pace's agitators who was always spouting the Red propaganda and trying to turn the BEF men to treason. "Hey, Trotsky! Is it true what I heard?"

"What's that?

"Lenin gave you a sickle and hammer up the ass."

Berkowtiz found a club and, eyeing the other veterans, took a step closer in threat. "I thought clowns only had big feet. You got a mouth to match 'em."

Lincoln kept taunting him. "You Communists share everything, don't you? Even hold each other's dicks at the latrine?"

"Why don't come over here and find out."

As the other BEF veterans gathered around to watch the confrontation with the Communist veterans, Lincoln took off his stovepipe and hung it on a post, careful not to get it damaged. "Let's meet halfway."

On the city side of the river, sheltered from the drizzle by the raised arm of the Eleventh Street drawbridge, Lt. Edwards sat on a concrete block enjoying a corned beef sandwich and a beer.

A young cop came running up to him. "Sir, we got a problem."

Edwards mocked the rookie's look of alarm. "What now? Did those pikers down there run out of corn cobs in the outhouses?"

"One of them is hurt pretty bad."

"What the hell are you talking about?"

"He's gushing blood. He got into a fight with Pace's Reds."

Edwards threw what remained of his sandwich to the ground in anger and walked to the edge of the bridge to get a better look at the camp. On the far bank, the BEF veterans were congregated around a man sprawled on a stretcher. The victim's shirt and scalp were drenched bloody. Edwards shouted across the river at the vets, "What the hell is going on over there?"

"We got a man dying here!" Ozzie shouted. "He's losing blood fast."

Edwards was skeptical. "Lift him up! Let me see him."

The veterans raised the stretcher, and Edwards recognized the victim as that ridiculous little Lincoln impersonator the government agents had roughed up on the night of the boxing match. "Have that Red nurse patch him up!"

"She's up on the Hill!" Ozzie shouted. "We ain't got no medics down here! If he dies, it'll be your name with his in the papers! I figure the headline will say something about manslaughter!"

Edwards cursed. He knew there'd be hell to pay with Glassford if he left the codger over there to bleed to death. "I'll send an ambulance over, on one condition! Only the wounded man goes across! Anybody tries any funny business, I'll give orders to shoot!"

Ozzie and the veterans nodded grimly. After a long hesitation, Edwards reluctantly signaled for the bridge to be lowered. When the two ends of the span finally met and locked, a police ambulance rumbled across into the camp. Two cops in the ambulance cab climbed out and lifted Lincoln into the rear of the ambulance. The ambulance splattered mud on the other veterans as it sped back across the bridge.

Edwards and his officers on the far banks watched with their hands on their weapons. When the ambulance was nearly halfway across, the officer smiled and eased his fingers off the trigger. He turned to the young cop who had reported the wounding and dropped a dollar into his hand. "Hightail it over to Magilley's and get us another case of beer. We'll have an Irish wake for the poor bastard. Doesn't look like he's gonna make it."

A couple of minutes later, shouts rang out from the riverbank. Edwards wheeled around and saw thousands of veterans rushing across the bridge behind the ambulance, hurrying to leap the gap before the arm was raised.

Shinault pulled his pistol. "Should we fire on them?"

Edwards couldn't bring himself to issue the order. He stood seething as the veterans poured across the bridge and surged toward the Capitol. Some of the escaping bums stopped the ambulance, hauled out the driver, and jumped inside the cab. At that moment, the lieutenant's lackey chose a bad time to arrive back at the bridge with just a lone bottle of beer in his hands. Edwards looked for the case he had ordered. "You got some change for me, Brister?"

The young cop, reddening with embarrassment, shook his head.

"What the hell happened to the other longnecks?"

"Just as I was coming out of Magilley's, some of those camp fellas stopped in to quench their thirst."

"And?"

"They said to tell you … thanks for the donation."

Edwards slapped the bottle from the rookie's hand, and stormed off.

On the Capitol steps, Glassford turned at a sudden commotion rolling up south Pennsylvania. A police ambulance was speeding toward the plaza from the east, followed by a horde of veterans who were wheezing and clutching their chests from the chase. The staggering BEF men shouted and hurried toward their comrades who had come up to the Capitol at dawn. Behind this invasion came a third wave—a dozen police cars with bubbles flashing. Glassford ran down the steps and fought his way through the throngs to reach the ambulance. He threw open the driver's door and found Hruska behind the wheel. "What the hell's going on here?"

Hruska stepped out. "You tell us, General."

The other veterans converged on the ambulance to find out what was happening. Before Glassford could make sense of the chaos, Lt. Edwards sped up in his police car and leapt out with his pistol drawn. Glassford shouted at his officer, "Holster that weapon!"

"These scofflaws violated a direct order!"

"What order?"

Edwards didn't answer him.

"Somebody better start talking," Glassford warned. "Or there'll be arrests."

Ozzie came huffing up and bent over his knees to catch his breath. "Chief, your cops here double-crossed us. They raised the drawbridge on us to keep us from coming up here and exercising our Constitutional rights."

The veterans in the vanguard on the Hill surrounded Edwards and the arriving cops, glaring threat at them. Calls from their throngs rang out to storm the Capitol building, and the BEF men began looking around for limbs and rocks, anything that could be used for weapons.

Glassford turned on Edwards. "You raised that bridge?"

Edwards set his jaw in defiance. "I used my best judgment. There was a mob preparing to come over that river."

"A mob?"

"I was provided intelligence indicating that some of these men were armed."

"Did you find any weapons?"

Edwards shifted his eyes. "No."

"You will issue an apology to these men."

Paling at that demand, Edwards glanced at his co-conspirators, assessing whether to mutiny against the order. Finding none of them willing to step to his side in protest, he muttered, "I may have misunderstood the situation."

"Report back to headquarters at once," Glassford ordered the officer. "You are relieved of field duty until further notice."

Edwards refused to move.

"Did I not make myself clear, Lieutenant?"

Edwards, sulking, walked a few steps away without answering him.

"Wait! Why are they driving one of our ambulances?"

Edwards turned on him with a sneer. "They've got a wounded man inside. Bloodied up by one of Pace's toughs that you let loose around the city."

Glassford located Anna in the crush of veterans and hurried with her to the ambulance to determine the condition of the wounded man inside. Assisted inside by a couple of the veterans, Anna closed the doors behind her.

Moments later, she stepped out, looking sullen.

"Will he make it?" Glassford asked.

She betrayed not a glint of emotion. "He'll survive ... unless he develops an allergy to chickens and diabetes from high blood sugar."

Glassford and the other cops frowned in confusion.

Anna threw open the ambulance door.

Streaked in what looked like blood, Lincoln popped out. Grinning, he brought his stained shirt to his mouth and licked the blood with his tongue. He waved at Lt. Edwards walking off, and shouted, "Hey, Lieutenant, we're running a little low on ketchup! You think you could roust up another case or two for us? The condiment goes pretty fast in a cockfight!"

The veterans roared with laughter at how the cops had been conned into lowering the bridge. With a great cry of jubilation, they lifted the red-splattered Lincoln on their shoulders and paraded him across the grounds. They sang *Hail, Hail, the Gang's All Here* and thumbed their noses at Lt. Edwards, who was forced to endure the mockery as he stormed off.

That hot afternoon, as the long, tense hours at the Capitol edged toward evening, the BEF veterans—many with no strength left to keep standing—sang songs of courage and gave speeches and prayed to the Christ who had promised the world to the meek. Inside the Senate chamber, the gallery was packed, and the senators droned on about fiscal responsibility and duty to country and burdens on the national treasury. Periodically, a messenger would be sent outside to report to the thousands of waiting BEF men on the progress of the debate, and the shadow-bearded oracles would pronounce their prophecies based on the latest utterance or nuance of rhetoric.

As the scheduled vote approached, the veterans veered from frenzied hope to forlorn despair. On the far side of the city, the White House stood on high alert, guarded by the Army and scores of non-uniformed agents. The newsrooms in the city remained fully staffed, waiting for what many feared would be an uprising should the Bonus go down in defeat. No one could ever remember such a night of fear in the District.

And then, at 9:30 p.m., Waters, looking drawn and shaken, walked through the west doors of the Capitol and came to the top step.

The men hushed.

"Prepare yourselves, men," Waters said. "The Bonus is defeated."

Glassford walked the perimeter listening for clicks of hidden revolvers, for angry words, for the trod of sudden footsteps surging toward the doors. If the vets turned into a mob, his career would be done. By now, the senators would be hurrying back to their offices through the tunnel. He had chosen to keep his officers out of sight to avoid provocation, but the calculated gamble meant that mustering them to fight off a riot might prove too late. He swallowed hard, wondering if he were about to go down in history as the man who had lost the nation's capital to a second revolution. The Great Appeaser, they would call him. The West Pointer who could not control an army of homeless men.

On the steps, he saw Anna trying to console the men, hugging them and begging them to return to the camp. She glanced worriedly at him. Was that terror in her eyes? What was she trying to tell him? Suddenly, a roar of anger shook the Capitol, and the veterans heaved up the steps toward the doors behind Anna, their shouts for revenge rising in vehemence.

Glassford braced for the worst. There was a tipping point in armies, he knew. Once a charge was mounted, individual soldiers moved in unison, trained to react without doubt. He realized, too late, that Pace and his Communists had infiltrated the crowds. The Reds were stoking resentments and whispering calls for violence. He hurried for his radio to send orders to bring up his armed police from their hiding places in the buildings surrounding the plaza. If the veterans moved fast through those doors, his call for reinforcements would be too late. Somehow he had to delay them. Smoke bombs, sirens, anything to confuse them and break the momentum. He pressed the button on his radio.

"Yes, sir," his officer on the other end reported.

Glassford muffled his mouth with his hand. "Bring them—"

Then, something caught his eye. Elsie Robinson, a Hearst columnist who had championed the cause of the veterans in the press, rushed to Waters's side on the Capitol steps. She whispered to the BEF leader.

Waters stood on the top step, looking frozen with indecision.

Anna, positioned near the Oregon veteran, overheard what the reporter had just said to him. She nodded and looked across the grounds at Glassford, as if to communicate a warning to him.

Robinson sang *America*, and Anna joined in.

Glassford was stunned. He knew that singing patriotic songs not only went against Anna's Mennonite faith, it cut against the very core of her antipathy against capitalist propaganda. Why was she doing it?

Waters seemed hypnotized as he looked down at his waiting veterans. Tears began streaming down his cheeks. He began singing with the women.

Blessed by the miraculous intervention, Glassford seized the moment and signaled to the Army band that he had arranged to play that evening. The bandleader, taking his cue, raised his baton to accompany the singing with a rousing brass overture. The soothing anthem transformed the men's rage into a melancholic longing for a better time. One by one, they joined in singing with the band, heaving with sobs and sliding to their haunches, every ounce of their strength drained by the disappointment. Even Hruska, his face still bruised from his beating, sang along.

The final stanza came to a choking finish, and the veterans began drifting off from the Capitol steps to make their way back to the camps. Waters was left standing on the top step, surrounded by Alford and his inner circle. Near him, Angelo aimlessly stroked the Distinguished Service Star on his lapel, as if by rubbing it he might alter the defeat of the vote.

Glassford walked across the lawn and climbed the steps. He put a hand on Waters's shoulder and softly encouraged him, "Let's go home."

Waters seemed unaware that Glassford was standing in front of him. Only when Angelo nudged him did he recover to the present and looked down with bloodshot eyes at Glassford. "What d-d-do we do now, General?"

Glassford clasped his hand to buck him up. "You fought a good battle. Go on down to Anacostia and rest with your troops for the night."

Nodding, Waters limped down steps with Angelo and Alford. Walking off, Alford glanced over his shoulder and shot Glassford an unnerving glare, one that suggested their next visit to these steps might not be so peaceful.

When the last of the straggling veterans had finally dispersed from the Capitol grounds, Glassford dismissed his officers for the night. Taking a seat on the steps near one of the fluted columns, he allowed himself a sigh of exhaustion, and lit up his pipe. From the shadows of the portico, Anna, wrapped in her nurse's cape, came hovering over his shoulder. A gentle rain began to fall again, and she raised her hood. He felt her judging presence behind him. "I'm surprised you knew the words."

"We had to learn them as children."

"But I thought..."

"For survival. My father was always afraid we would be stopped at night in the English towns and be challenged. At the start of the war, some of our people were lynched for not being American enough. Our only way to save ourselves was to sing the songs that the English didn't know themselves. You'd be surprised how many people in this country don't know the lyrics."

"So, I guess it's over for now."

"You really think that?" she asked.

He didn't want to tell her what he really thought. The city—no, the country—had narrowly escaped a close call that night. But another storm, one even more furious, was building over the western horizon. Earlier that morning, he had received a telegraph dispatch from the Los Angeles Police Department warning that a contingent of hard-boiled California veterans was on its way to Washington. And by all reports, this band of rail riders had a different strategy in mind to get their Bonus. Leading these reinforcements was a Hollywood actor named Royal Robertson, a charismatic orator who possessed all the polish and cunning that Waters lacked.

Anybody with a name like Royal, he figured, was likely to be trouble.

No, it was not over.

60

WASHINGTON, D.C.
JUNE 17, 1932

The new kingfish had finally arrived.

Waters hurried with his bodyguards across the Eleventh Street bridge, eager to check out his scout's report that Royal Robertson and his three thousand California veterans were setting up their tents at the Capitol.

Angelo stayed glued to his side. "What if he don't join us, Dubya?"

Waters was starting to feel like the catcher in a high-flying trapeze act, and he didn't like it. The newspapers around the country, always looking to start a fight, were now touting Robertson as the new hope for the veterans. Determined to assert his authority, he had sent several telegrams to Robertson inviting him to join the BEF, but the movie actor had not responded. He wondered what the fellow would look like. Tall and suave like Clark Gable? Or maybe he'd have windswept Irish features and thick wavy hair like Spencer Tracy. Tanned for sure, coming from Los Angeles. He brushed back his blond locks and sucked in his stomach as he strode up Pennsylvania Avenue toward the Capitol terraces. "Don't worry. He'll join us. He d-d-don't have a choice."

"Make him talk first," Alford counseled. "Like kings and queens do."

"Yeah," Angelo said. "He should kiss your ring, Dubya, if you had one."

Waters could hear the doubt in their hollow flattery. During these past three weeks since the Senate defeat of the Bonus, he had managed to hold the BEF together with little more than smoke and mirrors. He had even resigned three times, only to have the men beg him to come back when the camp fell into chaos. He didn't have anything to offer them now except a pledge to hang on and never leave the city until Congress took up the bill again. But they were becoming restless and increasingly disgruntled. He couldn't escape the whispers: That he was incompetent, that he was taking bribes from Hoover, that he was mentally unstable. Even the *BEF News*, the camp's newspaper, had been running editorials calling for his ouster. The mood all across the city was changing, too. Many of the residents, once supportive of their cause, were growing weary of the Hoovervilles and the constant reminders on their back porch of the country's miseries.

Everyone was looking for a new messiah. And all eyes were turning to this man from California with the regal name and Hollywood mystique.

Reaching the Capitol plaza, Waters searched the lawns and found a few pup tents hoisted near the sidewalks, set back far enough from the grass to avoid the sprinklers that the cops had turned on to dissuade stragglers from lingering near the steps. He estimated there couldn't be more than four hundred men scratching around there. Had Robertson taken the rest of his troops down to the White House to confront Hoover directly? These fellas must just be a few of his stragglers, surely, and they were a sad-looking bunch at that. Hell, one of them over there even walked with a peg leg. Every so often, the fellow would find an abandoned cigarette butt, blow the dust from it, and store it in a small compartment just below his knee. He had a regular tobacco store down there. At least he was making the best of his situation.

Next to the peg-legged man stood a bent, walleyed codger with a doughy face the hue of a rotting avocado and a puckered fish mouth. He wore a metal brace that rose high above his neck and was hooked to his chin by a leather strap. He looked like one of those dictionary drawings of a medieval torture victim.

Waters buttonholed him. "Hey, partner, what the hell happened to you?"

"War injury."

Angelo circled the queer-looking gimp. "What'd the Boche do to you? Put a radio antenna in your head and send code signals through your teeth?"

The trussed fellow kept shuffling his feet in percolating silence, picking nervously at his buttons like a chicken at the trough while constantly shrugging in an effort to shift the runners of his apparatus to the meridians that ran down the length of his vertebrae.

"If the government ever d-d-decides to execute you, they won't need a gallows," Waters said. "You can just jump up and d-d-down and hang yourself."

When the laughter finally died down, the braced man took a few pigeon-toed steps closer. Forced to remain humped over, he turned his head sideways to glare up at Waters like a modern Quasimodo. "I heard you mud rats were jokes, but I didn't know you told them, too."

"You might want to change your attitude, pal," Dolan warned. "Or you'll be walking ass-up in that tomato trellis."

Waters signaled for Dolan and the others to cool off. Then, he asked the mouthy newcomer, "You with the California brigade?"

"Who wants to know?"

"Commander Waters, that's who."

The neck-braced man gave Waters another squinting once-over from head to foot. "That explains a lot."

"Such as?"

"For one thing, why you teat calves have been letting that head flatfoot lead you around the barn by the nose for six months."

Angelo came up snorting fire. "I'll straighten that chicken neck for you!"

Waters held Angelo back. "We're all in the same army here."

The trussed man spat a wad of tobacco chaw. "The hell we are."

"Listen up, scarecrow," Waters said. "We'll let you get b-b-back to stewing in your own juices. Just tell us where we can f-f-find Royal Robertson."

The man tried to elevate his curved scoliotic back, but he only managed to loft his head a few inches higher. "You're talking to him."

Amid hoots of disbelief, Waters looked around with dropped jaw at the pitiful gathering behind the California ringleader. "What happened to the three thousand recruits you were s-s-supposed to be bringing?"

"We lost a few along the way."

Before he could question Robertson further, several police cars with sirens blaring sped up to the plaza and stopped. Glassford got out of the lead car and, accompanied by a dozen officers, walked up.

"Hey, General!" Angelo pointed to Robertson. "Look what the sewers washed in. Better let him know if any storms pop up. He's a walking lightning rod."

Glassford offered his hand in welcome. "I'm Chief Glassford."

Robertson refused to shake it. "So, you're the trainer of these monkeys."

Glassford's smile vanished. "You got a problem, mister?"

"Not as long as you stay out of my way."

Glassford refused to take the bait. Instead, he made a suggestion to Waters. "Commander, why don't you take Mr. Robertson and his men down to the camp and get them mustered in. We'll see if we can't get some extra coffee down there."

Waters nearly bit his lip trying to get the invitation out. "You're w-w-welcome to j-j-join us."

Robertson grinned. "You got a catch in your mouth there. Does that happen all the time, or just when a bigger rooster comes in the barn?"

Glassford stared down the angry Anacostia men, forcing them back.

Robertson traded derisive laughs with his California men, his eyes never leaving Glassford. "I think we'll wait a few days before we tour Camp Shithole. Take the bull by the tail up here, look the situation in the face, and plant our flags near the fount of freedom. We didn't come three thousand miles to hold a picnic down by the river. We're here to petition Congress. And the last time I checked, those tootin' birds roost below that dome."

Glassford studied the man who was fast rising on his problem list. "You've got a right to congregate. But the city ordinance bans sleeping within congressional boundaries. If you and your men lie down, you'll be arrested."

"We'll then, we'll just have to keep moving, won't we?"

Angelo guffawed. "How are you gonna manage that?"

Robertson motioned up several news correspondents who had been waiting for interviews. "Stick around and watch."

Floyd Gibbons stepped off the train from New York and hurried past the vaulted arches of Union Station. He had always made it a point to toast Bastille Day with a bowl of *vichyssoise* and an expensive Bordeaux at a venue evocative of Paris, such as the roof restaurant at the Ritz-Carlton. But this year's celebration with his expatriate French friends would have to wait.

Les misérables had thrown up their barricades right here at home.

He had just three hours to file his story with the *Literary Digest*, but if the rumors turned out to be true, he'd have the country extolling him as the new Victor Hugo in the morning's edition. Relying on his silver-capped cane to aid his arthritic knees, he hobbled up the sloping cobblestones of Delaware Avenue and made his way toward the Capitol. The July haze was so sopped with humidity that he was forced periodically to pause and wipe the beads of perspiration collecting under his eye patch.

He reached the Senate Office Building and stopped to catch his breath, only to lose it again in mid-inhale. These grounds of heat-burnt grass between the Capitol steps and First Street were ringed by hundreds of civilian spectators, all hollering and trading wagers as if rooting on their favorite jockey at Belmont Park. He elbowed a path through the cackling onlookers to discover what had captured their attention on such a miserably hot day.

The spectacle would have left even Hugo at a loss for words.

A staggering line of several hundred emaciated veterans snaked around the Capitol in a halting procession of misery and torpor. Driven by the lugubrious beat of a muffled drum, some of the veterans wore bandages on their heads; others held onto the shoulders of the comrades in front of them to avoid collapsing. He recognized a few of the men, having interviewed them in Anacostia, but most of these macabre faces were unfamiliar.

A squat little man in a neck brace marched down their ranks barking orders and threatening them with the humiliation of being dishonorably discharged if they faltered. The loudmouth came hovering over one of his veterans who had fallen to the grass, half asleep. "You come to Washington to sightsee?"

"No, sir," the veteran gasped.

"Then get the hell up!"

"I don't have it in me, Royal."

This slave driver screamed at the poor fellow until he staggered up to his knees. "You can sleep standing up, damn it! Every man keeps moving!"

Gibbons pulled out his notebook and began scribbling fast. If this tyrant in the neck brace had been armed with a whip and his veterans locked in chains, the scene would have been right at home in the antebellum South. What had happened to this city since he'd last been here?

The spectators buzzing around him were betting on which of the wretches would drop next. This was all a game to them now. His face reddened with anger, and he circled one of the laughing bastards, a federal apparatchik who no doubt owed his job to greasing some fat palm. When no one was looking, he whipsawed his cane and hammered the suited cad in the back of his knee, sending him crumpling to the ground.

"God damn!" the maimed man cried. "Who the hell clipped me?"

Gibbons circled to confront his victim. "You okay there, penitent?"

"Penitent?"

"You might as well say your confession while you're on your knees."

"I'm not a papist!"

Gibbons saw a water bucket being used to slake the thirst of the veterans. He picked it up and doused the kneeling man, rendering him sputtering and confused. "There you go, Martin Luther. I just baptized you."

The man wiped his eyes furiously. "You Irish fuck! I'll shove that cane up your—" He stopped in mid-threat, seeing his attacker clearly for the first time."

"Sorry, old boy. I didn't get the gist of that last blast from your Puritan prayer book. What'd you say your name was?"

The man, floundering on his knees, went bug-eyed with recognition. He backed away like a washed-up crab. "Now, hold on there, Gibbons. Don't you go blathering anything about me on the radio. I've got a family to support."

"Of course you do. We wouldn't want you to miss a meal. Like these fellows over there who fought in France so that you could make an ass of yourself."

The man turned tail and crawled into the crowd to escape.

His fighting blood up, Gibbons looked around at the stunned crowd and invited another challenge. The well-heeled onlookers retreated with contrite frowns and downcast eyes. He crossed a restraining rope and walked alongside the marching veterans, shaking hands and offering them cigarettes. As he neared the Capitol steps, he saw the two Anacostia nurses, Anna Raber and Lauretta D'Arsanis, attending to those veterans who were feeling faint.

Anna rushed over to him. "Thank God you're here, Mr. Gibbons. You must help us stop this. The men are putting their lives at risk."

"Whose idea was this ghost show?"

Anna angled her head toward the veteran in the metal neck brace. "His name is Royal Robertson. He brought four hundred more men from California. Some of the BEF men down at the camp have come up to join him. They're calling it the Death March."

Death March? That description made Gibbons shiver. The death march was a military tactic with a long history, used to brutalize prisoners and shock a besieged city or country into a crushing submission. The American government had forced the Choctaws, Muskogee, and Cherokee to suffer their own death marches, and after the European war, thousands of Armenians and Ottoman Greeks had met the same fate. But why would anyone insist that his own men to undergo such an agony?

"Robertson won't let them stop and sleep until the Bonus is passed."

"Where's Glassford?" he asked.

"Meeting with MacArthur and the commissioners. The White House has set tomorrow as a deadline for the veterans to be out of the city."

Gibbons gripped his cane in anger. The rug-pulling political tactics that he had warned the idealistic new police chief about months ago were being put into motion. "They're trying to force Glassford's hand. Why isn't Waters up here? He needs to stop this nonsense before it's too late."

Anna drew him aside, out of earshot of the veterans. "He's in bed at Evalyn McLean's house."

"In bed? While his men are out here suffering?"

"Something has happened to him."

"Is he ill?"

"He collapsed this morning. Mrs. McLean called a doctor, but Alford and his bodyguard won't let anyone in to check on his condition. I'm worried about him, Mr. Gibbons. Ever since this Robertson man arrived, Waters has been under a great deal of strain."

"You think he's having a nervous breakdown?"

She couldn't deny that possibility. "He has a habit of resigning and disappearing when a crisis arises. You can't write of this. You must promise me."

"Of course, but these men need steady—"

A distant shout interrupted their conversation. Several streetcars ground to a screeching halt, and a company of Marines in trench helmets and carrying rifles fixed with bayonets stepped off the cars. Dozens of flashbulbs went off, causing one of the veterans, groggy and confused, to stumble to the ground, as if avoiding gunfire. Others gathered around the arriving Marines, convinced they had come out to cheer them on and perform drills in support of their cause. The exhausted veterans saluted the leathernecks and waved their ragged flags in gratitude.

But Gibbons knew from his experience in the war that the Marines would never fix bayonets for parade drill. Motioning Anna back to safety, he hurried through the throngs and recognized the captain in charge of the company as one of the brass he had worked with on the Belleau Wood anniversary ceremonies. "Javil, what are you doing up here?"

"Curtis ordered us into action."

"The Vice President?"

"We were told the Capitol was being attacked."

Gibbons steadied against his cane. "My God, the inmates are running the asylum here. Does Hoover know about this?"

"I don't know. Half the men in the barracks refused to muster. They won't take up arms against the veterans. Between you and me, Gibbons, I'm not sure who *is* in charge of the government anymore."

"Hold off your men, for a few minutes, at least. Until I can get someone down here."

"I can't hold them long."

Gibbons limped as fast as he could over to two District cops who were watching the confusion from across First Street. "You need to get word to Glassford that all hell is about to break loose up here."

One of the cops grinned. "Maybe it's time some hell *did* break loose."

Gibbons looked down at the name on the cop's badge and wrote it into his notebook. "Call your boss now, or I'll make sure the entire country knows the name of the man who failed to act."

The cop lost his grin and nodded for his partner to call in the report to headquarters.

While Gibbons waited for Glassford to arrive and hopefully put a stop to this impending disaster, he jotted down some lines for his story:

> *Four abreast they marched—five thousand strong. Few uniforms tonight, and those ragged and wear-worn. The grease-stained overalls of the jobless factory workers, the frayed straw hats of unemployed farm hands.*
>
> *The shoddy elbow-patched garments of idle clerks.*
>
> *All were down at the heel. All were slim and gaunt, and their eyes had a light in them. There were empty sleeves and limping men with canes. They were five thousand hungry ghosts of the heroes of 1917. Not so young now …*
>
> *They did not march in the light of day. They marched in darkness … And they marched, proud and unashamed, carrying the flag they fought for.*

lassford sat in MacArthur's office in the War Department building and watched General Crosby pace in front of him.

"You had no authority to allow that California hustler to launch his publicity stunt at the Capitol," the commissioner said. "You've let them turn this city into a freak carnival."

Glassford resisted the urge to loosen his tie. The temperature in the room had to be over a hundred, and the sputtering ceiling fan squealed with every third revolution, causing his blood pressure to rise even more. He glanced over at his old friend for support, but MacArthur stood mute at the window, gazing off at the White House.

Crosby poked a finger into Glassford's chest. "Are you going to defend yourself, or just sit there?"

Glassford shoved Crosby's finger aside and thought about throwing a fist at the man's jaw. "Does the President feel the same way?"

"Yes."

"Then why doesn't he call me into the White House and tell me himself?"

Crosby just glared at him.

"You hired me," Glassford said. "If you and the President are not satisfied with my performance, you can fire me."

"Fire you? After you've curried the adoration of that Anacostia mob? That would set off a revolution."

"Revolution?"

"What the hell would *you* call an armed takeover of a country's capital?"

"Those men aren't armed. And they've been peaceful since the first day they arrived, despite the provocations of undercover government agents."

Crosby reddened. "What are you implying?"

Glassford stood and took a challenging step closer. "Somebody's been trying to stir them up and goad them into violence. Even a poor man can take only so many blows to his dignity."

MacArthur cleared his throat. "You've been dealt a tough hand, Hap. Nobody denies that. You've got to deal with the Capitol police, the Secret Service, and the Hill committees. I think what Commissioner Crosby is trying to convey is that we are constrained by the laws of Congress. We've found an 1882 statute that forbids anyone from parading or assembling on the Capitol grounds."

"Does that include Wall Street lobbyists?" Glassford asked.

Crosby got into his face. "There's some who think you've turned Bolshevik."

Glassford bristled at the slander. "I suggest they come forward and file a formal charge. But then maybe yellow doesn't match well with Red-baiting."

"Damn your insolence!"

MacArthur intervened. "Gentlemen!"

Crosby required a moment to regain his composure. "The President wants these squatters out of the city by tomorrow."

"If that's what the President wants, he should issue a formal order—"

The door opened, and Admiral Henry Butler, commandant of the Navy Yard, hurried in with a dispatch. "I'm sorry for the interruption."

"Not at all," said MacArthur. "How can I help you, Henry?"

Admiral Butler glanced coldly at Crosby. "It's with Chief Glassford I need to speak. Vice President Curtis has ordered a company of my Marines up to Capitol Hill."

Glassford rushed to the window to confirm that unlikely report, but the haze denied him a clear vantage of the Capitol. Incensed, he brushed past Crosby. "I am fed up with you and the rest of your hysterical meddlers!"

MacArthur called him back. "Hap, as always, if there's anything I can do to help, let me know, old friend."

Glassford, nodding uncertainly, hurried out.

Admiral Butler remained at the door, as if expecting an explanation.

MacArthur merely strode to his desk, sat down, and began examining several documents. He looked up to find the admiral still waiting. "Anything else, Henry?"

Butler turned to leave, perplexed by the casualness with which MacArthur had greeted the news of the Marine deployment.

"Henry?"

"Yes, Doug?"

"Close the door behind you, will you?"

Burned by that attempted twist of the Army knife, Butler left the door ajar in defiance. Crosby snorted his amusement as he watched the admiral huff off.

Alone again with Crosby, MacArthur buzzed Eisenhower. "Ask General Moseley to bring the file we discussed this morning."

Moments later, Moseley marched in and tossed a manila folder marked classified onto MacArthur's desk. "I saw Glassford leaving in a state. How'd the woodshedding go?"

"I think he got the message."

"I wouldn't count on it," grumbled Crosby.

MacArthur arose and lit his pipe. He offered Crosby a cigarette from his desk case. "Bert, I'll have to request your highest confidentiality on a matter that has come up."

"Of course."

He handed Crosby the file that Moseley had just delivered. "Yesterday the Adjutant General's office received this radiogram from one of our operatives."

Crosby's face paled as he read the correspondence.

"This fellow Bundell mentioned in the report is from New York," MacArthur said. "It appears that he is organizing another army of veterans to come down here. I think we need to take this surveillance very seriously."

Crosby kept staring at the report. "The BEF has machine guns?"

"It gets worse," said Moseley. "Bundell has been bragging that some of the Marines over at the Navy Yard are in on the conspiracy. They're preparing to hold the bridges around the city for the revolutionaries."

"That hack Gibbons has his handprints all over this," said Crosby. "Doug, do you really think the Marines would turn traitor on us?"

MacArthur blew a contemplative puff of smoke from his pipe. "George, didn't you tell me that half the Marines at the Navy Yard this morning refused to comply with the Vice President's order to form up?"

"Damn right," said Moseley. "Where there's fire, there's smoke. And those bastards have been opening up their clinics to the bums."

MacArthur nodded. "Just to be safe, I think it best we not coordinate with the Marines on the contingency defense plans."

"Right." Crosby said. "That's prudent."

"Speaking of the White Plan," Moseley said. "We've run into a snag on its implementation."

"What's the holdup?" MacArthur asked.

"The lawyers say we need a presidential proclamation."

"Draft one."

"Already done," said Moseley. "But that's not the problem. Hoover and his aides over there don't want to consider it."

"Submit the proclamation to Hurley. He'll grease that wheel."

"What about the tanks?" asked Crosby.

MacArthur looked to Moseley for the answer to that question.

"They're in place."

MacArthur waved them off to indicate the meeting was finished. Then, he walked to the wall and straightened the framed picture of his mother.

Hoover, sitting next to Lou in the rear seat, slouched down to avoid being seen as Walter Newton drove their unmarked car across Arlington Memorial Bridge. He had finally given in to his physician's demand that he escape the city's heat for a couple of days at Camp Rapidan in the Shenandoah Valley. Somehow he had to regain his strength for the grueling stump campaign that he'd soon be waging against the Democratic nominee, Franklin Roosevelt. As the car sped past pedestrians on the sidewalks, he pulled the brim of his hat over his eyes. If the press spotted him leaving while the Capitol was under siege, the editorials would pillory him.

"Bert, for heaven's sake," Lou said. "You think any of your comings and goings get missed? The reporters at the White House will know you're gone in ten minutes. You might as well sit up and enjoy the scenery."

"The scenery? You mean all the shantytowns?"

"Come on now, dear. You promised me you would try to relax."

Hoover glanced at the pile of morning newspapers that lay between them. A headline caused his angina to flare: *War Hero Smedley Butler Calls For BEF To Persist in Protests.* "Can you believe this?"

Lou looked over at the story that had set off his ire. "Smedley Butler was that nice Quaker Marine boy that helped us in China, wasn't he?"

"That nice Quaker Marine boy grew up and ran for the Pennsylvania Senate this year. Do you know what his platform was?"

"I suppose you're going to tell me."

"Hoover is out of touch with the country."

Lou reddened at the betrayal. "I thought he was a Republican."

"He *is* a Republican. And he's been telling everyone who will listen that I don't have a heart for the fighting man."

Lou let the silence extend, hoping to calm him. Glancing at the driver, she lowered her voice. "I received a letter from Bert Junior yesterday."

"How's he feeling?"

"Much better."

"Took a terrible toll on him, having to resign from Western Air Express," he said. "I warned him that people would claim he got the job because of me."

"That's all in the past. Let's thank God the tuberculosis has regressed."

"I suppose."

"Bert… he wrote something else. Something that concerns me."

"He's not thinking of running for office?"

"No, no. He mentioned a few things he's been hearing from his colleagues in the aeronautics business. Many of them have ties to the military, you know."

"If this has anything to do with approving contracts, I don't want to hear it."

"He overheard some talk…. Darling, can you trust these War Department people who advise you?"

"Of course I can trust them. What kind of rumormongering is Bert Junior up to now? And he's putting this scurrilous stuff in letters?"

"He's concerned about you."

"I can take care of myself. He needs to look after his own business endeavors."

"Why won't you take a meeting with Chief Glassford?"

Hoover threw the newspaper aside in a fit of pique. "I thought I was taking this trip to get away from all of that?"

"Please, Bert, hear me out this once. I promise I won't speak of it again."

"You are not privy to the intelligence reports that I receive."

"That's what worries me. Are you getting the full story about these veterans?"

"If I allowed Glassford to high-step into my office, it would be seen as evidence that I have kowtowed to his appeasement of these agitators. That police chief is turning into another Smedley Butler, holding hands with these squatters and demagoguing about Constitutional rights. Before you know it, Huey Long will have his barefoot rascals up here trying to open up the Treasury to pass out free money."

"Evalyn McLean says Glassford is a fine man."

"That woman is a fatuous, Red-leaning socialite who married into money and whose only talent is holding dinner parties. I might as well take policy advice from Trotsky's wife."

Lou patted his mottled hand to appease him. "I'm sorry I brought it up, dear. Try and get some sleep on the way."

"Glassford," Hoover muttered under his breath as he closed his eyes to try to ease his headache. "God help me."

Wilma Waters rushed into a second-floor bedroom of the Florentine-styled mansion owned by Evalyn McLean on Fifteenth and Eye Street. Arrived from Oregon that morning, she fell to her knees at her husband's bedside and took his hand. "Dubya, what happened to you?"

He slowly opened his eyes. "Wilma? Am I dreaming?"

"I'm here now."

"You came.... Where are the girls?"

Wilma glanced worriedly at Alford and Angelo, who were standing vigil over their leader. "I left them with my sister.... George here said you needed me."

"I just had a little spell, is all."

She nodded. "He gets those from time to time."

"Nothing to worry about," he insisted.

Evalyn McLean came into the room carrying a tray with a sandwich and milk for her bedridden guest. "How are you feeling, Commander?"

"Like I died and went to heaven, with all these beautiful angels around me."

Mrs. McLean blushed. "You rest up here, as long as you want."

Walter lifted to his elbows. "What's the situation with the men?"

Alford traded concerned glances with Angelo. "Wilma, I'll bet Mrs. McLean would love to show you her kitchen. She's got some right fancy kettles."

The hostess took the cue. "Yes, please, let me show you the house."

"Joey," said Alford. "Why don't you go with them, make sure none of those government spies lurking around give them trouble."

Angelo hesitated. "I need to talk to Dubya."

"Later. When he's more up to it."

Waters did not countermand Alford's order, so Angelo reluctantly followed the two women out of the room. Alford shut the door behind them.

"Is Robertson still up at the C-c-capitol?" Waters asked.

Alford nodded. "Some of our boys have joined him. Hoover's back from his little fishing holiday, so they decided to go over and serenaded him."

Waters sank dejected into the pillow. "I've lost them."

"You ain't lost them yet."

"I've lost the p-p-power, Georgie. My t-t-talking's traitoring me again. Somebody's been shooting at me. A bullet missed me by a foot two days ago. The boys are t-t-turning on me."

Alford glanced at the door. "You got to out-Robertson Robertson."

"But I p-p-promised the General—"

"Forget Glassford. He won't be around much longer anyway. You've been outflanked. Now you have to take up the tactics of the great leaders of Europe. Hitler was a trench rat, just like us. He don't have nothing you don't. You got to show these men that you still command them."

Waters stared at the ceiling, not convinced.

Alford grasped his friend's hand. "I didn't bring you all the way out here from Oregon to see you lose courage and fail. You were chosen by God to lead these men for a purpose. You know what you have to do."

"I d-d-don't…"

Alford walked to the closet and swung open its door. "We both knew this day would come. I had this sewn up for you about a month ago."

Waters marveled at the starched uniform hanging on the rod before him.

"Now get out of bed," Alford ordered. "You have a country to save."

The next morning, Glassford sped his motorcycle up Pennsylvania Avenue, bracing for whatever new crisis the day might bring. The asphalt leading to the Capitol was already baking under the cloudless sky, and the stench of the burning rubber from his tires transported him back to France and those awful moments before all hell would break loose on the trenches. Now, he felt that same grip of war nausea in his gut.

The city seemed on the verge of exploding.

He glanced at his watch. It was nearly ten. He had been rushing from hotspot to hotspot since before dawn. Hoping to capitalize on the Vice President's trigger-happy order to call out the Marines the day before, Royal Robertson was now threatening to take his Death March to the White House. And not to be outdone, John Pace and his ragged band of fifty Communists had launched a new strategy, trying to bait Robertson's veterans into joining their mischief by making sorties across Lafayette Park and taunting the Secret Service agents into a battle.

So far, Al Headley, his inspector in charge of that sector, had managed to repulse these attempts. But Hoover had overreacted by canceling his traditional visit to adjourn Congress scheduled for that night. The decision might have been logistically prudent, given the tension on the streets, but it was sending the wrong message to the country and would only serve to confirm the opinion held by the veterans that the president was a coward.

If those weren't problems enough, the bureaucrats at the Treasury, no doubt instigated by the Administration chickenhawks, were badgering him about a block of burned-out concrete buildings that surrounded the old District armory on Pennsylvania Avenue between Third and Fourth Streets. Desperate to find more housing for a hundred and fifty veterans and their families recently arrived from Texas, he had given the new arrivals permission to bed down on the exposed upper floors of the skeletal remains. In gratitude, the Texan veterans had dubbed their new abode "Camp Glassford," a dubious honor that caused him to cringe every time he heard it. Owned by the federal government, the burned-out block had been scheduled for months for the wrecking ball to make way for new office buildings. He suspected someone at the White House had accelerated the demolition as a way to incite a confrontation with the veterans.

The situation across the river in Anacostia was no better. The BEF leadership was splintering, making a consensus among the veterans nearly impossible to obtain. Royal Robertson, a master at self-promotion, was refusing to negotiate with authorities. In response, Waters, eclipsed by the Californian's overbearing personality, had turned reclusive, sending out his orders by mimeograph from his headquarters, which seemed to be situated in whatever house was on offer that week. Waters resigned his commandership at every perceived slight, only to be reinstated, and the BEF newspaper had been running editorials attacking the Oregon leader for failing to obtain the Bonus. The street poles were papered with flyers from anonymous sources claiming that Waters lived lavishly in Evalyn McLean's mansion while his men bedded down in the mud.

He knew Robertson didn't have the funds to finance such a sophisticated smear campaign. The instigators were likely undercover government operatives bent on fomenting dissension among the veterans. He actually felt sorry for Waters, knowing as he did, firsthand, what it was like to be the target of underhanded slander and sabotage.

He arrived at the Capitol plaza and saw that his officers had cordoned off the grounds as he had ordered. Several thousand veterans stood behind the ropes, some drinking coffee from their tins, others engaged in the usual debates about going home or staying until Congress returned. He nodded to Anna and her fellow nurse, Miss D'Arsanis, who were mingling among the men, asking about their health and warning them not to remain in the sun for too long.

Robertson didn't look to be around. That was one small blessing. At least he wouldn't have that gum-flapping troublemaker to worry about for a while. For once, everything up here appeared peaceful. He was about to crank the throttle to head back down toward the White House when a roar swept across the plaza. From the corner of his eye, he saw a blur of tawny movement, followed by a surge of the crowd like filings to a magnet. He blinked away the hazy sweat from his eyes.

A slender man clad in a crisp tan shirt, dark jodhpurs breeches, and black, knee-high boots strode determinedly toward the ropes. Ten men dressed in similar military attired followed him in what looked like a military entourage.

Glassford rode his cycle closer to the plaza to get a better look.

Is that Waters?

The crowds stilled, stunned by the BEF commander's transformation. The Anacostia veterans cheered wildly, but Robertson's men, standing apart from their rivals, were unimpressed.

"Well, if it ain't the string-bean Mussolini," scoffed a California veteran. "What'd you go and do, Waters? Turn Fascist on us overnight?"

Waters glanced around the plaza. Suddenly, as if prodded by an electric shock, he dashed across the cordon ropes and ran for the Capitol Steps

Glassford launched off his cycle. He caught Waters near the bandstand and, grabbing at the epaulets on the BEF leader's new uniform, spun him around. "What are you trying to pull?"

Waters stared right through him. "Nothing personal, General."

Glassford sensed that something had changed in the Oregon man, but he couldn't put his finger on just what. Confronted with a brewing riot, he pushed Waters up the Capitol steps and through the doors.

Outside, the veterans kept shouting, "We want Waters! We want Waters!"

He pinned Waters against the wall. "We had an agreement."

Waters refused to look at him directly.

A cop burst in. "Chief, we're losing control out there."

Too late, Glassford realized that Waters had schemed this confrontation to undercut his department's trust with the veterans. "Take him into the basement and hold him there until I come back."

His officer hesitated. "Chief, you shouldn't go back out there."

Glassford burst back out through the Capitol doors and fought a path to the bandstand. Below him, thousands of men, informed of Waters's arrest, were pouring up the slopes from Anacostia. He looked down into faces that held vehemence he hadn't seen since the war. The congressmen and senators might be endangered if the veterans breached the doors and made for the chambers and tunnels to the office buildings. Surrounded by jeers and threats, he climbed atop the platform and begged for silence. "Hear me out, men!"

"Turn Waters loose! Or we'll go in and get him!"

"I don't want any trouble!" Glassford shouted. "I've got a job to do! I promised I'd keep this plaza clear, and I'll do it!"

"Bring him out! Or we'll do it for you!"

Glassford could feel the spark about to be lit. He retreated from the bandstand and, grabbed at by a dozen hands, hurried back up the Capitol steps. The men were converging to attack him when Lauretta D'Arsanis raised a megaphone and began singing *America the Beautiful*. Anna hurried through the mob and joined her, following up with a rendition of *Over There*. The patriotic tunes washed over the men, and they became quiet. A few began singing with the nurses, and soon the plaza was filled with the chorus.

The quick thinking by the nurses had given Glassford enough time to hurry back into the Capitol. Moments later, he reappeared on the top step with Waters. The veterans roared at their victory.

Waters preened and puffed out his fascist chest pockets. "Men! We have just begun to fight! No more accommodation and negotiation!"

With control regained, if only for the moment, Glassford tried to wrestle Waters through the doors before he could make more incendiary statements.

But Waters escaped his grasp and continued his speech atop the steps. "I've made mistakes! I ain't per-perfect! I done the best I can to ge-ge-get you here and get your grievances heard! I'm hereby forming a new organization of veterans!"

"What's that, Dubya?" Angelo shouted.

"The Khaki Shirts!"

Lurking behind the strident faces in the crowd, Alford grinned. "Damn right! No more of Glassford's stew-and-beans mooching! When that vote came in, he raised the drawbridge so we couldn't mass!"

Glassford searched for the source of that false charge. He saw Anna hurrying from veteran to veteran, trying to convince them to pull back to the ropes.

Waters strutted across the top step of the portico like Mussolini atop the Capitoline terraces of Rome. "We're never leaving this city!"

"We'll follow you, Dubya!" shouted Ozzie.

Waters pointed down at his comrades. "I'll lead you under one condition!"

"You name it, Dubya!" cried Lincoln.

"I gotta have total power! What I say goes!"

Glassford tried to argue against this crass imitation of a dictator, but the cheers drowned out his attempt. Seeing that he had lost these men to this cunning scheme of doubling down, he took Waters aside. "What are you after?"

"We want to enter the chambers."

"That's not going to happen."

"Do you want an army of Khaki Shirts to storm it?"

Glassford resisted the urge to slam a fist into his gut. "You don't fool me, I know who you are. You're just a rail rider hiding behind a fancy uniform."

"It's not you I have to fool, General."

Stunned by that cold calculation, Glassford stole a glance at the boiling crowd below. The few dozen officers he had stationed here wouldn't be enough to prevent those thousands of men from flooding the entrances, and he didn't have time to call in reinforcements. "I'll allow you to occupy the plaza again."

"Not enough."

"You're trying to humiliate me. I won't have it."

"You've been leading us around by the nose for months."

Glassford played for time. "Not the chambers. You can deploy your men on the middle steps. That's farther than you've ever gone with the protests. You'll make your point. You've won the day."

"And a meeting with the Speaker of the House."

"I'll see what I can set up."

Not waiting for a handshake to seal the deal, Waters pushed through the doors and raised his arms to embrace the acclamation. "Men, we have won a great victory! I have demanded and won the right for us to use these center steps! But you've got to keep a lane open for the white-collar birds inside so they don't have to run into us lousy rats!"

Another roar shook the plaza, and Alford shouted, "Waters for President!"

Waters raised his fist. "We're gonna stay until I see Hoover in person!"

As the BEF leader strode down the steps basking in the adulation, Glassford hung back behind a pillar on the portico. The White House would skewer him for giving in to the challenge, but at least he had avoided bloodshed. He turned and saw Anna in the crowd of veterans. She looked at him, distraught, as if sharing his realization that Waters had contracted this city's most contagious and malignant disease—the lust for power.

61

WASHINGTON, D.C.
JULY 26, 1932

Clad in his crisp new Khaki Shirts uniform and black riding boots, Waters hurried up the interior staircase of the State, War and Navy Building. Accompanying him were two BEF staff men and Herbert Ward, a local attorney who had donated his time to help find housing for the veterans. Waters could almost taste the rarefied air of power here. For all of these many months, the president had adamantly refused to meet with him, not wishing to be photographed with the lowly of this world. Now, reaching the top floor, he realized that this was as close as he had ever gotten to that Quaker recluse. He paused at a window and searched the White House grounds across the way, hoping to catch a glimpse of the famous medicine ball. But all he saw were lines of armed Secret Service agents stationed around the perimeter fence to fend off the feared Communist attacks.

Never mind old Herbert. The man wasn't long for the Oval Office anyway, not with Roosevelt promising relief to the common folk. Today he would be negotiating with the real powerbrokers in the government. At long last, he was about to fulfill his dream of meeting his hero. That morning, General MacArthur's courier had personally delivered the invitation to Anacostia. He still couldn't quite believe that the Beau Brummel of the Marne was requesting a meeting with *him*. Generals ordered enlisted men to their headquarters, but they *requested* meetings with fellow commanders.

Mac must have finally discovered that another military man of consequence now resided in the city. Probably dawned on him last night, after that loud-mouth Royal Robertson conceded defeat and took off for California in his traveling gallows getup. Mac had taken long enough to come to his senses, that was for damn sure. Hell, the general had never even once come down to the camp to speak to the men.

But all was forgiven now. With Mac championing their cause, it wouldn't be long before they'd find a home, maybe even get their Bonus. He just wished Alford were with him to savor the triumph. But his trusted advisor had gone off again without leaving word of his whereabouts. Knowing Georgie, he was probably in Virginia or Maryland somewhere trying to forage spoiling hamburger for the boys.

He walked down the long hall and came to a set of mahogany doors that held a metal nameplate: *Office of the Chief of Staff.* Before knocking, he whispered the drill that he had practiced as a boy to smooth out his words. "Just *my* daggum luck…. Just my *daggum* luck…. Just my daggum *luck.*"

"Walter, are you okay?" asked Ward.

Waters nodded, holding his right hand to stifle its shaking.

Just then, Major Eisenhower, MacArthur's adjutant, turned the corner. "Gentlemen, General MacArthur and the Secretary are waiting. Follow me."

"Secretary?"

Eisenhower maintained a stony expression. "The meeting will be in Secretary Hurley's office."

Waters grinned as he and his BEF men were led to an office several doors down the hall. Hurley was Hoover's main mouthpiece, so that meant Hoover himself would be as good as in the room. Eisenhower escorted them into the Secretary of War's massive office and closed the door behind them. Across the room, Patrick Hurley sat behind a desk festooned with Indian arrowheads, stone tomahawks, and other New Mexico artifacts. The War Department chief took a pained look at his guests and set his jaw in disdain. With a snap of his wrist, he silently motioned them toward a row of chairs that had been set up in front of him as if ready for a seated firing squad.

Behind Hurley, a tall, erect man paced back and forth with his hands clasped behind his back. Several seconds passed before Waters realized that the meditating walker was General MacArthur in civilian clothing. Waters bounded up from his chair to offer his hand to his hero. "General, by God you gave 'em hell in the Argonne. You and I were in the same sector, from what I've been told."

MacArthur kept his arms behind his back, and continued pacing.

Waters figured the general didn't realize who he was, so he introduced himself. "I'm Commander Waters."

MacArthur grimaced at hearing that absurd honorific.

"Have a seat, Mr. Waters," ordered Hurley.

Confused by the frigid welcome, Waters took a chair whose legs appeared shaved down to force the occupant to sit lower than the desk.

Hurley stared down at him, as if wondering how such a slight, unimpressive man could have caused so much trouble. In a paternalistic tone, the War Secretary said, "It is time for you to leave."

Waters found it difficult to focus while MacArthur remained in perpetual motion. "But we just got here. We ain't even exchanged pleasantries."

"Your... " Hurley" stopped to search for the appropriate word, which he enunciated with dripping condescension. "It's time for you and your *people* to leave the city."

Blindsided, Waters stole a worried glance at his attorney and staffers, who had turned wan. "I thought we were here to discuss the Bonus."

"These veterans you've brought here are a threat to the government!" Hurley insisted. "The President wants you to go back home without delay!"

Waters edged up on his chair. "How come Hoover won't tell me that to my face?"

MacArthur, pacing faster behind Hurley, shot Waters a glare of worthy of Zeus examining a pitiful mortal about to be zapped.

"The President is a busy man," Hurley said. "He has no time to waste on local police matters."

Waters pressed a hand to his knee in protest. "Local police matters? Hell, this is a countrywide matter. The whole damn nation is starving."

Hurley yanked defiantly at the tips of his vest. "There is no one starving in this country! I have toured the nation, and I can assure you that there is absolutely no one starving. Any man willing to work hard can amass a fortune here. Look at me. A few years ago, I started with a cow and a pig on a poor piece of ground. Now I'm a millionaire."

"Come out to Oregon and I'll take you on another tour. I'll show you men who look worse than those German fellas the general and I saw crawling on the Boche streets after the war on the Rhine." He looked up at MacArthur, who was now turning to and fro like a wooden duck in a carnival shooting gallery. "You remember them poor fellows on their last legs, don't you, General?"

MacArthur could barely bring himself to deign an answer. "You dare to compare this country to Germany?"

"That's not what I meant now, General, and you know it."

Hurley's attitude turned even more belligerent. "You and this so-called Bonus Army have no business in Washington. It is the policy of the government to get you out of the city as quickly as possible. At the first sign of disorder—"

"D-d-disorder?" Waters felt his tongue quivering, betraying him the way it used to do when he was nothing but a vagabond. "We ain't hurt a f-f-flea since we been here!"

"We have the means to get you out," Hurley warned.

Dumbfounded, Waters leaned forward. "What are you t-t-talking about?"

The phone rang, and Hurley picked it up. He said to the other voice on the line, "Hold dinner. I may be here a while."

While the war secretary spoke to his wife, Waters glanced up with plaintive eyes at MacArthur. "General, many of my men out there fought for you."

Still in motion, MacArthur struck his favorite martial pose, protruding his chin and thrumming his right hand against his thigh. "Those malingerers across the river are not *my* men. None of *my* men ever turned Communist."

"There ain't a Red amid us!"

"Our intelligence confirms otherwise." MacArthur conducted a sneering inspection of Waters's uniform. "Did you also copy *that* from the Germans?"

"I g-g-gotta right to wear a uniform. We're a d-d-duly constituted army, with officers and r-r-ranks. Nobody objected in 1917 when we were issued —"

MacArthur turned his back, curtly cutting him off.

Finishing his phone call, Hurley slammed his palm against the desk to regain the BEF commander's attention. "Enough about the past, Mr. Waters. We've had reports that the Reds in your camp are plotting a new wave of violence."

Waters couldn't believe what he was hearing. "We can't please you politicians. If we b-b-bust the heads of Pace's troublemakers, the c-c-cops hound us for breaking the peace. And if we d-d-don't give them the knuckle sandwiches, you and the president call us Red sympathizers. Why d-d-don't you arrest the t-t-troublemakers if you know who they are?"

"*We* know who they are," said Hurley. "And so do you."

"My men will join up to f-f-fight 'em."

"Under no circumstances will you in any way ever again be associated with the Army," Hurley said. "We don't need you. We don't want you."

Waters felt his chest tighten. "We got nowhere to g-g-go."

"That's not our problem."

"We need to find a permanent camp before we can leave."

"This isn't Russia," Hurley said. "Americans don't live in communes."

"I can't tell go out there and just tell my m-m-men to walk off without giving them some hope of a p-p-place to put some shelter over their f-f-families. They won't heed me if I issue such an order."

Hurley glared at him. "You're not much of a commander then, are you?"

Waters turned to his staffers for support, but they had their heads down, slumped in defeat. He realized, too late, that he had severely miscalculated. These military men had never intended to help him. He had walked into an ambush. Seeing no alternative to surrender, he managed to ask weakly, "Can you at least s-s-spare us some tents?"

Hurley turned to MacArthur, "Is there any tentage available?"

"No."

"You see, Mr. Waters," Hurley said. "The War Department has no tents available. And even if it did, I would not place them at your disposal. So, let us agree upon a timetable for getting your people evacuated and returning this city to its rightful owners."

"I'll need a couple weeks—"

"Tomorrow night is the deadline."

Waters was breathing hard now, trying to find air above the miasma of pipe smoke. "I'm w-w-willing to try a gradual evacuation, but that's t-t-too soon. I got the women and children to think about. I can't just set them off d-d-down the road."

"I am not without feeling for the women and children," Hurley said. "Since you've now agreed to evacuate, let me call General Hines at the Veterans Bureau and see what can be done to help them." He ordered his secretary to place the call, and moments later he spoke into the receiver. After a cryptic discussion, Hurley dropped his voice and said to General Hines on the other line, "So you think that if Waters were out of the picture for forty-eight hours the thing would break up?" Hurley pondered for a moment, and then told General Hines, "Well, maybe you're right."

Waters turned inward, struggling to wrangle his wits. One enigmatic statement from Hurley's telephone conversation lingered in his ear.

If Waters were out of the picture.

Hurley hung up. "I was hoping we might utilize Fort Hunt for a few days to house the families, until they got on the road. Unfortunately, General Hines is closing the fort in August." He shrugged. "I tried my best."

Waters sat numb, unable to comprehend how he would tell the men that they would have to leave the city within hours. His lawyer and staffers, seeing the hopelessness of the situation, begged out of the meeting and left him abandoned. He sat there for four more hours, harangued and browbeaten on the specifics on the looming evacuation.

All the while, MacArthur never ceased pacing.

Late for dinner at his home in Georgetown, Hurley stood and announced that the meeting was over. "Mr. Waters," he said, donning his felt hat. "By tomorrow night, you can either be a big man, or a broken one." At the door, he turned and added, "You'll no doubt encounter newspapermen outside wanting to know what we talked about. Tell them that we discussed the economic situation in America, and leave it at that."

Hungry and exhausted from being double-teamed all afternoon, Waters felt his head spinning, unable to make sense of what had just happened. *We have the means to get you out…at the first sign of disorder or bloodshed.* Were they setting him up for a fall? *So you think that if Waters were out of the picture…*

If he went down to Anacostia and told the men they had to evacuate the camp by tomorrow night, there would be a riot. He had twelve thousand veterans scattered around the city in twenty-four camps. How was he supposed to muster them all with transport in twenty-four hours? He had been shot at several times during the past weeks. He'd always thought it was the Communists out to get him, or Robertson and his gang of intimidators, but now he wondered if undercover government agents had fired those bullets. Why was the Administration insisting on evacuating Camp Glassford on Pennsylvania Avenue first? Everyone knew those Texas boys bunking over there were stubborn and tough, easy to taunt into a fight.

Then it dawned on him. *This is what Hoover and Hurley want.*

Why hadn't he seen this before? They were trying to trick him into giving the Army an excuse to use their guns. He had been dealt a stinking hand, a couple of lousy threes against the government's full house. He was gonna have to pull off a hell of a bluff, or all was lost.

As he stood slowly, his legs threatened to fail. He braced against the back of the chair and saluted MacArthur. "General, will you p-p-promise to give us the opportunity to f-f-form in columns, salvage our b-b-belongings, and retreat in orderly f-f-fashion?"

For the first time since the meeting started, MacArthur stopped pacing. With a thin smile, he turned and assured Waters, "Yes, my friend. Of course."

WASHINGTON, D.C.
JULY 28, 1932

lassford watched the minute hand on his watch tick down to half past nine. Then, wiping the humidity from his eyes, he nodded for his hundred officers, accompanied by several dozen Treasury agents, to begin removing the defiant Texas veterans from the condemned armory.

While his cops fanned out to their assigned positions, he pulled the eviction order from his pocket and read it again, hoping to find some overlooked illegality that might allow him to abort its enforcement. For two long days, he had negotiated with the commissioners, arguing that his department had no authority to carry out such an unprecedented operation on federal land. But the White House had finally backed him into a corner with a cynical legal loophole: the Treasury agents would handle the clearing, while his officers were to remain at their sides to insure their safety and maintain the peace.

To avoid another spectacle like the Death March, he had ordered civilian spectators roped off and the morning traffic rerouted from the Pennsylvania Avenue site. Above him, the skyline crowning the partially demolished buildings of Camp Glassford formed a jagged cut of slate. His stomach tightened every time he saw that pitiful cluster of square caves named in his honor. The block with its four stories of exposed skeletal frame resembled a grotesque Hieronymus Bosch painting. The eastern walls of the edifice were missing, revealing precarious stairwells whose railings had been hammered away. Crane operators sat waiting nearby, eager to finish the destruction with their wrecking balls. The two thousand veterans billeted there stood along the floor edges, looking down in ominous silence. Many had dressed that morning in shabby white shirts and ties, as if sensing that something momentous was about to happen.

After a tense moment of delay, the Texas veterans finally accepted the inevitable and began peacefully filing in single lines down the stairwells.

He whispered a prayer in relief. All he needed to do now was escort the veterans to the trucks that he had leased to take them out of the city. But as he walked toward to the armory, he spied a slender figure threading the throngs of the descending veterans and pushing them back up the stairwells.

Was that Waters?

He hurried closer and heard the BEF commander haranguing the veterans about how the government had lied to him. Angered, hundreds of them began jeering and making threats at the police. They halted their voluntary evacuation and began returning to the condemned buildings. Waters climbed up the stairwells with the Texans, shouting a promise to defend the armory.

This is Crosby's doing.

With the White House's insidious blessing, the Machiavellian commissioner had undercut Waters, forcing his hand by reneging on the promise to allow him four days to find another camp. Accused now by many of being an Administration puppet, Waters had apparently decided to turn militant in a last-ditch attempt to retain command.

Did Hoover and his advisors *want* violence?

Waters stood atop a pile of bricks and pointed down at him. "You d-d-double-crossed me, General! You said they'd give us four days!"

Glassford sent an aide across the street to calm him down, but the Oregon man, in a white rage, wouldn't listen to reason. Sensing that the veterans were on the verge of an upheaval, he hurried through the surly scrum and pulled Waters aside. "I tried to get word to you. The commissioners changed the terms of our agreement at the last minute."

"No more t-t-talking! No more!"

He firmed his grip on the BEF leader's arm. "Keep your head. Let's work out a solution to this situation."

Waters broke away. Strutting off, he signaled for Bill Hruska to join him, but the Lithuanian veteran hung back. "You coming, Billy?"

"I think I'll hang up here, Dubya. These boys need some cheering up."

Waters glared at Hruska, as if suspecting his old friend from the rail rides no longer wanted to be seen with him. "Suit yourself." He marched off the site and headed toward Anacostia. Several steps away, he turned back and warned Glassford, "This ain't over, General."

Before Glassford could demand an explanation for that threat, Waters disappeared into the swarm of men surrounding the condemned block. The environs fell silent as the Texas veterans standing on the exposed floors waited to see what would happen next. The Treasury agents below them shifted impatiently, itching to get on with the operation. Glassford reluctantly motioned for his officers to climb the first flight of wooden stairs. The protesters on the upper decks waited with fists clenched as the cops and Treasury agents came to a black veteran who lay at the top step.

The officers ordered the man to stand up, but he refused.

Glassford had anticipated that passive tactic by instructing his ranks to use the minimal amount of force necessary. Two of his cops lifted the black veteran by the hands and legs as gently as they could and slid him slowly down the steps, plank by plank. The veterans were so impressed by the care being taken to help the lame man down that they eased their scowls and silenced their threats. They began walking down the stairs without additional prodding, shaking hands and slapping the backs of the officers, many of whom they had gotten to know over the past months.

As the veterans filed past and greeted him warmly, Glassford released a held breath. His careful planning and instruction were paying off. He had defused the outburst by Waters, and the eviction was back on track. With a little luck, he just might have this distasteful task finished before lunch.

In the Anacostia camp across the river, Anna was making her usual morning rounds, checking in on the sick and elderly. Lincoln and Taylor accompanied her, having offered to help bring to the clinic those residents who were too weak to walk. As they passed the speaker's stand in the center of the grounds, she noticed that the microphone on the pole that usually played soothing classical music from a donated Victrola was silent. Feeling the camp was sadder without it, she was struck by an idea. "Why don't you bring your oboe along?" she asked Ozzie. "Music is a great healer, you know."

Ozzie seemed embarrassed by the suggestion.

"He's plum out of reeds, Miss Anna," explained Lincoln. "Some of the boys offered to collect some coffee money for the purchase, but he won't abide it."

"How long have you gone without playing now?" she asked Ozzie.

"Maybe a month. It don't seem that important no more, to tell you the truth. I just keep it in the case these days. I don't much like to be reminded of Big Jim and the band. Nobody likes ragtime now anyway."

"That instrument gave much pleasure to your fellow soldiers. You must never abandon your calling. It's your talisman."

"Talisman? What's that?"

"An object that carries mysterious and supernatural powers."

Lincoln lifted his stovepipe hat to scratch his head. "I thought you Mennonite folk didn't believe in that kind of hocus-pocus."

"To be honest, I don't know what I believe anymore."

They continued walking until they came to a hovel at the far end of the camp. It's tin roof shook with the shrill wailing of an infant.

Lincoln knocked on the rotted baseboard that served as the door. "Miss Meyers? You got a visitor. The nurse is here."

A consumptive mother in a dirty calico dress swung open the wormy board attached to the frame by a single rusty hinge. She barely had the strength to speak. "Bernie's been colic all night, Miss Raber. He's in an awful state."

Lincoln and Taylor watched from outside as Anna crawled into the little cell and knelt aside the baby. She placed her palm on its red forehead and felt its distended belly. "He has an intestinal infection. Probably a bacteria. We need to get him some fresh milk. Where is your husband?"

"Cecil's up at the armory," the mother said. "All we got is some cornmeal."

"I'll see what I can find in the commissary. In the meantime, you need to get the child some fresh air. I know you're not feeling well yourself, but if you can, take a walk with your babe under the shade today. This fetid air in here inflames his throat."

The mother struggled to her elbows. "Yes, ma'am."

Lincoln reached into his pocket and offered the woman a sliver of rabbit jerky. "Gnaw on this, Fannie. It fools my innards for awhile when the aches starting attacking."

The mother bit on the pull with her rotted teeth. "Thank you kindly."

Anna heard a loud commotion. She crawled from the hovel and saw Waters marching across the Eleventh Street Bridge shouting orders. The camp suddenly sprang to life, and men rushed from their tents and shacks as if shaken from a beehive. They began forming up at the speaker's stand to learn why Waters was so agitated.

"The government's gone and d-d-done it!" Waters shouted. "Hoover's trying to d-d-drive us out of Camp Glassford!"

Lincoln clawed his way closer. "I thought those boys had four days yet?"

Waters rushed through the camp banging on doors. "I want every able-bodied man up to Camp Glassford right n-n-now!"

"Where's the Chief?" Anna asked him.

"He's up there leading the charge against us!"

She couldn't believe that Glassford would go back on his promise to find new housing for the veterans before they were chased from the city. Had he broken the vow he had made to her never to betray these men?

"Where the hell is Angelo?" Waters demanded.

"He's sleeping one off," Ozzie said.

Waters marched over to Angelo's bunkhouse and kicked the door. "Joey!"

Stumbling out shirtless and groggy, Angelo shielded his bleary eyes. "What's all the racket?"

"Pin your medal on and get up to the Front!"

It was nearing noon, so Glassford decided to give his eviction officers a lunch break. He was about to issue the order when he saw two trucks barreling down Pennsylvania Avenue. The trucks, with their tailgates down, blew through the rope cordons. A dozen men scrambled out of the rear beds. The arriving gang ran at him with fists balled.

The man leading their charge was waving a large American flag. "Give the cops hell!"

Glassford didn't recognize any of the attackers. The streets were teeming with onlookers, and hundreds more veterans were coming up from Anacostia on foot. He didn't have time to muster a defense line. His officers, who had just settled down to open their delivered sandwiches and iced tea, hustled to their feet and pulled their nightsticks. He rushed into the scrum. "Hold off!!"

Bricks and scrap iron filled the air. Outnumbered, he and his officers turned and took the brunt of the assault on their backs. One of the rioters rushed across the no-man's land of rubble and tore the badge off the chief's shirt. A cop grabbed the flag from the ringleader, but he was pummeled back with a lead pipe. Bricks flew in both directions. One officer, bleeding from a split skull, fell to the ground.

Angered by the theft of his badge, Glassford hurled himself into the midst of the brick throwers. He took a brick in the chest, and staggered. A collective gasp, followed by a tense hush, froze the fight. The veterans, stunned at seeing the chief take a hit, stopped their throwing. Regaining his breath, Glassford arose from one knee and forced a worried smile. "Come on, boys!" he pleaded. "Let's call an armistice for lunch."

The veterans, impressed by his courage and humor in the face of danger, nodded and backed off, their faces cast down in shame.

Glassford ordered Lt. Edwards to fan out through the new agitators and make arrests.

Edwards handcuffed one of the instigators and prodded him up. "Is he the one who hit you, Chief? He says his name's McCoy."

Glassford studied the man's features. The attack had happened so fast, he couldn't be sure who had nearly brained him.

"I didn't do it, General! I swear! I got hit by a billy club!"

"Who told you to come up here?"

The arrested man seemed genuinely addled. "I don't rightly know. Some of the fellas said everyone was heading to the armory. I just joined in."

"Are you a Red?" demanded Lt. Edwards.

"No sir!"

Glassford scanned the demolition site, determined to put down any more brewing attacks. He recognized a couple of faces, but most of these new arrivals were unfamiliar to him. Were they some of Pace's men from the Communist camp across the Mall? From the corner of his eye, he saw one of his uniformed cops slip away and hurry into the alley toward City Hall. He pointed to the retreating officer. "Who was that man?"

Lt. Edwards traded a knowing glance with a couple of his fellow officers. "Lieutenant Keck."

"What was he doing here?"

The lieutenant didn't look eager to answer that question, but finally he admitted, "He's been reporting to Commissioner Crosby."

Glassford's face drained. *They have a spy on my force.*

He walked a few steps away to gather his frazzled thoughts. How could he be sure who stood with him? Had Pace and his Communists instigated this attack? Or had someone else?

Officer Shinault came hurrying up from the communications car. "We just got an order delivered from Attorney General Mitchell's office."

"What does *he* want?"

Shinault looked elated. "We've been commanded to evacuate the veterans from all federal property, not just these buildings."

Glassford couldn't fathom that change in his orders. Surely the Attorney General wouldn't have issued such a sweeping and dangerous directive without White House approval. The screws were being tightened on him, minute by minute. He didn't have the force necessary to launch such an expanded operation, and Hurley and Crosby knew it.

Glancing with triumph at Shinault, Lt. Edwards pressed the chief, "What do you want us to do about these men we've arrested?"

Glassford studied the contrite veteran in handcuffs, trying to understand what was really happening. He had the situation back under control, but it was clear that someone was trying to undercut his operation. "Take them to headquarters and hold them. And call in for more reinforcements."

Summoned to the White House, MacArthur strode down the sidewalk from the War Department building and saluted the guard as he entered the West Wing.

In the corridor, Patrick Hurley rushed up to him. "He won't sign it."

"You told him of the situation?"

Hurley nodded. "You're the only one who can convince him."

Escorted into the Oval Office, MacArthur found Hoover and Secretary of State Stimson hovering over a draft copy of a speech. In the corner stood George Drescher, the president's personal Secret Service agent.

"Mr. President," Hurley announced. "The Chief of Staff has arrived."

Aggravated by the interruption, Hoover slapped his palm to the desk. "I don't have time for that now."

MacArthur took a step forward. "Sir, I'm afraid the situation in the city has seriously deteriorated. The nation's security is at risk."

Skeptical, Hoover shook his head in vexation. Then, reluctantly, he whispered a request to Stimson that they take a break. After the Secretary of State left the room, Hoover walked to the window and looked north toward Pennsylvania Avenue. Clutching at the ache in his left forearm, he demanded testily, "What it is now?"

Hurley nodded at MacArthur, cueing him to the task.

MacArthur set his brow in that famous leer of military authority. "Sir, there is a riot in progress at the old District armory. As we feared, Communist elements in the camps have taken root and are now bearing their venomous fruit."

"I will *not* sign a proclamation declaring martial law!"

"Sir, an insurrection," MacArthur insisted.

Hoover turned slowly, looking as if an announcement of the Apocalypse's arrival would have surprised him less. "What does Glassford say about this?"

MacArthur stole an uncertain glance at Hurley. "Glassford has lost control of the situation."

Hoover studied the two advisors hard. "Has he requested federal troops?"

"That would be an admission of defeat on his part, sir."

"Have you been down there to assess the danger?"

MacArthur hesitated. "I can personally attest to the need for troops."

Denied a direct answer, Hoover paced the length of the room, trying to make sense of these dire pronouncements. After nearly a minute of troubled contemplation, he told Hurley. "I will not sign a proclamation of insurrection."

The corners of Hurley's eyes twitched slightly. "With all due respect—"

"I will draft an order authorizing limited and humane use of federal troops to restore the peace on the condemned federal property along Pennsylvania Avenue. These troops will be placed under the direction of Chief Glassford. He alone will determine if they are needed to complement his police force. Women and children in the area must and will be accorded every consideration and kindness."

Hurley blanched at such constraining terms. "Sir, this unduly ties our hands. Army officers will not take orders from a civilian police chief."

"The man once commanded Army troops, did he not?"

"Yes, but—"

"Perhaps we should have the soldiers carry only police sticks. That would help prevent accidents."

Hurley was livid at having his counsel questioned. "I must protest this."

MacArthur circled the desk to force Hoover to look at him directly. "There is no time to arrange for the delivery of police sticks, Mr. President. I think we can manage under the conditions you've set forth."

Hurley glared at MacArthur, stunned that he would surrender so easily.

MacArthur slapped his hand to his thigh. "Now, if you will excuse us, Mr. President. Time is pressing."

Hoover waved them away. When the two men had left the room, Secret Service agent Drescher closed the door and returned to his station in the corner. Hoover tried to resume his editing of Stimson's speech, but after several minutes in distracted effort, he threw the paper aside. He looked over at Drescher. "George, am I doing the right thing?"

"Sir?"

"Giving MacArthur and Hurley these troops."

Drescher was reluctant to answer. "Sir, it's not my place."

"I trust you every day with my life. I'm no longer sure I can trust anyone else in this building except my wife. I'd welcome your opinion."

"Sir, between you and me, I don't see what good can come of it."

Hoover slumped into his chair. "Well, they say MacArthur was the luckiest man in the war. Maybe some of that luck will rub off on me today."

When Ozzie and Lincoln finally reached the old armory around one o'clock, their feet were blistering from the hot walk up from the river. Things looked pretty quiet, with most of the boys just milling around under the shade of the overhangs and scrounging for something to eat while the cops stood back along the newly planted trees on the Mall. The blocks on all sides of the demolished structures were filling up with the thousands of veterans that Waters had mustered from Anacostia and the other camps.

Ozzie squinted through the dripping haze, looking for a familiar face. "Hey, there's Billy! Maybe he knows where we can find some coffee."

He and Lincoln weaved their way through the claques of men lounging on the hardpan. They reached the old Ford showroom and found Hruska sitting against an exposed beam, chewing on a blade of sawgrass.

"Billy boy!" Ozzie cried. "Where's this war we heard about?"

"Yeah," Lincoln chimed. "Waters was yelling like the Boche had invaded."

"No war," said Hruska. "Infiltrators."

Ozzie blinked hard. "Infiltrators? What you talking about?"

"Bad types. Never see them before. They attack the General."

Ozzie searched the mounds of brick rubble and saw Glassford on the far side of the demolition site, mingling with his officers and talking to the veterans. "The Chief don't look no worse for the wear."

"Infiltrators try to blame us!" said Hruska, furious. "They come back, I will hang them from those beams up there!"

"You get a good look at them?" asked Lincoln.

Hruska nodded and pointed at his own nose. "I remember their ugly faces."

"Speaking of ugly faces," Ozzie said. "Have you seen Alford lately? Dubya is looking for him."

Hruska shook his head. "Alford never around."

"You're right about that," said Lincoln. "Ol' Georgie comes and goes like the ghost of Christmas past. I wonder if he's got a sweet floozy stashed uptown."

Ozzie waved off that possibility. "Georgie? With that old crow's frightful mug? He couldn't draw a mosquito with a pint of blood."

"I reckon you're right," said Lincoln. "Now that you mention it, he never impressed me as much of a ladies man. Me, on the other hand—"

A gunshot rang out.

Ozzie nearly leapt out of his overalls. Hunched on the concrete, he looked up to see hundreds of men rushing up the exposed stairwell above him to get a better look at who was firing across the block. Two more shots fired, and the men lounging around him erupted like a tornado and charged down the stairs.

"Let's get him!" someone shouted.

A sudden surge of men pushed Ozzie aside. Several veterans rushed at Glassford, who was climbing the stairwell to find the shooter. Garbage cans and bricks flew everywhere. Two police officers followed their chief up the stairs. A brick hit Officer Shinault, who was standing a few steps behind Glassford on the stairwell. Dazed from the blow to his head, Shinault drew his gun and fired into the crowd.

"Stop that shooting!" Glassford ordered.

Wild-eyed, Shinault aimed his pistol at Glassford.

The police chief dropped down behind a pillar. Moments later, he risked inching his head out. Shinault stood looking at his weapon, as if trying to convince himself that he hadn't discharged it.

Glassford rushed the officer and stole the pistol from his hand.

Stunned by the gunshots, the veterans fell silent.

Ozzie looked around to inspect the damage. When the smoke cleared, he saw Hruska lying against a rail in a pool of blood. "Billy!" He rushed to his friend and tried to revive him.

The men converged around Hruska, muttering threats.

Ozzie lifted Hruska's lifeless head. "They done killed him!"

"They got Carly too!" shouted another veteran.

The men turned to find Eric Carlson, one of Robertson's California men who had stayed on with them. He was thrumming helplessly on the ground, a bullet hole in his gut. Several of the men lifted Carlson and carried him toward an arriving ambulance while four injured police officers retreated to the protection of their comrades.

Glassford hurried among the angry veterans, trying to calm them. "Let's stop this now, before it's too late."

"The General's right!" shouted Lincoln. "Don't let the Reds and them government agents turn us against the police! The cops have been our friends!"

Hundreds of the veterans pressed against the cordon ropes, picking up rocks and promising vengeance for Hruska, whose blood was pooling into a halo around his head.

In the confusion, Jesse Essary, a reporter for the *St. Louis Post-Dispatch*, slipped under the cordon ropes. The reporter came aside a shaken Glassford. "Things are getting pretty hot down here. What happened to those fellas?"

Glassford waved off his small talk. "I don't have time for an interview."

"Mind if I tag along?"

"Suit yourself, but just stay out of my way."

"It's gonna be like the old days, eh?"

Glassford, confused, turned on the reporter. "Old days?"

"With the Army back in Sam Brownes and field leggings."

"What are you talking about?"

The reporter realized that the police chief hadn't been told the latest news. "A couple of infantry regiments are sailing up the river by steamer from Fort Washington. I just saw the cavalry on Memorial Bridge with tanks a half-hour ago. Mac's mustering them all down at the Ellipse. Looks like it's going to be a hell of a show. We were told you requested them."

Glassford ran past his officers and jumped on his motorcycle.

I n his War Department office, MacArthur pulled out a drawer in his desk and opened the lock box where he kept his awards and ribbons. He pressed a buzzer to summon Eisenhower, his adjutant. "Major, drive to my house at Fort Myer on the double and retrieve my uniform and boots. They're in my closet."

Eisenhower just stood there, gawking as if he had misheard. "Sir?"

"MacArthur is going into action. You'll need to change into your uniform, as well. I'll have to cancel lunch with Mother."

"I haven't had my uniform out of storage since the war."

"Let's hope you still fit in it." He saw his aide staring at the decorations laid out on his desk, ready to be appended. "Should I be ashamed of them?"

"No, sir, of course not." Stunned at learning that the troops were being mobilized within the city, Eisenhower delayed at the door.

MacArthur looked up. "Something else, Major?"

"Sir, with all due respect. Putting down a local disturbance is beneath the dignity of the Army Chief of Staff."

MacArthur fixed a withering stare on his adjutant. "Your naiveté, Major, disappoints me. We now find ourselves in the throes of a Communist conspiracy. This is a very serious test of the strength of the federal government against its enemies. MacArthur will be on the front lines, as he always has been. And you will be at his side."

"Sir, why don't you just fire me?"

"Fire you?"

"Permission to speak freely?"

"Granted."

"Goddammit, General. You do things that I don't agree with. And you know damn well I don't. Why don't you get another officer in this job who shares your…"

"My what?"

"Your philosophy of democracy."

MacArthur stared oddly at him, as if the observation had been offered in a foreign tongue. "Major, are you familiar with the fate of Themistocles?"

"Only vaguely, sir."

"He saved Greek democracy from the Persian hordes by turning Athens into a fortress under martial law. Once the danger from the East was repulsed, the Athenians showed their gratitude by ostracizing him and sending him into exile."

"I'm not sure I take the inference, sir."

"A military leader must be prepared to take the unpopular stand to save democracy from an inherent impulse to destroy itself. I will not fire you. You will do your duty."

Simmering at the vainglorious order, Eisenhower saluted stiffly and turned for the door.

"And Major, on your way back, stop by the Chastleton and tell Miss Cooper that MacArthur will be unavoidably detained."

Glassford sped Blue Bessie west down Pennsylvania Avenue. When he passed the Treasury Building, his heart sank. On the grassy slopes of the Ellipse, four hundred infantrymen in full battle gear were forming up columns and collecting gas canisters from a quartermaster wagon. A squadron of cavalry on their flank hurried with preparations, tightening saddle straps and wiping their gleaming sabers with oil cloths. Behind them, trucks sat loaded with tanks. So many of his old friends and officer acquaintances, including Lucian Truscott and George Patton, were assembling a force that looked like a reunion from the war.

As he approached the gathering on his cycle, he noticed several of the officers averted their eyes, refusing to acknowledge his arrival. In the midst of this impressive array of West Pointers, MacArthur stood in full dress uniform, conferring with General Perry Miles, commander of the Sixteenth Brigade, and giving orders to his aide, Major Eisenhower.

With that old war look of keen anticipation in his agate eyes, MacArthur saw his old classmate and motioned him over. "Just look at these crack troops, Hap. Seeing them now, I can't help but think back on my old Rainbow boys."

Glassford parked the cycle and got off slowly, turning in disbelief as if he were caught in a nightmare. "General, several of your Rainbow men are out there on that avenue. What are you planning to do?"

"I am going to break the back of the BEF."

"There's no need for these troops. We had some tense moments earlier this morning, but—"

"Deaths. You had deaths, not tense moments. The insurrection has exploded into street fighting. Four of your officers were injured in it."

"I've regained control of the area."

"Battle sector control is a mercurial thing, Hap. Once the enemy gets its fighting blood up, there can be no half-measures, or all will be lost."

Glassford's jaw dropped. "Enemy? General, there is no enemy. Those men are Americans. Americans who fought for *us* in France."

MacArthur slapped his riding crop to his thigh. "I have orders from the White House to drive the squatters out of the city."

"The President gave his permission for the dispersal?"

MacArthur became increasingly agitated, shooting impatient glances at the slowness of the troops to form up. "Within a short time, we will move down Pennsylvania, sweep through the billets there, and clean out the other two large camps. The operation will be continuous. It will be all done by tonight."

Standing there in shock, Glassford now understood from the reaction of the other officers that MacArthur and Hurley had been planning this military operation for weeks. "General, there are thousands of citizens on the streets down there. You'll put innocent people in harm's way."

"Hap, you'll have to excuse me now. I must address the troops."

Glassford stole a pleading glance at his watch. He'd give a king's ransom for the gift of darkness, but it was only four o'clock. This day was dragging on like none he had ever experienced, even those on the Marne. "General, give me ten minutes, at least. Let me at least try to clear the avenue of civilians before you send these troops."

"Yes, of course, my friend. I can hold my attack for ten minutes."

As they walked out of the District morgue down near the river, Ozzie Taylor and Charlie Lincoln needed a moment to regain their bearings in the damp heat. They finally found the Washington Monument in the sweltering haze, and keeping its tip in their sights, hoofed it back north up Seventh Street. They had followed the ambulance down here to the southwest waterfront, praying that Billy Hruska had miraculously resurrected himself after the shooting. But they had discovered their buddy laid out cold naked on a slab, with a bullet hole in his chest and his gut splayed open like a butchered steer.

Lincoln took several gasping breaths as he walked into the blasts of lethally baked air. He tried to avoid the morbid subject on both their minds. "It's hotter than a Turkish bath in Texas out here! I could've stayed in there a while longer. Coolest spot in the city."

Ozzie glanced over his shoulder, still fascinated by the morgue's steeple and arched, stained-glass windows. "I never seen a dead house built like a church."

"They build 'em like that to comfort the bereaved. Most of those fellas lying in state back there were just like us. Didn't have a dollar to press their eyes, let alone spend for a funeral. So that iced chapel does double duty."

Ozzie couldn't get the ghastly image of Billy's mutilated corpse out of his mind. "Why'd they have to filet him like that, Charlie?"

"That's what they do to murder victims. They gotta make sure the bullet is what got them."

"What else would have gotten him?"

"He could have been poisoned by that river mud coffee they make us drink. Then the shooter wouldn't have been the proximate cause of the death."

"Prox what?"

"Proximate cause," Lincoln said. "It's a term of jury prudence. If I was to waylay you here and leave you for a goner, but you was still lingering when a storm brewed up and a bolt of lightning came down and struck you all the way to Paradise, I wouldn't be criminally accountable for your demise. That would be what's called an act of God."

"Since when did you become Clarence Darrow?"

"I learned a little court sophistry during those thirty days I was incarcerated."

"You spent time in the pokey?"

Lincoln nodded as he picked up the pace. "Two years ago, in Abilene. The Jayhawker state doesn't take kindly to loitering. But I made the best of my situ-

ation, as I always do, and furthered my already extensive education by studying
under the tutelage of a cellmate who was in for the larceny of a five-and-ten.
Harry Collins was his name. Hell of a magician. During his arraignment, he
pilfered a Bartlett's Legal Dictionary from the clerk's desk and secreted it out
under his shirt. At night, we took turns catechizing each other on the nomen-
clature of the common law spoken since the signing of the Magna Carta."

"You're a right learned man, Charlie. I have to give you that."

"Despite what Alford says about my lack of education, my talent for self-
improvement has been passed down through the Lincoln clan's bloodstream."
He stopped on a nonexistent dime and stared down at an empty field that
bordered the river. "They did it right over there."

Ozzie looked around but saw nothing except empty garbage cans overturned by wild dogs. "Did what?"

"This is the very ground where they hung the conspirators that conspired
to murder my kinsman."

"How do you know that?"

"Sometimes I get visions sent from my forefathers. That poor woman they
swung was innocent as you and me. But the government had its bloodlust
up. They made her pay for just being around at the wrong time. She took her
damn time dying, too."

Ozzie was getting the scare chills from all this death talk. "Let's get outa here."

Lincoln shook off his ghost vision. "Yeah, Dubya probably thinks we went
AWOL by now."

"Speaking of Dubya, I'm a little hurt he didn't come with us to the morgue
to pay his respects to Billy."

"Dubya's got important things on his mind."

"That's right, I guess. Still, if it was one of us took the bullet, I'd hope the
commander would come see us off to our Maker."

They headed across the Mall toward Camp Glassford at the old District
armory. Ozzie slowed down as they passed the Communist camp at Thirteenth
and C streets. Pace's Red vets were all in a lather, hollering and running toward
Pennsylvania Avenue like banshees. In the vaporous distance, he saw a column
of cavalry cantering down the hallowed boulevard of inaugurated presidents.
Behind the mounts rolled four tanks. Hundreds of civilian workers and residents were coming through the doors in the Old Post Office and the hotels
along the avenue to see what the commotion was all about.

Lincoln squinted into the haze. "Is there a parade today?"

Ozzie quickened his faltering gait. "Look there, Charlie! That's infantry
behind the horse boys! They look right fine, don't they? Those tanks are a might
heftier than the cracker tins on wheels ol' Georgie Patton drove in France."

"By god, the regulars have finally come out to support us!" yelled Lincoln. "I told you those boys down at the barracks would get behind the Bonus!"

The two veterans hurried as fast as their sore feet would allow toward the spectacle up ahead. When they reached Pennsylvania Avenue, they found Chief Glassford riding his cycle up and down the lanes, pleading for the civilians to retreat north behind rope cordons that his officers were throwing up in front of the sidewalks. On the south side, thousands of their comrades had converged in front of their shacks to welcome the approaching troops.

"Hey, General!" shouted Lincoln. "Can we get across to join our buddies?"

Glassford, looking sick in the gills, waved him off. "Get out of here!"

Ozzie was thoroughly puzzled. "He's in a sour mood, huh."

Lincoln crawled under the restraining rope and stood on the pavement where the old streetcar rails still ran. He saluted the infantry, and motioned Ozzie over to join him.

Ozzie held back, fearful of disobeying the general's order. But Lincoln insisted, and finally Ozzie relented. They stood there together on the avenue at attention, basking in the memories of those days when they had marched across France with guns shouldered and tin hats flashing under the sun. All around them, their fellow veterans were waving American flags and singing patriotic songs. Lincoln removed his stovepipe hat in reverence for the Stars and Stripes. He hadn't seen a show like this since the good folks in Omaha had sent him and the other doughboys off on July Fourth of Nineteen-and-Seventeen. "By God, Oswald, it makes you proud to be an American, don't it?"

Ozzie nodded, mesmerized by the infantry column that came to a heel-thumping halt near Gilman's Drugstore, just beyond Sixth Street. An order was shouted from somewhere behind the regulars, and they executed a deft quarter turn. Half of them now faced the throngs of civilians to the north, and the other half stared down those veterans who were packed together along the rubble on the evacuation block below the armory. An Army officer shouted a second order, and the troops quickly fixed bayonets.

Lincoln started clapping and spurring everyone around him to join in the applause. "I ain't seen potstickers like that since the Marne. They're pulling out the stops for our entertainment, boys! Let's give them a hand!"

Ozzie suddenly got a sinking feeling in his gut. "Charlie... "

"Yeah?"

"I think they're meaning us some trouble."

Lincoln guffawed. "Trouble? You're dafter than a swinging screen door in winter, Oz." He commenced walking toward the lead soldiers in the column. "To put your hallucinating mind at ease, I'll start up a conversation with—"

"Halt!"

Lincoln frowned at the surly sergeant. "There's no cause for that."

The infantry lowered bayonets and moved forward on the double. A silence of disbelief and shock froze the civilian crowds and the veterans.

"They're attacking us!" shouted a veteran perched on the armory's top floor.

That bellowed warning broke loose all Hell.

The cavalry spurred to the chase and fanned out on both sides of the avenue. The riders drove their horses pell-mell into the crowds, pummeling panicked spectators with the flat of their sabers and threatening to stomp on them with the hooves of their chargers if they didn't move off.

The streets filled with screams and shouts of vengeance.

The infantry sergeant marched down the street yelling at the curious spectators, "You got three minutes to clear out! Three minutes!"

"This is America!" shouted Lincoln. "We got a right to be here!"

Ozzie backed away down the Avenue toward the Capitol, but hundreds of veterans scrambled over the rope lines and tried to form a human barricade. The soldiers pulled gas masks from their packs and pulled them over their heads. Moments later, the regulars threw gas canisters at the veterans, and the air filled with smoke carrying poisonous potassium nitrate. Veterans and civilians heaved, choking and vomiting. The unarmed veterans cursed the soldiers and taunted them with indictments of cowardice, and they were answered with a fusillade of gas canisters.

Remembering their training in the trenches, the veterans tried soaking their kerchiefs with what water they could find and pressed them against their mouths and noses. Many dropped to their knees, sneezing and tearing up and fighting for breath. Those who could still stand picked up the hot canisters and threw them back at the soldiers. The air became filled with lacing bricks, whizzing canisters, and any debris that the outgunned veterans could get their hands on.

The BEF line tried to hold, but it crumbled under the onslaught of sharp steel. Crying from the gas and the shock of betrayal, the veterans fell back as squads of infantry split off and descended on the abandoned federal buildings in Camp Glassford. The regulars drove the frightened families of the veterans out of the dark recesses at the points of the bayonets.

Lord help them poor folk, Ozzie prayed. *Lord help us all.*

The infantry column kept moving up the avenue and sweeping aside anyone who got in its way. The womenfolk of the veterans tried to run up to the Army officers and beg permission to retrieve what few belongings they kept in their huts, but the dragoons scattered them off with their sabers. Across the street, a cavalryman lashed with his saber at a reporter trying to call in the story on a phone at a gasoline station.

"If we had guns!" shouted Lincoln.

"Move it!" demanded a soldier who couldn't have been more than eighteen.

Shaking with rage, Lincoln saw an American flag abandoned on the ground. He picked it up and brandished it at the insolent soldier. "Hit me now, you yellow bastard! You hit me, you hit this flag!"

The young soldier whipped his rifle butt at Lincoln's chin. Spitting blood, Lincoln crawled off and curled into a ball to protect his head.

A few feet away, Ozzie was desperate for breathable air. He climbed a tree, but the clouds of tear gas just kept rising toward him. One thought kept coursing through his heated brain: What would Big Jim have done if he were here to witness this shameful devastation?

The wind began to turn, and the gas shot at the veterans wafted toward the civilians who were scrambling for the protection of the Mall. By now, Ozzie calculated, there had to be twenty thousand innocent people in the area, all drawn by the rumors of a battle. Below him, the American flags atop the shanties erupted in flames.

They're setting everything afire.

He held to the limb for dear life. The whole damn place looked like the Marne again. Wounded were staggering and dropping everywhere. Women and their children ran screaming and falling into holes in the rubble. Soldiers jabbed and thrust at stragglers with their bayonets. From his high vantage, he saw one infantry squad break off from the main column and head with bayonets flashing toward the Communist camp across the Mall.

By God, he muttered, he wouldn't want to be those Red boys right now. He searched the panorama of chaos below for Lincoln. His throat was burning, but he risked ruining his chords to yell, "Charlie! You hurt?"

There was no answer from below.

Had Charlie been worked over too badly to answer? On the Avenue, the soldiers kept marching up the canyon of heroes and raining down destruction upon anything in their path. Would they ever stop?

Lord God, protect me from this wrath of evil.

Why the heck did Dubya want him to bring the medal? Angelo shrugged off that mystery as he climbed the bluffs from the Anacostia flats and headed for the Capitol. The orders passed through the camp around noon had called for all able-bodied men to head on up to Camp Glassford for another rally. But he had decided to take the long way around, making a circuit past the Supreme Court first to pay a visit to a friendly popcorn vendor who always saved the unexploded kernels for him. Mashed and soaked for a few hours in vinegar, those little burnt balls produced a passable substitute for peanut butter, if your expectations weren't too lofty.

As he walked toward the shimmering dome, he felt his Distinguished Service Cross flapping against his chest. The pin holding it had frayed the wool lapel on his jacket so severely that he debated moving it down an inch. But he remembered the instructions of his mother, bless her soul, who had taught him as a boy that the accurate situating of holy medals, statues of saints, and other relics of veneration could mean the difference between divine protection and demonic misfortune. So, he decided against that breach of regulation.

He finally reached the Capitol plaza, now twice as famished for the effort. But the place was deserted. Hell, even the popcorn hawker was gone. Where was everybody? The air stung his nostrils, causing his nose to run. He wiped the snot with his sleeve.

Damn, that smells like the Marne.

He picked up his pace and hurried around to the west side of the Capitol. Below the statue of General Grant, the Mall looked like an ant farm sprayed with pesticide. Thousands of people were running and darting every which direction, and above them wafted a strange, bluish haze. He rubbed his eyes, but that only made them hurt worse. Cats were screeching and dogs were barking and howling. Pregnant women sat sobbing under trees. Mothers dragged mattresses and chairs across the Mall while crying children carried what ragged clothes they could salvage before the soldiers burned their shanties.

It looked like the Day of Judgment.

He hurried down the grassy slope toward the giant Esso gas station building, where the congressmen got their fancy Cadillacs filled and shined. When he reached the intersection of Pennsylvania and Constitution, a sea of rushing panic stopped him in his tracks. Hundreds of veterans and civilians were coughing and heaving and scattering for the abandoned Methodist Church on Fourth Street to find sanctuary.

Are those tanks down there?

He covered his mouth as he ran through the swirling gas mists to get a closer look. A few yards ahead, an open-bed truck carrying six veterans came wheeling up and braked to a skidding stop. The men behind this rolling barricade unleashed a barrage of bricks at the tanks, but their missiles bounced harmlessly off the iron plating. A squadron of cavalrymen retaliated by charging with their sabers drawn. Those khaki-clad hussars hammered at the exposed veterans, driving them to their knees and bloodying their scalps. One of the uniformed horsemen was yelping and grinning and swinging his blade as if it were Custer's ghost given a second chance at Little Big Horn.

He froze. Where had he heard that shrill shriek before?

Crissakes…that's Major Patton.

He ran toward his old superior officer, waving to get his attention. "Major! It's me! Joe Angelo!"

Patton turned with wild eyes toward his shout.

Angelo remembered that crazy look. *Can't he see me?*

As bricks rained down around him, Patton reined his spooking sorrel and, slapping its withers, spurred off for another attack on the retreating truck.

"Major! Over here! It's Joe—"

A bayonet pricked his chest. Staggered to the ground, Angelo looked up and found an infantryman aiming the deadly end of a rifle at him. His dander up, he scrambled back to his feet and pointed at the medal on his chest for the soldier's edification. "You see this? Have some respect for this!"

The private threw a hip into him. "Get moving!"

Knocked to the pavement, Angelo lurched to his scraped hands and knees. "You know where France is?"

The soldier raised the butt end of his rifle. "I know where Hell is, and you're gonna take the chute to it if you keep flapping that mouth."

"I was over there taking bullets when you were still in diapers!"

The soldier reached to his belt and unhooked another gas canister. "You're gonna need those diapers again if you stick around here much longer."

Angelo was madder than a fighting cock in a Camden pool hall. "Give us some weapons! Then we'll see who can shoot their mouths off!"

The soldier prodded him with his bayonet across the grass like a calf to slaughter. His tormentor yelled over to one of his fellow storm troopers who was chasing a woman out of her hut. "Hey, Jimmy! Take a look at this one! He ain't got enough flesh on him to put a hook through."

"Throw him back into the pool!" trilled the second soldier.

Angelo crawled away, cursing and promising vengeance. "The whole country's gonna hear about this!"

The soldier kicked at him again. "Yeah? Who's gonna listen to *you?*"

Tired of the one-sided tussle, the soldier moved on to look for more challenging game. From his humiliating position of battered prostration, Angelo risked a glance over his elbow. He saw MacArthur standing across the street, slapping his riding crop while pointing officers toward the remaining pockets of resistance. He thought he saw tears coming down the general's cheeks.

Was Mac crying from the shame of it all?

One of the soldiers yanked a flag from a retreating veteran. "Give me that, you crummy old bum!"

A few feet away, a civilian watching from behind the ropes shouted at the soldier, "The American flag means nothing to me after this!"

MacArthur turned toward the cursing spectator and ordered one of his officers, "Put that man under arrest if he opens his mouth again!"

Angelo realized that MacArthur was tearing up all right—not from emotion, but because, just like in France, he was too vain to put on a gas mask.

Twitching from fatigue and feeling faint, Waters remained fixed at the third-story window of his headquarters in the Ebbitt Hotel. For the past half hour, he had stood there watching in disbelief as the regulars scattered his battered BEF army across the city. "MacArthur lied to me, Georgie," he muttered. "He lied to me."

Alford kept watch on the door, in case any of the regulars came looking for them. He risked coming across the room to comfort his distraught friend with a hand to his shoulder. "They're all lying bastards."

"Ain't there nothin' at all a man can believe in anymore?"

"We're surrounded in this country by nothing but politicians and warmongers. We never had a chance against the big money of the Wall Street thieves who finance them."

Waters fought back tears. "I g-g-gotta go d-d-down there and lead them."

Alford restrained him from rushing for the hall stairs. "It's too dangerous, Dubya. Remember those government spies who've been trying to assassinate you for weeks? Only thing that's kept you alive was our moving you around each night. You go down there in that mayhem now, one of their trigger goons will sure as hell take aim at you. You're too valuable to us."

"But what d-d-do I do now?"

"We'll lay low for awhile. Soon as things quiet down in a few days, we'll get you out of town. They won't know you're even gone. Then we'll muster the Khaki Shirts and come back with thousands more."

Shaking from nerves and exhaustion, Waters staggered to the bed and pulled the covers over his head, trying to muffle the screams and shrieks in the street below. "Let me rest a moment, will you, Georgie?"

Alford closed the blinds. "Don't you worry, Dubya. I'll keep watch."

Hoover sat stewing at his desk with the overbearing gaze of Admiral Boone fixed on him like the all-seeing Masonic eye of the dollar bill. Holding his blood pressure cuff at the ready, the physician had insisted on remaining at his side since dawn to watch for signs of cardiac distress. He didn't know which was worse: waiting for Hurley to bring word of the military operation on Pennsylvania Avenue, or suffering the admiral's incessant pokings and ministrations. "Joel, go ask Joslin if there have been any injuries."

"Sir, I really shouldn't leave you."

"I can't take being cooped up in here like a veal calf. I need some air."

"That's not wise, Mr. President. There is gas—"

"Gas?"

"There are reports that the troops have deployed tear-gas canisters."

"My God."

Seeing his patient dangerously agitated, the admiral moved in on the biceps for another reading, but he was repulsed. "Sir, take a few long breaths."

Hoover erupted from his chair. "Where in the blazes is Hurley? He was supposed to report to me over—"

Ted Joslin opened to the door to the Oval Office. Before the press secretary could announce the arrival, Secretary of War Hurley marched in. The stoic New Mexican stood in silence before the president.

"Well?" Hoover demanded.

Hurley glanced at Admiral Boone to indicate that what he was about to say was for the president's ears only.

"Joel, will you give us a moment alone?"

Admiral Boone reluctantly retreated. "Deep breaths, sir. If you experience any discomfort in the chest—"

"Close the door behind you."

Hurley waited for an invitation to sit, but Hoover kept him standing. Finally, the war secretary reported, "The dispersal has proceeded as planned."

Hoover grimaced at the military lingo designed to mask the bald truth. He sensed that something was amiss. "Speak plainly, Patrick. Has anybody been hurt?"

"Minor injuries, is all."

"What does *that* mean?"

Hurley seemed to have difficulty looking at him directly. "Nothing you need to concern yourself with, Mr. President."

"Is General Miles remanding the troops to Fort Myer?"

"The troops are still engaged. General MacArthur is leading them—"

"MacArthur? What's he doing out there with them? You told me Miles would command."

"The Chief of Staff felt it was essential that he direct the mission."

Hoover felt his heart racing in his chest. "Where is MacArthur now?"

"Approaching the Eleventh Street Bridge."

Hoover flushed. "My orders were clear and limited. I told you to clear *only* the federal properties at Fifteenth and Pennsylvania Avenue."

"Sir, it is General MacArthur's opinion, and I agree with him, that we should expel all of the veterans from the city while we have the troops in motion."

"Absolutely not!"

"We must close the Anacostia camp tonight, sir. General MacArthur has received evidence from military intelligence of a Red conspiracy in the works. If we allow these traitors to regroup, they will have time to marshal their hidden weapons and mount a formidable counterattack in the morning."

The veins in Hoover's neck bulged. After a long silence, he managed to gather his composure and said in a low, tremulous voice boiling with emotion, "Mr. Joslin will draft an order under my signature. You will have it couriered without delay to General MacArthur by a member of your staff. That order will state in unambiguous terms that the Army is not to cross the Eleventh Street Bridge. Nor is it to enter the Anacostia camp by *any* means. Have I made myself sufficiently clear, sir?"

Forced to endure the lecture, Hurley replied in a clipped tone, "Yes, sir."

In Cleveland on another lecture tour, Floyd Gibbons opened a new bottle of whiskey and kicked up his heels atop the desk that the *Literary Digest* pooh-bahs had found for him in the offices of the *Plain Dealer*. With twenty minutes to spare, he had just handed in his copy for next week's column on the rise of Japanese militarism in Asia. The only problem on his mind now was which saloon to grace that evening with his raconteur wit.

He lit up a stogie, savoring its aroma, which brought to mind a lithe *señorita* in Havana whose hips could have launched a thousand ships. He wondered if she was still plying her magic in those rumba halls across from the Malecon. Maybe he'd go down in the fall and stake his flag again on the white sands of Varadero beach. There had to be some story worthy of an expense-paid—

"Damn," muttered one of the editors behind a circular copy desk. "There's a battle raging in Washington."

Gibbons enjoyed another sip of malt and toasted the eternal circle of life. "There's always a battle raging in Washington, Hayward, ol' boy."

The copy editor watched the tape spit out from the wire-service ticker. "No, Gib. I mean there's a *real* battle."

"What the hell are you blathering about?"

"MacArthur called out the Army this afternoon. He's attacking the Bonus vets. They're fighting right now on Pennsylvania Avenue."

Gibbons didn't bite on that shiny hook. "Little late for April First pranks."

The editor checked the wire photos and shook his head. "Come over here and take a look. Maybe this will convince you."

Gibbons ambled over to examine the photograph coming over the wire. His jaw dropped at what he saw. Infantry in soup-bowl hats were prodding unarmed veterans at the point of bayonets down a street littered with tear-gas canisters. He had seen those smoking cans up close in France. "God damn that preening peacock MacArthur! And God damn that coward Hoover!"

"Looks like you missed out on the story of the year, Gib. First time two American armies under the same Stars and Stripes ever squared off. I'd have loved to hear you burn up the airwaves on this one like in the old days."

Gibbons fumbled for his cane—and the bottle—and lumbered for the door. "It's not a story until I get there! Book me on the next flight to Washington! And call Benny Scalen at NBC in New York! Tell him I want the radio commentary spot for tomorrow!"

Glassford had never felt so helpless. He wasn't much more than a spectator now to the unfolding horror, relegated to tagging along with the rear of the main infantry column. Flanked by roving cavalry, the regulars had made their way up Pennsylvania Avenue and had now disappeared beyond the Capitol in the blue haze of tear gas and the summer heat.

Yet the tanks had turned south onto Third Street.

He thought it odd that the troops would abandon the site of the protest, but he had no time to investigate. He prayed that MacArthur had finally come to his senses and had ordered the tanks back to Fort Myer. He darted on his motorcycle from one pitched fight to another, deploying his officers has best he could to protect and control the thousands of civilians who had poured out onto the streets from their office buildings to watch the unthinkable. Their reactions on seeing the unfair battle turned from shock to outrage.

Several spectators glared at him and shook their heads in judgment, apparently believing that he had conspired in the attack. One woman persisted in trailing him while describing in detail the varied sceneries that he would meet on his way to perdition. "Shame! Shame on you, Chief Glassford!" she shouted. "Not since Pharaoh! Not since the Israelites were driven into the desert!"

He considered reminding her that the Israelites left Egypt on their own accord, a choice that the veterans could have made weeks ago, but he knew that reason stood no chance against this chaos. He merely tipped his hat in contrition and gunned Blue Bessie toward the Capitol dome. It was nearly nine in the evening, and the sun was blessedly slipping toward the Virginia horizon behind him. On reaching the Capitol plaza, he looked around for the vanguard of the infantry. Perry Miles should have been here preparing to disperse the regulars back to the barracks. Where had they gone?

My God, no.

He sped along the railroad tracks past the Navy Yard and spun a right onto Eleventh Street. The tanks sat on the banks overlooking the river with their barrels aimed at the veteran's camp in Anacostia. A company of infantry was marching across the span while MacArthur prowled the bridgehead, conferring with Mills and Eisenhower. Across the river, in the camp, women were screaming and children crying, and a desperate scrum of veterans appeared to be trying to form a line of defense with shovels and broom handles for weapons.

He gunned the cycle up to the officers and skidded to a stop.

MacArthur, in constant motion as usual, wielded his riding crop like a lecture pointer while resting his free hand on his hip at various angles, as if testing poses for a statue. "Hap, have your men move those civilians back."

"General, what are you doing?"

"I'm going to get this area cleared for you."

Alarmed, Glassford turned to Major Eisenhower, who held a sickened look. The adjutant turned his eyes askance, as if to indicate that he had already lost the argument. Before Glassford could beg an explanation for this variance from the plans he had been briefed on at the Ellipse a few hours ago, a staff vehicle sped toward the bridge and braked. General Moseley got out of the back seat and marched up with an urgent scowl on his face.

MacArthur glared at him. "I thought I told you to remain at the office."

"Hurley sent me down here."

Shifty-eyed, MacArthur quickened his pacing while mopping the sweat from the back of his neck with a kerchief. "I don't have time for this."

Moseley made clear by his vinegarish sneer that he shared the disdain for the message he was now required to deliver. "The President wants you to suspend the evacuation for the night. You are not to cross the bridge and enter the Anacostia camp."

MacArthur clenched his jaw and walked a few steps away. Finally, he turned back to Moseley and muttered, "Does that man not understand that we are in the midst of a military operation? I am too busy to deal with correspondence."

Glassford took a step forward and caught Moseley shooting him a suspicious glance, as if questioning what *he* was doing here in the midst of an Army field conference. Glassford angled his head to direct Moseley's attention toward the bridge, where an exploratory sortie of infantry was now crossing to test what opposition the veterans would try to throw up.

Moseley nodded his approval of the decision, making clear his eagerness to see the instigators get what they deserved. The deputy turned and caught up with MacArthur, who was now stalking the riverbank, his owlish eyes blinking with agitation. Glassford moved closer, just enough to overhear Moseley tell MacArthur, "I have to be able to confirm that I delivered the President's order to you. And that you received it."

MacArthur kept walking away, acting as if he had not heard the specifics of the White House command. He was talking faster now. "I will not allow me or my staff to be bothered by people coming down and pretending to bring orders. That will be all, General."

Moseley lingered, looking uncertain what to make of the ambiguous dismissal. Shrugging at the Byzantine ways of his immediate superior, he headed back to his car to report to the White House that he had performed his duty.

Glassford was about to plead with MacArthur to follow the presidential order when they spied a lone veteran crossing the bridge while waving a white flag. He recognized the bedraggled man as Eddie Atwell, the BEF staff officer that Waters had left in charge of the Anacostia camp. The poor fellow's hesitant manner reminded him of those Germans in 1918 who had climbed nervously from the Argonne trenches to surrender, not sure if they would be shot. He walked over and motioned Atwell across the bridge, hoping to reassure the veteran that he would not be harmed.

With worry in his eyes, Atwell nodded to him. "General."

"Are your people okay over there, Atwell?" Glassford asked.

"They're pretty shaken up."

MacArthur came strutting over. "Aren't you that mouthy fellow who said you were going to fight us to the death?"

Atwell, humiliated, hung his head. "You taught us that in France, sir."

MacArthur lorded an air of conquest over the defeated veteran. "I am quite certain no man who stepped foot in that insurrectionist mud pit ever fought for me. Are you giving yourself up to the mercies of the authorities?"

Atwell's hands were shaking. "I'm asking you to allow us to leave peacefully, with our dignity. It'll take us awhile to pack. The women and children—"

MacArthur stretched his chin. "One hour."

The punitive condition shocked Glassford. "General, my men can throw up a patrol around the camp tonight. If we give them until morning—"

"There have been too many prevarications and delays," MacArthur snapped. "I will not allow my troops to bivouac under the guns of traitors."

Glassford didn't know what was more disconcerting: that MacArthur thought the veterans were armed, or that he considered them traitors.

MacArthur glared with disgust at the cowering Atwell. "It is your choice. One hour, or not. Either way, this will all be over tonight."

Atwell looked over his shoulder toward the river, wondering how he could find the words to tell the families that they would be leaving with only those possessions they could carry. As the veteran debated the demand, additional infantry crossed the bridge and fanned out around the perimeter of the camp, taking positions for an attack if necessary. He turned and, glancing in despair at the police chief, reluctantly nodded his acceptance of the terms.

Glassford walked off down river to be alone with his troubled thoughts.

A hobbled veteran, driven from the incinerated shacks near the Mall, approached him. Assisted at the arm by his wife, he recognized the police chief and came closer. "General, you remember what the Belgian children said? They have burned our little beds. They have burned *Monsieur* Jesus Christ.'"

"Those were the Germans," Glassford reminded him in a weak defense.

"And *these* are tin soldiers," the veteran's wife insisted. "They come and burn us in the night. That's all we have to our name up there, going up in smoke."

Glassford was at a loss how to comfort the distraught couple. He dug into his pocket and found a few dollars. "I know it's not much, but the boarding houses north of the Capitol may have some rooms open."

The woman declined the offer. "We'll stay with our own people."

Anna rushed from shack to shack in the Anacostia camp, tending to the scared families and the old men who had stayed behind, many with maladies worsened by the panic of being cast homeless again. One of the last to remain before the evacuation deadline passed, she hurried to make sure all of the infirm had managed to walk out. All around her, she heard wailing and cries of confusion and empty shouts of vengeance. She ran to the commissary and shoved as many library books as she could fit into her shoulder bag. Then, she retreated to the hovel inhabited by the Myers family and found the wife still inside, trying to nurse her colicky infant. Mother and child had bloodshot eyes and were wheezing and coughing. She warned the woman, "You have to get out of here now!"

Mrs. Meyers was too weak to stand. "Bernie's having trouble breathing."

Anna didn't doubt that complaint, for her own lungs were burning from the gas. She took the baby in her arms and saw that he was in severe distress, red as a turnip and gasping. "We have to get him to a hospital." With her free arm, she lifted the mother up, and together they staggered down the rows of abandoned huts in the dark. She looked over her shoulder one last time and saw the hovel where Ozzie Taylor and Charlie Lincoln bunked.

The oboe.

With the baby in her arms, she turned to go back and save the precious instrument. She remembered that Ozzie kept it in his case and stored up on two slats, away from the rainwater.

A young soldier armed with a rifle came around the corner. He lowered his bayonet at her. "Get out!"

"I have to go back for one last thing. It's priceless."

"Orders. Take another step, and I will arrest you."

She thought about charging at the insolent soldier, but she remembered the baby. "What's your name?"

The soldier reacted with surprise at the question. "Calvin."

"Didn't your mother ever teach you manners?"

"My mother?"

She brought forward Mrs. Meyers, sobbing and distraught. "Take your hat off when you pass a lady."

The soldier was thrown on his heels by the odd demand.

"Do it!" she screamed.

The soldier slowly unbuckled his helmet and lowered it to his chest.

She leaned in to him, and the soldier flinched, as if expecting a slap. She pressed a kiss to his cheek.

Before the soldier could recover from the biblical gesture marking betrayal, Anna hurried off toward the river with the baby and Mrs. Meyers. Nearing the bridgehead, she turned around to take one last look at her home here. She saw the young soldier she had just kissed pull a tightly wrapped newspaper from his knapsack. He lit the wad with a match and held it against the cardboard roof of the house built by Ozzie Taylor and Charlie Lincoln.

In minutes, the hovel was aflame—with the oboe inside.

That night, President Hoover stood at the window of his second-floor office watching the distant fireball behind the Capitol dome.

The door cracked open, and his wife Lou stuck her head inside. "Bert, Secretary Hurley and General MacArthur are downstairs."

"Ask them to come up."

"It's 10:30. Can't this wait until the morning?"

Hoover ran his hand down the drapes, testing the richness of the fabric. "Those renovations we talked about for the Stanford house?"

Lou was perplexed that he would raise the subject he always tried to avoid, especially at this hour. "Yes?"

"I think you should go ahead with the contracts."

Realizing what he was admitting, Lou made a half-hearted protest for his sake, choosing not to reveal that she had already been making arrangements to send items to California. "But if we're not moving for four more years... "

He turned with his face so haggard and drawn that it startled her. "We shouldn't delay the preparations."

"You'll feel better tomorrow."

Shaking his head, he turned back toward the window.

Minutes later, an aide escorted MacArthur and Hurley into the upstairs office and shut the door behind them. The two men waited for their presence to be acknowledged, but Hoover remained frozen at the window. Hurley coughed to indicate their arrival.

The president kept his back turned to them. "General MacArthur, do they teach grammar at West Point?"

MacArthur shot an uncertain glance at Hurley, bewildered by the question. "Grammar was a part of our literature curriculum, yes, sir."

Hoover spun on the Army chief of staff with a fearsome glare. "In my order this afternoon, sir, did I misplace a comma, or leave a modifier dangling, that caused you to misinterpret my intent?"

MacArthur didn't answer immediately. Instead, weary after the long day, he followed Hurley to a sofa, and the two military men sat down to rest their legs while they explained their decision to rid the city entirely of the veterans.

"Remain standing!" Hoover ordered. "Both of you."

Stung by his harsh tone, the two advisors came slowly back to their feet.

Hoover walked the length of the room to confront MacArthur, drawing so close to the West Pointer's practiced, lizard-like gaze that he could smell the talcum on his insolent jaw. His voice thrummed with compressed fury. "Did my order reach you this afternoon?"

MacArthur refused to meet the president's bagged eyes. "Too late, sir. The operation was already underway."

"An operation that I expressly rejected in our previous discussions."

MacArthur slowly turned his withering glare directly upon the man that he had come to privately regard as a spineless mugwump. "With all due respect, Mr. President, you never served in the military. Field command must take precedence in the heat of battle."

"You call herding unarmed men like cattle… *battle*?"

"We found ourselves confronting a dangerous Communist insurrection out there today," MacArthur insisted. "To pull back my troops while they were in harm's way would have been gross malfeasance."

"They weren't your troops. They belong to the country."

"I command them."

"General Miles commands them in the field. You interjected yourself into the situation needlessly."

"I'm afraid I don't see it that way."

Hoover clenched his fists, incensed by MacArthur's smugness. "I should fire you both for insubordination."

Hurley bristled. "On the contrary, we have done you a great service, sir."

The blue vein in Hoover's right temple throbbed. "No, sir, you have not. You and your chief of staff here have dealt both the nation and me a grievous wound. A wound, I fear, that will not soon heal. Tomorrow the newspapers across the country will run headlines excoriating me for being the first American president to order regular troops to fight American veterans."

"Most of those *clochards* out there were covert Reds," insisted MacArthur. "You were on the verge of becoming another Kerensky."

Hoover set his jaw in disgust at MacArthur's insufferable penchant for sprinkling French into his bombast. "You will immediately issue a joint statement taking full responsibility for today's debacle."

Hurley took a defiant step forward. "I strongly suggest you rethink that course of action, Mr. President. With the election just a few months away, it would not be wise for your political future, or for the long-term future of our party. And it would only give our enemies cause for renewed hope. Condemn this long overdue cleansing of the city, and thousands more will descend upon us, heartened with the certainty that they will be met with appeasement."

Hoover pinched his brow into a tighter glare. "You expect *me* to take the blame for *your* disobedience?"

MacArthur thinned his diffident smile. *This ore salesman thinks he can intimidate me, after what I endured at West Point and in France?* He cleared his voice. "If history teaches us anything, it is that the American people reward boldness in their leaders and look with disfavor upon those who castigate subordinates for decisions made under their authority."

The president slouched from fatigue, offering no protest to that dire prediction. Dazed from the enervating effect of his heart medications, he walked to his desk and sat down, remaining there in agonized silence.

Hurley seized upon the president's inexplicable loss of resolve. "We will address the press tonight, before the BEF whiners can spread their lies to the reporters. Tomorrow the country will applaud you for saving the nation from revolution. That I can assure you."

The two architects of the expulsion operation waited tensely for the inevitable denial of that brazen proposal, but Hoover, after turning inward for several tortured moments, merely waved them from his presence.

Taking his persisting silence as acquiescence—just more of the same cowardice and indecision they had witnessed during the past two years—Hurley and MacArthur nodded to each other with suppressed triumph and walked briskly from the room before the president could change his mind.

On the entry lane outside the White House, Major Eisenhower sat waiting in the driver's seat of an Army staff car. Seeing his superior emerge, the aide jumped out and opened the rear door.

After conferring with Hurley on a plan to reconvene later that night, MacArthur climbed into the back seat and ordered Eisenhower, "Call all of the national reporters you can get hold of this late. Tell them to gather on the Anacostia bluffs in one hour. Arrange for a microphone to be set up."

"Sir, it's still pretty rough down there, sir. The fires are burning hot. And we haven't finished driving out stragglers."

"All the better. They will get to see for themselves the dangers that we were required to suppress today. I'm going to paint them a vivid picture of the battle. We have one bit of luck going for us, at least."

"What is that, sir?"

"That blowhard Gibbons is out of town at the moment. We won't have to put up with his mud-raking rants on the radio."

Eisenhower hesitated to turn the ignition key. "Sir, do you really think a press conference is prudent? Wouldn't it be the better part of valor, if not wisdom, for us to keep a low profile and let the politicians handle this now?"

MacArthur watched with satisfaction as the light dimmed and finally died in the window on the second floor of the White House above him. "Major, if you learn anything during your commission in my service, let it be this: Never allow *any* politician to handle the Army."

A few minutes before midnight, Glassford stood under the shadows cast by Navy Yard wall, trying to remain aloof from the crass publicity show. He watched from afar as MacArthur and Hurley, surrounded by nearly fifty reporters and back-dropped by the flames rising from the Anacostia flats below, held their *post mortem* press conference at the temporary military headquarters set up near the Eleventh Street Bridge.

Jesse Essary, the hard-bitten reporter for the *Baltimore Sun*, shouted to be heard above a volley of questions. "How come we can't take newsreels of the burning camp?"

MacArthur struck a Jovian pose of authority. "This is an ongoing military operation. The ban on moving pictures is standard Army regulation."

The *Sun* reporter's baritone voice boomed like a cannon. "They had cameras on the battlefield the day after Antietam! Maybe if people out in the country could see with their own eyes what you did to those veterans, they might have a different opinion on the matter."

"Those were insurrectionists out there today."

"How do you know that?"

MacArthur shot an admonishing glance across the street at Glassford, who slinked deeper into the shadows, trying to remain inconspicuous. "If there was one man in ten in that group today who is a veteran, it would surprise me."

Tracing MacArthur's eyes to Glassford in the shadows, the reporter shouted at the police chief, "What do *you* say about that?"

Glassford shook his head. "I'm not taking questions tonight."

Puzzled by that demurral, Essary turned back to MacArthur and Hurley. "Did the White House give the order to clear out the veterans?"

MacArthur refused to give the reporter the honor of looking at him directly. Instead, he projected his statement into the darkness, as if addressing an imaginary assembly at West Point. "The President proved himself a strong leader today. That mob down Pennsylvania Avenue looked bad. They were animated by the spirit of revolution." He glared down at the source of several disbelieving hoots in the crowd of civilians that had gathered along the banks. "The gentleness and consideration with which they had been treated had been mistaken by them as weakness, and they had come to the conclusion that they were about to take over the government in an arbitrary way or by indirect methods."

Paul Anderson of the *St. Louis Post-Dispatch* shoved his way to the front. "When did President Hoover issue the order to burn the camp?"

MacArthur was becoming visibly annoyed at these attempts to pin him down on specifics. "Had the President not used force, he would have been derelict indeed in his judgment regarding the safety of the country, because this is the focal point of the world today. Had he not acted with the force and vigor which he did, it would have been a bad day for the country tomorrow."

Anderson, who had earned his stripes investigating the race riots in East St. Louis while being subjected to repeated assassination threats, kept boring in. "Are you going to provide trucks for the veterans to leave town?"

"No," MacArthur said. "The Army had nothing to do with this problem."

"Did you hear the local residents booing your troops?" asked Anderson.

MacArthur turned prickly. "I have never seen greater relief on the part of a distressed populace than I saw today. At least a dozen people told me, especially in the Negro section, that a regular system of tribute was being levied on them by this insurrectionist mob."

Anderson scribbled on his notebook with such fury that he threatened to impale the pages with his pen. "Is that a fancy way of saying the veterans were asking for donations?"

MacArthur ignored the verbal jab and stepped away from the microphone. "Now we should hear from Secretary Hurley. He was instrumental in keeping President Hoover informed of today's success."

Hurley came forward and placed an approving hand on MacArthur's shoulder. "It was a great victory. Mac here did a great job. He is the man of the hour." The war secretary seemed to catch himself, and quickly added, "But I must not make any heroes just now."

63

WASHINGTON, D.C.
JULY 29, 1932

The next morning, Floyd Gibbons landed at Hoover Field in Arlington and took a cab along to the Eleventh Street Bridge. Strapping his portable radio pack over his shoulder, he paid the fare and stepped out onto the steaming asphalt.

A tableau of charred remains and swirling gas mists lay before him.

The first sound he heard as the taxi drove off was the doleful paradiddle of an Army drummer somewhere in the smoke-smeared distance. Behind him, on the west bank of the Anacostia, hundreds of veterans and their families milled about as if in a daze, searching for missing comrades and staring across the flotsam at what remained of the shacks that had once protected their now-lost Bibles and family scrapbooks.

After taking a minute to calm down enough to think twice about driving his fist into the nearest wall, he walked to a pay phone at the Navy Yard gate and called the NBC office in New York. "Morrie, I'm cranking up the transmitter in thirty seconds."

He returned to the bridge and found several dozen weary Army regulars patrolling the entry to the scorched flats. His old battle blood was now up, and he shambled a knee-hitching charge at the bridgehead, daring the soldiers to try stopping him.

A corporal recognized him. Breaking off an abased glance, the corporal motioned for his sentries to step aside and provide the correspondent some privacy for his radio report.

In one of his rare moments unscotched, Gibbons limped onto the concrete span and weaved his way with his cane through a litter of ragged togs, tin cans, and abject relics that had been dropped by the veterans in their haste to leave that night. This *via dolorosa* was a memorial to the Depression, galleried with the humblest of treasures: a smashed wooden crucifix, its vial of holy water inside its hollowed core cracked and spilled; a spray of painted flowers crafted with strands of rubber salvaged from punctured inner tubes; a fractured cookie jar containing a handwritten note remembering to future descendants how it had been used to hide the daguerreotypes of a once-proud Virginia family from General Sheridan.

Halfway across the bridge, he coughed the soot from his throat and began sending his commentary over the airwaves:

> "Ladies and gentlemen, this is your Headline Hunter reporting to you from a wasteland that would rival the darkest scape of the moon. I am not on the frozen steppes of Siberia. Nor am I crouching in the searing ghettos of Calcutta. Here, where I now stand, Lady Liberty hoists her gleaming torch above our own nation's Capitol. She hovers this morning in harsh judgment of those who do not deserve her blessings and protection. Like the goddess Athena, who abandoned her namesake city when the ancient Athenians chose dictatorship over the burdens of democracy, our Lady now turns her gentle gaze away in distress. For below her here lies a smoking scrabble, the few acres that once served as the only plot of ground those men who once fought for your freedoms were allowed to call home. Smoldering and steeped in tear gas, this camp of the Bonus veterans now resembles the Flanders no-man's land over which they once crawled. Anacostia, ladies and gentlemen, will go down in the annals aside the names that bring a shiver to the spine of memory. The Marne. The Meuse-Argonne. Belleau Wood. Yet none of those hallowed battlefields ever surpassed this blackened ground in shameful panorama of ruin and desolation.... "

Assigned the task of guarding the north end of the burned camp, Major George Patton sat on a bale of hay and regaled his fellow cavalry officers with his exploits on the previous day. "This one Red insurrectionist banshee came at me like Geronimo. I sliced off his ear without drawing blood. He loped away not knowing what hit him."

"Sure you did, George," said Captain Lucian Truscott.

"Damn it, Luke, I'm telling you I did it. It's all in the turn of the wrist. I learned the technique when I studied in France under the second finest swordsman in the world."

"I guess we don't need to ask who the finest is."

Patton rushed to his saddle and pulled out his precious blade from its scabbard. He strutted about like a matador making his *faena* passes before driving home the kill blow. "Did I ever show you Old Bessie, Luke?"

"Only about a hundred times."

The other officers smirked as Patton walked around flashing the curved saber with its broad hilt guard, which looked more Napoleonic than twentieth-century in pedigree. "Designed it myself. The secret of its superiority is in the taper. Front edge runs the entire length. Double-edged half-length. Allows for both thrusting and cutting."

Truscott smothered a grin. "You launched a lot of cavalry charges against the Marne trenches, did you, George?"

Patton only then realized that his fellow officers were making fun of him. "The art of the saber builds character. Some of you could use a little more instruction in both."

Truscott deadpanned, "I'm still trying to perfect the broad axe."

Patton cut the air with the saber, whipping up a whistling sound. "Laugh all you want. But this came in handy against those *routiers* out there yesterday. Peasantry always runs from armored horse and the blade. It's a fear passed down in their blood."

"Peasantry? Hell, George, whose service are you in? Henry the Fifth?"

Patton made a puffing sound full of derision as he looked toward the direction of the White House. "There is no Henry the Fifth in *our* castle. More like Edward the Second."

Truscott's mirth suddenly evaporated. "Watch yourself, George. If we *were* in merry old England, you'd have your head separated from your shoulders for talk like that."

Patton held a solemn gaze into the distant past. "I did."

Truscott was about to wave off Patton's belief in reincarnation when he saw a sergeant approaching the entry post with a short, scrawny fellow clad in a ragged black suit. He stood up and, walking to the edge of the camp, pointed at the little civilian. "Is he delivering lunch?"

The sergeant brought the nervous man forward. "He says he's a friend of Major Patton's."

Truscott gave the elfin fellow the once over. "You must be a jockey. Do you take care of the Major's horses out at his Virginia farm?"

The man shook his head. "Name's Joe Angelo. I saved Colonel Patton's life in France." He pulled out his medal from his pants pocket and displayed it. "I just want to talk with him a moment."

Truscott hesitated, as if not believing the man. He called over to Patton, who was still lecturing his captured audience several dozen yards away. "Hey, George. This fellow says he saved your life in France."

Patton squinted over at them, and his face flushed. "I don't know him."

"Says his name is Joe Angelo."

Patton turned away. "I don't know anyone by that name."

Humiliated by the rebuff, Angelo stood mortified, as if his former superior officer had just ripped the Distinguished Service Cross from his flesh.

"Take him away!" shouted Patton. "Under no circumstances allow him to return!"

Truscott, feeling bad for Angelo, could only shake his head to indicate that the attempted audience would not happen.

Angelo turned and, like a bird with a broken wing, hobbled alone back toward the Eleventh Street Bridge.

A s a city bus chugged up Massachusetts Avenue, the driver fiddled with the knob on his new dashboard radio, a Rogers Majestic Batteryless. He found an NBC news commentary in progress:

"First of all, let's get one thing clear. These veterans are not bums. Second, they are not agitators, although I can't think of anything more agitating to a fellow than sore feet and an empty stomach, and no job and a wife and kids, and the rent unpaid.... "

"Hey, buster," shouted a passenger. "Turn up the Headline Hunter, will ya?"

The driver complied, and all of the passengers sat riveted to the report:

"There's plenty of old, worn-out clothing and shoes in this army of men who represent a cross section of American life today. These men are citizens. They are veteran American soldiers. Some of them are disabled soldiers.... "

Approaching Scott Circle, the driver slowed to a stop at a military checkpoint that had been set up across from the German Embassy. An Army corporal with a holstered sidearm waved him over. The driver turned off the radio and cranked opened the door. "What's the problem?"

The corporal boarded. "We've got orders to search every bus in the city."

"Orders from whom?"

"Why don't you just keep your eyes on the cash till and leave the questions to me." The corporal walked down the aisle studying every passenger. He stopped at a white woman who carried a worn handbag and asked her, "You got identification?"

The woman refused to open her purse. "Is there a Constitution left in this country? Or did you burn that yesterday, too?"

"Ma'am, I'm going to ask once more."

"Appears to me that the government stopped asking and started demanding about twenty-four hours ago."

"Are you the wife of a veteran?"

"Is that a crime now?"

"All BEF veterans and their families must be out of the city by sundown." The corporal scanned the rear of the bus. His gaze fell on a slender black fellow slouched down in the last seat. "You there! Stand up!"

The black man rose slowly. "Yes, sir?"

"You look familiar."

"Don't think we ever met."

"What's your name?"

The bent man, crumpled fedora in hand, debated his fate. Finally, he muttered, "Taylor."

"Are you one of the BEF bums?"

Cornered, Ozzie dropped his bloodshot eyes toward his tattered shoes. Hungry and heartsick, he'd been riding this bus for ten hours trying to avoid the Army vigilantes, but now he saw that his attempt to avoid exile was doomed. He stepped forward. "Yes, sir, I am. I fought with the Three-Sixty-Ninth."

An elderly Negro lady in the seat across from Ozzie sassed the corporal, "Them was the Harlem Hellfighters, son. Doubt you ever heard of them, wet behind the ears as you are. They never gave up an inch of ground in France. No, sir, not one inch."

"They gave up some ground yesterday," the corporal smart-mouthed.

The passengers began whispering among themselves, and the corporal spun to search for the source of the insolent murmurs. Surrounded by surly glares, he pointed at the Negro fugitive from justice and motioned him forward. "You're coming with me."

The white woman he had questioned stood from her seat and stepped into the aisle. "No, he won't be coming with you."

The corporal felt for the pistol at his side. "I'm going to enforce my orders."

The woman refused to move. "You aren't taking that man off this bus. He risked his life for this country. You'll have to arrest me first."

The corporal unbuttoned the strap on his holster. "I'll do just that."

One by one, the other passengers arose and pressed into the aisle, denying the officer the door with his prisoner. Confronted by the protest, the corporal backed down and sneered a warning at Ozzie, "I'll remember your name."

The woman looked at the last name sewn on the breast of the corporal's uniform. "And we'll remember yours, Corporal Burns."

The corporal broke off their silent battle of stares. "General MacArthur is going hear about this."

"You tell General MacArthur that Henrietta Young works behind the cosmetics counter at Garfinckel's department store. If he wants to interrogate me further, he can find me there in the afternoons from noon to six. And tell the general that if I ever hear that the government laid a hand on this good man, I'm going to come and find *him*. And those medals he likes to hide behind won't do him much good if that happens."

The other passengers nodded their admiration for the woman's fortitude.

Crimson-faced, the corporal walked off the bus.

When the door slammed shut, the lady who had led the protest pulled five dollars from her purse and walked to the back of the bus. She handed the money to Ozzie. "Mister Taylor, it pains me to say this, but you won't be safe until you get as far away from this city as possible. Here's some help for a train ticket." She called up to the driver. "Turn this bus around and take him to Union Station. We'll walk with him to the platform and make sure he gets on it without being harassed." She pressed Ozzie's quivering hand between her palms and whispered, "God bless you, soldier."

Ozzie's eyes teared up as the passengers passed his hat down the aisle and collected money for his sojourn into the bleak unknown.

O n the second floor of the White House, Lou Hoover sat in her bedroom study listening to the radio. She turned the volume down so that her husband, who hovered over his desk in his private office across the hall, wouldn't hear the Headline Hunter's report.

"We called them heroes when they sailed for France. Called them that again when they limped back with the bacon after the armistice and found the country dry and some other fellow with their girl and somebody else in their old job.... "

She glanced across the hall again and saw him lower his head into his hands. She turned off the radio and buzzed in Maggie Rogers, the head White House maid.

"Yes, ma'am?" the maid asked at the door.

Lou stood and closed the door quietly. "Maggie, I think we'll start collecting a few personal items to box up and ship to California."

The maid quickly changed her perplexed expression. "Of course, ma'am."

Lou looked around the room and sighed. Trying to mask the reason for the request, she said, "We've got so much clutter here."

The servant smiled sadly, nodding to indicate that she understood. "You just give me the list, Mrs. Hoover, and I'll get started."

I n the Negro neighborhood of Columbia Heights, several blocks north-west of the Capitol, two white men in Khaki Shirt uniforms walked into a shadowed alley behind the Tivoli Theatre and found George Alford waiting for them. One of the men pulled an unmarked envelope from his pocket and delivered it to the BEF veteran. "You did a hell of a Red recruiting job for us down at the armory yesterday, Georgie boy. I suggest you spend a chunk of your windfall on a one-way ticket back to Oregon."

Alford counted out three hundred-dollar bills. He slipped the envelope into his hip pocket and, looking beyond their shoulders shiftily, whispered, "I was hoping you might be able to use my intelligence services on a regular basis."

"Intelligence?" The payoff man laughed scornfully. "You think we used you for your *intelligence?* Get one thing straight, Alford. There are two species of bums in this world. There's your typical scum hobo. And then there's the lower form of life, the kind that rats on his fellow rats and profits from it. A class of decrepitude of which you are now a card-carrying member."

Alford opened his mouth to protest, but he didn't get the chance. The other agent hammered him to the ground and drove a heel into his side.

"You ever open your fat lip about our arrangement," the thug said, "it'll be your last pronouncement before you hit the bottom of a pauper's grave. Do we have an understanding?"

Clutching his broken ribs, Alford could only nod.

"Now take your Judas pay and get the hell out of Washington."

Across the Potomac, a laborer father and his son took a break from digging a grave in Arlington National Cemetery. The radio in their truck parked on the paved path nearby blared Floyd Gibbons's commentary:

> "They were also voters. And workmen, just like you and me. And
> by golly, this morning, as they walk off into hopelessness, they
> are just as puzzled as we are about what is happening to this
> country...."

Wiping sweat from his forehead, the boy began digging at the hole again. "Who's this one for, Pa?"

His father checked the work order. "How about that. It's for that Russkie they shot the other day down at the old armory. Says his name's Hruska."

"They're burying a Red in here?"

The father shrugged as he lit up a cigarette. "I guess he managed to sneak into the Army somehow."

His son walked over to their truck and checked the engraving on the head-stone in the bed. "They spelled his name wrong."

The father waved it off. "Hruska. Hushra. Hushka. Who gives a damn?"

The boy stared at the stone, pondering this last indignity that the dead veteran was forced to suffer. "That's a heck of a thing, Pa."

"What?"

"This one finally got *his* Bonus. He was the first, I suppose."

"What are you talking about?"

"The fishwrap said this morning that those bums they drove out of town won't get their Bonus until they kick the can."

The father tossed his cigarette butt and drove his shovel into the hole. "Lot of good it's gonna do him down here."

The boy couldn't understand how the world seemed to work at times. "Maybe there's something to be said for getting what you set out for, even if it means having to die for it."

L ate that afternoon, Anna trudged north up Sixteenth Street with a few hundred bedraggled veterans and their families. Mickey Dolan limped along with them, as did Charlie Lincoln and Chief Running Wolf, carrying his quiver and bow. The bridge to Maryland, they'd been told, was finally reopened, and they had three hours to cross it. The air still stank with the peppery stench of gas, and the dark clouds of smoke from the burning camps had followed them overhead like the smoldering exhaust of Hell.

Anna hadn't slept at all that night, having spent a wracking vigil with the sick Meyers baby at the hospital, only to see it die that morning of an intestinal inflammation. The attending doctor had refused to confirm for the reporters that the Army had killed the infant, but off the record, he had muttered an aside to her that the tear gas "didn't do it any good."

As she and the veterans passed the rows of expensive homes, hundreds of residents came out to line the street to see them off. They stood in shamed silence mostly, some whispering prayers for the refugees, others languidly waving flags while watching warily for patrolling soldiers who might take the gesture as an act of insurrection. Taking refuge in gallows humor, Charlie Lincoln thumped a mournful beat against the top of his stovepipe hat and sang his own version of *The Battle Hymn of the Republic*:

"Mine eyes have seen the glory of the coming of the tanks,
They rumbled through the streets behind the infantry in ranks,
They were out to save the country for the rich men and the banks,
And the tyranny of Wall Street lives on."

Anna watched as Glassford rode Blue Bessie alongside the stumbling column of veterans and their families, keeping a lookout for outbreaks of violence. When he rolled up aside her, she found not the look of relief on his face that she expected, but despair etched into his dark-circled eyes.

"You don't need to go," Glassford told her. "There's plenty of work left to do here."

She walked closer to him and whispered over the purr of his engine, "That's not a very wise thing for a police chief to say to a Communist."

He quickly changed the subject. "Have you seen Waters?"

She shook her head. "Last I heard, he was heading to Pennsylvania to find another site for a camp." As they moved together in silence, she saw that he was struggling to say something more. She decided to spare him further agony. "I've never thanked you for all the money you gave these men out of your own pocket."

Glassford turned aside, too choked up to offer a response.

She caught him glancing at the books sticking out of her backpack, the ones she had salvaged before the soldiers burned the camp.

He shook his head at the books. "Empty ideas. That's what you're taking from all this?"

"Ideas are all some of us have left."

"Ideas are what got us into this mess in the first place.... Justice, freedom, pursuit of happiness." His voice trailed off in bitterness.

She smiled sorrowfully through a film of tears while looking around at the veterans who had now lost all hope. "At least I've never been gassed by an idea." When he failed to offer one of his usual comebacks, she risked placing her hand on his. "Everyone else has abandoned them. I can't."

It took him a moment to find his voice again. "Where will you go?"

"To the United States of America, I guess, wherever that is." She met his eyes one last time, and then walked away, refusing to look back.

He stopped at the District line and, cutting his engine, watched the wretched column shuffle listlessly into Maryland. As the last of the stragglers disappeared into the haze, he closed his eyes and listened to Ozzie Taylor's song fade into the breeze:

> "Over here, Over here,
> The Yanks are starving,
> The Yanks are starving,
> The Yanks are starving everywhere."

At his Hyde Park estate in the Hudson Valley of New York, the Democratic presidential nominee, Franklin D. Roosevelt, sat eating lunch on the veranda while listening to Floyd Gibbons on the radio:

> "... So, say goodbye to the doughboys, folks. Hoover's Sanhedrin of Pharisees and Sadducees over at the War Department have banished them from the New Jerusalem. Didn't even give them a mule to ride out on to the Dead Sea. And his legions used bayonets and gas

canisters instead of palm leaves. There used to be talk around this town about crucifying the common man on a cross of gold. The Wall Street bankers put a stop to that. Gold's too valuable these days to waste on crosses. The powerbrokers just shoo the culls and runts out of the barn and let them die of exposure and famine.... This is your Headline Hunter signing off."

The phone rang.

The governor's advisor, Rexford Tugwell, turned off the radio and answered the call. He handed the receiver across the table to Roosevelt.

"Yes, yes," Roosevelt said to the caller. "I just heard.... Well, I hope you're right, but we won't be taking anything for granted.... I appreciate your calling."

He hung up the phone and lit up another cigarette in his holder, clenching it between his teeth. He winked at Tugwell. "I just spoke to the second most dangerous man in the country."

Tugwell waited. "Are you going to make me beg?"

Roosevelt puffed away, enjoying his secret. Finally, he revealed the identity of the man who had called. "Huey Long."

Tugwell sat expectant while his boss studied the morning papers and cast more twinkling glances over at him, enjoying his mounting frustration.

Exasperated, the aide said, "I'm going to assume that the *most* dangerous man is Father Coughlin."

Roosevelt arched backwards with a roar of delight and transferred his cigarette holder to the other corner of his mouth. "Coughlin? No, no, no."

"Well, then, who?"

"Why, Douglas MacArthur, of course."

64

PORTLAND, OREGON
SEPTEMBER 4, 1932

Seated at the head table of the American Legion's annual convention dinner, Patrick Hurley dug into his thick cut of filet mignon, which he had ordered rare. He brought the dripping morsel to his mouth and—

"The Secretary of War always likes it bloody."

Hurley turned to find Floyd Gibbons sliding into the empty chair next to him. The War Department chief glared at the spot where a name card should have been, exasperated that the Legion leaders had committed such a blunder. Being forced to watch this patch-eyed hack give a speech to the full convention on the previous evening had been infuriating enough. The newsman's podium-pounding condemnation of the BEF eviction had drawn the wildest applause for any speaker at the convention. But now he was forced to endure the gadfly's insufferable presence again on the very night that he would be delivering his own defense of the military action.

Gibbons clapped him on the back, too hard. "Looks like a lot of veterans came dressed as empty seats for *your* speech, Hurley. I can't believe they scheduled you to follow me. I must have better connections with the fighting man."

The other guests hushed, anticipating a showdown.

"Poison Pen Gibbons," Hurley growled as he impaled his steak with his knife. "Shouldn't you be off in some sound booth preparing your Amos-and-Andy routine?"

With a shark's smile, Gibbons leaned in to Hurley, close enough to brush the secretary's shoulder. "Actually, I was hired to broadcast this convention for NBC. But somebody high up in the Washington politburo got me barred from the radio for exposing the truth about that little *putsch* you and MacArthur tried to pull off."

"What are you insinuating?"

"I don't insinuate. I bloviate. Remember? That's what you told G-Man Edgar down at the FBI when you ordered him to put a tail on me. You can read all about what I think in a file at the Bureau marked 'Suspected Communists.' Sherwood Anderson and I go to the White House to protest the Army burning the homes of innocent American citizens. Next thing we know, we've got shadows growing over us in alleys."

Hurley calmly wiped his mouth and set the napkin on the table. Refusing to honor Gibbons with a direct glance, he hoisted a combative chin and, in his croaking frontier twang, gave the other guests a preview of what he would say on the podium in a few minutes. "Mr. Gibbons here has told you that the soldiers set fire to the humble homes of these men. That is *not* the fact. Those fires were set by the veterans themselves."

Gibbons pounced on a plate of olives and popped one into his mouth. "Why *did* you and Mac call out the troops?"

Hurley bristled at being subjected to an inquisition. "Glassford lost control of the situation. Two of the instigators and several police officers had been shot at the old armory."

"What time were they shot?"

"Don't you read your own papers?" Hurley grumbled. "A few minutes before three that afternoon."

Gibbons snapped up another olive and arced it onto his tongue. "Here's the rub, Mr. Secretary. An anonymous patriot in your War Department provided me with a copy of Mac's order for the troops to be mobilized. It's time-stamped at 1:35 that day."

Hurley angrily clanged his fork to his plate. "I am not in front of a grand jury here!"

Gibbons removed the olive pit from his mouth and sent it spinning on the empty bread plate. "Now tell me where my logic goes awry. The way I've got it figured, you and Mac jumped the gun—bad pun—or you *knew* there'd be shooting and casualties down at the armory to use as a pretext." He leaned in again, this time close enough to smell the garlic salt on Hurley's breath. "Here's what I *really* think. I think you and Mac planned the operation to burn that camp in Anacostia all along."

Hurley was looking for a way to escape, but the radioman had edged up his chair to pin him against the table. The war secretary set his gold-capped teeth in anger and insisted, "No member of the Army would do that! All the fatalities of that day, of which you have heard so much, took place before the arrival of the United States Army! On my sacred word of honor, no soldier set fire to a house in Washington!"

Gibbons let Hurley's frothing defense sink under the weight of its emptiness. Then, the radioman pulled a small photograph from his inner jacket pocket and placed it on the table for all to examine. The guests gasped at what was depicted on the glossy: An Army private in full battle gear stood lighting a torch to one of the shacks in Anacostia. In the photograph's background, infantrymen were walking through the camp setting more roofs afire.

"Funny thing about a camera," Gibbons said. "It doesn't need a word of honor."

Hurley nearly choked on his steak cud. After finally managing to get the cut of meat down, he snarled, "Any Communist stooge can stage a fake photograph and send it to a reporter to plant a false story. This is clearly a fake."

"I thought you might say that. What's your opinion of General Moseley?"

"Fine officer. Beyond reproach."

Gibbons reached into his jacket again and pulled out a folded paper. He handed it to Hurley and thumped the document with his forefinger. Before the War Department chief could protest, Gibbons slid his hand under his jacket for a third time and produced a flask. He unscrewed its top and tinctured his glass of water with his favorite golden elixir.

Across the table, a raven-haired lady with *boudoir* eyes quipped, "You should be fitted for a magician's jacket, Mr. Gibbons. Do you have anything else hidden down there that would entertain us?"

Gibbons winked at her. "Just a couple of spare eyeballs."

Hurley turned pale as he read the document forced into his hands.

"Shall I do the honors?" Gibbons returned his flask to its marsupial repose. "Or would you like me to request the microphone so that you can address the entire hall?"

Hurley threw the paper to the table, deeming it unworthy of comment.

The lady who had been sending Gibbons seductive glances picked the page up. Her smile grew as she studied it.

"Well?" asked another guest. "Let us all in on the mystery."

The lady fluttered a mischievous eyelash while she performed her best imitation of a ditz. "Why, it seems that General Moseley issued a statement to the convention an hour ago. Whatever can this mean?"

"Enough with the theatrics, darling," said the man sitting next to her. "We're all dying with curiosity."

"I suppose that's better than dying from a bayonet wound." The lady held the document near the candle for light and read Moseley's statement loud enough for those guests at the tables around them to hear: "'We are making no apologies for anything that happened on July 28. The huts were fired by troops in reserve. They are under orders. The troops were in waves. The last wave was ordered to burn down the huddles when they had been evacuated and there was no danger to anyone.'"

A tense stillness fell over those guests eavesdropping from the surrounding tables—until somebody dropped a fork that clanged like a death knell across the marble floor.

Gibbons angled his chin toward the candle and, grinning boyishly at his female admirer, lit up a cigar. He leaned back in his chair and flipped the ashes, nearly singing Hurley. "In all the excitement, I nearly forgot to tell everyone the good news."

"You mean there's more?" the lady asked, flickering her hand like a palmetto fan to cool her face.

Gibbons blew a puff of come-hither smoke across the table at her. "The Legion has just named me an honorary member."

That was the final straw for Hurley. Furious, he stood abruptly and marched away.

"Oh, Mr. Secretary!" called Gibbons.

Hurley stopped and turned back, his narrow hound's face now redder than the flags over the Kremlin.

"Didn't you forget something?"

Hurley pressed a hand against his jacket pocket, checking for his *pince-nez* glasses.

"Your word of honor." Gibbons brushed his heel against the carpet. "You left it here on the floor."

A month later, Gibbons was in Manhattan giving a lecture on his new novel, *Red Napoleon*, when his fellow columnist Drew Pearson called from Washington to tell him that Herbert Crosby and the District of Columbia commissioners had finally done the inevitable.

That evening, armed with a bottle of Bruichladdich malt whisky that he had saved for a great moment of need, Gibbons sat down at the typewriter in his hotel room and composed his next radio commentary:

> There's another jobless veteran today.
>
> He's carried on the records as Brigadier General Pelham D. Glassford. The Boys Higher Up—right up to the War Department and the White House—have just squeezed down the thumbscrews until Brigadier General Glassford had to get out or be kicked out.
>
> The General, who served almost a full year as Chief of Police in the District of Columbia—the National Capital City—is jobless. He's

right down with Private Jones, who lost a leg in the service, and Bill Smith who dangles an empty sleeve, and Jimmy Jeeves, who peeps out of eyes burned to the nearsightedness of mustard gas.

Maybe the General has some money saved up, now that he's out of a job. Maybe he hasn't.

Anyway, he's just an unemployed soldier.

He lost his job, which was dictated by the administration in Washington, because he was a veteran and sympathized with other veterans.

The records don't show that. They show that he was forced to quit because he couldn't find out which of the hundreds of officials up on the Hill was the real Chief of Police. The General knew doggoned well he wasn't.

Gibbons took another swig, allowing the whisky to marinate the anger across his tongue. Several paragraphs later, he caught his stride again:

I can't help thinking of that hot afternoon, around the first of July, when I sat down beside his big, square desk and watched that long, rangy General pack his pipe and smile and laugh at my suggestions that the boys up on Pennsylvania Avenue were out to get his hide.

That towering Chief of Police—lithe as a fencer and as keen of visage as a commander of the line—dressed with the careless Summer graces of a Washingtonian gentleman—tamped his pipe again and tossed for the nub of the whole Bonus Army story. ...

He reached for the bottle and took another draught of inspiration.

Say, just figure out. If a banker held a call note on you, how long would he hesitate to camp out on your doorstep if he needed the dough? But, don't forget, these are war veterans asking this Bonus payment in advance of the year of maturity, 1945, when most of them will be dead.

That makes them "reds." ...

What he wouldn't give for a rusty Bowie knife and ten minutes in a foxhole with Patrick Hurley and Dauntless Doug and their bootlicker, George Moseley. He was hammering at the keys now, and the half-empty bottle was rattling on the desk:

Old Herr Hitler in Germany and Benito Mussolini in Rome must be getting the laughs of their lives. And Comrade Stalin, in Moscow, may be chuckling under his drooping mustache. I hate to guess what the grizzled Joe Pilsudski in Poland is laughing about.

With his lone eye blurring from the scotch and fatigue, he could barely see the copy:

Brigadier General Glassford. Chief of Police of the District of Columbia. The District George Washington intended to be without party politics. The district in which honorable men might be free to ply the honorable business of making and administering law for a great nation. Washington. The soft valley where the dome of our Capitol gleams white and hopeful in the sunlight.

Too much for a loved Brigadier General to police?

Yes, too much. Because, like Washington, he loved his soldiers.

Can't be done these days. Vale, *General Glassford.*

He hit the "pound" key three times to indicate the end.

He stared at the page, trying to focus the overworked eye that the doctors told him was going blind. With a heavy sigh, he tossed the copy into a folder marked *Unfiled*, which was full of stories that had never made it on the air.

No one would broadcast it, he knew. What passed for news organizations these days wouldn't give a damn about a has-been police chief who had quietly saved the country from revolution, only to be kicked out on his ass for his trouble. No, the world had long since discarded the doughboys of 1918. And soon enough, he'd be thrown into the trash bin with them. Years to come, when Americans, who always forget their history, asked when it had all went wrong, some old walnut face in the diner would gargle the phlegm of wisdom from his throat and say, "July of 1932." And the young tawpies would just wave the codger off as the queer turnip that got lost in the bottom of the pickle barrel.

He drained the bottle. Sorry condition he was in, he probably wouldn't be around to witness what new bloodthirsty leviathan was lurking over the moors. Just as well. War reporting was a young man's game now. He had left his youth and its vanities with his eyeball on those pitted slopes of Belleau Wood.

I should have been a baseball scout.

He picked up the phone and asked the hotel operator to place a call. When a gentle voice coated in Kansas dust answered, he let out a Weiser whoop and barked, "Too Much! It's Gibbons!... Hell no, I haven't touched the hard stuff since I caught that fluff you tossed at me in Idaho a hundred years ago.... I heard that fat bastard Griffith handed you your walking papers last week.... Yeah, there's a lot of that going around lately.... Cleveland? Hell no, you don't want to go to that sluice pit. They play in a goddamn morgue up there! Now, listen up, Johnson. I say you and I put together a barnstorming team and take it around the world. We'll get the Babe and Cobb, and I'll manage and... Hello, Johnson? You still on the line?" He slowly lowered the receiver to its hook.

The familiar ache was starting up in his chest again. Grasping at his shoulder, he looked around. *There has to be another bottle around here somewhere.*

EPILOGUE

NORMAN, OKLAHOMA
DECEMBER, 1941

When Walter Waters came to the end of his story, the young Navy volunteers around him sat in stunned silence, their thoughts lingering on the incomprehensible image of two American armies fighting each other while flying the same flag.

Lt. Keyes checked his watch and realized that the mess hall had closed for lunch over an hour ago. "All right, back to it! Let's get those forms handed in." He walked toward his desk, preparing to finish up the paperwork for the day, when he looked back and saw the recruits still mulling around the fire, whispering among themselves. "You boys have something else on your minds?"

Rising slowly to their feet, the recruits kept glancing with concern at the BEF veteran, who remained seated on the chair with his head lowered, lost in his own dark thoughts. Finally, one of the recruits dredged up the courage to ask Waters what all of them wanted to know. "What happened to your army after Mac kicked you out of Washington?"

Waters pawed at the ground with his worn heel. "Most of us hoofed it across the state line into Pennsylvania. Those folks there d-d-didn't much want us around either, so some of us got shipped d-d-down to Florida to dig dirt in rehabilitation camps. But the Almighty wasn't done casting His wrath, so He sent a hurricane at us. The government d-d-didn't think we were worth evacuating. Four hundred of my men d-d-drowned. The government burned their bodies on a big bonfire so they wouldn't stink up the place."

"Damn," muttered the recruit. "You fellas couldn't catch a break."

"What about Glassford?" another volunteer asked.

Waters shook his head in regret. "The General headed out west and d-d-did a stint as the head of the Phoenix police. It wasn't long before the oligarchs out there ran him out of that cow town, too. He had the goddam gall to suggest that legalizing whorehouses might be a better idea than spending taxpayer money hauling whores into n-n-night court. He ran for Congress with the support of us vets, but the Wall Street carpetbaggers defeated him. Last I heard, he'd sworn off p-p-politics and was working on a ranch and selling his paintings."

"I guess we know what happened to Hoover and Mac," said one of the boys.

Waters spat a jet of black juice. "I guess we do."

"This Headline Hunter fellow," said another recruit. "How come I ain't never heard him on the radio?"

Waters smiled sadly at how sheltered from the world these farm lads were— and how that was about to change in ways they could never imagine. "You'd have to hold a séance to hear old Floyd's voice now. His heart exploded on him three years ago, while he was g-g-getting ready to take the plane overseas to go tell Hitler to go to Hell."

"Sounds like he had one helluva a big heart."

Waters nodded wistfully. "Came matched with his grin and that flask he always carried." His chin fell to his chest from the weight of the memories. "Joey Angelo, I never saw that little Wop again. And I lost t-t-track of Charlie Lincoln and Ozzie Taylor, too. Nurse Raber is probably back in Indiana sowing the Lord's true message of social justice with the corn seed." He waited for the next question hanging unspoken, but no one had the temerity to ask about the government undercover agents who had infiltrated the camps of his veterans.

"You fellas ever get your Bonus?"

Waters picked at the hole in his sole, trying to measure how much more leather he'd have before the rocks started punching through it. "Yeah, we got it, four years later. The outrage over how we were treated in that hurricane massacre finally scared the politicians into d-d-doing what they shoulda done from the start. But it was too late to d-d-do some of us much good. Lot of the fellas were already under the sod by then."

Lt. Keyes gave him a moment to recover from that memory. "What about you?"

Waters kept tending to the bottom of his shoes, avoiding the judgment in the young faces around him. "What *about* me?"

"What brought you out here to Oklahoma?"

"Same reason that's taken me anywhere. Scrounging for a job." Waters stared off toward the snow-dusted horizon. "After the BEF dismantled, I resigned from the Khaki Shirts and headed d-d-down to Florida for a while. MacArthur was getting a lot of heat from the press, so he arranged me a job pushing paper in the War Department. I guess he felt guilty about lying to me. That d-d-didn't last long. I ain't no a bureaucrat."

The lieutenant tried to raise the old veteran's spirits. "You kept up the good fight, though, right?"

Walters brushed a hand across his eyes. "I let those doughboys down, let them all down. Joey. Mickey. Charlie. And General Glassford, I let him d-d-down the worst. When they n-n-needed me most, I just wasn't up to the job."

The volunteers lowered their gazes in respect, trying as best they could to afford Waters the dignity of solitude. After nearly a minute of silence, one of the recruits who had taunted the old veteran earlier that morning slowly stepped forward. "I'd be honored to serve with Commander Waters here."

Lt. Keyes shook his head. "Son, you know I can't do that."

"After what the government did to him," the young volunteer insisted. "He deserves a second chance."

The lieutenant was adamant. "We've reached our quota."

Another volunteer stepped up to support the suggestion. "Then give him my slot. Hell, I'll go join the Marines, if that's what it takes."

One by one, the recruits began raising their hands to indicate their wish to join in the request.

Stunned by their spontaneous petition, Lt. Keyes asked the BEF veteran, "Just out of curiosity, Mr. Waters, how come you're trying to join the Navy this time around, instead of the Army again?"

Waters's eyes misted. "That day the regulars drove us out, I saw from my perch on the hotel window a sailor on leave who was walking down the Mall. When Mac's troopers began throwing their tear-gas cans at my men, this sailor got so goddamn mad that he threw one of those canisters back at them and shouted, 'By God, we'll show the infantry what side the Navy is on!' His pals had to drag him away before he tried to take on the whole damned Army. Ten minutes later, that same sailor was right smack down there in the ranks of my veterans. He went and changed into his civilian clothes in order to help us out. I knew right then that I should have joined the Navy years ago."

The recruits nodded in appreciation for the unknown sailor's act of courage.

Seeing the determination in their faces, Lt. Keyes glanced at his ensign, who winked to indicate that it was the right thing to do. Shaking his head in amazement, the lieutenant gave up a resigned shrug and told Waters, "It'll be a desk job, you know that. And you can forget about being called 'Commander' and wearing those riding britches."

His ensign, eager to comply with the decision, scribbled a few words on a requisition invoice and handed it to Waters.

Waters stared at it, unable to read it without his glasses. "What's this?"

"Take it to the commissary," the lieutenant said. "You might want to be careful with that tobacco spitting in your dress whites."

Moved by cheers around him, Waters nearly broke down. Wiping his eyes, he began walking off toward the barracks when he was called back.

"One more thing," Lt. Keyes warned him. "If I ever hear that you've been passing around Red propaganda in camp, I'll make damn sure you're thrown into the brig for the rest of your life."

The recruits gasped at the officer's suggestion that the BEF veteran might be volunteering just to spread a Communist revolution through the ranks.

The lieutenant broke a wide grin.

The recruits realized that the officer had been pulling their leg. Laughing, they converged on Waters and shook his hand in congratulations.

Overcome, Waters pointed a shaky finger at the recruits and repeated the rules he had first issued to his rail riders years ago on their sojourn through Idaho. "All right, listen up, shavetails! No begging! No bug juice! No airing the lungs! And no indulgence in talk against the government!"

"Yes, sir!" the recruits shouted, coming to attention.

After cutting off a trembling salute, Waters blew a tooting blast on his trench whistle as if sending them over the top. "Now go kill some goddam Boche and Japs, fellas! And when you get over there, tell 'em the boys of the Marne send their goddam regards!"

AUTHOR'S NOTE

wo of the eight main characters in this novel deserve some elaboration. During my research for the novel, I came across a photograph of a black veteran sitting in a rocking chair in front of his shack at the BEF camp in Anacostia. Dated July 1932, the photograph was taken at the behest of a white female sightseer who posed in front of the veteran's shack, which featured a sign that read:

BONUS INN
369th Inf. of NY, 93rd Div

I was never able to identify the black veteran, but the photograph, included in this book, confirms that at least one Harlem Hellfighter joined up with the BEF in Washington during that tense summer. There were likely others. In his unpublished memoir of James Reese Europe and the Harlem Hellfighters, Noble Sissle briefly mentioned Lt. Europe's aide during the war, a young black volunteer referred to only by his last name, Taylor. I wanted to include the Depression-era experiences of the black veterans in this story, so I combined these two tantalizing remnants from the dusty archives to create Ozzie Taylor.

Anna Raber is also a composite character. Too few Americans know of the shameful treatment suffered by Mennonite and Hutterite conscientious objectors during World War I. Rather than take up arms, some served under duress in nursing and other noncombatant duties. American nurses were the unsung heroes with the American Expeditionary Force in France, and veteran nurses played important roles in the events leading up to the BEF expulsion from Washington. Although the newspaper articles of the period confirmed that nurses accompanied the protesting veterans, the names of these women were often left unreported. One exception was Lauretta D'Arsanis, the nurse from New York who was affectionately known as the Flower of St. Theresa. The identities of the others who ministered to the BEF men and their families have been lost to history. Anna Raber stands for them.

Of the many people who assisted me in the research and writing of this book, the following deserve special mention: Leslie Stapleton and Caitlin Donnelly at the Daughters of Texas Republic Library in San Antonio; the staff at the UCLA Special Collections Library; Sam Breyer, Barry Joseph, and Firth Bowden (grandson of Joe Angelo); Desiree Butterfield-Nagy at the Raymond H. Fogler Library, University of Maine; and Wilfred Wood of Portland. A special thanks to Alicia Rasley, John Jeter, and Deacon Solomon for their superb editing and suggestions, and to David Martin, Michelle Millar, and Stewart Matthew for their encouragement on the manuscript.

Finally, a special note of gratitude across the veil to Harry Essex, a marvelous Hollywood writer, teacher, and my late mentor. Harry, who served in the Signal Corps during World War II with J.D. Salinger and other heralded authors, told me how vividly he remembered the Bonus March and that tense summer of 1932. He passed away a few months after encouraging me to turn my film screenplay about the era into a novel.

About the Author

A graduate of Indiana University School of Law and Columbia University Graduate School of Journalism, **Glen Craney** is an award-winning novelist, screenwriter, and journalist. The Academy of Motion Pictures, Arts and Sciences honored him with the Nicholl Fellowship prize for best new screenwriting. He is a Chaucer Awards First-Place Winner, a two-time indieBRAG Medallion Honoree, and a three-time *Foreword Reviews* Book-of-the-Year-Award Finalist. His debut historical novel, *The Fire and the Light*, was recognized as Best New Fiction by the National Indie Excellence Awards and as an Honorable Mention winner for *Foreword's* BOTYA in historical fiction. His novels have taken readers to Occitania during the Albigensian Crusade, to the Scotland of Robert Bruce, to Portugal during the Age of Discovery, to the trenches of France during World War I, and to the American Hoovervilles of the Great Depression. He lives in southern California.

Also by Glen Craney

The Fire and the Light
A Novel of the Cathars

As the 13th century dawns, Cathar heretics in southern France guard an ancient scroll that holds shattering revelations about Jesus Christ. Esclarmonde de Foix, a beloved Occitan countess, must defy Rome to preserve the true path to salvation. Christianity suffers its darkest hour in this epic saga of troubadour love, monastic intrigue, and esoteric mystery set during the first years of the French Inquisition.

The Spider and the Stone
A Novel of Scotland's Black Douglas

As the 14th century dawns, the brutal Edward Longshanks of England schemes to steal Scotland. But inspired by a headstrong lass, a frail, dark-skinned boy named James Douglas defies three Plantagenet kings and champions the cause of his wavering friend, Robert the Bruce, leading the armies to the bloody field of Bannockburn. Here is the thrilling saga of star-crossed love and heroic sacrifice that saved Scotland and set the stage for the founding of the United States.

The Virgin of the Wind Rose
A Christopher Columbus Mystery-Thriller

While investigating the murder of an American missionary in Ethiopia, State Department lawyer Jaqueline Quartermane discovers an ancient Latin palindrome embedded with a cryptographic time bomb. Separated by half a millennium, two espionage conspiracies dovetail in this breakneck thriller to expose the world's most explosive secret: The true identity of Christopher Columbus and the explorer's connection to those now trying to launch the Apocalypse.

The Lucifer Genome
A Conspiracy Thriller
(John Jeter and Glen Craney)

Islam's holiest relic has has been stolen, and retired Defense Intelligence agent Cas Fielding must recover it before the Saudi royal family is toppled. Teaming with a sultry expert on meteorites, he sees his mission morph into a deadly race to locate the world's oldest human DNA, proving the old adage that nothing in the Middle East is ever what it seems.

More information at www.glencraney.com.

www.ingramcontent.com/pod-product-compliance
Lightning Source LLC
Chambersburg PA
CBHW021834010726
47493CB00005B/1389